IS YOUR MEMORY UP TO SPEED?

1. What is the baffling engineering miracle concerning the DS9 doors—in fact, the doors on all the *Star Trek* series?

2. What's wrong with the comet in the title sequence of every episode?

3. When is a captain not a captain?

4. How old is O'Brien's daughter, Molly?

ANSWERS:

1. *The doors seem to know just when to open. Sometimes a character barely makes a movement toward them and they obediently pop open. Gotta hand it to those ship designers. (Actually, this is a TRTS in nitpicker lingo. How did the doors know to open? "They Read The Script.")*

2. *The tail always points at a right angle to the light source. Tails of comets in space always point away from the nearest star.*

3. *When he's Sisko objecting during Worf's hearing in "Rules of Engagement." Suddenly the recently promoted captain only has three rank pips instead of the normal four.*

4. *Molly's age is an example of a "changed premise." In "The Nagus," Sisko says she is three years old. "The Nagus" episode has no star date, but Molly was born sometime after star date 45156 ("A Man Alone"). "The Storyteller," and episode three episodes after "The Nagus," has a star date of 46729.1—making Molly one and one-half years old. (Note: 1000 star date units per Earth year.)*

QUIZ YOURSELF. QUIZ YOUR FRIENDS.
LOOK WITH INTENSE SCRUTINY AT YOUR VIDEOTAPES.
FIND THE "AHA!" MOMENTS...
AND IF YOU CATCH ANYTHING THE NITPICKER'S GUIDE MISSES,
WRITE TO THE ADDRESS AT THE BACK OF THE BOOK
AND JOIN THE GUILD.

THE
NITPICKER'S
GUIDE

FOR

DEEP SPACE
NINE TREKKERS

PHIL FARRAND

A DELL TRADE PAPERBACK

A DELL TRADE PAPERBACK
Published by
Dell Publishing
a division of
Bantam Doubleday Dell Publishing Group, Inc.
1540 Broadway
New York, New York 10036

Developed and produced by Ettlinger Editorial Projects, New York.

Library of Congress Cataloging in Publication Data

Farrand, Phil,

Nitpicker's guide for deep space nine trekkers
Phil Farrand

p.   cm.
Includes index
ISBN: 0-440-50762-6
1. Star trek, deep space nine (Television program)
I. Title
PN1992.77.S7315F37   1996
791.45'72—dc20   96–22816
                                                            CIP

Printed in the United States of America
Published simultaneously in Canada
December 1996
10 9 8 7 6 5 4 3 2 1

*Dedicated to nitpickers everywhere in general
and members of the Nitpicker's Guild in particular—
eagle-eyed, brain-engaged, remote-twirling viewers of* Star Trek*—
without whom there would be no* Guides.

TABLE OF CONTENTS

Acknowledgments xi
Introduction xv

FIRST SEASON

Emissary 3
Past Prologue 13
A Man Alone 17
Babel 21
Captive Pursuit 25
Q-Less 29
Personal Favorites 33
Dax 35
The Passenger 39
Move Along Home 44
The Nagus 48
Vortex 52
Battlelines 56
The Storyteller 59
Romance Tote Board 62
Progress 64
If Wishes Were Horses 67
The Forsaken 71
Dramatis Personae 75
Duet 78
In the Hands of the Prophets 82
Bajor: Terok Nor 86

SECOND SEASON

The Homecoming 91
The Circle 94
The Siege 98
Invasive Procedures 102
Cardassians 106
Melora 110
Rules of Acquisition 115
Necessary Evil 117
Second Sight 121
Triathlon Trivia on Characters 125
Sanctuary 127

Rivals 131
The Alternate 134
Armageddon Game 137
Whispers 140
Paradise 144
Shadowplay 148
Playing God 151
Profit and Loss 156
Damage Tote Board 159
Blood Oath 162
The Maquis, Part I 165
The Maquis, Part II 169
The Wire 172
Crossover 175
The Collaborator 179
Tribunal 182
The Jem'Haddar 185
47 190

THIRD SEASON

The Search, Part I 195
The Search, Part II 199
The House of Quark 203
Equilibrium 207
Second Skin 211
The Abandoned 214
Civil Defense 217
Meridian 221
Defiant 224
Triathlon Trivia on Places 228
Fascination 230
Past Tense, Part I 234
Past Tense, Part II 239
Life Support 243
Heart of Stone 245
Destiny 248
Prophet Motive 251
Visionary 254
Distant Voices 258
The Boys in Wonderland Tote Board 261
Through the Looking Glass 263
Improbable Cause 266

The Die Is Cast 268

Explorers 273

Family Business 277

Shakaar 279

Facets 282

The Adversary 285

Sisko's Top Ten Reasons for Shaving His Head 290

FOURTH SEASON

The Way of the Warrior 293

The Visitor 300

Hippocratic Oath 303

Indiscretion 306

Rejoined 309

Little Green Men 313

Starship Down 318

The Sword of Kahless 322

Trek *Silliness* 325

Our Man Bashir 328

Homefront 332

Paradise Lost 336

Crossfire 340

Return to Grace 343

The Sons of Mogh 346

Bar Association.. 352

Accession 355

Hodgepodge Tote Board 358

Rules of Engagement 360

Hard Time 363

Shattered Mirror 366

The Muse 369

For the Cause 371

To the Death 374

The Quickening 377

Body Parts 380

Broken Link 383

Triathlon Trivia on People Groups 386

★ ACKNOWLEDGMENTS

Many, many people have contributed to make this book a reality, both intentionally and unintentionally. Obviously, there could be no *Nitpicker's Guide for Deep Space Nine Trekkers* without the continued, dedicated work of the *Star Trek* division at Paramount Pictures in branching out to create new vistas for our entertainment. To those who have served as executive producers of *Star Trek: Deep Space Nine,* Rick Berman, Michael Piller, and Ira Steven Behr, I thank you and the multitudes you oversee for creating a product worth watching. And, as I am fond of saying: Since it's worth watching, it's worth nitpicking.

As with the *Classic* and *NextGen II Guides,* Steve Ettlinger served not only as agent for this work but book producer as well. He and his assistant, Tim Smith, coordinated William Drennan's copy editing, Jeff Fitschen's typesetting, Margo Zelie and John Long's proofreading and Jane Farnol's indexing. This makes the fourth one we've put out the door together, Steve.

Kathleen Jayes came onboard as editor for this installment of the *Nitpicker's Guide.* (Eric Wybenga decided to pursue writing as his first love. I wish you all the best in all your endeavors, Eric.) As with Eric and Jeanne Cavelos before him, it's been a joy to work with you, Kathleen. My thanks also to Michelle Filippo for her help with the cover, and the rest of the able individuals at Dell Publishing.

My wife, Lynette, and daughter, Elizabeth, still stand beside me. They continue to lend me their strength and—as have said before—because of that I am privileged.

I am also profoundly grateful to Charles Gragg of Ozark, Missouri, for his help during the writing of this *Guide.* I can safely say that without his assistance at just the right time, the creation of this *Guide* would have been exceedingly difficult. In fact, only his graciousness kept me from wandering the interstate road system of the United States wearing a sign that read, "Will work for tapes of missing episodes of *Star Trek: Deep Space Nine.*" Thanks for keeping track of the episodes I missed, Charles. (So...um...Charles, was that profuse enough?)

Nitpicker Central's resident solar physicist Mitzi Adams still serves with distinction. She very kindly answered—or tracked down the answer—to all the quirky questions I compiled while writing this *Guide.* Thanks again for your help, Mitzi. Thanks as well to Dr. David Brown, a magnetospheric physicist and associate of Mitzi's. They played tag team on a few of the more interesting issues. (By the way, if you're interested in having a scientist speak at your convention you can contact the Public Affairs Speakers' Bureau at the Marshall Space Flight Center in Huntsville, Alabama.)

As always, "world-renowned, internationally acclaimed" gratitude needs to go to Larry Nemecek—authorized

Star Trek author of *The Star Trek: The Next Generation Companion*—for his personal assistance on the unauthorized guide.

And I am indebted to the many members of the Nitpicker's Guild who expended significant amounts of time and energy toward the creation of this *Guide*. I have done my best to give credit where credit is due—hence, the list of names that follows these acknowledgments. Unfortunately, space considerations did not allow the inclusion of all the nits that members of the Guild sent my way. To everyone who wrote, whether your nit made it in or not, thank you so much for sharing your discoveries with me. I enjoyed them all.

Finally, I am eternally grateful to you, Jesus Christ, for infusing my days with meaning and wrapping my future with hope.

GUILD ACKNOWLEDGEMENTS

Greetings fellow nitpickers! It's time once again to thank you for your letters. (A gratitude I never grow tired of expressing. If you're interested, I have received almost 6,800 letter at the time of this writing. And, that doesn't include e-mail.) I have read them all and I do appreciate you taking the time to send me your thoughts.

I wish I could list everyone currently in the Guild in these next few pages because all of you have made valuable contributions. Unfortunately since—at the time of this writing—there are well over 4,500 members, space simply does not allow it.

What follows then is a list of the individuals who sent in nits for the first four seasons of *Star Trek: Deep Space Nine*—individuals who were the *first* to send in a given nit that was *included* in this *Guide*. I would hasten to add that there are additional nits for the episodes that were not included due to space. There will be some who have sent in good nits that do not appear in this *Guide* and therefore your name might not appear on this list. I do apologize for that. Some nits were cut solely because they happened to take up just the right number of lines. (By the way, the number after a given name indicates that the individual sent in more than one nit that was included in this *Guide*.)

Hacky Nitpipping!

Sandy Anderson of Taft, CA
Eric Ian Armbruster of Hamilton Square, NJ (2)
Richard Arnold of West Hollywood, CA
Shane Arnold of Columbia, KY
Paul Astle of Larchmont, NY
Kristi Aulenbach of North Pekin, IL
Simone Bache of Rastattm Germany
Mark Bailey of Richfield, MN (3)
Mike Ballway of Evanston, IL
Rebecca Bare of Elkhart, IN
Eric Barker of Fairbanks, AK
Robin Bassett of Atlanta, GA (4)
Alissa Baumbach of Denver, CO
Aaron Beckley of West Haven, CT
Alison Beehr of Mt. Pleasant, MI
Mark Belanger of Butte, MT
Brian Bell of Shannon, New Zealand
Adam Bernay of Fresno, CA
Clive Bilby of Essex, Great Britain (5)
David Birch of Cote Saint-Luc, Quebec
Holly Bjorum of Corpus Christi, TX (3)
Lydia Blackman of Conway, AR
Evan Blaisdell of Groton, CT
Sandra Blom of Fredericia, Denmark
Judy Bonadore of Thornton, CO
Jonathan Bridge of Salt Lake City, UT (5)
Gail Brodie of Woburn, MA
Rachel Lynn Brody of WMSVL, NY (2)
Greg W. Brookshier of Knoxville, TN (2)
Robert E. Bowen of Santa Clara, CA
Eric J. Bowersox of Isla Vista, CA (2)
Diana Brown of San Ysidro, CA
Graham Buckingham of Thompson, Manitoba
Randy E. Burris of Celina, OH
Geoff Benton of Livingston, NY (2)
Rachel Lynn Brody of WMSVL, NY (2)
Nadene Brown of Chicago, IL
Mike Brunsdale of Sherwood Park, Alberta

Randy E. Burris of Celina, OH
Jospeh E. Buss of Cicero, IL
Deborah L. Butcher of Lawton, OK
Elizabeth Campion of Wixom, MI
Aric S. Campling of Haddonfield, NJ (2)
Pete Carter of Kirchener, Ontario (2)
Daniel B. Case of Clarence, NY (9)
Cliff Casselman of Ogdensburg, NY
Brian D. Catlin of Gaithersburg, MD
John Chapelhow of Lancaster, United Kingdom
Shannon Chester of Everett, WA
May Chin of Silver Spring, MD
J. Michael Clark of Defiance, OH (3)
Al Cofazzato of Houston, TX
David Conrad of Bixby, OK
Judy Cook of Batavia, IL
Robert Cook of Anacortes, WA
Al Corazzato of Houston, TX
Matt Cotnoir of Coventry, RI
Whitney Cox of Corpus Christi, TX (3)
Joanna Cravit of Toronto, Ontario (5)
Sandy Crutchfield of Oak Ridge, TN (5)
Frank M. Cunat of Chevy Chase, MD
Laura Dachenbach of Gahanna, OH
George H. Daley, Jr. of Owosso, MI (15)
Matthew Davis of Parkersburg, WV
Mike Davis (Location Unknown)
Stuart Davis of East Sussex, England (2)
Erin M. Dalahanty of Dracut, MA
George H. Daley, Jr. of Owosso, MI (7)
Lita J. Des Rochers of Durango, CO
Rick Donovan of Hutchings, KS
John S. DiGianno of E. Elmhurst, NY
Ian Dixon of Co. Durham, England (3)
Stanley Dunigan of Bethany, OK (2)
Jim Eastin of Wingate, NC (3)
Jonathan S. Edelman of Raleigh, NC
Tom Elmore of Myrtle Beach, SC (3)
Yoko K. Ema of Chicago, IL
Gail M. Eppers of Racine, WI (2)
Joshua Ethridge of Fayetteville, AR
Michael J. Evans of Sussex, England
Brendan P. Farley of Pittsburgh, PA
Adam Farlinger of Cornwall, Ontario (7)
J. Seth Farrow of Independence, MO (5)
Todd Felton of Victoria, British Columbia (8)
David J. Ferrier of Washington, DC
Jim Ferris of Holly, MI (9)
Christopher Ferro of Bridgewater, MA (2)
Richard Fisher of Sudbury, Ontario
Allan W. Fix of Minneapolis, MN
Christie Flynn of Hickory Hills, IL
Alexander Foertch of Nuernberg, Germany
Luanna Foster of San Diego, CA
Alex Frazer-Harrison of Calgary, Alberta (6)
Robyn Frazier of APO, AE
Katie Gallagher of Kapolei, HI
Emma Garland of Gloucestershire, England
Dianna C. Garrett of Weed, CA
Jennifer Gartner of Reistertown, MD
Linda Gill-Aranha of Vancourver, British
  Columbia (4)
Sean Gilpin of Sudbury, Ontario
Rande Goodwin of Windsor, CT
Jeni Gordon of Westlake Village, CA (3)

Geoffrey L. Gould of Verona, NJ
David Grattan of Port Huron, MI
Sara Green of Lake Elsinore, CA (2)
Elie Greenwald of Bloomsburg, PA (2)
Charles Gragg of Ozark, MO (4)
Stephen C. Guilfoyle of Spartanburg, SC (2)
Peter Gulka of Edmonton, Alberta
John C. Gunzburg of Victoria, Australia
Charles Gurkin of Williamston, NC (2)
Jason Allan Haase of Pierce City, MO (2)
Jennifer R. Hale of Takoma Park, MD
Jeffrey M. Hall of Springfield, MO (3)
Nathan Hampton of Pacific City, OR
John Handis of Pittsburg, PA
Brian Harrington of Co. Cork, Ireland
Jeff Hawley of Solon, OH
Kristyn Hayden of Manhattan, KS (4)
David B. Heagney, Jr. of San Carlos, CA
Sharon Henry of Las Vegas, NV
Alan Hewitt of Portsmouth, United Kingdom
Myles Hildebrand of Niverville, Manitoba (10)
Renie Hildt of Owings Mills, MD
Patrick C. Hodges of Glendale, AZ
Lori Hope of Austin, TX (2)
Ronn Hubbard, Jr. of Murray, KY
N. Adam Hughley of Tigard, OR
Darrin Hull of Willard, MO
Pete Isaacson of Hacienda Heights, CA
Martin Jack of United Kingdom
Griffin James of South Deerfield, MA
Rhonda L. Javine of Coweta, OK
Paul C. Jensen of La Grange, IL
Paul Jennings of Rock Rapids, IA
Doye Jernigan of Lawton, OK
Mikal C. Johnson of Kirkland, WA
Reid Joiner of Arkedelphia, AR (3)
Philip G. Jones of Mid-Wales, United Kingdom
Shira T. Karp of Wilmette, IL (7)
Jim Kenworthy of Needles, CA
Chris Kerr of Mountain View, CA (2)
Brad Kimak of Edson, Alberta
Sarah King of Chapel Hill, NC
Kristi L. Kuhlmann of St. Louis, MO
Chris Kuhn of Saint Heights MI (2)
Johnson Lai of Ajax, Ontario (24)
Erin Lale of Sonoma, CA
Francis Lalumiere of Montreal, Quebec
Marshall Lamm of Wilson, NC
Gordon Lawyer of Lancaster, VA (15)
Fred Learn of Commodore, PA (2)
Johnson Lee of Staten Island, NY
Murray J.D. Leeder of Calgary, Alberta
Paul LeGere of Rotterdam, NY (4)
Rob Levandowski of Rochester, NY (2)
Rick Lewis of Bellevue, WA (33)
Paul R. Lilly of Danbury, CT (3)
John Liming of Signal Hill, CA
Jeff Lockway of Tehachapi, CA
Brian Lombard of Gaithersburg, MD (4)
Kevin Loughlin of Kitcher, Ontario
Gain G. Lu of Little Neck, NY
Mark Luta of Eugene, OR (2)
C. J. Mack of Omaha, NE (9)
Steve Mack of Berkeley, CA
Vinny Magno of Framingham, MA

Gordon J. Malkowski of San Antonio, TX
Nora Malloch of Dartmouth, Nova Scotia
Linny Marcus of Brookline, MA (6)
Felix Mariposa of Oakland, CA (9)
Mike Mayers of Fairfield, NJ (2)
Alison McCaffrey of Roseburg, OR (5)
Robert A. McCormick, Jr. of Macon, GA
Laurie McGinn of Lockport, NY
John T. McKinney of Tacoma, WA
John McManus of Louisville, TN
Stephen Mendenhall of Ann Arbor, MI (5)
Drew Mercy of Camarillo, CA
Richard Merritt of Creve Coeur, MO
Merak Milligan of Seattle, WA
Colin Miller of Tucson, AZ (3)
Tracy Miller of Battle Creek, MI
Scott Minter of Chatsworth, GA
Debbie Mirek of Fullerton, CA
Becky Monsess of Vienna, VA
David J. Moody of Burke, VA (2)
Laura Morgan of Denver, CO
Anna Mracek of Creve Coeur, MO
Matthew Murray of Bellingham, WA (4)
Valerie K. Narehood of Center Valley, PA (6)
Yr Hen Nefoedd of Pembrokeshire, United
    Kingdom
Matt Nelson of Spokane, WA
Larry Nemecek of Pasedena, CA (3)
Walbert Ng of Elmhurst, NY (2)
Robert Nichol of Newmarket, Ontario
Andrew J. Nagel of Michigan City, IN
David Nittel of Nanaimo, British Columbia
Walbert Ng of Elmhurst, NY (5)
David Nurenburg of Northampton, MA (8)
Austen O'Kurley of Bruderheim, Alberta
Jim Orr of Northville, MI (2)
Steven Page of Tujunga, CA
Evan Parry of Dayton, VA
Sebastian Pauls of Kleve-Kellen, Germany (2)
Tim Pavey of Medina, OH
Joseph Pintar of New Hartford, NJ (8)
Susan Podkowinski of Syracuse, NY (12)
Ana Pope of Belen, NM
David D. Porter of River Ridge, LA (8)
Bob Potter of Tasmania, Australia
Matthew Powell of Nottinghamshire, England
Kathy Proffitt of Mattoon, IL
Matthew Pugsley of Spartanburg, SC
Lyanne Quirt of Kanata, Ontario
Adam Rackes of W. Cola, SC (5)
Brad Raimondo of Tenafly, NJ
Greg Reid of Toronto, Ontario
Kymberlee Ricke of Aurora, IL (3)
Eric T. Robinett of Venice, FL
Grace Robinson of Richmond, VA (3)
Jason Robinson of Las Vegas, NV (3)
Jason Rockwell of Wyoming, MI
Layla Rodgerson of Dartmouth, Nova Scotia
Matthew Rorie of McLean, VA
Martin Russ of Suffolk, United Kingdom
J. Robert Sawatzky of Mississauga, Ontario (2)
Benjamin Schak of Minneapolis, MN (2)

Glen A. Scheel of Washougal, WA
Alex Scrivener of Gambrills, MD
Bryan Scrivener of Gambrills, MD
Maureen Schroeder of Derry, PA
Myriem Seabron of Randallstown, MD (2)
Mine Sharpe of Taipei, Taiwan (2)
Michaela Schlocker of Stanford, CA
Steve C. Shives of Clear Springs, MD
Mark Shore of Staffordshire, England (3)
Abby Siuta of Racine, WI
Jason Simcoe of Katrine, Ontario
Aaron Smith of Carlsbad, CA
David Smith of West Trenton, NJ
Davis N. Smith of Arnold, MD
Larry Smith of Monroe, TN
Stephen Sparrow of Ajax, Ontario
Greg Spradlin of Madison, WI
Paul M. Steele of Ft. Belvoir, VA (2)
Christine Steichen of Ames, IA
Peter F. Stoll of Toronto, Ontario (2)
Jonathan Strawn of Albuquerque, NM (6)
Ian & Ruth Stuart-Hamilton of Worcester,
    United Kingdom
Chris Street of Suffolk, England
Vicki Strzembosz of Oak Lawn, IL
Bill Synnamon of Lafayette Hill, PA
Sharon Taggart of Rush, NY (2)
Daniel Taller of Flushing, NY
David L. Tayman of Springfield, MO
Lars Thomas of Valby, Denmark
Gerhard Thielman of Ridgecrest, CA (5)
E. Catherin Tobler and the First Light staff of
    Wesminster, CO (2)
Elijah Ton of Carthage, MO
Timothy B. Totthe of Gainesville, FL
Shane Tourtellotte of Rutherford, NJ (7)
Joshua Truax of Fridley, MN (22)
Sarita G. Taub of Redondo Beach, CA (7)
Pam van Allen of Memphis, TN
Martin F. Waddell of Indianapolis, IN
Kristen Wagner of Santa Clara, CA
Trevor Washington of Fort Fairfield, ME (2)
Edward Watson of Downington, PA (7)
Cary Bernadette Webb of New York, NY
Arija Weddle of Fairfield, CT (2)
Gary H. Weddle of Fairfield, CT
Philipp Weißßuß of Berlin Germany (2)
Kevin Weiler of Anchorage, AK
Bob Weiss of Bowie, MD
Kari M. Wendel of Dunkirk, NY
Ryan Whalen of Jacksonville Beach, FL (2)
Gregg Wiggins of Arlington, VA
Wesley H. Williams of Heavener, OK
Dave Wolff of Garden City, NY
Jeremy Wood of Sheffield, England
John Wyant of Hants, United Kingdom
Demarco Wynne of Alameda, CA
Jathaniel Velazquez of Las Vegas, NV (3)
Jennifer Velazquez of Las Vegas, NV (3)
Justin Yeoman of Whiteriver, AZ (2)
Doyle Steven Youngblood of Waldron, AR (4)
Lee Zion of San Diego, CA (3)

INTRODUCTION

reetings, fellow nitpickers! So now we turn our attention to *Star Trek: Deep Space Nine*. As you may know, three guides have preceded this one: *The Nitpicker's Guide for Next Generation Trekkers* (a.k.a., the *NextGen Guide,* released November 1993), *The Nitpicker's Guide for Classic Trekkers* (a.k.a., the *Classic Guide,* released November 1994), and *The Nitpicker's Guide for Next Generation Trekkers, Volume II* (a.k.a., the *NextGen II Guide,* released November 1995). You wouldn't believe how much we pay high-powered consultants to come up with these truly original titles!

By now, I would assume that most everyone reading this would understand the basics of this book. But for those unfamiliar with a *Nitpicker's Guide,* let me offer my usual quick tour. For each episode I list the title, star date, and a brief summary—in case you haven't seen that particular installment in the *Star Trek* universe. I also add a few ruminations along the way and offer picks for great moments. There are two trivia questions just to test your knowledge of the episode or movie. Then—as I say—it's on to the *good stuff*! I take the nits for each review and place them in one of four major categories: Plot Oversights, Changed Premises, Equipment Oddities, and Continuity and Production Problems.

Plot Oversights is a catchall. Any-

thing that concerns the plot, or won't fit anywhere else, goes here. Under Changed Premises, you'll discover that sometimes information given in one show directly contradicts information in another. In Equipment Oddities I'll point out any technical problems with the machinery of the *Trek* universe. Lastly, the section Continuity and Production Problems will expose errors in the actual creation of the show. (Speaking of Continuity and Production Problems, I've finally discovered *closed captioning*! Oh, for those of you in countries other than the United States and Canada, read that: subtitles. While I didn't set out to document *every* error between the closed captioning and the spoken dialogue, I did find a few that you might find interesting in the first four seasons of *DS9* and have noted them appropriately.)

If you happen to have the episodes of *Star Trek: Deep Space Nine* on videotape, pull them out and grab the remote as you work your way through this *Guide.* If you find something I missed, disagree with a nit I picked, or even find an error in the *Guide* itself, drop me a line at the address at the back of this book. This will make you a member of the Nitpicker's Guild.

The tote boards in this edition of the *Nitpicker's Guides* posed a challenge. The bulk of this book—including the tote boards—was submitted for publication at the end of February 1996. Sharp-minded readers will immediately recognize that several episodes in the fourth season had yet to be aired! Those episodes were later added to the book. However, the tote boards could not be updated, since they were already in production. Here's the part you need to read closely: The tote boards are only current through "Paradise Lost." In case you missed it the first time, let me say it another way: Question: How current are the tote boards? Answer: Only through "Paradise Lost." (Get the point? Wink, wink.)

As always, the Nitpicker's Prime Directive remains in full force. For those who don't remember, the main rule of nitpicking reads, "All nits picked shall derive from sources the creators consider canonical." In other words, anything that Paramount claims is authoritative can be nitpicked. As I understand it, any of the television episodes in any incarnation of *Star Trek* are canonical. So are the movies and the reference materials available from Pocket Books. On the other hand, the creators do not consider the *Star Trek* novels authoritative. Those stories have never actually happened. Trying to prove a nit by citing a passage from a novel violates the Nitpicker's Prime Directive. And, as you know, nitpickers *never* violate the Nitpicker's Prime Directive.

A final exhortation. Some of you may not know that there is a Nitpicker's Secondary Directive. It reads, "All nitpickers shall perform their duties with lightheartedness and good cheer." This whole nitpicking thing is about having some fun with our favorite television shows. It is not about pointing fingers and assigning blame. It is a celebration of being human. No matter what we're involved in as humans, no matter how hard we try, everything we do will have mistakes in it. As long as that's true, we might as well 'fess up to it and find some humor in our own imperfections. Let me give you an example. I once misspelled the title of a *NextGen* episode "Datelore" instead of "Datalore." John DiGianno of East Elmhurst, New York, responded, "Wasn't that a new television show hosted by Chuck Woolery?" See? Now, that's funny! I made a mistake and John found some humor in it.

"Lightheartedness and good cheer" should also be the way nitpickers approach fans of the *Trek* who aren't into nitpicking. If a person wants to watch their show without knowing what's wrong with it: *Let them watch their show!* A true nitpicker doesn't have to tell everyone everything he or she knows all the time. If you see a nit and are in a roomful of "non-nitters," just smile and drop me a note later.

Happy nitpicking!

FIRST
SEASON

EMISSARY

Star Dates: 46379.1—46393.1

The two-hour premiere of *Star Trek: Deep Space Nine* begins with a flashback to the Federation's battle with the Borg at Wolf 359 (See the *NextGen* episode "The Best of Both Worlds, Part II.") When the Borg destroy the USS *Saratoga,* Commander Benjamin Sisko flees the ship with his son, Jake, and a few other survivors—leaving his dead wife behind.

Three years later, Sisko accepts command of a Cardassian-built space station orbiting Bajor. For decades, the Cardassians exploited the resources of the planet and its people, leaving only chaos behind. Captain Picard of the USS *Enterprise* gives Sisko the responsibility of preparing Bajor for entrance into the Federation. Unfortunately, a report from Major Kira Nerys—Sisko's first officer and Bajoran liaison on the station— makes this possibility sound bleak. Bajor totters on the brink of civil war. Kira states that only Kai Opaka, the spiritual head of all Bajorans, can call for unity. Interestingly enough, Opaka soon asks for a meeting with Sisko.

During the meeting, Opaka tests

Trivia Questions

1. For what star system does the *Enterprise* depart from *Deep Space 9.*

2. Which Kai experienced a vision in the Denorios Belt?

Sisko's *pagh*—his life force—and proclaims Sisko "the emissary," a figure predicted by Bajoran religion. She also shows Sisko a "Tear of the Prophet"—one of nine hourglass-shaped, crystal orbs that have appeared in space near Bajor over the past ten thousand years. The Cardassians stole the other eight. Opaka fears that the Cardassians will use them to discover "the Celestial Temple"—home of Bajoran deities known as the Prophets. Before Opaka will call for unity, Sisko must find the Celestial Temple and warn the Prophets of possible Cardassian incursion.

With the help of his Trill science officer, Jadzia Dax, Sisko locates a stable wormhole near Bajor. The noncorporeal aliens who exist inside arrange an encounter, and Sisko soon learns that they live in nonlinear time, unaware that other species experience a past, present, and future. Originally these aliens dispatched the orbs as a way to contact other lifeforms like themselves. Amid a myriad of his own memories and through the metaphor of baseball, Sisko demonstrates the challenge of living with an unknown future. In the course of the

3

discussion, however, Sisko's memories return him again and again to the battle at Wolf 359 and the sight of his dead wife. With the aliens' help, he realizes that his life has also become nonlinear. He admits that he never has learned to live without his companion and finally begins to find closure for his grief.

Satisfied, the aliens agree to allow passage of vessels through the wormhole to a distant point in the Gamma Quadrant, 70,000 light-years away.

RUMINATIONS

This was a great beginning for the series. Nice, hard sci-fi edge to it. (Note the understated, classic sci-fi message: Advanced species will seem like gods to those less advanced—i.e., the Bajorans worship the aliens as "Prophets" when the aliens were simply sending out probes to contact other races.) Lovely intertwining of Sisko's "nonlinear" existence and the aliens' nonlinear existence. I especially like the usage of baseball as the tool Sisko finally uses to "drive home" the understanding of what it's like to exist in linear time. (Obviously I wouldn't be doing my job if I didn't point out the plot problems that arise from this plot idea, but I'll hold off on that for just a bit.)

And the foreshadowing! Really nicely done. The first allusion to baseball occurs very quickly after Sisko meets the aliens—giving us one of those "so that's what that was for" moments that are so much fun when the episode finally gets to the baseball analogy.

Also, here's a bit of cleverness from the creators. In the two-hour premiere

of "Emissary," the title sequence doesn't show the wormhole at the end (as the title sequence does from here on out). Since its existence hadn't been revealed yet, the creators didn't want to give anything away! (Thanks to David L. Tayman of Springfield, Missouri, for pointing this out.)

There is one aspect of this episode that bothered me the first time I saw it and still bothers me today, though it's not really a nit. I realize the creators were trying to set this series apart from NextGen. One way they did that was to pit Sisko against Picard. This episode has Sisko delaying his meeting with Picard. When he finally does report to the Enterprise he immediately brings up the fact that he fought Picard in battle at Wolf 359 while Picard was controlled by the Borg. Patrick Stewart does his usual wonderful job playing the scene with a compelling mixture of shame, regret, and distractedness after this revelation.

Now...remember the time frame of this episode. At this point we are halfway through the sixth season of NextGen and it is flying in the ratings. In the midst of this, the hero of NextGen, Captain Picard, has to face Sisko's hostility over the battle at Wolf 359. The first time I saw this scene, I immediately sided with Picard. I knew it wasn't his fault. I knew he had tried his best to fight the Borg's invasion into his life (see the NextGen episode "Family"). And yet this guy— this desk-hugging commander who got one bloody nose out in space and has been pushing a pencil at Utopia Planitia ever since—is beating up on my hero and making him endure the shame and humiliation of it...all...over...again!?

See the problem? I was ready for this episode to show me a person I could identify with, a person whose adventures I would want to enjoy for the next seven years, and suddenly I was mad at him because of the way he was treating Picard. Honestly, it took a while for me to get past those few seconds and the image they painted of Sisko. Yes, I knew that he was going through a bad time. I sympathized over the loss of his wife. And I was glad that he had started to work things out by the end of the episode. But I really, really would have liked to hear just a few words of apology from Sisko over the way he treated Picard in their first meeting. There were none. Which makes me wonder: Does Sisko still blame Picard for the death of his wife? (I haven't forgotten the handshake at the end of the episode, but, for me, that had all the flavor of "I know I was a jerk before but I'm not about to admit it to you.")

A few words on procedure. Normally I treat premieres gently. I have a slightly different viewpoint with this one, however. This show was put together by the same team as NextGen—*while* NextGen *was still on the air. It's more of an extension than a whole new start.*

GREAT LINES

"No, it is not linear."—Sisko to the aliens after the aliens demonstrate that he "exists" at the moment he found his dead wife and they observe that Sisko's own life is "not linear."

PLOT OVERSIGHTS

• During the flashback at the beginning of this episode, why are there civilians on board the starships that are attacking the Borg? Why hasn't Starfleet evacuated these people prior to the battle? (They could use escape pods if nothing else.)

• The caption shown after the battle at Wolf 359 claims that three years have passed. Actually, if the star dates are to be believed, it's more like two and one-half years. (Pick, pick, pick, pick, pick.)

• During his first encounter with the Tear of the Prophet, Sisko flashes back to the day he met Jennifer—the woman he would marry. He is standing on the beach, holding a tray of lemonade, when he realizes that the sand is burning his feet. He hops around, eventually kicking sand on his wife-to-be. They flirt for several moments and then take off on a walk down the beach. It looks like they are walking on dry sand—dry, *hot* sand, if I recall correctly. It no longer seems to be burning his feet. (One could assume that the sand had little to do with sending Sisko toward Jennifer in the first place. But it was a convenient excuse, eh?)

• In their first meeting, newly arrived Dr. Julian Bashir tells Kira that he took the position on DS9 because he wanted to practice "frontier medicine" on a remote outpost. He says heroes are made "right here...in the wilderness." Kira takes great exception to this characterization, and rightly so. Isn't it arrogant, presumptive Earth-centricity to characterize Bajor as "out in the sticks" just because it's on the edges of the Federation? With this in mind, why isn't Kira torqued about the new name for the station?

Wouldn't she be upset that Starfleet had named it "Deep Space 9"? *Deep space* from what?

• Okay, so let's talk about this whole nonlinear time deal. The aliens supposedly experience everything at the same time. They have no past or future. It's all present. I suppose this would be like sitting on a bluff looking down on a winding river. Anyone in a boat on the river could only see to the next bend, but the person on the bluff could see everything. More precisely, the person on the bluff would see the boat in every location along the river at the same time—like some kind of giant smear. Conceptually this has some problems when applied to this episode. The aliens shouldn't be surprised by Sisko's arrival. Neither should they have to learn about linear time. Neither should they suspect that Sisko is deceiving them. Neither should they think that Sisko is aggressive or adversarial. They should already know all this stuff because they should already know everything that's going to happen to them because they live in *nonlinear* time. Discovering all this stuff implies a past (before they met Sisko), a present (learning about linear time), and a future (sending Sisko back). (Granted...it would make for a short show if it were really written from a true nonlinear viewpoint: "About time you got here, Sisko. Your wife's dead. Get over it. You can use the wormhole. We love baseball, too. Now leave.")

• Seeing the strange-looking Cardassian terminals on DS9 causes me to wonder: When did every Starfleet officer suddenly become fluent in Cardassian?

• I'm confused about the effect that passing through the wormhole has on the aliens. When first discussing the issue with Sisko, the aliens claim that their existence is disrupted every time someone uses the passage. They add that his linear existence is inherently destructive. Yet at the end of the episode, the aliens agree to let ships use the wormhole. Have the aliens just decided to "take the pain," or did their conversation with Sisko help them figure out a way around it?

CHANGED PREMISES

• It's time to question the entire existence of the *Star Trek: Deep Space Nine* series! In "The Best of Both Worlds, Part 2" *(TNG)*, the *Enterprise* comes on the recently concluded battle at Wolf 359. The exact time between the battle and the arrival of the *Enterprise* is difficult to ascertain because we don't know how long it took the ship to travel to Wolf 359. But we can safely say that the battle scene is "fresh." On arrival, Data reports, "No active subspace fields, negligible power readings." Riker responds, "Life signs?" Data: "Negative, sir." *Data* is working the controls. *Data* says that no one survived the battle. Yet the premiere of *DS9* has Sisko, Jake, and many others surviving the battle. The only possibility is that the escape pods somehow managed to get out of sensor range between the time of the battle and the arrival of the *Enterprise*. This seems very unlikely. The *Enterprise*'s sensors can scan for light-years. Also, according to the *Tech Manual,* the *Enterprise*'s lifeboats only have impulse engines, so it's safe to assume that Sisko's ship, the *Saratoga,* had the same. It would take *years* to escape the *Enterprise*'s sensors by traveling at less than the speed of light. Besides, these escape pods must have subspace communication capability. Isn't the whole purpose of these crafts to survive the evacuation of the ship and then contact Starfleet for rescue?

The conclusion reached must be that *no one* survived Wolf 359! Sisko's dead. Jake's dead. And *someone* has replaced them with replicants and a fabricated story about escaping the battle alive. (Insert *Twilight Zone* music here.)

• While we're on the subject of the *Saratoga,* the *Tech Manual* has its registry as NCC-31911. You may recall that there was also a USS *Saratoga* in *Star Trek IV: The Voyage Home.* The registry of that ship was NCC-1937. I wonder why Sisko's *Saratoga* wasn't something like NCC-1937-C. (If it's good enough for the *Enterprise*...)

• Early on, Kira identifies DS9 as a "godforsaken place." Interesting choice of terms given that Bajorans don't worship a god, they worship the Prophets. (Maybe she was trying to give Sisko the willies?)

• In my review of "The Host" in *The Nitpicker's Guide for Next Generation Trekkers, Volume II,* I dealt fairly extensively with the major changes to the Trill between that episode and the start of *Star Trek: Deep Space Nine.* I will revisit some of those issues in my review of the episode "Dax" (an episode that supposedly gives us more information about the entire Trill "joining" thing). In addition—though they are first seen here—I will discuss the physiological differences in the implant process in my review of "Invasive Procedures."

• When first arriving on the station, Bashir tells Kira that he could have had his choice of any job in the fleet. He's exaggerating, but only a bit. In fact, he never had a chance at the chief medical officer position on the USS *Lexington* because Elizabeth Lense wanted that position. And what Elizabeth wanted, Elizabeth got because she—not he—was valedictorian of their class. (See "Explorers.")

• This episode begins a long series of problems with the conservation of matter and Odo's shape-shifting abilities. Quite simply, you cannot just lose and gain matter at will (unless you exercise aerobically or use steroids, of course). In "Vortex," Croden rescues Odo from a cave and later says that Odo is heavier than he looks. So, let's say that Odo is about 175 pounds. It doesn't matter what shape Odo takes, he will still weigh 175 pounds, period. Otherwise he is violating the known laws of the physical universe. Yet in this episode, Odo becomes a bag that Quark lifts with one hand! (I suppose that little Ferengi could be a lot stronger than he looks.) Then a Cardassian carries the bag filled with latinum onto his ship and throws it into a locker. Odo puddles out onto the floor and from a very small amount of matter seems to expand into his normal humanoid shape. To do this he would have to be hollow inside. But if he were hollow, he wouldn't weigh 175 pounds! (Unless he were really dense, but if he were dense, then Quark wouldn't be able to lift him with one hand. More to come in later episodes.)

EQUIPMENT ODDITIES

• *The Star Trek Encyclopedia* mentions that the *Melbourne* in "The Best of Both Worlds, Part 2" was a Nebula-class starship. The *Melbourne* in this episode—seen during the reenactment of the battle at Wolf 359—is clearly an Excelsior class.

• Speaking of the *Melbourne,* Locutus seems ill disposed toward this particular ship. When it approaches in battle, he sends out some kind of "weapon of mass destruction" that pulverizes it almost instantly. Gratefully, he's much less severe with the *Saratoga,* merely trapping it in a tractor beam and giving the inhabitants (i.e., Sisko and Jake) a chance to escape. Why the difference? Does the really big gun chew up too much energy?

• After trapping the *Saratoga* in a tractor beam, Locutus sends out some type of energy weapon that hits the underside of the *Saratoga*'s saucer section. Moments later a Bolian officer reports damage to decks one through four. What?! I thought deck 1 was the bridge on the *top* of the saucer section. How can the bubble on the underside of the saucer be deck 1?

• Obviously, Jake is a catch-and-release fisherman. Near the beginning of the episode he enjoys some time on a holodeck with a fishing pole. One wonders what happens to the fish he catches when he goes back to his quarters. (I committed a good deal of space to the issue of the permanence of holodeck matter once it leaves the holodeck grid in the *NextGen Guide* and the *NextGen II Guide*. For more information see the reviews for the *NextGen* episodes "Elementary, My Dear Data" and "Ship in a Bottle.")

• O'Brien has an odd definition of the term "value." Shortly after Sisko arrives on the station, O'Brien tells his new commander that the Cardassians stripped DS9 of "every component of value" when they left. A short time later, O'Brien beams Odo from a Cardassian ship using a Cardassian transporter still installed on the station! Obviously O'Brien doesn't believe that Cardassian transporters have any "value." In addition, the Cardassians seem to have left behind an incredible store of computer hardware. There are working monitors everywhere! But, then again, maybe according to O'Brien none of this has "value" either!

• This episode begins a long series of oddities with the doors on the station. As with all *Star Trek* television series, these doors seem to *know* just when to open. After Sisko threatens to put Nog in a Bajoran prison if Quark doesn't keep his bar open, the doors to the Security office pop open with barely a movement from the commander. Gotta hand it to those Cardassian designers! (Actually, this is a TRTS in nitpicker lingo. How did the doors know to open? "They Read The Script.")

• Cardassian internal sensors must not work as well as their counterparts in Starfleet. After discovering a possible sight for the Bajoran Celestial Temple, Sisko and Dax take off in a runabout. To ensure that Gul Dukat won't follow, Sisko arranges for Odo to be carried on board. (Hence the problems mentioned above under "Changed Premises.") Odo then disables the Cardassian ship, allowing Sisko and Dax to fly off undetected. So why didn't the intruder alarms sound on the Cardassian ship as soon as Odo returned to his humanoid form? Don't they have an intruder alert on a Cardassian ship like the one on the *Enterprise*?

• Eventually Gul Dukat follows Sisko through the wormhole. Soon three more Cardassian ships show up, demanding to know what happened to their comrade. O'Brien reports that his former ship, the *Enterprise,* is the closest ship that can come to their rescue. If memory serves, there were times in *NextGen* when two Cardassian warships seemed to give Picard pause (in "Ensign Ro" and "The Chase," for instance). Yet here we have three Cardassian warships against a defenseless space station, and the crew pins their hopes on the *Enterprise*?

CONTINUITY AND PRODUCTION PROBLEMS

• At the beginning of the episode, Locutus's body suit seems browner than it was in "The Best of Both Worlds, Part 2," but it's hard to tell. Could be a lighting problem.

• According to "The Drumhead" *(TNG)*, thirty-nine Starfleet vessels were destroyed at Wolf 359. I wonder why they didn't attack at the same time? In the footage of the battle at the beginning of this episode, there are only a few ships engaging the Borg.

• Speaking of that battle, when the *Saratoga* approaches, the camera swivels to show it flying toward the Borg. Off to the left is an Excelsior-class ship that we later learn is the *Melbourne*. Then the camera angle changes and suddenly the *Melbourne* seems farther away.

• Arriving at DS9 for the first time, Sisko and Jake stand in front of a window to get a glimpse of the station as the ship in which they travel prepares to dock. A log entry follows. Sisko states that the *Enterprise* arrived two days ago, bringing O'Brien and three runabouts. The creators then show us a lovely picture of the *Enterprise* docked at DS9. Wait a minute: If the *Enterprise* has been hanging around for two days, why didn't we see it when Sisko and Jake enjoyed a bonding moment staring out the window at the station? Did Data take the *Enterprise* for a spin around the sun because he needed a few more frequent-flier miles to earn that free trip to Risa? (Just for your own information, none of the dialogue indicates that the *Enterprise* left.)

• When Sisko finally decides he's good and ready to meet with Picard, the view out the observation lounge on the *Enterprise* isn't correct. An establishing shot shows the *Enterprise* facing away from Bajor. Since the observation lounge is on the aft side of deck 1, the planet should fill the windows. It doesn't. Only a piece shows on the side nearest Picard.

• During this meeting, Picard pours Sisko a drink, picks up the cup, and sets it down on the table. Sisko refuses it and later leaves. Afterward, Sisko's cup, has somehow returned to the tray. (There is time for Picard to move the cup, but it made a definite "chinking" sound the first time Picard moved it. Presumably it would do so again if moved a second time. By the way, several nitpickers found Picard's pronunciation of "Bajor" at the beginning of this meeting less than satisfying!)

• There is a gorgeous matte painting of a Bajoran landscape in this episode—apparently featuring the Bajoran equivalent of the Vatican. It causes one to wonder, though. How did it escape with so little damage during the Cardassian withdrawal? (I know Kai Opaka apologizes for the condition of the area, but it sure looks fine to me!)

• Just after Kai Opaka tells Sisko that finding the Celestial Temple is the journey he has always been destined to take, the episode cuts to a commercial. When it returns, the establishing shot of the station shows only the *Enterprise* docked. Bajor seems to have moved someplace else! (Unless the station rotates. But that's a whole other discussion that we will visit in the coming episodes. According to the stars in the windows, Sisko's office rotates but the rest of the station doesn't!)

• When Quark's bar reopens, we see a woman in a very familiar costume. It is made from a gold lamé-type fabric and is missing a strategic portion of cloth in the midriff area. Specifically, the outfit exposes the lower third of the woman's breasts. Interestingly enough, this same outfit appears on one of the elbow babes

who accompany the fat Ferengi trader in "Unification II" *(TNG)*. A Ferengi design, perhaps?

• Not a nit, just one of the those "strange but true" items. (The term "SBT" was first used in nitpicking by Sara Green of Lake Elsinore, California.) For some reason red is the color of choice in the future for medical operating gowns. Starfleet uses red, and—during Dax's flashback with the orb—we discover that Trill doctors do as well.

• Just prior to Sisko's meeting with the aliens, an orb grabs Dax and takes her back to DS9. Evidently she could move around inside the thing because when she disappears she is holding her tricorder, but when she reappears on the station the tricorder is in its holster.

• At one point, as Sisko explains linear time existence to the aliens, he sits on a blanket with Jennifer in a park. The camera pans from Jennifer's face over to another blanket on which duplicates of Sisko and Jennifer recline. They then sit up and replay a conversation from Sisko's memory. If you watch carefully, you'll see the bodies "shimmer" a bit as the footage cuts from the stunt doubles to the real actors.

• Apparently the Frunalians buy their ships from the Talarians. At the end of the episode Dax tells Sisko that three Frunalian ships are requesting to dock, but the external visual shows ships that look just like the Talarian ships in "Suddenly Human" *(TNG)*.

• Boy, those custodians sure cleaned up the station fast after the big battle with the Cardassians!

• Why do the Starfleet personnel

have different-style uniforms on this station? The personnel on Starbase 74 had standard uniforms in "11001001" *(TNG)*.

• Editing the original two hour premiere into two one-hour episodes, the creators made several syndication cuts. Only a few are worth noting:

Right after Dax has her encounter with the Tear of the Prophets, the creators deleted everything until the next commercial break—consisting of O'Brien's farewell visit to the *Enterprise* and saying goodbye to Picard. This edit actually takes care of a nit. Picard identifies the woman who operates the transporter as an ensign (a commissioned rank). Yet moments earlier, she addresses O'Brien as "sir." Either she is doing this out of courtesy or it indicates that O'Brien is a commissioned officer. In the military, it is not normal practice for commissioned officers to address noncommissioned officers as "sir." The problem is this: We will see in subsequent episodes that the creators of *DS9* take great pains to bolster their notion that O'Brien is a noncommissioned officer. For instance, at the end of "Facets," O'Brien says that as soon as Nog graduates the academy (and becomes an ensign), he will have to call him "sir." This makes sense only if O'Brien is a noncommissioned officer. But, if O'Brien's rank is such that he calls ensigns, "sir," why then does the ensign transporter chief in this episode call O'Brien, "sir"?

Also, the creators made two other cuts that were unfortunate. I'll explain why in a minute. The first occurs af-

ter Gul Jasad gives Kira one hour to prepare to surrender and subsequently hails the station. At this point in the two hour version, O'Brien tells Kira that once the Cardassian penetrate the thoron field with their sensors, what they find will raise a few eyebrows.

The second cut comes with an additional commercial block inserted just after O'Brien tells Kira that he wouldn't want to play a game of Roladan Wild Draw with her. Returning from the commercial break, Part II of this episode has Dax reporting that the lead Cardassian ship is sending out a call for reinforcements. A section prior to this in the original two-hour episode has the Cardassians penetrating the thoron field and thinking that *DS9* has somehow acquired 5000 photon torpedoes and integrated phaser banks on every level. Gul Jasad responds to the report by saying that it must be a trick—that somehow the crew on the station has created a massive illusion of duranium shadows (which, of course, is *precisely* what O'Brien did).

Here's why these were unfortunate cuts. The creators had no way to know that three years later—for the premiere of the fourth season—they would revisit this exact scenario. In "Way of the Warrior," Gowron receives a similar report from his sensors. At this, General Martok tells Sisko that the 5000 photon torpedoes are merely an illusion. To this, Sisko responds, "It's no illusion." And in moments— when part of the Klingon task force attacks—we see that *DS9* really *does* have 5000 photon torpedoes and in-

tegrated phaser banks now! The dialogue provides a nice closure to the
original scene. Since "Emissary" probably will always be shown as two one-
hour episodes from now on, however,
many fans will miss the connection
unless they saw the original two-hour
episode when it aired in 1992 (or unless a friend tells them about it or they
read this *Guide*—wink, wink).

TRIVIA ANSWERS

1. The Lapolis System.
2. Taluno.

PAST PROLOGUE

Star Date: unknown

As a Cardassian vessel pursues a badly damaged Bajoran scout ship into Bajoran territory near DS9, Sisko orders O'Brien to beam the scout ship's only inhabitant to Ops. After materializing, the injured man introduces himself as Tahna Los. The Cardassians soon arrive—demanding Sisko turn Tahna over to them and accusing the Bajoran of being a member of a radical terrorist group called the Kohn-Ma. When questioned by Sisko, Tahna admits that he is a member of the Kohn-Ma but claims to be finished with the organization. However, Garak the tailor—the station's only Cardassian merchant—informs Sisko that Lursa and B'Etor, the sisters of Duras (see "Redemption," "Redemption II," "Firstborn," and *Star Trek Generations*), have arranged to sell Tahna a cylinder of bilitirum. In addition, Tahna has stolen an antimatter converter from the Cardassians. Combined, the two items would become a powerful explosive device.

Trying to uncover Tahna's plan, Kira agrees to grant his request for a runabout. To her horror, she discovers that Tahna intends to collapse the entrance to the wormhole. Tahna wants Bajor for Bajor alone, and the wormhole is bringing more and more outsiders to the area. A fight ensues, and Kira manages to stop Tahna just as Sisko arrives with reinforcements.

Trivia Questions

1. What is the name of the admiral with whom Kira speaks in this episode?

2. What is the name of Gul Danar's ship?

PLOT OVERSIGHTS

• So let's talk about Odo and conservation of matter once again. This time Odo shape-shifts into a small rodent, somehow compacting all his mass into an object no more than four or five inches long. It is possible—I suppose—but it would be one very hot and very heavy rat. (Hot because of the compression, doncha know!)

• Speaking of rats, methinks that our dear Constable Odo is only feigning incompetence when it comes to creating a humanoid nose. The rodent he becomes is perfect—whiskers and all! I have a hard time believing that making a rodent's nose is substantially easier than a humanoid's nose. I think Odo just doesn't *want* to make an accurate representation.

• Tahna's logic could stand a bit of scrutiny. He tells Kira that once he

13

closes the mouth of the wormhole, the Federation will leave. Just how did he arrive at this conclusion? The Federation established a presence on the station *before* the discovery of the wormhole. Obviously the Federation's interest extends beyond Bajor's one true asset.

• O'Brien has an interesting definition for the words "dead quiet." To catch Tahna with the evidence they need to charge him, Sisko and O'Brien take a runabout to Tahna's rendezvous point with Lursa and B'Etor. They hide the runabout behind a moon, and Sisko tells O'Brien to cut main power. Afterward, O'Brien mutters "dead quiet." In the background, all the panels continue to chirp and peep.

• After Tahna buys the cylinder of bilitirum from Lursa and B'Etor, Sisko and O'Brien give chase. Tahna heads directly for DS9, making Sisko fear that the terrorist is going to blow up the station. Desperate, Sisko even appeals to Gul Danar to see if the Cardassian warship coming to capture Tahna can intercept the runabout instead. One question: Why doesn't Sisko call the station and have them launch the third runabout toward Tahna to head him off?

• As the runabout approaches DS9, Kira tells Tahna that they are 100,000 kilometers from the station. Then the two talk for another 40 seconds or so before they drop out of warp. First of all, I'm assuming that the runabout is running at maximum warp. Otherwise Sisko's runabout could overtake them. And how long would it take for a runabout zipping along at warp 5 to traverse 100,000 kilometers? (Strike up

the math music, maestro!) According to *The Star Trek Encyclopedia,* warp 5 is 214 times the speed of light. Light travels approximately 300,000 kilometers per second. That means the runabout is traveling just over 64 million—*million* with an "m"—kilometers per *second.* In other words, it should reach the station in just over 0.0015 second, not 40 seconds.

• Of course, this all begs the more obvious question: When did Kira—a member of the *Bajoran* military—learn to pilot a *Starfleet* runabout?

• Toward the end of the episode, Tahna and Kira tussle. At one point Kira resorts to pulling Tahna's leg in an effort to keep him from punching this big red button mounted on the ceiling of the runabout (more on that in a minute). Let me get this straight: Kira—the freedom fighter, the feared terrorist—can't come up with a better strategy than sitting on the floor and *pulling the guy's leg*? Wouldn't a well-directed blow to the guy's knees be a bit more effective?

CHANGED PREMISES

• Wanting to talk with Odo about Tahna, Kira goes to the Security office and starts asking about security arrangements for the upcoming trip to Bajor. Odo cuts through this pretext and moves to the heart of the matter. Along the way he states that he's never been good at pretense. Kira says that's one of the things she likes about him—no pretense. In this context, "pretense" seems to indicate a process where the person states one purpose or intention to cloak the real state of affairs. I knew these statements about Odo's nature were trouble for the creators the moment I heard them. Sure enough, Odo's "pretense" starts cropping up again and again. I'll document them along the way, but here's one for starters. In "Dax," Odo wants Quark to let Sisko use his bar for an extradition hearing. When Quark refuses, Odo begins talking about how Quark might be in violation of certain building codes. Obviously he hopes that Quark will make the connection that if he doesn't allow Sisko to use the bar for the hearing there will be trouble. That sounds an awful lot like pretense to me. I guess it's just a nasty habit Odo picked up from these Federation types. After all, he lived with Cardassians for several years and never learned this skill.

EQUIPMENT ODDITIES

• The doors on DS9 continue their baffling behavior. Distressed over her competing loyalties to the Kohn-Ma and the Federation, Kira decides to have a heart-to-heart talk with Odo (actually, it would be more like a heart to *JellO* talk, maybe?) During the discussion, she strides right up to the doors, but they refuse to open. No doubt they sense her need to complete the conversation.

• Interestingly enough, after the above discussion, Odo taps his combadge and calls Sisko. It looks like the same combadge he was wearing when we saw him shape-shift from a rodent to a humanoid. So Odo can create a functioning combadge? Wow!

• And what about this *big red button*? Tahna pushes it to launch his bomb from the runabout. It's mounted on

the ceiling of the runabout. Clearly you have to stand up to slide open a panel to access it in the first place. Just what is this button normally used for? We *never* see it used again in the first four seasons of *Star Trek: Deep Space Nine*. It's almost like the designers of the runabout put this "thing" in a really awkward place and then started a disinformation campaign to ensure that any dastardly person who wanted to use the runabout for nasty business would be convinced of the button's importance, thereby giving the hero or heroine a chance to stop them. It certainly worked in this case. Good thing, too. The series would have ended rather quickly if Tahna could have launched his bomb from a flight panel (in the same way he could control *every other function on the entire ship*)!

CONTINUITY AND PRODUCTION PROBLEMS

• An observation. Evidently Kira decided she wanted a more severe look, so she chopped off most of her hair.

• The stars in the window of Sisko's office intrigue me. When Gul Danar shows up to complain about the docking procedures, the stars move. Later, when Odo gives Sisko a report on the arrival of Lursa and B'Etor, they don't. Now, dear friends, either the station is turning or it isn't (unless someone in Ops is bored and they decided to play with the rotational speed control).

• Not a nit, just a wonderment. At one point, Kira checks over Bajoran Intelligence's latest report on Kohn-Ma activity. Oddly enough, the Cardassian monitor uses "Chicago" font, the same font used by default in the menu bars and dialogue boxes of Macintosh computers. (Just a strange coincidence? I'll let you decide!)

• Purchasing the cylinder of bilitirum, Tahna hands B'Etor a bag telling her it contains thirteen kilos of gold-pressed latinum. Thirteen kilos is almost thirty pounds. There is no way that fluffy little bag that they are tossing around has thirty pounds in it. (By the way, this is the last time gold-pressed latinum is measured by weight. From here on out it's bars, strips, or slips, except in "Rivals," where it's isiks.)

TRIVIA ANSWERS
1. Rollman.
2. *Aldara.*

A MAN ALONE

Star Dates: 46384—46421.5 [see below]

When an old nemesis named Ibudan shows up on DS9 and is subsequently murdered in a holosuite, Odo becomes the prime suspect. Only hours earlier, Odo had scuffled with Ibudan and angrily ordered him off the station. Also, the holosuite containing Ibudan's dead body recorded only one entrance—Ibudan's—and only one subsequent exit—obviously to allow the murderer to escape. Supposedly only a shape shifter could account for this oddity by squeezing through the cracks in the door to gain entrance to the holosuite. In addition, Bashir can find no other DNA traces beside those of the victim and the investigative team. Unfortunately, Odo has no alibi because at the time he had returned to his liquid state and sat in a bucket in his office.

A thorough examination by Bashir of the quarters used by Ibudan while traveling to the station finally uncovers the truth. Working with Dax, Bashir realizes that Ibudan had created a clone of himself. Wanting to frame Odo for murder, he took this clone to the holosuite and then killed it—constructing the crime to implicate Odo. Before the real Ibudan can flee the station in disguise, Odo arrests him for murder.

Trivia Questions

1. What type of bugs do Jake and Nog use to play their practical joke on the couple in the promenade?

2. With whom did Ibudan have lunch on the day he arrived on the station?

RUMINATIONS

The creators used Ibudan's diary to pay homage to a few folks. On star date 46383, he has lunch with Della Santina. (Robert della Santina is listed as the unit production manager in the credits of this episode.) On star date 46384, the diary also has the entry "Subspace Teleconference (GOCKE)." (Bill Gocke is listed as sound mixer.) Thanks to Colin L. Miller of Tucson, Arizona, for pointing this out.

PLOT OVERSIGHTS

• It's amazing what love can do to you. Looking for something to do, Nog and Jake use bugs to play a practical joke on a couple seated at a table in the promenade. To pull off this undertaking, Nog has to walk right up between the pair and place a box on the floor. I don't know about you, but I'd be watching this kid pretty closely if he strolled up and knelt down at my feet. The Bajor couple seem oblivious to Nog's presence. Just love-numbered, I guess.

17

• To discover the murderer of Ibudan's clone, Bashir sweeps the holosuite, looking for—among other things—"hair follicles." Hair follicles. Those little, tiny blips on the root end of a strand of hair? (Okay, I realize that the follicle is the part that potentially contains DNA, but is he really just going to look for the follicles? I can just hear Bashir now, "Oh, here's a hair. No, wait...this one doesn't have a follicle, either. I guess I'll just throw it away because it's useless in this investigation.")

• Interestingly enough, Odo boards a Bajoran transport, uses a Bajoran computer to access Ibudan's files, and the date is given in star dates—the Federation standard. Not really a nit, I suppose but it brings up another question. Just from watching this episode, how much real time on the station do you estimate it covers? One day, two days, a week? The star date for Ibudan's arrival, according to his diary, is 46384. Sisko ends the episode with a star date of 46421.5. That's a difference of 37.5 units. Using our handydandy conversion of 1000 star dates to an Earth year, we find that almost two weeks have elapsed in Earth days during this episode. Somehow that doesn't seem right.

• The substory of this episode deals with Keiko finding something to do on the station. She starts a school for the children. While this is noble, it makes one wonder. Are the computer programs for education in the future so advanced that a teaching certificate is no longer required? It's sounds like teaching is just something that Keiko has always wanted to try, so she decides to give it a go! (Then again, maybe the situation is so bad on the station that anything would be better than nothing.)

• As the story progresses, the fact that Ibudan entered the holodeck, locked the doors, and then was killed increasingly points to Odo's guilt. Supposedly no one else could have come into the holodeck and done the deed. It is assumed that Odo could have slipped through the cracks in the door. But wait: The records also show an exit from the holosuite after the murder. Now, if Odo committed the murder, you would think he would be consistent. If he oozed in, wouldn't he also ooze out—leaving an even more mysterious situation behind? (I suppose you might surmise that Odo panicked and fled the crime scene, but Odo doesn't seem like the panicky type to me. As premeditated as the crime was—as well-concealed as it was behind closed doors—the murderer's exit from the holosuite carries as much weight for me as his or her "nonentrance." Yet the team seems to ignore this.

• Quark uses an odd turn of phrase when coming to Odo's defense in the bar. When a Bajoran comments that Odo has been Quark's worst enemy, the Ferengi bartender replies that may be the closest thing Odo has "in this world" to a friend. Which "world" would that be?

• In a sadder moment during this episode, Odo enters Quark's and sidles up to the bar, only to have everyone around him take off and leave him sitting there alone. (Even Morn! Gasp.) But why is Odo in Quark's in the first place? He doesn't drink. He's not checking on Quark, because he's been relieved of duty. He's not exactly the social type—at least not yet. Just force of habit, maybe?

• These twenty-fourth-century humans sure do grow up quickly. Molly O'Brien was born sometime after star date 45156 according to "Disaster" *(TNG)*. (You remember, "I *AM* PUSHING!") We see her in this episode sometime around star date 46421. She's speaking fluently and looks about three years old. According to the star dates, she's only about fifteen months old. (A difference of about 1265 units converted using 1000 star dates to represent one Earth year.)

CHANGED PREMISES

• Odo's recitation of Ibudan's former criminal record seems suspect. Odo tells Sisko that Ibudan was a black marketeer who killed a Cardassian and was imprisoned on Bajor during the Occupation. Yet in "Tribunal," O'Brien is scheduled for execution for simply being suspected of smuggling weapons to the Maquis. And in "Defiant," Tom Riker's initial sentence for his crime of invading Cardassian space was to be execution as well. One wonders how Ibudan escaped with only imprisonment.

• Attempting to cool Bashir's continued advances, Dax states that Trills do not look for romance the same way humans do. In fact, they find it quite a nuisance. A weakness of the young, if you will. They may have *those* types of feelings occasionally, but they make the effort to "live on a higher plane."

Yeah, right! This from a Trill who was ready to chuck her entire Starfleet career just a few days after meeting a guy named Doral in "Meridian." If I recall correctly, that guy had her toes curling within hours after they met, and Dax even offered to let him *count her spots.* (I guess the cool, aloof female types don't play that well in the ratings!)

• In the discussions about setting up the school, Sisko tells Keiko that it won't be easy. That he can't guarantee that anyone will come. That even if they do, everyone will have a different culture, a different philosophy. (Sage advice.) Keiko, in her enthusiasm, readily agrees that she will have to be innovative. Once she's in the grind of it, Keiko apparently forgets Sisko's admonishments. The episode "In the Hands of the Prophets" has Keiko toeing the Federation line, adamantly refusing to make allowances for the Bajoran religious mind-set.

• At one point Odo tells Kira that he must regenerate every eighteen hours. By the time of "The Storyteller," this figure has changed to *sixteen* hours.

• At the end of this episode Odo says that killing your own clone is still murder. That's funny. I could have sworn that Riker killed his own clone in "Up the Long Ladder" *(TNG)* and never faced charges. Maybe this "killing clones is murder" thing is just a Bajoran law.

EQUIPMENT ODDITIES

• Are holosuites self-cleaning? Bashir states that he only finds DNA evidence for Ibudan and the investigative team. What about all the other customers who used the holosuite that day? According to Ibudan's appointment calendar, the murder occurred sometime well after lunch.

• During a Bajoran riot outside Odo's office, someone throws a brick and shatters the glass in the doors. Granted, it doesn't actually break—just crinkles like safety glass—but wouldn't a Security office have something a bit more sturdy, like a thick panel of Lucite or transparent aluminum?

CONTINUITY AND PRODUCTION PROBLEMS

• Personally, I think there should be some "truth in advertising" stipulations when it comes to previews. In the preview for this episode, Sisko says, "You're not going to take the law into your own hands!" To this, Odo replies, "Watch me." In the actual episode, the conversation proceeds like this: Sisko tells Odo that he can't arbitrarily force Ibudan to leave. Odo replies, "Watch me." Then Sisko chides Odo for attempting to take the law into his own hands. Odo comes back, saying that laws change but justice is always justice. Bringing the conversation to a close, Sisko tells Odo that if Odo can't follow the rules he'll find someone who can. This is substantially different from what's portrayed in the preview.

• Just after the title sequence, Odo and Quark spar in the bar. Odo comments that Quark is almost making an honest living, to which the Ferengi agrees that there are a lot of new faces. Quark glances over at a Dabo girl passing by, the camera angle changes, and suddenly he's looking down—pouring a drink.

• During the opening credits, the actor who plays Nog is listed as "Aron Eisenerg." His last name is actually "Eisenberg." (No doubt the creators fixed this in subsequent rebroadcasts. They usually do with typos in opening sequences.)

• I don't suppose this is a nit, but Odo really doesn't sound like Odo when he's giving Sisko the preliminary report on Ibudan's death in the holosuite. I didn't know who was talking until the camera pulled back. Maybe he's experimenting with different types of vocal cords?

• After discussing Nog's schooling with Keiko, Rom—who seems *very* Ferengi in this episode, by the way (not at all like our lovable, goofball Rom)—turns back to the gambling tables and begins encouraging the patrons to place their wagers. Then he says, "Get this lovely young lady a drink." The closed captioning adds, "on me." Obviously that little bit of dialogue was deleted for not adhering to the Ferengi Commerce Authority's strict guidelines for running a gambling casino.

TRIVIA ANSWERS
1. Garanian bolites.
2. Moudakis.

BABEL

Star Dates: 46423.7—46425.8

When an overworked and exhausted O'Brien begins speaking gibberish, Bashir diagnoses him with aphasia—a neurological disease that scrambles the brain's ability to send and receive information. Then Dax comes down with the same symptoms. By comparing brain scans, Bashir isolates the cause as a genetically engineered virus. Backtracking O'Brien's steps, the crew finds a device attached to the command-level replicators. It was interfaced with the materialization portion of the replicators and had been building the virus into everything it created. Unfortunately—while waiting for his own replicators to be fixed—Quark has been using an infected replicator and subsequently selling the food and drink it manufactured in his bar. Consequently the virus has spread to the rest of the station.

Bashir determines that the virus has a Bajoran origin and sets to work on an antidote. Believing that the virus was an attempt to sabotage DS9 while it was in the hands of the Cardassians, Kira contacts Bajor, only to discover that the virus's creator, Dekon Elig, died many years ago. In desperation, Kira kidnaps Elig's uncooperative assistant in the affair, Surmak Ren. Once exposed to the virus as well, Ren combines his knowledge with Bashir's research and develops an antidote.

PLOT OVERSIGHTS

• After coming down with the aphasia virus, O'Brien is taken to the infirmary. At one point, frustrated over his lack of ability to communicate, he taps out a message on a padd (more on this in a minute). Part of the message reads, "STRIKE LIMITS VICTORY FROSTED WAKE SIMPLE HESITATION." Yet later O'Brien says, "victory strike limits frosted wake...simple hesitation." Note that this is the only time O'Brien uses the words out of order from what he's written. At times he only quotes snippets of the message, but every time the words are in exactly the same order as what he has written. (Granted, it may not be a nit, but I thought I'd bring it to your attention.)

• After catching Quark red-handed stealing food from a command-level

Trivia Questions

1. What does Captain Jaheel hope to transport to Largo V?

2. Of what did Dekon Elig die?

21

replicator, Odo tells the Ferengi that unauthorized access to crew quarters is a crime. At the end of the episode, however, Quark receives no punishment. (Maybe he plea-bargained his way out of getting charged by working in Ops during the crisis?)

• Gotta give Sisko credit for knowing his station. When Jake comes down with the aphasia virus, Bashir tells Sisko that he has converted some empty crew quarters to a hospital ward. Sisko immediately says that he will escort his son there and leaves before Bashir can tell him *which* crew quarters now house the hospital ward. Either most of the crew quarters are filled, or Sisko and Jake just wandered around the habitat ring until they heard people shouting, "Stomp the dark light! Fantastic comes ugly!"

• Toward the end of the episode, freighter captain Jaheel freaks out and decides he's going to leave the plague-infested DS9 no matter what the cost. He fires his aft thrusters even though the mooring clamps are still locked. One problem complicates another, and soon Sisko determines that Jaheel's ship will explode in fifteen minutes. Then Sisko blacks out with the virus, and Odo is left alone in Ops. The episode cuts away for a time to Kira and Surmak Ren in the runabout. (You remember good old Surmak. He's got a brother named "Stimpy.") When it returns, Odo is still in Ops. Thankfully, Quark shows up to volunteer his services and beams Odo out to the docking ring so Odo can manually blow the mooring clamps and get Jaheel's ship away from the station before it explodes. Just before

transporting, Odo reports that they have only five minutes left. So, in other words, he just sat there for ten minutes? (I'm okay with the fact that Odo may not know how to work the transporter even though he's been on the station for *years*. But I don't understand why he didn't just take off in a turbolift for the docking ring. Yes, that would leave Ops empty. But doesn't an exploding ship take precedence?)

• This virus sure affects people differently. Sisko doesn't come down with it until the very end, but when he does, he immediately goes sleepy-time. Everyone else is conscious well after they became aphasic.

• Arriving on the station, Surmak looks through Bashir's files on the virus. One of them looks like the progress report Bashir kept on his investigation. One section begins with, "17:45 [sic] Contacted Chief O'Brien, requested environmental engineering data for last twenty-four hours. First, military time is normally written without the colon (at least in the twentieth century). Second, contacting O'Brien for environmental engineering data would be a real trick, since his aphasia started the investigation in the first place. (Bashir: "Chief, I *need* those data!" O'Brien: "Salt way link, way *link*!")

CHANGED PREMISES

• Rom has yet to attain his "mechanical genius" status at this point in the series. In this episode, Quark must wait for O'Brien to fix his replicators. Later, Odo comments that Rom couldn't fix a bent straw. Yet by the time of "Heart of Stone," Rom is servicing Quark's replicators. Maybe after the bad experience with O'Brien's team in this episode Quark decided it was time to enroll Rom in one of those correspondence courses. ("Yes, friends, you, too, can be plasma-conduit-certified in just fifteen weeks using our patented...")

• In the last episode, Dax told Bashir that Trills do not look for romance the same way humans do. She went on to say that they find it a nuisance; a weakness of the young. Trills, she claimed, made the effort to "live on a higher plane." One episode later, she's walking down the hall with Kira and the boys are giving her the big smile and she's smiling back! She even tells Kira that she had forgotten what it was like to be a female, and she finds the attention quite enjoyable. Now, pray tell, what is the purpose of this attention? Would it not be that these men are looking for a little *romance*? Granted, no one expects Dax to be a cold fish (though she definitely leans that way in the first few shows). But if she's going to go around telling Bashir that she lives on a "higher plane," what's she doing making googly eyes on the promenade? (Personally, I think Dax reserves that "higher plane" junk for Julian Bashir alone.)

• Dax's eating habits are slipping as well. Last episode, she and Sisko went to Quark's for supper, and she ordered steamed azna. The conversation that followed definitely gave the impression that Dax eats steamed azna almost exclusively because it's good for her. Of course, in this episode, Quark offers her a double whipped I'Danan spice pudding, and she happily accepts.

EQUIPMENT ODDITIES

• In the episode's teaser, O'Brien works on a replicator and then orders hot coffee (black, double sweet). Note that this is the only thing we see O'Brien consume from a replicator during the entire show. After he takes a swig, the camera angle changes to show us the maintenance area behind the replicator. Ominously, the shot pulls back to Dekon Elig's nasty little device. As we watch, the device turns on. Later in the episode, Kira says that O'Brien came down with the virus right after working on the replicators. Apparently we're supposed to think that O'Brien got the virus from the cup of coffee he had at the beginning of the episode. There's only one problem: The device turned on *after* O'Brien got his cup of coffee. That cup of coffee wasn't infected. O'Brien must have gotten the virus from somewhere else. (Of course, with as much coffee as O'Brien drinks...)

• After hearing that the command-level replicators are working, Quark wanders over to his computer terminal and asks for a station layout. Nothing happens as he pauses. Then he asks to see the location of all the replicators on the command level. The computer asks for security authorization, Quark supplies it, and the screens change to show the information. What I want to know is how the computer knew that Quark was going to make an unauthorized request. Surely, simply asking to see a station layout isn't restricted. But Quark asked, and the computer doesn't do anything—somehow prescient that the second half of the request would render the whole request in need of an access code. (Gotta hand it to those Cardassian designers!)

• The user interface for manual input on the Starfleet padds (those little rectangular slabs of plastic that work like a laptop computer) is nothing short of amazing. In the infirmary, an aphasic O'Brien gets frustrated because he can't communicate. He grabs a padd, taps it about twelve times, and produces a message *fifteen words* long!

• Here's another equipment oddity for you concerning Odo. Sneaking into empty crew quarters to get some food and drink for his bar, Quark uses a hand-held device to open the door. He sets this device down on the cart he has brought with him and orders a Ferengi starduster from the replicator. Just as Quark picks up the drink, Odo morphs from the cart back into his humanoid shape. The device on the cart morphs at the same time! In other words, Odo had shape-shifted into a working electronic device! Even more odd, the device is not in physical contact with Odo, yet it retains its shape. It doesn't revert to its gelatinous state as it should (ac-cording to dialogue in "The Adversary").

• After taking a runabout to Bajor to kidnap Surmak, Kira hits the flight panel in front of her to initiate a conversation. The panel bows in noticeably. I would have thought Starfleet designs sturdier than that.

CONTINUITY AND PRODUCTION PROBLEMS

• I knew it! I *knew* it! I knew there was a "rotational speed control" for the station in Ops. You can actually *see* it in action in this episode. At one point, Sisko, Kira, and Odo discuss the fact that the aphasic device must have been installed eighteen years ago, when the station was built. They decide that Kira should try to find the Bajorans who invented the virus and get the antidote from them. Odo pipes up and remarks, "That's assuming they ever bothered to create one." The camera angle cuts back to Sisko, and behind his head you can see the stars clipping along and then *slowing down*!

TRIVIA ANSWERS
1. A shipment of tamen sasheer.
2. Neural trauma from phaser fire.

CAPTIVE PURSUIT

Star Date: unknown

As the episode begins, a damaged ship comes through the wormhole. Inside, O'Brien finds a being who will identify himself only as Tosk. Curious to learn how Tosk's ship was damaged, Sisko suggests that O'Brien show the visitor around the station and ply him for information. However, once Odo catches Tosk attempting to access a Security junction, Sisko can no longer afford the subtle approach. After imprisoning Tosk in a cell, Sisko demands to know what he was doing. Though Tosk refuses to answer, O'Brien deduces that his newfound friend was attempting to access the weapons locker.

A short time later, another ship appears from the Gamma Quadrant. Several armed individuals beam aboard and blast their way into Odo's Security office. One of the men locates Tosk and informs the others that the hunt is over. Pressed by Sisko for an explanation, the hunter reveals that his race has bred the Tosk for blood sport—that they have made the Tosk sentient to increase the challenge and danger to themselves. The situation appalls Sisko, but he agrees to turn Tosk over to his captors because the Prime Directive forbids his interference. At this, O'Brien arranges for Tosk to escape so the hunt can begin again.

PLOT OVERSIGHTS

• After coaxing Tosk off his ship, O'Brien takes him on a jaunt around the promenade. At one point, Tosk walks into the infirmary and asks O'Brien if it is a health center. As far as I can see, there are no patients on the beds, and Bashir stands, talking with a woman. So ...what led Tosk to suspect that it was a health center? Do hospitals still have that antiseptic smell in the twenty-fourth century? (I realize the beds might have given Tosk a clue. But for all he knew, Bashir might be running a house of ill repute!)

• Tosk sure gets the royal treatment from O'Brien. The quarters supplied for Tosk actually have a thick foam pad for the bed. Three episodes ago, in "Past Prologue," Kira escorted Tahna to a room that only had some thin, lumpy, vinyl-looking bumps for a bed.

• Shortly after O'Brien takes Tosk to the bar to have a look around, Quark

Trivia Questions

1. What is the name of the Dabo girl who accuses Quark of sexual advances?

2. Where does Tosk's captor get jolted backward by the weapons sensors?

tries to tempt the visitor with a trip to the holosuite. He suggests a holosuite program created by the "Brothers Quark." Boy, poor old Rom gets no respect at all. "Quark" is Quark's given name. If anything, Quark and Rom's family name would be "Keldar"—the name of Quark's father.

• Does everyone get free repairs once they get to DS9, or just visitors from the Gamma Quadrant? No wonder O'Brien Is always busy!

• Ex-feared terrorist and experienced fighter Kira Nerys makes a pitiful showing when the hunters first appear on the station. First, she allows one of them to flank her position by walking—*walking*(!)—around her. Then she gets off a good shot that shoves the guy into a wall but she lets him stand up, swing his weapon into position, and fire in her direction. (The whole time the guy was leaning back upright I was shouting, "Shoot him again! He's getting up! Shoot him again!")

• Speaking of this little exchange— when the hunter fires and blows up the doors of Odo's office—the blast throws Kira into the shape shifter's arms. Is it just me, or does Odo have his hand wrapped around an inappropriate place on Kira's upper torso?

• As Odo prepares for Tosk and his captor to leave DS9, O'Brien walks into the Security office and announces that Sisko told him to come down and escort the pair to a transporter pad. Understandably incensed at this intrusion into his area of responsibility, Odo storms off to talk with Sisko. Let's say that again: Odo *storms off* to talk with Sisko. Odo probably just forgot he was wearing a combadge. (Of course, if Odo used the combadge, then Sisko would have stopped O'Brien from carrying out his plan to assist Tosk, and it would have been a short show. Wink, wink.)

• I wonder what Sisko did with the hunters' ship. Obviously it only had a crew of four or five, and Tosk killed them all as he fought his way off the station. I say "obviously" because when Tosk flies away, the hunters' ship makes no effort to stop him (no missiles, no phaser fire, no tractor beam...). The only conclusion I can come to is that it's empty.

CHANGED PREMISES

• Evidently Starfleet has revised its information on the Gamma end of the wormhole. In "Emissary," Sisko claimed that he and Dax had traveled 70,000 light-years just after they traversed the passage for the first time. Yet, in this episode, Sisko tells Tosk that he has traveled 90,000 light-years.

• As O'Brien first takes Tosk for a walk on the promenade, Quark hustles a Bolian female out of his bar. He has caught her cheating, and she is no longer allowed in his bar. Interestingly enough, he says that he will give her money back! Apparently he has forgotten that the first rule of acquisition is "Once you have their money, you never give it back," as revealed five episodes later in "The Nagus." (I know. It was a cheap shot!)

EQUIPMENT ODDITIES

• Tosk seems to fly his ship sidesaddle. When O'Brien gives it the once-over, it appears that his pilot's stool is about forty-five degrees to the right of center. I don't suppose this is really a problem. I guess Tosk has gotten used to looking out the front window of his craft by turning his head to the left. It just seems odd. (On the other hand, this setup does allow O'Brien to go directly to the access panel in the floor, and maybe when you're being hunted it's more important to get to your damaged systems quickly. Besides, Tosk doesn't impress me as the kind of guy who would get a crick in his neck.)

• The doors on DS9 once again have read the script. Just before O'Brien leaves Tosk's quarters, the doors pop open with nary an anticipatory move from our kindly chief of Operations.

• After O'Brien leaves his quarters, Tosk goes to the computer and asks it to tell him where the weapons are stored. The computer tells Tosk the exact location (Habitat Level 5, Section 3) but then adds that a security clearance level of 7 is required to access it. Does this seem right? If this is such a sensitive area that it requires a security clearance, why blab its location to every Tosk, Dick, and Harry who comes along?

• Okay, let's talk about the Universal Translator. First, there's no question that language is a horrific problem when writing true *science* fiction. *Star Trek* tries to solve this problem by appealing to an ethereal, ubiquitous device that somehow automagically makes everyone speak Federation Standard (which to us sounds suspiciously like English, but in Japan—for instance—it sounds like Japanese). In this episode, you've got this guy named Tosk who is the first visitor

from the Gamma Quadrant. It is possible that some exploration mission from the Alpha Quadrant has encountered a race with a language that is similar to the one used by Tosk, so I *suppose* we could say it is *possible* that the UTs on DS9 already have a translation matrix. Indeed, they must, because Sisko can immediately communicate with Tosk. Later, however, we see O'Brien attempting to learn enough about the terminology of Tosk's ship to fix it. Tosk speaks of "arva nodes" that O'Brien eventually deduces are "ramscoops." Then, after this deduction, Tosk speaks of the arva nodes again. My question is this: If the Universal Translator can convert Tosk's language so spectacularly well—as it does in this episode —why doesn't this wonderful device automatically convert "arva nodes" into "Bussard ramscoops" in the first place as O'Brien and Tosk discuss his ship? And even if we allow that the UT didn't have that piece of information, surely it is eavesdropping on this conversation, right? (We see this eavesdropping in action during "Sanctuary.") When O'Brien makes the connection between the two terms, the UT would also make the connection. Yet Tosk still can refer to the units as "arva nodes." (I know this is grungy nitpicking and I know there's really no way to fix this, but I do find it interesting! Note also that at one point Tosk says, "seventeen minutes per rotation." "Minutes" would be Earth-specific—unless we're talking about degrees in a circle. "Rotation," on the other hand, could refer to any planet. So which is it, O mighty Universal

Translator? Are you going to give it to us in ambiguous terms or Earth-specific? Snicker, snicker, snicker.)

• I'm less than impressed with Cardassian access panels when Tosk works at the Security junction. He opens the hatch and the whole thing wobbles around like it's going to fall off the wall.

• Odo's Security office received an upgrade at some point since "A Man Alone" (two episodes ago). In that episode, the doors that lead back to the cells had octagonal windows. In this episode, the doors are solid.

• I'm confused. I thought I had that big table display in the center of Ops figured out, but evidently not. Just after O'Brien starts helping Tosk escape, Kira announces that a fight has broken out on the promenade. She then identifies the location of the altercation by pointing to the spot on the big horizontal table display. It's a bit difficult to tell exactly where she's pointing because someone walks in front of the camera (I hate it when that happens), but it looks like she's pointing into space! Either that or she's pointing at the docking ring. That's why I'm confused. I thought the prom-

enade was in the center core, just under Ops.

CONTINUITY AND PRODUCTION PROBLEMS

• The creators saved themselves an optical. Normally, when the crew of DS9 engages a tractor beam, an exterior shot illustrates this action. In this episode O'Brien puts a tractor beam on Tosk's ship and we never see it happening.

• This Tosk guy isn't used to having anyone else work on his ship. As he crawls out of the access hatch he accidentally *kicks* O'Brien in the head! (You can see Colm Meany look up at the guy and almost hear him say "Hey! Quit kicking me!" Then Colm realizes the director is going to keep rolling, so he continues with his part.)

• The hunter's ship looks like a refit of the Zalkonian vessel in "Transfigurations."

• Once again the stars move in Sisko's office but remain still in the window of Tosk's ship.

TRIVIA ANSWERS
1. Miss Sarda.
2. Security Checkpoint 4.

Q-LESS

Star Dates: 46531.2–46532.3

After a powerless runabout limps back to DS9, Sisko and crew find not only its crew but Vash as well (see the *NextGen* episodes "Captain's Holiday" and "Qpid"). Though she admits living in the Gamma Guadrant for two years, Vash refuses to give any details on how she arrived there in the first place. A short time later, O'Brien spots Q on the promenade and hurries to inform Sisko. The omnipotent being has had a falling out with Vash after promising to show her the universe ("Qpid"). He's back to make good on his pledge, but Vash no longer desires his company.

Meanwhile, power-er fluctuations— similar to those experienced on the runabout—begin buffeting the station as damaging graviton pulses erupt from seemingly nowhere. Q hastily denies any involvement, and even Sisko has to admit that the oddities aren't really "Q's style." With the station in peril, the crew finally traces the problem to Vash's collection of artifacts from the Gamma Quadrant and a particular crystal container. Once beamed off the station, the container

hatches and the embryonic being races into the wormhole and home. As life on DS9 returns to normal, Q tries one last time to reconcile his differences with Vash, but she refuses.

GREAT LINES

"Picard and his lackeys would have solved all this techno-babble hours ago."—Q to Sisko as he and his crew struggle to find the answer to the power fluctuations. This line is hysterical to me because, at the time in the series' life, the operative phrase on board the station seemed to be, "I don't know."

GREAT MOMENTS

As usual, John de Lancie packs this episode full of wonderful moments in his portrayal of Q. I know it's just silly-cute, but I love the fisticuffs scene between Q and Sisko.

PLOT OVERSIGHTS

• Early on, Sisko sets Dax to work trying to discover how Vash got to the Gamma Quadrant. Either Sisko never bothered to talk with O'Brien about this, or our good chief of Operations was in a snit about something and decided not to be forthcoming. Later we

Trivia Questions

1. Where does Vash store her artifacts in the assay office?

2. Who buys Vash's Gamma Quadrant dagger, and for what price?

discover that O'Brien knows that Vash met Q on the Sherwood Forest jaunt ("Qpid"). So let's see: You have a human in the Gamma Quadrant with no possible way to get there using known means. And you have this really powerful being who has shown on numerous occasions that he can cover large distances in a single bound. (In case you are wondering: Yes, Sisko would know this because he attended a Starfleet debriefing on Q.) Now, doesn't it seem that a reasonable hypothesis might be that Q might have had something to do with Vash's little trip to the Gamma Quadrant? (I know that we have the benefit of having been privy to the events of "Qpid," but this deduction seems pretty basic.)

• And while we're on the subject of basic deductive reasoning, let's talk about the power drains. The runabout lost power as it came back from the Gamma Quadrant. Shortly thereafter, the station started losing power. Oh, my; oh, dear; oh, me. How *shall* we figure out what's happening? O'Brien responds to this dilemma by griping about the terrible Cardassian internal sensors. Come on! Are we to believe that the best and the brightest in the twenty-fourth century are so dependent on machinery that they have lost the ability to do some simple problem-solving? You don't *need* sensors to solve this. First, you subtract everything that isn't common to the two occurrences and you have the crew of the runabout, Vash, and her artifacts. (I suppose we could add Q to this list because he could have been hanging around, even though Dax couldn't see him. But let's say for a moment that Sisko is right: It

isn't Q's style. You could always add Q back into the list if everything else failed.) Presumably the crew of the runabout returned to the station before and nothing happened. That leaves Vash and her artifacts. In other words, we now have a working hypothesis: The power outages have something to do with Vash and her artifacts. Testing this hypothesis is just as simple. Take Vash and her artifacts and put them on a runabout. Tractor-beam it out, away from the station. See what happens. If you get a power drain, tractor the runabout back to the station and start removing Vash and the artifacts one at a time until the power drains stop. Problem isolated. Case closed. (Granted, it's not very exciting, but that *is* how it would be done!)

• These Starfleet types sure do whine about the Cardassian mattresses a lot. In this episode, O'Brien takes Vash to her quarters and starts up with the "Cardassians make the lousiest beds in the whole galaxy" bit. Strangely enough, Vash's quarters show a thick piece of foam rubber on the bed, and it doesn't look all that uncomfortable when Q sits on it. (I suppose Cardassian foam rubber could be substantially less comfortable than the Federation kind. Maybe it has big rocks in it?)

• This episode commences a practice by females concerning Quark that I find somewhat shocking. Quark comes to Vash's quarters, offering to auction off her artifacts from the Gamma Quadrant. Unhappy with the percentage split Quark initially suggests, Vash grabs his ears and begins to give him *"oo-mox"*—a procedure first observed in "Ménage à Troi" *(TNG)*. It involves rubbing the considerable cartilage of Ferengi ears. According to "Ménage à Troi" *(TNG)*, the Ferengi consider their ears one of their most erogenous zones. *Oo-mox* is considered sexual foreplay. Attempting to put this little scene in its proper context without offending your sensibilities, my gentle readers, I am forced to ask: If Vash were negotiating with a human male and she wanted a better deal for herself, what part of his anatomy would she grab? And how would we as the viewers react if she did? (Granted, Vash seems the type who might actually try this, but I had a difficult time believing that Dax would do so—until she exhibited precisely the same behavior in "Facets.")

• After inviting Vash to dinner, Bashir waits for her in what looks like the replimat—an interesting choice given that they agreed to meet in Quark's, and, in fact, Vash goes there for their rendezvous.

• Near the end of the episode, the graviton waves send the station hurtling toward the wormhole. Kira reports that they have only eighteen minutes left before they enter it and the station is ripped to shreds. Yet Sisko never bothers to call for an evacuation.

• I realize that I may not measure up to the brave and valiant standards set for Starfleet officers, but—at the end of the episode, when Sisko tells O'Brien to beam the container 500 meters off the docking—I think I would have told O'Brien to transport it out a wee bit farther. (The maximum range of a transporter is 40,000 kilometers, after all.)

EQUIPMENT ODDITIES

• Soon after the episode begins, Sisko and Kira desperately struggle to get the door of the powerless runabout open after it has docked at the station. O'Brien and Bashir arrive moments later, and—as Bashir drones on ominously about the life support levels—the chief scrambles for a power capacitor to charge the energy system just enough so Sisko and Kira can pry open the hatch. In a truly amazing display of technoamnesia, no one even brings up the possibility of *transporting* the occupants of the runabout to safety.

• The assay office has a Cardassian MK-12 retinal scanner with an L-90 enhanced resolution filter. Bajorans run the assay office. Where did they get the scanner? Did Bajorans buy a piece of Cardassian technology? Not likely at this point in the series. At this point in the series the Bajorans *hate* the Cardassians. (And I'm sure Starfleet must make a decent retinal scanner. We saw one in *Star Trek II: The Wrath of Khan*.) More likely, the assay office inherited their scanner when the Cardassians vacated the station. That's interesting, because O'Brien told Sisko—when the commander first arrived in "Emissary"— that the Cardassians took "every component of value."

• For some reason, the computer in the assay office doesn't catalog Vash's last item—the crystal container. On all the other items, the computer chirps to signal the entry. But on the last item, it doesn't. (Actually, this whole process is a bit twitchy. Somehow the computer knows exactly when the assay guy is done describing an item. The only thing

I can figure is the computer is watching him and whenever he hands the item to his assistant, the computer assumes the description is complete. Unfortunately, this protocol doesn't hold for the first and last items.)

• After Quark visits Vash's quarters, the doors only open three-quarters of the way to let him out. Moments later, Bashir enters and the doors open all the way.

• While trying to find out what went wrong with the powerless runabout, O'Brien tells Sisko that the warp core is on the verge of collapse. Interestingly enough, the runabout is still docked at DS9. (If I remember correctly, when a warp core collapses, bad things happen. Sure wish Commander Deanna Troi was around so I could find out for certain. See my review of the *NextGen* episode "Disaster" in the *NextGen Guides*.)

• The crew must have always suspected that the wormhole might try to suck them in someday. As soon as DS9 heads in that direction, Sisko calls for thrusters to stabilize their position. We immediately see the thrusters firing, and evidently they are exactly where they must be to do the needed job. That's very, very fortunate. You might remember from "Emissary" that the station only has *one* set of thrusters, and they are all clustered on *one* side of the station.

CONTINUITY AND PRODUCTION PROBLEMS

• While storing her artifacts in the assay office, Vash shows the head guy a crystal container. He responds, "Beautiful. I've never seen anything like it." Obviously the guy has never seen an Albeni meditation crystal. (Riker gave one to Beata in the *NextGen* episode "Angel One.")

• This is a good one! At one point, Sisko pays O'Brien a visit in the powerless runabout. The chief is trying to figure out what happened. The floor access panel directly in front of the transporter station is open when Sisko first arrives. When O'Brien closes the hatch, pay close attention to the area between Sisko's legs and the left side of the screen. Just beyond the transporter station you'll see what looks like a microphone cord snake into the picture.

• For the last item in the auction, Vash displays the crystal container by opening its box only about halfway. In fact, from one camera angle, you can't even see the crystal—only the box. What's really interesting is that one of the high bidders looks at the box from just about this same angle. Why doesn't Vash just open the box all the way so the guy who's bidding can see the crystal?

• It's hard to tell because of the less than stellar quality of my recording of this episode, but: Do Dax's spots look really light at the end of this episode?

TRIVIA ANSWERS
1. Cubicle 19.
2. Quark's cousin Stoll for 105 bars of gold-pressed latinum.

★ PERSONAL FAVORITES

As I've said in the previous guides, I'm not sure why these nits and "odd little moments" are some of my favorites. Most of the ones listed below didn't jump out at me the first time I watched the episodes. But after the third or fourth viewing, my eyes happened to wander over the right part of the screen at the right time. Others were pointed out by members of the Nitpicker's Guild and confirmed with a smile as I finally saw them, too. I hope you find them enjoyable as well!

1. *Spock's Visage.* I freely admit that this one is difficult to see. And even if you can see it, you'll agree that it's not a nit. If it really exists, it's a lovely homage. Watch carefully during the title sequence for *Star Trek: Deep Space Nine.* Just after the comet passes, focus a bit to the right of the center of your television screen. You might be able to make out the face of Spock—angled to the left—in the comet dust. It seems to form from nowhere and then travels quickly to the left before dissipating.

2. *She's Pulling His Leg...for Real!* At the end of "Past Prologue," Kira and a former associate named Tahna Los tussle in a runabout. Tahna is attempting to launch an explosive that will collapse the wormhole and keep Bajor for Bajorans. To launch the explosive, Tahna must press a big red button mounted on the ceiling of the cockpit. Kira is on the floor. Tahna is standing. So what strategy does Kira—ex-freedom fighter, ex-feared terrorist, ex-"really nasty person on a bad day"—employ? Well, she doesn't direct a blow to Tahna's legs. She employs a tactic from the Winnie-the-Pooh martial arts system. She sits on the floor and pulls his leg!

3. *Kung Fu Repair Philosophy.* Speaking of martial arts, "Captive Pursuit" features a "bred for the hunt" individual named Tosk. When his ship limps up to the station, O'Brien lends a hand, helping Tosk repair it. Then, while climbing out of the bowels of the ship, Tosk accidently kicks O'Brien in the head!

4. *Must Be One of Those Cardassian Mic-Cord Snakes.* During "Q-Less," Sisko visits O'Brien as the latter attempts to repair a powerless runabout. Just after O'Brien closes a floor hatch, a microphone cord snakes into the picture on the left side of the screen.

5. *Kentanna, Final Resting Place for Hippie Outcasts.* The Skrreeans make up the aliens-of-the-week for the episode "Sanctuary." Having found freedom

from their cruel oppressors the T'Rogorans, the Skrreeans now seek "Kentanna"—their promised legendary home. Three million strong make this pilgrimage, and DS9 soon fills with the dazed refugees. Although no decipherable audio exists above the crowd roar as a particularly large group enters the promenade, closed captioning give us some indication of the Skrreeans' true origin. The subtitles read: "This is great!" "This is incredible." "This is pretty far out." "Dig this place."

6. *The Colonists of Eternal Doom.* Some legends are almost too sorrowfully strange to tell. The creators give us the briefest hint of one such legend in "The Maquis, Part I." During this episode, we see an exterior shot of a colony. In the background, an aqueduct snakes up a mountain. It just so happens that this exterior shot is a reuse from the episode "Ensigns of Command" *(TNG).* Since nitpickers don't deal in reality, we must conclude that these poor colonists first crashed on a planet bathed in hyperonic radiation. Many died, but they finally adapted, only to have the *Enterprise* come and evacuate them because their world was deeded to the Sheliak. (We know this from "Ensigns of Command.") *Then* ...these poor people moved to another world, started all over, built an exact replica of their old colony...only to have the Federation deed their planet to the Cardassians!

7. *Miles "Jackson" O'Brien.* I usually don't comment on the costuming of *Star Trek.* After all, who knows what people will be wearing *hundreds* of years from now? For "Tribunal," however, I made an exception. In this episode O'Brien stands trial on Cardassia Prime. The prisoner outfit that O'Brien must endure for the entire episode consists of a shirt and pants wrapped with strip-mesh belts. As I say in my review of "Tribunal," the costume makes O'Brien look like a reject from a Michael Jackson video.

8. *Yet More Evidence of Time-Traveling Incursions.* In "Visionary" Bashir uses a "tool" that is actually the warp nacelle from the plastic model kit of a Romulan warbird! The only question is: Why would Starfleet travel all the way back to our time just to acquire the packaging for this instrument? Is plastic exorbitantly expensive in the twenty-fourth century?

9. *Nothing Serious, Just a Fluff Piece.* "Facets" features a Dabo girl named Leeta. At the very end of the program—just after Rom announces that a newly attired Nog is "coming"—Leeta stands in the background near the Dabo table in her low-cut, skin-tight Dabo girl outfit. Unexpectedly, she reaches up, grabs both sides of her outfit, and gives her cleavage a quick fluff.

DAX

A past host's life intrudes on Jadzia Dax when Ilon Tandro attempts to kidnap the Trill for extradition to Klaestron IV. When thwarted by Sisko, Ilon reveals that Dax will stand trial for the betrayal and subsequent murder of his father, General Ardelon Tandro, thirty years ago during a civil war. Though the Federation treaty with Klaestron allows unilateral extradition and Ilon's papers *are* in order, Sisko uses the fact that DS9 is a Bajoran station to stall the process and arrange a hearing. Before it commences, he sends Odo to Klaeston IV to investigate the charges, since Dax will not discuss them.

A Bajoran arbiter arrives, and the extradition hearing begins. Sisko argues that Jadzia Dax and Curzon Dax—the host during the alleged incident—are two different people, that she should not stand trial for someone else's crimes. Obviously, Ilon disagrees. Even after many witnessess, the arbiter's decision still seems unpredictable. Then Odo arrives with Tandro's widow. She tells the arbiter that the hearings are unnecessary—

Trivia Questions

1. What airlock does Ilon Tandro use when making his escape with Dax in tow?

2. What is the widow Tandro's first name?

that she knows Curzon did not betray General Tandro, nor was he responsible for her husband's death because Curzon was in her bed at the time. The arbiter suggests that Ilon reexamine his request for extradition and ends the hearings.

PLOT OVERSIGHTS

• In one scene, Odo blackmails Quark into letting Sisko use the bar for the hearing. Odo claims there's no other suitable place on the station. Really? I find that hard to believe. This is a huge station. What about the wardroom—seen later in "The Search, Part I"?

• Starfleet protocol can sometimes produce the oddest actions. Just after the arbiter calls the final one-hour recess, an officer walks up to Kira and hands her a padd that states a message is coming in from Odo on Klaestron IV. She looks at it and hands it to Sisko, who is about two feet away and wasn't doing anything when the officer first appears. So...why didn't he just hand the padd to Sisko?

• Klaestron IV must lie very, very close to DS9. "Emissary" establishes that DS9 is 160 million kilometers from Bajor. That may sound like a

35

lot, but in cosmic terms, it's nothing. It's only about 9 light-minutes—approximately the same distance as Earth is from the sun. Hold on to that piece of information while I discuss the location of Klaestron IV for a few moments. After the arbiter calls a final 1-hour recess, Sisko receives a call from Klaestron IV. It's Odo, and he's uncovered the affair between Tandro's widow and Curzon Dax. Following this conversation, Odo meets with the widow, and the two of them fly to DS9. They interrupt the extradition hearing *2 minutes* after it reconvenes. Let's say that Odo could run over to the widow's house, have the conversation, decide to bring her to DS9, beam her up to the runabout, and start for home in about 12 minutes. (I think you'll agree that those activities probably would take a bit longer, but let's be generous for the creators' sakes.) That leaves about fifty minutes for the runabout to get from Klaestron IV to DS9. From the dialogue in this episode, we know that the maximum speed of a runabout is warp 5. The question is: Assuming a speed of warp 5 (214 times the speed of light, according to *The Star Trek Encyclopedia*) and a travel time of 50 minutes, what distance will the runabout cover? (We are, of course, completely ignoring docking time and the like.) Given that the speed of light is approximately 300,000 kilometers per second, the runabout would traverse 192.6 billion kilometers (300,000 times 214 times 60 times 50). Yes, that's right. More than 19 trillion—with a "t"—kilometers. Now, that may seem like a

bunch at first. But in space? Well, space is big! For instance, Alpha Centauri—the closest star system to our own—is more than 4 light-years away. Using this same terminology, Klaestron IV would only be about 7.5 light-*days* away from DS9. Since DS9 sits so close to Bajor, that means the Bajoran system and the Klaeston system are almost within rock-throwing distance in cosmic terms!

CHANGED PREMISES

• In "Past Prologue," both Kira and Odo make the unqualified statement that Odo's never been any good at pretense. I mentioned in my review of that episode that I knew the statements were going to be trouble for the creators. In "Dax" we see Odo using pretense to convince Quark to let Sisko use the bar for the hearing. When Quark refuses the direct approach, Odo begins talking about building codes and how walls will have to be moved. Definitely pretense.

• The Trill were first introduced in the episode "The Host" *(TNG)*. In that episode Dr. Crusher falls in love with a Trill named Odan. Everything about the episode indicates that the Trill humanoid hosts are little better than robotic extensions for the slugs that possess them. In my review of the episode in *The Nitpicker's Guide for Next Generation Trekkers* (Volume I), I did a little rant about my dismay over Crusher's quick acceptance of this exploitation of humanoids. I noted that the Trill symbionts didn't have the gumption to get off their backsides and evolve opposable thumbs—choosing instead to steal their use from another species. Of course, then *Deep Space Nine* started up and this episode came along—supposedly "explaining" the real relationship between Trill host and symbiont. First, let me say that if people want to compete to have a slug stuck inside them, it's fine with me. My problem is that the Trill race first introduced in "The Host" bears little resemblance to the Trill race shown in *Star Trek: Deep Space Nine*. There are deep, fundamental differences that I discussed in depth in *The Nitpicker's Guide for Next Generation Trekkers, Volume II*. Here's the quick summary: Odan's host had lumps on his forehead, Dax's host has spots; Odan's relationship to its host was one of parasitism, Dax's relationship to its host is one of mutualism; Odan's race was relatively unknown to the Federation, Dax's race is well known to the Federation. (Curzon Dax went to Klaestron IV as a Federation mediator thirty years ago, and Jadzia Dax is a Starfleet officer.) And then there's the transporter thing, but I'll save those comments for "The Alternate." (*And* what about that thingamawidget that Odan ran across his stomach at the beginning of the *NextGen* episode "The Host"?)

• When discussing Curzon's indiscretion with Tandro's widow, Jadzia Dax seems genuinely embarrassed by it. She talks to Sisko about "one of her kind" stumbling—speaks of Curzon acting "shamefully with another man's wife." Her statements all appear to orginate from a high moral conviction. Oddly enough, in a later episode, Jadzia Dax gives Sisko ad-

vice that seems diametrically opposed to this high moral conviction. In "Second Sight," Sisko falls for a married woman, and Dax encourages him to pursue the relationship.

EQUIPMENT ODDITIES

• Ilon's ship does initially depart from the station, but Sisko captures it in a tractor beam. Interestingly enough, the tractor beam erupts from the same location as the station's phasers in "Emissary." Must be that versatile Cardassian design.

• Speaking of tractor beams, it looked like the ship was fleeing the station at a high rate of speed. What happens to the inhabitants of the craft when the tractor beam grabs hold? Do they all tumble forward and crash into the windshield?

• Sisko evidently grew tired of using Cardassian technology for his desktop terminal. In this episode he sports a shiny, new Starfleet-issue model.

CONTINUITY AND PRODUCTION PROBLEMS

• During the kidnapping at the beginning of the program, one of Ilon's people knock Dax to the floor. She lands semiconscious on her stomach with her face looking to the left. A few moments later, the kidnappers stoop to pick her up, and—though she's still on her stomach—now her face looks to the right.

• If memory serves, the model used for the Klaestron ship originally came from the episode "Darmok" *(TNG)* and belonged to the Children of Tama. I believe it also serves again as a T'Lani vessel in "Armageddon Game."

• The matte paintings first seen in "Angel One" *(TNG)* serve yet again! This time they are a cityscape on Klaestron IV. These matte paintings also appeared in "Samaritan Snare" *(TNG)*, "First Contact" *(TNG)*, and "The Mind's Eye" *(TNG)*. (And they appear as well in the *Voyager* episode "Ex Post Facto.")

• Tandro's widow and Data's mom from "Inheritance" *(TNG)* bear a striking resemblance to each other. Mere coincidence? I wonder.

• During the scenes in Sisko's office the stars just barely creep by in his window. During the scenes in Dax's quarters, the stars stay rock-solid still. (And so it goes.)

TRIVIA ANSWERS

1. Airlock 5.
2. Enina.

★
THE PASSENGER

Star Date: unknown

Traveling back to DS9, Kira and Bashir intercept a distress signal from a transport ship. Beaming over, they find the vessel on fire. While Kira runs off to check the central power linkage, Bashir ministers to a woman overcome by the smoke. Then—detecting vital signs behind a locked door—Bashir rushes in to help. With his dying breath, the severely wounded man inside grabs Bashir by the throat and says with a hiss, "Make me live."

Back on the station, the woman introduces herself as Ty Kajada, a Kobliad Security officer. She identifies the dead man as Vantika, a ruthless criminal whose sole focus had been to extend his life. Though Vantika's body is in Bashir's morgue, Kajada knows the criminal has faked his death before. She also knows that Vantika had set out for DS9 before she apprehended him. She worries that Vantika plans to steal a secured shipment of deuridium that will soon arrive at DS9. Surprisingly enough, Vantika almost succeeds by using the body of...Julian Bashir. In the last moment of his life, Vantika transferred

his consciousness to Bashir by using a microscopic generator hidden under his fingernail. Just in time, Sisko and crew find a way to thwart the theft and return Bashir to normal. (Well, maybe. See below.)

Trivia Questions

1. What is the name of the Kobliad transport at the beginning of this episode?

2. What is the name of the mercenary who wants a 70 percent payment in advance?

RUMINATIONS

It's always nice to see Starfleet personnel moving up in the ranks. This episode introduces a lieutenant named George Primmin. You may not know this but he served on the Enterprise *as an ensign! He works with La Forge in Main Engineering during "Brothers."* (Thanks to George H. Daley, Jr., of Owosso, Michigan, for pointing this out.)

PLOT OVERSIGHTS

• Following Ty Kajada's appearance on the station, I can find no evidence that the crew even bothered to call Kobliad Security to ask if they had an officer by that name working for them. (They must have done it when we weren't looking because I can't imagine they would just take her word for it.)

• At one point, Dax discusses with Bashir her hypothesis that Vantika was working on transferring his consciousness to another humanoid. The

---

39

good doctor responds that there is "plenty of room." He says, "A humanoid only uses a small portion of the brain." This statement sound suspiciously similar to "humans only use 10 percent of their brains"—something I've heard many times over the years. Somewhere along the way, however, I had also heard that the statement was just folklore. Jon Liming of Signal Hill, California, was kind enough to do some research for me. After consulting numerous professors, colleagues, and texts, he concluded that the statement about humans using only 10 percent of their brains is "one of the most overused, undersupported myths that has been accepted as canon by the general public."

• At one point, Lieutenant George Primmin meets with Odo to discuss the security arrangements for the deuridium shipment. Oddly enough, Odo leaves his door open! (Of course, if he didn't leave the door open then Kajada couldn't make her dramatic appearance after the database service goes down and announce that Vantika did the same thing on Rigel VII—which, by the way, must be the most inhabited planetary system in the galaxy. Look it up in *The Star Trek Encyclopedia* sometime!)

• Amazingly—even after Dax discovers that Vantika transferred his consciousness through touch—Sisko doesn't bother to ask either Kira or Bashir if Vantika touched them before he died.

• I'm a bit confused over Vantika's continued efforts to steal the deuridium shipment. Kajada claims that Van-

tika is obsessed with prolonging his life. As a Kobliad, it makes perfect sense for him to attempt to acquire the shipment because he needs it to survive. But by the time the actual theft occurs, Vantika has transferred himself to Bashir's body. He doesn't need the deuridium any longer, and if he's really obsessed with self-preservation, one would think he would want to quietly escape from the station and make the most of his newfound health.

• Near the end of the episode Dax uses a transporter to remove the Vantika-affected brain cells from Bashir and places them in a container. A few comments about this process. First, Dax says that she has programmed the transporter to isolate any "glial cells with Vantika's neural pattern." While the understanding of neurobiology is certain to change over the next four hundred years, at the time of this writing glial cells are thought to provide only a supportive role within the mature human brain. Dax probably should also be transporting Bashir's affected "neurones." Second, when the processes concludes, she whips out a tricorder and pronounces, "He's clear." Given that humans don't just use a small portion of the brains and Dax has just removed an unknown percentage of Bashir's brain, I couldn't help but think, "Yeah, he's clear, all right. He's also Forrest Gump!" (One also wonders if Dax has finally grown weary of Bashir's sexual advances and decided to use this opportunity to make a few minor adjustments.)

• After taking custody of what's left of her prisoner, Kajada pulls out her weapon and disintegrates the container—leaving a *lovely* scorch mark on the equipment! If I were Bashir I'd be ticked about this. The good doctor—obviously still recovering from Dax's gentle lobotomizing ministrations—simply stares with a blank look on his face.

CHANGED PREMISES

• The number of previous hosts for Dax was still in flux at the time of this episode. Odo tells Quark that Dax has lived ten lifetimes, and he says it very emphatically. The very next episode, "Move Along Home," revises the figure to seven.

EQUIPMENT ODDITIES

• This episode opens with a discussion in the runabout between Kira and Bashir. Apparently Bashir had just revived a woman after Kira's tricorder clearly stated that the woman was dead. After Kira expresses her amazement, Bashir pops off with a comment to the effect that tricorders are very accurate when it comes to the living but not so accurate when it comes to the dead. In other words, you can't always tell that a person is dead just by using a tricorder. Surprisingly enough, only moments later, Bashir pronounces Vantika dead by using...you guessed it...a *tricorder*! (I knew this bit with the tricorder and dead people would be a recurring bit as soon as I heard Bashir's statement. As you will see, it is! After all, that's the main tool Bashir uses for diagnostics, and he's the doctor guy, and—in the greatest tradition of *Star Trek*—that means he *is* going to be around dead

people. "He's dead, Sisko.")

• Arriving on the transport, Kira and Bashir seem genuinely surprised that it is on fire. Wait a minute: Didn't they scan the interior before beaming over?

• Coming back from her investigation of the central power linkage on the transport ship, Kira carries some kind of newfangled fire extinguisher. I must say that I am really impressed with this device because the fire seems to die down considerably before *anything* comes out of the tube. (I can just hear the flames now: "Oh, no! She's got one of those new fire suppression systems. Quick! Everybody duck and cover!" This, of course, causes the flames to commit suicide and die of oxygen deprivation as they dive under the rug, but then, no one ever said fire was that intelligent.) Seriously, the effects guys *did* try to cover this up by making the sound of the extinguisher begin as the flames start to dissipate, but I've watched it several times and it looks like Kira's extinguisher doesn't start working until well *after* the fire disappears on its own!

• In the excitement of the moment with the fire and all, Kira contacts the runabout and says, "Computer, four to transport." Nothing happens. Apparently Kira has forgotten that the runabout can transport only two people at a time (as we learn in "The Homecoming").

• Shortly after the episode begins, Quark serves Dax an iced raktajino with extra cream and makes a pass at her. Odo tells Quark that he doesn't have a chance. He says every man on the station would like to buy Dax a raktajino. Quark agrees to this but notes that he has the raktajino machine. Aside from the fact that Dax seems to have abandoned her steamed azna (see "A Man Alone"), I distinctly recall others ordering raktajinos from the replicators. Is there something special about making the "iced" version?

• During a scene in the infirmary, Bashir ministers to a patient and then reminds him to lift with his back straight and use "the antigrav degenerator." First, the closed captioning says "antigrav generator," which makes a lot more sense. Second, according to "Melora," antigrav technology doesn't work on DS9. That's why Bashir had to replicate an old-fashioned wheelchair for Melora.

• Man, this Vantika guy is something. According to Sisko and Dax, this guy stored his entire consciousness in a *microscopic* generator. If he could really do this, how do you know he's really dead? He could have made thousands of these things—literally sprinkling them everywhere. Anyone who touched one would have his neural patterns imprinted on their brains. (Yikes!)

• Seems to me that I remember the Borg attempting to lock onto the *Enterprise* with a tractor beam in "The Best of Both Worlds" *(TNG)*. It also seems to me that they couldn't because the *Enterprise*'s shields were up. Yet, in this episode, Vantika/Bashir raises the shields on the freighter, and Sisko still manages to lock onto the vessel with a tractor beam. (Must be a new design.)

• Vantika/Bashir's phaser seems to have some sort of odd targeting filter on it. On the freighter, Vantika whips it out, firing it at one of his mercenaries, but the beam travels away from the phaser at a really weird angle.

• DS9 definitely needs more transporter stations. After temporarily restoring Bashir's control of his body, the crew beam him to Ops. A *dangerous* criminal. They beam him into *Ops*. Right.

CONTINUITY AND PRODUCTION PROBLEMS

• Kajada sure looks an awful lot like a mercenary named Vekor from "Gambit, Part I" *(TNG)*, doesn't she?

• During a meeting with Sisko, Dax mispronounces Vantika's name as "van-TEE-kah." She corrects herself moments later. (It's a minor point, but, hey, aren't they all?)

• Finding herself shut out of the security preparations for the shipment, Kajada storms into Odo's office. When Odo won't allow her to access the file, Kajada leaves in a huff. Watch carefully as she goes. Odo's doors close, Kajada walks off in a straight line. Then, thinking she's clear of the shot, she stops, turns around, and walks back a few steps before finally wandering off to her left.

• Beaming onto the freighter that carries the shipment of deuridium, Vantika's mercenaries kill the three crew members who are on the bridge. A very strange thing happens to both the male crew members when they are hit with the energy weapons. Although the blasts catch both of them in the chest, sparks erupt from the region near the zipper on their pants! (I have made a conscious decision *not* to speculate on the reason for this because *anything* I said at this juncture would no doubt be misinterpreted.)

• After coming to himself on the freighter, Bashir struggles to drop the shields. In one shot we see his hand hovering over two large rectangular buttons. In the close-up, his hand is suddenly over a cluster of small buttons.

• This isn't really a nit, just a surprise. Did you realize that the men's uniform pants have *stirrups*? When Bashir comes back from the freighter and is rolled underneath the transporter you can clearly see them going around the bottom of his right foot.

TRIVIA ANSWERS
1. *Reyab.*
2. Durg.

MOVE ALONG HOME

Star Date: unknown

Expecting to conduct a "first contact" with a new race from the Gamma called the Wadi, Sisko spends the next six hours sitting at Quark's bar, listening to the Wadi play—and win—Dabo. The Wadi love games. Eventually Sisko calls it a night. That's when Quark decides he's had enough. He attempts to cheat the Wadi out of their winnings, only to be caught by Falow, the Wadi leader. With menacing seriousness, the Wadi leader produces a box. When opened, it creates a three-dimensional playing area.

As Falow assigns four players to the second level of the board, Sisko, Kira, Dax, and Bashir awake to find themselves in a maze of corridors and rooms. All too soon, Quark discovers that the dangers he chooses for his game pieces are simultaneously delivered to Sisko and the others on the life-size playing area. Forced on by the Wadi, a worried Quark manages to play the game through to the last level, only to lose all his pieces in the final round. The Wadi then close the box and depart, leaving Quark to ponder the deaths of his friends. (No, not really. Just joking. Actually, Sisko and the others appear in the bar, safe and sound. The Wadi say it was just a game and then leave.)

GREAT LINES

"Yes...yes...yes...now where are the games?"—Falow to Sisko, dismissing the commander's formal introductions in favor of the information he really wants. I love the look on Sisko's face here. He's gone to all the trouble to get ready for first contact with Falow and his associates and all they want to do is go to Quark's!

GREAT MOMENTS

The look on Sisko's face when he realizes that he will have to hop around and say a rhyme to get through a force field is truly priceless. (I'm told that Avery Brooks was less than enthusiastic about this scene!)

PLOT OVERSIGHTS

• Early on, Sisko tells Jake that first contact is one of the most important missions. By implication he seems to refer to the upcoming meeting with the Wadi. Yet moments earlier, Sisko explains that Vulcans made contact

Trivia Questions

1. What is Falow's position among the Wadi?

2. Who wrote the revised first contact procedures for Starfleet?

with the Wadi three weeks ago in the Gamma Quadrant. I'm confused. The Vulcans are a part of the Federation—one of the founding members, in fact. Didn't *they* make "first contact"?

• Speaking of the Vulcans, they are apparently the only source of information that the Wadi have on the Alpha Quadrant. But when they disembark their ship they immediately ask about Quark's. So...the *Vulcans* recommended Quark's?

• These Wadi know a whole lot more about Starfleet than they are letting on. When Falow first meets Sisko, he sees two officers in dress uniforms: Kira in her Bajoran uniform and Bashir in his normal uniform. Then Falow begins the game. The scene shows Sisko in his pajamas rolling over and waking up in his standard uniform. Presumably the situation was similar with Dax. How did Falow know that Sisko and Dax should be dressed in their normal uniforms and not dress uniforms? Along the same lines, Falow also manages to supply them with working combadges (sort of, see below) and working tricorders. All this from a "first contact" situation?

• There seems to be a bit of a time problem in this episode. Follow the sequence. As Sisko prepares to leave for the meeting with the Wadi, Jake arrives at their quarters. They talk. Sisko goes to meet Wadi. Sisko spends six hours watching Wadi play games. Sisko goes back to his quarters. Jake is still up. Sisko tells Jake to go to bed. Sisko goes to bed. My guess is that it's no later than two or three in the morning. That would mean the Wadi arrived at about 2200 hours. (Remember

that there seem to be twenty six hours in a Bajoran day.) True, 2200 hours for an arrival seems a bit late—ten o'clock in the evening to you and me—but putting the Wadi arrival any earlier makes the time problem even worse. Okay, so Sisko goes to bed. The episode seems to indicate that shortly after this Quark tries to cheat the Wadi. They get mad. They start setting up their game. Sisko wakes up in the game. Jake shows up at the Security office and tells Odo that his dad is missing—that they were supposed to talk first thing in the morning, but when he got up, his dad was gone. Odo goes up to Ops and meets with Primmin. Primmin greets Odo with "Good morning to you." It's got to be several hours later, doesn't it? Is there any way that Jake would be at Odo's office any earlier than six in the morning? The action then returns to Quark's. Falow calls for last wagers—stating, "The board is ready." Did it really take *hours* to set up this board?

There are only a few places where the time could have gone. Possibly the Wadi arrived very late at the station and Sisko actually spent the entire night in Quark's. But if that's true, then Jake would have stayed up *all night* as well, and I have a hard time believing the young man would be awake enough to notice that his dad was missing until sometime in midmorning. By then, Odo would already know that the commander and his senior officers had disappeared. Or...possibly Quark let the Wadi win for several more hours before trying to cheat them. This seem just as unlikely, given Quark's disposition just before Sisko left. Finally, it is *pos-*

sible that the Wadi game actually takes several hours to prepare (though I can't see why it would). This would mean that Sisko and the others wandered around aimlessly inside the game for *hours* with nothing to do. (No wonder they are not amused!) Unfortunately, this possibility seems just as unlikely as the other two. Would you want to participate in a game where you were placed on the playing field and then had to twiddle your thumbs for hours while everything else was set up? Doesn't seem very "playable" to me!

CHANGED PREMISES

• Dax sets the record straight in this episode. Last time, Odo claimed she had lived ten lifetimes. In the caves at the end of this episode, Dax says seven.

EQUIPMENT ODDITIES

• With Sisko approaching the airlock, Bashir frantically explains to Dax and Kira that he can't find his dress uniform. Is it against Starfleet policy to replicate a new one? (And yes, Cardassian replicators can make more than just food. O'Brien replicated a new racket in "Rivals" and says that Keiko has been replicating longer dresses in "Paradise.")

• Speaking of replicators, why are gems valuable to Quark? (The Wadi use them for currency when playing games.) In "Catspaw" *(TOS),* Kirk claims Starfleet has the technology to manufacture the baubles at will. (This brings up another question: What is this gold-pressed latinum, anyway? Can it be replicated? If not, why? Is there a law against it?)

• Okay, so let's talk about the com-

badge situation. Sisko, in his pajamas, rolls over in bed and wakes up lying on the floor of the life-size playing area of the Wadi game. He's dressed in his uniform, and it has a combadge. Sisko stands, slaps his chest, and says, "Sisko to Ops," followed by "Sisko to Security." He receives no answer to either hail. The commander then locates Bashir. Kira and Dax soon arrive. So the group can split up and search more area, Dax tests to see if the combadges are working. She slaps her chest. The combadge chirps. Kira's communicator chirps, and Kira slaps it. From this, it appears that Dax concludes the combadges are working. A bit later—after hearing the little girl saying her "Allamaraine" lines—Sisko hits his combadge and calls for the others. They quickly arrive. Obviously the combadges are working. So why didn't anyone answer Sisko when he initially tried to use his? Granted, he directed the call to Ops and Security, but when Dax slaps her combadge in the test, Kira's chirps *immediately*. This leads me to believe that in a remote situation where a master computer is not controlling the combadges, all combadges chirp when one of them is tapped. (This actually makes sense.) But if the combadges chirped when Sisko first tried to use his, why didn't Dax or Kira slap theirs and respond to Sisko's page? (I *know* why Bashir didn't respond: He was too busy screaming, trying to wake himself up from the dream he thought he was having!)

CONTINUITY AND PRODUCTION PROBLEMS

• This episode begins with Sisko in a

dress uniform. Interestingly enough, it appears to be based on the *NextGen* uniform style, not the *DS9* uniform style.

• To move from the second shap of the game to the third shap, Sisko and the other must solve a riddle. It involves a little girl saying a rhyme in cadence and hopping across the floor toward an exit. A force field blocks the way to the exit. To get through, our heroes must say the rhyme, hop on the right squares, and do the hand motions all at the same time! (I bet Starfleet Academy never had a course on this!) No doubt the scene was very difficult to produce. Under the dialogue, the little girl keeps saying the rhyme, and at strategic times, the actors have to join her. The timing must have been critical. Surprisingly enough, there's really only one spot where the creators had to fudge to make the scene work. (We'll get to it shortly.) Unavoidably—with this much movement and rhythmic speaking and a child actor to boot—the scene does have a few problems.

Just for review, the rhyme goes like this: "Allamaraine, count to four (hands on hips). Allamaraine, then three more (three fingers on the right hand raised in the air). Allamaraine, if you can see (right hand saluting). Allamaraine, you come with me (right thumb pointing to self.)" Starting our count from the moment the door opens, the second time through, the girl forgets to salute on "if you can see." The fifth time through—on "then three more"—the girl salutes

and then corrects herself by raising three fingers. On the seventh time, the overhead shot is not synced with the girl's speech. Her salute comes between "then three more" and "Allamaraine, if you can see." Finally, on the eighth time, the creators had to fudge to make the scene work. The little girl only says, "Allamaraine, count to four" and "Allamaraine, then three more" before starting over with "Allamaraine, count to four."

• To move from the third shap to the fourth shap, Sisko and company must drink an antidote to poison gas. Falow then points to a door to show them the exit. The next camera angle shows the door opening. Then an overhead shot shows the door closed. Sisko and company begin walking toward the door. The camera angle changes, and the door is suddenly open without any accompanying sound.

• Quark suffers from "wigglehead" in this episode. At one point Falow states that Quark must choose which of his players will be lost so that others may survive. Quark says he can't do it and then begins pleading for someone else to make the choice. As he implores, "Pleeeeease... pleeeeeease," his head shudders, setting up sympathetic vibrations in the actor's prosthesis. (Once you know what to look for, it's quite funny!)

TRIVIA ANSWERS
1. Master Surchid.
2. Captain McCoullough.

THE NAGUS

Star Date: unknown

Quark's world turns upside down when Grand Nagus Zek—the leader of the Ferengi—suddenly appears at DS9 with his son Krax. Over dinner, Zek asks to use Quark's bar for a very important meeting. In short order, high-ranking Ferengi begin arriving at the station. At the meeting, Zek laments over the limited opportunities left in the Alpha Quadrant, contrasting it with the incredible potential of the Gamma Quadrant—virgin territory untouched by the Ferengi notoriety for greed. Then Zek makes a surprise announcement: He steps down from the role of grand nagus, appointing Quark instead.

At first, Grand Nagus Quark enjoys his role as leader of the Ferengi—until he receives his first death threat. Frightened, Quark hurries to Zek for advice. Unfortunately, Zek dies during their talk. Quark turns to his brother Rom for support, only to find that Rom and Krax have conspired to flush him out an airlock. Rom wants the bar. Krax wants to be Nagus. Just in time, Zek reappears with Odo to save Quark's life. He had faked his death to deter-

mine if Krax was ready to become Nagus. Seeing Krax's crude grab for power, Zek deems the test a failure. Afterward, Quark congratulates Rom for his ruthlessness.

RUMINATIONS

This episode is amazingly well formed for so early in the series. Many of the elements of Ferengi culture are here, full-blown: the lovable, hapless Rom, Grand Nagus Zek, the Rules of Acquisition; vacuum-desiccating the bodies of the dead. The creators could show this episode in any of the four seasons, and the Ferengi portions of it would fit right in from the standpoint of characterizations. The formula for Ferengi culture—first hammered out here—works! And it works well enough that the creators used it effectively throughout the first four seasons.

GREAT LINES

"It's like...it's...it's...it's like talking to a Klingon!"—Zek to himself, grumbling over his son's thickheadedness. I believe this is the first indication that we get that Klingons and Ferengi do not hold each other in high esteem.

Trivia Questions

1. Why is O'Brien late for school?

2. According to Krax, which planet in the Gamma Quadrant has rich deposits of miszinite ore?

48

This theme is later fully developed in "House of Quark."

PLOT OVERSIGHTS

• In this episode, O'Brien serves as substitute teacher at school while Keiko's away on Earth. From the sounds of it, he's been at it for some time and still has two more weeks to go. Is he doing this every day of the week for the length of a normal school day (six hours or so)? Doesn't he have anything else to do with his time? Isn't this the same O'Brien who's usually running ragged, trying to keep the station functioning properly?

• When setting up the meeting in Quark's bar, Zek says it will begin at nine o'clock sharp. Evidently the grand nagus doesn't like using a military time format (even though it is more efficient when dealing with planets that differ in their rotational periods). For instance, Bajor apparently has twenty-six hours in its day—using "o'clock" would result in two hours of the day being labeled "thirteen o'clock." And what about a planet with twenty-nine hours in its day? Wouldn't you have to go from "half past fourteen o'clock" to "one o'clock"?)

• I'm a bit confused over the succession order for becoming grand nagus. Zek appoints Quark. From everything I can see, Quark is the legally appointed leader of the Ferengi. But when asked who would benefit from his death, Quark states that Krax would become nagus next. Why Krax? If being nagus is passed by bloodline, wouldn't it pass to Rom, since Rom is Quark's nearest male relative? Granted, Quark doesn't have a male heir,

but doesn't Rule of Acquisition 139 say, "Wives serve. Brothers inherit."?

• Shortly after Zek "dies," we see Krax selling chunks of his vacuum-desiccated body. Of course, we learn later that Zek didn't really die. One wonders just *whom* Krax was selling!

CHANGED PREMISES

• In this episode Sisko says that O'Brien's daughter Molly is three years old, and O'Brien seems to agree. As I stated in my review of "A Man Alone," Molly was born sometime after star date 45156 (according to the *TNG* episode "Disaster"). Unfortunately, there's no way to tell the star date when Sisko makes this statement because the creators never bothered to give us one for this episode. However, "The Storyteller"—an episode that occurs three episodes after this one—has a star date of 46729.1. Using our handy-dandy conversion of 1000 star date units per Earth year, Molly would be about one and one-half years old. (I *suppose* if you really wanted to stretch the point you could say that the O'Briens decided to use the Eastern system of setting a person's age at one on the day they were born and celebrating everyone's birthday at the beginning of the new year. But even that would make Molly only two.)

• While performing his duties as nagus, Quark holds a pet that looks like a fat, little, leafless tree trunk. If memory serves, the little creature looks exactly like a Corvan gilvos. According to "New Ground" *(TNG)* only fourteen specimens remained of this creature on star date 45376.3. Obviously the breeding program on Brentalia is going spectacularly well, because now they are so plentiful that Quark had somehow managed to get one shipped in for his amusement!

• In this episode we learn that Nog can't read. Since Rom won't allow him to attend Keiko's school any longer, Jake decides to tutor him in the evenings. Upset that Jake has missed dinner again, Sisko arrives at Cargo Bay 14 during one of their sessions to drag his son back to their quarters so they can enjoy a meal together. As an aside, I'm really surprised that Jake and Nog didn't hear the cargo bay door opening. But more importantly, the textbook from which Rom read appears to have some serious factual errors. As Sisko closes on Jake and Nog's position, Nog reads aloud the following sentences: "The largest planet is Bajor. It has three moons." Four episodes from now, during "Progress," we will learn that Bajor plans to tap the molten core of its *fifth* moon, "Jeraddo." (Sounds like that textbook committee needs some nitpickers!)

EQUIPMENT ODDITIES

• Shortly after arriving, the nagus avails himself of Quark's holosuites. At one point the scene returns to the bar and we hear Zek cackling. Apparently when sitting at the bar in Quark's you can hear the delighted cries of someone enjoying a holosuite program on the second floor! Now, *there's* an interesting way to advertise. "Hear that, friends? That's another satisfied customer!" (Personally... if I were going to use a holosuite—and I did say *if*—I definitely would *not* want anyone to hear what was going on in there.)

• I must say I am becoming more and more impressed with the doors on DS9. They are so intelligent it's almost spooky. After a hard day of granting audiences and favors in his quarters, Grand Nagus Quark decides to go for a stroll to his bar. He strides between Rom and Krax and nearly reaches the doors. When they don't open, he stops, turns, and rudely rips the grand nagus scepter from Krax's hand. Almost immediately, the doors open. (My theory is the doors knew that Quark would be *a lot* happier in his wandering if he had his scepter to flash around, so they decided not to open until he took it from Krax. They were just looking out for Quark's best interest!)

• After Jake fails to show up for dinner, Sisko asks the computer to locate his son. The computer immediately places Jake in Cargo Bay 14. Wait a minute: Jake isn't wearing a communicator. (He doesn't get one until "Shadowplay.") Wearing a communicator is the only way we have seen the computer locate a person up to this point in the series. For instance, in "Dax," kidnappers leave Dax's communicator in a hall, and the computer identifies that as her location. So how does the computer find Jake? And if it has another method besides using the communicators, why didn't Sisko use it in the episode "Dax"? (I suppose—as a precautionary measure—Sisko could have tagged his son while he was sleeping. "Hey, Dad, what's this big yellow thing that's stapled through my ear?" "Oh, don't worry about that, son. That's just something I brought back from Bajor for you. It's all the rage.")

CONTINUITY AND PRODUCTION PROBLEMS

• After an attempt on his life, Quark recovers in the infirmary. Sisko and Odo pay him a visit to ply him for information on the attack. Quark brushes them off, saying it's an internal matter of Ferengi politics. He then gets up and starts to leave. Helping Quark put on his grand nagus coat, Rom leans the grand nagus's scepter against the medical bed, and Sisko holds it in place. Sisko! *Sisko*...holding Quark's scepter so it won't tumble to the floor. Now, there's a twist! (From the look on Avery Brooks's face, you can almost hear the director telling him, "Okay, now, when Max puts the cloak on Armin, make sure you steady the stick.")

TRIVIA ANSWERS

1. The transporter in Ops needed an adjustment in its upper molecular imaging scanner.
2. Stakoron II.

VORTEX

Star Date: unknown

After being locked up by Odo—on charges including the murder of a Miradorn raider—a man from the Gamma Quadrant named Croden intrigues the constable with stories of a "Changeling" colony. Meanwhile, Sisko and Dax travel to Rahkar, Croden's home planet, to inform the authorities of his arrest. They find that Croden is wanted there for crimes as well. Upon returning to the station, Sisko dispatches Odo in a runabout to take Croden back to Rahkar. Unfortunately, the slain Miradorn's brother, Ah-Kel, wants his revenge and follows them into the Gamma Quadrant.

To evade Ah-Kel, Odo allows Croden to pilot the runabout into a sensor-obscuring nebula. Once there, Croden quickly sets the craft down on an asteroid, proclaiming that they have reached the colony of the Changelings. They haven't. Croden has come to the caves on the asteroid to retrieve his daughter—the only other person to survive a brutal and unprovoked slaughter of his family by Rahkarian Security forces. Ah-Kel soon locates and attacks the

asteroid. When falling rocks knock Odo unconscious, Croden drags the shape shifter to safety. Working together, the pair then destroy the Miradorn's ship. Convinced of Croden's innocence, Odo arranges passage for them on a Vulcan science vessel that happens by.

PLOT OVERSIGHTS

• More problems with Odo's shape shifting and the known laws of the universe! At the beginning of this episode, Quark meets with the Miradorn raiders in a holosuite. They have an art object they wish to sell, and Quark is acting as intermediary. (Unknown to them, Quark has arranged for Croden to barge into the meeting with a Ferengi phaser and steal the object. In the ensuing scuffle, one of the Miradorn is killed.) Realizing the meeting is about to begin, Odo shape-shifts into a glass that Rom carries on a tray with four other glasses and a flask up to the holosuite. In other words, Rom carries Odo. Yet later in the episode, Croden carries Odo from the caves on the asteroid and then tells the shape shifter that he is heavier than he looks. Odo looks like a standard-

Trivia Questions

1. What drink does Quark order Rom to bring to the initial meeting with the twin Miradorn?

2. With whom does Sisko speak on Rahkar?

52

size adult male. That would make him at least 175 pounds. Since weight is directly related to mass, Odo would weigh the same no matter what his shape. In other words, *Rom* carried at least 175 pounds on that flimsy little tray. This seems unlikely.

• In the Security office, Odo tells Quark that he finds it interesting that Croden was carrying a Ferengi phaser. Quark replies that Ferengi phasers are available in many ports. True, but Croden hasn't been to many ports; he's from the Gamma Quadrant. And besides, if Croden had brought the weapon with him, the Security sensors would have gone off when he tried to carry it onto the promenade (see "Captive Pursuit"). And if the phaser didn't set off the sensors on the promenade, then it was obviously smuggled in by someone who knew all about the sensors; someone who had been on the station for some time; someone *just like Quark*. Of course, Odo never pursues this line of reasoning.

• To prove his claims of a Changeling colony, Croden displays a locket he wears around his neck. Once opened, the contents of the locket morph into a key and then return to their original shape. Odo sure has some interesting policies when it comes to incarceration. He allows prisoners to keep their jewelry. (Maybe it's just another example of a silly Starfleet regulation. No wonder Odo is always griping about them.)

• To return Croden to his home planet of Rahkar, Sisko dispatches Odo in a runabout. First, when did Odo learn to pilot a runabout? Second, Sisko knows that the chance exists

Ah-Kel will discover this plan and go after Odo. If that happens, it will be a dangerous confrontation in which the runabout will be at a disadvantage. Sisko knows this, but he doesn't bother to send someone with Odo who has a bit of combat experience. (We know Odo doesn't have the necessary skill because he says so. In a manner that's *very* reminiscent of our beloved Dr. McCoy from the original series, Odo complains, "I'm a Security officer, not a combat pilot!") Why doesn't Sisko send Kira along? Answer: Kira probably could outfly Ah-Kel and then there would be no need to go into the nebula. This would lead to the infamous "short show syndrome."

• In the nit above I expressed my amazement that Odo could fly a runabout. Guess what? Shortly after Ah-Kel fires on them we discover something even more amazing: *Croden* can fly the runabout. Croden...from the Gamma Quadrant. The guy who's only been on the station a short while and was brought there by the Klingons. *That guy*...can pilot a runabout?

• This "asteroid" has a breatheable atmosphere and Earth-like gravity. Doesn't this sound suspiciously like...a *planet*?

• More "strange but true" facts about our favorite shape shifter. Near the end of the episode, Odo gets hit on the shoulder with a rock, and it knocks him unconscious. Later, in the runabout, he awakes and feels his head as if it's hurting. Wait a minute: This is the same guy who was thrown across a holosuite at the beginning of this program and smashed against a wall, the same guy who immediately rose up from that abuse fully conscious. Besides, just where is Odo's consciousness stored? Wouldn't it be interlaced throughout his entire body? He's really a liquid, after all, isn't he? (I know it's a bit gruesome, but I see no reason why you couldn't chop off Odo's head and still have his body function. With that in mind—or "in head," if you prefer—I'm thinking that Odo was faking it just to see what Croden would do.)

• At the end of this episode, Odo arranges passage for Croden and his daughter on a Vulcan science ship. Um...are we *missing* something here? Croden is a *criminal*. I don't care what happened on his home world. On DS9 he took Quark's phaser and barged into a meeting with intent to steal. While intending to steal, he killed a Miradorn. Unless the Federation has substantially altered the norms of common jurisprudence, killing someone during the commission of a crime is murder...period. I don't think you can claim self-defense under those circumstances. What does this say about Odo's sense of justice? ("Oh, I know he was a bad man, but he gave me a *beautiful* locket that had my cousin inside, so I let him go!")

• On top of all this, Odo admits that he will have to lie to everyone back on the station. (Sure hope he remembers to delete the conversation with the Vulcan captain from the communications log of the runabout.)

EQUIPMENT ODDITIES

• Oddly enough, Bashir uses a tricorder to quickly assess that the Miradorn is dead in the holosuite. (In "The Passenger," Bashir claimed that tricorders aren't very accurate on dead people.)

• The sensors on the doors to the Security office must be calibrated only to Odo. At one point Ah-Kel and his thugs wait outside the Security office, blocking the entrance, and demanding that Croden be given to them. Odo wanders over from Quark, tells them to get back to their ship, and promptly walks into his office without touching anything! We know the doors didn't open when Ah-Kel and his team arrived because I can't see any reason Ah-Kel would hesitate from marching into the cell block and executing Croden on the spot. So *somebody* must have set the door to open only when Odo arrived.

• The handcuffs used on Croden as Odo escorts him onto the runabout appear to be (gasp!) Cardassian in design. (We see similar ones used on Picard in "Chain of Command, Part 1" and on Sito in "Lower Decks.") In "Past Prologue," earlier in this season, we saw a different style of handcuffs used on Tahna at the end of the episode. Why the change? (Has Starfleet ripped off the design? Or did the Bajorans finally, begrudgingly grant that those bad old Cardassians really do know how to build a good pair of restraints?)

• For some reason, Odo is taking Croden back to Rahkar on impulse! Watch the windows. The stars are just creeping by. Remember that Rahkar is at least 5 light-years from the wormhole! (Dialogue between Sisko and Dax in "Emissary" indicated that the closest star to the Gamma end of the wormhole was 5 light-years away.) Funny, I got the distinct impression that Odo wanted to complete this mission as quickly as possible, but traveling to Rahkar on impulse will take *years*.

• So how come the runabout computer is in a snit? Odo and Croden are flying along minding their own business when all of a sudden the ship rocks from an explosion. Surprise! They're under attack! Isn't the onboard computer supposed to warn you about things like this? (Odo must really be doing a lousy job piloting this craft to make the computer this mad.) Interestingly enough, in the final confrontation, the computer sounds all sorts of warning sounds as Ah-Kel's ship prepares to attack.

• Croden has this locket. When opened, the goo inside transforms into a key. Well...sort of. The first time Croden opens the locket, the goo becomes a key and immediately changes back to goo. Yet at the end of the episode, Croden opens the locket and the goo changes into a key *and stays in that shape*. How did it know to do that?

• In the final confrontation between Odo and Ah-Kel—mentioned above— Croden gives Odo a moment-by-moment update on the status of Ah-Kel's ship. At one point Croden says, "His starboard photon bank is armed." When Ah-Kel fires, however, the torpedo comes from directly in the center of the ship. I would have expected it to come from an outcropping on the starboard side of his ship.

CONTINUITY AND PRODUCTION PROBLEMS

• After Croden fails in his attempt to steal from the Miradorn, a Security guard comes into the holosuite and escorts him away. Away "where" I do not know, because the guard and Croden walk parallel to the exit of the holosuite and head directly for a wall! (In the first four seasons of the *DS9* series I do not believe we ever see more than one exit on a holosuite.)

• While in the cell on DS9 Croden takes a spoonful of his gruel twice. He lifts out a spoonful of it. Then the shot changes. Now his spoon is empty and he must refill it. (Drat those cell block gremlins. You would think Odo would keep them fed so they wouldn't steal the prisoners' food!)

• I'm sorry, but...these Miradorn outfits? They make the actors look like they are wearing women's underwear on the outside of their clothing (or worse yet, diapers).

• Odo's shape-shifting capabilities are nothing short of amazing at times. During the first attack by Ah-Kel, a lock of hair on the right side of Odo's head comes loose and flops around. (Watch for it just after Croden tells Odo to give him the flight controls.) It sure looks like normal humanoid hair. And it fixes itself moments later!

TRIVIA ANSWERS
1. A flask of his special Langour.
2. The exarch of Nehelik Province.

Star Date: unknown

Over the hesitations of Sisko and crew, Kai Opaka—spiritual head of Bajor—talks herself onto a runabout scheduled for an exploration mission in the Gamma Quadrant. Drawn by an odd subspace signal from a moon in an unexplored system, Sisko, Kira, and Bashir discover a satellite network that promptly attacks the runabout. Kai Opaka is fatally injured in the crash.

Sisko and the others then meet Golin Shel-La, leader of the Ennis—one of two warring factions on this moon. The Ennis and the Nol-Ennis were banished to this moon centuries ago by their government when they refused to abandon their blood feud. The true nature of their punishment becomes clearer when Opaka suddenly appears, alive and seemingly healthy. Shel-La explains that no one can die on the moon, and Bashir soon uncovers the reason. Tiny biomechanical devices infest the bodies of the Ennis, the Nol-Ennis, and even Opaka. These devices repair any physical damage when a person dies. They also make the infected individual completely dependent on the continued operation of the devices and a prisoner to the environment of the moon. When O'Brien and Dax arrive in another runabout to effect a rescue, Opaka stays behind to attempt to bring peace to the warring factions.

Trivia Questions

1. On the moon of which planet does the *Yangtzee Kiang* crash?

2. According to Sisko, how many planets are in the Federation?

PLOT OVERSIGHTS

• Just before the satellite system attacks the runabout, Bashir reports humanoid life signs on the surface—stating that they are all confined to an area of 12 square kilometers. Then the runabout crashes, and—lo and behold—Sisko somehow manages to put it down near the only inhabitants on the planet. Even more amazing, there isn't one piece of dialogue to indicate that he did it on purpose. The runabout *just happened* to crash on a large moon in exactly the right spot! (Of course, it wouldn't be much of a show if Sisko, Kira, and Bashir sat around Kai Opaka's dead body for forty minutes!)

• After extricating Opaka out of the wreckage, Bashir pulls a tricorder and determines that the Kai's upper thoracic vertebrae have been crushed—among other injuries. He then proceeds to attempt to resuscitate her.

Now, I may not know much about that there doctoring thang, but it sure don't seem like a good time to be pumping on her chest when her back's broke. (Then again, from the way Sisko and Bashir yanked her out of the runabout, I would imagine all the damage has already been done!)

• Adrenaline can do wondrous things for the body. Just after the crash, Kira is frantically scrambling around trying to ensure that Kai Opaka is all right. She uses both arms to support her weight. She flops down on Opaka's body and weeps. Yet, after Opaka dies, Kira sits in a cave holding her left arm as if any motion causes her intense pain.

• At one point Golin Shel-La tells Sisko that the Ennis stopped using directed-energy weapons centuries ago. Then the Nol-Ennis attack, and both sides fire weapons that look just like...*directed-energy* weapons!

• Shel-La tells Sisko that no one can die on the planet. Bashir discovers that tiny robots—like nanites—repair all damage. So...what would happen if you chopped one of these guys' heads off? These Ennis seem to have no compunction against taking a Nol-Ennis and chopping him into teensy-tiny bits. How would the robots deal with *that* situation? Or, how 'bout *fire*? Could these robots take a cremated body and reanimate it? (The point is this: There should be any number of ways to defeat the reanimation process. Yet these two groups have apparently been fighting for just about forever. Personally, I don't think they're really trying.)

• At the end of the episode, Bashir

tells Sisko that he might be able to program the robots to stop their regeneration cycle. He thinks it might be kinder to let the inhabitants of the planet live only one more life and then finally die. Shel-La jumps on the idea, suggesting instead that the reprogramming would be the ultimate weapon on this world. Of course, when our fearless Starfleet officers hear Shel-La's response, they decide against supplying Shel-La with this ability. At this point O'Brien prepares to transport Sisko, Kira, and Bashir from the surface. Surprisingly enough, Shel-La lets them go! As ruthless as he appears, I would have expected him to put a knife to somebody's throat. Yes, I realize that the Nol-Ennis had just commenced another attack. But wouldn't this seem like a once-in-a-lifetime opportunity to Shel-La? (If you'll pardon the pun.)

EQUIPMENT ODDITIES
• Ya know, if the runabouts had harness restraints, then Kai might still be alive.
• Guess what? Bashir pronounces Kai Opaka dead using...a tricorder! (See "The Passenger.")

CONTINUITY AND PRODUCTION PROBLEMS
• After the crash, the camera angle pans up slowly from the ground to reveal the damaged runabout. One of the nacelles lays broken off nearby. At least it's supposed to be one of the runabout's nacelles. It actually looks a lot more like something off a shuttle craft from *NextGen*. Johnson Lai of Ajax, Ontario, wrote to say it was the

nacelle from a Type 6 Shuttle as seen in episodes such as "The Outcast" *(TNG)*, "Rascals" *(TNG)*, and "Parallels" *(TNG)*.

• The creators left the door wide open for another episode at the end of this one. Kai Opaka tells Sisko, "...your *pagh* and mine will cross again." Now, if you want to have a little fun, check out this scene again with closed captioning on. It reads, "your *power* and mine will cross again"! *And*—if you look directly at the word "power" when Kai Opaka says *"pagh"*—for a brief moment it sounds like she has just developed a very thick southern accent.

TRIVIA ANSWERS
1. The third planet in an uncharted binary star system.
2. More than one hundred.

THE STORYTELLER

Star Date: 46729.1

Summoned by medical emergency to a village on Bajor, Bashir and O'Brien find only one person ill: "the sirah." The magistrate claims that if the sirah dies, the village will be destroyed. That evening, the sirah struggles from bed to face the Dal'Rok—a great foaming cloud that appears in the sky. As the sirah speaks of the villagers' unity, lights appear over their heads to shrink the Dal'Rok. Before it completely disappears, however, the sirah collapses. Renewed, the Dal'Rok fires on the village. Hovath, the sirah's young apprentice, runs to the old man's side, but the sirah calls for O'Brien instead. Hovath failed a few nights earlier, unable to control the Dal'Rok. The sirah makes O'Brien the new sirah and with his dying instructions helps O'Brien vanquish the Dal'Rok.

Facing another encounter with the Dal'Rok, O'Brien uncovers the truth. The Dal'Rok comes from the villagers' fears focused through a fragment of an orb from the Celestial Temple. The sirah tells the story so the people will find unity to vanquish their fears. Un-

> **Trivia Questions**
>
> 1. Who is the village magistrate?
>
> 2. What is the border between the Paqu and the Novat?

fortunately, O'Brien cannot inspire the people when the Dal'Rok attacks. Just in time, Hovath takes over and succeeds where he failed a few nights ago, thereby winning back the villagers' confidence—as the old sirah planned all along.

PLOT OVERSIGHTS

• According to "Emissary," the wormhole is 160 million kilometers from Bajor. Yet in this episode, dialogue indicates that Bashir and O'Brien have been in a runabout together on their way to Bajor for 2 hours. Even on impulse, the runabout flies at approximately 75,000 kilometers per second (one-quarter the speed of light). This time, I'll let you do the math, but by my calculations it should only take about 36 minutes! And remember: This is a medical emergency. (I wonder if O'Brien could do a controlled high-warp jump and get the runabout there in significantly less time.)

• The subplot of the episode concerns two clans on Bajor called the Paqu and the Novat. A land dispute brings their negotiators to DS9 to a conference with Sisko. On the way to welcoming the Paqu delegate, Kira expresses concern to Sisko about his ability to deal with these two groups. She says that Bajor has the saying "The people and the land are one." She then points out that the territory occupied by the Paqu and the Novat is some of the harshest on the planet. Kira seems to imply that these people will be tough. The first time we see the Novat leader Woban he's scarfing down a piece of Larish pie and complimenting Cardassian replicators. Pardon the snide comment, but he appears to have had one too many pieces of Larish pie in his time. As for Varis Sul—the young female tetrarch of the Paqu—she seems contemplative: torn by her responsibilities, weary of the adult role she must play. I'm having a hard time labeling either of these leaders "tough." (If you want tough, look at Mollibok's friends in the next episode.)

• Not a nit, just a ponderment. So you've got this Dal'Rok that forms in the sky for five nights in a row every year. I wonder if the Bajoran government ever investigated this phenomenon? That high up in the sky, it's got to be visible for a long way. And what about the Cardassians? How well did the Dal'Rok play during the Occupation?

• Maybe I missed some subtlety here, but how many times has this Dal'Rok thing happened? ("Oh, we're afraid, the Dal'Rok is going to get us." "Yea, we beat it!" "Oh, we're afraid, the Dal'Rok is going to get us." "Yea, we beat it!" "Oh, we're afraid, the Dal'Rok is going to get us." "Yea, we beat it!" *Ad nauseam.*) One would think that the villagers would reach

the point where they'd say, "Dal'Rok? What Dal'Rok? Oh, you mean that fluffy thing in the sky? Ha! Piece of pie!" (Larish pie, that is.)

• Starfleet needs to teach its people a bit more about cultural sensitivity. This episode clearly establishes that two items are part of the sirah's costuming. The first is a bracelet—worn on the hand—containing the fragment of an Orb of the Prophets. The second is a cloak. This cloak is so closely identified with the office of the sirah that when O'Brien attempts to palm the job off on Hovath midway through the show by placing the cloak on Hovath's shoulders, the village magistrate immediately reacts and takes it away. So what does O'Brien do at the very end when Hovath is proclaimed the new sirah? He throws the cloak *on the ground* before he and Bashir escape!

• And speaking of this escape, I wonder why O'Brien and Bashir didn't just call the runabout for transport instead of making their way willy-nilly down the crowded stairs of the outdoor platform.

CHANGED PREMISES

• In "A Man Alone," Odo states that his regeneration cycle occurs every 18 hours. In this episode, Jake states that Odo regenerates every 16 hours. I'd be willing to chalk this statement up to misinformation on Jake's part, but Odo himself confirms the new regeneration time in "The Forsaken."

EQUIPMENT ODDITIES

• Trying to impress Varis, Nog decides to play a practical joke on Jake. First he talks Jake and Varis into stealing Odo's bucket. Then, once he has the pair in the Security office, he fills the bucket with oatmeal and "accidently" spills it all over Jake. Jake reacts with shock, believing that Odo is dribbling down his pant leg. The scene finally gives us a quick pan of the left side of Odo's office ("left" if you are standing at the doorway looking in). This side of Odo's office now has a display of wanted criminals, some Security monitors, and finally the door to the cell block. "Emissary" showed this area, but in that episode the left wall featured a third door instead of the wanted-criminals display. Obviously this wall has been remodeled—probably about the same time the station personnel took out the octagonal windows on the cell block access doors (See "Captive Pursuit.")

CONTINUITY AND PRODUCTION PROBLEMS

• During the negotiations, Kira comes into Quark's for a drink. Just as she enters, Quark tells that lovable barfly Morn, "So I sold him a whole herd of Klingon targs." Morn laughs. Interestingly enough, the closed captioning reads, "So I sold him a whole herd of Klingon *talk*." (Emphasis mine.)

• It's getting to be an old problem, but the stars creep by in Sisko's office while remaining stationary everywhere else. Also, the first time Varis speaks with Sisko in his office, watch the star field closely. It looks like the shots featuring Sisko came from two completely different takes. The star field jumps

back and forth between two different configurations. (Just pick out a cluster of stars whose shape you can remember and then watch for it.)

• Finding Varis sitting on the upper level of the promenade with her legs draped over the edge, Jake and Nog join her and offer their encouragement. At one point Nog has his hands about one foot apart on the railing under his chin. The shot changes and suddenly his hands are close together.

• When Nog slings Odo's bucket toward Jake, some of the oatmeal inside lands on the upper portion of Jake's right leg. Yet moments later, when Jake walks out of the Security office, the area is completely clean! (Yes, I know that this was practically impossible to get right given that the scenes were probably shot on different days. But if I didn't make note of it, I wouldn't be doing my job! And I take this job *very* seriously. Wink, wink.)

• Stepping into his role as the new sirah, Hovath passionately recounts the story—igniting the villagers' faith in themselves and vanquishing the Dal'Rok once again. Apparently the creators thought Hovath got a bit too carried away because they deleted the audio on his last two lines. At the very end of Hovath's speech, the closed captioning adds, "There's nothing we cannot do. No foe we cannot conquer."

TRIVIA ANSWERS
1. Faren Kag.
2. The River Glyrhond.

★ ROMANCE TOTE BOARD

1. Number of women who kiss Sisko: five
2. Number of men who fall for Kira: seven
3. Number of men who date Dax: three (for sure)
4. Number of times Bashir and Dax sleep together: two
5. Number of women who are attracted to O'Brien: three
6. Number of times Odo puddles with another Changeling: four
7. Number of times we see a couple having a spat: five
8. Number of times Ferengi males touch females in an uninvited way: six
9. Number of times we see or hear about Jake and Nog watching the girls: four
10. Number of women who rub at least one of Quark's ears: eight
11. Number of men who rub at least one of Quark's ears: two
12. Number of times Quark rubs his own ear: six

REFERENCES

Note: This tote board is current only through the first eighty-four episodes, ending with "Paradise Lost."

1. Jennifer Sisko in "Emissary." Fenna in "Second Sight." Dax *and* Kira in "Through the Looking Glass." Yates in "The Way of the Warrior."

2. Quark expresses his interest in her in "Emissary" and many other episodes. Vedek Bareil is obviously drawn to her in "The Circle." Zek in "Rules of Acquisition." Garak accuses Dukat of pontificating for Kira's attention in "Civil Defense" and seems interested in it himself. Tiron makes his feelings clear in "Meridian." Odo confesses his love in "Heart of Stone."

3. Dax mentions a date she has with a Gallamite captain named "Boday" in "The Maquis, Part I." During this conversation, Kira makes an offhand comment about the fact that Dax dates Ferengi. (Rom, perhaps?) In "Meridian," Dax dates Doral. Also, honorable mention should go to Morn. According to dialogue in "Progress," he asked Dax out and she was considering it.

4. Dax comes to spend the night in his quarters on the *Defiant* during "Equilibrium." She took the lower bunk. And they sleep together in the turbolift during "Starship Down." (Had you going there for a minute, didn't I?)

5. Keiko, even though the first time we see them together they are arguing. (See "A Man Alone.") Neela during "In the Hands of the Prophets." Just watch the conversation they have together in the airlock. Gilora in "Destiny."

6. He does it twice with the female Changeling in "The Search, Part II." Also, he puddles with the adversary in "The Adversary" and one of the Changelings on Earth in "Homefront." (Granted, this may not seem like romance to us, but let's not let our speciescentricity cloud us to the habits of metamophic beings.)

7. O'Brien and Keiko argue in "A Man Alone." O'Brien and Keiko fuss in "Fascination." Leanne storms away from her date with Jake because of Nog's comments in "Life Support." Sisko and Yates have a disagreement during "Indiscretion." Dax and Kahn raise their voices at each other in "Rejoined."

8. Quark has his hand on Kira's hip in "Emissary." Miss Sarda relates to Sisko that she told Quark to keep his Ferengi knuckles to himself in "Captive Pursuit." Quark puts his hand on Dax's thigh in "Rules of Acquisition." Zeks pats Kira on the bottom twice in "Rules of Acquisition." In "The House of Quark," Grilka says that she's so grateful for Quark's help that she's going to let him take his hand off her thigh instead of shattering every bone in his body.

9. They go to Airlock 3 during "Move Along Home" to watch the girls arriving on a transport. They admired a blue cat-suited Vulcan who strolls by in "The Nagus." They watch the promenade in "The Storyteller" just before Nog spots Varis Sul. They go to Docking Bay 1 to watch the girls in "The Maquis, Part I."

10. Vash in "Q-Less." An imaginary trollop in "If Wishes Were Horses." Pel in "Rules of Acquisition." Dax in "Playing God" and "Facets." Natima in "Profit and Loss." A Dabo girl in "The Collaborator." A Boslic freighter captain in "The Abandoned." Emi in "Prophet Motive."

11. Zek in "Prophet Motive." Odo-Curzon grabs Quark's ears and kisses him on the forehead in "Facets."

12. After Zek makes him the new nagus in "The Nagus." When meeting with Yeto in the bar during "Invasive Procedures." After Zek gives him a percentage of every deal in the Gamma Quadrant in "Rules of Acquisition." After Mrs. Vaatrik agrees to give him five bars of latinum to recover her list in "Necessary Evil." After tricking Bashir and O'Brien into a racquetball match in "Rivals." He rubs his ear against Keiko's head in "Fascinations."

PROGRESS

When the provisional government and the Federation work together to tap the core of Bajor's fifth moon—thereby making the surface uninhabitable—a stubborn old man named Mollibok refuses to leave. Used to fighting for the underdog, Kira finds herself charged with the uncomfortable job of convincing Mollibok to abandon the home he made on the moon forty years ago, when he escaped Cardassian occupation. Though the project will supply energy for thousands of Bajorans, reason fails quickly with Mollibok. Reluctantly, Kira tries an armed evacuation, but that only results in Mollibok being injured. In the time it takes for Mollibok to heal, Sisko pays Kira a visit. His words help clarify her feelings, and a short time later she forces Mollibok to leave with her.

Meanwhile, Jake and Nog have an adventure in profit. After acquiring five thousand unwanted wrappages of Cardassian yamok sauce from Quark, Jake and Nog trade the lot for one hundred gross of self-sealing stembolts. Then they trade the bolts for seven tessipates of land on Bajor only to discover that the provisional government wants to buy the land for a reclamation center. At this point the pair advise Quark of their acquisition, and he gladly steps in to handle the negotiations.

Trivia Questions

1. What is the name of the fifth moon of Bajor?

2. What are the names of Mollibok's two companions?

GREAT MOMENTS

Mollibok and Kira share some delightful moments in this episode. I love it when Mollibok tells her that she walks like a carnivorous rastipod and instead of flying off the handle Kira realizes that he's just trying to make her mad. It shows that Kira really is more than just a fireball waiting to explode (as she seemed to be in the early episodes). And, Kira's story about the old tree is well put (even if metaphor is not Kira's strong suit as the creators ably illustrate).

PLOT OVERSIGHTS

• Again, I wonder if "truth in advertising" should apply to episode previews. The preview for this episode has the following narration: "A remote moon on the brink of destruction. A rebel leader refusing to surrender. And the Federation faces a mutiny within its own ranks."

Presumably "a rebel leader" refers to Mollibok. Now, I *suppose* you could say that Mollibok was the leader of his little group of three, but that's a stretch. And the Federation faces "a mutiny within its own ranks"? When did this happen during this episode? Is this referring to Kira? Kira isn't a part of the Federation, she's Bajoran!

• Jake and Nog sure are up late. The beginning of this episode shows them playing cards in Quark's. Either Quark has run out of customers for the day or he's closed for the evening. This is a bar. I believe Quark's doesn't close until about 0200 hours.

• Let's spend a few moments talking about this plan to tap the moon's core. First, gravity looks Earth-normal. That means the "moon" would have to have the equivalent mass of Earth. The moon also has a breathable atmosphere. Sounds like a planet, not a moon. Second, Minister Toran acknowledges that there is another method available to tap the energy in the moon's core without poisoning the atmosphere. Does Bajor have so much space, such a surplus of resources that it can afford to destroy a perfectly habitable moon? For the record, the answer according to "Sanctuary" and "Shakaar" is a resounding "No!" Both episodes state that the Cardassians poisoned the farmlands before leaving. Yet Mollibok grows a beautiful crop. If Bajor needs good farmland, why is it throwing this moon away? And besides, if the Federation is willing to help Bajor with its energy needs, why isn't it just providing fusion reactors?

• Originally Quark gets the yamok sauce because one of his Ferengi flunkies orders the stuff even after Quark left specific instructions to the contrary. Quark tells the flunky that he's going to dock his pay for the next six years because of the mistake. Nog and Jake overhear this conversation and begin their adventure. Knowing his uncle is irritated about the situation, Nog brings up the yamok sauce in conversation and then casually offers to dispose of it. Quark readily agrees. Nog and Jake then trade the sauce for the stembolts. I realized it would be a short show if Nog couldn't get the sauce from Quark, but does this seem right? Quark's a horse trader from a long way back. Does it seem likely that he couldn't find *some* way to unload that sauce? (Especially since we discover in "The Wire" that Quark has *Cardassian* friends, and Cardassians are the ones who eat yamok sauce in the first place.)

• Mollibok claims that he was the first person ever to settle this moon. Initially I thought this was just more bluster, but then Minister Toran states that there were only forty-seven other people on the planet. Yet according to Sisko in "Explorers," Bajorans were using solar sailing ships to visit the planets in their system and beyond eight hundred years ago. In other words, eight hundred years ago, Bajorans *could* have reached this beautiful moon. So why didn't anyone ever settle there?

• When Mollibok is injured, Kira orders a Security officer to beam back to the runabout, call the station, and contact Bashir. Wait a minute: This is one of *Bajor's* moons. According to the last episode it takes at least two hours to fly from DS9 to Bajor even during a medical emergency. Surely, a doctor from Bajor could get there more quickly. Then, after arriving and ministering to Mollibok, Bashir says he is going to take him back to the station. Same problem. Aren't there any good hospitals on Bajor?

• It's a *good* thing Mollibok never had a grease fire in that little house he built on that moon. At the end of the episode, Kira sets fire to it in six places, and one minute later, the house is engulfed in flames.

CHANGED PREMISES

• Bajor seems to have acquired two more moons since the episode "The Nagus." In that episode, Nog read from a padd that stated that Bajor had three moons. In this episode, Bajor is preparing to tap the core of its *fifth* moon.

EQUIPMENT ODDITIES

• After acquiring a hundred gross of self-sealing stembolts, Nog and Jake seem a bit uncertain what to do next, especially since they don't know who actually uses self-sealing stembolts or what they do. I suppose it would be too much trouble to ask the computer?

CONTINUITY AND PRODUCTION PROBLEMS

• Just after making the deal to trade the yamok sauce for the stembolts, Nog says, "Now the question is, what are we going to do with a hundred gross of self-sealing stembolts?" Watch the background on the left side of the screen when he starts this sentence. There's a woman dressed in a red Starfleet uniform who is standing still and staring straight ahead until Nog says, "Now the question is..." Then she immediately begins moving from left to right on the screen and out of the picture—almost like she was waiting for a cue. (Hmmm.)

• When Sisko comes to talk some sense into Kira, Mollibok meets him at the door. Moments later, Mollibok begins to tell Sisko the story of Kira's gnarly tree. As he raises his left hand, you can clearly see a black watchband.

• Old Mollibok can really work when he sets his mind to it. After doctoring Mollibok all night, Kira awakes to find him working on his kiln. Through the window we see him tapping the row he's just completed. He has two more rows—five tiles in all—to go before he's through. Kira strolls outside and we hear Mollibok continue his tapping. Then the shot changes and Mollibok is applying mortar to a tile that he then places at the end of the next-to-last row. Now he has only one row—two tiles—to go. Somehow, in the space of only a few seconds, he manages to plaster up two tiles!

TRIVIA ANSWERS

1. Jeraddo.
2. Baltrim and Keena.

IF WISHES WERE HORSES

Star Date: 46853.2

The episode opens with O'Brien reading "Rumpelstiltskin" for a bedtime story to his daughter Molly. Moments later, O'Brien is shocked to find an actual incarnation of the mythical character in her room. Sisko experiences similar confusion when Jake comes home from the holosuite with Buck Bokai—the greatest baseball player of all time. He's supposedly been dead for centuries. At the same time, Bashir awakes to find a doppelgänger of Dax hovering over his bed, completely infatuated with him.

Reports come in from all over the station as the real Dax searches for an answer to these puzzling anomalies. Somehow, whatever people imagine now comes to life. At first the subspace scans show nothing, but then a small, expanding rift appears. The senior staff attempts to seal the rift with photon torpedoes but fails. With the situation looking catastrophic, Sisko realizes that the rift is a figment of their collective imaginations. Once they refuse to believe it exists, the rift disappears, as do all the other anomalies. Buck Bokai then

reappears for a final farewell, telling Sisko that he is part of a band of explorers traveling the galaxy. They find the concept of imagination fascinating and have used the personnel on the station as a case study.

Trivia Questions

1. What did Dax and Bashir order in Quark's bar before the episode began?

2. What does Quark desire to show the "trollops" that he has conjured?

RUMINATIONS

After watching this episode several times, something about it started feeling familiar. This is another storyteller episode! (See "The Storyteller.") Sisko plays the role of the sirah at the end, marshaling the "villagers" to overcome their fears of the "Dal'Rok" (i.e., the rift). I'm also intrigued in this episode by what must be going on in Bashir's mind when the episode is over. The show opens with our good doctor trying to convince Dax that he is hopelessly in love with her. Then a new and improved Dax appears that's everything he's ever fantasized. Just as he decides to yield to the moment, Sisko calls him to Ops, where he discovers the other incarnations of the station's inhabitants. One thing leads to another. Bashir never does get to spend any "quality" time with his version of Dax. At the end of the episode, she fades away. You can almost hear his mind screaming. As for what he's really thinking...that's what holosuites are for. Maybe he should talk with Quark.

PLOT OVERSIGHTS

• Just before the Dax kitten appears in Bashir's quarters, we see DS9's chief medical officer asleep on his bed, wearing his uniform. Did he fall asleep while reviewing some reports, or is the good doctor just this dedicated?

• This next nit is perfectly understandable, but I wouldn't be doing my job if I didn't note it. With the Dax kitten crawling all over him, Bashir attempts to find a reason for her amorous behavior. First he thinks she may have the flu. Then he wonders if he might be having a reaction to the "replimated antipasto" he had for lunch. "Replimated"? Would that be "replicated" (as the closed captioning reads)? As I said, it *is* understandable. If you had a Dax kitten crawling all over you, you'd be talking gibberish, too. (Ladies, feel free to change "Dax kitten" in the previous sentence to "Sisko kitten" or "Bashir kitten" or "Odo kitten" or even "Quark kitten" if you prefer.)

• In discussing the possible ramifications of the rift, Sisko says, "If the rift collapses, the implosion would overtake us immediately." Doesn't "implosion" refer to an inward motion? If the motion is inward, how is it going to overtake the station? Is the implosion going to cause an "explosive" wave of some sort?

• Where does Buck Bokai get his baseball? Does it originally belong to Jake, or does it come off the holodeck

with Buck? There's no way to tell, but the next-to-last time Buck disappears, he takes it with him, and no one seems to care. On the other hand, if the baseball is part of the whole Buck Bokai thing, why does he throw it to Sisko at the end? Did the alien make sure it retained its form even after they left? Was that the excuse Buck was going to use to return? ("Hey, guys. I left my baseball back there. Let's pay them another visit!")

CHANGED PREMISES

• In this episode Quark has to explain to Odo that Jake plays baseball in a holosuite every afternoon. Obviously Odo has improved his intelligence techniques by the end of the third season. In "Facets" Odo knows what Bashir has for breakfast.

• In her attempt to mollify Bashir's embarrassment of his version of Dax, the real Dax tells him that she was a young man once. Actually this might be true, but later episodes reveal that the Dax symbiont has had at least three male hosts that Jadzia should be aware of at this point. In "Facets" we see O'Brien receive Tobin's memories, Bashir receive Torias's memories, and Odo receive Curzon's memories. I suppose we could say that two of these three men received the Dax symbiont when they were middle-aged, but the episode "Dax" establishes that most hosts receive a symbiont in their twenties.

• In this episode, Buck Bokai—dressed in a "London Kings" uniform—asks Sisko if he's got room on his team for a switch-hitting third baseman. Also earlier in the episode, Bokai says he remembers breaking Joe DiMaggio's record. The *NextGen* episode "The Big Good-bye" first mentions the player who broke DiMaggio's record. However, in that episode, Data—speaking of DiMaggio's streak—tells Picard, "The record will stand until the year 2026, when a *shortstop* for the London Kings..." *The Star Trek Encyclopedia* tries to cover up this error by stating that Bokai started out playing shortstop but later switched to third base. That may be. But did Bokai break the record when he was a shortstop then? (If he broke the record after becoming a third baseman, Data would have said "third baseman," no question about it. Pick, pick, pick, pick, pick.)

EQUIPMENT ODDITIES

• In "The Storyteller" I mentioned that Odo's office had changed. In "Emissary," a door shown near the main entrance of the office on the left side—as you are looking in—is now a Federation's Most Wanted display. In this episode there's actually a better pan of the left- side wall just before Odo imagines Quark in jail. The door frame still exists. As Odo walks into his office you can see that it's identical to the door frame for the access door to the cell block. The creators simply walled the opening and used it for the wanted "posters."

• O'Brien can do the handiest things from his console in Ops. Toward the end of the episode he tells Sisko that he is "installing pulse wave devices in the [photon] torpedoes" as he pecks away at his terminal. Somehow I thought this would take a hands-on

approach like we saw at the end of *Star Trek VI: The Undiscovered Country* when Spock and McCoy worked on the torpedo together.

• Those small, teethlike projections on the habitat ring of DS9 are really versatile. To date we have seen them used for firing phasers in "Emissary," for sending out a tractor beam in "Dax," and in this episode they are used as photon torpedo launchers!

• Just after the explosion, Kira works to reestablish the comsystem. Watch and listen carefully when O'Brien walks behind her. The red alert Klaxon sounds, but the red alert lights above the workstations don't illuminate. (And they aren't broken! They're flashing in the shot just before this one.)

CONTINUITY AND PRODUCTION PROBLEMS

• After reading Molly "Rumpelstiltskin," O'Brien steps outside her room and closes the door. He and Keiko share a nice moment together. Then Molly comes out of her room to tell her dad about the appearance of the dwarf. Just before O'Brien walks over to Molly, his sleeves are pushed up to his elbows. As he walks over to console his daughter, the camera angle changes, and the sleeves are suddenly much lower.

• Following Bashir's arrival in Ops with his Dax kitten, the real Dax appears. Moments later she walks behind the happy couple to get to a workstation. As she does, the camera focus blurs on the real Dax. It's almost like the creators were trying to cover up the fact that the person walking behind Bashir is a body double for Terry Farrell. Also, the person walking turns her head conveniently away from the camera to further obscure her identity. (If this person is a double body, she's an excellent one. She looks *a lot* like Dax.)

• At one point, Rumpelstiltskin fiddles with the controls on O'Brien's workstation. Irritated, the chief of operations slaps his hand. The closed captioning at this point reads, "Stop it."

• On the promenade, Odo claims to be chasing a large bird called a gunji jackdaw. Funny, it looks exactly like an emu to me. (An emu is an Australian flightless bird related to but smaller than an ostrich. Just a couple of miles down the road from my house, there's a family who raised emus and ostriches, among other things.)

TRIVIA ANSWERS
1. Two raktajinos.
2. His Tartaran landscapes (though it sounds like he says "Tartarus").

THE FORSAKEN

Star Date: 46925.1

Visiting DS9, Lwaxana Troi quickly becomes enamored with Odo. Meanwhile, O'Brien discovers that the station's computer has suddenly improved following a download from an unidentified probe that recently came through the wormhole. Then the station experiences a series of odd systems failures, one of which traps Lwaxana and Odo in a turbolift at a most inopportune time. Odo is close to the start of his regenerative cycle and soon will revert to a liquid.

O'Brien finally comes up with a working theory. The probe evidently contained some type of mechanical life form that has now jumped into the station's computer. It's behaving like a lonely puppy, causing trouble just to get attention. Back in the turbolift, Odo reveals that his regeneration is a deeply private matter. He is quite distressed over being trapped with another person when it happens. To even the score, Lwaxana removes her wig and allows Odo to see her "ordinary" self—a self she lets no one else see. Grateful for her understanding, Odo melts into the lap of Lwaxana's dress. In Ops, O'Brien creates a "doghouse"—an area of the computer with a great deal of nonessential activity. As the now satisfied puppy moves in, all station functions return to normal.

Trivia Questions

1. What is the name of O'Brien's Bajoran engineering assistant in this episode?

2. Lwaxana asks Odo if he's ever been to the fourth moon of what planet at dawn?

RUMINATIONS

Evidently Kira didn't think her uniform fit tightly enough to really show off her figure. Commencing with this episode, she wears a catsuit instead of the two-piece unit she used for the first fifteen episodes.

GREAT LINES

"You are not at all what I expected."—Odo to Lwaxana after she willingly abandons her wig, disclosing her "ordinary" self, so he will feel more comfortable when he reverts to a liquid. This was such a nice change of pace for the character of Lwaxana. Up to this point, she had been mostly self-absorbed. Yet here, we see her humble herself for Odo's benefit.

GREAT MOMENTS

All of the interchanges between Lwaxana and Odo in this episode

71

are wonderful—well written and well executed.

PLOT OVERSIGHTS

• Odo originally proves himself worthy of Lwaxana's affection by recovering her brooch. When it is lifted by a thief in Quark's, Odo suggests that Lwaxana sweep the room with her telepathic sense. She senses nothing but casts an accusatory glance at Quark, stating that Betazoid cannot read Ferengi minds. Odo responds with the tangential insult that Quark usually doesn't have to resort to *petty* theft to fleece his customers. Odo then looks around the room and lays hold of a Dopterian. The Dopterians are distant cousins of the Ferengi, and Odo wonders if the Dopterian might be opaque to Lwaxana's telepathic sense as well. Sure enough, when the Dopterian empties his pocket, Odo finds a small pile of pilfered items, including Lwaxana's brooch. Odo then hauls the Dopterian off to the Security office and leaves the rest of the stolen items behind on the table!

• At one point an Arbazan ambassador tells Sisko that she can't stand the thought of spending another night in a Cardassian bed with gargoyles staring down at her from the wood poles. Both "Past Prologue" and "Q-Less" show us the guest quarters on DS9, and I do not recall seeing any gargoyles. (Bashir probably tried to do the ambassador a favor and put her up in the station's honeymoon suite. Knowing Cardassians, it probably also has handcuffs, leather restraints, and whips decorating the walls!)

• When Odo finds out that Lwaxana has reserved a holosuite for them with Quark he exclaims, "Good Lord!" Which "lord" would this be? Odo has grown up around Bajorans. They worship the Prophets. (Just another one of those pesky human habits Odo is absorbing much too quickly. First it was pretense—see "Past Prologue." Now it's exclamatories!)

• Discovering that Odo has been in a turbolift for four hours, Sisko asks Kira if she knows his regenerative cycle. Kira replies that she does not. Now, let me get this straight: This guy is your chief of Security, and you have no idea when he will be out of commission? Does this seem right? Who wants to wager that Quark knows exactly when Odo will regenerate?

CHANGED PREMISES

• Making a pass at the station's chief of Security, Lwaxana asks him if Odo is his first or last name. Odo simply answers, "Yes." Now, I realize that Odo's under some pressure at this moment and probably would say anything to get away from Lwaxana, but in "Heart of Stone," Odo reveals that his full name is Odo Ital. Given the Bajoran format, that would make Odo his family name and Ital his given name.

• In this episode Odo confirms that his regenerative cycle is sixteen hours long, not eighteen hours long as he stated in "A Man Alone."

EQUIPMENT ODDITIES

• Complaining about the fusion reactors on the station, O'Brien says that he would trade it in for a Federation model tomorrow if he could, but it's all they've got. Wait a minute:

Doesn't O'Brien fix every broken ship that wanders by? What does he use? Cardassian parts? Bajoran parts? Wouldn't he use Federation parts? And in "The Survivors" *(TNG)*, Picard *gave* a fusion-powered replicator to Kevin Uxbridge and his faux wife. The Federation has never seemed stingy when it comes to its equipment. So why can't O'Brien get a couple of fusion reactors?

• I'm confused. I seem to have misplaced the windows in Ops. When the rift gets mad in the previous episode— "If Wishes Were Horses"—one shot shows the main viewscreen. Several circular windows rest above it. And in this episode, several shots show that the windows extend all the way around to at least the edge of Sisko's office. Also, the footage of this episode establishes that these windows are *above* the level of Sisko's office. Now come with me to the exterior shots of DS9. I think I've figured out where the promenade windows are. In the center section there's a series of outward-sloping solid plates with large circular buttons near their tops. Above these plates is a series of vertically elongated oval windows. They look just like the windows on the promenade. So far, so good. But where is Ops? I'm guessing that Ops is at the very top of the center stack—that little pod thing that hovers over the promenade. In fact, there is a horizontally elongated window, shown quite often in the exterior shots of DS9, that would correspond perfectly with the window in Sisko's office. This is where the trouble begins. According to the interior sets, there should be a ring of win-

dows *above* Sisko's window. *I have never been able to find them on the exterior shots!* (There is a series of small windows below Sisko's window, but those would be in the wrong place according to the interior footage shown in this episode.)

• Early on, O'Brien complains about the Cardassian computer system and how he is going to have to rebuild it from the ground up. That's funny; I thought in "Emissary" that O'Brien said that the Cardassians took "every component of value." (Then again, from the way O'Brien is talking, I suppose this would be a true statement!)

• There is a beautiful visual when Odo and Lwaxana board the turbolift. More than once, nitpitckers have asked why there is only one set of doors on the turbolifts of the *Enterprise*. Rightly so; nitpickers know that there should be an inner set of doors and an outer set of doors—one set to stay with the deck and the other to ride along with the turbolift. The creators solved this problem on DS9 by showing in this episode that the turbolifts have only one set of doors. After Odo and Lwaxana board we actually get to see the decks zipping by. Bravo! Beautifully done. Well...almost. Odo and Lwaxana board the turbolift on the promenade. As far as I know, the promenade sits in the center section of the station, under Ops. Going upward from the promenade leads only to Ops. If you go up any farther, you go out into space. A rough visual estimation puts the distance between Ops and the promenade at no more than five or six decks. Amazingly enough, after Odo and Lwaxana board the turbolift, it goes up some twenty-eight decks...*in a straight line*!

• There's some confusion concerning which turbolift Odo and Lwaxana inhabit. Odo says it's Turbolift 7. Yet later, Sisko identifies it in his log entry as Turbolift 4. (Here's an odd little thought: Together, these two numbers make "47." A coincidence? I wonder. See the sidebar "47.")

• Evidently the Cardassians never expected anyone to get stuck in one of their turbolifts. They don't have an emergency exit, like a Starfleet turbolift, or Odo would have long since used it.

• I realize that the transporters on the station are down and that's why Sisko's team doesn't just beam Odo and Lwaxana out of the turbolift, but why doesn't anyone mention the transporters on the runabouts? Are they out of commission, too? And if so, why? Are their computer systems connected to the main system on the station?

• Once again—as was the case on the *Enterprise*—when the computer is unhappy, great arcs of electricity erupt from the terminals. One has to wonder why the designers of these death traps constructed them to run on 50,000 volts instead of the normal low-power method used today.

• At the end of this episode, Bashir and three ambassadors find them-selves in a plasma-flame-engulfed corridor. Wisely, Bashir leads them into a conduit. Several minutes later, Sisko and company charge to the rescue. After coming to the conclusion that Bashir and the ambassadors must be dead, Sisko happily watches as the hatchway to the conduit flies off and everyone emerges a bit singed but safe. Aren't these conduits interconnected? Why didn't Bashir lead them to safety on another level? Was the conduit blocked off in some way?

CONTINUITY AND PRODUCTION PROBLEMS

• Nearing the start of his regenerative cycle, Odo begins to do his impression of the Wicked Witch of the West. ("I'm melting. I'm melting.") Oddly enough, though his face and hands look like they are ready to drip, his clothes look just fine. Yet every time Odo morphs we see that his clothes are actually part of him. So why aren't they melting, too?

• The corridor plasma explosion seen in this episode looks amazingly similar to the plasma explosion seen only last episode in "If Wishes Were Horses."

TRIVIA ANSWERS

1. Anara.
2. Andevian II.

DRAMATIS PERSONAE

Star Dates: 46922.3—46924.5

A Klingon vessel that returns early from the Gamma Quadrant and subsequently explodes before it reaches DS9 commences a bizarre adventure onboard the station. A sole Klingon survivor beams into Ops before proclaiming, "Victory!" and then dying from his wounds. Dax and O'Brien retrieve the vessel's mission record, but the logs are badly scrambled, and it will take time for the computer to sort them out. Gradually the senior staff begin polarizing over a seemingly minor incident. Kira wants to investigate a Valerian transport she believes is running weapons-grade dolamide to the Cardassians. Sisko refuses. O'Brien sides with Sisko. Dax sides with Kira.

As hostilities escalate, Odo turns to the Klingon ship's logs—finally deciphered by the computer. He learns that the Klingons discovered telepathic spheres on a world they surveyed. The spheres recounted an ancient power struggle. Shortly after they were opened, the Klingon ship erupted in the same type of power struggle. Realizing that the senior staff are also reenacting that same

Trivia Questions

1. Who served as first officer on the Klingon vessel *Toh'Kaht*?

2. What drink does Quark make for Dax in this episode?

struggle, Odo tricks Bashir into creating a field that can purge the telepathic energy from the senior staff. He then lures everyone to Cargo Bay 4, where he activates the field and flushes the resulting telepathic energy into space.

PLOT OVERSIGHTS

• At one point the telepathic matrix attempts to infiltrate Odo but fails. His face "butterflies" and he collapses. After the commercial break, Odo wakes in the infirmary. He wonders if he's back to normal. Well, actually, no. He now suffers from the dreaded "Tasha Yar syndrome." (Aaaaaaaah!) This syndrome—named for the original chief of Security of the *Enterprise*-D—causes otherwise competent officers to become grammatically challenged. (Tasha Yar exhibited this disease with statements such as "What have bright primary colors got to do with it?") Worried over his state of being after collapsing, Odo says, "I don't remember anything. But I back to normal?"

• There's a big-time skip in this episode. In the middle of his investigation of the senior officers' strange behavior, Odo goes to Sisko's office

75

and finds O'Brien. They chitchat and, among other things, O'Brien says the data interpolation on the logs won't be complete for another seven hours. Odo goes to Sisko's quarters to visit the commander. Then the episode takes a commercial break. Coming back, we see Odo returning to his office. Kira is waiting for him, and they chitchat about the mutiny. She leaves. Odo asks the computer about the logs and the computer says that the data interpolation is complete! (My, that was a *fast* seven hours!)

• During the aforementioned chitchatting between Odo and O'Brien, O'Brien says that Sisko is in his quarters "where he's safe." Oddly enough, Sisko is back in his office. Funny, I thought tensions were escalating *if anything*.

CHANGED PREMISES

• Once again Odo attempts to use pretense to extract information from Quark. Trying to determine if the Klingons revealed anything to Quark about their mission, Odo chats with the Ferengi bartender about the problems he had with the Klingons the last time they came through. Quark talks about how hard the Klingons are on holosuites. Odo comments that they do tend to bluster. Quark takes the bait at first, freely sharing what the Klingons told him about their mission. Then he realizes Odo's keen interest in the conversation. Quark turns and observes, "Crafty tonight, aren't we, Odo?" My point? In "Past Prologue," both he and Kira made adamant statements that Odo had no pretense.

EQUIPMENT ODDITIES

• After the Klingon ship comes through the wormhole and explodes, O'Brien says he is reading a transport signal. He adds that somebody may have beamed off the ship just as it exploded. So...Klingon transporters can continue to function *after they blow up*? Now, that's engineering for you! (This would be like a computer uploading a file to an Internet server, shorting out halfway through the process, and the file arriving at the server completely intact!

• Pardon me for bringing this up, but—once again—Bashir uses his tricorder to determine that a person is dead, this time a Klingon. (See "The Passenger.")

• Sometimes this crew really misses out on the easy solutions to their problems. If Sisko and friends had understood the Klingon mission logs early on in the episode, a lot of needless conflict could have been avoided. They sit there in Ops watching this badly garbled transmission, and no one—*no one,* mind you—even thinks to turn on the closed captioning! Granted, the picture quality is poor—and sometimes when you have really poor picture quality the closed captioning doesn't come through—but shouldn't they at least *try it*? I mean, *I* turned on the closed captioning in my backward old twentieth-century television and I could read *everything* the Klingon guy was saying!

• Someone upgraded the Cardassian transporters on DS9. Prior to this episode the annular confinement beam of the transporters featured a series of swirling dots. In this episode the beam also includes circular arcs.

CONTINUITY AND PRODUCTION PROBLEMS

• According to the star dates on this episode, it precedes "The Forsaken."

• After Odo "butterflies" and then comes back to normal in the infirmary, Kira visits Sisko. She waltzes into his office, and a few shots later we see the doors have closed—*without* making their usual sound.

• Kira's earring seems to have a cloaking device in this episode. She visits Dax in Quark's and tells the lieutenant that she's going to get rid of Sisko. Quark reacts with shock. As she moseys over to Quark's position behind the bar, we see that Kira wears her earring on her right ear. Then the scene cuts to a close-up and the earring is gone! Then Kira throws Quark into the bar, and the earring is back! Then Kira says "Good," and the earring is gone!

• Escaping from Kira, Sisko pulls off his and O'Brien's communicators and tosses them into a hallway. Then the entire senior staff end up in Cargo Bay 4—the result of Odo's maneuvering. Once Bashir's field purges the telepathic energy from everyone, Odo opens the cargo door and blows it out into space. After the scene shows the cargo bay door closing, it cuts to a medium-wide shot of Sisko, and somehow his communicator is back! Thankfully, order returns to the universe moments later when a subsequent shot shows us that the communicator has had the grace to disappear once again. (This was one of the most submitted nits.)

• Odo's hair seems to be blowing the wrong way in the cargo bay. As he opens the door and exposes the cargo bay to the vacuum of space, he stands directly opposite the opening. The evacuating air seems to be hitting him in the face, however, when it should be rushing away from him.

TRIVIA ANSWERS
1. Hon'Tihl.
2. A Modela aperitif.

Star Date: unknown

The episode opens with a Kobheerian freighter captain requesting medical attention for one of his passengers. He says the individual suffers from Kalla Nohra. Kira reacts immediately. The only known victims of Kalla Nohra suffered it because of a mining accident at a Cardassian labor camp named Gallitepp. Kira helped liberate that camp. Ready to find an honored Bajoran in the infirmary, she instead finds a Cardassian whom she immediately arrests. Kira believes he is a war criminal, though his name, Aamin Marritza, doesn't appears on any warrants.

In the course of the investigation, Kira uncovers evidence that Marritza is actually Gul Darhe'el—former head of the labor camp and known as the "Butcher of Gallitepp." As Kira interrogates him, the prisoner lets slip that he knew she was in the Shakaar resistance group. Having difficulty believing that a labor camp supervisor would remember this, Odo digs deeper. He discovers that the Cardassian is actually Marritza posing as Darhe'el, hoping to be captured, wanting to

Trivia Questions

1. Who is the minister of state on Bajor?

2. What drink does Odo bring Kira from Quark's private stock?

stand trial for the atrocities at Gallitepp, believing it will help Cardassians to face their guilt. Humbled by Marritza's sentiments, Kira lets him go—only to have a bitter Bajoran stab him to death on the promenade moments later.

RUMINATIONS

This is a great episode. Well formed. Beautifully executed. Elegant in its simplicity. No need for two plots going at the same time here. The story has enough substance to carry it nicely throughout. Each time it looks like everything is figured out—the creators twist the plot once again to keep us interested. Kudos.

GREAT LINES

"What you call genocide, I call a day's work."—Marritza to Kira. (Not that I agree with the sentiment, you understand. It's just that when he said it, I thought, "Yikes!")

PLOT OVERSIGHTS

• I am ever amazed at Starfleet procedures for dealing with disease. Out of the blue, Bashir gets a call from Kira stating that a patient will be beaming on with a malady the good doctor knows nothing about. Bashir's response? While the patient is beaming on board he's going to look it up in the database! Wouldn't it make more sense to look it up *first* and then beam the guy aboard? What if the guy's disease is contagious? (Yes, it would be nice to believe that the Kobheerian freighter captain would have alerted DS9 to any potential danger, but what if he isn't versed in the disease either?)

• I guess military terminology is the same all over the galaxy. At the beginning of this episode Kira calls for Security to come to the infirmary "on the double." Then again, maybe the Universal Translator just substituted this little slang phrase to make the Starfleet Security officers feel more at home.

• Kira speaks of "liberating" the forced labor camp known as Gallitepp. Yet apparently this "liberation" was accomplished without Kira ever seeing the camp's Cardassian leader's face, because she doesn't know Gul Darhe'el on sight. (Hmmm.)

• Learning of Marritza's detention, Gul Dukat and Sisko have a little chat. During one exchange, Dukat states that he will hold Sisko personally responsible if any of the Bajoran hatemongers gets their hands on Marritza. I wonder: Did Dukat hold Sisko responsible? After all, a hatemonger did get his hands on Marritza *and killed him*!

• The final revelation of Marritza's true identity begins when Odo refuses to believe that Marritza would know Kira was in the Shakaar resistance cell. Marritza, posing as Darhe'el, fluffs off Kira's questions on the mat-

ter, stating that he read it in a report that came across his desk. Interestingly enough, later revelations about Cardassians make me wonder why Odo would doubt Marritza on this matter. According to Sisko in "The Maquis, Part I," the Cardassians are famous for their *photographic* memories, cultivated by an intense mind-control program that begins at age four. Wouldn't Odo have had some exposure to these particular Cardassian skills? And if so, why does he seem surprised that Gul Darhe'el would remember that Kira belonged to the Shakaar resistance cell? It would take only one report mentioning this fact, wouldn't it?

• Having become suspicious that the prisoner who claims to be Gul Darhe'el is actually someone else, Odo has a conversation with Gul Dukat. In it they argue over whom Odo has incarcerated. Gul Dukat's position is that it cannot be Darhe'el because he attended Darhe'el's funeral six years prior. So why doesn't Odo just show Dukat a picture of the guy in the cell? He looks exactly like Darhe'el, doesn't he?

• And speaking of pictures, why isn't Darhe'el's picture shown on the death certificate that Odo presents to Sisko?

• As Sisko and crew close in on the fact that the prisoner is actually Marritza, Bashir reports that the Cardassian is under treatment for Kalla Nohra and a few other minor ailments "related to his age." Whose age? Marritza's or Darhe'el's? In the one image that shows both men at Gallitepp, Marritza looks *decades* younger than Darhe'el. If this is the case, why would Marritza be suffering from ailments related to old age? Conversely, if Bashir means to say that the prisoner suffers merely from the ailments of middle age, then doesn't that lend credence to the fact that the Cardassian in custody is too young to be Darhe'el?

• Odo puts in a pitiful showing as chief of Security at the end of this episode. The Bajoran killer approaches from behind Odo and has to overtake the shape shifter to get to Marritza. I have always been stunned that Odo didn't sense the guy coming up behind him. This brings up another point. Those eyes that Odo simulates aren't real eyes, right? In addition, we find out in "The Alternate" that Odo demonstrated his sentience to Dr. Mora by becoming a beaker. (This was just before Odo ran off to join *The Muppet Show*. Just joking.) To become a beaker, Odo had to *see*— or at least perceive—the beaker. Since Odo had not formed a humanoid face yet, we must conclude that Odo can analyze and interpret patterns of light without the benefit of his fake humanoid eyeballs. If that's true, I see no reason why Odo wouldn't have the ability to see out his back—given that we have seen on numerous occasions that his uniform is actually formed by his shape shifting. Unfortunately, the high probability that Odo can see in any direction only worsened his incompetence at the end of the episode!

• Finally, why doesn't anyone call for Dr. Bashir after Marritza is assaulted? It's only a knife wound, for crying out loud! This is the twenty-fourth century!

CHANGED PREMISES

• At the end of the episode, a Bajoran "hatemonger"—to use Dukat's terminology—stabs Marritza in the back. I could have sworn that Odo said in "Emissary" that he doesn't allow weapons on the promenade. I also could have sworn that he told the Duras sisters in "Past Prologue" that they could leave their weapons or leave the station. I also could have sworn that "Captive Pursuit" showed us that the promenade has Security sensors that sweep for weapons. So how did this lone knifeman get past all that security? (I suspect there was a second Bajoran, also armed with a knife, standing on the grassy knoll.)

EQUIPMENT ODDITIES

• Part of the evidence that initially implicates Marritza as Gul Darhe'el, "the Butcher of Gallitepp," comes from a photograph that shows both Marritza and Darhe'el. The sequence in Ops showing Sisko and crew analyzing this photograph deserves some scrutiny. First—before the crew can begin—O'Brien must manually patch the image enhancement routine directly into Dax's console. So why doesn't Dax have access to image enhancement routines from her console in the first place? Second, the console that O'Brien identifies as Dax's console is not the one she usually uses! It is off to the side of her normal workstation. Why didn't O'Brien just patch the routines into her normal workstation? (Because then Dax wouldn't have been in the shot. With her standing at the little auxiliary console, the creators could frame the picture better.) Third, the image enhancement that Dax runs on Marritza's out-of-focus blowup seems to take a long time. Granted, it is only a few seconds before the image sharpens, but this is supposed to be the twenty-fourth century. In our backward twentieth century we already have computers and image processing software that can "deblur" graphic images. With the current rate of increase in sophistication of both hardware and software, I have a hard time believing that image enhancement software would still take a few seconds to execute in the twenty-fourth century. (Of course, the previous sentence opens up a huge discussion that I will not indulge in here, namely that none of the computer hardware and software shown on *Star Trek* can ever begin to simulate the level of sophistication that will be available in synthetic intelligence by the twenty-fourth century. The whole field of computer science is moving so rapidly, it's mind-boggling!) Fourth, to their credit, however, the creators *do* show us incredible sophistication with respect to the image processing done on Darhe'el's portion of the picture. Zooming in and extrapolating, the computer's camera gives a perspective that actually drifts around an individual to get to a complete view of the Gul's face. It rotates three-dimensionally in a two-dimensional image. That's pretty impressive. (Although I have no doubt that somebody out there reading this has some knowledge of leading-edge image processing software that already has the beginnings of this kind of capability.)

TRIVIA ANSWERS
1. Kaval.
2. Maraltian Seev-Ale.

IN THE HANDS OF THE PROPHETS

Star Date: unknown

Vedek Winn—leader of a relatively unimportant orthodox sect within the Bajoran religion—pays a surprise visit to DS9 to protest Keiko's instruction of Bajoran children on the scientific explanation for the wormhole. Winn believes the "passage" to be the location of the Celestial Temple and considers Keiko's secular teaching methods blasphemous. For her part, Keiko stands on her convictions about truth, justice, and the Federation way, steadfastly refusing to allow any religious beliefs to be taught in her school.

Seeking a compromise, Sisko meets with Vedek Bareil—the favored successor to Kai Opaka and leader of a more liberal sect. Initially Bareil declines Sisko's request for help. The Vedek Assembly is divided over the role the Federation should play in Bajoran life. Some even label Sisko and the Federation "godless." With the election of Kai approaching, Bareil is hesitant to speak out on the controversial issue. However, when a bomb goes off in Keiko's school, Bareil decides to act. He travels to DS9 to attempt to cool passions and bring unity. This is precisely what Winn planned. She has already convinced Neela—one of O'Brien's Bajoran coworkers—to kill Bareil when he arrives. Just in time, Sisko prevents the murder. Unfortunately, the assassin refuses to implicate anyone but herself.

Trivia Questions

1. What was Vedek Bareil's greatest ambition while he was a gardener?

2. What code does O'Brien use to access the file A.N.A.?

RUMINATIONS

Kudos to the creators for not choosing a nameless Bajoran-of-the-week to play the part of the assassin. Obviously aware of this episode's approach, they cast Neela early and gave her a bit part in the previous episode, "Duet," to establish her relationship with O'Brien.

PLOT OVERSIGHTS

• The preview of this episode has the following narration: "A religious extremist sets off a wave of terror—a holy war that could divide the station and bring the Federation to its knees." A bit "over the top," don't you think? (Of course, I may not be one to talk!) Was there ever any chance that this picayune conflict would "bring the Federation to its knees"?

• This isn't so much a nit as it is an

"I wish they would have." After refusing Winn's demand that she teach the Bajoran belief about the wormhole to the Bajoran children in her school, Keiko changes her lesson plan to review the events of Galileo and his trial by the Roman Catholic Church. Fresh from this experience, Jake comes to talk with Sisko, convinced that this whole problem with the Bajoran belief about the wormhole is "stupid" and "dumb." Sisko defuses his son's newfound intolerance by stating that the aliens who built the wormhole see the past and the future with equal ease. He asks why they couldn't be considered "Prophets." He explains that it's a matter of interpretation; that it may not be what Jake believes, but that doesn't make it wrong; that if Jake begins to think that way, then he'll be acting just like Vedek Winn, only on the other side. I agree! But "I wish they would have" had Sisko go one extra step during this discussion. He already *has* someone on the station who is acting just like Vedek Winn, only on the other side, and I wish he would have identified her—namely...*Keiko*! Now, I understand that she's mad and hurt over the way Vedek Winn has handled this issue. I also understand Keiko couldn't say anything that would make any difference in this situation. Winn's agenda really isn't about teaching Bajoran beliefs in school, it's about getting Bareil to the station. Keeping these facts in mind, let's backtrack just a bit.

In "A Man Alone," Keiko decides she wants to start a school. She talks with Sisko about it, and he outlines the difficulties she may encounter. He says

he cannot force the children to come. He says that even if they do come, everyone will have a different culture, a different philosophy. Awash in optimism for her new project, Keiko excitedly agrees that she knows she will have to be innovative. By the time of this episode, Keiko seems to have lost her "innovativeness." What's wrong with saying something like this: "This is an artifically created wormhole. Our scientific studies have shown that a race of aliens who live a nonlinear existence used vertiron particles to construct it. These aliens are revered by Bajorans as the Prophets, and Bajorans believe that their Celestial Temple exists inside the wormhole."? And *then*—in addition to being less than innovative—Keiko steps over the line by pulling out one of the worst examples of conflict between science and religion. (Misguided application of belief on the part of the Roman Catholic Church, I might add. They were off-base when it came to Galileo, and they did admit it centuries later.) What is Keiko's purpose in pulling out this example? To convince the students to see things *her* way—which, of course, she does! After all, she *is* the teacher. Personally, I think Sisko needs to have a small talk with Mrs. O'Brien.

• I take it all back. Everything I have ever said questioning anything to do with the competence of Federation medicine. *I take it...all...back!* Bashir pulls off the most amazing analysis in this episode that I have ever seen in all my years of watching *Star Trek*. As the episode unfolds we learn that Neela intended to use a runabout to effect her escape after killing Bareil. Evidently Neela took O'Brien's "E-J-7 interlock" to access the Security seal on Runabout Pad C. Unfortunately, Ensign Aquino discovered her in the process, and she killed him with a phaser. (Note: She didn't *vaporize* him, she just killed him.) Neela then dumped the guy and the interlock in a plasma conduit, turned on the power, and reduced both to one medium-sized, burned blob of ash. She thought she had covered her tracks and made it look like an accident, but she didn't account for the intrepid Dr. Bashir and his magical, mystery autopsy skills. After analyzing the residue, Bashir reports to Sisko. He states that the reconstructed DNA definitely belongs to Aquino, but the power flow in the conduit didn't kill him. Then he says, "You see the plasma disruption in his cellular membranes indicates that he was exposed to a directed energy discharged before he was placed in the conduit." You may recall that Aquino's burned goo was not found in some Jefferies tube look-alike, it was a *plasma* conduit. For hours it had hot *plasma* running though it—cooking Aquino to a crisp. Yet Bashir can determine that a *plasma* disruption from a phaser killed the guy after his body has been reduced to ashes by the *plasma* in the conduit. This is *truly* a stellar piece of work! (Sort of like determining that a man was burned to death after his body has been cremated.)

CHANGED PREMISES

• Meeting with Sisko for the first time, Winn tells the commander that the Prophets have spoken to her through the "orbs." She must be speaking "evangelastically"—a term sometimes applied to a television preacher who stretches the truth. According to "Emissary," the Bajorans only have one orb. The Cardassians have the rest, and I can't imagine they gave any of them back!

• I've been trying to pin down the shift schedule for DS9. In "The Forsaken," Sisko schedules a briefing for 0400 hours. That's four in the morning for nonmilitary types. It seems a bit early for a briefing, but in space there is no day or night, so it doesn't really matter what the clock says once an officer's body adjusts to a specific cycle. From this I surmised that Sisko and his senior staff work what we would call the graveyard shift. In this episode, however, the senior staff discusses the missing interlock, and Kira suggests that whoever took it might not have wanted to wake O'Brien to ask permission to borrow it. She reminds the chief that it was "four in the morning." (Don't ask me why she doesn't say "0400 hours.") Evidently O'Brien was asleep at 0400 hours. Since we usually see the senior staff working together, it's safe to assume that they work the same shifts. But that would mean that 0400 hours would be the middle of the night for Sisko, so why would he schedule a briefing then? (I suppose that the schedules might be rotating a human twenty-four-hour day against a Bajoran twenty-six-hour day, but this seems needlessly complex. It's also possible that Sisko and the senior staff rotate through the different shifts—working graveyard one week, swing shift the next, and so on. I'm told this is really hard on the human constitution, however, and it's got to be murder on family life.)

EQUIPMENT ODDITIES

• After a bomb detonates on the promenade, a Bajoran officer runs up with a hose and starts to put out the fire. No sprinkler system? No fire suppression system? Not even any protective gear for the poor, hapless fireman? Just a *hose*? (If you think about it, I think you'll agree with me that fire is a *bad* problem on a space station. One would think that the designers would have lots of safety features built in to put a fire out quickly!)

• Someone needs to send a note of acknowledgment to the company that manufactured the flooring for DS9. At the end of the episode, Sisko tackles Neela. In the process, her phaser dips down, and the beam hits the floor. The energy discharge—strong enough to kill a humanoid—doesn't even singe the carpet!

CONTINUITY AND PRODUCTION PROBLEMS

• At one point, the computer in Ops locates what's left of the E-J-7 interlock in a conduit on Level 12, Section 8. The resulting graphic shows a wire frame of the DS9 moving in a fixed three-dimensional pattern, with the location of the E-J-7 remains marked by a dot. The dot doesn't look like it's moving exactly the same as the wire frame of the station—making it appear that the remains of the E-J-7 are wandering in circles!

• The day after Winn arrives on the station, Keiko and O'Brien find her standing in front of the school with the Bajoran families who have children who attend. Watch the boy on the far right of the screen. He keeps looking at the camera.

• When a bomb goes off in the school, O'Brien believes that Keiko may be inside. He runs to the location, and Odo must restrain him from charging inside. In one shot we see Odo extend his arm completely around O'Brien's chest. Then the shot changes and Odo is suddenly holding O'Brien's arms.

• For some reason the Bajorans have begun buying their ships from the Wadi! The footage used for the arrival of Bareil on the station comes from "Move Along Home."

• The graphic showing Neela's program to establish an escape route from the promenade to Runabout Pad C comes from "Dramatis Personnae."

• At the end of the program, a close-up shows Sisko leaping into the air to tackle Neela and prevent her from killing Bareil. This close-up features an "elephanthead" individual off to Sisko's right who is not present in either the preceding or the succeeding shots. (He's one of those guys who has what looks like an elephant trunk sprouting out the top of his head and looping down his back.)

TRIVIA ANSWERS
1. To grow the loveliest Feloran on Bajor.
2. 4100RLX.

THOUGHTS AND RUMINATIONS ON *STAR TREK: THE NEXT GENERATION*'S SUCCESSOR

I've done enough of these *Guides* that I use a simple, methodical system. The first step is the "crash session." I sit and watch eight episodes a day—making notes as I go—until I watch every episode reviewed in the book. It helps me "get my arms around" the series and get an overview of the material. I began this *Guide* prior to the start of the fourth season, so I had only seventy-two episodes to watch. The crash session took me nine days. Something came out of those nine days that changed the way I watch *Star Trek: Deep Space Nine.* And frankly, it allowed me to enjoy the program much more. What follows is just my humble opinion. I don't necessarily expect you to agree with it, but you might find something here that makes sense. (And you'll probably find something here that you thought of *years* ago! I admit it. It takes a while for certain thoughts to seep into my brain.)

By the start of the third day of the crash session for this *Guide,* I was *not* happy. And I was not happy that I was not happy. I have a great deal of respect for the creators of *Star Trek.* I believe them to be some of the most talented in the business. They do good work. I'm a fan of their work. I think I understand their work and what they attempt to accomplish. It follows, then, that I should enjoy sitting all day and watching their work. (It is, after all, a *fabulous* job to have.) But after two days of *DS9,* I wasn't enjoying it. I had watched sixteen episodes, and I just didn't *get* it.

For years prior to the crash session, I had done my Trekly duty—tuning in to watch and record *DS9* almost every week. I had assumed my dissonance with the show came from the casual way I had approached its viewing. Although I enjoyed the show, I had never really connected with it. Going into the crash session, I had expected to give myself a good, stiff dose of *DS9, finally* figure out what the creators had in mind for the series, *finally* lock onto their vision, and immediately become *very* impressed over how that vision was implemented. I wasn't locking.

Then, as I watched "Dramatis Personae" on the morning of the third day of the crash session, it hit me! As I watched Kira fight for Bajoran interests yet again—albeit *this* time under the influence of a telepathic sphere—I wrote in my notes, "This really is more like *Bajor: Deep Space Nine.*" For two days I had tried to fit the series into my *Star Trek* mind-set and it just wouldn't work. I suddenly realized there was a reason for that dissonance.

Let me see if I can illustrate my conundrum. Suppose a guy named George Staffengrape started a company back in 1966 to manufacture mechanical wristwatches. Wanting his customers to know that he manufactured quality watches, he named his company Seventeen Jewels. Every watch had the logo *Seventeen Jewels* inscribed on it, and in fact all the watches he manufactured had seventeen jewels. (I talked with the proprietor of a local clock and watch repair shop here in Springfield, and if I understood correctly, a "jewel"—with respect to wristwatches—is a device that reduces friction—not a gemstone!) Eventually the original watches became successful and Staffengrape decided to design another set of watches—a next generation of watches, if you will. (Wink, wink.) These watches were also mechanical and did indeed have seventeen jewels. They also bore the inscription *Seventeen Jewels*. However, once Staffengrape died, the new owners of the company decided to modernize. Quartz-based watches were all the rage, and Seventeen Jewels was soon happily manufacturing a whole new line of quartz-based digital watches inscribed with the logo *Seventeen Jewels*. True, the watches didn't have seventeen jewels, but the company had a long list of loyal customers who bought the watches anyway.

This was the difficulty I faced with *Star Trek: Deep Space Nine*. I had spent a lot of time watching *Star Trek* and *Star Trek: The Next Generation*. To me, "Star Trek" wasn't the name of a franchise, it was a formula for a television show, a formula whose elements I had deduced by watching more than one thousand hours of *Star Trek*. Every time the words "Star Trek: Deep Space Nine" flashed across the screen, those first two words would invoke the formula, and my brain would try to pattern-match elements of the formula with what I saw in the episode. When it couldn't, I would start buzzing. A few quick examples:

Until *Star Trek: Deep Space Nine, Trek* episodes featured "trekking through the stars." Remember the opening? "Space: the final frontier. These are the voyages of the starship *Enterprise*. Its continuing mission: To explore strange new worlds, to seek out new life and new civilizations. To boldly go where no one has gone before." Right after this pronouncement in both the *Classic* and *NextGen* television series the words "Star Trek" zoom onto the screen. (Yes, I realize that the opening to *Classic Trek* is a few words different.)

Until *Star Trek: Deep Space Nine, Trek* episodes featured the *Enterprise*. (Actually, with the advent of *Star Trek: Voyager,* I found this was the easiest part of the formula to abandon.)

Until *Star Trek: Deep Space Nine, Trek* episodes featured Starfleet personnel in the lead roles. This configuration said something about the characters featured. It revealed a common purpose in them, a shared experience, a unity of framework. On *Star Trek: Deep Space Nine,* Kira, Odo, and Quark represent three very different agendas from those of the Federation. The "team" doesn't exist.

Until *Star Trek: Deep Space Nine, Trek* episodes featured Federation technology. Every week I could scan the displays and feel reasonably comfortable that I knew who did what and—sort of—how they did it. I could make some sense out it. (I *still* don't have the foggiest notion how the Cardassian displays in Ops work. Nor have I figured out who does what from where!)

Until *Star Trek: Deep Space Nine,* almost every *Trek* episode featured a log entry with a star date. I admit it. It's a *small* thing, but the log entries and star dates always gave me a feeling of continuity and some sense of progression since the previous episode. (However, I should note that there is one thing worse than no star date in an episode: It's when the creators have someone make the *first* log entry of a show with the dreaded star date "Supplemental.")

I tried ignoring the formula. I tried telling myself that "Star Trek" is only a name and since *DS9* is set in Gene Roddenberry's universe, it rightly deserves the title. Although that line of reasoning is legally correct, it didn't help. But on that third day of the crash session, I finally found a way to see certain episodes of *DS9* for what they were, not what the formula in my head said they should be. I made up a new title for them. I call them *Bajor: Terok Nor* episodes! (*Bajor: Deep Space Nine* would be hopelessly Earthcentric, since the station isn't in deep space from Bajor's perspective.) For instance—as I write this sidebar—my local Fox affiliate has advertised that it will air "Crossfire" tomorrow night. From the preview, the episode appears to be about a love triangle among Kira, Odo, and Shakaar. In my opinion, that's a *Bajor: Terok Nor* episode because it revolves around individuals who are not Starfleet. Since it's a *Bajor: Terok Nor* episode, I won't expect to see any strange new worlds or new life or new civilizations. Neither will I expect it to have any "boldly going." It will be about life on board a space station. Period. Please understand: That *doesn't* make it a wrong or a bad episode. It just makes it *different*. (Before you write, read that statement again. *I'm not saying it's wrong or bad*. I'm just saying it's different!) For me, calling it a *Bajor: Terok Nor* episode will actually increase my enjoyment of the episode because it will rearrange my expectations.

Now, I could list all the episodes I consider *Bajor: Terok Nor,* but I know how much nitpickers love to debate stuff like this, so I'll leave it to you to come up with your own list! (Here's a hint, though: Many of the *Bajor: Terok Nor* episodes end with an emotional outburst from Kira.)

SECOND

SEASON

THE HOMECOMING

Star Date: unknown

When a Boslic freighter captain brings Quark a Bajoran earring from Cardassia IV, Kira discovers that it belongs to Li Nalas—a legendary resistance fighter who was thought to be dead. She asks Sisko for a runabout to stage a rescue in spite of Cardassia's continued claims that it no longer holds any Bajoran prisoners. Sisko reluctantly agrees. A new faction has appeared on Bajor called the Circle. It is a militant group that wants Bajor for Bajorans only. Sisko hopes that the return of Li Nalas will rally all Bajorans to peaceful unity.

The rescue is successful, but Li Nalas isn't what Sisko expected. The resistance fighter reveals that his only claim to fame is shooting Gul Zarale as the Cardassian emerged in his underwear from a lake. The incident quickly became a legend of fierce hand-to-hand combat. From then on, almost every Bajoran resistance victory was credited to his account. Li is tired and simply wants to be left alone. Sisko convinces him otherwise. He tells Li that Bajor needs him as a symbol of honor and decency. A short time later, the provisional government posts Li Nalas to DS9 as liaison officer even as Minister Jaro informs Sisko that Kira has been recalled to Bajor.

RUMINATIONS

I love this Li Nalas character. He shoots a Cardassian in his underwear and becomes a national hero!

PLOT OVERSIGHTS

• These Bajoran prisoners have been in the Cardassian labor camp *too long*. During the breakout, Kira knocks down one Cardassian and stuns another in close range of the prisoners, yet no one thinks to grab their phaser rifles. As it turns out, they would have come in handy.

• This episode commences a practice by Quark that I find highly dubious. He divides his profits for the week out in the open without securing his doors! Does this make the least bit of sense, considering this guy is a greedy barkeep?

• During this counting process, several bad-boy Bajorans come into the bar and brand Quark with the symbol

91

of the Circle separatist group on Bajor. You may recall that earlier in this episode, Sisko told Odo that there were no longer any low-security areas on the station. So, in other words, these terrorists broke into a medium-to high-security area on the station and branded Quark? (Bet that won't look good on Odo's job review.)

CHANGED PREMISES

• Either educational standards have fallen dramatically in the past few years or Jake is "math challenged." In this episode Sisko congratulates him for passing his algebra test. In "When the Bough Breaks" *(TNG)*, Harry—a boy many years younger than Jake and who wanted to be an artist—vociferously complained about having to take *calculus*.

• When tending to Li's injuries, Bashir claims that he is a "history buff." He must have become one recently because he didn't know anything about the Setlik III massacre during "Emissary."

EQUIPMENT ODDITIES

• Snatching Li's earring from Quark's hands, Kira marches out to find Sisko. He asks her to join him in the replimat. As Kira impatiently waits, Sisko first orders a raktajino with a jacarine peel. Then he walks over to another replicator and orders an icoberry tort. Why couldn't he order the tort from the same replicator? Better yet, why couldn't he order both at the same time? Was he just trying to get on Kira's nerves?

• Speaking of replicators, they must have some type of automatic credit-

ing system. I can't imagine why anyone would go into Quark's and order food when he or she could walk around the corner and get it free!

• At the beginning of the first season I noted several statements made about characters that I knew were trouble when I heard them (i.e., Odo's lack of pretense, Bashir's denial of tricorders to judge the dead). This episode has another such statement that seems ill-planned. Approaching the Hutet labor camp on Cardassia IV, O'Brien reports that the sensors read "about" a dozen Bajoran prisoners. Kira then asks if there is any way of beaming up more than two at a time. O'Brien says, "'Fraid not." Now, I realize that the characters haven't *technically* said that a runabout can beam only two people at a time. Yes, there might be special considerations because of the labor camp. But it sure *sounds* like that's what O'Brien just said, and the transporter pad in the runabout is configured for two people to stand side by side. Unfortunately, there are a few problems with this equipment restraint. First, the shuttles on the *Enterprise* had emergency transporters that could beam *three* people at a time. We saw one in action when Data and Worf retrieved Picard in "The Best of Both Worlds, Part 2." Runabouts should be *more* advanced—not less—than shuttles. Second, the creators quickly found the "two people at a time" transport rule too confining. In the very next episode, they violate it! (As we shall see.)

• Fleeing for safety, Kira, O'Brien, and the Bajoran prisoners come under attack. Four of the Bajorans volunteer to stay behind (with only *one* phaser!) to hold off the Cardassians so the others can get back to the runabout. Reaching the runabout, Kira makes O'Brien wait for a few minutes before lifting off. The tension increases when O'Brien reads two Cardassian warships approaching. Finally Kira gives up on the valiant four, who stay behind, and tells O'Brien to take them home. One question: Why don't they just beam up the four guys as the runabout is taking off from the planet? A transport cycle requires only about five seconds to complete. (This is yet another example of technical sophistication thwarting good storytelling. There are too many easy ways to solve problems in the *Star Trek* universe.)

• Continuing on with this transporter theme, Li Nalas takes a phaser hit during the escape. With worried expressions, Kira and O'Brien help him out of the airlock on DS9. Bashir takes one look and has Dax beam Li directly to the infirmary. So...why didn't Kira have Dax beam Li to the infirmary as soon as the runabout was within 40,000 kilometers of the station?

• The doors that lead to Sisko's office never fail to amaze and confound. Sometimes people waltz right in. Sometimes they ring Sisko's doorbell. Sometimes they stand and wait. This episode has a prime example. Kira comes barreling in just after the rescue while Sisko is on the horn to Dukat. From his expression and tone, it appears that Sisko is miffed about Kira's rude entrance. The question is: How did Kira know Sisko's doors would open? It looks like she heads through them full force, yet there doesn't seem to be any way for a person to *know* that the doors will open automatically. Is there an indicator on the doors to tell entrants when the doors are configured for automatic opening?

CONTINUITY AND PRODUCTION PROBLEMS

• The first time we see Kira in the second season she has her arms raised in meditation. The scene begins with a tight shot of the side of the head and right shoulder, pulling back to almost full length. Interestingly enough, Kira's shoulder features a round scar that looks exactly like a smallpox vaccination mark. Since this is the age of hypospray, it's obviously the result of some fiendish Cardassian torture technique. (Then again, anyone who has endured a smallpox booster might make the same claim!)

• Shortly after Li's rescue, Minister Jaro Essa visits DS9. One shot shows him exiting the airlock while Kira waits to greet him. Oddly enough, the side of the ship shown in the airlock looks exactly like a Starfleet runabout!

• There's a small continuity glitch as Quark and Rom discuss what's fair when it comes to distributing the profits from the bar. From one camera angle, Quark holds six bars of latinum with both hands. From another, he holds them in his right hand only.

TRIVIA ANSWERS
1. Laira.
2. Romah Doek.

THE CIRCLE

As Kira packs her things to leave DS9 for her new posting on Bajor, Vedek Bareil comes to her quarters and invites her to his monastery. He knows she needs some time to reflect on her life. A short while later, Bareil brings Kira to a room that contains the third orb—the Orb of Prophecy and Change. She sees herself surrounded by members of the provisional government, all shouting incomprehensibly. She also sees Minister Jaro and Vedek Winn offering to help her understand. Bareil appears and urges her not to listen to them. Then the scene changes and Kira finds herself naked, with Bareil—also naked—standing behind her.

Meanwhile, Quark informs Odo that the Kressari are supplying weapons to the Circle. A further investigation reveals that the Cardassians are secretly acting as the true source for these weapons, hoping that the Circle—led by Minister Jaro—will topple the provisional government and expel the Federation from DS9. The Cardassians could then retake Bajor and the station, thereby gaining control over the wormhole. As the episode ends, the plan seems to be working. Two Bajoran assault vessels approach, demanding that all non-Bajorans evacuate. Starfleet deems it an internal affair and orders Sisko to withdraw.

Trivia Questions

1. What does Dax try to return to Kira before Kira leaves the station?

2. What is the name of the Kressari vessel that docks at DS9 during this episode?

GREAT LINES

"*A party!*"—Quark upon entering Kira's quarters and seeing that Odo, Dax, Bashir, and O'Brien have come to wish her well.

PLOT OVERSIGHTS

• In the previous episode—after seeing the emblem of the Circle spray-painted in a Habitat ring corridor—Sisko told Odo that there were no longer any low-security areas on the station. Near the beginning of this episode, Jake calls Sisko to the hallway outside their quarters. Someone has spray-painted another Circle emblem—this time on Sisko's door. In other words, someone managed to sneak into a medium- to high-security area, and Odo didn't catch the person?

• The bad science continues with Odo's shape-shifting abilities. In this episode Odo becomes a thin label on

94

the side of a container that O'Brien carries onto the Kressari vessel. For Odo—who is described as heavier than he looked in "Vortex"—to become light enough to carry, he would have to lose a portion of his mass. From dialogue in "The Adversary" we know that this detached portion would revert to its liquid state. There is no indication in this episode that Odo has left a portion of himself behind when he morphs into the label. According to physics, Odo the label should weigh the same as Odo the humanoid.

• As mentioned above, O'Brien carries Odo onto the Kressari vessel. Sisko and company want to find out if the Kressari are smuggling arms from the Cardassians to the Circle. Just before the vessel leaves, Dax tells O'Brien that the ship will return to DS9 "day after tomorrow." It appears that Odo will be on board the entire time. I wonder if he brought his bucket along. He *will* pass through at least one regeneration cycle while he's away.

• At one point Jaro has Kira kidnapped and tortured. He wants to know what the Federation will do once he mounts a coup against the provisional government. Hearing of her disappearance, Sisko stages a rescue, taking along Li Nalas, Bashir, O'Brien, and two nondescript Bajoran Security officers. Oddly enough, Sisko leaves Odo on the station. Wouldn't he be ideal on a covert rescue operation like this one? It's not like Odo's *doing* anything on the station. There have been two security breaches in the past two episodes alone!

• And speaking of the rescue of Kira, our good Dr. Bashir seems to suf-

fer a major brain cramp during its execution. Beaming down into the labyrinths beneath the Perikian Peninsula, Sisko tells his team, "Anyone who finds Kira, pin this on her and call for transport immediately." By "this" Sisko refers to the combadges he hands out. The commander's plan is simple: Blast your way in. Find Kira. Slap a combadge on her. Holler for O'Brien to transport everyone to safety. Seems straightforward enough, doesn't it? So what does Bashir do? He finds Kira and stops *to take the time to untie her* before moving around to her side. Then—as he begins to place the combadge on Kira—a member of the Circle shoots him in the back. (Serves him right for not following orders.) Kira—intuitively understanding what Bashir was *supposed* to do in the first place—sweeps the combadge from the dirt just as Bashir calls for transport, and O'Brien beams everyone up to the runabout.

• And speaking of Bashir getting shot in the back, the phaser must have just barely grazed him, because he seems "fit as a fiddle" only a short time later as he takes care of Kira's injuries back on the station. (This brings up another issue: According to "The Storyteller," it takes at least two hours to get from Bajor to DS9 in a runabout. Bashir knew he was going on a rescue mission. One would think he brought a full slate of emergency medical equipment. So what was he doing all the way back from Bajor if he wasn't working on Kira's injuries? Was Sisko doctoring him so he could finally get around to doctoring Kira?)

CHANGED PREMISES

• During the episode "In the Hands of the Prophets," Sisko came to Ops, glanced around, and proclaimed to Kira that they seemed to be short-handed although several officers were milling around. Kira reported that three of the Bajoran crew members had caught the DS9 version of the "blue flu." I noted at the end of that episode that tension still appears high because only *one* crew member inhabits Ops. This situation is almost as bad in this episode. Kira comes to Ops to say her farewell, and it looks like there are only two people manning the stations.

• Realizing that Bareil has brought her to the orb room at the monastery, Kira shudders and says she has dreamed of this moment all her life. Obviously she is excited about being in the presence of an orb and receiving a vision from it. This makes sense. For the Bajorans, the orbs represent a most physical manifestation of their "gods." Such an object would engender a great sense of devotion and wonder. So...why didn't Kira bop on down to Dax's lab when Sisko had the orb on the station in "Emissary"? Did he neglect to tell Kira that he brought it with him?

• At the end of this episode, Sisko has evidence that Cardassia is supplying the Circle with weapons. Yet Admiral Chekote (not to be confused with Commander Chakotay on *Voyager*) orders the withdrawal of Starfleet personnel from DS9. I wonder if Starfleet Command is going to set up some sort of blockade to ensure that no further weapons shipments make it from Cardassia to Bajor. Starfleet Command allowed Picard to do so in the case of the Romulans supplying weapons for the House of Duras in "Redemption II" *(TNG).* And that blockade eventually lead to Gowron's victory as the rightful leader of the Klingon Empire. (The point is this: Starfleet Command's response in this situation seems passive. They have options here. They just don't exercise them. Of course, that allows Sisko to play the rebellious hero by finagling a way to violate the intent of Chekote's orders.)

EQUIPMENT ODDITIES

• Great confusion surrounds the user interface of the turbolifts on DS9—specifically the turbolifts in Ops. Most of the time, crew members just hop into them and they start sinking. At other times, however, the turbolifts wait for the rider to state a destination. Most intriguingly, the turbolift always seems to wait for a destination when the rider—or another individual remaining in Ops—has dialogue to say before the scene concludes. (Wink, wink.) This happens twice in this episode. When Kira disembarks, the turbolift waits for her to say, "Docking Bay 3." Also, when Sisko departs to rescue Kira, the turbolift waits for him to say, "Docking Bay 1."

• In "Dax" Odo spoke with Gul Dukat via the large monitor built into the surface of the desk in his office. At some point after that episode, O'Brien and his busy bees installed a new communications device for the chief of Security. In this episode Odo talks with a Security officer on Bajor by using an upright flat panel display that rises and falls out of a slot in the constable's desk. (I believe that this upright panel is never seen again!)

• In the previous episode, O'Brien seemed to say that a runabout can transport only two people at a time. At the end of Kira's rescue, five people beam out at the same time (six, if the second Bajoran Security officer didn't get killed in the raid).

CONTINUITY AND PRODUCTION PROBLEMS

• At the beginning of the previous episode, Quark visited Kira in her quarters. When Kira retired to her bedroom to don her uniform top, Quark wandered over to take a greedy peek. Bright light streamed from the off-camera room, and Quark appeared to be gazing straight ahead. Also, When Kira retired to her bedroom she seemed to walk straight in and straight out. Obviously this little incident greatly disturbed Kira because she had Maintenance erect a wall just inside the doorway to her bedroom during the previous episode. You can see this new addition at the beginning of this episode. Now Kira must loop around the wall to get from her bedroom to her living area.

• Vedek Bareil causes a small continuity problem as he and Kira discuss her encounter with the orb. A medium-wide shot shows Bareil's hands clasped. The scene cuts to a wide shot, and Bareil's hands are suddenly at his side.

• I know they're cheap shots, but I *love* misspoken words! After Kira's rescue, Sisko and company discuss the latest situation on Bajor in the station infirmary. At one point Li refers to Minister Jaro as "Charo"! Completely unbidden, the image leaped into my mind of Minister Jaro—outfitted in a flamboyant peasant dress and plastic-fruit-topped hat—swaying to Latin music and shouting, "Reepa, reepa, reepa, oochi, coochi, de Circle is de best!"

TRIVIA ANSWERS

1. A bottle of epidellic lotion.
2. The *Calondon*.

THE SIEGE

Star Date: unknown

After loading their families onto runabouts that will take them to safety, Sisko and crew defy Starfleet's order to evacuate the station and stay behind. They intend to stall the Circle's takeover of DS9 until Kira and Dax can deliver evidence of Cardassian involvement in the coup to the Chamber of Ministers on Bajor. Sisko believes this will cause the Circle to fall and encourage the military to change its loyalty back to the provisional government.

When the attack cruisers arrive from Bajor, the military forces find DS9 empty. Colonel Day quickly declares the station secure. However, General Krim does not believe Sisko or Li would abandon the station so easily. In fact, Sisko and company have sabotaged the internal sensor net and are hiding in the conduits—with Li Nalas and several other Bajoran officers by their side. After an extended game of cat and mouse, Sisko tries a more direct approach: He arranges for Li to speak with Krim and convince the general of Cardassian involvement. At the same time, Kira and Dax accomplish

Trivia Questions

1. Which Federation officer is engaged to a young Bajoran male?

2. On what runabout does Nog leave the station?

their mission with the help of Bareil. With the restoration of the provisional government, Krim turns the station back to Sisko. Enraged, Day tries to kill the commander. Li leaps in, takes the blast, and dies.

GREAT LINES
"Oh! Whoa! What's that!? Is that a spider or a dog?!"—Dax to Kira, while nearing the Lunar V base in search of a sublight fighter upon seeing a Bajoran paluckoo. I believe this is one of the first "hintings" of the more relaxed, new and improved Dax who makes a grand entrance in "Playing God."

PLOT OVERSIGHTS
• To get the proof of Cardassian involvement to the Chamber of Ministers on Bajor, Li suggests Kira try to resurrect a fighter on the "Lunar V base." Later, while nearing the Lunar V base, Dax spots a huge, furry spider that Kira identifies as a "paluckoo." Kira adds that the Bajoran moons are full of them. From this I surmise that the Lunar V base is actually on a moon of Bajor. (Seems reasonable, doesn't it? After all they are going after a sublight fighter. Depending on how "sub-

light" these fighters are, it would take a long time to make it to back to Bajor if the base were elsewhere in the planetary system.) Interestingly enough, this Lunar V base isn't on the fifth moon of Bajor! We know that because Kira and Dax can breathe the atmosphere, and in "Progress" we learned that Bajor was about to tap the core of its fifth moon and the operation would make the atmosphere unbreathable.

• Taking advantage of the station inhabitants' desperation, Quark starts selling nonexistent seats on the runabout that will soon leave DS9. Odo catches him in the act, and Sisko must go down to the airlock with Li to talk a bunch of Bajorans into staying. Call me moralistic, but don't Quark's actions amount to *fraud*? (Of course, by the end of the episode everyone has forgotten all about this humorous little trick pulled by the ever-lovable but incorrigible Ferengi barkeep.)

• (I hesitate to mention this next one because there's a certain whimsy to Michael Pillar's writing that I really enjoy. But...nitpickers do notice these things.) As Kira pilots the fighter into a high orbit over Bajor, Dax discovers that the navigational sensors aren't working. To this Kira replies, "We'll have to fly by the seat of our pants." Amazing how colloquialisms crop up virtually unchanged from culture to culture, eh? (Having grown up in the Republic of the Philippines, I might add that I cannot recall ever encountering even *one* colloquialism that had sprung up spontaneously in both the American and Filipino cultures. Having said that, however, I think the "seat

of the pants" exchange between Kira and Dax is a lot of fun.)

• About halfway through the episode, O'Brien and Li get pinned down in the Security office. I wonder why they didn't use the back door, as Nog did when he snuck into Odo's office in "The Storyteller."

• As their fighter begins its decent, Dax tells Kira that there's an opening "six kilometers ahead at two o'clock." *Two o'clock?* Would that be "two o'clock" on an Earth clock or a Trill clock or a Bajoran clock? (Remember, it appears that Bajor has twenty-six hours in their day. Their clock—if it divided the day into halves, as some Earth clocks do—would have *thirteen* hours on the face.

• During a major portion of this episode, Quark lugs around a suitcase supposedly filled with his gold-pressed latinum. Aside from the fact that the suitcase is obviously not as heavy as Quark wants everyone to believe—I suspect a ploy for sympathy—this sad picture of a man and his wealth causes me to wonder. Have the Ferengi never heard of electronic funds transfer? (Or "subspace" funds transfer as the case may be.) Do all the Ferengi actually keep their considerable fortunes in hard currency? (Actually, the fourth season episode "Homefront" may shed some light on this mystery. In that episode Quark speaks of a "great monetary collapse" on Ferenginar. If the Ferengi experienced some type of economic catastrophe, they *may* all keep their fortunes in bars of gold-pressed latinum!)

• Somehow—while at the monastery

with Vedek Bareil—Dax manages to get "nosed" and "despotted" so that she looks like a Bajoran! Did Bashir send along the ridge nose appliance in case she needed to "make like the natives"? Certainly I never suspected that a *monastery* would have this capability. ("The name's Bareil...Vedek Bareil." Insert James Bond theme music here.)

• Li Nalas's phaser injury must be really bad at the end of the episode. Evidently Bashir can instantly tell that there's no point even trying to attend to the war hero's wounds. The good doctor does nothing but stare at his tricorder. ("If Wishes Were Horses" establishes that there is an emergency medical kit on the bridge. Or did Bashir already pack it away with the rest of his supplies?)

CHANGED PREMISES

• As Jake tries to say good-bye, Nog assures him that they'll be back together in school in no time. When did Nog go back to school? In "The Nagus" Rom decreed that Nog wasn't allowed to attend the school any longer.

• Quark must have sunk to even lower depths of criminal activity following "The Forsaken." In that episode Odo pays Quark a backhanded compliment, telling Lwaxana Troi that the Ferengi barkeep usually doesn't resort to petty theft to fleece his customers. Sadly—as Quark departs Ops on his way off the station—Odo says he'll miss the barkeep. He says he'll miss "the aggravations, the petty theft, the bad manners."

EQUIPMENT ODDITIES

• Let's see: Sisko says he's got two

hundred people to get off the station and only three runabouts. You know, I never imagined that you could cram more than sixty people into one of those craft. (I guess it's just another "strange but true" fact.)

• There's probably some sort of Lucite covering the outside, but it sure looks like the cockpit hatch cover on the fighter that Kira and Dax use to get to Bajor has *vents* cut into its side. As in...*air* vents. As in...all the oxygen in the cockpit will leak out into space as you leave the moon. *That* kind of vents!

• At the beginning of the episode Sisko addresses an African-American Starfleet crew member as "Ensign Kelly." Later we see Ensign Kelly in the conduits with the rest of the Starfleet officers who decided to stay behind and defend the station. Oddly enough, Kelly carries a *Bajoran* phaser. Sisko didn't have enough *Starfleet* phasers to equip his officers? Or are the Bajoran phasers actually better?

• At one point during the cat-and-mouse game on the station, Odo gives Sisko a report on Colonel Day's search parties. We see our favorite Changeling's upper torso lean out from a wall, and then a reverse angle shows us his face as he continues his report. Evidently the lower half of his body has taken on the appearance of the wall and is spread thinly all around him. Here's what's interesting: The bottom edge of his combadge appears to be distorted, as if it's shape-shifting as well. This would seem to indicate that Odo's combadge is part of Odo. But if it is, how is Odo communicating with Sisko? (I guess he really can make working electronic components!

See "Babel." Of course, that doesn't explain how Mareel can remove his combadge at the beginning of the very next episode!)

• The fighter craft that Kira pilots is amazing. It sustains seven—count 'em, *seven*—phaser hits from newer, more advanced fighters, and then Dax gets off one lucky shot with the old fighter's phasers and knocks a new and improved model to the ground!

• And speaking of this fighter, not only do its shields hold up extraordinarily well, not only do its phasers perform admirably, but also its navigational sensors seem to know exactly when to start working. Once the fighter's thrusters fail, Dax suddenly can use the previously nonfunctioning sensors to tell Kira that there's a good place to land "six kilometers ahead at two o'clock." (Must be built right into the fail-safe circuits. "If the thrusters go out, engage the emergency navigation sensors. But until then, let the pilots fly by the seat of their pants.")

• I find Sisko's plan to hold out on the station refreshingly primal. He stages lots of hit-and-run attacks. Captures a few Bajoran here. Captures a few more there. Sure glad Picard wasn't the head of this station. He would just have used the transporters and force fields to lock up the Bajor strike force within two minutes of their arrival on the station. Then it would have been

a short show. (For an example, see the *NextGen* episode "Rascals.")

CONTINUITY AND PRODUCTION PROBLEMS

• Well, there's at least one set of twins on the station. Directly after the title credits and commercial break, the camera pans down a spiral staircase on the promenade and we see people pouring into an airlock. One woman is a light brunette, her hair piled on top of her head in tight curls. She appears to wear a red turtleneck shirt under a jumper. After she enters the airlock, the shot changes, and another woman, who looks identical to the first woman—wearing exactly the same clothes—walks across the screen escorted by a Starfleet officer in a blue uniform.

• There is a lovely visual in this episode as three Bajoran attack cruisers approach and dock at DS9. At the end of the previous episode, too bad O'Brien said there were *two* approaching!

• While dressing Kira in a religious order robe for safe transit to the Chamber of Ministers, Dax pulls a length of fabric through a ring and begins to secure the fabric. Then the shot changes, and Dax pulls the fabric through the ring a second time!

TRIVIA ANSWERS
1. Lieutenant Bilecki.
2. The *Rio Grande*.

INVASIVE PROCEDURES

Star Date: 47182.1

During a plasma storm that forces the evacuation of DS9, a shuttle approaches, feigning damage and asking to dock. O'Brien and Odo meet it at the airlock, only to be taken prisoner by its four inhabitants—a Trill named Verad, two Klingon mercenaries, and a pleasure girl from Khefka IV named Mareel. The band force Odo into a sealed container and then compel Bashir to place the box in a stasis chamber. They assault Ops next, where Verad announces that he has come to steal the symbiont Dax. Under threat of injury to the others, Jadzia convinces Bashir to perform the transfer, though he knows Jadzia will die in hours once the symbiont is removed.

Afterward, Verad becomes Verad Dax—inheritor of the memories of Dax's previous hosts, including those of Curzon and Jadzia. Like an old friend, Sisko tries to talk Verad into relinquishing the symbiont to spare Jadzia's life. Verad refuses and—when the plasma storm clears—heads for the docking bay and safety in the Gamma Quadrant. Thankfully, Bashir

and Quark have already freed Odo, who releases the shuttle before Verad can reach it. Desperate, Verad heads for the only remaining runabout. He finds Sisko waiting for him. As the show concludes, Bashir returns Dax to its rightful host.

Trivia Questions

1. Where did Sisko and Curzon Dax first meet?

2. What does Mareel bring O'Brien from the replicator?

GREAT MOMENTS

I love the look on Quark's face when the Klingon whom Bashir drafts to play nurse jams a medical device into Quark's supposedly injured ear. (Be safe. Remember Quark's agony. Don't play doctor with a Klingon!)

PLOT OVERSIGHTS

• The preview for the episode has the following narration: "A desperate outcast plots the ultimate theft—the life force within Dax. Now, to save her shipmates, will she make the ultimate sacrifice?" The creators seem to have forgotten a minor structural detail about Deep Space 9. There *ain't* no ship! (At least not yet. Wink, wink.) I believe the correct term would be "stationmates."

• Once again, "heavier than he looks" Odo is carried with one hand after he pours himself into a container. Both

Mareel and Bashir swing the box around with ease.

• Bringing most of the prisoners to Ops, Verad and company cluster them around the center table. O'Brien even takes a seat in front of a workstation built into the side of the table. He also places his arm over the control pad area. It almost looks like he is trying to enter some covert command code—which, of course, would be a *great* idea—but unfortunately, he doesn't.

• Jadzia Dax makes the statement in this episode that only one Trill in ten is joined. Later Kira says that there are thousands of symbionts on Trill. Something is wrong here, because that would mean that the population of the entire Trill home world would be only about 100,000. (Presumably Kira would have used "tens of thousands" if there were that many—or "hundreds of thousands" if more. Okay, okay. For the sake of argument let's say that there are 999,999 symbionts on Trill. That still puts the entire Trill population at just under 10 million. This seems small for an entire planet.)

• Kira puts in a pitiful showing in hand-to-hand combat during this episode. She actually gets beaten up by Mareel! Let's review. Kira: Began fighting the Cardassians when she was twelve. Mareel: Grew up on the streets of Khefka IV. Worked in an "accommodation house" until Verad took her to the Trill home world. Khefka IV must have some really rock-'em, sock-'em houses of ill repute!

• This episode reveals an important aspect of Trill psychology. Evidently the symbiont has little or no moral con-

straints. Verad is *killing* Jadzia, and all Verad Dax can say is he feels bad about it. Obviously the symbiont Dax doesn't feel bad enough to force him to undo the act. It's true that this is supposed to be a joining—a sharing—but doesn't it seem likely that if the symbiont was truly aghast at the events, the joining wouldn't take? In this episode the combined attitude of both Verad and Dax seems to be: "Oh, that's too bad about Jadzia. Well...on to the Gamma Quadrant!" One must assume that Verad feels *some* sorrow over the events. If he does, then what is the symbiont contributing to the mix of grief? (Answer: Not much at all. Evidently as long as it's got a body with opposable thumbs, it's happy!)

• If Quark is going to fake an injury, he really should remember what's supposed to be injured. After attacking a Klingon, Quark lands on his right ear. He makes a great commotion about being injured, holding his right ear as if in pain. Verad tells Mareel to take him to the infirmary. On the way out, you can see Quark holding his *left* ear. (Nothing touched it in the scuffle, in case you're wondering.)

• Once Verad discovers that Odo has escaped his box, he orders T'Kar—one of the Klingon hirelings—to escort him to the airlock. Inside, Verad finds a table that he ignores as he hurries to the second door. The table turns out to be Odo. Remember that Verad as Verad Dax now has Jadzia's memories. Do work crews usually leave tables lying around inside airlocks? How can Verad—with Jadzia's experience— not suspect that this table is Odo?

• Verad misses another piece of vital information when walking up to the second airlock door. The transparent portions of the door clearly show that there is no ship docked there. Yet Verad seems surprised by this information moments later. (By the way, the transparent portions of the door also show that there is no plasma storm outside the station when there's supposed to be at least the remnants of one. Hmmm.)

• Sisko misses a prime opportunity for a good left cross at the end of this episode. Only Sisko and a phaser stand between Verad and a runabout. Verad gloats that Sisko won't shoot him, that Sisko knows the phaser might damage the symbiont. For some of this discussion, Verad stands—with weapon dropped—a few feet from Sisko. I kept yelling, "Hit him! Hit him! Knock him out into the corridor! That way the symbiont will be safe!" Instead, Sisko shoots him with the phaser.

CHANGED PREMISES

• There are several changes concerning the implanting of the symbiont between this episode and "The Host" *(TNG)*. (You may recall that in that episode, Dr. Crusher implanted a symbiont named Odan in Commander Will Riker so Odan could finish peace negotiations between two moon colonies.) When Riker was joined with Odan, Crusher told the commander that he needed to be awake during the operation. In this episode, Bashir initially insists that Verad go to sleep. In "The Host" we get a good look at Odan's stomach, and it appears to be a normal humanoid stomach. In this

episode, the Trill have little kangaroo pouches. (I know that Bashir later calls it an incision, but he can't fool me. I *know* a kangaroo pouch when I see one!) Finally, the Trill symbiont itself looks substantially different in "The Host." The one in "The Host" is bigger. It's got a real tail, and it pulls itself into the incision.

EQUIPMENT ODDITIES

• Evidently the difficulty of evacuating the station last episode spurred Sisko to consider a more efficient method for removing the population from DS9. In this episode the station is evacuated as well, but the dialogue refers to "evacuation shuttles." These would be *new*.

• Near the beginning, Mareel removes Odo's combadge! So, there you go. It *is* a real combadge. (Because it didn't turn to goo in her hand as it should—according to "The Adversary"—if it was actually part of Odo. Now the question becomes: What does Odo do with his combadge when he morphs into another object? (Like a mouse, for instance, as he did in "Past Prologue.") And when Odo leaned out of the wall in "The Siege," why did the bottom part of the combadge look like it was distorted if it was a real combadge? (Hmmm.)

• In the infirmary, Bashir has an intriguing machine that sits near Dax. The top portion of the machine looks like the standard Bajoran/Cardassian junk that's littered around the station, while the bottom half has the sleek, clean, efficient displays of Starfleet equipment. (Ya, I know. I'm prejudiced.)

• Fleeing the station, Verad runs up

to an airlock and presses a button on the lighted control panel to open the door. A bit later he runs to a runabout airlock and presses the long oval button on the door control *beneath* the lighted panel to open the door. Why the difference?

CONTINUITY AND PRODUCTION PROBLEMS

• Not a nit, just record-keeping. Tim Russ—who now stars as Tuvok in *Star Trek: Voyager*—plays T'Kar in this episode. (Even though I often list multiple roles for the same actor as nits, I don't consider this particular role a nit because Tim Russ is barely recognizable. This character is such a departure from Tuvok or the mercenary Russ played in the *TNG* episode "Starship Mine" that you really have to look closely to see the resemblance.)

• At one point, Quark closes the lid on a box of liquid data chains and then places both hands on the bar. The shot changes, and Quark is suddenly gesturing with his right hand.

• Amazingly enough, receiving a symbiont can change your spots! As Verad leaves Ops, the camera gives us a close-up of his right ear. Notice the pattern on the ear flap. It almost makes the tab look like it has a dimple in it. Now come forward in the episode when Sisko reminds Verad Dax that Jadzia is bleeding to death in the infirmary. As Verad says he'd rather not discuss it, take another look at the tab on his right ear. Hasn't the pattern changed?

• It might just be my tape, but at the end of the episode, as Sisko stands in front of the runabout door, all the wide shots show two stripes, each composed of a large dark section and then a lighter section. But when Sisko shoots Verad, a close-up shows him sliding down the runabout door and there's only one dark section per stripe.

TRIVIA ANSWERS
1. Pelios Station.
2. A container of Senarian egg broth.

CARDASSIANS

Star Dates: 47177.2–47178.3

After an adopted Cardassian boy named Rugal bites Garak on the hand, Gul Dukat immediately contacts Sisko, claiming a deep concern for the Cardassian orphans left behind on Bajor. Of even greater interest, a DNA scan soon reveals that Rugal is the son of Kotan Pa'Dar, a high-ranking member of the civilian assembly on Cardassia. Eight years ago, Pa'Dar served as exarch for a Cardassian settlement on Bajor. Terrorists supposedly attacked his home, killing both his wife and son.

Garak suspects a greater game is being played and recruits Bashir's help. They discover that Rugal was originally brought to an orphanage on Bajor by a female Cardassian officer attached to DS9, then called Terok Nor, commanded by Gul Dukat. Evidently Dukat arranged for Rugal's dispatch and now his recovery. Family is everything to Cardassians. If it became public that Pa'Dar had allowed Bajorans to raise his son, it would end his political career—an event Dukat would find comforting. The civilian government on Cardassia is about to investigate the

military's role in the failed attempt by the Circle to seize control of Bajor. When Bashir reveals this information at a custody hearing for Rugal, both Dukat and Pa'Dar agree to bury the matter quietly.

GREAT LINES

"Really, perhaps we have met!"—Garak to a volunteer at the Tozhat Resettlement Center when she admits that she was in the underground. Isn't it great how Garak turns this situation around? The Bajoran woman proclaims her involvement in the Resistance, obviously trying to heap guilt on Garak by reminding him of the awfulness of the occupation and all he does is conjecture that they might know each other!

PLOT OVERSIGHTS

• Garak seems inconsistent in his attitude toward the orphaned Cardassian children of Bajor. After visiting the Tozhat resettlement center, Garak tells Bashir that orphaned children have no standing in Cardassian culture. And while leaving the center, a young Cardassian girl asks Garak if he's come to take her back to Car-

Trivia Questions

1. What beverage does Bashir drink at the beginning of this episode?

2. What is the name of Rugal's adopted Bajoran father?

dassia. Garak gives her an uncomfortable "No" before scurrying away. Oddly enough, at the beginning of this episode—when first laying eyes on Rugal—Garak is immediately taken with the Cardassian boy. He even wanders over to his table to say hello. This leads to the infamous hand-biting scene and sets the rest of the episode's events in motion. It almost makes one wonder if Garak *intentionally* greeted Rugal—knowing the young man's hatred of Cardassians—simply to stir up trouble.

• After the hand-biting incident, Bashir reports to Sisko. Bashir rides a turbolift up to Ops, hops off, and apologizes for being late. Sisko, Kira, Dax, O'Brien, and Odo stand around the center table, apparently having a meeting. When Bashir explains that Garak has just been bitten by a Cardassian child, Odo immediately leaves Ops. So...they weren't having a meeting? (Or was the meeting optional for Odo?)

• At one point Bashir questions a businessman over the Dabo table about Rugal's upbringing. The man is on a winning streak and periodically interrupts his conversation with Bashir to yell, "Dabo!" Yet the last time we hear the wheel slow to a stop, nothing happens. The man doesn't yell, "Dabo!" but neither does he moan, and the crowd is strangely silent as well. Is there some combination in Dabo where everything just stays the same?

• Cardassian children must grow up fast. Rugal supposedly went to the orphanage when he was four. That was eight years ago. The first thing

he remembers is his Bajoran adoptive father teaching him how to swim. One could surmise that he was adopted fairly quickly after arriving at the orphanage. That means Rugal is twelve, on the outside thirteen. He carries himself like a fifteen- or sixteen-year-old human.

• After Bashir interrupts his conversation with Gul Dukat, Sisko tells his CMO that he wants to meet with Garak at 2100 hours. Did this meeting ever take place? There's no subsequent mention of it.

• The entire premise of this episode deserves some scrutiny. Supposedly Gul Dukat has brought up the issue of the orphans to embarrass Kotan Pa'Dar—a high-ranking member of the civilian assembly on Cardassia—because hearings are about to starting over the military's involvement in the Circle's attempted coup. (See "The Homecoming, "The Circle," and "The Siege.") I fail to understand how this *conveniently* embarrassing situation came about in the first place. Does Gul Dukat have some dirty little secret on *every* low-level civilian officer who ever worked on Bajor? Remember that this scenario began eight years ago when Pa'Dar was exarch of a Cardassian settlement on Bajor. This does not sound like a prominent position to me. In other words, Pa'Dar was a "nobody." It seems unlikely then that Dukat would single this particular person out—to murder his wife and turn his son over to a Bajoran orphanage—just in case the guy ever made it to the upper echelon of the Cardassian civil government. How could he possibly know

Pa'Dar's destiny? (The only conclusion is that Dukat was indeed a very busy boy all through his years on Bajor, collecting dirt and creating indelicate situations to later use as leverage against anyone who might possibly become a threat in the distant future!)

CHANGED PREMISES
• O'Brien claims that Molly is four. Well, let's see. She was born very near star date 45156.1 during "Disaster" *(TNG)*. This episode begins on star date 47177.2. Wouldn't that make her just over *two* years old?

EQUIPMENT ODDITIES
• Soon after Rugal bites Garak, Gul Dukat contacts the station. Sisko stands in Ops. Kira announces that he has a call. Sisko says, "In my office." Then the commander walks up the stairs and through his doors. He sits on his desk, facing a monitor on his back wall. Beside Sisko, we see his desk terminal. The message comes up on the monitor on the back wall. Why didn't the message go to the desk terminal? Is it standard practice for Kira to watch Sisko and route the message differently depending on where he sits, or did the computer do this automatically?

• Here's some picayune nitpicking for you. O'Brien comes home to find Keiko setting the table for supper. Large decorative plates are already on the table. Keiko has three dinner plates in her hands. O'Brien takes them and sets them on top of the decorative plates. Next, Keiko calls Rugal to the table. Both he and O'Brien sit.

Keiko walks over to the replicator. We hear the replication cycle completing, and she picks up some bowls of Zabu meat stew. When she sets them down in front of O'Brien and Rugal we can see that the bowls match the dinner plates. It appears that the stew constitutes the entire meal. Did Keiko replicate the plates just so the bowls would look nicer on the table? Wouldn't this be considered—gasp—*wasteful*!? (Aaaaaaah! How could high and noble twenty-fourth-century humans do such a thing?)

• Garak and Bashir travel to the Tozhat resettlement center to investigate Rugal's origins. Once there, Garak fixes the orphanage's computer and downloads the files for all the adoptions into a Cardassian "data-clip." In a stunning display of supreme standardization we see that the "data clip" looks *exactly* like the small panels that are used all over DS9 to open doors! I tell you what: Those Cardassians are efficient.

CONTINUITY AND PRODUCTION PROBLEMS
• Well, at least this episode answers one neurotic question left unsolved from the episode "Progress." In that episode Mollibok had two mute friends named Baltrim and Keena. Nitpickers everywhere were biting their nails in irritation at the end of this episode because the creators never told us if Baltrim and Keena were their family names or their given names. (Nitpickers know that Bajorans, unlike Vulcans and Klingons, have two names, just like humans.) We can all breathe a collective sigh of relief now

that this episode has aired. Baltrim is the male's given name, and his family name is...(Sorry. I can't tell you that because it would ruin the second trivia question.) How do I know this about Baltrim? Because his twin brother is the man who adopted Rugal eight years prior to the episode!

• Apparently Quark replaced one of his Dabo girls and kept the costume. This episode feature an alien female in a gold lamé outfit that has a large section of cloth strategically cut from the midriff area, exposing the lower third of her breasts. As I mentioned in my review of "Emissary," this outfit first appeared in "Unification II" *(TNG)*. However, in "Emissary"...um...the top portion of the dress was...shall we say "filled to capacity"? In this episode there's a wrinkle down the center of it.

• This episode contains another prime example of the station's "rotational speed control." (Mostly likely this knob is located in Ops.) Sisko is awakened by Bashir. The stars in his window do not move. Ops calls with an urgent message from Gul Dukat. Sisko takes it. In the medium-side shots of the display terminal the stars do not move. Then the scene cuts to a close-up of the display terminal, and two things have happened simultaneously. First, the display terminal instantly lurches to the left several inches and the stars begin to move in the background. (Obviously the inertial damping field was malfunctioning in that area of Sisko's quarters.) Then Sisko gives Bashir a runabout, and guess what? The stars stop moving!

• The closed captioning has an additional phrase in Sisko's station log, star date 47177.2. After he says, "...that we are being manipulated in some manner," the closed captioning reads, "but how and for what purpose?"

TRIVIA ANSWERS
1. Tarkalean tea.
2. Proka Migdal.

Star Date: 47229.1

The first Elaysian to join Starfleet, Melora Pazlar, comes on board DS9 to perform a cartography survey in the Gamma Quadrant. Her situation is made difficult by the fact that Melora's home world has very low gravity. Consequently she must use muscular supports that allow her to walk only with great effort. In addition, Bashir has replicated a wheelchair for her, since standard Federation antigrav units won't function on the Cardassian station.

At the same time, Fallit Kot arrives on the station, looking to avenge a betrayal by Quark eight years ago. Attempting to mollify Kot, Quark brings him along to a sale of forty-two "Rings of Paltriss" for 199 bars of gold-pressed latinum. Quark intends to give Kot the latinum from the sale. Instead Kot seizes both the rings and the latinum before taking Quark, Dax, and Melora hostage and escaping in a runabout. When Sisko traps the runabout with a tractor beam, Kot convinces the commander to let them go by shooting Melora. Left for dead in the rear of the pilot's compartment,

Melora crawls to the back wall, shuts off the gravity, and quickly subdues Kot. A short time later, Sisko, Bashir, and O'Brien arrive in a second runabout and escort everyone back to the station.

Trivia Questions

1. Who did the original work on neuromuscular adaptation thirty years ago?

2. Melora requests the music of what Vulcan composer in the runabout?

RUMINATIONS

Erin Lale of Sonoma, California, noted the similarity between Melora's race, Elaysian, and Elaan's race, Elasian (see the Classic *episode "Elaan of Troyius"). Erin suggested that this might be a case for the Galactic Court for Race Name Conflict Resolution—featured in "The Creator Is Always Right" section of the* NextGen Guide *on pages 350–55.*

PLOT OVERSIGHTS

• Fallit Kot comes from a race that somehow managed to "evolve" a nosepiece that connects directly to his chin. This seems *exceedingly* inconvenient. Moments after he comes into the bar, Quark offers him a drink. One wonders how the poor guy manages to imbibe it. Does he drink sidesaddle? The same would apply for eating. The pieces would have to be cut up and shoved in with a utensil. Fine, but what did this race do before forks were invented? Feast on sticks? (I can't imagine how the guy manages to get his mouth open wide enough to eat something like an apple. I suppose all the food on his world could have been courteous enough to evolve in a manner suited to be consumed.) And wouldn't it be horrible to catch a cold with a nose like that? Ick. I suspect Fallit Kot and his people are victims of a race of cruel practical jokemasters who roam the galaxy looking for civilizations to terrorize. "Hey, what say we go down to that planet with the protohumans and modify their genetic structure so their noses connect to their chins. Then we can give them a perpetual sinus infection and really have some fun!

• Given that Kot makes his intentions known very early on in the episode (i.e., that he's going to kill our favorite Ferengi "host"), one wonders why Quark hasn't arranged for a little bit of preemptive incapacitating. We've seen in other shows that Quark knows *plenty* of thugs.

• Boy, Bashir really turned on the charm in this episode! He must have taken a "Troi" pill before Melora arrived.

• Okay, so Melora invites Bashir into her quarters because she's about to turn down the gravity. He's nervous and says that he can't tell her how curious he is about low gravity. First, I believe that what we see in this episode is better termed "microgravity" than "low gravity." Low gravity is what the astronauts experienced on the moon. Though they could hop a lot farther than on Earth, they didn't float away. Floating around—as seen during

space shuttle missions—requires microgravity. Second, Melora turns down the gravity and Bashir goes flipping through the air just like he's never been in microgravity before. Does this make sense? Starfleet doesn't train their officers in microgravity environments? *Starfleet?* As in "the fleet that flies...to the stars"? The fleet that uses artificial gravity on their ships? The fleet that must account for the possibility that their artificial gravity might quit working? (I do have to admit that the Starfleet gravity system seems remarkably stable. I can think of only one time in the entire history of *NextGen* that a gravity problem was even mentioned aboard the *Enterprise*.) On the other hand, Sisko brings along "zero-gravity rations" during his solar sailing adventure in "Explorers." This indicates that Starfleet *does* have a microgravity training program!

• One wonders how life began on Melora's world in the first place. If the planet has so little mass that it generates only microgravity, how did it retain an atmosphere?

• There's a whole intertwining mesh of issues concerning Melora's performance in microgravity. For instance, if Melora grew up in microgravity, wouldn't her muscles be adapted so that this very low gravity would feel to her like Earth-normal gravity feels to us? In other words, wouldn't she walk around the room after turning down the gravity just as we walk around a room with Earth-normal gravity? Doesn't Bashir float because his musculature is accustomed to Earth-normal gravity and therefore he possesses the strength to overcome

Melora's "normal" level of gravity? (Rumor has it that the reason Vulcans are so strong is that their planet has much higher gravity than Earth-normal.) Along the same line, if you subscribe to the theory of evolution, why would life on Melora's planet develop to equip her to overcome the level of gravity on her world while leaving humans bound by the level of gravity on their world? (I should let you know that I can argue both for and against Melora doing cartwheels through her room. Just some things for you to think about!)

• *Technically* this is not a nit, but it crops up in several places in *DS9* and you might find it interesting. To set a direction of travel, Starfleet uses an established navigational system that employs two angles: an azimuth angle and an elevation angle. If the *Defiant* was lying flat on a clock face, the numbers on the clock face would be the azimuth angle of the ship (after conversion to degrees, of course). The elevation angle would be another clock face perpendicular to the first. (Wesley explains this to Lore in the *NextGen* episode "Datalore.") Traveling straight ahead with the system would be "000 mark 000." Traveling in the same flight plane but turning to starboard would be something like "045 mark 000." Traveling up at a 45-degree angle but going in the same direction would be "000 mark 045." Back to the episode. After coming through the wormhole in a runabout, Melora tells Dax she is setting a course "28 mark 142." This is *technically* a legal course, since both numbers are in the range 0 through 360. On the other hand, the course is needlessly complex. At first glance it appears to set a course for the ship that is forward and off to starboard. It doesn't—because of the second number. In reality, the course is more backward and off to port! That's because the elevation is not given in the range 0 through 90 or 270 through 360. If the elevation angle doesn't fall in these ranges, the course "folds back" from the direction set by the first angle. (If I've done my math correctly, "028 mark 142" also can be expressed as "208 mark 052." This seems much clearer to me!)

• When Melora first arrives on the station she claims that she will be surveying a sector in the Gamma Quadrant. Later, she and Dax take a runabout to the Gamma Quadrant. The entire time we eavesdrop on them in the Gamma Quadrant the runabout travels at impulse or less. The only way this would make sense is if Melora is surveying the sector in which the wormhole lies. Hasn't this sector been surveyed already? No wonder Melora feels like she's being patronized. It looks like Starfleet is just drumming up things for her to do!

• Part of the plot of this episode deals with Bashir's attempt to augment the signals from Melora's brain so she can operate freely in Earth-standard gravity. After the first treatment, Bashir and Melora come to Ops with her first report from the Gamma Quadrant. As she appears on the turbolift, O'Brien expresses his surprise. Either O'Brien makes a stunningly quick deduction, or he's just being nice. Granted, he's never seen her walking around without her wheelchair, but she has done it using her muscle enhancers. I fail to see how the sight of her in a turbolift could inspire such shock. Now...*after* she walks off the turbolift, that's another story! (Personally I think Bashir called up to Ops ahead of time and encouraged everyone to make a big deal over Melora when she arrived. As I said, O'Brien's just trying to be nice.)

• Odo seems strangely lax in his duties when it comes to protecting Quark. Remember, this is the guy who always manages to shape-shift into just the right object so he can be at just the right place at the right time. In this episode he's lollygagging around in the Security office while Kot attacks Quark in the Ferengi's quarters. (Then again, maybe Odo's slacking off on purpose!)

EQUIPMENT ODDITIES

• This is a cheap shot. In this episode Melora is confined to a wheelchair. It limits her access to the station. Wouldn't you think that, by the twenty-fourth century, cyberneticists would have invented practical multilegged walking machines? (I know, too expensive to simulate on TV.)

• Bashir claims that Melora will need to use a wheelchair because the standard antigrav units won't work with the Cardassian technology of the station. Evidently, someone upgraded the system because just two episodes from now—in "Necessary Evil"—Bashir will order an antigrav stretcher to take an injured Quark to the infirmary.

• When Melora invites Bashir into her quarters, the door switch on the wall is mounted upside down. (Of course, this *could* just be another ex-

ample of the famed Cardassian standardization witnessed in the previous episode, "Cardassians.")

• Somehow Kot's phaser managed to elude Odo's Security sensors. (I'm telling ya—Odo is just not trying when it comes to this guy!)

• Somehow Kot also manages to elude all the force fields we have seen Odo erect at a moment's notice when faced with a fleeing criminal. (Getting the picture here yet?)

• While chasing the runabout containing Kot, Quark, Dax, and Melora as it travels at warp, Bashir asks O'Brien if they could beam the occupants off the craft. O'Brien says he wouldn't advise it. Did O'Brien just forget that he beamed an away team to the Borg ship while at high warp in "The Best of Both Worlds, Part 2" *(TNG)*? (I suspect Odo had a chat with O'Brien before he left the station.)

• I love twenty-fourth-century musical instruments! We get to see one of Klingon design at the end of this episode. The "singing" Klingon favors Melora and Bashir with a selection. With his right hand, he strums away on this thing, which looks just like an electric violin. Only it can't be a simple twentieth-century electric violin because the guy never changes fingerboard position with his left hand—never touches the strings at all—and the instrument knows exactly when to change chords! Gotta admire that twenty-fourth-century engineering.

CONTINUITY AND PRODUCTION PROBLEMS

• The preview for this episode features graphics from "The Chase"

(TNG) in the lower left-hand corner. True, they look cool, but what do they mean in this context?

• Writing scrolls by in the upper left-hand corner during the preview for this episode. At one point the words "SECUIRTY BREACH" appear. That probably should be "SECURITY BREACH."

• Those sneaky creators tried to pull a fast one on us. After getting past Melora's defenses, Bashir invites her to a Klingon restaurant and he orders *gagh*. You may recall that *gagh* is serpent worms, first seen in "A Matter of Honor" *(TNG)*. At the end of the meal

the camera gives us a close-up of the plate. Bashir grabs the final worm and drops it slowly into his mouth. Just who are they trying to fool? First, it's obvious the thing is dead. Melora wanted a plateful of live *gagh*. Second, it's obviously not *gagh,* it's a gummy worm! Come on! If the script calls for serpent worms, we want to see *serpent worms. Live* ones! *Eaten* by the crew! We watch this show for realism! Am I right or am I right?

TRIVIA ANSWERS
1. Nathaniel Teros.
2. Delvok.

RULES OF ACQUISITION

Star Date: unknown

rand Nagus Zek shows up at the station and commissions Quark to negotiate a deal for the purchase of ten thousand vats of tulaberry wine from a Gamma Quadrant race called the Dosi. Fearing that Zek is looking for a scapegoat should the negotiations fail, Quark takes on a consultant named Pel—a recent addition to his staff at the bar. He doesn't know she's actually a Ferengi female. Then Zek suddenly ups the purchase to one hundred thousand vats. Stunned, the Dosi angrily storm back to the Gamma Quadrant. Quark and Pel follow and soon discover that the Dosi simply don't *have* one hundred thousand vats. However, one of the negotiators agrees to introduce them to the Karemma—an important power in "The Dominion." She says that everyone must do business with the Dominion in the Gamma Quadrant.

This is the piece of information Zek really wanted from the negotiations. He rewards Quark with a percentage of the profits from the Gamma Quadrant. Unfortunately, Rom has discovered that Pel is a female, and a short

time later Pel herself reveals this scandalous fact to Zek. In Ferengi society, females are not allowed to wear clothes and acquire profit. Only Quark's intervention keeps Pel from going to prison, but it costs him his Gamma Quadrant percentage in return.

Trivia Questions

1. What does Pel suggest Quark serve in the bar to boost beverage sales?

2. What is the name of the female Dosi negotiator?

RUMINATIONS

I love these episodes with Grand Nagus Zek. Both the writing and the execution are just superb when it comes to the leader of the Ferengi. Also, Pel's makeup is great in this episode. One moment she has male Ferengi ears and then—rip— female ears!

GREAT LINES

"A little late, aren't we?!"—The grand nagus to Maihar'Du after the servant fails to provide a handkerchief in time to catch a violent sneeze. (Sisko and Kira's reactions to Zek blowing his nose are priceless and I've always thought that Wallace Shawn does a superb job playing the part of Zek.)

PLOT OVERSIGHTS

• Rom discovers that Pel is a female after he searches her quarters in a fit of jealousy. He finds the case where she keeps her extra pair of synthetic

115

ears and the tools she uses to put them on and take them off. I wonder why she didn't take this along on her trip to the Gamma Quadrant with Quark. What if her lobes had been damaged?

• I guess the old saying that men sometimes marry women just like their mothers holds true. In this episode Quark falls for an independent-minded, profit-seeking Ferengi female. Though he refuses to pursue a relationship with Pel, he does give her a stake of ten bars of latinum to start a new life. Interestingly enough, in "Family Business," we discover that Pel is just like Quark's mother. (The only difference is: Quark can stand his mother!)

EQUIPMENT ODDITIES

• Near the beginning of the episode, Zek secures Sisko's permission to use the station for negotiations with the Dosi. Afterward Zek walks toward the doors. We hear them open. Then he stops and walks all the way back to Sisko's desk. Amazingly, the doors know he will be leaving soon and remain open until he does leave.

• Bringing a gift for Kira, Maihar'Du rides the turbolift for Ops and walks right up to the center table. Does this seems right? Can anyone waltz onto a turbolift and ride it to the command center for the station?

• The pattern used when Quark and Pel return to Zek's shuttle from the Dosi doesn't match the transporter pattern used by the Ferengi in *NextGen.* For instance, in "The Battle," the Ferengi transporter featured

a spiraling bolt of energy that surrounded the person being transported. The transporter patterns seen in this episode are much more similar to those of a Cardassian transporter. Perhaps the Dosi beamed them back to the shuttle or Zek bought his transporter at a discount.

CONTINUITY AND PRODUCTION PROBLEMS

• Once again, the graphics in the lower left-hand corner of the preview come from *NextGen.*

• The grand nagus appears to be reading his lines when he first contacts Quark over subspace.

• When first broadcast, the episode's title read, "Rules of Aquisition." In subsequent "encore performances" (now, *there's* a euphemism if I've ever heard one) the creators corrected it to "Rules of Acquisition."

• After learning that Pel is a female, Quark comes to her quarters to give her ten bars of gold-pressed latinum and send her on her way. To this Pel responds, "But you need me, Quark, I'm the only one you can trust." At this point the closed captioning reads, "I thought we were partners."

• Rom's teeth seem to be a little loose. Toward the end of the episode he chows down on what looks like a dark-colored baby crab. As he bites into it, his teeth move.

TRIVIA ANSWERS
1. Gramilian sand peas.
2. Zyree.

NECESSARY EVIL

Star Dates: 47282.5—47284.1

When Quark is shot, Rom admits to Odo that he and his brother had just retrieved a list of Bajoran names from the opposite side of a wall plate in a shop on the promenade. The information reopens an unsolved murder case for the shape shifter. During the Cardassian occupation, the shop with the hidden list belonged to a Bajoran named Vaatrik. Five years ago, Gul Dukat brought Odo to the station to investigate Vaatrik's murder. At the time, Mrs. Vaatrik accused Kira Nerys of a crime of passion. Though admitting that she worked for the resistance, Kira claimed innocence. Instead, she confessed to sabotaging some ore-processing equipment on the station at the time of the murder. Interested only in finding Vaatrik's killer, Odo let her go.

Trivia Questions

1. Where does Odo threaten to send Rom if he doesn't cooperate with the investigation?

2. According to Kira, what type of ginger tea did Vaatrik have in his shop?

GREAT LINES

"Ohhhhhhh, irony of ironies! I finally get the bar and I'm falsely accused of my brother's murder."—Rom to himself as Sisko and Odo play the good cop/bad cop routine trying to ply the Ferengi for information about the as-

sault on Quark. (The real surprise here was that Rom was literate enough to use a phrase like "irony of ironies"!)

PLOT OVERSIGHTS

• After Quark is shot, Rom takes Odo to the shop where they found the list. Rom even offers to show Odo which panel they removed. That wouldn't be too hard! If you look in the background, you'll see the panel is still off and all the flashing lights of the conduit are streaming through!

• I'm intrigued by the Cardassians' behavior toward Odo. He shows up in the Denorios Belt during the Cardassian occupation of Bajor ("Emissary"). Presumably the Cardassians knew of Odo's existence early on. Yet, for some reason, they allowed a Bajoran scientist to work with him. And when Odo left the research center, evidently no one complained. It seems to me that Odo is a life form with great potential. If you could unlock the secrets of his shape-shifting abilities, that knowledge might prove very useful. Instead, this episode has Gul Dukat bringing Odo to the station to investigate a murder when he could be shipping him off to

117

Cardassia for further study. Or does the Obsidian Order have absolutely no interest in our friendly Changeling?

• At one point Odo—trying to pressure Rom into disclosing what he knows—tells the Ferengi that he's not as stupid as he looks. To this Rom replies, "I am *too*!" Personally, I'm inclined to agree with Odo. The mysterious list in this episode is written in Bajoran script. Rom looks at it for only a short while. Later, under Odo's urgings, Rom identifies the first letter of the first name as "C," the last letter as "O," and says the name has a mark in it. This tells us that Rom reads Bajoran—and he knows Odo does not—so Rom transliterates the Bajoran script into Federation standard letter names so Odo can succeed in his investigation. (One would expect Rom to say something like, "The first letter in the name was 'Kwa,'" since the list was written in Bajoran.) Amazingly enough, Rom accomplishes this linguistic sleight-of-hand while doing a perfect impersonation of a bumbling idiot. (On the other hand, maybe the ubiquitous Universal Translator took care of the conversion and Rom really *is* an idiot.)

• Supposedly Gul Dukat originally put Odo on the case of the murder of Vaatrik because Vaatrik was his link to a network of Bajoran sympathizers and Dukat didn't want to be associated with the case. All fine and well. However, it appears that Odo never solved the case. So what does Gul Dukat do? He keeps Odo on as an investigator! Does this make sense? And another thing: What did Dukat do about this murder? Did he go ahead

and execute ten Bajorans, as he threatened to do at the beginning?

CHANGED PREMISES

• Having assembled the names on the list, Odo disgustedly tells Sisko that they were all collaborators, that they were "selling out their home world for profit." He goes on to say that even a Ferengi wouldn't do that. Excuse me! I believe that Rule of Acquisition 6 states: "Never allow family to stand in the way of opportunity." (See "The Nagus.") I also believe that Rule 111 reads: "Treat people in your debt like family, exploit them." (See "Past Tense, Part I.") In addition, Rule 102 reads: "Nature decays. Latinum lasts forever." (see "The Jem'Haddar.") Given these rules, does it seem likely that Ferengi would have some aversion to selling their home world for profit?

EQUIPMENT ODDITIES

• This was one of those nits that I didn't spot until I had seen the episode five times. It's very odd. The mind gets used to seeing certain things and then suddenly the old synapses start firing and you think, "*Wait a minute!*" At the beginning of the episode, Quark visits with Mrs. Vaatrik on Bajor. The room is romantically lit with candles, and she makes a passing comment that at least the Cardassians could keep the power on. Later Odo pays Mrs. Vaatrik a visit on Bajor as well. He notes that her power had been terminated for lack of payment. He also informs her that he knows she transferred the necessary funds to the power company that morning. In other words, when Quark visited, the candles weren't just for atmosphere; Mrs. Vaatrik's house didn't have any power. Oddly enough, when Quark leaves, the doors open and close! (Must be some of those gerbil-powered doors!)

• Possibly it happened before this episode and I just missed it, but Odo's office has inherited a replicator. It sits in the cubby right behind Odo's desk. Here's what's interesting. Some of the flashbacks in this episode are set in a room that looks just like Odo's Security office, *and* the flashback room also has a replicator built into the wall of the cubby. Now, I know for sure that the replicator was not there for most of the first season. If the room in the flashback is Odo's current office, then the Cardassians installed the replicator, somebody ripped it out, and O'Brien installed it again later.

• The same would apply for the doors that lead to the cell block in Odo's office. The doors in the flashbacks look identical to the current doors, but the current doors didn't appear until "Captive Pursuit."

• After the experience with Melora, Bashir must have chewed on O'Brien for not having any decent antigrav units available. In "Melora" Bashir had to replicate an old-style electric wheelchair for the gravity-challenged ensign to use because the standard antigrav unit wouldn't work due to the Cardassian construction of the stations. In this episode Bashir hollers for an antigrav lift to take Quark to the infirmary, and one shows up seconds later! (And it looks like a Federation model.)

• Speaking of taking Quark to the infirmary, I wonder why Bashir didn't have him beamed there. After all, the

Enterprise beamed the away team directly to sick bay when Picard was shot with a compressed teryon beam in "Tapestry" *(TNG)*.

CONTINUITY AND PRODUCTION PROBLEMS

• To gain access behind the wall panel, Rom uses magnesite drops. Four bolts secure the panel to the wall. In order, Rom places drops on the upper left, upper right, lower left, and lower right. Soon the bolts spark and the panel falls off. Interestingly enough, the lower right bolt sparks before the lower left bolt even though Rom put the drops on the lower left bolt first.

• The list of Bajoran names appears to be in Bajoran script. This would make sense. However, the first name on the list looks like it's composed of three separate words, the first one fairly short. This is the name that Kira later identifies as "Ches'sarro." Bajoran script must really be compact for Ches'sarro to be the short series of characters seen for the first word on the list. Also, Rom remembers a mark in the name. Unfortunately, I can't find it.

• I love the "flying backward" stunts that the creators use in *Star Trek*. In this episode, Quark gets hit with a weapon and goes flying backward for fifteen feet before thumping to the ground. The only problem is that Quark appears to "rebound" at the end of the stunt. The double flies through the air with the greatest of ease, making a beautiful prostrate landing, slides backward a bit, and then *slides forward* a bit—almost as if he's tethered to a rope. (Wink, wink.)

• At one point Odo travels to Bajor

to interview Vaatrik's widow. In the establishing shot you can see a coffee table that features a cylindrical pot. Both the lid and the body of the pot protrude horns that serve as handles. Isn't this the same pot that Picard's faux wife in "The Inner Light" *(TNG)* used when she dished him out

some supper? Wow! Now, that's weird! Could it be that the Bajorans visited the Kataan system before its star went nova?

TRIVIA ANSWERS
1. The lunar prison on Meldrar I.
2. Pyrellian.

SECOND SIGHT

Star Date: 47329.4

The day after the anniversary of Jennifer Sisko's death, Benjamin meets a mysterious, red catsuit-clad woman named Fenna. She seems to know nothing of her past, disappears at the most inopportune moments, and is very attracted to Sisko. The feeling is mutual. Meanwhile, the flamboyant Gideon Seyetik prepares for the crowning achievement of his impressive terraforming career. He intends to bring a dead star, Epsilon 119, back to life. The USS *Prometheus,* currently docked at DS9, will carry out the mission.

When Seyetik invites Sisko and staff to dinner, the mystery of Fenna deepens. Seyetik's wife, Nidell, looks exactly like Fenna (minus the catsuit), but she denies any knowledge of Sisko. Accompanying Seyetik on the mission, Sisko learns that Nidell is a Halanan and has psycoprojective capabilities. In times of emotional distress, Halanans lose control of this ability and create other individuals from their unconscious. Nidell has come to despise her husband, but Halanans mate for life. Because of this, Nidell's emotions have turned self-destructive—pushing her into a lethal coma as Fenna comes to life once more. To free his wife from her oath, Seyetik uses the regeneration experiment to commit suicide while rebirthing the star. Nidell then awakes without any remembrance of Fenna or her attraction to Sisko.

Trivia Questions

1. Odo wants to be notified the moment what person arrives on the station?

2. Where did Bashir see an exhibit of Seyetik's paintings?

RUMINATIONS

In the category of "Great Lines We'll Never Hear," at the end of this episode—as Nidell walks away from Sisko—I kept wishing the commander would say, "Nidell ...Nidell...if you don't mind...could you put on that red catsuit one last time before you leave?"

GREAT LINES

"She was wearing...red!"—Sisko to Odo, rounding out his sparse description of Fenna so the constable can search the station for her.

PLOT OVERSIGHTS

• Ain't love grand? Sisko goes to Odo's office to solicit the constable's help in finding Fenna. Odo asks for a description and—in fits and starts—Sisko eventually ends up with the following: female, humanoid, 1.6 meters tall, brown skin, dark hair. Oh...and let's not forget, "She was wearing ...*red*!" However, there's one particularly helpful detail missing in this description. Sisko evidently has forgotten that she also has double-tipped, pointed ears! Obviously he hasn't been spending much time looking at Fenna's *ears*. (No doubt his gaze has been distracted elsewhere. But seriously, just how many races are there with this type of ear? One would think this little detail would greatly assist Odo in his quest. I guess Sisko was just too love-numbed to notice.)

• Something very, very weird is going on aboard the *Prometheus*. Note first that Odo claims Seyetik is the only person to disembark while docked at DS9. I realize this was said to build tension and confuse the living daylights out of Sisko because at this point he thinks Nidell is wiggling into her catsuit and leaving the *Prometheus* to surprise him with an unexpected rendezvous. But it raises an obvious question: Does *none* of the crew of the *Prometheus* wish to sample the pleasure of the promenade? When the *Lexington* docks during "Explorers," Starfleet officers are all over Quark's. Odder still, the *Prometheus* has no medical staff! When Nidell falls into her deep coma, only Dax is available to provide some advice. By far, the most unusual aspect of the *Prometheus* comes, however, when Lieutenant (J.G.) Piersall takes the center chair! This starship is commanded by a lieutenant?! *What is going on here?* (I'll tell you what's going on. The structure of *Star Trek: Deep Space Nine series* had a problem at this point in its life cy-

cle. If the *Prometheus* showed up configured as it would be normally configured in the *Star Trek* universe, Sisko would immediately be relegated to second fiddle. The captain would hold command over the last twenty-five minutes of the episode. Of course, the creators couldn't have that. So they created this stripped-down starship so its personnel wouldn't outshine the stars of the show!)

• After taking a tricorder reading of Fenna, Dax pronounces her "pure energy." So...is she like a benign force field or something? How does one touch pure energy? How does one *French kiss* pure energy, as Sisko does in this episode?

• Traveling to Epsilon 119, Seyetik quotes from G'Trok's "The Fall of Kang." Sisko finishes the quotation after stating that it was required reading at the Starfleet Academy. Near the end of the episode, as he is about to crash into the dead star, Seyetik explains his motivation to Sisko. "Remember 'The Fall of Kang'?" he says. "Well, this is one warrior who refuses to be pitied." At this point, Lieutenant (J.G.) Piersall—who captains the *Prometheus* for some unknown reason (see above)—spouts off with, "What's he talking about?" If "The Fall of Kang" was required reading at the academy, shouldn't Piersall *know* what Seyetik is talking about? (Or did Piersall *sleep* through Klingon Poetry Appreciation 101?)

• When Seyetik's shuttle hits Epsilon 119, we see the dead star igniting almost instantly. It makes for good television but not good science. Stars are ancient things. You don't turn them on and off at will. They live for age upon age—burning with the fury of fusion—oblivious to little dustballs like us. Mitzi Adams tells me—according to our current understanding of stellar evolution—that once the core temperature of a star reaches 15 million degrees Kelvin, the fusing of hydrogen atoms into helium atoms commences. The individual photons (packets of energy) produced by this fusion then begin a dance to the surface of the star that will take one *million* years to complete! One *million* years! So even if Seyetik could turn on the star, it would be quite a while before Sisko and company would see any result.

CHANGED PREMISES

• At the beginning of this episode, Sisko gives a star date of 47329.4 and says the fourth anniversary of his wife's death at Wolf 359 occurred yesterday. According to "Emissary," the battle at Wolf 359 happened on star date 43997. If 1000 star date units constitute one Earth year, the confrontation with the Borg would have occurred fewer than three and one-half years ago. (On the other hand, maybe Sisko's using Bajoran years?)

• At least Jake is making some progress with his math. At the beginning of the season, in my review of "The Homecoming," I noted that the young man was taking an algebra test. I found this interesting because "When the Bough Breaks" featured a lad many years younger who was complaining about taking calculus. In this episode, Jake has a calculus test as well. (Pretty impressive to go from algebra to calculus in just a few months.)

• Just prior to Sisko meeting Seyetik for the first time, Dax gives her commander some advice about terraformers. She says that you can't tell a terraformer anything, that humility and common sense aren't part of the job description. That's strange because the terraformers in "Home Soil" *(TNG)* didn't seem like Seyetik at all.

• Protomatter has somehow refurbished its soiled reputation. In *Star Trek III: The Search for Spock,* we learn that Dr. David Marcus used protomatter in the Genesis device. We also learn that protomatter is unstable and unethical and no self-respecting physicist would even go out and have a drink with the stuff! Yet, in this episode, Seyetik uses protomatter in his device to revitalize the star.

• After discovering that Fenna is Nidell, Dax has a little talk with Sisko, suggesting that he needs to get her alone and find out what's going on. Sisko responds that Nidell is a married woman, to which Dax shoots back, "That would have never stopped Curzon." It almost sounds like Dax is encouraging Sisko to go after Nidell. This is very strange because in "Dax," Dax expressed her profound regret that Curzon had slept with General Tandro's wife.

EQUIPMENT ODDITIES

• For dramatic purposes, the creators have Seyetik doing something dangerous just before Sisko meets the famed terraformer. He is in the flux generator in the science lab. This is a dangerous place that supposedly can kill him. Oddly enough, it appears to have a complete workstation *inside* the generator. If the place is so dangerous, why put a terminal in there? Wouldn't this be like putting the on and off button on the interior wall of a reactor core? (Of course, you can never tell about those Cardassians. They do do the strangest things.)

• After eating a meal with Sisko, Dax says that she needs to meet with O'Brien. They are going to boost the maximum speed of the *Prometheus* to warp 9.5 just in case Seyetik's experience fails and the star goes supernova. Obviously both Dax and O'Brien have forgotten that a starship can outrun a supernova even at warp 1. A supernova is a natural phenomenon, and as such it must travel slower than the speed of light. (In addition, I hate to bring this up, but the Federation has a new warp 5 speed limit that became effective at the end of the *NextGen* episode "Force of Nature," star date 47314.5. I sure hope *somebody* is going to contact Starfleet command and ask permission if they are planning on violating the new directive.)

CONTINUITY AND PRODUCTION PROBLEMS

• I know it was supposed to look that way, but I couldn't help but chuckle over Nidell's costume at the very end of the episode. As she walks out of Sisko's life forever, we see that one of her sleeves is a good six inches longer than the other! At first I thought, "Man, that lady needs a better tailor!" But then it dawned on me: She probably bought that dress from Garak's shop on the promenade! No wonder Bashir refuses to believe the guy is a simple merchant.

TRIVIA ANSWERS
1. Villus Thed.
2. The Central Gallery on Ligobis X.

TRIATHLON TRIVIA ON CHARACTERS

MATCH THE CHARACTER TO THE DESCRIPTION TO THE EPISODE

CHARACTER	DESCRIPTION	EPISODE
1. Alenis Grem	A. Accused of cheating the Wadi	a. "A Man Alone"
2. Altrina	B. Gave Kira one hour to surrender	b. "The Abandoned"
3. Arlin, Lysia	C. Adviser to the House of Quark	c. "Battlelines"
4. Ashrock	D. He budded	d. "Captive Pursuit"
5. Bilecki, Lieutenant	E. Blessed Quark's pens (maybe)	e. "Cardassians"
6. Broik	F. Bought the first item at Vash's auction	f. "The Circle"
7. Boday	G. Recruited Kira for the resistance	g. "Civil Defense"
8. Borath	H. Captain of a Kressari vessel	h. "Dax"
9. Draxman, Admiral	I. Commander, Proxima	i. "Defiant"
		Maintenance Yard
10. Frin	J. Did a study on Elemspur	j. "Emissary"
11. Garland, Nurse	K. Leader of the Nol-Ennis	k. "Equilibrium"
12. G'Trok	L. Engaged to a young Bajoran male	l. "Fascination"
13. Hogue	M. Gallamite captain who dated Dax	m. "Heart of Stone"
14. Inglatu	N. Gave oo-mox to Nog	n. "The Homecoming"
15. Jasad, Gul	O. Had lunch with Ibudan	o. "The House of Quark"
16. Kahn, Nilani	P. Helped Tom Riker on the Defiant	p. "Indiscretion"
17. Kolos	Q. Married to Torias Dax	q. "Invasive Procedures"
18. Leanne	R. Helped Verad steal Dax	r. "Life Support"
19. Lorit Akrem	S. Tried to buy Rings of Paltriss	s. "Little Green Men"
20. Malko	T. Accused Quark of sexual advances	t. "The Maquis, Part I"
21. Marayn, Gul	U. Invented by Kira	u. "Melora"
22. Muniz	V. Left his son Rugal on Bajor	v. "Meridian"
23. Okalar	W. Male Dosi negotiator	w. "Move Along Home"
24. Pa'Dar, Kotan	X. Trill guardian	x. "Past Prologue"
25. Peers, Selin	Y. Bolian Jumja kiosk proprietor	y. "Past Tense, Part I"
26. Redab, Vedek	Z. Marta made him lose at Dabo	z. "Profit and Loss"
27. Santina, Della	AA. Attempted to blow up the wormhole	aa. "Progress"
28. Sarda, Miss	BB. Negotiated for the Novat	bb. "Q-Less"
29. Sirco Ch'Ano	CC. Owns thirty bars	cc. "Rejoined"
30. Tahna Los	DD. Wrote "The Fall of Kang"	dd. "Rules of Acquisition"
31. Tamal	EE. Posed as a founder	ee. "The Search, Part II"

32. Timor	FF. She *was* dating Orak	ff. "Second Sight"
33. Tiron	GG. Testified at Dax's extradition hearing	gg. "Second Skin"
34. Tumek	HH. Worked in a Jefferies tube with Dax	hh. "Shadowplay"
35. Varis Sul	II. Tetrarch of the Paqu	ii. "The Siege"
36. Vilix'Pran, Ensign	JJ. A student of Natima Lang	jj. "Starship Down"
37. Woban	KK. Traded land for stembolts	kk. "The Storyteller"
38. Yeto	LL. Vomited all over a table	ll. "The Way of the Warrior"
39. Zef'No	MM. Wanted a hologram of Kira	
40. Zlangco	NN. Gave Dax a massage	

SCORING

(BASED ON NUMBER OF CORRECT ANSWERS)

0–10	Normal
11–19	Good
20–29	Excellent
30–40	Beyond excellent

CHARACTERS ANSWER KEY: 1. J gg 2. LL gg 3. Y hh 4. S u 5. L ii 6. A w 7. M t 8. EE ee 9. I y 10. CC g 11. N s 12. DD ff 13. JJ z 14. W dd 15. B j 16. Q cc 17. F bb 18. FF r 19. G p 20. NN ll 21. U n 22. HH jj 23. Z b 24. V e 25. GG h 26. E l 27. O a 28. T d 29. KK aa 30. AA x 31. P i 32. X k 33. MM v 34. C o 35. II kk 36. D m 37. BB kk 38. R q 39. H f 40. K c

SANCTUARY

Star Date: 47391.2

After a damaged ship comes through the wormhole, O'Brien beams its four occupants directly to Ops. The woman Haneek, her two husbands, and a son are Skrreeans, finally freed by the Dominion from the oppression of the T'Rogorans. Hearing about a "tunnel" recently discovered in space, the Skrreeans decided that it must be the "Eye of the Universe"—a momentous discovery to be sure, since—according to the Skrreean sacred texts— the true home of the Skrreea, "Kentanna," lies just beyond it. Three million Skrreeans have taken flight in ships looking for the Eye, and Haneek has finally found it. Sisko immediately sends out ships to find the other Skrreean vessels and guide them through the wormhole to DS9.

In short order, Skrreeans begin pouring into the station. Since the T'Rogorans killed all their leaders, the Skrreeans vote in Haneek as their new leader. As Sisko and Dax search for a planet to give to the immigrants, Haneek begins her own investigation and decides that Bajor is Kentanna. Predictably, the provisional government turns down the Skrreean request to settle there. Disappointed, Haneek tells Kira that they are farmers and could have made Bajor bloom before she acquiesces and departs for her new home on Draylon II.

PLOT OVERSIGHTS

• At the end of the program, Haneek speaks of a "famine" on Bajor. I assume that this is a Universal Translator glitch. A famine would mean "an extreme general scarcity of food." Surely the Federation—knowing the devastation caused by the Cardassians to the farmlands when they left— would move in and assist with food replicators until the farm ecology could be reestablished. And if there really is a famine on Bajor, shouldn't we see more people sneaking onto the station in search of food? Haneek must mean instead that Bajor cannot produce enough food for its own inhabitants. (In other words, Bajor has a crop shortage. I know. Picky, picky, picky.)

• There's more to these Skrreeans than meets the "eye." They are supposedly just farmers, but they have a fleet of ships that can transport 3 *mil-*

Trivia Questions

1. Who is the Reegrunion listed in Odo's office and wanted in seven star systems for illegal weapons sales?

2. What food item does Jake recommend to Haneek's son Tumak?

127

lion refugees. Evidently these ships are warp-capable and can defend themselves. (Does this sound like an invasion fleet to anyone else?)

• Shortly after coming on the station, Haneek tells Kira and Sisko that the Dominion recently conquered their oppressors, the T'Rogorans. This little tidbit promptly falls to the floor and goes unnoticed for the rest of the episode. Too bad Sisko didn't bother to question the Skrreeans a bit more about the Dominion. It might have helped later in this season when the Jem'Haddar make their first move. Now, I realize it's easy to look back and say Sisko should have done this or should have done that, but the Gamma Quadrant is new, isn't it? Don't you want to find out as much as you can about it? Especially with regard to an evident aggressor?

CHANGED PREMISES

• In "Home Soil" *(TNG)* we witnessed a group of terraformers who would spend their lives on a hot, dusty rock, turning it into an Earth-like planet. Yet in this episode, Sisko locates an M-class planet with apparent ease. This raises the following question: If there are available M-class planets, why are there still terraformers? Are they all just loners and love a good challenge? (Yes, I do remember Gideon Seyetik from the previous episode and do remember that he was a terraformer as well. Somehow his work struck me as different—more like the Magratheans from Douglas Adams's trilogy *The Hitchiker's Guide to the Galaxy*.)

• Haneek tells Kira that there were fifty years of Cardassian rule. Actual-

ly, according to Kira in "Emissary," it was sixty. But hey, ten years more or less of spirit-crushing humiliation and servitude...who's counting?

EQUIPMENT ODDITIES

• There are some elements of science fiction on television that will never be easy to deal with. For instance, we all know that sound doesn't travel in a vacuum; not only is space cold and dead, it's also achingly silent. "Silent" does not play well on television! And so we all wink when the creators put in the sound effects of ships exploding in space, and the "whooshing" of high-warp travel, and we welcome the gritty firing of the *Defiant*'s phasers. Personally, I think we should all just wink at the Universal Translator (UT) as well. Yes, we all know that everybody speaks a different language and they shouldn't all be able to communicate. But do we really want to listen to alien garble every week and read subtitles? At least for my part, I vote no. So what say we all just agree that there's this magical, mystical, ubiquitous *thing* out there called the Universal Translator and it *somehow* just takes care of it?

Unfortunately, the creators apparently feel some obligation to demonstrate how the UT works. And—it seems to me—every time the creators try this with the UT, they insult our intelligence. Take this episode, for instance. Haneek and her boys beam onto the station speaking Skrreean— really speaking Skrreean. O'Brien says that the UT is working but is having a hard time establishing a translation matrix. Sisko says to keep them talking, and a short time later—lo and *behold*—the UT starts working and Haneek begins speaking in Federation standard. *But* not only does she begin speaking in Federation standard, her lips and tongue also form every word in Federation standard precisely correct! The only explanation I can come up with is the UT also has holographic projectors that operate all over the station and automatically create some type of facial mask that is reconfigured to look like it's speaking Federation standard. (This high level of technology was obviously developed by a team of engineers who had very horrific experiences with badly dubbed movies from the Orion Sector when they were young and so set themselves on a quest to eliminate bad dubbing throughout the entire galaxy!) Even more amazing, the UT accomplishes this magic for thousands of Skrreeans simultaneously when the station fills up!

• This episode gives us the first look at Jake and Nog after the engineers decided to make the promenade less safe. For some reason, the powers-that-be removed the lower railing on the second level of the promenade. Now only one railing exists; it sits about waist high for the average station inhabitant. Previous episodes have established that Jake and Nog like to sit on the promenade with their feet dangling off the edge. In the past the lower railing gave them something to hold. Now nothing sits between them and a dangerous fall.

• I wonder who footed the bill for all the replicator food that the Skrreeans ate. One scene shows them lined up

in the replimat. (Before you say "Well, it's free because it's just replicated," remember that Quark's is just around the corner. Why would anyone eat at Quark's if there was free food next door? Dabo girl ambience?)

• At the end of the episode, Haneek's son steals a ship and attempts to go to Bajor. Two interceptors meet him and accidently destroy his ship. During the tension-filled moments before this occurs, Sisko, Kira, and Haneek stand over a monitor, watching the drama unfold. For some reason, however, the monitor doesn't keep the three ships in the center but instead allows them almost to drift off the end when the fatal accident occurs. I guess Kira forgot to lock the sensors onto the targets because of the stress of the situation.

CONTINUITY AND PRODUCTION PROBLEMS

• This episode also features a Bajoran musician named Varani. Prior to the episode, Kira arranged for Quark to allow Varani to play in his bar for a month. The first time we see Varani he turns to the camera while playing his wind instrument. He appears to take a breath, but the instrument just keeps sounding. (Obviously this instrument is some Bajoran derivative of the bagpipe.)

• The creators decided to have a little fun with the Skrreeans. When a large group arrives on the station, several shots show us the shocked refugees wandering through the promenade. Although there's plenty of background conversation, nothing really stands out in the audio. The closed captioning is another story. Instead of just saying "(Skrreeans talking)," it reads—and I am *not* making this up:

"Man: THIS IS GREAT!"

"Man: THIS IS INCREDIBLE!"

"(all talking at once)"

"Man: THIS IS PRETTY FAR OUT."

"Man: DIG THIS PLACE."

• Sometimes ya gotta feel a little bad for Rom. His son gets nabbed by Odo for spraying foul smelling vapors on a Skrreean boy. Then Odo pages him to come to the Security office, but he can't go because Quark has him doing an inventory. That means Quark comes to the Security office instead. So not only does Quark cut him out of his fatherly duty, but Rom also loses his one shot in this episode to have a little screen and earn some extra money!

• This one is really tough to see, but I've watched it several times and I think you'll agree. At the very end of the episode, Kira stands in an airlock. Haneek walks through, and the door on her ship closes. The camera angle then reverses to show us Kira, and the airlock door rolls shut. Watch the reflection very carefully in the airlock door. To me it looks like Haneek is still standing in front of the airlock door, off-camera, when she's supposed to be inside already.

TRIVIA ANSWERS

1. Plix Tixaplik.
2. An icoberry torte.

RIVALS

As the episode begins, Odo arrests an El Aurian named Martus. A Pythron couple has charged that he swindled them out of their savings. In the cell with Martus, a sickly old male plays with a small gambling sphere, claiming that he once had it all but luck turned against him. Playing the game once more, the old man finally comes up a winner...and dies. Intrigued, Martus "inherits" the sphere. However, everytime *he* plays it, he wins. Quickly, his luck changes. The Pythron couple drop the charges. Martus finds a financial backer to help him open a gambling establishment on the promenade based on larger versions of the sphere. It does a thriving business. Then his luck begins to change as well.

Reports of minor accidents begin coming in from all over the station. At "Club Martus" all the gambling devices hit the jackpot at the same time. Files randomly appear and disappear from the computer. O'Brien suddenly never misses a shot in a racquetball match with Bashir—a much better player. Dax traces the problem to the gambling devices. Somehow they change the laws of probability. Sisko promptly destroys them. The Pythron couple refile their charges, and Martus goes back to Odo's cell.

Trivia Questions

1. What is the name of the woman who cons Martus out of 10,000 isiks?

2. What anesthetic does Quark attempt to administer to Bashir?

GREAT LINES

"Kick his butt."—Keiko to O'Brien just before O'Brien heads into a racquetball match with Bashir in which Bashir is the odds-on favorite. I like this section because it gives us a chance to see the O'Briens function as a real unit. Keiko must know that O'Brien doesn't stand much of a chance but she's for him anyway and is willing to hope beyond hope that he can thrash Bashir.

PLOT OVERSIGHTS

• Not really a nit, just a wonderment. Odo identifies Martus as an El Aurian. In *Star Trek Generations* we learned that this is Guinan's race! That makes three individuals we've come to know from this group of humanoids. At this point Guinan appears to be the only worthwhile one of the bunch. Remember, her fellow El Aurian Soren—also of *Generations*—was a maniac! Must have something to do with being ripped from the Nexus.

131

• Evidently Odo never inventories the old male's possessions before putting him in the cell. When the geezer dies, Martus keeps the bauble! What is this? The old West? ("Ya ol' hackin' Bob died with his boots on, he did. *You* want 'em?")

• In this episode a female con artist takes Martus for 10,000 isiks. When Martus delivers the funds it looks suspiciously like many bars of gold-pressed latinum. Now, I can understand how the female con artist might have a different name for her currency. But at the end of the episode, Quark offers Martus 500 isiks to leave the station. Why isn't Quark talking about strips or slips of latinum?

• So...these machines alter the laws of probability, eh? Now, *that's* quite a trick. I've been thinking about this and I can't image how this would be done without active *continual* intervention. For instance, Dax gets "lucky" when a file she has been searching for suddenly appears. Then she gets "unlucky" when the file disappears. Computers, dear friends, do not work on luck. They work from a series of commands. Someone or something had to bring that file to the surface. Someone or something had to send it away. And that someone or something had to know *exactly* what they were doing. In the same train of thought, consider the big match between O'Brien and Bashir. Supposedly no matter who hits or throws the racquetball, it always bounces to O'Brien. There simply *has* to be some type of active intervention by *someone* or *something*. The way a ball bounces is dictated by physics (angle of attack,

velocity, wind resistance, density of the surface, etc.). Although there is some chaos involved, that chaos will never lead to a programmed response like we see here. Evidently the machines send out little gremlins that are making these things happen. (Unless, of course, you would prefer that *Star Trek* was set in the universe invented by Douglas Adams in *The Hitchhiker's Guide to the Galaxy* trilogy. Then this episode would make perfect sense.)

• Having said all that, I am stunned and astonished at the apparent lack of scientific interest in these machines displayed by Sisko and Dax. Think of the potential if one could unlock their secrets and rig them always to flood the station with good luck! (How about that for a weapon to use against the Jem'Haddar? "I'm sorry, founder, but every time we attack the station, one of our engine nacelles falls off or the soldier at Tactical has a stroke or ...")

• Great confusion surrounds the system of justice utilized by Odo on the station. Near the end of the episode, Odo arrests Martus because a Pythron couple has filed charges. Then Quark comes into the cell block and starts negotiating to pay the guy to leave the station. Excuse me? Isn't the guy going to stand trial on the charges? Or is Quark encouraging the guy to become a fugitive? And, if so, is Odo listening in on this conversation?

EQUIPMENT ODDITIES

• After arresting Martus, Odo places him in a cell with a sickly old male. (I believe this is the first time we've ever seen two to a cell, but that's okay because it's essential to the plot. Wink, wink.) The cell doesn't appear to have any rest-room facilities. Maybe they are built into the wall?

• Interestingly enough, Martus replicates larger versions of the gambling sphere without knowing how it works. The replicator even reproduces the spheres' internal power units! (Is there a problem here with perpetual motion? Could you replicate a replicator with new power cells before the power cells on the old replicator failed?) Given the amazing success at replicating a machine that actually changes the laws of probability, I'm having a hard time believing a replicator would have much difficulty reproducing gold-pressed latinum. Why doesn't Quark just take a bar of latinum to the replicator and make a whole bunch more? Obviously the replicators on DS9 are really sophisticated.

CONTINUITY AND PRODUCTION PROBLEMS

• Bashir causes a small continuity error. Early on, O'Brien strolls happily down the hall to his newly completed racquetball court. The doors open and he finds Bashir inside going through a warm-up exercise. The good doctor has his hand raised, palm facing outward, fingers spread in the American numeric representation for five. The shot changes and suddenly Bashir's hand turns palm in—now showing the American numeric representation for two. (Of course, it's possible Bashir really *can* move this fast. That would account for his ex-

traordinary racquetball capability.)

• After his first match with O'Brien, Bashir discusses the situation with Dax in the replimat. To add some motion to the scene, the creators have Bashir get his sandwich from the replicator, sit down, attempt to add sauce, find the sauce bottle empty, get up, retrieve a second sauce bottle from another table, sit down, find the bottle empty, get up, retrieve a third bottle from yet another table, sit down, and finally pour sauce on the innards of his sandwich. Amid all this motion there is something very, very odd going on at the table directly behind Dax—the table that holds the third bottle of sauce. When Bashir picks up his sandwich, you can see a Bajoran man and a woman seated there. Moments later, the scene cuts to a front view of Dax. Now a Starfleet officer and a man in civilian clothes sit at the table. A few seconds pass, Bashir gets up to get the second sauce bottle, and you can just barely see the edge of a woman's dress. Then the scene goes back to Dax, and the Starfleet guy and his buddy reappear. Bashir goes to the table for the third sauce bottle. Now the man and the woman are back! And when the scene cuts back to Dax? You guessed it! Starfleet and his buddy return. (I suspect Changelings have already infiltrated the stations. Aaaaaaaaaaah!)

TRIVIA ANSWERS
1. Alsia.
2. Hyvroxilated quintethyl metasetamin.

THE ALTERNATE

Star Date: 47391.7

D r. Mora—the Bajoran scientist assigned to Odo after his discovery near the wormhole—comes to the station to ask for Odo's help. A Bajoran probe has detected a substance similar to Odo on a planet in the Gamma Quadrant. Mora wants Odo to ask Sisko for a runabout to investigate. Both Odo and Sisko agree.

On the planet, Mora, Odo, Dax, and a Dr. Weld find a metamorphic substance. They also encounter a ground tremor that releases paralyzing volcanic gas. Seemingly unaffected by the gas, Odo beams everyone up to the runabout. That night on the station, however, something destroys the lab containing the substance, allowing it to escape. The substance soon dies, unable to live without a higher carbon dioxide count. Sixteen hours after the incident in the lab, a giant blob attacks Bashir in the infirmary. He manages to fend off the blob with a laser scalpel, but this time it leaves an organic trace behind. It is Odo. Somehow the volcanic gas has affected him, and every time he regenerates, a violent personality takes over.

With Mora's help, Sisko and crew lure Odo onto the promenade during such an incident and trap him in a force field. Bashir then purges the volcanic gas from Odo's system (with Rolaids, I would imagine).

PLOT OVERSIGHTS

• The episode piqued my interest in Federation archaeological policies concerning once-inhabited worlds. Dax, Odo, Mora, and Weld beam down to the remains of a village. A large stone monolith stands near the center of the ruins. Dax thinks it looks interesting, so she beams it back to the runabout. Obviously there isn't any law against doing this, but this type of pilfering must drive archaeologists nuts.

• After Odo attacks the lab, Dax strolls in and looks around. Sisko wonders if she should be released from the infirmary yet. Dax says that she snuck out wearing a gown that didn't close in back. Two questions: Doesn't Bashir have the authority to keep her in the infirmary if he wants to? And why was Dax wearing a gown that didn't close in back when O'Brien appears in a gown only two shows later that does? (I suppose the easy answer to both of

Trivia Questions

1. What beverage does Dr. Mora order from Quark?

2. On what planet is Odo's "cousin" found?

134

these questions is Bashir arranged for Dax to wear a gown that didn't close in back and so thoroughly enjoyed watching her sneak out of the infirmary that he judged her healthy enough to leave. "All I can say, Commander, is: She looked perfectly fine to me!" Sorry, sorry. I apologize for that last remark.)

• I am constantly amazed at the high level of DCD (Descriptionally Challenged Disorder) among members of Starfleet—even members of the Bajoran military. Not only must we endure such informative phrases as "I think you better get up here, Commander," but we also often see personnel at a complete loss of words at the simplest times. I first noticed DCD in the *NextGen* episode "Hide and Q" when Worf labeled Q's hairy pig-faced humanoid "animal things." O'Brien comes down with DCD in this episode when he's crawling through a conduit. He hears a noise and says, "It almost sounds like...I can't describe it." How about, "a low moaning accompanied by a clinking sound"?

• At the end of this episode, Dr. Mora—seeing Odo's distress—says, "Dear God, what have I done?" Not to be nitpicker, but don't Bajorans believe in "The Prophets"?

• Let's see. At the end of the program, Odo collapses in exhaustion. Specifically, he's a large, blobby monster, and then he morphs into a humanoid shape as he falls to the floor. Wouldn't it make more sense for him to turn into a liquid if he's really that worn out? (I know, I know. It wouldn't have nearly the same emotional impact for Mora to scoop up a handful

of goo and choke out his "We have a lot to talk about" line.)

• And speaking of collapsing into a humanoid shape, Odo does a really respectable impersonation of gasping for air for someone who doesn't have a respiratory system.

CHANGED PREMISES

• At the beginning of the episode one might make the case that Odo is using pretense as he talks with Quark about his interest in death rituals. The entire conversation seems to be a ruse to draw out the truth that the pieces of Plegg that Quark is selling aren't really Plegg because Plegg is still dead. Of course, Odo can't be using pretense because, according to "Past Prologue," Odo never uses pretense.

• Evidently Nog really *is* back in school. In "The Nagus," Rom pulled him out. Then in "The Siege," Nog assures Jake that they'll soon be back together as they bid each other goodbye during the evacuation of the station. Now in this episode, Jake and Nog are studying for the same test.

EQUIPMENT ODDITIES

• The transport from the surface of the planet contains several oddities. Dax beams up the stone monolith. The ground starts shaking. She tells the computer to realign the transport and lock on to their combadges. The ground shakes. The ground shakes some more. The away team stumbles around. The ground shakes even more. The computer calls down and says it's ready. Odo calls for beam-out. First, it seems to take a *really* long time for the computer to realign the transporter.

Second, the runabout transports four people at once, but "The Homecoming" seems to indicate that you can beam only two people at once with a runabout transporter. Third, the transporter beams Dax, who is a Trill; but "the Host" *(TNG)* indicated that Trill symbionts are damaged by transporters.

• I am heartened to see that the creators finally ordered some real pillows for the poor station personnel of DS9. In previous episodes such as "Cardassians," we've seen station personnel trying to sleep with their heads resting on triangle-shaped wedges that looked really uncomfortable. In this episode, Sisko has a more normal-looking pillow.

CONTINUITY AND PRODUCTION PROBLEMS

• It's a valiant attempt. When Dax, Odo, Mora, and Weld beam down to the planet, the creators use a large matte painting to make it look like they are outside. It almost does.

• In my review of "The Forsaken," I found it odd that Odo's face would melt but not his clothes, since his clothes are supposedly part of him. In this episode the creators went to the extra trouble of "melting" Odo's hair, but the clothes still look laundry-fresh.

TRIVIA ANSWERS
1. Deka tea.
2. L.S. VI.

ARMAGEDDON GAME

Star Date: supplemental (see below)

Orbiting above T'Lani III, Bashir and O'Brien help the T'Lani and the Kellerun destroy their stockpiles of "harvesters," deadly biomechanical genetic disrupters that were used by both races during their war. Neither officer is aware of the depth of the commitment that the T'Lani and Kellerun governments have to ensure that no one can re-create the hideous weapons. As the last few cylinders await destruction, Kellerun assassins burst in, intending to kill every person involved with the project—including Bashir and O'Brien. The pair escape to the war-torn surface of T'Lani III, but not before O'Brien is infected by the final batch of harvesters.

Meanwhile, the T'Lani and Kellerun ambassadors visit DS9 and tell Sisko that Bashir and O'Brien have died. They bring a data clip showing O'Brien accidentally setting off a defense mechanism that vaporizes everyone in the room. Keiko doesn't believe it. She sees her husband drinking coffee—something she insists that O'Brien never does in the afternoon. Sisko and Dax investigate, locating Bashir and O'Brien just in time to save them from a second wave of assassins. Back on the station, Bashir stops the harvesters from killing O'Brien before leaving him alone to enjoy a reunion with Keiko. That's when Keiko discovers that her husband drinks coffee in the afternoon all the time!

Trivia Questions

1. Which test sequence succeeds in destroying the harvesters?

2. What does Sisko order at Quark's just before learning that O'Brien and Bashir are dead?

PLOT OVERSIGHTS

• Bashir begins this episode with "Medical log, supplemental." I find this *extremely* unsatisfying! It's like reading Chapters One and Two of a book, then turning to Chapter Three, only to find the next section titled "Supplement to Chapter Three." It leaves me feeling like I've missed something.

• When the assassins burst into the lab to kill everyone on sight, aren't they just a tad early? After all, Bashir hasn't dispensed with the last batch of harvesters yet.

• Just after arriving on the surface of T'Lani III, Bashir and O'Brien find refuge in an abandoned building. Bashir finds a cache of supplies and starts to open a box. Quite wisely, O'Brien rushes over to tell him it might be booby-trapped. He tells Bashir that Cardassians would often rig the supplies they left behind with pressure grenades. O'Brien then checks the supplies with his tricorder and pronounces them clean. Moments later, O'Brien finds a communication device. Almost immediately he rips the top off the thing. Wouldn't it be a good idea to check this device for booby traps as well?

• Bashir must be a traditionalist. Prior to the episode we learn that he had given his diaries from medical school to Dax so she would understand him better. Believing that Bashir is dead, she wonders to Kira if she should send them back to his parents. Wouldn't they be stored as optical data in a computer? Why not just transmit a copy of the files? Did Bashir actually write out a diary using pen and paper?

• The recording brought to Sisko by the T'Lani and Kellerun ambassadors shows the radiation pulse that supposedly vaporizes everyone in the room occurring at 15:28:55. Later, Dax discovers a remote transport request erased from the logs. When she tells Sisko that the request came at 1534 hours, he reacts by saying, "That's a full three minutes after the accident on the T'Lani cruiser." No, Commander, that would be a full *five* minutes! (At least we know why Jake is struggling with math. Apparently Sisko has a bit of trouble with it himself!)

• Once Sisko beams Bashir and O'Brien up to his runabout from the surface of T'Lani III, the T'Lani cruiser blocks all transmissions and short-range sensors to prevent them from contacting Starfleet. Since the inversion field put out by the T'Lani cruiser has blinded its own sensors as well,

Sisko beams everyone to the runabout used by Bashir and O'Brien when they came to the system. He then remote-pilots the other runabout to make it look like he's trying to run away. Of course, the T'Lani cruiser gives chase and fires a warning shot at the empty runabout. Sisko then hails the cruiser—probably using some kind of subspace relay on the fleeing runabout—and tells the T'Lani ambassador that firing on the vessel will be an act of war. Moments later, the T'Lani ambassador destroys the empty runabout, supposedly giving Sisko and company time to escape. Was Sisko just blustering, or is the Federation now at war with the T'Lani and the Kellerun?

• And speaking of Sisko and company making their escape, why didn't the T'Lani cruiser go after them? Their ambassador says the cruiser is no match for a runabout. Sure, the runabout has a little bit of a head start, but couldn't the cruiser close the gap before the runabout made it back to DS9?

EQUIPMENT ODDITIES

• The episode opens with Bashir struggling to find a way to destroy the harvesters. Here's a novel idea: Why not use the transporter? Could these harvesters survive if they were dismantled into their quantum particles and sprayed into space?

• Bashir and O'Brien fend off the first wave of assassins, only to find that they can't contact the computer on their runabout. Initially they wanted to beam back to the ship and escape. Instead they use the lab's transporter to beam down to the surface of the planet. Ultimately this proved to be the correct thing to do, but why didn't they use the lab's transporter to beam to the runabout?

• This episode predicts an end of an era for actors and actresses. To prove their concocted story about the death of O'Brien and Bashir, the T'Lani and Kellerun ambassadors present Sisko with a faked visual record. One must assume that Dax or somebody checked the record to make sure it was authentic as part of the routine investigation into the death of a Starfleet officer. Amazingly enough, the record is so flawless that everyone buys into this story until Keiko finds what she believes is a nit in it! In other words, someone took footage of our heroes, rearranged it to fit their scenario—even added whole sentences to O'Brien's dialogue—and no one could tell. Can virtual actors be far behind? (As a side note, this also may mean that we nitpickers will have real jobs in the future ascertaining the veracity of visual records! "It appeared to be authentic, Your Honor, until I watched it for the twenty-third time. That's when I noticed that the shadow from the victim's index finger rested at a slightly different orientation than the shadow from his thumb.")

CONTINUITY AND PRODUCTION PROBLEMS

• The T'Lani cruiser design is amazingly similar to the design of the Children of Tama's ship in "Darmok" *(TNG)*.

• After the harvester droplet falls on his forearm, O'Brien starts to get up. Then the shot changes and suddenly he holds a phaser rifle.

• Yet more proof that the station has rotational speed control in Ops. (See "Past Prologue" and "Cardassians.") When the T'Lani and Kellerun ambassadors talk with Sisko, only the corner of his window shows at first. The stars are moving in the shot. Then the scene cuts to a wider shot of Sisko standing in front of the window, and the stars definitely are *not* moving.

• Investigating the "death" of Bashir and O'Brien, Sisko beams aboard the T'Lani cruiser that houses the lab where the harvesters were destroyed. As Sisko questions the T'Lani ambassador, Dax pages the commander from a runabout. Listen carefully and you'll hear Sisko's communicator chirp three times in a row!

• Apparently, the Ferengi sold some supplies to the T'Lani. When O'Brien asks Bashir if he's talked with his former girlfriend lately, there's a box in the lower left-hand corner of the screen that has a Ferengi logo on it.

• If you look very carefully using freeze frame, you'll see that the runabout cockpit shows the damage caused by the T'Lani phasers *before* the T'Lani phasers finish cutting through the hull.

TRIVIA ANSWERS

1. Number 375.
2. Alterian chowder, uttaberry crepes and a slice of...

Star Dates: 47569.4—47581.2

As the episode begins, O'Brien races back to the Paradan system in the Gamma Quadrant. He intends to advise the Paradans to call off the peace conference scheduled for DS9. Several days prior, O'Brien had traveled to the Paradan system to discuss security arrangements, but when he returned he found almost everyone on board DS9 subtly changed. Keiko had seemed strangely distant. Bashir had insisted that O'Brien come to the infirmary for a complete physical. Sisko and the others had even approached him with weapons drawn, but the chief was ready and quickly escaped in a runabout.

In fact, the O'Brien who is attempting to warn *both* sides in the conference is a replicant constructed by scientists of the Paradan government to commit an act of violence against Paradan rebels *during* the peace conference. (Is this confusing, or what?) The real O'Brien is still in the Paradan system. The rebels discovered the government plan and informed Sisko before the faux O'Brien returned to

Trivia Questions

1. One of O'Brien's favorite meals includes what for dessert?

2. Who comes to DS9 on star date 47552.9 to assess Cardassian movements along the border?

the station. Even stranger, when Sisko attempts to retrieve the real O'Brien, the replicant bursts in and accuses the commander of siding with the rebels. Sisko tries to keep everyone calm, but a rebel fatally wounds the replicant—leaving the commander to ponder that the scientists did their job too well. This O'Brien had the same commitment to duty as the original.

PLOT OVERSIGHTS

• At the beginning of the episode, O'Brien sets a heading of "410 mark 32." According to the *Tech Manual,* headings are set using the degrees of a circle. Since there are 360 degrees in a circle, the first number should be in the range 0 through 359.

• O'Brien begins to sense that something is wrong when he finds his wife awake at 0530 hours. Then he tries to say hello to his daughter Molly, and the little girl snaps at him. Presumably Molly knows that this O'Brien is not the real O'Brien. How does she know this? Surely, Keiko didn't tell her. Four-year-olds are not exactly the best secret keepers in the galaxy. Besides, why terrorize your daughter by trying to explain that Daddy is not Daddy but a replicant? I suppose Molly could have *sensed* that this O'Brien wasn't the real O'Brien, but—for a replicant— he seems very complete in both his verbal and nonverbal mimicry. Furthermore, Molly only had a few seconds to make this determination if she came to it on her own. (It's not like he went to the replicator and ordered a batch of Talarian hook spiders for breakfast or anything!)

• During a voiceover, O'Brien mentions that his birthday is in September. Many nitpickers took exception to this, since Alexander gives his birth date as a star date in "New Ground" *(TNG)*. Maybe O'Brien's a traditionalist?

• At one point O'Brien goes to the bar. Quark comes up and begins an enigmatic conversation with "the odds are against you." He also plies O'Brien with questions about the Paradan. When O'Brien asks the reason for his interest, Quark says it's always good to know about new customers before they come through the door. Gruffly, O'Brien asks which Rule of Acquisition states that sentiment. To this Quark says he's not sure; maybe it's one of the high ones. I realize that the creators put this in to heighten the drama of the episode and make even Quark seem odd. Unfortunately, this is completely out of character for the Ferengi. He knows these rules forward and backward, inside and outside. Every other time we see Quark display any knowledge about these rules, it is very precise. It is his *religion,* after all! (I suppose you could make the case that he knows this isn't the real O'Brien, but why would Sisko give Quark this delicate piece of information?)

• Sometimes Security procedures on DS9 just baffle me. O'Brien is on the run. Ops locates him and erects force fields around his position. Unfortunately, they leave a terminal running inside the area defined by the force fields, so O'Brien can escape. Does this make sense? Isn't this like putting an escape artist in stocks and then making sure he has a set of lock-picking tools?

• And while were talking about Security procedures, how many times are the Security officers going to *forget* to check the conduits when someone disappears from a hallway? After Jake notifies Security of his position, O'Brien runs down a hall and jumps in a conduit. Security personnel soon trot by without even giving the conduit a glance.

• Maybe Sisko couldn't have done anything about the replicant O'Brien getting killed at the end of this episode, but this seems like a very bad strategic blunder by the commander. Look at it from his viewpoint. He's sitting in his office. He gets a calls from the Paradan rebels. They say that the O'Brien coming back to the station is a replicant. Sisko tells the senior staff and Keiko. O'Brien arrives. Bashir gives him a complete physical and can't find any indication that the guy is a replicant. At this point don't you have to consider the possibility that this is the real O'Brien and the Paradan rebels are trying to get you to substitute a fake one? Any technology can be stolen. Maybe the Paradan government does have an exact replicator technology. How does that stop the rebels from using it? It's absolutely crucial at this point to secure the safety of *both* O'Briens, since you have only the rebels' word that this O'Brien is fake. Sisko should have transported the O'Brien on the station into one of Odo's cells when he had the chance and then gone to the Paradan system and retrieved the other O'Brien (if the rebels had another O'Brien in the first place). But you absolutely, for sure, come hell or high water, do *not* want to let either of these guys get killed.

CHANGED PREMISES

• Several times this episode indicates that DS9 received transmissions from the Paradan System. There is no question that the Paradan System is in the Gamma Quadrant. Yet in "Destiny," Sisko and company work with a team of Cardassian scientists to place a communications relay in the Gamma Quadrant. That episode says that the relay will finally make it possible to communicate with the Gamma Quadrant!

EQUIPMENT ODDITIES

• While enduring a physical exam by Bashir, O'Brien wears a hospital gown with ties in back. As I mentioned two episodes ago in "The Alternate," O'Brien fares better with regard to the distribution of hospital gowns than Dax. In that episode, Dax complained that her gown didn't close in back. And while we're on the subject of hospital gowns that close in back with ties, does this seem very twentieth-century to anyone else? One would think that the seamless closure technology would have been extended to these garments as well.

• Searching for the cause of every-

one's strange behavior, O'Brien has the computer scan for signs of telepathy. Somebody upgraded something somewhere in the past years! During "Night Terrors" *(TNG)* Troi had to deduce that aliens were trying to communicate with the ship telepathically because the sensors couldn't register telepathic transmissions.

• All that racquetball has improved O'Brien's reflexes. Just after Sisko and company draw phasers on him in Odo's office, O'Brien takes out one Security officer and *dodges* a phaser blast from another!

• To hide from a pursuing runabout, O'Brien takes his vessel into the magnetic pole of a moon. Sensors soon quit working, and the computer informs O'Brien that he must switch to manual navigation. So...the runabout's computer can't navigate with visual systems when its sensors go dead?

• After losing O'Brien, Sisko takes his runabout from Parada IV to Parada II. Amazingly enough, he does this at impulse in fewer than twenty-five seconds! I don't know about you, but that seems really, really fast to me. (The other option would be to say that the planets were only 1.875 million kilometers apart. Remember that we are talking about Parada II and Parada IV, so there's bound to be a Parada III in there somewhere. I talked with Mitzi Adams about this. She said it's possible but unlikely. After all, the distance from just Earth to Venus—without another planet between—is approximately *40* million kilometers! And Earth to Mars? It's *78* million kilometers.)

CONTINUITY AND PRODUCTION PROBLEMS

• Try this one on for grungy nitpicking. Just before a commercial break, O'Brien makes the dramatic statement, "This was not my Keiko." Coming back from the break, O'Brien asks the computer to play back his last entry, and we hear the line again: "This was not my Keiko." Except...the intonation on "my" is different. It's more elongated the second time. In other words, it was quicker for the creators to have Colm Meany read the line twice than it was to have him read it once and then dub it once!

• Attempting to flee the station, O'Brien rips the combadge from his chest. If you look closely you'll see something left behind. (It's either a piece of Velcro or a tear in the uniform.) It disappears in the next shot.

• Just before returning from the flashback, the episode shows us O'Brien's runabout entering the wormhole, heading for the Gamma Quadrant. As the scene fades to a commercial, O'Brien expresses his bewilderment that someone or something had started to infiltrate Starfleet. The closed captioning adds, "I decided the only alternative left was to go back to the Paradan System to warn them and maybe to find some answers."

TRIVIA ANSWERS

1. Sweet flan.
2. Admiral Gupta.

PARADISE

Star Date: 47573.1

Discovering a human colony on a supposedly uninhabited world, Sisko and O'Brien beam down, only to find that their equipment has stopped working. The colony leader, Alixus, explains that the same thing happened to them when they were forced to land there ten years ago. Consequently they've learned to grow their own food, weave their own clothing, and even discover their own medicines by scavenging the forest for herbs and fungi. Alixus welcomes them into the community, asking only that they contribute.

After watching a young woman of the community die of an insect bite, however, Sisko orders O'Brien to find a way to communicate with the runabout. Alixus catches O'Brien "wasting time" and sentences "cool hand" Sisko to the "box"—a metal container left all day in the sun. Eventually O'Brien locates the reason none of the equipment works: A duonetic field generator is buried in the woods. Alixus helped invent the device and created the problems on the transport to bring the colonists to the planet ten

years ago. She wanted to test her theories about the reinvigoration of the human spirit. After turning off the device, O'Brien frees Sisko. The pair then take Alixus and her son into custody before returning to the runabout. Believing that they've gained more than they've lost, the rest of the colonists voluntarily stay behind.

PLOT OVERSIGHTS

• This episode occurs on star date 47573.1. The previous episode, "Whispers," began on star date 47569.4 and ran through 47581.2. In other words, right in the middle of preparations for the Paradan peace talks, Sisko took the replicant O'Brien out in a runabout to scout for habitable planets and had this little adventure?

• Sisko and O'Brien make an interesting choice in this episode. They arrive at the planet, pick up human life forms, try all hailing frequencies, and get no response. O'Brien says he's picking up a low-level duonetic field that may be blocking communications. So what do they do next? They both beam down, and—sure enough—that duonetic field *was* blocking commu-

Trivia Questions

1. What was the original destination of the colonists?

2. Admiral Mitsuya is diverting what ship to DS9 so he can play poker with Sisko?

144

nications, and now they can't get back to the runabout!

• Giving her first rousing speech to Sisko and O'Brien about what the colony has accomplished, Alixus proclaims that they have learned to "plow the crops and harvest the fields." I believe that would be "plow the *fields* and harvest the *crops*." If you do it Alixus's way you end up harvesting dirt! (This may be why the winters have been so bad for them.)

• While the plot summary above is accurate—at least I think it is—it doesn't tell the whole story of the episode. At some point Alixus turns off the duonetic field, beams up to the *Rio Grande*, sets the controls for it to fly into the system's star, beams back down, and turns the duonetic field back on—feeling confident that the runabout is gone for good. In fact, the *Rio Grande* misses the star. Kira and Dax later corral the runaway vessel and return to the colony to pick up Sisko and O'Brien.

There is a myriad of problems in the preceding paragraph, but we'll go through them one at a time in the course of this review. Let's start with a simple one. Kira and Dax initially locate the *Rio Grande* when the Romulan vessel *Gasko* reports seeing it flying at warp uninhabited. Personally, I find it very considerate of the Romulans to notify DS9 of this small fact instead of commandeering the runabout, taking it back to Romulan space, and stripping it of any technological secrets it might possess.

• Joseph—one of the colonists— has been living on an isolated planet for too long. At the end of the episode,

he makes a speech and comments that the colonists will have to decide if they want to establish contact with the "outside world." Just *which* world would that be?

• Some nitpickers found it inconceivable that not one colonist would want to get back to civilization. I understand their point.

CHANGED PREMISES
• At the beginning of this episode, Sisko asks O'Brien to allow Jake to work with him. Sisko is hoping to get his son ready for Starfleet Academy. The commander is worried because Jake placed in the lower third of his age group in mechanical aptitude. O'Brien thinks that's great because he did the same. O'Brien then goes on to tell Sisko that he discovered his talent for engineering when he had ten minutes to fix a field transporter on Setlik III or become a Cardassian prisoner. He says he didn't know a transporter from a turbolift at the time but he accomplished the task, became the tactical officer on the *Rutledge,* and "got the gold suit."

This bit of "history" gives the impression that O'Brien never really understood mechanical things until that fateful day on Setlik III. Yet in "Samaritan Snare" we learned that O'Brien built ships in bottles as a child. In the previous episode, "Whispers," we learned that O'Brien played with inverters for subspace transceivers as a boy. Do these sound like the activities of a young man who didn't get mechanical things? Also, the first time we see O'Brien on the *Enterprise* in "Encounter at Farpoint" *(TNG),* he wears a red uniform, not a gold one. That means O'Brien went from wearing gold on the *Rutledge* to wearing red on the *Enterprise* and then back to gold. Having a little trouble making a career decision, are we?

EQUIPMENT ODDITIES

• I should have mentioned this in the last review because it happens there as well. Those clever creators found a way to save themselves some headaches when it came to matching the star fields in the runabout's side windows to what should be occurring at any time in the script. They fitted the runabouts with shutters that completely block the windows! (I guess that takes care of that!)

• Let's talk about Alixus and the *Rio Grande*. First, how did she contact the runabout in the first place? Has she been hiding a communicator all these years? Second, after first contact, how did Alixus get the computer to beam her up? Are we to believe that these runabouts will offer a ride to any stranger who happens by? Can anybody just get on the right frequency and say, "Computer, one to beam up"? Third, after she made it to the *Rio Grande,* how did she set a course? In "The Jem'Haddar" Jake and Nog tried to get a runabout back to DS9, but the little ship just kept asking for the correct codes. The pair eventually ripped enough stuff out of the console to disable the autopilot but leave manual navigation intact. But that was only because Jake had been working with O'Brien. Alixus is *ten years* out of the loop on technology. How did she pull this off? (Or did O'Brien integrate

the autopilot safeties into the runabouts after this little adventure? If so, it seems like a huge design flaw to let anybody waltz up and take control of a ship.)

• Contacting DS9 after sighting the *Rio Grande,* the *Gasko* reports the vessel flying at warp 2. When Kira and Dax catch up to it, Dax reports that it is running at warp 1.3. Why did it slow down?

• After finding the *Rio Grande* running at warp 1.3 without any inhabitants, Kira and Dax must devise a plan to recapture the ship. Now, friends, this is *not* the first time in the *Star Trek* universe that we have seen our heroes take remote control of a ship. In *Star Trek II: The Wrath of Khan* we saw Kirk use prefix codes to shut off the *Reliant*'s shields. In "Unnatural Selection" we saw Picard take remote control of the bridge functions of the *Lantree* using a Security override request code. Just a few episodes ago, Sisko remote-piloted the *Ganges* to its death. *Obviously* it's possible to seize control of this type of Starfleet vessel using command codes. Or if for some unknown reason that wouldn't work, why couldn't they hail the *Rio Grande* and tell it to stop? It evidently listens to just about anyone!

• Continuing on with this theme, Kira first suggests beaming over to the *Rio Grande* at warp. Dax immediately pooh-poohs this idea as too dangerous. Excuse me! O'Brien did it just fine in "The Best of Both Worlds, Part 2."

• So what does Dax eventually suggest to stop the *Rio Grande*? An untried, potentially destructive and lethal maneuver using a tractor beam to lasso the runabout and drag it out of warp! I have to hand it to the Utopia Planitia guys. Somebody over there significantly improved the tractor beam technology in the past few years. In "Samaritan Snare," the *Enterprise*—a Galaxy-class starship, mind you, the biggest in the fleet— couldn't use its tractor beam to tow a barge any faster than at half impulse. Yet in this episode—not only does Dax pull the *Rio Grande* out of warp using the tractor beam, but also, moments later, she tells the computer on board the *Rio Grande* to lock a tractor beam on their runabout, the *Mekong,* and prepare for a *warp* tow. (I guess it would make too much sense to reduce the stress that a warp tow is bound to cause on the hulls of both the *Rio Grande* and the *Mekong* by having Kira and Dax pilot the ships separately.)

• Surprisingly enough, no one seems to conclude that this duonetic field would make a great weapon. Just get it close enough to an enemy vessel and you can shut it down completely!

CONTINUITY AND PRODUCTION PROBLEMS

• After the colonists haul Sisko out of the "box," he asks how long he was in there. The spoken dialogue indicates "since yesterday," but the closed captioning says, "since this morning." Evidently someone thought that "since this morning" didn't sound punishing enough.

• Alixus brings Sisko out of the box to see if he's ready to cooperate. She pours him a glass of much-needed water and then shows him some normal clothing. She tells him, "Once you've changed, you can have this water." Interestingly enough, the closed captioning adds, "and when you drink, everyone will be allowed to drink."

TRIVIA ANSWERS
1. Gemulon V.
2. The *Crockett.*

SHADOWPLAY

Star Date: 47603.3

Investigating an unusual particle field in the Gamma Quadrant, Dax and Odo beam down to find a village in crisis. Twenty-two people have disappeared—the most recent, a woman named Anetra, only six hours ago. At first held as suspects, Odo and Dax eventually convince village protector Colyus that they are innocent and offer their help. Interviews with the villagers yield only one piece of odd information. None of them has ever left the village. Then Anetra's daughter, Taya, takes Odo and Dax to the farthest point she's ever been from the village. The pair continue, but when Taya tries to follow, her arm disappears. The entire village is a hologram, maintained by an aging generator in the middle of town. With the villagers' permission, Dax shuts it down, planning to upgrade the generator and then restore everyone—even those who have disappeared.

An old man named Rurigan remains. He came to this planet thirty years ago, fleeing Dominion oppression. He programmed the village, giving its inhabitants the ability to reproduce. Now he wants to go home and tells Dax to leave

the generator turned off. Odo convinces him otherwise, helping Rurigan to see that the villagers deserve to live.

PLOT OVERSIGHTS

• Attempting to prove his innocence, Odo assures Colyus that he could depart the village protector's watchful eye anytime he chooses. To prove his point, Odo calls for beam-out and quickly disappears. Colyus seems genuinely astonished—as if he had never seen such a thing before. A bit later, however, Odo asks Colyus if he checked for transporter activity after the people disappeared, and Cloyus assures him that he did. So why did Colyus seem so astonished when Odo transported? And if Rurigan designed the villagers to never leave the village, why would they need—or know about—transporter technology in the first place?

• During the subplot of this episode, Kira thwarts Quark's attempt to buy stolen Cardassian bone carvings from his cousin Kono. At one point Kira asks Bashir to keep an eye on Quark. Bashir readily agrees, stating Garak has been lecturing him on surveillance techniques. *Garak* has

Trivia Questions

1. Who is the Bolian woman who runs the jumja kiosk on the promenade?

2. What province on Bajor has a new nature preserve?

148

been lecturing him? "Plain, simple" Garak? Garak the tailor? Garak, who has never admitted being a spy? That Garak? Granted, the creators have gone to great lengths to insinuate that Garak is or has been a spy up to this point in the series, but the creators also have gone to lengths till now in the series to have Garak obfuscate when it comes to discussing his past. I suppose we could say that Garak changed his approach when we weren't looking, but "The Wire"—six episodes down the line—will show a Garak who is still cagey about his past.

• Some nitpickers found it odd that Rurigan couldn't fix the holographic generators himself, since he claimed to have designed the program in the first place. They also expressed amazement at the level of sophistication in the villagers. They fall in love. They marry. They have children. I would humbly suggest a solution for both these problems. Yes, Rurigan "designed" the program in the first place—much like someone today writes a macro for an existing computer program. All the "designer" is doing is stringing together complex modules. He doesn't really know how the modules work. Certainly, if anything goes wrong, he couldn't fix them. On the other hand, the macro makes him *look* very proficient at the program because the real programmers built in a friendly interface that allowed him to access their genius!

CHANGED PREMISES

• In this episode Odo tells Taya that his face looks the way it does because he doesn't do faces very well. The mouse faces he did in "Past Prologue" and "The Circle" were exquisite.

• Contrary to the information presented in "The Host" *(TNG)*, Dax the Trill transports just fine in this episode.

EQUIPMENT ODDITIES

• When first approaching the planet, Odo reports no life sign. Dax responds that the omicron field on the surface may be interfering with the sensors. Thankfully, though the sensors aren't working, the transporter seems to function just fine! The point is this: The transporter has to use some sort of sensor to pinpoint the destination site for the transport. So the main sensors don't work (which means that Dax and Odo can't tell there is only one real guy down there), while the transporter sensors do. (This, of course, allows them to arrive on the surface safely.) In other words, we just happen to have a very selective interference field that selectively inhibits or allows just the right sets of sensors to move the plot forward.

• Supposedly Rurigan created the village with a holographic generator thirty years ago. Presumably in that time he changed his underwear. At least one would hope that the man isn't wearing the same set of clothes he brought with him to the planet all those decades ago! Why, then, is he still clothed when Dax turns off the generator? Wouldn't his clothes be holographic as well, just like Colyus's cape? (Kristi L. Kuhlmann of St. Louis, Missouri, surmised that the creators wanted to keep the show rated "G.")

CONTINUITY AND PRODUCTION PROBLEMS

• Wonders will never cease when it comes to the theory of doppelgängers. Here you have a holographic village in the Gamma Quadrant. A little girl named Taya is developed somewhat randomly by a holographic generator, and she looks and sounds identical to a young girl on the *Enterprise* named Clara Sutter!

• Dax changes the way she holds a piece of equipment just in time for a visual effect to work. Since her tricorder won't function in the village due to the omicron field, Dax borrows a sensing device from Colyus. Normally she operates the unit with both hands, but just before approaching the edge of the holographic generator's influence she switches to an open-palmed, one-handed approach. This allows for a very nice visual effect in which the sensing device dissolves from her hand.

TRIVIA ANSWERS

1. Lysia Arlin.
2. Hedrikspool.

PLAYING GOD

Star Date: supplemental

A Trill initiate named Arjin comes to DS9 for field training. As part of the program, an initiate must spend time with a joined Trill who serves as "field docent." For the initiate it is a time to see how a joined Trill lives and interacts with those around them. For the docent it is a time to evaluate the initiate. The symbiont Dax has a reputation for being hard on Trill initiates. In fact, when Curzon Dax served as field docent for Jadzia, he recommended her termination from the program. Because of this, Jadzia intends to go easy on Arjin, though she finds him unfocused and a bit arrogant.

The next day Dax and Arjin travel to the Gamma Quadrant to conduct a survey. While there, the starboard nacelle of the runabout snags a strange energy formation from a subspace interphase pocket. They return with it to DS9, only to find that it is an expanding protouniverse and will destroy the station if they don't get it back where it belongs. In the midst of this crisis, Dax confronts Arjin about his goals in life. The young initiate reacts badly at first but eventually comes around and even plays a key role in helping Dax take the energy formation back to its home.

Trivia Questions

1. What is the name of the self-exiled Romulan composer whose music Dax enjoys?

2. What did Arjin's father do?

RUMINATION

I'm thinking that O'Brien finds a way in this episode to exact a little vengeance on Quark for all of the Ferengi's shenanigans that he's had to put up with since arriving on the station. The subplot deals with a Cardassian vole infestation. Voles are cat-sized rodents that are attracted to energy fields and have a nasty habit of making themselves a galaxy-sized nuisance. Seizing the opportunity, O'Brien creates a directional sonic generator—ostensibly for the purpose of driving the voles out of hiding. However, after listening to Quark's complaints in Ops over the growing vole infestation, O'Brien "accidently" exposes the Ferengi to the wonders of his new device. Almost instantly, Quark disappears behind a piece of equipment howling in pain and soon leaves Ops banging the side of his head. O'Brien looks very contrite but I think I know what's really going on here!

PLOT OVERSIGHTS

• Arjin first encounters Dax playing Tongo with Quark and his pals. He enters the bar just as she makes a big win. At first an unhappy Quark grouses at him to leave. Then Dax comes to his rescue, and Quark invites the initiate to join the game. When Arjin demurs, Dax offers to escort him to his quarters. Quark immediately protests her departure, evidently wanting to regain some of his losses. What's really odd is that Dax *leaves her winnings behind on the table*! Personally, given the Ferengi reputation for sticky fingers, I would have filled a bag with latinum before I sauntered out.

• Arjin's knowledge about Jadzia seems to fluctuate with the moment as needed. At one point he reveals that he knows she completed only third-level flight experience in her last year of training. On the other hand, he doesn't seem to know that Curzon recommended her termination, that she reapplied, and only then was accepted. If I recall, this was a *big deal*. I believe "Equilibrium" establishes that Jadzia was the *only* Trill ever to wash out of the program, reapply, and be joined. If Arjin could discover a fairly obscure fact like when Jadzia completed her flight training, how could he not know the major event in her path to joining? Was all the information about her reapplication buried by the Symbiosis Commission?

• At one point Dax confronts Arjin over his lack of goals. She tells him that the influence of the symbiont is very strong and the host must be equally as strong. Otherwise the symbiont will overwhelm him. I find Dax's advice intriguing because apparently it is given from firsthand experience! Let's review. Jadzia describes her pre-joined self as the "quietest, shiest, most withdrawn woman you've ever known." While it is true that this changed a bit after she was challenged by Curzon's recommendation for dismissal, I would still classify Jadzia as reserved, polite—even a bit aloof—when she arrived at DS9 after her joining. In her own words, she was attempting to live on a "higher plane" (see the conversation she had with Bashir in "A Man Alone"). In fact, up until this episode— with a few hints dropped here and there—Jadzia Dax has operated well within the boundaries of the descriptors "reserved" and "polite." So what gives with the sudden emergence of the towel-clad, Galeo-Manda-style wrestling, black-hole drinking, Ferengi-ear-flicking version of Dax in this episode? My guess is that the symbiont memories finally have started to overwhelm her. (She admits as much, by the way, at the end of the episode in her final talk with Arjin. Please understand. *I am not complaining.* It's about time this character got some life. In fact, I hereby vote to christen this Dax the "new and improved.")

• Does anyone else find it interesting that this rare opportunity for joining would be extended to a person like Jadzia, who would then spend her life doing really dangerous stuff practically every week?

• When Dax first determines that the protouniverse poses a threat to the station, Sisko takes steps to destroy the protouniverse. Dax then makes an astounding discovery: She comes to believe that there may be intelligent life within the energy mass. She begins her road to revelation when the sensors confirm a "localized entropy decrease." The term "entropy" can mean one of two things. It can be the measure of the available energy in a system. It also can be the final state of inert uniformity in any system, as predicted by the second law of thermodynamics. (In other words, according to the second law, all the energy in our universe is winding down and will eventually end up as useless background heat. This is known as increasing entropy.) No matter which definition Dax uses, her puzzlement over the "localized entropy decrease" has no foundation. Earlier in the episode she stated that the protouniverse was "highly structured but it doesn't seem to conform to any of our physical laws." If it doesn't conform to our physical laws, why does Dax find the entropy decrease odd?

• In this episode, while trying to decide the fate of the protouniverse, Sisko makes a log entry (with the ever-illuminating star date "supplemental") in which he ponders the indifference of the Borg during their wanton slaughter of Starfleet personnel at Wolf 359. Sisko goes on to ask himself if it would be any different to destroy another universe just to preserve his own. Well ...*yes*! The Federation didn't pose an immediate threat to the existence of the Borg. Yet the Borg came in with guns blazing to assimilate a culture they knew represented a high degree of sophistication. In this episode Sisko

is faced with a protouniverse guaranteed to destroy his own unless he takes action, a universe that may contain intelligent life. I have a hard time establishing more than a tenuous connection between these two situations.

• There has to be a time skip near the end of this episode, but I can't find a good place for it. Sisko decides to send the protouniverse back to the Gamma Quadrant. O'Brien beams it on board the *Rio Grande*—positioned right next to the station. Arjin says he's firing thrusters. An external shot shows us the runabout moving away from DS9. The scene cuts to an interior shot of the cabin. We hear O'Brien say that energy readings are holding. Dax tells Arjin to take the vessel to 50 "kph." Arjin replies that they will reach the wormhole in 17 seconds. For the sake of argument, let's forget about acceleration. (Any acceleration factor would only make the wormhole closer, and we want to establish a maximum distance to the wormhole based on these figures). Presumably "kph" stands for kilometers per hour. I suppose it's possible it could mean something else, but I doubt it. If the runabout is traveling 50,000 meters an hour, it's traveling approximately 833 meters per minute and approximately 14 meters per second. Since the runabout started out at the station and flew for 17 seconds, the wormhole is only 238 meters from DS9. That's about half the width of the saucer section on the *Enterprise*. This *cannot* be right! Think back when we saw the *Enterprise* docked at DS9 during the premiere, "Emissary." The saucer section was a bit smaller than the habitat ring (that's the middle ring). According to this episode the wormhole is about the same distance from the station as Ops is from the habitat ring. If DS9 is only 238 meters from the wormhole, it is in constant danger of a ship emerging from the wormhole and running into it! (There's a simple solution to this conundrum. The episode loses time somewhere in this sequence. But where?)

• There are two back-to-back navigational heading problems as Arjin attempts to negotiate his way through the wormhole while avoiding those gigantic vertiron nodes (which, of course, we've never seen before, but they look really cool). First Dax tells Arjin there's a node to starboard at "037 mark 7." This is close enough to be correct. Then she tells him there's a node to port at "030 mark 51." This is not correct. If the node was to port, the first number should be in the range 181 through 359—assuming a relative orientation (which seems appropriate, since they are in the middle of a wormhole having traveled who knows how far from DS9). Then Dax tells him there's an opening in the vertiron nodes at "130 mark 47." Note that the opening is somewhat in front of them. A relative bearing of "130 mark 47" would be back over your right shoulder!

• So exactly what did Dax and Arjin do with the protouniverse at the end of the episode? Was the "subspace interphase pocket" still there? Did they beam the protouniverse back inside it? Did they leave a little space buoy with flailing accordian-tube arms that transmitts the continual message, "Dan-

ger! Danger! This area can destroy your version of reality!"? (Methinks the creators ran out of time and opted to show the tense hero scene with Arjin over wrapping up the story line.)

CHANGED PREMISES

• Just after coming on board the station, Arjin tells Bashir that more than five thousand candidates qualify for the training program each year but on average only three hundred symbionts are available for joining. That's a ratio of at least one in sixteen. During "Invasive Procedures," Dax said that only one Trill in ten is joined. Note that she *did not* say that only one Trill *candidate* for joining in ten gets a worm. Aside from the fact that the numbers are off, does everyone on Trill become a candidate for the program at one time or another?

• After telling Arjin about her dismissal as an initiate, reapplication, and the eventual assignment of the Dax symbiont, Jazdia tells him that she isn't quite sure why Curzon didn't object to her receiving his slug when he died. Wait a minute: The episode "Dax" establishes that the new host gets the memories of the old host. Why doesn't she know why he didn't object?

EQUIPMENT ODDITIES

• After the runabout snags the strange energy formation, Arjin calls Dax's attention to something on one of his screens. She gets out of her chair, sidles over, and bends forward to peruse his monitor. Obviously she just wanted to stretch her legs because I find it unthinkable that she couldn't just hit a few buttons and transfer the image to one of her displays. (Either that or she just wanted to get close enough to Arjin to rattle him with her perfume.)

• Although the whole subplot dealing with the Cardassian vole infestation is delightful, O'Brien must continually overlook the obvious and easy solution. Why can't he program the transporter to look for Cardassian voles and just beam them off the station? Kira picks one up on her tricorder, so obviously the voles are "sense-able."

• Twenty-fourth-century musical instruments continue to amaze and astound. In "Melora" I noted that the Klingon food bar proprietor strummed on a string instrument that changed chords without anyone touching the fretboard. In this episode the singing Klingon is back—this time with an autochord-o-magic accordion! All he has to do is pump the thing and it plays along precisely in tempo with the song the Klingon croons. (No doubt the two instruments came from a single manufacturer.)

• Great confusion surrounds the levels on DS9. At the beginning of the episode, the computer tells Bashir that Dax is on Level 7 in Section 5. Moments later we find out that's Quark's. Later in the episode, the protouniverse blows through the hull in the docking ring (the outermost ring). Everyone identifies this location as Level 22, Section 14. Yet, in the external shots

of the station, it certainly does not look like there are *fifteen* levels between the plane that intersects the promenade and the plane that intersects the hull breach. (I suppose that each of the major sections could have their own numbering schemes. Level 1 on the docking ring might be at the tip of the upper pylons, whereas Level 1 in the central core would be Ops. This seems needlessly complex, unless, of course, the Cardassians purposefully designed it that way so they'd have trick questions to use during Bajoran interrogations: "You're on Level 21 on the docking ring and you take Crossover Bridge 5 to the habitat ring: What level are you on?" "Um...*21?!?*" "WRONG!" *SWACK!*)

CONTINUITY AND PRODUCTION PROBLEMS

• Taking the protouniverse back to the Gamma Quadrant, Arjin decides to release the inertia dampers to give him more maneuverability. An exterior shot shows the runabout moving forward. Then the scene cuts inside to show Dax and Arjin bouncing up and down in their seats as the camera jiggles. Oddly enough, if you watch very closely, you'll see the camera begin to jiggle *before* the scene cuts to the interior shot of the cabin.

TRIVIA ANSWERS
1. Frenchotte.
2. He was a pilot instructor at the Gedana post for forty years.

PROFIT AND LOSS

Star Date: unknown

In a damaged shuttle, three Cardassian dissidents arrive at DS9—Professor Natima Lang and two of her students, Rekelen and Hogue. As O'Brien repairs their ship, the trio take a stroll on the promenade and promptly run into Quark, who is still smitten by Lang, though their relationship ended bitterly seven years ago. Still in love with Quark as well, Lang tries to hide because her life has taken a new direction. She is convinced that her students represent the future of Cardassia—a free and democratic future.

Unfortunately, Garak also recognizes Lang and her students. He quickly informs Cardassian Central Command, hoping to curry some favor. A Cardassian warship soon arrives at DS9. In response, Bajor negotiates a prisoner swap, and Odo is forced to arrest the trio. Later he releases them. He knows they don't deserve death. At the same time, Gul Toran recruits Garak to kill the dissidents. In exchange, Toran promises Garak a return to Cardassia. Garak quickly agrees, cutting off the trio's escape in a cargo bay. That's when

Toran butts in, determined to take credit for the assassination himself. Incensed, Garak kills Toran and allows the dissidents to depart safely—courtesy of a small cloaking device from Quark.

PLOT OVERSIGHTS
• Two small items concerning the ending of this episode: First, I have a hard time believing that Garak would stand off to the side in the cargo bay and wait around while Quark says his gushy "so longs" to Lang. And second, whatever happened to the Bajoran prisoners? Were they returned, or did Odo's actions result in the condemnation of one-half dozen prisoners to lives of continued pain and suffering? (And, if you were the provisional government and you lost the opportunity to get a half dozen of your people returned because of some loose-cannon Security officer, what you would do to him?)

CHANGED PREMISES
• "Plain, simple Garak" returns at the beginning of this episode. Once again, Bashir attempts to discover—over his regular luncheon with the Cardas-

Trivia Questions

1. What was the first holosuite program Quark and Natima enjoyed together?

2. What book does O'Brien loan to Odo?

156

sian—what Garak's true role is on the station. This is very odd. After all, just two episodes ago, Bashir said that Garak had been lecturing him on surveillance techniques.

• I find it extraordinarily intriguing that Bajor arranges a prisoner exchange during this episode. Cardassia agrees to swap "half a dozen" Bajoran prisoners for the wanted trio. Paint me blue and call me silly, but I could have sworn that Gul Dukat said *all* Bajoran prisoners had been released during "The Homecoming"!

• Jumping in to take credit for the assassination of Lang and the others, Gul Toran taunts Garak—amazed that our beloved tailor would believe that this one act would curry him renewed favor with Cardassian Central Command. Obviously, at this point in the series, the creators didn't know that Garak wasn't with Central Command in the first place. He was with the Obsidian Order—as yet unintroduced into the *Star Trek* universe. (We learn of Garak's background four shows later, in "The Wire." At least we gather enough facts to infer his background.)

EQUIPMENT ODDITIES

• At one point Quark brings the cloaking device to Lang's quarters. Somehow I was expecting more. This little chunk of metal—apparently only a bit larger than a softball—can hide an entire ship from everyone's sensors?

• There seems to be an overabundance of Cardassian phasers on the station during this episode. Lang has one. Garak has one. Toran has one. Obviously Odo needs to tighten security a bit.

CONTINUITY AND PRODUCTION PROBLEMS

• At the beginning of the episode, Bashir and Garak discuss General Yiri's execution of his brother for the good of the state. (Don't ask me *who* General Yiri is or *what* state we're talking about!) Garak, of course, sides with Yiri, believing that nothing is more important than the good of the empire. Bashir takes the opposite view, saying that before you can be loyal to someone else, you must first be loyal to yourself. Garak scoffingly wonders who he should thank for that pearl of wisdom, "Sarek of Vulcan?" Interestingly enough, the closed captioning has "Miseric of Vulcan?" (The creators probably felt that name was a bit too obscure.)

• The stars in Ops again play their odd little game of "Now We'll Move, Now We Won't." When O'Brien brings a damage report on Lang's ship to Sisko, the stars stand rock still in the upper windows in Ops. Just a short time later, when Lang speaks with Sisko in his office adjacent to Ops, the stars are moving.

• It always amazes me how well things work out for the creators. Take this episode, for example. You've got Lang's ship docked at the station, and a Cardassian warship approaches. Obviously, at some point the episode will use an external shot of DS9. That's a problem if both Lang's ship and the Cardassian warship are both in the shot, because then it's a completely custom shot and can't be reused. Thankfully, Sisko had the presence of mind to tow Lang's ship to the opposite side of the station. In that way, when the exterior shot of the station did occur, the creators could take a stock shot of the station and slap a Cardassian warship over it.

• Usually Quark's coats have some sort of ornamentation near the center of his chest. For instance, the outfit he wears in this episode has an elongated loop of stiff wire that terminates in a circular pendant. When Quark arrives in Lang's quarters with the cloaking device, the ornament rests in its normal, straight-up-and-down position. He puts the cloaking device on the table and walks over close to Lang. She brushes past him, and when the shot changes, the ornament is suddenly crooked. Then Quark decides to leave. The shot changes as he walks toward the door and the ornament is straight again. Lang pulls out a phaser. Quark turns. Now the ornament is crooked! It stays crooked until Lang shoots him with the phaser. Finally, as Quark tumbles

over a bed on his way to the floor, the ornament rights itself!

• Finally deciding to unilaterally release Lang and her students, Odo accompanies Quark back into the cell block behind the Security office. He walks over to the release panel for the force field as Quark greets Lang. If you watch Odo carefully, you'll see it almost looks like he's *waiting* for Quark to finish his line before dropping the force field. Hmmm. I wonder why.

• At the very end of the episode, Lang gives Quark a good-bye *oo-mox* before boarding her ship. What's really weird is that Quark seems to have a delayed reaction. She starts rubbing. He stares blankly. Then he seems to remember and goes into the moaning thing. (Could Quark be faking it all this time?)

TRIVIA ANSWERS
1. Picnic on Rhymus Major.
2. *I, the Jury* by Mickey Spillane.

DAMAGE TOTE BOARD

1. Number of times the station explodes: six
2. Number of individuals who punch Sisko in the face: four
3. Number of times life weighs heavily on Kira at the end of an episode: eleven
4. Number of episodes in which Jadzia's life is endangered solely because of the Dax symbiont: four
5. Number of episodes in which Bashir pronounces someone dead by using a tricorder: five
6. Number of times someone throws up on O'Brien: one
7. Number of times Odo gets flaky, drippy, or goopy: four
8. Number of times someone tries to kill Quark: seven
9. Number of times we see Rom using his ear cleaner: two
10. Number of times characters bang their heads: at least ten
11. Number of runabouts lost: four

REFERENCES

Note: This tote board is current only through the first eighty-four episodes, ending with "Paradise Lost."

1. (Some of these are twitchy and open to debate but ...) A locator bomb goes off in Quark's during "The Nagus." Corridor H-12-A, guest quarters, sustains a plasma explosion in "The Forsaken." A fire bomb goes off in the promenade school during "In the Hands of the Prophets." The protouniverse expands on Level 22, Section 14 in "Playing God." A time-traveling O'Brien witnesses the station's destruction in "Visionary." Garak blows up his shop in "Improbable Cause."

2. Q in "Q-Less." Vedek Bareil in "Fascinations." A "ghost" in "Past Tense, Part I." Dax in "Facets."

3. "Past Prologue," "Battlelines" (probably), "Progress," "Duet," "In the Hands of the Prophets," "The Homecoming," "The Siege," "Necessary Evil," "Sanctuary," "Second Skin," "Life Support."

4. "Dax," "Invasive Procedures," "Blood Oath," "Equilibrium."

5. (For an explanation on why this is unusual, see "The Passenger.") "The Passenger," "Vortex," "Battlelines," "Dramatis Personae," "House of Quark."

6. Molly does at the beginning of "Fascination."

7. With Lwaxana in the turbolift during "The Forsaken." In the presence of Dr. Mora during "The Alternate." Under Garak's interrogation in "The Die Is Cast." In Bashir's mind during "Distant Voices."

8. Rom and Krax try to kill him with a locator bomb and then try to blow him out an airlock in "The Nagus." Kira in "Dramatis Personae" (if Quark is to be believed). Mrs. Vaatrik's thug shoots him in "Necessary Evil." Kozak pulls a knife on him in "House of Quark." D'Ghor attempts to slay him with a bat'leth in "House of Quark." The Lethean in "Distant Voices" (if Bashir's mental version of Quark is correct).

9. Just before Quark demands that Rom clean up his quarters in "Prophet Motive." After Quark spends the night checking "Moogie's" acquisitions in "Family Business." (Hey, that thing has got to hurt!)

10. O'Brien bangs his head just after Tosk appears in "Captive Pursuit." Dax bangs her head in the sublight fighter during "The Siege." In "Melora," O'Brien says that he had bumps on his head to prove Melora's quarters are ready. ("Bumps" would imply that he hit his head more than once.) Quark bangs his head upon learning that Pel is a female and promptly faints in "Rules of Acquisition." O'Brien bangs his head while looking for Cardassian voles in "Playing God." Quark bangs the side of his head after begin exposed to O'Brien's ultrasonic tool in "Playing God." Quark bangs his head when Odo comes into his quarters on the *Defiant* during "The Search, Part I." Jake bangs his head in the ore-processing tube during "Civil Defense." O'Brien bangs his head just before greeting Riker in "The Defiant." O'Brien bangs his head when Gilora makes a play for him in a *Defiant* Jefferies tube during "Destiny." (Honorable mention: In "Rivals," Bashir reports that O'Brien was knocked unconscious when he stepped on a racquetball that fell to the floor.)

11. The *Yangtzee Kiang* crash-lands in "Battlelines." The *Ganges* is destroyed by the T'Lani in "Armageddon Game." The *Mekong* is abandonded at the end of "The Die Is Cast." The *Orinoco* explodes at the beginning of "Our Man Bashir."

For those of you who would like a bit more information, DS9 starts out with three runabouts in "Emissary": the *Rio Grande,* the *Yangtzee Kiang,* and the *Ganges.* (The *Ganges* is not specifically mentioned until the next episode,

"Past Prologue.") In "Battlelines," the *Yangtzee Kiang* crash-lands. At some point the *Orinoco* arrives at the station. (It is not mentioned until the second-season episode "The Siege.") As of "The Siege," then, DS9's three runabout are the *Rio Grande,* the *Ganges,* and the *Orinoco.* The T'Lani destroys the *Ganges* in "Armageddon Game." The very next episode, "Whispers," mentions the *Mekong.* (Current runabouts as of "Whispers": the *Rio Grande,* the *Orinoco,* and the *Mekong.*) An unidentified runabout is abandonded at the end of "The Die Is Cast." (This *has* to be the *Mekong,* because the *Orinoco* appears in "Our Man Bashir" and the *Rio Grande* appears in "The Sword of Kahless.") In "Family Business," Sisko names the replacement runabout the *Rubicon.* (Current runabouts as of "Family Business": the *Rio Grande,* the *Orinoco,* and the *Rubicon.*) Then the *Orinoco* explodes at the beginning of "Our Man Bashir." In "The Sons of Mogh," the *Yukon* is mentioned. Assuming that this is the replacement for the *Orinoco,* as of "The Sons of Mogh," DS9's three runabouts are the *Rio Grande,* the *Rubicon,* and the *Yukon.*

BLOOD OATH

Star Date: unknown

Three ancient Klingon warriors—Kang, Koloth, and Kor—rendezvous at DS9 looking for Curzon Dax. About eighty years ago, an Albino killed the trio's children by infecting them with a genetic virus. At the time, Curzon Dax, the godfather of Kang's son, joined the three Klingon warriors in swearing a blood oath to find the Albino, cut his heart from his chest, and eat it as the villain watched with dying breath.

Kang has called the band together because he has finally located his nemesis, but he wasn't aware that Curzon had died. At first reluctant, he eventually agrees to allow Jadzia Dax to fulfill Curzon's oath. On the way to the Albino's stronghold, however, Dax realizes that something is wrong. She confronts Kang, and he admits making a deal with the Albino. The warriors will attack without strategy and die glorious deaths. "It is a good day to die," he says. Instead, Dax convinces him that it is a good day to live. She disables the Albino's weaponry, and the quartet attack with bat'leths, slaying every defender of their opponent. By the time the battle ends, Kang and Koloth lay dead, as does the Albino—slain by Kang's own hand—while a wounded Kor sings of their victory and Dax grieves for the friends she's lost.

PLOT OVERSIGHTS

• In case you didn't gather it from the trivia question, the episode represents a reunion of sorts. All three Klingons appeared in *Classic Trek* episodes. While it was delightful to see the old guys again, many nitpickers had the same questions. First, how come these guys looked like humans in their original episode but somehow grew turtle heads and nose ridges in this episode? (I suspect bad TV reception in the 1960s. The ridges were always there, but you just couldn't see them.) Second, are Klingons supposed to get this old? In "All Good Things" *(TNG)*, the action zipped twenty-five years into the future. That made Worf approximately sixty, and he looked just as old as these guys, who supposedly were over a hundred. (Must have something to do with being a Klingon Dahar master.)

• Sometimes Odo cracks me up.

Our favorite shape shifter puts Kor in a cell and retires to his office. A slow camera pan shows the outer doors open before finding Odo reading with his back to the door. He suddenly spins and looks up to find Koloth staring down at him. "How did you get in here?" Odo huffs. Well, maybe he walked through *the open doorway*!

• Trying to endear herself to Koloth, Dax pronounces that she used to call him "d'Akturak." Oddly enough, she then turns to Kor and translates the title to Federation Standard: "iceman." Obviously Dax knows that these events are being recorded in a visual log, and she wants to make sure future generations won't miss the meaning of her words. Certainly Kor didn't need the translation.

• Discovering that Dax is going on the quest to kill the Albino, Sisko comes to her quarters to dissuade her. He tells her that he never understood why Curzon made the blood oath in the first place. He says that whatever else Curzon was, he was fundamentally moral. Then Sisko asks, "What about the laws of the Federation?" Dax replies that the Klingons have their own laws and that this quest is justice to them. She adds that she respects their ways. Yeah? Well, respect is one thing. Going along for the hunt is something altogether different. At least when Worf killed Duras in a rite of vengeance during "Reunion" *(TNG)*, he was a Klingon to begin with. Dax has nothing to hide behind. The behavior guidelines established by both her race and her chosen organization simply do not allow this. Sisko should have slapped her down hard and been done with it.

(Of course, then it would have been a short show.)

• Boy, Sisko really wimps out at the end of this episode. His science office has just openly defied him and tramped all over Federation standards for an officer in Starfleet. And what does he do when she sneaks back into Ops? He gives her a really severe *glare*! (I bet that hurt!) At the very least he should have informed her of the reprimand that would appear on her permanent record, just as Picard did to Worf in "Reunion." (Or did Sisko really let her get away with this scot-free?)

CHANGED PREMISES

• Shortly after the conclusion of *Classic Trek,* Leonard Nimoy felt the urge to write a book called *I Am Not Spock.* Decades later he decided to pen the sequel, *I Am Spock.* Jadzia Dax seems to have the same difficulty. At the end of "Playing God," she proudly proclaimed, "I am not Curzon." Yet, in this episode, she seems to be doing everything to say, "I am Curzon and bound by his blood oath."

• The episode "Heart of Glory" *(TNG)* went to great lengths to show us the Klingon death ritual. The eyes of the slain warrior are held open while those still living howl at the ceiling. Supposedly this warns the dead that a Klingon warrior is about to arrive. This tradition must have started sometime after Kor got set in his ways. Being the only Klingon survivor of the battle, it would have fallen to him to perform the ritual. Instead, he begins singing. (The death howl is probably a private thing for him and he was waiting for us to leave before performing it.)

EQUIPMENT ODDITIES

• I know I've mentioned this particular oddity before, but it bears repeating. At the beginning of the episode, Quark and Odo walk up to a holosuite and you can hear Kor inside shouting. I reiterate: If *I* were using a holosuite, I definitely *would not* want people *outside* the holosuite to hear what was going on *inside* the holosuite!

• So...um...why isn't the famed Universal Translator working when Kor comes roaring out of the holosuite after Quark turns off the power? (Oh, wait. I said we weren't going to talk about the UT anymore. Sorry.)

• To even the odds against the Albino's forces, Dax suggests using the disrupter banks and flooding the area with tetryon particles. This will render all phasers useless. Several points of interest here. This seems like a really good tactic. I wonder why it's never been used before and never is used again. (Is it considered naughty?) Also, it's amazing that the Albino's home team fails to notice that their phasers have quit working until it's too late. Is this such an unknown tactic that no one scans for tetryon particles? Finally, Dax uses the disrupter banks on the *Bird-of-Prey* to create this wonderful field while the craft is cloaked. I believe it is well established that cloaked ships cannot fire their weapons—so much so that one of the key components of *Star Trek VI: The Undiscovered Country*

was a new experimental ship that *could* fire while cloaked.

• The Albino evidently buys his computer systems from the Cardassians. In the main battle area, there are two units—one on either side of the big staircase—that look just like the one Garak worked on during "Cardassians." This same piece of equipment also showed up on the surface of T'Lani III during "Armageddon Game."

• At the end of this episode, Kang goes after the Albino with his bat'leth. When the Albino dodges one of Kang's lunges, the bat'leth strikes a stone surface and shatters. Does this seem right?

CONTINUITY AND PRODUCTION PROBLEMS

• As Kang's *Bird-of-Prey* approaches the Albino's location, Dax suggests that they cloak. Kang agrees, but the next exterior shot shows the ship blazing ahead uncloaked.

• It's a minor thing, but at the end of the episode, when Dax returns to Ops, a low-placed shot clearly shows that her pants do not have stirrups. This is a change. A close-up of Bashir's feet during "The Passenger" clearly showed stirrups on his pants.

TRIVIA ANSWERS

1. "Day of the Dove" (Kang), "The Trouble with Tribbles" (Koloth), and "Errand of Mercy" (Kor).
2. The Korvat colony.

THE MAQUIS, PART I

Star Date: unknown

hen the Cardassian vessel *Bok'Nor* explodes after departing DS9, Gul Dukat comes to the station to help Sisko launch an investigation. It quickly uncovers serious problems within a newly created demilitarized zone (DMZ). A recent treaty deeded some planets containing Cardassian colonies to the Federation and other planets containing Federation colonies to Cardassia. (See the *NextGen* episodes "Journey's End" and "Preemptive Strike.") All of these problem areas were then lumped into an area supposedly off-limits to weaponry. Yet upon entering the demilitarized zone, Sisko and Dukat find civilian ships of both Cardassian and Federation design—modified with phasers and photon torpedoes—firing on each other.

The pair arrive in time for a tense meeting in the Volan colonies between Commander Calvin Hudson—the Federation's attaché to their colonies in the demilitarized zone—and Gul Evek, Hudson's Cardassian counterpart. Before leaving, Evek announces that the Cardassians have found the

Trivia Questions

1. Where was William Patrick Samuels born?

2. According to Dukat, what did the *Bok'Nor* deliver to the Regulon System?

Federation terrorist responsible for the *Bok'Nor*'s destruction and promptly produces a confession from a colonist named William Samuels— now dead, supposedly by suicide. Incensed, Sisko returns with Dukat to DS9, only to have the Gul kidnapped by the Maquis—a resistance group made up of Federation colonists and renegade Starfleet officers, including Hudson. Claiming the Federation has abandoned them, the Maquis has formed to protect the endangered colonies.

PLOT OVERSIGHTS

• It amazes me every episode but— once again—Quark counts his profits in plain sight.

• During this episode, a Vulcan female named Sakonna arranges to buy weapons from Quark for the Maquis. Smitten, Quark invites her to dinner at "eight." I guess Bajor does manufacture a clock with thirteen indicators on the dial. (See "The Nagus.")

• When sensors pick up a skirmish between Federation and Cardassian colonists in the DMZ, Sisko sets course and engages at warp 3. An external shot shows the runabout jumping to warp. Why isn't the runabout already at warp? Sisko is escorting Dukat to the DMZ, right? They began their journey at DS9. One would think that the edge of the DMZ is at least the next star system over. Normally there's light-years of distance between star systems. But evidently the runabout has been puttering along on impulse.

• At the end of this episode, Dukat is kidnapped by Maquis terrorists. Personally, I think he wanted it to happen. First, examine the scene where four Maquis attempt to get him to board a vessel. Dukat knocks two of them unconscious while the other two watch. Then he turns his back and starts walking away even though one of the two guys still standing is reaching for a weapon. I would have expected Dukat to tear through all of them before strolling off if he really wanted to get away. Second, after stunning Dukat with a phaser, the Maquis drag him onto their ship. As they attempt to negotiate the two stairs up to the airlock, the stunned Dukat helps them by putting his foot on a stair and shoving upward!

• To gain access to Dukat, a man in a Starfleet uniform approaches the guard outside Dukat's door. As the man distracts the guard, Sakonna reaches up from behind and gives the guard the famed Vulcan neck pinch. Interestingly enough, the guard later describes both the man in front of him and Sakonna, who appeared to be well out of his peripheral eyesight range.

• In this episode, O'Brien tells Sisko that the ship believed to be carrying Dukat left DS9 on a bearing of "216 mark 177." This is technically correct,

but it seems much simpler to me just to call the bearing "36 mark 87." (See the discussion of this particular type of problem in "Melora.")

• Both Sisko and Kira put in pitiful showings as infantry soldiers at the end of this episode. They run off to find Dukat. They arrive at an M-class asteroid (an *M-class* asteroid?). They know there are humans on the surface. They beam down without tricorders. They stroll along, and there are people running by in the bushes beside them. And then they seem surprised when they are captured!

CHANGED PREMISES

• When Hudson visits Sisko, we learn that Hudson knew Curzon Dax as well. Hudson wonders if Sisko finds the arrangement with Jadzia Dax a bit uncomfortable given the prior relationship Sisko had with Curzon. Sisko replies, "Oh, no, she's a good officer." I kept waiting for him to add, "Of course, the last week she ran off in direct violation of my wishes—and Starfleet policy—to hunt down and kill an Albino in cold blood but...that was just a phase, and she's over it now." (See "Blood Oath.")

• Great confusion surrounds the new Federation/Cardassian treaty with respect to colonies along the DMZ. This whole saga begins with the *NextGen* episode "Journey's End" (which aired in the production week beginning March 28, 1994). In that episode Picard must evacuate colonists from Dorvan V because their planet has been deeded to the Cardassians as part of the new treaty. The colonists refuse to leave. Picard pleads their case with Starfleet Command. Starfleet Command says they had a representative from the colony at the treaty deliberations, but this was the best deal they could strike, so...the order stands: Get them off the planet. A scuffle breaks out. Picard comes up with a deal. The colonists will renounce their citizenship in the Federation and will hold no expectations for the Federation to protect them. *This makes sense.* If you are going to establish a border and you leave your people on the other side of the border, you are inevitably going to have problems. In *The Nitpicker's Guide for Next Generation Trekkers, Volume II,* I commented on this same thing in my review of the episode "Preemptive Strike" (which first aired in the production week beginning May 16, 1994). In that episode the colonists in the DMZ were suddenly Federation citizens again! And guess what? They were having problems, and their problems were threatening to drag the Federation and the Cardassians back into war! (Big surprise!)

In reality, though, this particular changed premise with respect to the citizenship of these colonies didn't start in "Preemptive Strike," it started with this episode "The Maquis, Part I." This episode first aired in the production week beginning April 23, 1994. And in this episode the creators attempt to have Sisko explain why the Federation made special arrangements for the colonists to remain in the DMZ and retain their Federation citizenship. Supposedly they had roots. Supposedly they'd built something on these planets. Supposedly

they deserved to stay. Sounds just like the guys on Dorvan V to me. So did Starfleet Command go back to the colonists on Dorvan V and tell them they could be citizens again? Or were those guys just out of luck? In addition, I still am *unconvinced* that you couldn't just redraw the boundary so everybody is in their own territory. These colonies are in separate star systems, aren't they? Isn't there *a lot* of space between star systems? And what's with the Federation, anyway? Why did they sign a treaty in the first place with these kinds of problems? Couldn't they run their fancy projections on this scenario and see where it was going to lead? (Okay, okay. Sorry. I'm ranting now.)

• Sisko scrambles his races when talking with Hudson about the events in the trilogy of episodes at the beginning of this season ("The Homecoming," "The Circle," and "The Siege"). He tells Hudson that Cardassians were supplying the Circle with weapons through a third party, the Yridians. Actually—unless the creators forgot to mention something in the first three episodes of this season—it wasn't the Yridians. It was the Kressari!

EQUIPMENT ODDITIES
• I gain more respect for Cardassian engineering with every show. At the beginning of this episode we see the *Bok'Nor* dip slightly down after detaching from an upper pylon on the station and then explode. It is clearly within DS9's defensive shield bubble, so the station had no protection from the force of the explosion or the impact

of flying debris. Yet not one piece of dialogue indicates that there was *any* damage to the station!

• Ya know, in this episode the headrests on the runabouts look *really* uncomfortable. When you lean your head back it bangs into this metal band. O'Brien should really adjust those things.

• Taking Dukat aboard a runabout to travel to the DMZ, Sisko turns off Dukat's control panels so he can't steal any Federation secrets. Of course, Sisko doesn't bother to shut off the side panels that line the walls. They're flashing information to beat the band!

• To replay a confession by Samuel—coerced by the Cardassians—Hudson inserts a Cardassian isolinear rod into a Federation communications device. The *Federation* communications device must have been modified by the colonists because it has a *Cardassian* isolinear rod receptor built right into its *front* panel. Oddly enough, it doesn't appear to have a corresponding slot for a *Federation* isolinear optical *chip*. A bit strange—wouldn't you say—for a *Federation* device?

CONTINUITY AND PRODUCTION PROBLEMS

• Boy, you really do have to feel for some of these colonists. Their story begins almost a century ago. Radiation drives their colony ship off course and lands them on Tau Cynga V, a planet bathed in hyperonic radiation.

Many died, but they struggled on, adapting to the radiation and even building an aqueduct up the side of the mountain to bring water to their colony. Then Data shows up and tells them they've got to move because the planet belongs to the Sheliak. So they move. They find another mountain. They build another aqueduct. In fact, they replicate the colony on Tau Cynga V in virtually every detail. Only one problem: Now the Federation has come along and given their land to the Cardassians! Talk about rotten luck! I'll explain. The composite outdoor scene used for a colony in this episode is actually from "Ensigns of Command" *(TNG)*. You can even see Gosheven standing beside the water reservoir! I can hear him now: "Give up our colony to the Cardassians? Do you see that mountain? My grandfather died on a mountain that looked just like that mountain to bring water to this colony..."

• When Sisko gets back from his excursion into the DMZ, Kira waltzes into his office to give him her opinion on the situation. Listen close as she says, "And you don't think you might be playing into their hand?" Does it sound like the microphone was in the next county when the creators filmed this scene?

TRIVIA ANSWERS

1. Bergen, Norway.
2. Fourteen metric tons of golside ore.

THE MAQUIS, PART II

Star Date: unknown

Calvin Hudson—now a member of the Maquis—tells Sisko that he believes the Cardassian Central Command is supplying their colonists inside the demilitarized zone with weapons. Since Starfleet refuses to violate the recent peace treaty with Cardassia by doing the same, the Maquis have kidnapped Dukat to learn more about the weapons shipments. They intend to stop them—even though Dukat previously swore to Sisko he knew nothing of them. Then Legate Parn—a high-ranking official in Central Command—pays an unexpected visit to DS9. He claims Dukat *was* responsible for the shipments. The legate also says the shipments have been stopped, and the Maquis are free to do with Dukat as they like. Sisko quickly concludes that both Dukat and Hudson were telling the truth.

After locating and rescuing Dukat, Sisko relates his conversation with Parn. Painfully aware that his standing with Central Command has slipped, Dukat makes a deal with Sisko. He will help Sisko prove that Central Command is supplying the weapons if Sisko will stop the Maquis. Sisko agrees, and in short order the pair catch a Xepolite vessel loaded with weapons bound for the DMZ. In exchange, Sisko heads off an attack by the Maquis on a suspected Cardassian weapons depot.

Trivia Questions

1. Who is the hetman of the Xepolite vessel?

2. Where is the weapons depot the Maquis intend to attack?

PLOT OVERSIGHTS

• In the opening discussion between Sisko and Hudson, the renegade commander proclaims that a treaty is just a "piece of paper." I guess these Maquis guys really are out there on the edge of the frontier. When was the last time you saw a piece of paper on DS9? (Then again, maybe it's just one of those expressions that refuses to die.)

• I find it interesting that Legate Parn would come all the way to DS9 to talk with Sisko for fewer than five minutes. I also find it interesting that Sisko would send Kira to greet him at the airlock. (A Starfleet officer would seem more sensible. Then again, perhaps Sisko meant it as an insult.) And finally, I find it interesting that Legate Parn would board a Bajoran station without at least a couple of bodyguards.

• There's a great exchange between Quark and a Vulcan female named

Sakonna in this episode as both in-habit a jail cell. (A coed jail cell. Now, there's an idea! Certainly would make the confinement a bit more pleasant.) In the aforementioned exchange, Quark explains why peace is cheap to acquire at that particular moment. It's very well written, but it raises a question: Why is Quark working so hard for peace? Yes, I know that Rule of Acquisition 35 is "Peace is good for business." But don't forget Rule of Acquisition 34: "War is good for business." Especially for a Ferengi like Quark who can arrange weapons sales. Or is this part of his parole requirements?

• Space is big. Really big. Really inconveniently big when it comes to shooting a science fiction series. At the end of this episode Sisko determines to take three runabouts and stop two Maquis ships from attacking a Cardassian colony. The establishing shot of the runabouts shows them clustered together, hanging in space. Yes, I remember that they've got sensor probes scattered around the system. And yes, maybe they could split off and intercept Hudson and his friends, though the runabouts look like chickens huddling for warmth. What I *can't* figure out is Hudson and friends. The two Maquis ships fly right up to the runabouts before turning. Then Hudson seems frustrated that Sisko has locked a tractor beam on his ship. Well, maybe if you hadn't flown into tractor beam range they wouldn't have been able to do that!

• I wonder how Dukat fared after this episode. Central Command had already decided to convict him for the sale of weapons to the Cardassian colonies in the DMZ. Then he went out and embarrassed them by exposing Central Command as the real source of the weapons sales. Somehow I don't think that helped his standing.

• At the end of this episode Sisko tells Kira that Starfleet Command has congratulated him. She says he deserves it—he prevented a war. Sisko isn't certain of that at all. He wonders if he just delayed the inevitable. If it's any consolation, Commander, let me give you my take on this deal: *You only delayed the inevitable.* Granted, it might have helped if you would have captured Hudson instead of letting him get away. But setting that aside, the real problem isn't you. The real problem is the dingleweed diplomats who negotiated this agreement in the first place and didn't have the guts to fix this problem before they signed the *stupid treaty*! If it's really the best they could do, then tell those colonists in the DMZ that they are on their own and they are no longer Federation citizens. Period.

EQUIPMENT ODDITIES

• A bit of history will expose this equipment oddity. In the previous episode, the Maquis kidnap Dukat. The crew on the station determine that only two ships departed the station during the appointed time. One went through the wormhole. The other didn't. Sisko guesses that the one that didn't go through the wormhole is the one that had Dukat. O'Brien then locates the ship's warp signature and gives Sisko the bearing of departure for the vessel. To locate the ship, Sisko then has O'Brien send out a general alert that includes the warp signature of the ship, hoping someone will spot the craft and help determine its destination. On the way to the DMZ, Sisko receives a call from O'Brien, who says that another vessel has spotted the ship in question. From this, Sisko and Kira determine the ship's destination—an M-class asteroid. Dukat isn't there, however, because he was transferred to a shuttle and taken away. With me so far?

Okay, now we start this episode. After returning to the station, Sisko has O'Brien begin searching for the shuttle that left the asteroid with Dukat. Alone in Ops, on the station, far away from the DMZ, without *any help* from *any other* vessel, O'Brien reconstructs the flight path of the shuttle that scurried away with Dukat by using its warp trail. Hold it! Wait a minute! If O'Brien can find the shuttle by himself, why did he need the help of other vessels in the previous episode?

• Odo arrests Quark for a short time during this episode for his role in arranging for weapons to be sold to the Maquis. At one point Sisko jokingly suggests that Odo keep Quark in the cell "forever." Odo sure picked the right cell for it. A wide shot at the end of the scene shows that the cell has no button to lower the force field!

• I'm a bit puzzled by the airlocks on the promenade. Are they like giant turbolifts of some kind? Leaving the station, Legate Parn marches into an airlock. Then he turns around and stands as the door rolls shut. It's al-

most like he expects the room to start moving. Then again, maybe that's how the Cardassians say good-bye.

• While interrogated by members of the Maquis—supposedly Federation citizens—Dukat wears Cardassian-design handcuffs. (I suppose given Cardassian proclivities, their handcuffs would be more sturdy than ours, but still I say, "Buy Federation, use Federation for all your restraining needs!" We're talking jobs here!)

• Trying again to convince Hudson to come back into the Starfleet fold, Sisko takes a bag containing the man's uniform to Volan III. Hudson refuses to repent, pulls a phaser from his pants, and disintegrates the bag and the uniform. So this Hudson guy walks around with a phaser set on disintegrate and stuck it down into his pants. Right.

CONTINUITY AND PRODUCTION PROBLEMS

• Legate Parn in this episode bears a striking resemblance to the Klingon ambassador at the beginning of *Star Trek IV: The Voyage Home*. Hmmm.

• Kira must have had some wild party after she returned to the station. When she visits Sisko after his encouraging exchange with Admiral Nechayev, we see that not only is her collar insignia backwards, but also her combadge is upside down. (I'd say she got redressed in a hurry!)

TRIVIA ANSWERS
1. Drofo Awa.
2. The Bryma colony.

THE WIRE

Star Date: unknown

After an irritable Garak collapses with a seizure while in Quark's, Bashir discovers an implant in the brain of DS9's only Cardassian merchant. The doctor presses Garak for an explanation until the tailor finally reveals its purpose. On Cardassia he was entrusted with certain information too sensitive ever to reveal. Because of this he was given an implant that could release vast amounts of pleasure-causing endorphins, thereby ensuring that he would never break under torture. For the past two years Garak has used them constantly to cope with life on the station. Now they're breaking down, but his body has become accustomed to the higher endorphin levels.

Bashir convinces Garak to turn off the device, promising to help him through whatever happens afterward. In the delirium that follows, Garak weeps, rages, and spins tales of the reason for his exile. In one he mentions the person who gave him the implant, Enabran Tain, former head of the Obsidian Order—Cardassia's covert intelligence agency. Desperate to help the rapidly deteriorating Garak, Bashir goes to see Tain for the information he needs. Tain gladly supplies it, stating that he wants Garak to live a long, miserable life. In short order, Garak recovers.

Trivia Questions

1. Who does Quark contact on Cardassia concerning Garak's implant?

2. Who wrote the Cardassian novel *Meditations on a Crimson Shadow?*

PLOT OVERSIGHTS

• In this episode Garak hires Quark to procure another implant along with schematics for its installation. Presumably Garak is going to try to replace his defective implant. While Bashir does not know what Garak is attempting to procure from Quark, he does see the two talking, and the good doctor mentions this fact to Odo. Odo says that would explain why Quark has sent several coded messages to Cardassia Prime. Early the next morning, Odo and Bashir eavesdrop on a subspace conversation between a Cardassian named Boheeka and Quark. During the conversation Quark tells Boheeka that he needs a piece of Cardassian biotechnology. Boheeka asks what it is. Quark has only the requisition code. After punching the requisition code into his terminal, Boheeka is aghast because the implant and even its requisition code are clas-

172

sified by the Obsidian Order. This conversation helps the plot along. Obviously now Odo and Bashir know what Garak wanted. Also, the conversation introduces us to the Obsidian Order. It does evoke a certain puzzlement, however. Why did Quark make all those other coded calls to Cardassian Prime? Couldn't he find anyone else who was even willing to punch in the requisition code and look up the device in the computer? (When Quark hears the name "Obsidian Order" he seems frightened by the prospect of muddling in their affairs, so we must assume that no one in his previous conversations made this discovery.)

• At one point Garak tells Bashir that living on the station is torture for him. It's too cold. It's too bright. Obviously Bashir wasn't listening because as Garak convalesces we see all the lights in his room on full, and Bashir appears to be comfortable enough to wear his uniform tunic. If he was really concerned for his patient wouldn't Bashir dim the lights and turn up the heat?

• Near the end of this episode Bashir takes a runabout into Cardassian space to the Arawath colony to find Tain. This raises many questions. First, what did Bashir say to Sisko to convince him to allow the good doctor to borrow a runabout? (Did anyone else notice that Sisko seems strangely absent during this episode?) Second, how did Bashir expect to waltz into Cardassian space unhindered? (True, Kira and O'Brien did it in "The Homecoming," but that required extensive modifications to the runabout.) Third, how did Bashir find Tain's house? He lives at the Arawath *colony*. If the last

word in the previous sentence means anything, it probably contains more than one domicile. Has Bashir been beaming up and down into Cardassian homes all evening? This does not seem like a healthy practice!

• You have to feel a little bad for this Boheeka guy. Quark calls him out of the blue. Gives him a requisition code. The code turns out to be classified. Boheeka says he's ruined. Only one chance remains: Maybe no one will trace the quest back to him. Then Bashir goes to visit Tain. After Tain demonstrates his somewhat intimate knowledge of his uninvited visitor, the good doctor pops off with, "That Cardassian Quark was talking to—Boheeka—I supposed he really did have reason to fear the Obsidian Order." Great, just great! Bashir saw how frightened the guy was. He knew Boheeka was trying to hide out, to keep it a secret that he requested the information on the implant. And yet our good doctor blabs the guy's name to the former head of the Obsidian Order! *Really* smooth, Bashir. (I realize that Tain is *supposed* to be retired, but he doesn't seem very retired to me.)

CHANGED PREMISES

• There seem to be different versions of the Cardassian drink kanar. At one point Garak imbibes quite a large portion of the stuff in Quark's from somewhat normal-looking bottles. Also, at the end of the show, Tain orders a glass of kanar from his replicator. In both cases kanar looks light blue. (Or at least some derivative of blue. I'm lousy with colors.) Yet in "Destiny," Quark brings complimentary bottles of kanar to the quarters of a visiting Cardassian scientist. In this case the kanar is packaged in an exotic, spiral-shaped bottle, and the liquid appears to be quite dark. (I realize that this kanar has gone bad, but if you could tell that the kanar is bad simply by its color, Quark should have known it before ever bringing the bottles in the first place.) Also, the last time we saw a spiral-shaped bottle like those shown occurred during "The Maquis, Part II." Sisko rescues Gul Dukat and returns him to the station, after which Dukat indulges in a hearty meal. The scene joins him as he pours a thick, dark, molasseslike liquid from a spiral-shaped bottle. Is this kanar? If so, it's very different from what is shown in this episode. Finally, kanar makes its first appearance in the *NextGen* episode "The Wounded." A Cardassian orders a glass in Ten-Forward. In this scene it's clear.

• Continuing on with this theme briefly, in the scene that features a drunk Garak in the bar, Quark tells Bashir that the Cardassian drank up half his stock. Surely this is hyperbole, but Quark seems genuinely perturbed by this. Oddly enough, in "Destiny," Quark bemoans that he's had three cases of kanar sitting in his storeroom since the occupation ended. If the stuff is that hard to get rid of, one would think Quark happy to have Garak drinking up his stock.

EQUIPMENT ODDITIES

• When Garak collapses in Quark's, Bashir orders an emergency transport to the infirmary. This make sense. A bit later, Garak collapses in his quarters, showing much the same type of teeth-gritting seizure as we witness in Quark's. This time, however, Bashir calls for a medical team instead of an emergency transport. (And yes, they do take Garak to the infirmary.) Why the difference? Was Garak offending the sensibilities of Quark's customers and Bashir wanted to get him out of there as quickly as possible?

CONTINUITY AND PRODUCTION PROBLEMS

• Speaking of Garak collapsing in his quarters and subsequently being taken to the infirmary, if you just watch the episode, it looks like the action moves quickly from Garak's quarters to the infirmary. Bashir calls for a medical team, and the next thing we see is Bashir calling for cardiostimulation, as if they are in an emergency situation. All well and good. But if they are in an emergency situation, why did they change Garak's clothes? In his quarters he is dressed in his own attire. In the infirmary he's in a medical gown.

TRIVIA ANSWERS

1. Boheeka.
2. Preloc.

Star Date: unknown

Traveling back from the Gamma Quadrant, Kira and Bashir discover a plasma injector leak as they enter the wormhole. The problem causes a disruption that catapults the runabout into a parallel universe. In this reality, the Alliance rules. Principally composed of Cardassians and Klingons, Bajor was accepted for membership some years ago and has risen to become a major influence. A ruthless version of Kira rules the Bajoran sector from *Terok Nor,* a.k.a. DS9. Of interest, the Alliance Kira tells our Kira that this is the same alternate universe visited by Kirk and company in the classic episode "Mirror, Mirror." (At the end of that episode, our Kirk challenged the "imperial" Spock to consider the illogic of an empire that rules by fear and intimidation—to consider that the Empire would most certainly fail. Evidently Spock took our Kirk's words to heart. After rising to commander in chief of the Empire, he instituted noble reforms. Unfortunately, these reforms left the Empire unprepared to fend off the Alliance. Humans, called "Terrans," now serve as ore-mining slaves.)

Trivia Questions

1. With whom did Bashir study rhythmic breathing?

2. According to Bashir, Tor Jolan's music is slightly derivative of whom?

Spurred on by the stories of life in our universe, a hooligan named Sisko helps Kira and Bashir make it back to their runabout. Passing through the wormhole a second time, the pair make it home.

RUMINATIONS

Next time you're at a convention that features Nana Visitor, ask her about the famed milk bath scene in this episode. It's a great story featuring spirit gum, essence of orange oil and "armor."

PLOT OVERSIGHTS

• What is wrong with Bashir at the beginning of this episode? Did he double up on his daily dosage of obnoxious pills or something? First Kira tries to meditate quietly, and he launches into a panting fit. Then Kira suggests some music, and Bashir launches into a snooty review of Bajoran composers. Granted, Bashir has always had a touch of this arrogance, but the writing for the teaser of this episode puts him way over the top.

• Shortly after arriving at Terok Nor, our Kira makes a comment about the wormhole. Garak reacts instantly, since this alternate reality has never heard of the wormhole. Oddly enough, Garak never takes the opportunity to explore this topic further with either Kira or Bashir.

• Humans in this episode are identified with a designation that includes a Greek letter for classification. For instance, O'Brien in this episode has a theta designation. Many nitpickers found this very strange. Why would a conquering army establish a system of designations based on an ancient language of the conquered? Wouldn't the conquerors instead base the designations on one of their own languages? Usually conquerors attempt to deculturalize their slaves to increase their feeling of isolation and dependency.

• I realize that ore processing was a function carried out on the space station even in our reality, but it doesn't seem very efficient. Usually any type of processing refines a material, doing away with the dross. Why would you transport tons of rock up to a space station only to refine it down? Why not just build a processing plant next to the mines?

• The Alliance must be really hard up for slaves. Remember that we call this station Deep Space 9. From Earth, it's out in the sticks. Why then has the Alliance dragged these humans all the way out here? Aren't there planets closer by that could be conquered? (Of course, if the Alliance didn't drag humans all the way out to Terok Nor, Sisko and O'Brien wouldn't be in this episode; Bashir would have died a slow, agonizing death on the promenade; and Kira would have spent the rest of her life as the love toy of her alternate self.)

• It's an easy mistake to make. Twice the creators slipped with dialogue that was habitual for our reality but out of place for the alternate reality. In the alternate bar, Alt-Quark speaks with our Kira. At one point he asks, "Do you have a way back to your side, Major?" Only Bashir has referred to Kira as "Major" in this alternate reality, and only then in a whisper. Alt-Kira is called "intendant." Also—while fleeing from Alliance forces—Bashir asks Alt-O'Brien to tell him how to get to the "runabout pads." Alt-O'Brien seems to understand this term. Since the Federation developed the runabouts, Alt-O'Brien shouldn't know what a runabout is. One would expect Alt-O'Brien to respond to Bashir with, "You mean the *landing* pads?"

• In this episode Alt-Quark is a good guy who cares little for profit but rather gives his life helping humans escape the station. Or does he? When Alt-Garak comes to the bar to arrest the Ferengi, Alt-Quark whips out a phaser rifle. Alt-Garak knocks it away as Alt-Quark fires, and the beam flies over the Cardassian's shoulder . Now watch the scene again closely. Alt-Quark grabs the phaser rifle, swings around, jams the rifle into Alt-Garak's chest, waits for Alt-Garak to react, and—once the rifle has moved out away from Alt-Garak's body—only then does Alt-Quark pull the trigger. It almost looks like Alt-Quark purposefully kept himself from shooting Alt-Garak. Maybe this was all just for show. Maybe Alt-Quark is really working for the Alliance to destroy any resistance from the inside. My guess is Alt-Garak really didn't kill him. He simply relocated Alt-Quark.

• I'm amazed how long Alt-Kira lets Alt-O'Brien talk at the end of this episode. Here's a guy who has always been a good little slave, and suddenly he starts helping Bashir. Alt-Kira wants to know why. In the bar, filled with humans, Alt-Kira lets Alt-O'Brien talk about how glorious it is in the alternate reality, how *anything* would be better than this. Guess what happens next? The humans rebel, and Alt-Kira seems stunned. (Well, ding, ding, dollface, what did you expect?)

• Kira and Bashir make it back to their runabout. They blast away from the station and go straight to impulse. The episode cuts to the interior of the runabout and Kira announces, "Forty-five seconds to the wormhole." *Hold it!* Near the beginning of this episode, Kira and Bashir came flying out of the wormhole and were shocked to see the station gone. Kira quickly located it in orbit around Bajor. The whole point of these crossover episodes is that our reality and the alternate reality are parallel. Celestial stuff is in the same place. Remember that it routinely takes at least two hours on impulse to go from Bajor to the station near the wormhole. Since Terok Nor is orbiting Bajor, it should take Kira and Bashir at least two hours to get back to the wormhole, not forty-five seconds, unless, of course, there was a big time skip when we weren't looking. But opting for the time skip has its own problems. If it took two hours to get back to the wormhole, how did Kira and Bashir manage to evade the patrol ships?

• The wormhole behaves strangely in this episode. At the beginning, Kira and Bashir enter in the Gamma Quadrant and fly through to the Alternate-Alpha Quadrant. At the end, they enter the wormhole in the Alternate-Alpha Quadrant but fly through to the *Alpha* Quadrant. Shouldn't they come out in the Gamma Quadrant?

• At the end of the episode Kira tells Sisko that she and Bashir have been "through the looking glass." This from a *Bajoran* woman who didn't know the human expression "bury the hatchet" when Bashir used it at the beginning of this same episode.

• I am constantly amazed at the imperturbability of Starfleet officers. Does nothing give these guys pause? Look at it from Sisko's position. He's lost two officers. Then suddenly they reappear. He opens a channel to them, and their images flash onto the main display in Ops. Think about what he sees at this point. He's got a first officer, dressed in a purple floozy dress, leaning over so the Prophets and everyone else can look *straight* down her cleavage, and a chief medical officer who looks like he's been *mud wrestling!* Yet Sisko carries on like he sees this sort of thing every day, simply asking the strangely attired couple where they've been.

CHANGED PREMISES

• Alt-Kira tells our Kira that Spock rose to "commander in chief" of the old human Empire. In "Mirror, Mirror" *(TOS),* however, Kirk's woman, Marlena Moreau, refers to being the "woman of a Caesar." Moreau says it as if this is the highest rank possible in the Empire.

CONTINUITY AND PRODUCTION PROBLEMS

• At the very end of this episode, I was screaming, "Look out! Look out! Everybody off the promenade! Run for your lives!" If you watch the final approach of the runabout, you'll see it pass the runabout landing pad and continue straight for the central core of the station!

TRIVIA ANSWERS

1. Isam Helewa.
2. The great Boldaric masters of the last century.

THE COLLABORATOR

Star Date: unknown

As the election of the new Kai on Bajor approaches, an exiled Bajoran levels a disturbing accusation against the front-runner, Vedek Bareil. Kubus Oak, former member of the Cardassian occupational government, comes to DS9 and meets privately with Vedek Winn. Furious to learn that Winn has granted him sanctuary, Kira presses the Vedek for an explanation. Winn reveals that Kubus claims Bareil gave the Cardassians the location of a rebel encampment some years ago. This information led to the Kendra Massacre—a massacre that claimed the life of Kai Opaka's son. Until now, everyone thought Prylar Bek gave the Cardassians this information and then killed himself. But Kubus says Bareil ordered Bek to do it.

Since the evidence is only circumstantial, Winn asks Kira to conduct a quiet investigation. At first Bareil seems guilty. When confronted by Kira, he quietly withdraws his name for consideration as kai, leaving Winn to be elected to that post. But then Kira discovers that Bareil was on a personal retreat at the time and couldn't

have sent the information. In fact, Bareil has been protecting Kai Opaka. She ordered Bek to give the Cardassians the location of the rebel encampment—though it meant the death of her son—to save the lives of twelve hundred Bajorans.

PLOT OVERSIGHTS

• The episode opens with Vedek Bareil weirding on the Tear (i.e., sitting in front of one of the Orbs of the Prophets and experiencing a vision). As the show progresses, he does this several times and—though the information conveyed is very symbolic and disjointed—everything that happens during these sessions eventually comes true in some way. This seems like a very, very tempting proposition. Open the box, have a vision, get a glimpse of your future. I'm wondering why there isn't a line around the entire temple waiting for an encounter with this orb. (Remember that there are nine of these "Tears of the Prophets," but the Cardassians took the other eight.) I'm wondering also if the experience with the orbs is addicting. People seem to come out of their vision with a slug of adrenaline shooting through

Trivia Questions

1. Under what document was every Bajoran member of the Cardassian occupational government exiled?

2. Where did Vedek Bareil enjoy a personal retreat during the week leading up to the Kendra Massacre?

179

their system. (Maybe there's a whole class of "extreme" weirding Vedeks out there that we haven't seen yet!)

• Let's talk about the Bajor religion. Usually religious systems infuse meaning into the mundane. One of their main functions is to contextualize existence—to give people a reason to do what they do; to establish guidelines for behavior; to demonstrate a benefit for compliance with the guidelines. In general, religious systems fall into three basic categories: asceticism, hedonism, and a hybrid that for want of a better term I will refer to as dualism. (Before you write to correct me: Yes, I understand that there are a lot more flavors to this mix, but for my purposes here, these will do. Asceticism infuses meaning into action by placing restraints on the physical to enhance the spiritual. Adherents deny themselves physical pleasures that are outside the bounds of behavior for the religious system. They employ self-denial to gain strength in the spiritual realm. Hedonism, on the other hand, exalts physical pleasure as the goal of life. If it acknowledges a spiritual realm at all, it purports that the way to that spiritual realm is self-indulgence. Dualism tries to find a middle ground. It separates the spiritual from the physical, placing the spiritual on a high plane and—for all practical purposes—rendering the physical existence immaterial. This allows for an interesting side effect: You can do whatever you want in the physical realm because it doesn't really matter! In other words, you can do your thing and have your halo, too.

So what is the Bajoran religion? Well,

they have monasteries and monks and something like a pope. Monastic lifestyles usually indicate an ascetic religious structure. Those involved draw themselves away from the normal pressures of day-to-day living to concentrate on building spiritual strength. On the other hand, we have Vedek Bareil, who is obviously playing pleasure games with Kira, and he's a Vedek! This would lead us to believe that the Bajoran religion has certain hedonistic elements to it. (There's also the statements made by Vedek Winn to Minister Jaro at the end of "The Circle." It sounds very much like they've had an affair as well.) Okay, so maybe the Bajoran religion takes a more dualist approach. As long as you meditate, "weird on the Tear," and walk around with that faraway look on your face, you can do whatever you want.

There's only one problem with making the Bajoran religion dualist in nature. If you recall during "Shadowplay," Vedek Bareil tells Kira that Prylar Rhit's gambling debts have caused quit a stir in the Vedek assembly. So obviously there is an element in Bajoran religion that is ascetic—that says you should deny yourself from running up a gambling debt. But if denial is part of Bajoran religion, why is Bareil playing footsies with Kira? (It's almost like this religion allows for anything that the creators want to do! But obviously, *that* couldn't be true, could it?)

• It's amazing how similar philosophies crop up in cultures separated by so much space. In this episode Quark recites Rule of Acquisition 285: "No good deed goes unpunished."

Oddly enough, Geordi La Forge—while stuck on the surface of Galorndon Core during "The Enemy" *(TNG)*—muttered to himself, "Galorndon Core, where no good deed goes unpunished."

• Twice in this episode, Kira speaks with Bareil concerning very sensitive information about the Kendra Massacre and Kai Opaka. I don't think she realizes how her voice must carry through the stone halls of the monastery. Personally, if I were Bareil I'd be telling her to keep it *down*.

• Okay, this next one's needlessly obsessive nitpicking, but I thought I'd mention it. At one point Bareil says twelve hundred innocent lives were at stake. Later he says "a thousand" when he probably should have said "more than a thousand."

CONTINUITY AND PRODUCTION PROBLEMS

• In my review of "The Maquis, Part II," I noted that one scene shows Quark in one of Odo's cells, but the button to lower the force field on the cell is missing. I joked that Odo intended to keep Quark in the cell for some time. In this episode, when Kira comes in to speak with Kubus—similarly confined by Odo's hospitality—we see that none of the cells has the release button any longer.

(Someone's been redecorating.)

• Another prime example of the station rotational control in Ops. Vedek Winn comes to Sisko's office to speak with the emissary. When we first see out the window, the stars creep along very slowly. Then the stars start moving faster. Then Sisko comes around his desk and the stars go back to creeping slowly!

• At one point Kira and Odo enlist Quark's help to break into the files of the Vedek Assembly. As they enter the bar, Quark grabs his box of latinum and clutches it to his chest. When the shot changes, he suddenly holds the box lower, in his left hand and out from his body. The sequence happens again as the camera angles alternate.

• At the end of the episode, Kira pays her respects to Kai Winn. She walks up and stops within inches of Bajor's new spiritual leader. The shot changes. Now Kira looks like she's back at least a foot from her previous position. Kai Winn reaches up to take Kira's ear. Winn's arm is almost fully extended. The shot changes. Winn completes the gesture, but now her arm is bent.

TRIVIA ANSWERS
1. The Ilvian Proclamation.
2. The Dakeen Monastery.

TRIBUNAL

Shortly after O'Brien and Keiko depart DS9 on a much-deserved vacation, a Cardassian patrol ship approaches. Gul Evek demands to search the runabout and—thinking he has nothing to hide—O'Brien agrees. Evek beams on board and promptly arrests O'Brien, hauling him off the runabout as Keiko screams. On Cardassia, O'Brien is quickly process-ed and confined to a cell, all without knowing the charges against him. Under Cardassian jurisprudence, the ac-cused is informed of his or her crime only at the trial—a trial whose verdict and associated punish-ment have already been determined. As with all Car-dassian trials, O'Brien's court-appointed counsel—"Conservator" Kovat—admits that the verdict will be "guilty."

Meanwhile, Sisko and crew work first to discover the charges and then prove O'Brien's innocence. They find that someone has stolen twenty-four photon warheads from a weapons locker opened with a forged voice-print from O'Brien. They also uncov-er a man named Boone on the station.

Trivia Questions

1. What com-poser's music does O'Brien request in the runabout?

2. Sisko extended O'Brien's accommodations at what loca-tion?

Though he looks like an old friend of O'Brien's, a DNA test reveals that he is a Cardassian spy. Evidently the Car-dassians engineered the theft and subsequent arrest of O'Brien to sub-stantiate a claim that the Federa-tion is still supporting the Maquis. With their plan exposed, the Car-dassians release O'Brien.

PLOT OVERSIGHTS

• When introducing him-self to O'Brien, Gul Evek merely says, "My name is Evek." It's a little thing, but Cardassians seem to be very proud of their rank. I would have expected him to say, "My name is Gul Evek."

• Just before beaming away with O'Brien, Gul Evek tells Keiko that he will be taken to Cen-tral Prison on Cardassia Prime. Yet later—while trying to explain to Keiko why he isn't charging to the rescue—Sisko says they don't even know where O'Brien is being held on Car-dassia Prime. Did Keiko forget what Evek told her?

• During processing, O'Brien claims that his rank is "chief of operations, Starfleet." I realize that O'Brien is prob-ably frightened out of his wits, but "chief of operations" is not a rank, it's a title.

O'Brien's rank—according to "Hippocratic Oath"—is chief petty officer. (At least it is on *Star Trek: Deep Space Nine*. For most of his tenure on board the *Enterprise* he was a lieutenant.)

• Also, during processing, a Cardassian reaches into O'Brien's mouth and extracts a molar. As the tooth is placed in a receptacle, you can see that it is perfectly intact. Gary Holmes of Morrow, Georgia—a D.M.D., no less—assures me that the tooth would have broken off at the root.

• Does Starfleet take stupid pills every so often to even the odds with their enemies? We have a long—and cherished—history in *Star Trek* of people faking voiceprints. And yet—apparently—DS9 still allows access to vital areas of the station using *voiceprint alone!* What happened to the access codes to ensure that the guy talking is really who he says he is? What happened to retinal scans? What happened to handprint identification? What happened to DNA tracing? What happened to combadge cross-referencing? (At ease, Phil...at ease.)

• Evidently court proceedings on Cardassia are broadcast *live* to the entire planet. Now, there's a daring idea. Hasn't an activist ever used this system to disseminate his views before he's sentenced? (And lest you're wondering if there is some type of time delay protection built in, Sisko—at the end of the program—seems to think that his ability to embarrass the High Command before the entire planet led to the release of O'Brien.)

• Just as Chief Archon Makbar—O'Brien's judge—is about to sentence him to death at the end of this episode,

Sisko waltzes into the courtroom on Cardassia Prime with Boone. Sisko says nothing, but Makbar immediately comprehends the precariousness of the situation and proclaims mercy for O'Brien. I want to know who helped Sisko. I find it inconceivable that Sisko could have just hopped in a runabout, flown all the way through hostile Cardassian territory, transported down to Cardassia Prime, and strolled into this courtroom without *somebody* running interference for him. (My guess: Gul Dukat lent a hand.)

CHANGED PREMISES

• O'Brien and Keiko should really spend as much time as possible with Molly, because she is growing about twice as fast as a normal human child. Last time we heard her age, O'Brien claimed she was four, in "Cardassians." In this episode Kira says she's five! Let's try this again. She was born very near star date 45156.1 during "Disaster" *(TNG)*. This episode begins on star date 47944.2. By my reckoning that would make her just under three years old!

EQUIPMENT ODDITIES

• Shortly into their vacation, Keiko discovers that O'Brien has brought a few technical update manuals along. She drops into the portside pilot chair on the runabout in a huff. O'Brien finally takes the hint, setting aside the manuals and ordering some music. He wanders over and begins kissing her lightly. As they attempt to slouch down, Keiko bursts into laughter. She asks him if the chair reclines, and O'Brien must admit that it does not.

During this entire exchange a monitor flickers over Keiko's right shoulder. It looks like it has a problem with horizontal hold, which—strangely enough—is precisely the same problem that Keiko and O'Brien are experiencing. A coincidence? I wonder.

• Makbar, the judge during O'Brien's trial, certainly has her monitor oddly situated. It rests *below* her knees. Maybe she operates it with her feet?

• In the scene in the weapons locker, we see opened boxes that should contain photon warheads. Instead, they are loaded with scrap metal. When Sisko comes in, he looks at an opened box and asks if they are all like this. Kira replies in the affirmative. Supposedly some transporter guru beamed the scrap metal into the boxes at the same time he or she beamed the warheads out. Interestingly enough, when Gul Evek presents the warheads found on the runabout during O'Brien's trial, we don't see these warheads. We see only their boxes! Where did the Cardassians get boxes for these warheads? Does Starfleet maintain a free box replacement service for their weapons customers? ("Starfleet Customer Service: How may I help you? You say you've got twenty-four photon torpedo warheads and you can't find your storage boxes? No problem! I'll get those right out to you by warp courier this afternoon. Have a nice day!")

CONTINUITY AND PRODUCTION PROBLEMS

• During processing, O'Brien bolts from the restraining chair and is quickly thrown back into it. The closed captioning at this point reads, "Sit down. Get back. Hold him."

• Most of the shots of O'Brien after the Cardassians cut off his clothes give us the impression that he is naked. This would correspond with similar treatment given to Picard in "Chain of Command, Part 2." However, as the Cardassians extract one of O'Brien's molars, a camera pan reveals that he is wearing the standard gray Starfleet boxers (first seen in "Paradise"). By the time Chief Archon Makbar arrives to greet him, the boxers have been removed. (It's possible the Cardassians initially let O'Brien retain his boxers, but I can't imagine why.)

• O'Brien's prisoner oufit consists of a shirt and pants wrapped by beltlike objects. These objects are made from some sort of strip mesh that wraps around O'Brien's chest, down around his waist, and between his legs. I usually don't comment on costuming, but in this case I gotta say that O'Brien looks like a reject from a Michael Jackson video. I kept waiting for him to break into a moonwalk or something!

TRIVIA ANSWERS
1. Minezaki.
2. The Lagoon.

THE JEM'HADDAR

Star Date: unknown

oping to get to know Sisko better, Quark cons his way onto a runabout bound for the Gamma Quadrant. Jake and Nog are going to do a planetary survey science project together, and the commander will pilot the runabout. That night, Quark's obnoxiousness drives Nog into the woods. He's deeply embarrassed by his uncle's behavior. Jake goes after him. Then the unexpected occurs: A humanoid female named Eris runs into the camp and is quickly captured by several savage-looking soldiers, who capture Sisko and Quark as well. In a temporary holding cell, Eris explains that the soldiers are the Jem'Haddar— enforcers of the Dominion.

Meanwhile, a Jem'Haddar soldier delivers an ultimatum to DS9, stating that the Dominion has detained Sisko and will no longer tolerate intrusions into their Gamma Quadrant territory. In short order, Starfleet sends a Galaxy-class starship, the *Odyssey,* to investigate the Jem'Haddar threat. On the planet, Sisko, Quark, and Eris escape, only to watch the Jem'Haddar destroy the *Odyssey.* Then Sisko discovers that Eris is actually a spy for the Dominion. To everyone's amazement, she beams off the station and vanishes. As the episode ends, Sisko comments that if the Dominion comes through the wormhole the first battle will be fought at the station, and he intends to be ready for them.

Trivia Questions

1. Sitting by the fire with Jake reminds Sisko of a camping trip they took to what planet?

2. What is the name of Eris's home world?

RUMINATIONS

This episode has much to commend it: A powerful, technologically advanced, well-characterized new enemy called the Jem'Haddar. (Great name, too!) Lots of fun moments as Quark endures the "nature" of the planet and rubs Sisko the wrong way. Beautiful visual effects showing correct perspectives on the Galaxy-class starship versus the runabouts. A spectacular explosion at the end after the Jem'Haddar attack ship performs its suicide run.

But—while this last sequence was very well done—it came at an unfortunate time as far as I'm concerned. I remember watching this episode, thinking how great it was to see a Galaxy-class starship in action again. Just a few weeks prior, "All Good Things" (TNG) had aired, bringing the seven-season run of Star Trek: The

Next Generation *to an end. I was still missing the show, still getting used to the fact that there wouldn't be any new television episodes. But...at least I'd get a small reprieve seeing a good old Galaxy-class starship in action during the finale for the second season of* Star Trek: Deep Space Nine! *You already know the end of this story. The episode is going along pretty well: and then the* Odyssey *takes a pasting. All the time I'm thinking, "Man, they need Picard on that bridge." Then the* Odyssey *gets* blown up! *I know it wasn't really the case, but I came away from the episode with the distinct impression that the creators were saying, "See, we can do whatever we want! We can cancel your favorite show and we can blow up your favorite ship* anytime we feel like it!" I'll grant you that my reaction was simply part of a larger Posttraumatic NextGen Cancellation Disorder. However, even to this day—every time I watch this episode—I get this little feeling that there was more to destruction of the* Odyssey *than just demonstrating the power and commitment of this new enemy. (Of course, the loss of the* Enterprise-D in Star Trek Generations *certainly didn't help my paranoia any, but that's another story! And, we certainly aren't going to discuss the burning of the* Enterprise-D's bridge set when it could have been donated to the Smithsonian.)*

PLOT OVERSIGHTS

• One has to wonder about Sisko's performance while confined by the Jem'Haddar in this episode. Granted, the dialogue was needed to move the

plot along, but was it really wise to talk with Quark about Jake and Nog when anyone could overhear this conversation with a transmitter hidden inside the confinement area? And what about telling Eris of the runabout in orbit when she asks what they will do if they can escape? Does this seem wise?

• I realize the creators did it for dramatic effect, but I think they went a tad overboard with the Jem'Haddar pronouncements of Dominion policy in this episode. Before we tackle that topic, let's take a moment to review the capabilities of the Jem'Haddar. These guys apparently have some sort of personal cloaking device. They can beam onto DS9 with the station's shields raised. They can walk right out of a containment field. They can drill through a Galaxy-class starship with impunity. And—if that's not bad enough—they have a behavioral code that allows them to commit suicide just to prove a point (i.e., in this episode, one of their vessels crashes into a *retreating* enemy ship). In addition, the Dominion evidently also has some type of cloaking technology for their *ships,* since Eris beamed off the station without a trace. Get the picture? These are not guys you want to fool around with. Now let's look at Third Talak'Talan's pronouncements to the DS9 staff. We'll pick up the scene shortly after he beams into Ops on the station.

Third Talak'Talan: "Commander Sisko will serve as an example of what happens to anyone who interferes with the Dominion."

Kira: "What kind of interference are you talking about?"

Third Talak'Talan: "Coming through

the anomaly is interference enough. Unless you wish to continue to offend the Dominion, I suggest you stay on your side of the galaxy."

Sounds pretty definite, doesn't it? If the Federation sends a ship through the wormhole, the Dominion will be offended. Period. So what's the response from the station crew? Dax says that the Jem'Haddar are making a mistake if they thinking kidnapping Sisko will stop the Federation from exploring the Gamma Quadrant. Hold it! *Wait a minute!* The Jem'Haddar have just laid claim to an area of space, and the Federation isn't going to respect that? If the Federation wandered into a new area of space in the Alpha Quadrant and a race came flying out to meet them with guns blazing, the Federation would still push on and keep exploring in that region though it was claimed by another group?! Is this really Federation policy? Talk about a blueprint for continual conflict! No wonder the Federation has been at war with all its neighbors at one time or another! It evidently takes bloodshed before the Federation backs off. (Or is the problem the *Gamma* Quadrant? Without the *Gamma* Quadrant, Bajor loses all its significance, and the members of the Starfleet staff on DS9 become minders of a useless wormhole. Is that the real motivation for Dax's remark? Is she worried about losing her status as the science officer of an important station?)

One last word on this subject: I reproduced Third Talak'Talan's dialogue for an important reason. In the third and fourth seasons, we are going to revisit these words *several* times, and I wanted to have an episode review I could reference later. As you probably already know, the creators conveniently *forgot* what Third Talak'Talan said here as the next two seasons progressed.

• Preparing to fly into the Gamma Quadrant, Captain Keogh says that Starfleet orders are simple: No traffic through the wormhole until Starfleet can investigate the Jem'Haddar threat. Then the *Odyssey* gets blown to bits and—next season—we'll see ships going back and forth through the wormhole again. ("Well, they destroyed one of our Galaxy-class starships. Yup, I'd say they're a real threat, all right. Okay...traffic can resume through the wormhole now.")

• This episode begins a practice that we'll see often in the coming seasons. The entire senior staff leaves the station to rescue Sisko. Is this a good idea, given the Dominion threat?

• When effecting the jailbreak, Sisko tosses a phaser rifle to Quark and then grabs a phaser pistol for himself. (Personally, since there is another guard who came in with a second phaser rifle, I would have taken the more powerful weapon but, then again, I'm not a hero.) Oddly enough, when we see the trio fleeing in the woods later, Quark still has his rifle, but Sisko is *sans* weapon. (I don't think this is a good time to discard a phaser pistol, do you?)

• At one point during the battle, a damage control team is sent to "Level 7" on the *Odyssey*. Since we are talking about a Galaxy-class ship, shouldn't that be "Deck 7"? (I know. Picky, picky, picky.)

• The first time I saw this episode, I snorted after Sisko said his final line. Kira says that Eris will be back, and the only question is who she'll bring with her. To this, Sisko responds that if the Dominion comes through the wormhole, the first battle will be fought at the station and he "intends to be ready for them." My response to Sisko's response was, "Hello? *Hello!* Reality check. These guys can blast right through your shields. Your weapons have little or no effect. They'll make suicide runs if they have to. They have cloaking technology. Your tractor beams don't work. They walk right out of confinement fields, and if they board your station, they can move so fast you can't even see them! And you're going to be 'ready for them'?" (I admit that my reaction was due in large part to Post-traumatic *NextGen* Cancellation Disorder. But even if we allow that Sisko had already decided to go back to Mars and get the *Defiant,* would he really believe that one ship could make the difference against this new threat? Or is he just loath to admit defeat and felt like the troops needed a rousing rallying cry? "We'll be ready. Yes, we will! We'll be ready! Yes, we will..." To which the Jem'Haddar—if they really wanted to—would answer: BLAM, BLAM, CRUNCH, POW, *BLAM*!)

EQUIPMENT ODDITIES

• So what's the deal with these runabouts anyway? We've had two episode in a row now where Starfleet officers use them for *personal* trips. Wouldn't this be like an Air Force pilot borrowing an F-16 to fly to the Bahamas?

• The rifles used by the Jem'Haddar have been seen several times before with one modification or another. The hunters used them in "Captive Pursuit." The Albino's Security forces use them in "Shadowplay." The Kellerun assassins use them at the beginning of "Armageddon Game." (Just to name a few. Somehow I would have expected a technologically advanced race like the Jem'Haddar to have a weapon of their own design.)

• Shortly after coming back to camp and finding it deserted, Jake hits his communicator and calls his dad. I wonder if Sisko's Jem'Haddar captors heard that, since they would have had the communicator at this point in the episode.

• This episode features a telekinetic suppressor. In other words, a device that can block telekinetic emanations. Quark says he has seen them before, but not so compact. So...does telekinesis operate on a different frequency than telepathy? I ask because Data in "Night Terrors" *(TNG)* said there was no known technology to block telepathic transmissions.

• I mentioned this in "Paradise," but it bears repeating here. In this episode Jake and Nog have a terrific struggle getting the runabout out of orbit because they don't have an access code. Yet in "Paradise," Alixus—having been isolated from Federation technology for a decade—manages to beam up to a runabout and set it on a course that very nearly flies it into a star. (As I said in my review of "Paradise," maybe O'Brien got the hint and installed better security routines?)

• In "Heart of Glory" *(TNG)*, Worf said that the *Enterprise* became a better warship once relieved of its bulky saucer section. Presumably the same would hold true for the *Odyssey,* yet Captain Keogh goes into battle with the saucer section of his vessel intact. (I *do* remember the dialogue in "The Best of Both World's" that seems to indicate the saucer section would be handy in battle. But doesn't it seems like the "Battle Bridge"—the auxiliary bridge that's supposed to be used for the star drive section when the saucer separates—should be called the *"Battle Bridge"* for a reason?!)

• The *Odyssey* seems to be missing the standard markings on the saucer that we enjoyed on the *Enterprise* for almost seven seasons. Just what *is* this ship's registry number? (By the way, several nitpickers wrote to say that they recognized the registry "NCC 1701-D" in certain frames of this episode. I've looked, but I can't find it. My screen is either too blurred, or the numbers are missing altogether.)

• Is there some reason that none of the Starfleet vessels fires photon torpedoes at the Jem'Haddar ships?

CONTINUITY AND PRODUCTION PROBLEMS

• Near the beginning of this episode,

Sisko reacts when Jake reveals that Nog will be his partner in the science project. "Partner?" Sisko questions. The closed captioning at this point reads, "Pardon?"

• When Nog identifies the saying "Nature decays. Latinum lasts forever" as Rule of Acquisition 102, the closed captioning has 103.

• Okay! Um...so there's still a collar on Eris in the holding cell that suppresses her telekinetic ability, right? Aaaaand Sisko decides that he thinks it would be good to take the collar off because then Eris could use her power to knock out the force field that imprisons them. With me so far? Good. He asks Eris if he can pry off the casing to get at the locking mechanism, and she says okay. Then the shot changes—and so help me, I am not joking about this— it looks like he starts unbuttoning her *blouse*! Did I miss something in this conversation? Why is he working on her shirt?!

• Kira seems to be a long way from a microphone when she starts talking with Odo in a corridor near the end of this episode.

TRIVIA ANSWERS

1. Itamish III.
2. Kurill Prime.

THE ANSWER TO LIFE, THE UNIVERSE, AND EVERY-
THING! (OH, WAIT: THAT'S FORTY-TWO)

my first encounter with the forty-sevens of *Star Trek* came when a letter from Paul LeGere of Rotterdam, New York, arrived just after the release of the *NextGen Guide* in November 1993. Paul asked if I had my book on computer. He wondered if I could do a search for the number "47." He had noted that it was quite popular with the creators (used for things such as a holoprogram, a starbase, a "captain's eyes only" transmission). The next day, I received another letter from Paul. Just for the fun of it, Paul had flipped through the *NextGen Guide* and—sure enough—he had quickly pulled out nine different manifestations of the number "47."

Frankly, I didn't think much about it. It could have just been coincidence. There are lots of numbers mentioned in *Trek* scripts. If you're looking for a particular one, you're bound to find it over and over. But then I started noticing 47's cropping up in a lot of places as well. And from the notes I kept on the episodes of *NextGen* it quickly became clear that the incidence of "47" was too high to be accidental. Sure enough, sometime later at a convention, I heard Ronald D. Moore explain that Joe Menosky started the trend. Seems he has an affinity for the number and tries to work it into every script he writes. The trend caught and has continued to this day.

In time I had the good fortune of meeting Michaela Schlocker of Stanford, California. She had been collecting the 47s of *Trek* as a case study in obsession. She kindly allowed me to combine her research with mine to produce this sidebar. Of course, with 178 episodes, *NextGen* has many more "47"s than DS9. But since this is a book about Sisko and crew, I will only list the "47"s that we've currently found in the first 84 episodes of *Star Trek: Deep Space Nine*.

Here then for your viewing pleasure are the known "47"s through the episode "Paradise Lost."

"The Passenger"
Just after receiving the Kobliad vessel's distress signal, Bashir says that he's just picking it up on long-range sensors, bearing "347 mark 08."

"Progress"
Forty-seven other people were living on the fifth moon of Bajor besides Mollibok and company. They left willingly.

"Rivals"
This episode reveals the Rule of Acquisition 47: "Don't trust a man wearing a better suit than your own."

"Whispers"
O'Brien's first destination in the runout is Parada IV. The computer tells O'Brien that Parada IV has seven moons.

"Playing God"
Toward the end of the episode Dax and Arjin navigate through the vertiron nodes of the wormhole. Dax tells him there's an opening in the nodes at "130 mark 47."

"The Search, Part II"
As Sisko makes his commander's log over the opening credits, the camera pans across a flicker display with the numbers "947."

"Meridian"
After Dax spends six hours having her molocules scrambled in the transporter, O'Brien says that according to Doral's calculations, the dimensional shift should occur within the next forty-seven minutes.

"Defiant"
To unlock the bridge stations on the Defiant, Kira uses the code "Kira Delta 547." Also in this episode, the Defiant destroys Cardassian Outpost 47.

"Visionary"
When Kira moves the Romulans to new quarters she puts them in Section 47, Level 2.

"Family Business"
On the promenade, Sisko begins to tell Bashir and O'Brien, "I'll be in Cargo Bay— Four?" O'Brien interrupts. "Uh...seven," Sisko corrects.

"Shakaar"
At one point Quark encourages O'Brien to come into the bar the next day for his forty-seventh straight victory.

"The Adversary"
There are forty-seven people on board the ship. At one point Kira says that they have altered course. Their new heading is "015 mark 47."

"The Visitor"
The first time we see young Jake, he's working with a padd that has "4747" at the top.

"Hippocratic Oath"
The first time we see Worf, he's working with a padd that has "4747" at the top.

"Little Green Men"
Nog guesstimated that he and Jake have spent 2,147 hours at their spot on the second level of the promenade. Coincidentally, a close-up on a pinup calendar shows the date as "July 1, 1947."

"Homefront"
Several exterior shots show a transport tube. Two tubes join, and the junction is labeled "47-48."

"Paradise Lost"
Red Squad returns to base at 1947 PST on the night of the twenty-third.

THIRD

SEASON

THE SEARCH, PART I

Star Date: 48467.3

After weeks of meetings, Sisko returns to DS9 with an over-gunned, overpowered prototype warship called the *Defiant*. Sisko has volunteered to take the ship into the Gamma Quadrant, attempt to locate leaders of the Dominion—the "Founders"—and start a dialogue. Of interest, the *Defiant* has a cloaking device courtesy of the Romulans. Two new individuals have returned with Sisko: a Romulan subcommander named T'Rul, to keep an eye on the cloak; and Lieutenant Commander Michael Eddington, to oversee all Starfleet Security matters. Odo reacts with resentment to the arrival of the latter. Believing Starfleet wants him to replace him as chief of Security, he resigns. Only with Kira's urgings does he agree to come on the mission.

At first the cloak seems able to hide the *Defiant* while Sisko searches for the Founders. Then the Jem'Haddar adapt: They attack and board the ship. Belowdecks, Odo and Kira fight hand-to-hand with Jem'Haddar soldiers as Sisko and the rest of the crew do the same on the bridge. Knocked uncon-scious, Kira awakes in a shuttle piloted by Odo. His report holds little hope for anyone else's survival. But instead of heading back to the wormhole, he has acted on a strange urging and taken Kira to Omarion Nebula. Once there, Odo finds a colony of Changelings who welcome him home.

Trivia Questions

1. What does Jake greedily order from a replicator soon after returning to the station?

2. Who do the Karemma take orders from in the Dominion?

RUMINATIONS

I like the Defiant*! (Even if it was an obvious gimmick to garner more viewers for the series by changing the formula and making it closer to what viewers have come to expect from a show called* Star Trek*.)*

PLOT OVERSIGHTS

• The episode opens with Kira and the senior staff unhappy with their chances for survival during a Jem'Haddar attack. Kira says they have run seven simulations, and in every one the Jem'Haddar overwhelm the station in two hours. If you watch "The Jem'Haddar" immediately followed by this episode, you get the impression that very little time has passed. In fact, *weeks* have gone by. What have they been doing all this time? Well, Dax got a new hairdo. And, from the sounds of it, the senior staff got up every morn-

195

ing and comforted themselves with the thought that if the Jem'Haddar attacked that day, at least it would be over in two hours!

• Speaking of what station personnel have been doing since we last saw them, Commander "I Intend to Be Ready for Them" Sisko takes an interesting tack. Just after the revelation of the greatest threat ever to the Federation (according to the hype talk from Paramount), he leaves for Earth! Now, wouldn't this inspire your confidence if you were a member of his senior staff? You're staring down the barrel of the wormhole. You've just watched the Jem'Haddar blast through a Galaxy-class starship, and the next thing you know your commander is saying, "Listen, I need to go to Earth for some debriefings. I'll be gone for several weeks. Keep things together until I get back." (If I were stationed on DS9 I think I'd be suggesting that he send his reports over subspace!)

• One wonders why the *Defiant* doesn't have a registry number of NCC 1764-A in honor of the Constitution-class vessel that disappeared near Tholian space in "The Tholian Web." (If it's good enough for the *Enterprise* ...)

• This mission to find the Founders of the Dominion in the Gamma Quadrant reminds me *a lot* of the way penguins determine if water is safe. I've been told that when it's time to take a swim, a herd of penguins will begin shuffling toward the water. They'll keep pushing forward until a few of the penguins in front drop into the water; then the rest watch to see what happens next. If the penguins in the water aren't

attacked, the others join them! ("Okay, Sisko. You go over there and tell the natives we're friendly. Yeah, that's the ticket. Take this ship that needs lots of work and see what you can find out; Okay, buddy?")

• Somehow I have a hard time figuring out how Sisko is supposed to communicate a message of peace to the Dominion when he's sneaking into their territory with a cloaked warship that has gonzo phasers. Wouldn't a diplomatic envoy be more appropriate?

• According to this episode it takes only about a week to get from Earth to Bajor. As Sisko attempts to figure out when he started to think of DS9 as home, Jake offers that it occurred "last Thursday around 1700 hours" when Sisko pulled his "stuff" out of storage on Earth. In other words, Jake and Sisko were on Earth "last Thursday." At the most, this "stuff-pulling" could be only thirteen days past. Remember that Bajor is supposed to be in the sticks. After all, the station *is* named Deep Space 9. Here's what's interesting. According to *The Star Trek Encyclopedia,* the Federation is 10,000-light years across—a distance that would take more than seven *years* to travel at warp 9. Granted we don't really know where Earth is in the Federation. (Yes, there are maps available, but nothing canonical at this point.) For all we know, Earth may be slung off to one side and to reach Bajor requires only a short hop in intragalactic terms. Still—at warp 9—Bajor would have to lie approximately 50 light-years from Earth for the trip to be possible in the allotted time. At warp 7, Bajor would have to be approximately 25 light-years distant. Does this seem right for a "deep space" station? (Of course, we know that Jake and Sisko really had to travel at warp 5 between Earth and Bajor because of the warp 5 speed limit, right? See the *NextGen* episode "Force of Nature" for more information.)

• I'm a bit puzzled by Sisko's decision to bring "one of the finest collections of ancient African artifacts" back to the station with him. Yes, he wants to make his quarters feel like home. But, by his own admission, the chances of success for the coming mission are "slim" (translate that: "the chances of coming back alive are slim"). And the chances of the station withstanding a Jem'Haddar attack are practically *nonexistent*. Wouldn't it be a bit more prudent to let Jake live with his Grandpa Joe for a few months and leave the artifact collection in storage as bit longer until events play out? Of course, if Sisko left the collection in storage, the creators would miss the chance to have him act out the "I'm here to stay—and so is this series—because I brought my stuff" scenario.

• Before leaving for the Gamma Quadrant, Dax tells Sisko that she presumes Starfleet has already run two hundred probability studies on their mission. She wants to know how they came out. Given the *only* encounter Starfleet has had with the Jem'Haddar, I'd say this is a no-brainer. ("Let's see what we can deduce from our last encounter with the Jem'Haddar. They seem very hostile. They have very advanced weaponry. They seem very happy to use it. And—if that fails—they seem willing

to crash their ships into yours. Offhand...I'd say the probability that you're coming back alive is just about zero.")

• Once again, the senior staff goes traipsing off on a mission leaving the station in the hands of underlings.

• I wonder why Sisko doesn't use his phaser on the Jem'Haddar when they board the *Defiant*?

• I wonder why Kira survives a Jem'Haddar phaser blast; in the last episode Eris said everything about the Jem'Haddar was fatal. Was that just fearmongering propaganda?

• I wonder why the Jem'Haddar aren't better at hand-to-hand combat. Sisko takes out several in their attack on the bridge.

• The Changelings' home world is described as a rogue M-class planet. How does an M-class planet stay M-class once it moves away from a star? Mitzi Adams tells me that the atmosphere would condense on the ground!

• Several nitpickers have wondered why the Changelings at the end of this episode look just like Odo. See my explanation in the review of the next episode, "The Search, Part II."

CHANGED PREMISES
• In the previous episode, Quark told Eris, "The Ferengi have been trying to open up trade negotiations with the Dominion for over a year now." In this episode Sisko reminds Quark that he established a trade agreement with the Karemma *eight months ago* for tulaberry wine. Sisko goes on to say that the Karemma are part of the Dominion. Though he tries to downplay their importance in the organization because he doesn't want to go on the

THE SEARCH, PART I

mission, Quark *does* admit that the Karemma are part of the Dominion. So haven't the Ferengi already concluded a trade agreement with the Dominion? In "The Jem'Haddar," did Quark mean that the Ferengi were still trying to open negotiations with the Founders of the Dominion?

• After arriving in the Gamma Quadrant, Sisko engages the *Defiant* at warp 7. Either (a) he got permission to exceed the warp speed limit set in "Force of Nature" *(TNG)* or (b) he couldn't give a rip about the fabric of space in the Gamma Quadrant or (c) the creators would just as soon forget that they brought up that silly warp speed limit thing in the first place!

• After helping Sisko get the information he needs from the Karemma, Quark stays behind on the Karemma home world. He tells Sisko that he will book passage on the next ship going through the wormhole. In the previous episode, Captain Keogh of the *Odyssey* said that Starfleet orders were simple: No traffic through the wormhole until Starfleet could assess the Jem'Haddar threat. So what happened next? The *Odyssey* got blown to shreds. Now either Quark is going to have a long wait for a ride, or Starfleet really *did* decide they had accurately assessed the threat and let traffic recommence! ("It's bad. Go on in.")

EQUIPMENT ODDITIES

• This isn't really a nit, since the *De-*

fiant is a whole new class of ship. It's merely an observation. On the *Defiant,* Tactical and Weapons are controlled from two different consoles. On the *Enterprise,* Worf did both.

• Good to see Starfleet is still using those 50,000-volt interfaces on their display terminals. This is the first episode for the *Defiant,* and in the first battle the death-trap displays manage to kill at least one person.

CONTINUITY AND PRODUCTION PROBLEMS

• Evidently Odo decided that his outfit needed some accessorizing. He shape-shifted a belt for the beginning of the third season.

• I couldn't resist this one because it's my favorite kind of nit. While talking to Kira in his quarters over Starfleet's decision concerning Odo, Sisko receives a call from the bridge informing him that the ship has reached the Callinon System. Sisko gets up, as does Kira, and you can see the reflection of an angled tube in the panel on Sisko's desk. Is that the boom for a microphone? (I *love* Starfleet ships with all their reflective surfaces! I have really, *really* missed this sort of thing in the first two seasons of *DS9*!)

• The closed captioning is missing on Sisko's supplemental log entry.

TRIVIA ANSWERS
1. I'Danian spice pudding.
2. Vorta.

THE SEARCH, PART II

Star Date: unknown

A spokesperson for the Changelings tells Odo that they came to this planet to escape persecution many years ago. Wanting to learn about the universe, the Changelings then sent out one hundred infant explorers with genetic programming to return home after a time. Because of the wormhole, Odo is three hundred years early. The spokesperson quickly finds that Odo's isolation has stunted his maturation as a Changeling. She says he has much to learn before he is ready to take his place in the "Great Link"—a merging and sharing unique to shape shifters.

Meanwhile, Sisko and Bashir limp back toward the wormhole in a shuttle. Rejoining Dax and O'Brien on DS9, they discover that the Federation and every other Alpha Quadrant power except the Romulans are negotiating an ill-fated treaty with the Dominion. In desperation, Sisko and the others steal a runabout and collapse the entrance to the wormhole. Back on the Changeling planet, Kira attempts to contact Sisko, but her transmissions are jammed. She traces the problem to a room where Sisko and the others are hooked up to a machine that is generating their experiences so the Dominion can test their responses. In fact, the Changelings are the Founders, and they invite Odo to join them. Appalled, Odo refuses, using his influence to arrange his friends' release.

RUMINATIONS

This is another one of those hard-to-nitpick episodes, since most of it occurs as part of an adventure of the mind put on by the Dominion to test the resolve of Sisko and company. I've attempted to note it anytime a nit might be explained by a glitch in the holo-mind machinery.

PLOT OVERSIGHTS

• At the beginning of this episode Odo stares longingly at the Changelings who have just emerged from their lake and says, "You really are just like me...." And they are! They have the same ill-formed features as Odo. But wait: Odo has said on many occasions that he finds it difficult to make a humanoid face. In later episodes we will discover that these Changelings are very skilled at imi-

Trivia Questions

1. To what ship is Dax transferred in this episode?

2. What bird does Odo become while in the Changelings' arboretum?

tating *everything*. In "Heart of Stone" the spokesperson for the Changelings will turn into an exact duplicate of Kira. In "The Die Is Cast" we'll see a Changeling who looks just like a Romulan. In "The Adversary" a Changeling assumes the appearance of several different humanoids with ease. In "Paradise Lost" a Changeling who looks just like O'Brien approaches Sisko. What's going on here? Why *do* these Changelings look just like Odo? My guess is they don't want to make Odo feel bad. As Odo and Kira approached the lake at the end of the previous episode, the shape shifters must have looked up while doing that wild and crazy linkin' thing and thought, "Great Changelings! Look at that nose! And those ears! Is that Odo? What race has he been hanging around with? The Molders from Puttyface IV?" Then they realized that their poor infant Changeling had been isolated too long and was so underdeveloped that he simply *couldn't* make a decent humanoid face. So they all decided to imitate his face to make him feel at home.

• Although the DS9 scenes during this episode actually occur in the minds of the captured Starfleet officers and their Romulan associate, they do reveal an interesting attitude on Sisko's part. As the negotiations proceed between the powers of the Alpha Quadrant and the Dominion, Sisko tells Jake that he feels "out of the loop." Now, why do you think that would be, *Commander*? You're in charge of a "Cardassian monstrosity" of a space station slung off at the edge of Federation space. You're not even a captain in rank, let alone an admiral. When Starfleet appointed you to this position they had no idea there was even a wormhole out there that would add some prestige to your position. If you recall, DS9 definitely was not exactly a *plum assignment,* so obviously you weren't on Starfleet's "A" list. It's true, you've had a couple of good years here being the belle of the ball, but let's get real: You're an underling! You've got no say when it comes to setting Federation policy or negotiating Federation treaties. (Wait, wait, wait. Before you get your hackles up, I'm just joking!)

Now that I've got your attention, though, let me explain this in less emotive terms. The *DS9* Series has *always* had a problem with scale. In previous incarnations of *StarTrek* we've watched captains in action on the edges of Federation influence. These captains had difficult choices to make, and they couldn't always get the good word from their superiors on how to proceed. They were supposed to be explorers, adventurers—the first "into the breach" and all that stuff. In contrast, Sisko's role has always been one of a middle-level-management *administrator*. Yes, the creators have attempted to add some status to his position by giving him a wormhole and making him the emissary to the Bajoran people—and most recently by giving him the *Defiant*—but he's still a middle-level-management *administrator*. Why should he even *expect* to be included in treaty negotiations between the Federation and the Dominion? Did the Federation consult him when they negotiated the treaty with the Cardassians? Of course not—treaties are outside Sisko's area of influence. (This brings up another interesting point: What should Starfleet *really* do at this point? Should they continue to let the station hang at the entrance of the wormhole like bait? Or should they bring in an armada of ships to serve as a first line of defense for the Alpha Quadrant? To me it makes a whole lot more sense to bring in an armada of ships to serve as a first line of defense. There's only one problem. Starfleet would base them out of DS9. They would put an admiral in charge, and they would kick Sisko out of his office!)

• Just before attempting to collapse the wormhole, Sisko, Dax, Bashir, and Garak stand in the Security office and discuss their plans. Not exactly the best place, given the easy view from the promenade; but hey, it's only happening in their minds.

• At one point two Jem'Haddar get the drop on Sisko and company as they head for the runabout. Garak pretends to have captured the Starfleet officers and then shoots the two Jem'Haddar. There's plenty of time for the second Jem'Haddar to shoot Garak, but he waits patiently to take the phaser blast; but hey, it's only happening in their minds.

EQUIPMENT ODDITIES

• Here's one of those very odd occurences. The Changelings have lamps in their arboretum that look just like lamps seen on Ligon II in the *NextGen* episode "Code of Honor." (The true cause of this conundrum is just too strange to ponder.)

• At one point Kira attempts to send a message to Sisko. The computer tells her it is unable to do so because of external interference at all frequencies. Kira asks about the source of this interference, and the computer replies that the interference comes from "thermal radiation" generated by a subterranean power source. In other words, the computer can't send a message because it's too hot!?

• I believe Odo's office got an upgrade between the second and the third seasons. Now there's a boxful of phasers on the wall inside the little cubbyhole behind his desk. (This is very convenient because our beloved officers need weapons when they are standing in the Security office just before they make a break for the runabout.) What's interesting is that this sequence occurs in their minds. So either the box was added prior to this episode when we weren't looking, or Sisko liked it so much after seeing it in the fantasy that he had O'Brien install it there.

• At the end of the episode Borath, a member of the Dominion, tells Sisko that the *Defiant* is in orbit. One wonders what shape the *Defiant* is in after taking a pounding from the Jem'Haddar. One also wonders why the Jem'Haddar bothered to bring the ship to the planet in the first place. From the sounds of it, Borath didn't expect Sisko and the others to leave the room alive. Did the Dominion intend to study the *Defiant* and unlock the secrets of its gonzo phasers? If so, why would that work be done on the Founders' home world? Surely the Dominion has other worlds on which to carry out this type of research.

• And what about the shuttle that Odo and Kira bring to the Founders' home world? At the end of the program Odo and Kira beam up to the *Defiant*—apparently leaving the shuttle on the surface. Did they remote-pilot it back to the ship?

CONTINUITY AND PRODUCTION PROBLEMS

• To collapse the wormhole, Sisko tells O'Brien, "Attack pattern theta, hard aport." We see the photons firing, but the wormhole stays in the center of the runabout window. I suppose I could wonder why the runabout isn't turning to the left, since Sisko ordered "hard aport"; but hey, it's only happening in their minds!

TRIVIA ANSWERS

1. The *Lexington*.
2. An Arbazan vulture.

THE HOUSE OF QUARK

Star Date: unknown

When a drunken Klingon named Kozak falls on his knife in the bar, Quark decides it is an opportunity for profit and rewrites the event as a fierce battle—a story heartily endorsed by Kozak's brother D'Ghor. Unexpectedly, Kozak's widow Grilka then kidnaps Quark to the Klingon home world, holding a knife to his throat as they wed.

Kozak was head of a great Klingon house. If he had died by accident, the Klingon High Council might have allowed Grilka to become the new head of the house. Using Quark's story, D'Ghor has certified that Kozak died honorably. By Klingon law, the house will pass to him, since Kozak left no male heir. Desperate, Grilka has married her husband's slayer, thereby making it the House of Quark.

Interestingly enough, while looking over the house's records, Quark discovers that D'Ghor has used despicable financial means to weaken the house. When Quark brings this charge before the High Council, D'Ghor challenges him to personal battle. Knowing he can never defeat D'Ghor, Quark throws his bat'leth to the ground, taunting the Klingon to rise to headship over the house by slaughtering an unarmed Ferengi. D'Ghor attempts to do so but Gowron stops the fight, declares D'Ghor without honor, and assigns the house to Grilka. Quark then asks for and quickly receives a divorce.

RUMINATIONS

This is a great episode. It's one of my favorites in the first four seasons of Star Trek: Deep Space Nine. I love the way it thrusts Quark into a situation where he becomes more than his culture and upbringing; the way Grilka's estimation of Quark grows, then turns downward only to be reborn again; the way the creators use the diametrically opposed cultures of the Klingons and the Ferengi to create a setting that allows the characters to move effortlessly through the plot. Very nicely done. (I especially love the culture shock on Gowron's face as Quark tries to explain how D'Ghor has financially undermined the house of Kozak by discussing "gross adjusted assets" and "devaluation of capital income.")

Trivia Questions

1. What is the name of the trusted adviser to the House of Kozak/Quark?

2. Quark claims that his father would wash Rom's mouth out with what if he heard him say that money wasn't everything?

203

By the way, Quark must have ordered one of those personalized screen savers for the terminal in his bar. As he schemes to bring people into his bar by claiming he killed Kozak in a fierce battle, watch the right-hand monitor behind the bar. The word "QUARK'S" wanders by! (Thanks to Jason Allan Haase of Pierce City, Missouri, for pointing this out.)

GREAT LINES

"It's a gift."—Quark to Grilka after she comments that he must be quite a liar.

PLOT OVERSIGHTS

• Many nitpickers found it interesting that no one on the station seems to notice that Quark is missing during this episode! Of course, we don't really know how long he is gone. And maybe he has a habit of disappearing for a day or two at a time. I suppose if we were actually going to pick this nit we would have to consider how long it takes to get from DS9 to the Klingon home world. At least with that piece of information, we'd have some indication how incredulous we should be over the senior staff's apparent indifference toward the disappearance of the station's most prominent "civic leader." Let's see what the episode has to offer concerning clues dealing with the travel time from DS9 to Kronos. Before kidnapping Quark, Grilka injects the Ferengi with a drug to knock him unconscious. In the very next scene, Grilka's adviser Tumek injects Quark with a drug to wake him up. It appears that Quark was asleep throughout the trip. Also, once Grilka

shows up in Council chambers with Quark, D'Ghor decides to reveal Quark's lie about the fierce battle he fought with Kozak. A very short time later—seemingly only a day, possibly two—he has Rom marched into Council chambers. Now, even if we allow that D'Ghor had a ship stationed near DS9 that could pick up Rom and bring him to Kronos, that still allows only a few days for travel time. And a few days would seem about right for Quark's trip to Kronos as well, since he was drugged the entire time. (Unless Grilka put him in stasis, of course.) Here's the problem: If it takes only a few days to get from DS9 to Kronos—even if we assume that the ships carrying the Ferengi are traveling at warp 9—Bajor has to be really close to the Klingon home world in intragalactic terms. Two days at warp 9 will get you only about 10 light-years down the road. What's really interesting is that "The Search, Part I" put Earth only about a week's distance from the station. I guess it's a small galaxy after all. (I know many of you have seen maps drawn of the Federation, the Klingon Empire, the Romulan Empire, and the Cardassian Empire that flat out indicate there is no way the travel times in this episode could be correct. But to the best of my knowledge at the time of this writing there is no canonical map available. If we're going to follow our rules as nitpickers we just have to accept that these territories are really packed this tightly together!)

• With the ever-present Dominion threat, Bajorans begin moving off the station during this episode. Keiko is left with only two students—Jake and

Nog—and makes the painful decision to close the school. To give her something to do, O'Brien initially seeks Sisko's permission to set up an arboretum on the station. The commander agrees, and in short order we see O'Brien designing the arboretum on a padd in the replimat. If this is going to be Keiko's arboretum, wouldn't *she* want to design its layout?

• For a race that despises financial matters and considers ledgers "filthy," they sure do keep accurate records of their transactions. Quark apparently has no trouble tracing back the audit trails on D'Ghor's underhanded dealings with the House of Kozak. (They must buy their accounting software from the Ferengi and hire young Cardassian nubiles to punch the figures in for them.)

• Does anyone else find it odd that the Bajorans have had a civilized society for 500,000 years—according to Picard in "Ensign Ro" *(TNG)*—and yet O'Brien tells Keiko that the Janitza mountains on Bajor have *never* been surveyed before? What have these people been doing all this time!?

CHANGED PREMISES

• Evidently Odo is falling down on the job. According to "Emissary" and "Past Prologue" he doesn't allow weapons on the promenade. Yet, in this episode, Kozak carries a knife into Quark's and it looks like it's in plain view.

• There is an issue that crops up over and over and over again concerning the color of Klingon blood. *Star Trek VI: The Undiscovered Country* clearly establishes that Klingon blood is purplish or lavenderish or

whateverish (I'm not great with colors) but definitely *not* red. In fact, the video version of *Star Trek VI* includes footage of a human assassin dressed up to look like a Klingon. When this assassin dies, Colonel Worf immediately identifies him as non-Klingon because his blood is red. For whatever reason, the creators of the television series have never felt compelled to accede to this convention. In every case, when we see Klingons bleed on television they *always* bleed red. For instance, in this episode, when Kozak falls on his knife, Quark comes away with red blood smeared all over his hand.

• Wow, Bashir certainly has improved his interpersonal communication skills! Just six episodes ago, at the beginning of "Crossover," he was an obnoxious twit who couldn't even take a less-than-subtle hint that Kira didn't want to talk to him. Now he's spouting advice to O'Brien in the replimat that would make Counselor Troi proud.

EQUIPMENT ODDITIES

• While designing the arboretum, O'Brien moves a stylus over the padd. A sound effect indicates that some type of input is being processed, but the screen appears completely static!

CONTINUITY AND PRODUCTION PROBLEMS

• Boy, ya gotta say one thing about D'Ghor: He has really nice lower teeth for a Klingon. His upper set is as gnarly as normal, but that lower set is bright and shiny and white as white can be! If the lower teeth started out like his upper teeth he's had some masterful dental work done on the lower teeth.

I suppose it's just another one of this guy's despicable vices.

• When ruling that Grilka's wedding to Quark will be recognized, Gowron wears his leader's robe. Then the scene cuts to Grilka and D'Ghor for a reaction shot. When it comes back to Gowron he suddenly stands without his robe to pronounce that Kozak's house will now be called the House of Quark. (Yes, there is time for him to shrug it off his shoulders, but there is no sound to indicate the robe hitting the ground, and this is the *only* time in this episode that he appears in the Council chambers without his robe. It almost looks like footage that was hastily reshot.)

• As O'Brien designs Keiko's arboretum in the replimat, Bashir wanders by and peeks over the chief's shoulder. O'Brien notices Bashir's attention and drops his right arm. The shot changes, and suddenly O'Brien's arm is raised.

TRIVIA ANSWERS
1. Tumek.
2. Galcor.

★ EQUILIBRIUM

Star Date: unknown

Trying to discover the reason for Dax's erratic mood swings and disturbing hallucinations, Sisko and Bashir take her back to the Trill home world. Unfortunately, Dr. Renhol, the Symbiosis Commission scientist who works with Dax, can't provide much help. For some reason, Jadzia seems to be rejecting the symbiont. If that happens, the commission will remove the symbiont and place it in another host. Within hours, Jadzia would die.

Dax's problems come from a previous, unknown host named Joran Belar. The commission purged all records of this joining when—six months later—Belar killed one of their doctors. The experience defied the commonly accepted belief that an unsuitable joining would result in the quick death of both host and symbiont. This belief has kept the symbionts from becoming traded merchandise in the Trill culture—since in reality half the population could be joined, not just a very small percentage. In an effort to hide the truth, the commission took the symbiont from Belar, erased its memory, and placed

it in Curzon. Now, after many decades, the memory block is wearing off. Sisko learns the truth and threatens to expose the commission's secret. With no other choice, Dr. Renhol agrees to let Jadzia live and attempt to integrate Jolan's memories.

PLOT OVERSIGHTS

• This episode commences an interesting use of the *Defiant* that will continue through the rest of this season of *Star Trek: Deep Space Nine.* I find nothing in the previous episodes that indicates the Dominion threat has somehow wafted away. Yet, when the mood strikes, Sisko hops on the *Defiant,* takes a few crew members with him, and strolls off to other star systems. Given the poorly armed nature of the station, does this seem right? Doesn't Sisko have a responsibility to protect the lives of the individuals on the station with the best tools at his disposal? How in the galaxy does he know that the Dominion won't try something while he's away? (Yes, I realize that "The Search, Part II" established that the Dominion found out how stubborn Sisko and company could be. Yes, I realize that the Do-

> **Trivia Questions**
>
> 1. What is the name of Joran Belar's brother?
>
> 2. What is the name of the doctor who will prep the new host for Dax?

207

minion knows that if they tried to establish a foothold in the Gamma Quadrant, Sisko would collapse the wormhole. Obviously the Dominion and I don't think alike, because if I were in charge, I would send a fleet of Jem'Haddar ships through the wormhole to blast the station and the *Defiant* to kingdom come—thereby wiping stubborn Sisko and his stubborn company off the face of the galaxy—and then seize control of the entire sector. But then, there wouldn't be a show, would there?)

• The recharacterization of Julian Bashir that began with "The House of Quark" continues in this episode. Now—according to Dax—he's "a very dear man."

• While talking with Joran Belar's brother, Sisko claims that he is "of the Federation Starbase Deep Space 9." In the very next episode he 'fesses up that the station is really a Bajoran space station under Federation control.

• Not a nit, just a further bit of interesting information on Trill psychology. During my review of "Invasive Procedures," I noted that the moral framework for the consciousness of the joined Trill seems to derive solely from the host. This episode provides additional proof for that theory. Dax is placed in Joran, and six months later Joran *kills* a man. The symbiont's response? "Oops, sorry. I guess it's time for a new host." (It's interesting that the Symbiosis Commission seems to completely miss the possibility that the problem might be Dax!)

• I'm a bit confused about what actually happened with Joran. His brother says that the official report from the Symbiosis Commission went as follows: Joran applies for the initiate program. After two years, a doctor on the Symbiosis Commission recommends that Joran be dropped from the program. After being dropped, Joran finds the doctor and kills him. Then Joran is killed while trying to escape. But the brother also says that Joran called him six months before he died and claimed to be joined. From this Sisko deduces that Joran was joined and then killed the doctor. Presumably, after the murder, the Symbioses doctors moved Dax from Joran to Curzon, thereby ending Joran's life.

First, did Joran get a trial before he was put to death? I can't imagine that the Symbiosis Commission would want the publicity such an event would bring, but nothing indicates that Joran was in any danger of rejecting the symbiont. That means the commission took a perfectly healthy—though emotionally disturbed—individual and murdered him by removing the symbiont. Pretty broad powers, don't you think? Second, what *really* happened between Joran and the doctor? Why *did* Joran kill him? (The Symbiosis Commission story is obviously a fake. Joran wasn't dropped from the program. He carried Dax for six months! If the doctor gave Joran a bad recommendation, how did Joran stay in the program? He could not have been dropped and then reapplied. This episode states that Jadzia is the *only* initiate ever to successfully reapply. Also, one bad recommendation from Curzon got Jadzia booted. Wouldn't one bad recommendation from a Symbiosis Commission doctor get Joran booted as well?)

CHANGED PREMISES

• At the beginning of this episode Sisko says that his father owned a restaurant in New Orleans. This piece of information does fit with dialogue in other episodes that describe his father's culinary skills. However, in "A Man Alone," Sisko says that his father used to have supper with his family every evening and try out new recipes. If you own a restaurant, isn't supper one of your busiest times of the day? Did Sisko's father assign the responsibility for his dining establishment to someone else during this time so he could eat with his family? (If so, it is very, *very* commendable. We need more fathers like that in the world.)

• What a difference a season makes. Toward the beginning of the second season—during "Invasive Procedures"—Dax said that only one Trill in ten is joined. In this episode Bashir guesses that only one Trill in a thousand is a *candidate* for joining.

• The dialogue of this episode seems to indicate that Sisko made a deal for Jadzia's life. He wouldn't blab that half the Trill population could be joined if the Symbiosis Commission would allow Jadzia to live. So far, so good. Now, the Symbiosis Commission officially has Joran listed as a murderer, right? If Joran is recognized as a murderer, you probably don't want people to know that he once hosted Dax, right? So the Symbiosis Commission probably asked Sisko, Dax, and Bashir to keep quiet about it, right? Evidently one of these "rights" is wrong because Quark knows about Joran in "Facets."

EQUIPMENT ODDITIES

• The user interface in the infirmary seems to know just when Bashir is pressing a panel because he wants to do something, and when he is just resting his hand there for support. Wanting to look over Dax's medical history, Bashir walks over to a panel, places his hand flat over a cluster of buttons, and the display changes immediately. Moments later he picks up his hand, moves it just a bit, lays it back down on all but two of the buttons, and the display stays the same. Are those the only two buttons that do anything?

• The system software on the Trill home world monitors could really use a "window resizing" feature. Several times we see large monitors, but the display fills only a small portion of the screen. The *twentieth-century* Macintosh operating system allows the user to zoom out a given window to fill the available screen real estate. (Actually, this resize feature is available on most windowing software systems—even Windows 95!)

CONTINUITY AND PRODUCTION PROBLEMS

• Instead of using the established *Star Trek* tradition of three-dimensional chess as a game Sisko and Dax can play, the creators of *DS9* opted to return to the same game of chess that we play today. I believe "Playing God" is the first time we see this happen. Frankly, it's a nice change. The game of chess has been around for well over a thousand years. No doubt it will be around for at least another four hundred. In "Equilibrium" the creators return to a chess game between Sisko and Dax to highlight Dax's odd behavior. After Sisko makes a valid move that puts her king in check, Dax first accuses Sisko of cheating and then sweeps the pieces off the board before storming out. Interestingly enough, the chess board is oriented the wrong way! According to the traditional setup, the corner square to the right of each player should be white. If it's black, the king and the queen won't be placed in the correct orientation at the start of the game for their respective colors. (The easy way to remember this is: "White on the right and queen on her color.") In case you're wondering if the rules have changed in the future, the board is oriented correctly in "Playing God."

• Just before entering a pool where the symbionts breed at the end of this episode, Jadzia drops her cover-up on the ground. She walks down into the pool to have a psychic meeting with Joran and welcome his memories into her own. As she looks straight ahead—with her wrap visible behind her—the camera angle changes to show Joran emerging from the water. When the scene returns to Jadzia, we see that the cover-up has disappeared. In fact, once the camera pulls out a bit we find that Jadzia—at some point when we weren't looking—executed a quarter turn to the right! (There is time for her to do this. It just looks funny.)

TRIVIA ANSWERS
1. Yolad Belar.
2. Dr. Torvin.

Star Date: unknown

Kira awakes on Cardassia to find herself transformed into an Obsidian Order agent. A Cardassian named Entek tells her that, ten years ago, the Order kidnapped a Bajor resistance fighter named Kira Nerys. They took the woman's memories and transferred them to one Iliana Ghemor. After surgically altering her to look like Kira, the Order sent her to Bajor. Entek claims the Order has given Kira a drug that will cause Iliana's memories to reemerge. Then he introduces Iliana's father, a high-ranking member of Central Command: Legate Tekeny Ghemor. Of course, Kira steadfastly refuses to believe what they say, and Iliana's memories do not reemerge even after she watches a recording made by Iliana to assist with the debriefing. At this, Entek says he must have the information Kira possesses and hints at an Obsidian Order interrogation.

Ghemor refuses to allow it, arranging for Kira to covertly leave Cardassia. Discovering that Ghemor is a dissident, Kira deduces Entek's plan. The Obsidian Order official brought her here not to extract information but to use Ghemor's love for his daughter to trick the legate into helping Kira escape and thereby incriminate himself. Immediately Entek bursts in to arrest them, but Sisko, Odo, and an initially reluctant Garak come to the rescue—returning Kira and Ghemor safely to DS9 .

Trivia Questions

1. What is the exhibit number of Kira's fake corpse in Obsidian Order Central Archives?

2. Who grants Ghemor political sanctuary?

RUMINATIONS

*T*his episode begins with Kira receiving a message from a Bajoran woman named Alenis Grem. She is conducting a study on the Elemspur Detention Center for the Bajoran Central Archives. She wants to talk with Kira about the time Kira spent at Elemspur. Kira doesn't remember being at Elemspur, but she eventually tracks down an Elemspur cellmate who supposedly remembers her. Uncertain why her memories do not correspond to the records, Kira goes to Bajor to investigate. At this point the Cardassians kidnap her. At the end of the episode, Kira theorized that her "cellmate" was actually a Cardassian agent and that he was the one who altered the records. Some nitpickers found this a less than satisfactory wrap-up. They found the scheme to kidnap Kira needlessly convoluted. They assumed that the cellmate planted records at some time in the long-ago past and then had to wait until they were discovered randomly. I think the answer might be a bit simpler while at the same time demonstrating how fiendishly clever the Obsidian Order can be. Wanting to lure Kira from the station, the cellmate found an ongoing research project and studied the archivist to determine what records she would review next. Then he simply planted the records for the archivist to find—records that put Kira at Elemspur and himself in confinement with her. In short order he knew Kira would call. No doubt you're thinking: Why is Phil spending all this time explaining away a nit for the creators? Rule of Acquisition 76: "Every once in a while, declare peace."

PLOT OVERSIGHTS

• As noted in the rumination above, the episode opens with an elaborate scheme to lure Kira off the station by confusing her with records and testimony to show she was interred at the Elemspur Detention Center when her memories of that time place her in the hills of Dahkur Province. For some reason, Kira doesn't try to locate her fellow freedom fighters and get their recollections. No doubt they would substantiate her story. (We learn that they are still alive in the episode "Shakaar.")

• The capabilities of the Obsidian Order really do astound. Evidently they can change a Cardassian into a Bajoran. One would think this process difficult. The large neck support struc-

tures would have to be completely removed surgically and rebuilt with Bajoran musculature. The forehead would have to be belt-sanded smooth, as would the ears, chin, and nose. And the hair! Hair would have to be surgically implanted to bring the hairline down on the forehead to match the Bajoran configuration. Of course, the whole issue of hair does raise a question with Kira. She speaks of surgical alteration to describe the process the Obsidian Order used to turn her into a Cardassian. Does this mean that the Order regrafted her scalp so that the thick black mane she wears all during this episode is actually her hair and not a wig? (For the deception to work, it would almost have to be, wouldn't it?) No wonder Kira is torqued. Thankfully, Bashir is just as skilled as the Cardassians. By the end of the show, Kira is back to her radiant self. She even has her hairline lowered to its appropriate place. (This type of mission must be murder on the old body!)

• Although no piece of dialogue indicates that it happened, the Obsidian Order must have used drugs to extract information from Kira before they brought her to Ghemor's home. It's the only explanation for the following scene. Entek is trying to convince Kira that she's a Cardassian. He has the corpse of Kira Nerys transported to his location. As expected, this shocks Kira. Then Entek tells Kira about the time she was doing long-range recognizance in the Bestri woods and she shot a mother hara cat nursing its young because she thought it was a Cardassian. Even more stunned, Kira says she never told that story to anyone, at which point Entek gloats that the Order created the memory and placed it in her mind. See the problem? Since Bashir supposedly certifies that Kira *is* Bajoran at the end of the episode, the simplest explanation is that the Obsidian Order drugged her and extracted the story before they brought her to Ghemor.

• Once again, Sisko flies off with DS9's only real defense—though the station is still under threat of Dominion attack.

• The creators set aside the laws of physics when it comes to our shapeshifting constable yet another time. At the end of the episode Sisko walks in with a bag in one hand and throws the bag behind Entek. This bag then morphs into Odo. Need I remind you of the "You're heavier than you look" comment from "Vortex"? Mass is mass. If Odo took his mass and squashed it down to the size of a handbag, he'd still weigh the same.

• Speaking of the scene where Odo makes like a bag, Sisko enters and walks toward Entek. Entek stands facing Sisko. Kira is behind Entek and off to Entek's left. One of Entek's men stands on the opposite side of Kira with a weapon pointed at her left side. His entire body is rotated to face Kira so he has a clear view of the area behind Entek. Interestingly enough, this is precisely the area where Sisko throws Odo and precisely the area where Odo shapeshifts into humanoid form. Yet for

some reason, this guy stands, watching Odo morph, and *never* thinks to warn his superior!

EQUIPMENT ODDITIES
• These Cardassians build really smart doors. Shortly after Kira arrives on Cardassia, Entek escorts Ghemor into a room to meet his daughter. The doors open. The pair enters. The doors stay open. Conversation follows. Entek leaves. The doors stay open. Conversation follows. Ghemor leaves. *Now* the doors close. (As I said, smart doors.)

CONTINUITY AND PRODUCTION PROBLEMS
• As the *Defiant* makes its way into Cardassian space, Gul Benial of the Eighth Order hails Sisko and demands to inspect the ship. With a holofilter in place on the communications channel, Sisko announces that the *Defiant* is actually the Kobheerian freighter *Rak-Miunis*. The footage showing the Kobheerian captain announcing this fact actually comes from the beginning of "Duet."

• Linny Marcus of Brookline, Massachusetts, found it amazing that Kira—confined for at least two days while undergoing intense emotional pressure—would take the time every morning to craft her hair into the same beautifully intricate pattern it had when she first awoke as a Cardassian.

TRIVIA ANSWERS
1. S1983l.
2. The Mathenite government.

Star Date: supplemental

When Quark finds a baby among some salvage he's purchased, Bashir's preliminary exam reveals a very high metabolic rate, but everything else seems normal. By the next day, however, the baby has grown to the size of an eight- or nine-year-old humanoid and shortly afterward matures to a young man. He is a Jem'Haddar—the product of very advanced genetic engineering by the Founders of the Dominion. He is strong, quick, intelligent, and resourceful, totally focused on fighting and killing. He is also genetically addicted to a very specific enzyme. Apparently the Founders did this to ensure the loyalty of the Jem'Haddar, although this appears to be a last line of defense. The Founders have also genetically imprinted on the Jem'Haddar a deference for Changelings. Only Odo can control him.

Feeling responsible for what the Founders have done to the Jem'Haddar, Odo tries to encourage the Jem'Haddar soldier to become more than his programming. It doesn't work. The young man is only interested in

Trivia Questions

1. What is the name of the nurse who calls Bashir to the infirmary when the young Jem'Haddar runs onto the promenade?

2. What ship is coming to pick up the young Jem'Haddar?

returning to his people, certain that everyone else is his enemy and should be killed. Though Starfleet wants the Jem'Haddar soldier for study, Sisko lets Odo take him home to the Gamma Quadrant.

PLOT OVERSIGHTS

• Although the episode doesn't say for sure, it seems to indicate a fairly short amount of time—half a day or so—for the Jem'Haddar soldier to go from an infant to the size of a stocky eight- or nine-year-old. One of the first things this child says is, "I need food." No doubt! In fact, to maintain that type of growth, one would think that the child would have to be shoveling in the nutrients almost constantly! My neighbor's son, James Strathdee, is about the size of the actor who plays the young Jem'Haddar lad. If their weights are comparable, this Jem'Haddar person has gained about one hundred pounds in half a day! That mass has to come from somewhere. You can't just breathe it out of the air. (Although I have heard several claims from women that even the smell of chocolate makes them gain weight. I consider this apocryphal.) Even allowing for the complete metabolization of everything ingested, can you imagine eating *one hundred pounds* of food in twelve or thirteen hours?

• Obviously I'm not as bighearted as Sisko. The subplot of the episode deals with Jake's dating relationship to a Dabo girl named Marta. Jake's sixteen. Marta's twenty. Picking up a plot thread begun the previous season, Sisko invites her to dinner. He intends to end the relationship. When dinner arrives, Sisko learns that his son writes poetry and plays domjot. Apparently this is enough to convince him that Jake's relationship with Marta isn't such a bad thing after all. If it were me and I found out my teenage boy was dating a twenty-year-old woman who worked in a gambling establishment wearing the outfits we routinely see on Dabo girls, I can guarantee you it wouldn't matter if he was writing *War and Peace* and could run the table in a hyperspace juan'chi tournament playing against fifth-level temporal stasis masters. That relationship would end. *Immediately!*

• When Bashir is unable to replicate the specific enzyme that young Jem'Haddar needs, O'Brien finds a supply of it among the wreckage that Quark purchased. The damaged box contains a pump—worn on the chest—and ten vials of the liquid. In short order, Bashir attaches the pump and surgically implants the feeding tube into the young man's neck. Evidently the Founders *dramatically* improved the humanoid circulatory system when designing the Jem'Haddar. Supposedly the tube patches di-

rectly into the young man's carotid artery. Yet every time we see the clear tube it has bubbles running through it! With humans this would be almost instantly lethal. Amazingly enough, the young Jem'Haddar seems fine.

• Attempting to find the correct dosage for the enzyme, Bashir starts with 2 milligrams per minute and then increases the dosage to "3 cc's." I believe "cc" stands for cubic centimeters. Why is Bashir switching measurement systems in midstream?

• Whatever the measurement system, that stuff seems to be pumping through that tube at a pretty good clip if the bubbles are any indication. It appears to be pumping a lot faster than 3 cubic centimeters a minute. At the rate it seems to be moving, the pump would blow through one of those little vials of liquid in no time.

• So in other words—since the Jem'Haddar are absolutely dependent on this drug, all you have to do is yank out this feeder tube and the guy is in trouble? Does this sound familiar? Sorta like the inherent weakness we discovered about the Borg in the *NextGen* episode "Descent, Part II"?

• Toward the end of the episode, Sisko tells Odo that a starship will soon arrive for the Jem'Haddar soldier. At this point the young man comes flashing into Sisko's office in a blur, apparently invisible until he slows down. The creators probably will answer this question in the future, but I wonder: Is this ability physically inherent, or does the pump have something to do with it?

• Leaving Sisko's office, the young Jem'Haddar takes Odo with him, suggesting that both of them return to the Gamma Quadrant, where they belong. Odo goes willingly and tries to convince the young man one last time to rise above his genetic programming. He even offers to flee with the Jem'Haddar into unexplored space to give him the chance to be something other than a killer. During this discussion, Sisko and a Security team materialize near an airlock. Sisko tells his team to wait for his command to fire. Why? Isn't this the reason phasers have a stun setting? Shouldn't "shoot first and ask questions later" be the policy when dealing with a dangerous individual like this?

• Eventually Sisko lets Odo leave with the young man. Sisko agrees with Odo that if the Jem'Haddar soldier boards the starship that's coming to get him, the young man will either kill a lot of innocent people or be killed himself. Doesn't the transporter work on this guy? Why can't you just beam him into confinement? And what about drugs?

• During a log entry—heard at the end of this episode with the ever-illuminating star date "supplemental"— Sisko says that Starfleet has expressed "disappointment" over the missed opportunity to learn more about the Jem'Haddar. *Disappointment?!* I would imagine Admiral Nechayev had a wee bit stronger response than mere disappointment. The Jem'Haddar must be on the "A" list of potential threats to the Federation. The possibility of learning more about this threat was *invaluable*. (No doubt Sisko is being a bit euphemistic in his language.)

CONTINUITY AND PRODUCTION PROBLEMS

• If the closed captioning is to be believed, Marta changed the spelling of her name since the previous season. In "Sanctuary" and "Playing God" her name was spelled, "Mardah." (Of course, Marta might be a completely different Dabo girl from the Mardah mentioned in the second season. But...*two* Dabo girls in as many years?! As O'Brien mutters to himself during this episode, "Godspeed, Jake.")

TRIVIA ANSWERS

1. Hortak.
2. USS *Constellation*.

CIVIL DEFENSE

Star Date: unknown

O'Brien accidently initiates a Cardassian Security program, locking himself, Sisko, and Jake into an old ore-processing unit on the station. They find a way out, but not before the program becomes convinced that revolting Bajoran workers have escaped from ore processing. It puts the entire station on alert—locking doors, engaging force fields, cutting off communications. When the crew in Ops tries to help their commander, the program decides that Bajorans have commandeered the station. As designed, it initiates an autodestruct sequence.

Unexpectedly, Gul Dukat beams on board. He received a recorded communiqué transmitted by the Security program and has come over to take a look. Having designed the program, Dukat offers Kira a trade. If she will allow him to post a garrison on DS9, he will terminate the autodestruct. She refuses. When Dukat tries to beam back to his ship, the program traps him on the station as well. It informs him that he has lost control of the situation and is obviously attempting to flee in an act of cowardice. It also deletes all his override codes. Dukat wasn't aware of this addition to the program by Central Command. Working together, Dukat, Kira, and Dax reinstate communications and drop the force fields, thereby allowing Sisko to nullify the effects of the autodestruct.

Trivia Questions

1. O'Brien plans to convert Ore Processing Unit 5 into what?

2. Which of Quark's uncles owns thirty bars?

RUMINATIONS

This is a fun episode. It has some very nice turns in it—especially when Dukat discovers that he is trapped on the station as well!

PLOT OVERSIGHTS

• After becoming trapped in ore processing, Sisko, O'Brien, and Jake must escape through a maintenance hatch near the ceiling. Since the hatch latches from the inside, Jake goes into the machinery. Of course, he eventually gets the hatch open, but not before the computer begins releasing deadly neurocine gas. Up to this point, Sisko and O'Brien have waited to climb up to the maintenance hatch. I realize that I may not measure up to the brave and valiant standards of a Starfleet officer, but I think I would have climbed to the maintenance hatch while Jake was dorking around with the release lever so I'd be ready to get out of there in a hurry. (I suppose I could mention that Sisko seems to consider his life more important than O'Brien's. When the hatch opens, Sisko immediately starts climbing, as opposed to letting his subordinate go first!)

• After escaping from the neurocine gas, Sisko, O'Brien, and Jake climb up to a small room where Bajorans used to separate uridium ore from rock. The three find a locked door and attempt to use an ore cart to bash it open. When that fails, Sisko looks down into the cart and asks if they can do anything with the ore inside. He picks up a piece and comments that uridium is very unstable. Wait a minute! Let me get this straight. Sisko knew that the ore inside the cart was unstable and he left it in there while the trio used it as a *battering ram*?! (Granted, O'Brien adds that unprocessed ore needs a strong electrical charge to set it off, but Sisko seems oblivious to this fact at first.)

• After the computer clamps down on the station, Garak wanders up to Ops and uses his access code to temporarily drop the force field on the door. Since he can move around the station, Kira suggests he help evacuate the habitat ring. The computer is about to release neurocine gas and kill everyone in their quarters. Garak makes the weak excuse that the force fields reinstate the moment he goes through them. That may be, but couldn't he turn sideways and allow at least one person to go through with him? Or will the computer sense that he's cheating and not allow it?

• To escape the ore separation room,

Sisko, O'Brien, and Jake stack uridium ore against the door. The rocks sit in a long, flat row at the base of the threshold. Interestingly enough, when the uridium detonates, it leaves a nice circular hole in the door. Uridium must have a fascinating blast pattern to it!

• After igniting the uridium ore with a live electrical wire, Sisko crawls forward with said wire in hand. Just before exiting into the next room, he drops the end of the wire into a bunch of uridium ore chunks. Does this seem like a good idea? If an electrical charge ignites this stuff, why would you want to put the end of a live wire next to the ore? (Yes, I realize that the trio pulverize the rocks to make a fuse, and it *is* possible the electrical charge won't ignite the uridium unless it's pulverized. But is Sisko *absolutely* certain that no uridium dust remains around the blast site?)

• I am ever astounded by the halcyon attitude displayed by Starfleet officers facing certain death. Near the end of the program, Kira tells Sisko that the station will explode in about ten minutes. In that time he must disable the main fusion reactor. After hearing this disturbing piece of news, Sisko, O'Brien, and Jake walk purposefully down a short hall and turn right. The next time we see the trio, they are strolling along in a hall, wondering if they'll have time to disable the reactor. Then they get some equipment and start walking only a tad faster. Then they find that the corridor is blocked. When Jake suggests going around, Sisko says they don't have time. Does anyone wish to venture a *guess* why they don't have time? Could it *possibly* be that they should have been *sprinting* down the halls instead of strolling? Do you think *that* might have made some difference? I suppose they know that even if they did sprint down the halls they would still save the station just in the nick of time, so they might as well conserve their energy.

• Gul Dukat arrives in a warship and beams over to the station. Oddly enough, that's the last we ever hear of the warship. I wonder what the crew was doing the entire time Dukat was trapped on the station. (Maybe hoping for his demise and waiting to celebrate their promotions?)

CHANGED PREMISES

• After arriving in Ops, Garak comments that it is ironic that the only place in the galaxy that still recognizes his codes is a Bajoran station. Either Garak is experiencing a bit of short-term memory loss or he's just grousing. His codes worked to deflect the attentions of a Gul as the *Defiant* snuck into Cardassian territory during "Second Skin" only two episodes ago.

EQUIPMENT ODDITIES

• Didn't O'Brien say in "The Forsaken" that he was going to give the computer a "root canal"—that he was going to rebuild it from the ground up? It's interesting that he never came across this anti-insurgency program. (I also could wonder why no one has come across all the extra force field generators and poison gas emitters that the crew finds so surprising, but...I believe I shall postpone.)

• At one point a force field catches Dax's hands in Ops; Bashir grabs the medical kit and diagnoses her with second-degree burns. A bit later he says he wishes he could do more, but he'll have to wait until he can get her to the infirmary. This is very odd. In "Invasive Procedures," O'Brien gets shot with a phaser. Bashir grabs the Ops medical kit and pulls out a dermal regenerator to help the wound heal. Doesn't it seem like a dermal regenerator would work on energy burns if it worked on a phaser blast wound?

• Trying to override the anti-insurgency program, Garak comments that even if he could change Dukat's Security codes to his own, the computer would scan his DNA and realize that he isn't Dukat. This seems like a very sensible feature for the computer to have given how easy it is for someone to steal a Security code. But what about "Tribunal"? Did the Cardassian spy disable this feature when he used O'Brien's voice to gain access to the weapons locker?

• I find it strange that all the other doors in the station have force fields over them, but when Sisko, O'Brien, and Jake blast a hole out of the ore separation room door, they can crawl through. (Of course, if they couldn't, DS9 would blow up and that would be the end of the series!)

CONTINUITY AND PRODUCTION PROBLEMS

• At one point Kira gets tired of playing nicey-nice with the station and she blasts a door release. Bashir pushes the lever of the door up and then moves to push the door open. In the very next shot, the lever is back down again. (Well...maybe it flopped down.) What's really interesting is this: In the process of opening the door, Bashir's left shoulder clearly goes all the way across the threshold into the hallway, but when Kira tries to go through, a force field stops her cold at the door. (Do the force fields stop only Cardassians, Bajorans, and Odo? Is there ever a place in this episode where we see a force field impeding a human? Can Bashir stroll out of Ops anytime he feels like it?)

• Believing that rebel Bajoran workers have broken into Ops, the program uses the replicator to materialize some type of phaser weapon in the replicator. (By the way, the sequence showing the replicator first making the weapon and then *charging its power cells* is very nicely done!) This weapon targets any non-Cardassian in Ops, sending out energy beams that crash into walls and hit terminals. It's very exciting, but it seems like there are a few places where the beams shoot across Ops in the wrong direction. (Before I begin, I will admit that I'm not an expert on the location of everything in Ops. Just to get a feel for the room, I finally had to break down and draw a map whose details were gleaned from several different episodes. I am more than willing to admit that there might be another wall-mounted replicator in the main area, but I've never seen it, and the rest of

this nit *depends* on the fact that only one exists. Okay? On to the nit.) For instance, shortly after the weapon materializes, we see Garak and Bashir at Dax's station. An energy bolt flies toward them, shooting over their right shoulders and hitting the region of the transporter station. This is most unusual, since the replicator that houses the weapon is on the same wall as the transporter station. In other words, it is behind and to the right of Garak and Bashir, yet the blast comes from in front of them. Moments later, Bashir crawls down to the center table in Ops. He is huddled on the side opposite the transporter station and using the table as a barricade. He tries to reach for Kira's phaser when an energy blast angles in from the left side of the screen and strikes behind him. Yet as nearly as I can tell, the wall-mounted replicator should be directly in front of him and a bit to the right. Are these energy beams ricocheting off the walls?

• When Dukat prepares to flick Sisko's baseball, his index finger rests horizontally. Then the shot changes and suddenly his finger is vertical.

• Odo finally worked through his "belt" phase. In this episode his uniform goes back to the style we saw for the first two seasons. (See "The Search, Part I.")

TRIVIA ANSWERS

1. A deuterium refinery.
2. Frin.

Star Date: 48423.2

While exploring the Gamma Quadrant, Sisko and crew detect an odd gravometric disturbance. Arriving at the source, they watch a planet materialize before their eyes. It is Meridian, a planet that periodically shifts between this dimension and a noncorporeal one. Only in this dimension do the thirty inhabitants on the surface age, and only in this one can they reproduce. Unfortunately, the time spent in this dimension has been gradually shrinking for some unknown reason. This time they will have only twelve days before shifting back. If the trend continues, Meridian will cease to exist.

Sisko offers to help investigate the phenomenon. With information gathered from a probe, the *Defiant*'s crew trace the problem to an imbalance in Meridian's sun and devise a method to stabilize the time between two worlds. In the meantime, Dax and a Meridian inhabitant named Doral fall in love. At first Doral talks of going back to DS9 with Dax, but with Meridian's new lease on life he feels compelled to stay and help the others rebuild their society. Dax decides to stay behind with him. Sadly, a six-hour quantum scrambling of Dax's molecules in the transporter fails to produce the proper matrix for shifting, and Dax is left behind when the planet disappears.

Trivia Questions

1. What is the vintage on the Kandora champagne Quark gives to Kira?

2. To whom does Kira give her free holosuite visit?

PLOT OVERSIGHTS

• Near the beginning of the episode Sisko makes a log entry in which he states that despite the Dominion threat, he has convinced Starfleet that exploration of the Gamma Quadrant should continue. First, I believe Third Talak'Talan of the Jem'Haddar in "The Jem'Haddar" told the crew of DS9 that the Dominion would be offended if anyone came through the wormhole. (If you doubt it, you can refer to my review of that episode for a direct quote. See, I told you I'd be referring to it! Wink, wink.) Evidently neither Sisko nor the Federation care about offending the Dominion. This is terminally stupid. Second, why has Sisko—once again—left the station he commands *undefended*? (A bit bored with DS9, are we? Not enough excitement to keep the commander happy, maybe?) Third, why are Sisko and company performing a star system mapping mission? Doesn't Starfleet have science ships to do this stuff? (Oh, wait: I guess Starfleet probably wouldn't *want* to send a science vessel into the Gamma Quadrant because it wouldn't stand a chance if it encountered a Jem'Haddar patrol. I guess if you are going to do a mapping mission in *heavily guarded enemy territory* you really *do* need a warship!)

CHANGED PREMISES

• At one point Doral comes to the *Defiant* for the launch of a probe to investigate Meridian's star. Studying Dax as she studies her console, Doral asks his newfound love if she always bites her lower lip when she concentrates. Dax says she supposes she does. Obviously this is just oogly-googly love talk because yours truly has checked and I cannot find one instance prior to this episode where Dax bites her lower lip in concentration! (I admit it. That one was needlessly excessive picayune nitpicking. But hey, it was fun doing the research! *Just* ...joking!)

• So Dax beams down to this planet, meets this guy named Doral, spends a little more than a week with him, and she's ready to abandon her career and leave all her friends? This seems like a far cry from the Dax we met at the beginning of this series. (A pleasantly improved "far cry," I'll grant you, but a far cry nonetheless.) In "A Man Alone" Dax gave Bashir the cooldown routine by stating that Trill don't view romance the same as humans do. Trill—according to our lovely science officer—attempt to live on a higher plane. (I suspect that it is some kind

of "spot-counting" plane, since that topic comes up several times during this episode!)

• My estimation of Quark's covert intelligence-gathering ability dropped several notches during this episode. In "The Collaborator" Kira and Odo ask Quark to break into the Vedek Assembly's records. Quark appears to accomplish this task with great subtlety. Yet in this episode Quark approaches a similar problem in a very blatant and obvious manner. A bit of explanation. The subplot of this episode deals with an individual named Tiron. Tiron is smitten with Kira. He tried to initiate a relationship with the real Kira, but she gave him the brush-off—claiming that she already had a lover, Odo! (By the way, I believe Odo's reaction in this episode to Kira taking his hand during this little charade is the first hint we get that our dear shape shifter has fallen hard for the feisty Bajoran freedom fighter.) Discouraged only slightly by the news that Kira is "taken," Tiron goes to Quark and orders a custom holodeck program featuring a true-to-life reproduction of Kira. (At least physically. Tiron presumably wants Quark to reprogram her so that she finds him attractive.) At first Quark attempts to capture Kira's image with a holoimager. When that fails, he breaks into the station records and extracts her personal information. One would expect a bit more finesse. Odo and Kira have already apprehended him for attempting to take Kira's picture. They are obviously suspicious about his plans. Why steal only Kira's information? Why not copy the information on all the senior staff?

• Just before Dax runs off with Doral, Sisko comes to her quarters on the *Defiant* to talk with her about her departure. At one point he consoles himself with the statement that he's never known Jadzia to do anything without thinking it through. Sisko must have forgotten about the events in "Blood Oath." In that episode Sisko tries to talk Dax out of running off with three Klingons to wreak vengeance on their blood enemy. (Just so you get the drift of what's involved here: Part of the ceremony will involve cutting out the Albino's heart and eating it as he watches.) During this conversation, Sisko asks if Dax thinks she's really capable of murdering in cold blood. Dax replies that she doesn't know—that there's only one way to find out. Does this sound like the response of a person who doesn't do anything without thinking it through? Isn't Dax merely acting on the emotions of the moment and hoping that everything will turn out for the best?

• This episode establishes once and for all that the Dax symbiont has no problem with transporters. You might recall that the Trill symbiont Odan in "The Host" *(TNG) couldn't* be transported without fatal injuries. In contrast, the Dax symbiont in this episode spends six hours getting its molecules scrambled in the transporter and it's fine.

EQUIPMENT ODDITIES

• The doors on the *Defiant* demonstrate their sensitivity in this episode. In the last scene, Sisko comes to tell a grieving Dax that—once they beamed her back to the ship—Merid-

ian shifted normally into its noncorporeal dimension. Dax opens the door to her quarters, receives the information, and tells Sisko that she needs some time. Considerately, Sisko leaves. Almost immediately, Dax—who was standing right next to the door during this entire conversation—begins moving to the other side of the room. Oddly enough, the door closes, even though Dax is moving right beside it. (It must have sensed her despair and realized that she couldn't possibly turn and walk out into the corridor. By the way, several nitpickers have wondered why the creators don't put sensors on the doors and make them truly automatic instead of manually operated by stagehands. If the doors were automatic, they would open at the wrong times and disrupt dialogue! No doubt it would drive both the actors and the directors crazy.)

CONTINUITY AND PRODUCTION PROBLEMS

• Near the end of the program, Sisko, Bashir, and O'Brien—standing on the bridge of the *Defiant*—watch Meridian begin to phase. From behind, we see Bashir lean sideways and place his left elbow on the headrest of the chair occupied by O'Brien. Then the shot changes, and Bashir suddenly stands upright.

TRIVIA ANSWERS

1. 2368. (Kandora champagne must age very rapidly. According to the established chronology, this episode occurs in the year 2371, making the champagne only three years old.)
2. Ensign Quintana.

DEFIANT

Star Date: unknown

osing as Commander Wil Riker, Thomas Riker (see the *NextGen* episode "Second Chances") kidnaps Kira and hijacks the *Defiant*. Apparently Tom has become involved with the Maquis and intends to use it for their cause. Now a real danger exists that Cardassian Central Command will send ships into the demilitarized zone, using the incident to destroy the Maquis once and for all. Because of this, Sisko goes to Cardassia Prime with Gul Dukat to help him locate the ship.

On the *Defiant*, Tom heads for the Orias System. The Obsidian Order has been covertly building a fleet of warships there, though Cardassian law prohibits them from doing so. Tom intends to expose their activities. Much to Gul Dukat's surprise, several mysterious warships blockade the *Defiant* once it comes within sensor range of the system. At this, Sisko and Dukat strike a deal. In exchange for allowing the *Defiant* to return to DS9 with Kira and Tom's coconspirators, Dukat will receive the ship's sensor logs of the Orias System. The logs will give Central Command evidence to use against the Obsidian Order. Also, Tom Riker will stand trial on Cardassia for leading the raid, receiving a life sentence. Tom agrees to the deal, and Kira returns the *Defiant* to the station.

Trivia Questions

1. What is the name of Dukat's son?

2. Who commands the *Kraxon*?

RUMINATIONS

To hijack the Defiant, *Tom talks Kira into giving him a tour of the ship. On board, they find chief O'Brien. O'Brien begins his usual merry greeting, but Tom angrily cuts him off, stating that he has nothing to say to the chief. "I think you know why," Tom then asserts. O'Brien leaves, bewildered. Many nitpickers expressed similar feelings, uncertain what O'Brien had done to Tom or Wil Riker to garner such a response. Personally, I don't think there was anything O'Brien had done in the past. Tom just needed some way to throw O'Brien off balance until he could steal the ship. He had obviously been avoiding O'Brien, but once faced with a meeting, he just barked at the chief, knowing that O'Brien would respect his superior officer and leave quietly.*

PLOT OVERSIGHTS

• Paul C. Jensen of La Grange, Illinois, assures me that during his Navy days, a ship never had fewer than 25 percent of its personnel on board no matter what was happening. Yet when Kira gives Tom the tour, it appears that the ship is deserted—aside from the soon-to-be-leaving O'Brien.

• After admitting that the *Defiant* has a cloak, Sisko is quick to inform Dukat and the Obsidian Order observer Korinas that the Jem'Haddar were able to penetrate the cloak using an antiproton beam of some type. This seems to be a very handy piece of information, and the Cardassians use it to their benefit. Strangely enough, Sisko fails to mention that a cloak ship traveling at warp emits a slight subspace variance (a fact revealed in "The Search, Part I").

• Apparently Sisko is bilingual. On Cardassia Prime he asks to see sensor information on a ship that the Cardassians believe is the *Defiant*. The information comes onto the screen in what looks like Cardassian script, yet Sisko can read it and deduce that the ship is not the *Defiant*! (Actually, the ability to read Cardassian *would* be very helpful in Sisko's present position. Still, I found this revelation surprising—given that the creators have never had a bit of dialogue to support this proposition.)

• Having unhappily discovered that the Cardassians can penetrate the cloak of the *Defiant* with an antiproton beam, Tom tells the woman at the helm to adjust the cloak so this won't be possible. Evidently she does this with ease. Maybe she would be available to give O'Brien a few pointers. In "The Search, Part I," this antiproton beam seemed to confound everyone.

• To gain control of the *Defiant,* Tom asks Kira to release the bridge stations. She does so with a simple verbal command. Later, however, Tom allows her to sit behind him on the bridge, free as a bird and apparently free to speak her mind anytime she feels like it. Did Tom change *all* the emergency codes for this ship? Did he actually have the clearance to do that? Wouldn't there be a possibility that Kira could pull the same thing Riker did in "Power Play" *(TNG)* and "Rascals" *(TNG)* when he gave the computer a simple order that thwarted the *Enterprise*'s presumed hijackers? Note also that a bit later Tom allows Kira to walk up beside his chair and actually place her fingers on the control panel that sits on the port side of the captain's chair. This does not seem wise.

• Disclosing his real plan, Tom whispers it to Kira. Why? Is there anyone on this ship who doesn't know what he or she is there to do?

• At one point Sisko deduces that Tom and the *Defiant* are heading toward the Orias System. He suggests that Dukat send a ship there just in case. Dukat agrees. Then Obsidian Order observer Korinas tells Dukat that any ship entering the Orias System will be destroyed. Dukat's reaction? He asks if the Obsidian Order would really fire on Cardassian ships. This seems a very strange response, given a tidbit of information revealed several minutes later. According to Dukat—in dialogue toward the end of the episode—the Obsidian Order is "expressly forbidden" from having military equipment of any kind. If the Obsidian Order is forbidden to have military equipment, they shouldn't be able to fire on ships entering the Orias System in the first place, right? So instead of amazement that the Obsidian Order would fire on Cardassian ships, shouldn't Dukat be stunned that Korinas would claim that the Obsidian Order even has the *ability to fire on anything* in the first place?

CHANGED PREMISES

• During "The Maquis, Part II," Sisko made a deal with Gul Dukat. Dukat would help Sisko stop the weapons smuggling from Central Command to the Cardassian colonists inside the demilitarized zone; in return, Sisko would stop the Maquis. Apparently Sisko has yet to live up to his end of the bargain because the Maquis are still viable.

• This episode provides some background concerning the relationships of the Detapa Council (Cardassian civilian leadership), Central Command (the Cardassian military), and the Obsidian Order (the Cardassian spies). After Korinas threatens that any ships entering the Orias System will be destroyed, Dukat consults with Central Command, but no one can get any information out of the Obsidian Order. After receiving this report from Dukat, Sisko asks to whom does the Obsidian Order report. In theory, Dukat says, they report to the Detapa Council, but in reality everyone just runs their own show. Sisko comments that the system doesn't seem very efficient. Dukat replies that it had functioned for more than five centuries. Dialogue from

"Chain of Command, Part 2" *(TNG)* seems to contradict this statement.

During Gul Madred's torture of Picard, we learn the following: Two hundred years ago, the burial vaults of the First Hebitian civilization were unearthed. They contained many beautiful artifacts made of jevonite—a rare, breathtaking stone. Madred says that the tombs were plundered because Cardassia was an impoverished society. Also, when Picard comments that once the Cardassians were a peaceful race with a rich spiritual life, Madred counters that people starved by the millions, bodies went unburied, disease was rampant, and the suffering was unimaginable. When Picard notes that hundreds of thousands have died since the military took over, Madred angrily asserts that the military is feeding the people, has acquired territory and new resources, and has instituted building programs and mandated agricultural programs. The picture "Chain of Command, Part 2" paints is of a peaceful society that has recently turned militant—with "recently" being defined as within the past two hundred years (since Madred considered Cardassia "impoverished" at the time the First Heibitan burial vaults were unearthed). But the "recentness" of the rise of the military can be brought even closer to the time of the episode by examining further comments by Madred. At one point he tells Picard of living as a starving six-year-old child on the streets of Lakat. Since Madred earlier claims that the military feeds the people, his starvation as a child would seem to indicate that the military has risen to power within his lifetime. Since Picard describes the Cardassian people as peaceful with a rich spiritual life prior to the rise of the military, this would seem to contradict Dukat's statement that Central Command and the Obsidian Order have functioned separately and efficiently for five centuries.

• Obviously *someone* forgot to tell Kira about the new warp speed limit imposed on all Starfleet vessels at the end of "Force of Nature" *(TNG)*. At the end of this episode she sets course for the Federation at warp 8. There's no emergency and no dialogue to show that the *Defiant* has been given some special dispensation when it comes to this rule that no starship should exceed warp 5.

EQUIPMENT ODDITIES

• During Kira's tour of the *Defiant,* Tom asks her to unlock the bridge stations. Once she uses her access code to do so, Tom whips out a phaser and shoots her. One question: Where did he get the phaser? One moment he appears unarmed, the next he has a weapon!

• In this episode we discover that the *Defiant* still has a cloak! I had assumed that the Romulans removed the cloak after their officer disappeared from the show (last seen at the end of "The Search, Part II"). Evidently not! After disclosing its existence to Dukat, Sisko says that their agreement with the Romulans dictates that they can

use it only in the Gamma Quadrant. Does this seem right? With the recall of the Romulan officer assigned to the *Defiant,* have the Romulans really said, "Sure you can keep using the cloak! In fact, you can study it all you want: Just make sure you don't *use* it unless the ship is in the Gamma Quadrant."?

• The first time we saw the *Defiant*'s phasers in action during "The Search, Part I," they devastated a Jem'Haddar warship in no time flat. Oddly enough, a Cardassian warship takes pounding from them in this episode but loses only 30 percent of its shields! Does that mean that Cardassian ships are tougher than Jem'Haddar ships?!

CONTINUITY AND PRODUCTION PROBLEMS

• At one point—according to the dialogue—the *Defiant* has ten Cardassian ships chasing it from behind and three Cardassian ships approaching from the front. Neither the Cardassians' nor the *Defiant*'s displays show this. On both displays there are three ships closing from the front, but the number of ships chasing from behind is off. (Perhaps the other two or three ships are off the screen?)

TRIVIA ANSWERS
1. Mikor.
2. Gul Ranor.

TRIATHLON TRIVIA ON PLACES

MATCH THE PLACE TO
THE DESCRIPTION TO THE EPISODE

PLACE	DESCRIPTION	EPISODE
1. Andevian II	A. The inhabitants call Q "The God of Lies"	a. "The Adversary"
2. Bajor	B. Aamin Marritza's prior domicile	b. "Armageddon Game"
3. Balosnee VI	C. Bashir and O'Brien's hiding place	c. "Babel"
4. Blue Horizon	D. Contains the Great Erg	d. "Blood Oath"
5. Brax	E. Location of labor camp that held Li Nalis	e. "Dax"
6. Calondia IV	F. Quark visited in 1947	f. "Defiant"
7. Campor III	G. Croden's home planet	g. "Dramatis Personae"
8. Cardassia Prime	H. Dawn is wonderful on its fourth moon	h. "Duet"
9. Cardassia III	I. For it, Seyetik created Da Vinci Falls	i. "Emissary"
10. Cardassia IV	J. General Tandro's home	j. "Family Business"
11. Cestus III	K. Has rich deposits of miszinite ore	k. "Fascination"
12. Davlos III	L. It's near Draylon II	l. "The Forsaken"
13. Dayos IV	M. Original location of *Terok Nor*	m. "Hippocratic Oath"
14. Draylon II	N. Jaheel's tamen sasheer destination	n. "The Homecoming"
15. Earth	O. Souce of Zek's orb	o. "Improbable Cause"
16. Ferris VI	P. Kalens cornered Curzon and Sisko there	p. "Invasive Procedures"
17. Gemulon V	Q. Orellius Minor colonists' original destination	q. "Life Support"
18. Japori II	R. Where O'Brien went on trial	r. "Little Green Men"
19. Khefka IV	S. Kang and Dax had bahgol together there	s. "Meridian"
20. Klaestron IV	T. Location of Dakora Assan's murder	t. "The Nagus"
21. Kora II	U. Makes a "replicator to transporter" device	u. "Playing God"
22. Korvat colony	V. Bashir and O'Brien do a biosurvey	v. "Profit and Loss"
23. Largo V	W. Mareel's accommodation house locale	w. "Prophet Motive"
24. Ligobis X	X. It has a good science academy	x. "Q-Less"
25. Meridian	Y. Its massacre became a holosuite program	y. "Sanctuary"
26. Merik III	Z. Nidell fell into a coma there	z. "Second Sight"
27. New Halana	AA. O'Brien used its moon to hide	aa. "Second Skin"
28. New Mecca	BB. Bashir will set up a field hospital there	bb. "Shadowplay"

29. Orias III	CC. Obsidian Order's planet for shipbuilding	cc. "Tribunal"
30. Parada IV	DD. Locale of Quark and Lang's holopicnic	dd. "Visionary"
31. Rakhar	EE. Rurigan's home planet	ee. "Vortex"
32. Regulas III	FF. Seltin Rakal's home planet	ff. "Whispers"
33. Rhymus Major	GG. They play baseball there	
34. Rochani III	HH. Trajok's destination	
35. Sefalla Prime	II. Where Kang met the Albino's ex-wife	
36. Solais V	JJ. Bashir visited the Central Gallery	
37. Stakoron II	KK. Where Seyetik met Nidell	
38. Terosa Prime	LL. Yates's duridium ore destination	
39. T'Lani III	MM. It's near Sefalla Prime	
40. Yadera Prime	NN. Zek considered it for his vacation	

SCORING

(BASED ON NUMBER OF CORRECT ANSWERS)

0–10	Normal
11–19	Good
20–29	Very good.
30–40	Too good for words

PLACE ANSWER KEY: 1. H I 2. NN t 3. M i 4. I z 5. A x 6. HH u 7. BB f 8. R cc 9. O w 10. E n 11. GG j 12. U dd 13. II d 14. MM y 15. F r 16. Y q 17. Q y 18. T o 19. W p 20. J e 21. B h 22. S d 23. N c 24. JJ z 25. FF s 26. V m 27. KK z 28. D aa 29. CC f 30. AA ff 31. G ee 32. X k 33. DD v 34. P g 35. L y 36. LL a 37. K t 38. Z z 39. C b 40. EE bb

★
FASCINATION

Star Date: supplemental

While making final preparations for DS9 's celebration of the Bajoran Gratitude Festival, Kira discovers that Vedek Bareil will soon arrive on the station. The same shuttle brings Keiko and Molly home to O'Brien after two months on Bajor. Lwaxana Troi arrives as well. Officially she has come as the Betazed representative to the Gratitude Festival, but she quickly informs Odo that her real purpose here is to comfort him over the distressing revelations that his race actually founded the Dominion.

Soon odd fascinations grow among the crew. Jake decides he's in love with Kira. Vedek Bareil can't keep his hands off Dax. Dax, in turn, plays the kitten with Sisko. For no apparent reason, Bashir and Kira fall madly in love with each other. Eventually Vedek Bareil becomes so distraught over Dax's rejection that he hits Sisko. Furious, Dax steps in and knocks Vedek Bareil to the floor. Then Sisko sees Lwaxana wince in pain, after which Quark suddenly becomes enamored with Keiko. An exam by Bashir reveals that Lwaxana

has Zanthi fever—a virus that affects the empathic abilities of older Betazoids. She has inadvertently been spreading her attraction for Odo all over the station. Once Bashir treats her condition, everyone returns to normal in a few days.

Trivia Questions

1. Who did the portrait of the station on the pens sold by Quark?

2. What is the name of the zoologist who befriends Keiko on Bajor?

RUMINATIONS

Isn't this a fun episode? Just a pleasant romp after all that serious stuff with the Dominion. The actors look like they had lots of fun doing this one! (Except for Colm Meany and Rosalind Chao, who had to spend most of the episode as the "petty-fighting O'Briens.")

GREAT LINES

"Peldor Joi!" — Dax to Sisko after she gives him a little tweak on the posterio.r This is *definitely* the new and improved Dax! (See Plot Oversights in "Playing God.")

GREAT MOMENTS

I love it when Bareil tries to prove his manhood by taking on Sisko. Sisko obviously isn't under any imminent threat of physical harm, but he's not sure how to get out of the situation gracefully. Bareil is, after all, a Vedek— a Bajoran religious leader. Then Dax

230

steps in and knocks Bareil clean off his feet and onto the floor before explaining to Sisko that Bareil had started to annoy her! (As I said, this is definitely *the new and improved Dax. Granted, she's under Lwaxana's influence but I can't imagine her doing this during the first season!)*

PLOT OVERSIGHTS

• The appropriateness of the station's title comes into question again at the beginning of this episode. Jake says that Marta has gone to a science academy on Regulus III. You may not be aware of this, but Regulus is a real star, so this gives us some idea of the distance between Earth and DS9 . Regulus is only about 80 light-years from Earth. (The sources I checked said everything from 77 to 84, so we'll take the middle ground.) If the station is 300 light-years from Regulus, the absolute maximum distance that Earth could be from DS9 is 380 light-years. (The three would have to be aligned: Earth, Regulus, and DS9.) Considering that the Federation is supposedly 10,000 light-years across, "Deep Space" 9 doesn't seem to be very deep in space, does it?

• At the beginning of this episode we learn that O'Brien hasn't seen Keiko or Molly for two months. Why? According to "The House of Quark," it only takes three hours to get to Bajor in a runabout. Didn't O'Brien find *one* weekend in all that time to get away and beam down to the survey encampment? (Or better yet, beam Keiko up to the runabout!)

• Isn't it amazing that only the main

characters of the episode seemed to be affected by Lwaxana? Even more amazing, Sisko stands right next to Jake when Jake gets zoned, but the good commander never comes down with an attraction to anyone! (This poor guy needs to get out more. Are the creators telling us that there isn't *anyone* on the station whom Sisko finds remotely attractive?!)

• Wow! Good old Odo is really getting into this Bajoran Gratitude Festival thing. Normally very reserved, we see him at one point "directing" a group of Bajoran musicians—something that delights Lwaxana no end!

• At one point Kira corners Bareil to steal a kiss in a hallway. Bareil—intent on finding Dax—mumbles that people might see them. Kira—intent on having her way with Bareil—says that the two of them are the only people there, claiming that everyone else is on the promenade. Well...not really! There's a couple looking out the window behind Kira. True, they wander off very quickly, but they *are* there when she says it. (Personally, I think she's just impatient with Bareil's reticence and wants to get on with the show.)

• At the end of this episode Keiko tells O'Brien that she will see him in a few months. I asked before, I'll ask again: Why would O'Brien wait that long to see his wife again? It's only three hours to Bajor!

CHANGED PREMISES

• And speaking of Regulus being 300 light-years from the station, Jake also indicates in "The Search, Part I" that it took no more than two weeks to get from Earth to DS9. (See my review of that episode for more information.) If Regulus is 300 light-years from the station and Earth is about 80 light-years from Regulus, the absolute *minimum* distance from the station to Earth must be about 220 light-years. Now, *The Star Trek Encyclopedia* says traveling at warp 9.6 will take you about 20 light-years in 4 days. That means it should take Sisko and Jake about 44 days to get from Earth to DS9, not 13 or fewer!

• The spots on the upper chest of our favorite Trill make another appearance in this episode. For most of this episode, Dax wears a low-cut dress that shows her spots proceeding down from her neck, arcing out to touch her shoulders, and then arcing back in as they traverse the upper portion of her chest. All other episodes showing this particular set of spots, both before ("Emissary," "Invasive Procedures," and "Playing God") and after ("The Way of the Warrior"), have the spots descending from Dax's neck and then going more or less straight down. ("The Way of the Warrior" shows that the spots wrap out to Dax's sides as they continue down her body.)

EQUIPMENT ODDITIES

• Sometimes the placement of equipment in the infirmary is just a mystery to me. As Bashir doctors Lwaxana, we see that her bed is shoved up against a wall that contains a series of elongated octagons. We've seen these octagons at work in at least two episodes: "Q-Less" and "Invasive Procedures." Both times the octagons were actually the

front end of a chamber. If the same holds true for the octagons we see in this episode, wouldn't it be really inconvenient to have a bed shoved up against them?

CONTINUITY AND PRODUCTION PROBLEMS

• Shortly after arriving on the station, Keiko puts Molly to bed. She walks out of Molly's bedroom carrying two stuffed animals tucked under her left arm. Exhausted, she flops down on the couch with her back to the camera. The angle changes to a front view of Keiko, and suddenly one animal has disappeared and the other has jumped to Keiko's *right* arm. No wonder Molly enjoys playing with them!

• The closed captioning contains some dialogue that's never spoken. When describing her trip in from Bajor, Keiko tells O'Brien that it was a disaster, that she thought it would never end. Then the closed captioning adds, "Molly was miserable the whole time." Also, as Kira steps up to the platform to begin the Gratitude Festival on the station, the closed captioning has Bareil saying, "And now to begin this year's Gratitude Festival, the presider, Kira Nerys."

• When we first see Miles and Keiko sitting at "their" table in Quark's, O'Brien has his left hand along the edge of the table, outside a glass filled with some type of beverage. The shot changes and instantly O'Brien has his hands clasped together.

• Just after O'Brien yanks Quark to his feet by his ears, the lower half of the Bajoran earring worn by the Ferengi barkeep comes loose and flops to his chest. Amazingly, no one seems to notice!

• I could comment on my amazement that the *Defiant* always seems to be parked on the *other* side of the station whenever we see an exterior shot of DS9, but I believe I will postpone. (For those of you who don't realize I'm being a smartaleck: The creators of the *DS9* series face a small problem. With the original series and *NextGen,* the creators could take a bunch of external shots of the *Enterprise* and splice them in as needed. They did the same in the *DS9* series,

but to make them as generic as possible they had to do it without any ships docked at the station. So...we rarely ever see the *Defiant* docked at the station even though it's permanently assigned there! Of course, we also could talk about the fact that, during the first three seasons, we rarely ever see more than *one* ship docked at the station, but that's another topic altogether.)

TRIVIA ANSWERS
1. Ermat Zimm.
2. Sebarr.

★ PAST TENSE, PART I

Star Date: 48481.2

When the *Defiant* returns to Earth, a transporter accident throws Sisko, Dax, and Bashir backward in time to the year A.D. 2024. A patrol soon takes Sisko and Bashir in custody. Without ID or credit chips, they are delivered to a "sanctuary" district—America's early twenty-first-century response to unemployment and homelessness. Sanctuary districts consist of many buildings surrounded by a high wall. Inside, the inhabitants are promised food, shelter, and job training, though in reality their needs are barely met. Dax manages to avoid this fate. She is awakened by a media tycoon named Chris Brynner, who helps her acquire the needed ID.

Meanwhile, Sisko realizes that the particular sanctuary where he and Bashir await processing will soon experience the Bell Riots—a turning point in Earth history, one that led to the dismantling of the sanctuaries and the start of reforms. Those reforms culminated in the high standard of living enjoyed by humans in the twenty-fourth century. The riots were named for Gabriel Bell, who saw to the safety of the workers taken as hostages. Unfortunately, Bell is killed before the riots begin while trying to help Sisko and Bashir. Realizing Bell's importance in history, Sisko assumes his place as the riots flare, determined to protect the hostages though he knows Bell was shot dead when authorities retook the building.

Trivia Questions

1. What is the number on the building where Chris Brynner works?

2. What is the temperature in San Francisco according to the wall calendar in the processing office of Sanctuary District A?

PLOT OVERSIGHTS

• Once again we have Sisko hopping on the *Defiant* and wandering off—this time with the entire staff to Earth under pretense of a conference on the Dominion! In other words, Starfleet Command has decided to remove Bajor's only protection from the Dominion because Starfleet Command wants to *talk* about the Dominion. Couldn't this be done over subspace?

• And while we're on the topic of the entire senior staff, who's in charge of the station? Quark?!

• One wonders if San Francisco rests on some odd transjunction in the omniverse. At the time of this writing *every* set of main characters within the *Star Trek* franchise has experienced some

234

type of time-traveling anomaly in conjunction with San Francisco. The original cast went there in *Star Trek IV: The Voyage Home*. The *NextGen* cast went there at the end of "Time's Arrow, Part II." The DS9 cast did it in this episode. And Harry Kim of the *Voyager* crew awoke there in "Non Sequitur" *(VOY)*.

• After transporting backward in time, Sisko and Bashir land unconscious just outside a stairwell on the streets of San Francisco. The sanctuary guys haul them off, and the camera pans down into the stairwell. The angle reverses and we see Dax sitting unconscious on the floor with her back against the wall—right hand on the first step. (Did I mention she was *unconscious*?) My question is: How did she end in this position? She probably materialized at the same level as Sisko and Bashir. That means she had a ten-foot drop to the floor—possibly a bit less if she landed on the last few steps. So this *unconscious* woman drops several feet, lands either on some stairs or the floor, and stays standing long enough to stumble backward, hit the wall, and then slouch down? (Must be that amazing Trill physiology.)

• Several nitpickers wrote to commend Dax on the speed with which she adapts to her new surroundings after a grog-filled awakening. Unlike Sisko, she almost instantly deduces that she isn't in San Francisco at the right time and switches into her "damsel in distress" mode to evoke the sympathy of rich media tycoon Chris Brynner, who has just happened by. (And in the next episode, we'll find

even more good fortune connected with this chance meeting. The residents of Sanctuary District A need Net access and...guess what? Chris Brynner can get it for them! Hmmm.)

• Several nitpickers also wrote to commend Dax on her abilities to use an unfamiliar computer system so well that she can create a persona for herself, thereby avoiding the potential of being admitted to Sanctuary District A herself.

• I personally find it fascinating that Kira is apparently in charge of the *Defiant* in Sisko's absence. Bajor isn't even part of the Federation, Kira hasn't even visited Starfleet Academy (at least as far as we know), and she commands one of Starfleet's most powerful vessels? (In the next episode she makes a "first officer's log.")

• Sometimes the creators have to go a very, very long way to come up with a "plausible" explanation for plot contrivances. For instance, in this episode listen to O'Brien's recitation for why Sisko and company were swept backward in time: "The temporal surge we detected was caused by an explosion in a microscopic singularity passing through this solar system. Somehow the energy emitted by this singularity shifted the chroniton particles in our hull into a high state of temporal polarization." I don't know about you, but every time I read these two sentences, I burst out laughing. I especially love Kira's response to O'Brien's explanation. She looks him straight in the eye and says, "Which means what?" (That Kira, she's a kidder, doncha know!)

• I wanna know what happens between now and A.D. 2024 to create the environment we see in this episode. Note that people are being detained against their will simply because they don't have an ID! Apparently if you are just strolling down the street, a policeman can walk up to you and demand to see your identification, and if you don't have it, you get hauled off and interned *without* a trial for an *indeterminate* amount of time! What happened to the Bill of Rights? Is the United States of America under martial law at this point? It would almost have to be. That *would* explain the fact that freedom of the press apparently has been rescinded as well. (I have an extraordinarily difficult time believing that the media simply have no interest in what goes on within these sanctuaries.)

• The *Classic Star Trek* episode "The City on the Edge of Forever" deals with a proposition similar to the plot of this episode. McCoy goes through the Guardian of Forever. McCoy keeps Edith Keeler from dying. History is changed. Starfleet never emerges, and consequently the *Enterprise* never gets built. However, that episode treats time much differently than this one. In "The City on the Edge of Forever," time proceeds like a straight line. Kirk and his landing party watch McCoy go through the Guardian of Forever, and *instantly* the *Enterprise* disappears! Why instantly? Because McCoy saved Keeler's life more than three hundred years ago! All the history between then and now had already been rewritten.

For "Past Tense, Part I" the creators take a different approach to time. In

this episode Sisko, Dax, and Bashir are transported into the past, but the present for Kira, O'Brien, and Odo putters along just like normal until Bell gets killed. It's almost as if the creators have postulated a model of time where everything is happening on parallel tracks—that is, Sisko and Bashir are experiencing Sanctuary District A at the same time as O'Brien is figuring out what happened to them, even though Sisko and Bashir are currently living more than three *hundred* years earlier than O'Brien. That's really the only way to rationalize that Starfleet doesn't disappear the instant Sisko, Dax, and Bashir beam into the past. It's almost as if time is some kind of spiraling corkscrew that curls...um... back...(I could go on trying to come up with an explanation for this, but frankly it's giving me a headache! I just don't get how this is supposed to work. But in six episodes we'll see that time travel no longer responds to rational thought. (See "Visionary.") This is unfortunate, because Jeremy Wood of Sheffield, England, wrote me a great letter about this episode detailing the time travel problems.)

• Several nitpickers found it interesting that one guy in one city (a city in California, no less) could make all the difference in the development of the United States of America, and that, in turn, would make all the difference in the development of Earth, and that, in turn, would make all the difference in the development of the Federation and Starfleet. (Hmmm. Do I sense a bit of Ameri-centricity on the part of the creators, here? Of course, there is a *Star Trek* tradition here. The same *could* be said for "The City on the Edge of Forever.")

• Also, the established chronology of *Star Trek* states that Earth endured a third world war late in the twenty-first century—a conflict that killed *thirty-seven million* people. Where does that fit in with this episode's statements that the Bell Riots were a watershed that led to reform and eventually to the utopian existence enjoyed by Earth in the twenty-fourth century? Doesn't it seem likely that World War III "postatomic horror" would set all reforms back to zero? Somehow I have a hard time imagining the late twenty-first-century populace—eking out a day-to-day existence in the middle of a nuclear winter—saying to itself, "When we get things back to normal, the first thing we're going to do is make sure everybody has jobs!"

• Speaking of everything changing, O'Brien says the only signals he's picking up come from the vicinity of Alpha Centauri, and they are Romulan. I wonder why the Romulans didn't come over and look at this unknown warship suddenly orbiting a nearby star system.

CHANGED PREMISES

• Once and for all, the creators decided to settle the issue of O'Brien's rank by having him state that he is an enlisted man in this episode. I guess it was just a mistake when Riker called him "Lieutenant" in "Where Silence Has Lease." And I guess it was just a mistake that O'Brien wore the rank pips of a lieutenant in every episode in which he appeared until the sixth season of *NextGen*. (Don't get me wrong. The creators have every right to change *anything* they want with *any* character they choose. I just get tickled with the type of response I heard from a creator on this issue: "O'Brien has *always* been an enlisted man." No, he hasn't. *"Yes, he has!"* Ooookay!)

EQUIPMENT ODDITIES

• The big digital wall calendar in the processing center of Sanctuary District A has an interesting omission. It shows the day, date, and even the temperature, but it seems to be missing a clock! (Would this be because the creators didn't want to deal with the continuity problems caused by clocks, or did the Sanctuary District Purchasing Department get the calendars at a discount?)

• After spending the night in a stairwell-like enclosure, Bashir tells Sisko that if they return to the station, he'll never complain about Cardassian beds again. Wait a minute: Starfleet has commanded this space station for two and one-half years and no one has changed the mattresses yet?

CONTINUITY AND PRODUCTION PROBLEMS

• The closed captioning for this episode gives a star date of 48521.4. (In case you're wondering which is more authoritative, Sisko's spoken star date or the written one on the closed captioning, I vote for Sisko's.)

• Attempting to find their way out of Sanctuary District A, Sisko and Bashir decide to go up to the rooftop of a building to look around. As they approach a flight of stairs, a man turns with a knife to protect his injured son. Sisko walks forward for a few feet and then stops beside a hall light. There's a small detent in the hall behind him to the right. The man with the knife orders them to step forward into the light. A waist-up shot of Sisko and Bashir shows them stepping forward, and Sisko moves again into the spot beside the light, just ahead of the hall detent. Moments later, the scene cuts back to the original wide shot of the hall, and we see that Sisko is standing exactly where he was when he stopped the first time! In other words, he hopped backward when we weren't looking

and then walked forward again.

• Since I am no expert on fashion, I will defer to Linny Marcus of Brookline, Massachusetts, who wrote to predict that the feathers Dax wears in her hair during this episode probably would be expensive and tasteless by the year A.D. 2024. (I've made it a policy in life never to argue with a woman over fashion. I just wear whatever my wife tells me to wear. It's easier that way!)

TRIVIA ANSWERS
1. 599.
2. Fifteen degrees Celsius.

PAST TENSE, PART II

Star Date: supplemental

As Sisko and Bashir do their best to protect the guards and workers taken hostage during the sanctuary riot, Dax finally pinpoints their location, only to discover that Sanctuary District A is under siege by the police. Undeterred, Dax crawls through sewers to meet with them. Sisko quickly sends her back out. Although Dax has the only combadge and the trio needs to stay together in case Kira and the others find a way to return them to the future, Sisko doesn't want to put her in danger. Besides, the police have cut off media access, and Dax's friend Brynner might be able to provide it. According to history, the sanctuary residents must get on the Net and tell their stories—a key activity that led to reforms.

Back on the *Defiant,* Kira and O'Brien search through time, looking for the lost trio. Running out of chances, they make one final attempt, traveling to A.D. 2024. where they contact Dax. At the sanctuary, the National Guard moves in and secures the buildings by force. Grateful that Sisko and Bashir saved their lives, two of the sanctuary guards arrange

for the pair to escape from the sanctuary in time to rendezvous with Dax.

RUMINATIONS

There were a few things in this episode that I was very confused about until I watched it for the fifth time! The first concerned the actual process of getting Sisko, Bashir, and Dax back to the Defiant. I misunderstood what O'Brien was saying at first. Near the end of the program, O'Brien and Kira transport to the year 2024. Kira establishes contact with Dax and gives her their location. Kira tells Dax that the transporter is set to retrieve them in "about a minute," so she better deactivate her combadge. At this point O'Brien and Kira hit their combadges twice and O'Brien says, "We can reactivate them tomorrow in time for the next beam-out." Kira adds, "This should be interesting." In other words, O'Brien had set up the transporter so that if it couldn't find anyone to transport, it should wait a set number of hours and try again. Evidently, all five of our heroes spent the night in San Francisco! (There's still the small matter of Sisko and Bashir transporting without their combadges, but

Trivia Questions

1. What is the name of Danny Webb's sister?

2. According to Biddle Coleridge, where was Errol Flynn born?

239

maybe O'Brien brought some along or they all just had a big group hug.)

I was also confused initially by Sisko's picture appearing in the history books beside the name Gabriel Bell. Let's backtrack. Bell is the hero of the Bell Riots. Unfortunately, he gets killed helping Sisko and Bashir. Sisko takes Bell's identification card. Sisko then poses as Bell and helps with the negotiations. The troops storm in and shoot Sisko. A sanctuary guard takes Bell's identification card from Sisko and places it on a dead guy to make it look like Bell died when the riot police "pacified" the building. At the very end of the episode, Bashir comes to visit Sisko with a padd that has the official history of the Bell Riots, and there—big as life—is Sisko's picture. Many nitpickers found this unsatisfactory. After all, the whole point of putting the identification card on a dead guy was to make it look like Gabriel Bell died. I understand their complaint. However, Sisko as Bell did participate in the negotiations. No doubt these negotiations were taped. Later, the guards who were held as hostages were probably asked to identify the men who negotiated for the sanctuary residents. The guards would say that Sisko was Bell, and it's possible that the picture in the history books comes from the surveillance tapes of the negotiations. (Unfortunately that doesn't explain why the police didn't notice why the dead guy carrying Bell's identification card didn't look like the guy in the tapes!)

PLOT OVERSIGHTS

• Attempting to discover the "when-abouts" of Sisko, Dax, and Bashir, O'Brien narrows the search to ten dif-

ferent destinations in time. Then he and Kira begin making random visits into the past, scanning for transporter activity and attempting to make contact through their combadges when they arrive. This seems extremely inefficient on a number of counts.

First, there is still a twenty-fourth-century Earth below them. And it seems capable of supporting life. If it still has humans living on it, it's possible they have historical records. In addition, it seems likely that the *Defiant* has historical records in its computer memory. (And even if historical information isn't available from the *Defiant*'s memory banks, O'Brien appears to have knowledge of Earth's past.) So why isn't O'Brien scanning the planet's surface for civilization? Using the *Defiant*'s sensors, he could locate a library, beam in at night, and grab a few history books. The crew could then compare the corrupted historical accounts in the books with the uncorrupted memories of O'Brien and the ship's computer for the major events of the past three hundred years on Earth. It seems likely that this would help localize when the change occurred, doesn't it?

Second—if the historical research tack doesn't thrill you—there is a much more sensible way to go about searching for Sisko and company than just guessing. Before exploring that method, however, let's look at O'Brien's choices of destinations.

The first time we see O'Brien and Kira materialize, it's very close to the year 1930. How do we know that? Because of the boxing poster that hangs on the wall behind them! I keep thinking that it looked familiar, and suddenly it hit me. It's very, *very* similar to the poster that Kirk and Spock materialize in front of during "The City on the Edge of Forever." If you'll look closely you'll see that the same guys are scheduled to fight in the main *and* the secondary events! (In fact, I have no doubt that the creators sent O'Brien and Kira to this destination as a homage to that great *Classic Trek* episode. One additional "fun bit" of information before we proceed. There was one small problem the creators faced in reusing this poster. In "The City on the Edge of Forever," the very top of the poster read, "Madison Square Garden." Most appropriately, you will notice that the creators changed it for this episode, since O'Brien and Kira are supposedly materializing in *San Francisco,* not New York City!)

For the next trip into the past, O'Brien chooses some time in the decade of the 1960s. We know this from the appearance of hippies and peace signs. (One wonders if the creators didn't choose this time as a homage to the original *Star Trek* series as well. It aired from 1966 through 1969. And as long as we're on the topic, I would hereby like to nominate my entry for the category "Greatest Line Ever to Be Unincluded in Any *Star Trek* Episode." When O'Brien and Kira dematerialize in front of the two hippies, I kept waiting for the guy to say, "Whoa! Beam me up, Scotty!")

After the trip to the 1960's, O'Brien chooses to go to A.D. 2040. On return, he states that Earth was never that rough, and Kira suggests that they concentrate on dates prior to this year. This is *precisely* the approach O'Brien should have used *all along*! Think about the problem for a minute. You have ten possible locations. You can make only five attempts. You know that somewhere in there, Sisko and company changed history. How do you go about cracking this problem in a systematic way with the highest possible potential for success? For me—as a person who used to make a good living as a computer programmer—this is a no-brainer! It's actually one of the more ubiquitous problems in programming (i.e., how do you quickly locate the piece of information in a file that is sorted but does not have any type of key file?). Answer: You start in the center! By examining the center of the file you can determine if the data you are trying to find is in the first or the second half of the file. If it's in the first half of the file, you then go to the center of the first half of the file and go through the same process. This type of searching is very efficient. Of course, if O'Brien started with a date like 2040, the creators couldn't do the homages to *Classic Trek*. (One last thing. I was one of those self-taught "illegitimate" programmers. I never did have any training, just a knack for it. Because of that, I made my own names for stuff like this searching technique. I used to call it a "half search" because you just keep splitting your search area into halves. This is actually called a "binary sort.")

• The Earth rotates around the sun, right? Our sun rotates around the center of our galaxy, right? Our galaxy is moving through the universe, right? So wouldn't the Earth be in a substantially different position in space over the course of three hundred or so years? If you transported down to the position of Earth in the twenty-fourth century, wouldn't you wind up floating in space in the twenty-first century?

• One wonders why Dax—having retrieved her combadge—places it on the outside of her jacket after it was already stolen once. It could function just as well in her pocket, could it not?

• At the end of this episode Dax convinces Brynner to use his net access to give the sanctuary residents a voice. Brynner says that it will cost him his license, but he does it anyway. Obviously, Brynner did not make this sacrifice in the original timeline. At the very least, Dax can't know if Brynner provided this service in the original timeline. Yet she encourages him to do so anyway. In other words, the death of Bell completely rewrote history, but no one seems concerned that the ruination of Chris Brynner will do the same. (And why should they? After all, he's just the evil, sell-out millionaire, media tycoon who's lost touch with the common folk but still has a tender place in his heart that can be reinvigorated by the right words from a beautiful, long-legged incarnation of his terribly neglected conscience.)

• Sure is a good thing the invading hordes of riot police shot Sisko only once when they shot everyone else in the room multiple times.

• Evidently the real Bell didn't have any family or friends. Apparently Sisko's picture and Bell's name became quite well known after the riot. Why didn't anyone come forward and say, "That's not Bell!"?

EQUIPMENT ODDITIES

• Did O'Brien make some adjustment to the transporter before he and Kira took off for the past? When Sisko and company transported into the past, something happened to knock them unconscious, but O'Brien and Kira don't have any trouble at all.

• Just for the record, it does no good to keep pumping a shotgun without firing it first! In this episode both Sisko and "BC" pump their shotguns multiple times but never pull the trigger. The action of pumping this type of weapon ejects the spent cartridge and loads a live round of ammunition into the firing chamber. If you pump a loaded weapon, all you will do is eject the live shell! Yet our heroes just keep pumping away, but nothing happens. (Personally, I don't think they've got any ammunition!)

CONTINUITY AND PRODUCTION PROBLEMS

• At the beginning of this episode one of the sanctuary residents listens to a news report. It speaks of "Governor Chen," but the closed captioning reads "Governor River."

• Many nitpickers found it amazing that Dax could crawl through sewers to get to Sisko and Bashir and emerge her normal, radiant, *spotless*—and apparently clean-smelling—self.

TRIVIA ANSWERS
1. Jeannie.
2. Tasmania.

LIFE SUPPORT

Star Date: 48498.4

A Bajoran transport accident fatally injures Vedek Bareil, forcing Bashir to use extraordinary means to bring him back from the dead. At the time, Bareil was traveling with Kai Winn to conduct secret negotiations with Legate Turrel. The negotiations promised to bring a final peace between Bajor and Cardassia and possibly even the issuance of a formal apology for the atrocities of the occupation by Cardassian forces. Bareil has been the primary catalyst for the negotiations, and—though he is still recovering from the accident—Winn insists on moving the negotiations to DS9. She believes they must continue quickly to maintain momentum.

Unfortunately, Bashir's method for recovering Bareil has damaged his circulatory system. Bashir tells Bareil that a drug named Vasokin may allow him to assist Winn during the talks, but it can cause damage on its own. Bareil tells Bashir to proceed. As feared, the drug first destroys Bareil's internal organs and then the left side of his brain. Bashir replaces everything with artificial implants. In the end,

Turrel signs the treaty, but during the celebration the right half of Bareil's brain becomes damaged as well. At this, Bashir refuses to do any more, choosing to allow the vedek to die as a man—not as a machine.

Trivia Questions

1. What does Riska's uncle do?

2. What is Quark's "Kai Winn"?

RUMINATIONS

This episode opens with Odo and O'Brien running—running, mind you—to an airlock to meet a damaged incoming Bajoran transport. Since I mentioned Sisko, O'Brien, and Jake's stroll on the edge of disaster during "Civil Defense," I thought it only fair to mention this instance as a case where urgency is dictated and the crew actually responds in an urgent manner.

Of course, one has to wonder why Ops didn't just beam the emergency teams to the airlock. (Snicker, snicker) Also—if my estimates are correct—it's at least one-half mile from the promenade to the docking ring. That's a pretty good little jog, but our heroes aren't even winded when they get there! (For more information, see "Crossfire.")

PLOT OVERSIGHTS

• There's a race that crops up several times in *NextGen* called the Tarel-

243

lians. I had some fun with this race in *The Nitpicker's Guide for Next Generation Trekkers, Volume II,* since it's really confusing to try to fit together all the references to the Tarellians in some meaningful way. (See "Liaisons" in the *NextGen II Guide* for more details.) In this episode Nog tells Jake that he's set up a domjot match with three Terrellians—a race whose name is pronounced the same way as Tarellian! I think the creators are having a little fun with us. Either that or it's a job for the Galactic Court for Race Name Conflict Resolution. (See "The Creator Is Always Right" feature from *The Nitpicker's Guide for Next Generation Trekkers.*)

• In his log entry Sisko claims that he is sitting in on the Cardassian/Bajoran peace talks as an impartial observer. However, minutes later, he gives advice to Kai Winn. Since when do "impartial observers" give advice to one side in a negotiation?

• At one point the Cardassian representative to the peace talks, Legate Turrel, suggests that Cardassia will make reparations for all Bajoran property damaged in the occupation provided Bajor returns all Cardassian property. Winn is uncertain how to respond, and later she tells Sisko that she suspects Turrel is up to something. Well...wouldn't this "property" include the station? If Bajor had to return the station, wouldn't that put a kink in their ability to lay claim to the wormhole?

• After the above exchange, a frustrated Kai Winn tells Sisko that she was chosen by the Prophets to lead her people but not to sit in a room with a Cardassian debating legalisms and diplomatic nuances. This is actually a very sensible statement. After all, Bajor does have a provisional government. Wouldn't peace negotiations with Cardassia Prime fall in the purview of the *civil* government? Why is Kai Winn conducting these negotiations in the first place?

• Language can be a real bear sometimes. In this episode Bashir talks of Bareil's "humanity." While the term seems a tad racist (in keeping with Azetbur's comments around the captain's table in *Star Trek VI: The Undiscovered Country*), the alternative—"Bajoranity"—seems very awkward.

EQUIPMENT ODDITIES

• In this episode Bashir replaces the left side of Bareil's brain with a positronic implant. Evidently Bashir can also transfer the content of the left side of Bareil's brain into this implant. In addition, Bashir seems to be able to replace the right side of Bareil's brain using the same method. Wouldn't this result in a stable positronic matrix with at least *some* of Bareil's intelligence? Isn't this getting dangerously close to Data? I thought we couldn't make more Datas because Starfleet couldn't create a stable positronic matrix. Maybe the Cybernetics Department at the Daystrom Institute should look up our good doctor on DS9!

TRIVIA ANSWERS
1. He runs a bar on Osinar VI.
2. A chocolate soufflé with Haligian tongue sauce.

HEART OF STONE

Star Date: 48521.5

Kira and Odo chase a Maquis terrorist to a moon in the Cardassian badlands. Finding the wreckage of a ship, they begin searching some nearby caves—splitting up to complete the search more quickly. Soon Kira calls out for help. Odo returns to find her foot stuck in a rapidly growing crystal formation. If the crystal keeps expanding at the present rate, it will completely cover her in only hours. With both communication and the transporter inhibited by the moon's atmosphere, Odo attempts to shatter the crystal with an ultrasonic resonator. It doesn't work. The crystal seems to be constantly changing. When the crystal encloses all but her chin, Kira tries to get Odo to leave. He refuses, saying that he can't because he loves her.

Surprisingly, Kira returns Odo's love, and he suddenly realizes that something is wrong. He knows Kira doesn't love him. She would never say so just to make him feel better. He points a phaser at what looks like Kira encased in a pillar, and both morph into a female Changeling who staged the entire incident to discover Odo's link to

the "solids." She hoped that Kira's death would cause him to return to his race. Once again, Odo refuses. Just before leaving, the Changeling tells Odo where to find the real Kira.

GREAT LINES

"He's particularly fond of one called 'Louie, Louie.'"—Odo to Kira, explaining that when he and O'Brien go kayaking together in the holosuites, the chief likes to sing ancient human sea chanteys to help keep a steady rhythm. (Katie "The Cloudminder" Gallagher of Kapolei, Hawaii, tells me that her kayaking group in high school *did* use this song to keep a steady rhythm.)

PLOT OVERSIGHTS

• The episode begins with Kira and Odo coming back from Prophet's Landing—the Bajoran settlement nearest the Cardassian border. Odo's in a huff, answering Kira's attempts to make conversation with one-word answers or grunts. Finally she asks if something is bothering him. "What makes you say that?" Odo replies. Kira answers, stating that—for one thing—he hasn't said *five words* to her since they left Prophet's Landing.

Trivia Questions

1. Which officer is budding?

2. Which runabout brings Kira and Odo to the moon?

245

I think he just did! Count 'em up. "What makes you say that?" Five words. (Hey, I don't write the dialogue, I just nitpick it!)

• Odo needs to debrief Sisko concerning the extent of the Changeling's knowledge about life on the station. Obviously they have already infiltrated. Look at what the Changeling—posing as Kira—knows. She knows that "kayaking" means getting in a boat and paddling. (No doubt there are many places on Earth today that if you told the local inhabitants you wanted to "kayak" you would either get tossed out on your ear or quickly find yourself in a very compromising position.) She also knows that the real Kira hasn't read any of the detective novels O'Brien has given to Odo. She also knows that Kira doesn't know how Odo got his name. This is not the kind of information you get by intercepting subspace transmissions. The stuff requires *on-site, continuous* surveillance. The revelation that the Changelings have implemented this type of surveillance should send the station into a state of high alert. But, of course, it doesn't. (At least not that we know.)

• I've said it before, I'll say it again. Obviously the Changeling in this episode has no trouble at all creating a humanoid face. Her "Odo-like" appearance at the end of the episode must be a concession to Odo's more primitive skills.

• So...if the Changeling intended all along for Odo to see Kira die, why didn't the Changeling kill Kira instead of putting her in a stasis chamber?

CHANGED PREMISES

• Kira seems to have had a change of heart when it comes to her feelings about the Maquis. When she and Odo detect the Maquis vessel attacking a Lissepian supply ship, I really expected her to turn to the constable and say, "I don't see any Maquis ship. Do you?" After all, at the beginning of "The Maquis, Part II," she gave Sisko an impassioned speech on the rights of the Maquis to defend themselves. She said she knew what they were going through. She said she knew the Cardassians couldn't be trusted. She must have changed her mind since then, because at the beginning of this episode she chases after the Maquis ship like it houses a criminal. Maybe it has something to do with the new peace treaty between Bajor and Cardassia?

• In this episode Rom fixes Quark's replicators in the bar. I guess Quark got tired of waiting for O'Brien's teams to handle the repairs around the bar so he palmed the maintenance responsibilities off on his hapless brother. In "Babel" Quark stole food from command-level replicators because his were broken and O'Brien couldn't spare anyone to fix them. Also in that episode, Odo says that Rom is an idiot—that he couldn't fix a straw that was bent.

EQUIPMENT ODDITIES

• After her foot supposedly becomes trapped, the fake Kira picks up a phaser and fires at the crystal growing around her foot. You will remember that the crystal and Kira are both part of the Changeling. The phaser has no effect. So phasers don't affect Changelings? That's an important piece of information! (I realize that Kira may have set the phaser on the lowest setting, but even light stun affects humans. And in case you're wondering if the phaser was part of the Changeling as well, you will remember that the phaser was physically separated from the Changeling at one point and remained a phaser. According to "The Adversary," anytime part of a Changeling's body becomes separated from the whole, it reverts to its gelatinous state.)

• Attempting to send a distress signal to DS9, Odo launches a probe and asks the computer—under optimal conditions—how soon he and Kira can expect help from the station. The computer replies that it will take two days for the signal to reach DS9. First, that's not what Odo asked! He asks how soon they could expect help. The computer should have continued with its answer, estimating the length of time it would take for a second runabout to fly from the station to this moon, shouldn't it? Second, is it really going to take *two days* for the signal to get to the station? Doesn't the probe use a subspace transmitter? According to *Star Trek: The Next Generation Technical Manual,* subspace communications travel about 60 times faster than the fastest starship. Now, the *Enterprise* could do warp 9.6 in a pinch. According to *The Star Trek Encyclopedia,* at warp 9.6 the *Enterprise* could cover about 10 light-years in 2

days. So for the subspace signal to take 2 days to get to the station from the moon, the distance between them would have to be something like 600 light-years! (That's 10 multiplied by 60 since subspace can travel 60 times faster than the *Enterprise.*) Any idea how long it would take a runabout— whose maximum velocity is warp 5— to cover 600 light-years? Answer: about 2.5 *years*! How in the galaxy did Kira and Odo get that far away from the station? They would have had to start out just as the series began! (Wink, wink.)

• By the way, the upright rods that Odo places around faux Kira are first seen in "Power Play" *(TNG).* In that episode they were used as pattern enhancers for the transporter.

• The stasis chamber that holds Kira at the end of the episode looks very similar to the one shown at the end of "Vortex," but maybe everyone in the Gamma Quadrant buys them from Statis-Mart or something.

CONTINUITY AND PRODUCTION PROBLEMS

• Star date difference! Audio says 48521.5. Closed captioning says 48543.2.

• I believe the external visual showing the runabout resting on the surface of the moon originally came from the episode "Vortex."

TRIVIA ANSWERS

1. Ensign Vilix'Pran.
2. The *Mekong.*

DESTINY

Star Date: 48543.2

With the new peace treaty in place (see "Life Support"), Bajor, the Federation, and Cardassia work together to place a communications relay at the mouth of the wormhole in the Gamma Quadrant—though some on Bajor oppose the project. For one, Vedek Yarka believes that thousands of years ago a Bajoran named Trakor foresaw these events and penned a warning about them to the emissary. He tells Sisko that Trakor's third prophecy speaks of three vipers attempting to peer through the temple gates, a sword of stars appearing in the heavens, and the temple burning as the gates are cast open. Since adherents to the Bajoran faith believe that the Celestial Temple resides in the wormhole, Yarka fears that the relay project will destroy the wormhole and cut off the Bajoran people from the Prophets.

Unconvinced, Sisko proceeds with the project. Soon fragments from a comet (the "sword of stars") release a "burning" compound while passing through the wormhole. This compound "casts open" the "temple gates" just a

bit. Thankfully the wormhole is not destroyed, but the resulting subspace filament allows the relay to communicate with DS9. Now the station can keep in contact with ships traveling in the Gamma Quadrant.

PLOT OVERSIGHTS

• This entire episode deals with setting up a communications relay in the Gamma Quadrant. Does Starfleet also intend to station on armada of ships beside it to protect it from Dominion attack? If I were the Founders and the Jem'Haddar had told Starfleet to stay on their side of the galaxy—as Third Talak'Talan did in "The Jem'Haddar"—I would just wait until the *Defiant* went back to the Alpha Quadrant and then I'd blow the stuffing out of that puny communications relay. What I can't figure out is: How does Starfleet know that the Jem'Haddar aren't going to obliterate this piece of equipment?

• This episode features a "rogue comet" near the wormhole. We know from "Emissary" that the nearest star to the wormhole is 5 light-years distant. Yet this comet has a tail! In deep space, comets do not have tails. The

Trivia Questions

1. What dam on Bajor was just put back into operation?

2. Who is Dax's favorite poet?

248

tails form only as a nearby star heats the outer shell of the comet, releasing gases and particles that then drift in the direction opposite from the star. This "rogue comet" that approaches the wormhole should be nothing but a big ball of rock and ice. (But then we couldn't call it a "sword of stars," could we?)

• Evidently there is more to Trakor's third prophecy than we've been told. From the dialogue, this is what I pieced together. "When the river wakes stirred once more to Janir's side three vipers will return to their nest in the sky. When the vipers try to peer through the temple gate a sword of stars will appear in the heavens. The temple will burn and the gates will be cast open." But at one point Kira talks with Sisko about the prophecy and points out the elements in it that she believes are coming true. She mentions the three vipers, the sword of stars, and finally she says that Sisko—the emissary— has a decision to make, just as in the prophecy. Also, at the end of the episode, Kira speaks of the emissary *using* the sword of stars. So, what's the rest of Trakor's third? Where are the parts that say the emissary has a decision to make and he'll use the sword of stars? (Doncha just hate it when you only get half a prophecy?)

• During the testing of the communications relay, the wormhole opens and its gravity well increases by 300 percent. This changes the trajectory of the comet and puts it on a collision course with the wormhole. Amazingly enough, the communications relay that is sitting right next to the wormhole seems unaffected! (Yes, I heard

Sisko telling Dax to keep the *Defiant* in position, but I didn't hear him say anything about locking a tractor beam on the communications relay.)

• At least twice during this episode, Cardassian women have access to very sensitive areas of the *Defiant*. You may recall that the *Defiant* is Starfleet's experimental prototype of a warship, the same warship that— according to Gul Dukat—is the most heavily armed vessel in the sector. In one scene we see O'Brien crawling around in a Jefferies tube with Gilora, and later we learn that an Obsidian Order operative named Dejar somehow managed to depolarize an emitter coupling on the *Defiant* when no one was looking. What happened to all the security arrangements we saw in place at the beginning of *"Defiant"*?

•So we've got this comet flying toward the wormhole (tail and all), and the *Defiant* hits it with the gonzo phasers, supposedly shattering it into three pieces. Note the visuals of the phasers hitting the center of the comet and the resulting explosion. Amazingly enough, when the dust clears, the three remaining chunks are traveling parallel to each other and *still* heading toward the wormhole. Hold it! Wouldn't the force of the explosion—which was strong enough to shatter the comet—change the trajectory of the three pieces? Shouldn't each fragment be moving away from the others? (I'm willing to grant that maybe the gravity of the wormhole might eventually draw them back inside, but I can't see any way that the comet could endure an *explosion* with the resulting fragments running perfectly parallel to each other. Of course, if the chunks behaved according to the known laws of physics, the prophecy wouldn't come true. Maybe the Prophets had something to do with keeping them on course?)

• Originally Vedek Yarka claimed that the "three vipers" referred to the three Cardassians who were coming to the station. But at the very end of the episode, Kira reinterprets the prophecy. After helping Sisko guide the three comet fragments safely through the wormhole, Kira is suddenly convinced that *they* are the three vipers Trakor spoke of in his third prophecy. Me? I vote for Yarka's original interpretation, at least in regard to the three vipers. The prophecy reads, "When the river wakes stirred once more to Janir's side three vipers will return to their nest in the sky. When the vipers try to peer through the temple gate a sword of stars will appear in the heavens." How are the three comet fragments returning "to their nest in the sky"? The comet fragments are inherently destructive to the wormhole. How can that be their nest? Likewise, how are the three comet fragments trying to "peer through the temple gate"? The return of the three Cardassians to DS9—attempting to set up a communications relay—seems a much better fit.

EQUIPMENT ODDITIES

• Supposedly this relay will allow communications with the Gamma Quadrant for the first time. That's odd, because in "Whispers," Paradan

rebels send a message to DS9, and the Parada System is definitely in the Gamma Quadrant.

• During a discussion of the prophecy in his quarters on the *Defiant,* Sisko walks right up to his door but it refuses to open. It must have one of those "this is a really serious conversation and it's not over" sensors.

• Ya know, the communications relay in this episode looks a whole lot like the Amargosa observatory from *Star Trek Generations*. (Must be that standardized Federation design!)

CONTINUITY AND PRODUCTION PROBLEMS

• Star date discrepancy. Audio says "48543.2." Closed captioning reads "48XXX.X."

• I wanna know what that Bajoran guy is doing in the background when the Cardassian scientists Ulani and Gilora disembark their ship. He seems to wait until Ulani and Gilora begin speaking with Sisko and Kira. Then he skulks into the Cardassian ship! At least one more time you can see him wandering around in there. (I'm wondering if he's actually a member of the Maquis! Aaaaah!)

• When we first see the *Defiant* and communications relay, the two appear very close together. Then the wormhole opens and we get another external shot, but now the *Defiant* and the communications relay are quite far apart

TRIVIA ANSWERS
1. Qui'al.
2. Iloja of Prim, a serialist poet from the First Republic

PROPHET MOTIVE

Star Date: unknown

When Grand Nagus Zek suddenly appears on the station and authors a revised version of the Rules of Acquisition, Quark realizes something is terribly wrong with the leader of the Ferengi. His new rules are completely contradictory to established Ferengi business practices. In addition, Zek creates the Ferengi Benevolent Association—an organization dedicated to helping those in need—making Quark and Rom its cochairmen. At this, Quark takes the grand nagus to Bashir for a complete exam. The doctor finds nothing wrong, but Zek does mention that he will give the Bajoran people a present on the following night.

With the help of Zek's servant Maihar'Du, Quark and Rom gain access to Zek's shuttle and discover an Orb of the Prophets. Zek's log records that he was trying to contact the aliens in the wormhole. He wanted to know the future so he could profit from it. Instead the aliens removed his greed—a quality they considered adversarial. Quark returns to the wormhole with Zek and meets with the aliens. At first they decide to remove Quark's greed

as well, but he convinces them that if they do, it will only cause more suspicion and more investigation. Desiring as little contact with corporeal life forms as possible, the aliens return Zek to his normal avaricious self.

Trivia Questions

1. What is the name of the young woman who wishes to buy Quark's stembolts?

2. What is the name of the Andorian nominated for the Carrington Award?

RUMINATIONS

This episode answers one of the great burning questions of Deep Space Trekdom: For what are self-sealing stembolts used? According to a young female at the beginning of this episode, they play some part in the production of reverse racheting router planers! Glad we got that cleared up! (Speaking of stembolts, one hundred gross sounds awfully familiar. Did Jake and Nog's deal during "Progress" fall through?)

I also want to compliment the creators on their reference back to the game of baseball when Quark meets with the aliens who live in the wormhole. During the series premiere, "Emissary," Sisko taught the aliens the concept of linear time by using the example of the game of baseball. It was a very effective moment in the episode, and it was great to see it repeated here. (In case you don't remember, Quark meets with the aliens. They talk of Sisko and Zek, and then an alien in the form of Sisko—carrying a baseball—comments that Zek wanted to know the outcome of the game before it was played.

PLOT OVERSIGHTS

• As with "Emissary," there's a problem trying to write a story about aliens who live in nonlinear time—especially if the aliens learn something. (See "Emissary" for more details.) For instance, in this episode the aliens change Zek—not realizing that Quark will come to find out why. In his conversation with the aliens, Quark convinces them that if they change him as well, *more* Ferengi will come. So the aliens change Zek back. Well, if the aliens truly live in nonlinear time, they should already know that Quark will come if they change Zek. Since they desire as little contact with corporeal life forms as possible, one would guess that they wouldn't change Zek in the first place!

• By the end of the episode, Bashir apparently believes that his chances have improved for winning the Carrington Award. When he's first nominated he tells Dax that he'll get excited when he's nominated again in seventy years. At the end of the episode, when someone wishes him luck next time, he comments that it won't be for forty or fifty years.

CHANGED PREMISES

• In "Heart of Stone" Nog convinces Sisko that he wants to join Starfleet because he doesn't have the lobes for business. He says he gets this from his father. For someone who

purportedly doesn't have the "lobes for business," Rom seems to put in a pretty good showing as Ferengi in this episode. Not only does he steal from Quark, he also embezzles a large sum of latinum from the grand nagus himself while acting as the cochairman of the Ferengi Benevolent Association!

EQUIPMENT ODDITIES

• When the nagus first appears, Quark entertains a young female. Zek and Maihar'Du enter Quark's quarters. The young female leaves. Quark and Rom stare dumbfounded at this turn of events. Apparently the door is dumbfounded as well, because it forgets to close!

• These orbs seem to change how they operate. Or maybe the Orb of Change and Prophecy just works differently from the Orb of Wisdom. In this episode Quark opens the box on the Orb of Wisdom and is immediately swept into a vision. In previous episodes, however, there was a time lag between the opening of the box and the beginning of the vision. For instance, both Sisko and Dax stare at the orb for several moments before their visions begin in "Emissary." The same is true for Kira in "The Circle."

• This isn't really a nit, just a wonderment. When the name of the winner of the Carrington Award is broadcasted, we see a close-up of the screen, and the announcer is shown in a wide format from the shoulders up. Then the scene cuts to a roomful of station personnel who have gathered to wish Bashir luck. The next time we see the screen, the announcer is shown from the waist up, flanked by Starfleet medical symbols. The final time, the screen is back to the shoulders-up view. Oddly enough, the screen never shows *portraits* of the nominees. Since it's such a prestigious award, wouldn't it be nice to show the nominees' picture on the screen as their name is read? (It is interesting that the waist

shot occurs during the reading of the names of the nominees. There is room on either side of the announcer for the pictures. It almost looks like the creators purposely made space for them. Hmmm.)

TRIVIA ANSWERS
1. Emi.
2. Chirurgeon Ghee P'Trell.

VISIONARY

Star Date: unknown

As the show opens, O'Brien recovers from a plasma conduit accident that has flooded his system with radiation. Bashir administers the appropriate treatment, but a short time later the chief begins jumping back and forth in time. Dax traces the problem to a quantum singularity orbiting the station. The unknown singularity is sending out temporal waves that are reacting with the radiation in O'Brien's body. The time jumps—normally five hours into the future—show increasingly chaotic conditions on DS9, culminating in the station's destruction.

Meanwhile, a Romulan delegation arrives at the station for a debriefing on the Dominion. When the Romulans loaned Starfleet a cloaking device for the *Defiant,* the Federation promised complete disclosure of all information gathered in the Gamma Quadrant.

Hoping to discover the reason for DS9's destruction, O'Brien has Bashir create a device to control his time jumps. It allows him to travel only three and a half hours into the future and learn that the Romulans have a

cloaked warbird orbiting the station. It is the source of the temporal waves and—very soon—it will destroy DS9 before collapsing the wormhole, thereby precluding the possibility of a Dominion invasion. Armed with this information, Sisko confronts the Romulans and sends them on their way.

GREAT MOMENTS

The destruction of the station in the episode is really gorgeous.

PLOT OVERSIGHTS

• Near the beginning of the episode, Kira informs Sisko that the Romulans have arrived. Sisko tells her to bring them into Cargo Bay 12 and, in short order, the pair leave Ops in a turbolift. The next scene shows them wandering through the promenade, evidently still on their way to Cargo Bay 12. This is very fortunate, because it gives Sisko a chance to discover that Klingons have just arrived on the station as well. (Wink, wink.) But it does raise a question: Do you really have to go through the promenade to get from Ops to Cargo Bay 12, or was Sisko just taking the scenic route?

Trivia Questions

1. What is the name of the female on the Romulan delegation?

2. Where was the device manufactured that the Klingons use on the replicator?

254

• So...did anybody call Keiko while O'Brien endured this ordeal? She's only three hours away by runabout (less by subspace), yet our beloved chief has to face this crisis alone!

• Those playful creators are having some more fun with us. In this episode Odo mentions that he's going to investigate the visiting Terrellians. (See "Life Support" for more information.)

• Several nitpickers found it less than satisfactory that the crew of the station wouldn't immediately recognize the possibility of a cloaked Romulan ship as soon as they identified the presence of a quantum singularity orbiting the station.

• During a time jump, O'Brien meets himself piloting a runabout away from DS9 in an attempt to get a few people to safety before the station is destroyed. His future self says that he doesn't know what happened. He was asleep in his quarters when the station was rocked by an explosion. Before he could get to Ops, the evacuation alarm sounded and the comsystem was down, so he just hurried to the runabout. Later in the show we see O'Brien wearing pajamas to bed, so we can assume that this future O'Brien wore pajamas to bed as well, but now he pilots the runabout in a uniform. Did he really take the time to change *after* the station was rocked by an explosion and *before* he started toward Ops?

• It's interesting that the first four times O'Brien jumps forward in time he blacks out on the return trip but the fifth time he doesn't.

• In the time jump mentioned above, O'Brien rides in a runabout—piloted by his future self—as it dashes away from the exploding station. The side windows of the runabout are closed. The front window is facing away from DS9. Yet somehow O'Brien manages to describe the stages of the station's destruction. Did he see it happening on a monitor in the cockpit of the runabout?

• In my humble opinion, this episode illuminates—in the *Star Trek* franchise—a major shift in time travel theory for the creators. It's true we saw the inklings of this major shift in "Past Tense, Part I" when the creators delayed the effects of a corruption in the timeline to improve the drama of the episode (see my comments for that episode). But "Visionary" is the first time in the DS9 series that time becomes *irrational*. Interestingly enough, this trend begins not with DS9 but with *Star Trek: Voyager*.

Come with me to the *Voyager* episode "Parallax." In this episode *Voyager* is tooling along when they receive a distress call. They stop to investigate and become trapped in a singularity. In actuality, the distress call came from themselves trapped in the singularity several hours in the future. When this is finally revealed near the end of the program, the creators have Paris and Janeway exchange some very telling dialogue.

Paris: "Wait a minute. Wait. Wait a minute. Let me get this straight. We were cruising along at warp 7. Then we pick up a distress call and moved in to investigate. But now you're saying that the other ship is actually just a reflection of us and that the distress call is actually just the captain's opening hail. But we picked up the distress call before she sent the hail. How could we have been seeing a reflection of something we hadn't even done yet? Am I making any sense here?"

Janeway: "No, but that's okay. One of the more difficult concepts to grasp in temporal mechanics is that sometimes effect can precede cause. A reaction can be observed before the action that initiated it."

In other words, within the *Star Trek* universe the creators have now decided that time doesn't make sense—that it does not respond to logic and reason! The very next *Voyager* episode provides a prime example of this new attitude. In "Time and Again" *Voyager* unexpectedly encounters a shock wave emanating from a planet in a red dwarf system. Janeway diverts course to investigate. The crew finds that an explosion has wiped out all life on the planet. On the surface, Janeway and Paris are swept back in time due to subspace fractures. At the end of the episode we discover that a rescue attempt by the crew *caused* the explosion. We also discover that *Voyager* would not have gone to the planet in the *first* place had the explosion not occurred. In other words, there's no way to get the scenario started! Since the explosion originally draws *Voyager* to the planet, *logically* there would have to be some reason for *Voyager* to boldly go to the planet in the first place because the explosion is caused by the rescue attempt! But Janeway states at the end of the program—after the explosion is averted—that they have a policy *not* to visit prewarp civilizations. This

makes no sense from a cause-and-effect standpoint! (You can't rescue somebody who *ain't there,* and Janeway *can't get there* without the explosion, but the explosion is what *gets them there* in the first place, and it's caused by the *rescue attempt,* meaning Janeway had to be there already.) I have no problem with effect preceding cause as long as the relationships can eventually be established. But this is *irrational.* According to the creators' new premise, *anything* can happen in *any order,* and it can have *any* effect the creators choose. My, this certainly is *convenient!* It frees the creators from all that nasty work of having to figure out the cause-and-effect relationships in the plots of time travel episodes and lets them concentrate on writing good emotive scenes.

And what's the result of all of this? Well, since true nitpickers play by the creators' rules, we have to accept this new premise. Frankly, it explains *a lot* of things about the DS9 episode "Visionary" because there are several places where O'Brien's time jumps simply don't make sense. (I could list them all, but it would chew up at least a page, and—since they're not really nits because time is *irrational*—there's not much point to it, is there?)

CHANGED PREMISES
• And here all this time I thought the Borg were a vicious foe. After all, they kidnapped Picard, assimilated him, used his knowledge to wipe out thirty-nine or so Starfleet ships, and came within a hairbreadth of obliterating Earth. Apparently the Romulans were

not impressed. In this episode the head of the Romulan delegation tells Sisko that the Dominion is the greatest threat to the Alpha Quadrant in the past century.

EQUIPMENT ODDITIES

• During one of his time jumps, O'Brien sees himself die from a booby-trapped wall panel. Returning to the present, he leads Sisko and Odo to the location. (This is pretty amazing in itself. All the hallways on the station look the same to me, almost as if they were all shot with the same set! Grin.) Odo examines the wall panel but finds nothing. He then tells Sisko that he will position a surveillance device in the hall to monitor the panel. Does this seem right? Wouldn't the Cardassians have built the station with surveillance devices in *all* the hallways?

• Evidently the infirmary has some sort of voice-operated comsystem like Ops. When O'Brien comes back from his final time jump he pages his commander, saying, "O'Brien to Sisko," and Sisko responds, even though O'Brien isn't wearing a communicator.

CONTINUITY AND PRODUCTION PROBLEMS

• At one point Sisko, O'Brien, and Odo stand in a hallway discussing a booby trap that will be placed in a wall panel during the next five hours. Sisko

wonders why the device will be put there. All the quarters are empty, and—among other nonqualifications for importance—the area has no "crucial defense systems." The closed captioning translates this as "no 'cruiser' defense systems." (I sure hope the station has "cruiser" defense systems somewhere. You never know when the Love Boat might wander by!)

• Those clever creators gave us a hint at the true culprits in this episode well before revealing them. The device Bashir and O'Brien use to control the chief's time-jumping is an armband with a squat cylinder attached. To activate the device, Bashir uses another tool, this one rectangularly shaped and three and fifteen-sixteenth inches long by one and seven-eighth inches at its widest point. How do I know its measurements so precisely, you ask? Well, I happen to have one! It is actually a warp nacelle from a plastic model of a Romulan warbird. (I got mine in a model kit from AMT called "3 Piece Adversary Set." Aside from the warbird it also included a Klingon *Bird-of-Prey* and a Ferengi Marauder.) The creators were probably just giving us a clue that the quantum singularity came from a cloaked Romulan warbird!

TRIVIA ANSWERS
1. Karina.
2. Davlos III.

DISTANT VOICES

Star Date: unknown

After refusing to sell biomemetic gel to a Lethean named Altovar, Bashir falls prey to a telepathic attack. He awakes to find himself on a devastated DS9. Main power is out, and the Lethean is tearing up the station. In addition, when a rapidly aging Bashir locates four members of the senior staff, they all act strangely. Dax wants decisive action. O'Brien doubts it will help. Odo is suspicious of everyone. Kira seems constantly angry. (Okay, so maybe *that's* not very strange for Kira.) Eventually Bashir convinces O'Brien to work on the communications system. Once connected, the group listens to Sisko and Dax discussing Bashir's medical condition.

Though Dax stands nearby, Bashir hears Dax's voice say that Julian is in a coma, suffering from telepathically induced brain damage. From this and subsequent tricorder readings, Bashir determines that he *is* in a coma. The officers in the corridor with him represent different aspects of his personality. The station is really his mind, and if he can repair it, he'll recover.

After a failed attempt in Ops to re-pair the station, Bashir goes to the most important area on the station for him, the infirmary. Once there, he traps the mental image of the Lethean in a quarantine field and sterilizes it.

Trivia Questions

1. What type of holosuite program does Garak give Bashir for his birthday?

2. What liquid runs from the broken replicator?

PLOT OVERSIGHTS

• At the beginning of this episode Bashir worries that he's turning thirty. He tells Garak that the age of thirty signals the end of youth and a slow march into middle age. In "Emissary" we learn that Bashir is twenty-seven. "Emissary" begins on star date 46379.1. Although we do not have a star date for this episode, it succeeds the episode "Destiny," which carries a star date of 48543.2. It's safe to assume, then, that this episode has a star date later than 48543.2. Guess what? Bashir really *could* be turning thirty! If he had a birthday shortly after coming to the station, this would make perfect sense. (Yes! *Yes!* Way to go, creators! Clap, clap, clap, clap.) It is fascinating, *however,* to see how traditions continue for hundreds of years even though the reason for them has disappeared. In our day and age, the average life span is about seventy years. A thirtieth birthday really does signal the start of middle age.

But in *Star Trek* humans apparently live full and productive lives of well over one hundred years. Yet apparently the stigma of thirty has remained.

• I suppose Bashir is just being a nice guy when he doesn't immediately report Altovar's attempt to buy biomemetic gel from Odo. True, it is a *felony* even to *attempt* to obtain the substance, but he's a doctor, not a policeman, right?

• Bashir really should know very quickly that the reality he's experiencing is an illusion. Shortly after awakening, he looks in a mirror and sees that his hair is starting to turn gray. Note that the length of his hair has not increased, nor does the graying occur only at the roots. A large number of hairs have instantly turned gray over their entire length. As a doctor, Bashir should know that this cannot happen naturally. Even a virus cannot do this. Hair must *grow* out gray from the roots. Bashir should have suspected the work of a prankster makeup artist.

• Though this is all happening in Bashir's mind, you would expect it to conform to his knowledge of medical science, wouldn't you? Fleeing from the Lethean in Quark's bar, Bashir falls down and promptly pronounces that he has broken his hip. (This occurs just before a commercial break and heightens the tension of the show—no doubt to help ensure that viewers won't go channel surfing and forget to return.) As the episode continues, however, Bashir seems to improve, and eventually, he walks again! (Maybe in the twenty-fourth century broken hips mend themselves?!)

EQUIPMENT ODDITIES

• At one point Bashir finds a malfunctioning replicator. A liquid pours from the top like one of those hot-beverage vending machines that's out of cups. This surprised me. I guess Cardassian replicators work differently from Federation replicators. In "Evolution" *(TNG)* we see a Federation replicator malfunction. A glass sits on the materialization grid, and liquid bubbles out of it—as if it is constantly being materialized inside the glass. (Then again, this *is* happening in Bashir's mind.)

• The doors on the wardroom where Bashir first meets Kira, Dax, O'Brien, and Odo don't open all the way. (Then again, this *is* happening in Bashir's mind.)

• Trying to determine his status, Bashir takes a reading by punching a few buttons on a tricorder. He must know of a little-used "reverse scanning" feature built into the tricorder because he has the device pointed *away* from himself as he uses it. Moments later we see that even O'Brien doesn't know about this feature. When using the same tricorder, O'Brien flips the device 180 degrees in his hand to point the front of the tricorder at his torso to determine if he is showing any life signs. (Then again, this *is* happening in Bashir's mind.)

• Bashir must be a traditionalist when it comes to tennis. He and Garak lob a ball back and forth with twentieth-century rackets. In "Suspicions" *(TNG)* Crusher gives Guinan a tennis racket and it's very futuristic-looking. (Then again, this *is*...oh, never mind.)

• At two different times Bashir sees

a monitor readout on his condition. The first time, he comments that his pulse is thready. The second time, the Lethean says Bashir is dying. Yet both times, the right side of the monitor shows a strong regular pulse. (Do I need to say it?)

TRIVIA ANSWERS

1. An adaptation of one of Shoggoth's Enigma Tales.
2. Tarkelean tea.

THE BOYS IN WONDERLAND
TOTE BOARD

I n the *Classic* episode "Mirror, Mirror" a transporter accident sends Kirk, McCoy, Scott, and Uhura to a parallel universe where everything is opposite. Officers on the *Enterprise* step up in rank by assassinating their superiors. "Agonizers" are used to discipline crew members, and the Federation is an empire that rules by terror. At the time of this writing, the creators of DS9 have returned twice to this scenario, in the episodes "Crossover" and "Through the Looking Glass." (The rumors say that more are on the way. At the time of this writing, I've only seen through the episode, "Paradise Lost.") The first time "Crossover" aired I thought, "My, oh, my, oh, my! The boys out at Paramount certainly had fun with *this* episode!" (Only a few minutes into the episode evil Kira made her appearance in a leather catsuit!) The creators had taken the opportunity to create a dark, sensual version of the series' setting and apparently enjoyed every minute of it. A year later, "Through the Looking Glass" confirmed my initial reaction: Dominatrix Kira was back, and now we had Mistress Dax and Ruffian Bashir to boot. As I was doing my initial overview of these episodes for this *Guide*, I decided it would be fun to do a tote board just on these two episodes—a tote board that would concentrate on items not normally seen in an episode of *Star Trek: Deep Space Nine*. Given the allusions in both episodes to *Alice in Wonderland,* I thought the title above would be appropriate.

1. Number of times Sisko has his way with Kira or Dax: two, perhaps three
2. Number of times a main character dies: three
3. Number of times Garak sends a kiss Kira's way: one
4. Number of times we see Kira's bare back: two
5. Number of times a main character hits Bashir: four
6. Number of times we see Kira taking a milk bath: one
7. Number of times Garak interrogates a prisoner with Kira's permission: three
8. Number of times Kira orders someone's death: four
9. Number of time we see Quark taking a milk bath: zero
10. Number of times Sisko calls O'Brien "Smiley": twelve
11. Number of times Kira's leather-clad posterior saunters away from the camera: eleven

REFERENCES
1. "Crossover": When he goes to "discuss" his recent mission with Kira. "Through the Looking Glass": After mistress Dax tells Sisko that she's going to make him glad that he's alive. And after arriving on the station and being taken to Kira's quarters (perhaps).

2. "Crossover": Kira orders Quark's death and Bashir kills Odo. "Through the Looking Glass": Rom is impaled on an airlock door.

3. Just after he presents his plan to kill the intendant in "Crossover."

4. In "Crossover" during the milk bath. In "Through the Looking Glass" as Kira receives a massage.

5. Odo slaps him three times when instructing Bashir in the Rules of Obedience in "Crossover." Sisko punches Bashir in "Through the Looking Glass."

6. During "Crossover."

7. In "Crossover" he interrogates 0413-Theta and Quark. In "Through the Looking Glass" he interrogates Rom.

8. "Crossover": She tells Garak to kill Quark. She tells Garak to kill Bashir slowly on the promenade. "Through the Looking Glass": She picks three Terrans at random to slaughter. She orders everyone's death except Jennifer Sisko's near the end of the episode.

9. The scene in the holosuite at the end of "Meridian" featuring Kira's body and Quark's head was bad enough!

10. "Crossover": Four times in the bar. When he invites O'Brien onto his crew at the end of the episode. "Through the Looking Glass": Just before beaming down to meet the rest of the resistance. After O'Brien says they could use a scientist in the resistance. When O'Brien meets up with Sisko during the escape. Before asking O'Brien how far it is to the ore processing center. When he tells O'Brien to seal the door to ore processing. When he tells Jennifer to ask O'Brien for the details of who he is. When he tells O'Brien to take him home.

11. "Crossover": After reassigning 0413-Theta to the mines. After she tells Garak that she thinks he enjoys setting examples too much. Just before she agrees to allow Garak to interrogate 0413-Theta. Just after she tells Garak that she will make Garak her example if 0413-Theta dies under interrogation. As she enters her office in Ops. "Through the Looking Glass": After her conversation with Garak in ore processing. After she tells Garak to bring Sisko to her quarters. After she agrees that Sisko will die but not a moment before. In her quarters as she walks over to a reclining Sisko. After she tells Sisko that she has to think about what she will do with him. As Sisko tells her that she would be making a mistake by killing him.

THROUGH THE LOOKING GLASS

Star Date: unknown

Unexpectedly, O'Brien pulls a phaser on Sisko in Ops and forces him onto a transporter pad. The pair rematerializes in the alternate universe first visited during the *Classic* episode "Mirror, Mirror." After the visit by our Kira and Bashir in "Crossover," this universe's Captain Sisko began a rebellion to free Terrans from the rule of the Klingon-Cardassian Alliance. Recently the Alliance blew up Captain Sisko's ship before he could complete an important mission.

Jennifer Sisko—a Terran scientist and estranged wife of Captain Sisko—has been working to complete a transspectral sensory array that will allow the Alliance to scan the Cardassian Badlands for the rebellion's ships. Captain Sisko was attempting to stop her—to kill her if necessary. Our Sisko agrees to complete the mission, unwilling to see his wife die a second time when he could save her. The pair arranges for Rom to "betray" them to Intendant Kira and be brought to Terok Nor (a.k.a. DS9). Once there, Sisko convinces Jennifer to join the rebellion. Unfortunately,

Trivia Questions

1. How many Cardassian voles does Odo find in Quark's storeroom?

2. What is the command access code for Terok Nor?

Garak "persuades" Rom to disclose how Sisko intends to escape before impaling the Ferengi on an airlock door. Desperate, Sisko uses his knowledge of the station's command codes and sets Terok Nor's self-destruct sequence—forcing Kira to allow the Terrans to return to the Badlands unharmed.

RUMINATIONS

Well! Sisko has quite the time in this episode, doesn't he!? First he gets to have his way with Dax! Then it appears that he gets to have his way with Kira! (Possibly not, but she seems very happy to see him. Besides, "Crossover" gave every indication that they were intimate before, and if they were intimate before, why wouldn't they be again?) And then—as the pièce de résistance—he makes up with his dead wife and gets a kiss on the cheek! I wonder if Sisko told our Dax and Kira about this experience. (Philip G. Jones of Mid-Wales, United Kingdom, wondered this as well.)

PLOT OVERSIGHTS

• After transporting Sisko off the station, Alt-O'Brien materializes with his captive on a ship sitting in space—apparently quite close to the relative position of our DS9 in the alternate universe. How did Alt-O'Brien know where to position his ship? You might recall from "Crossover" that Terok Nor orbits Bajor in the alternate reality. In our reality, DS9 sits near the wormhole. (During "Emissary" the crew moved DS9 160 million kilometers so that Bajor could lay claim to the wormhole.) You also might recall that during "Crossover" Kira and Bashir discovered that the people in the alternate universe didn't know about the wormhole, and they quickly concluded that it should remain a secret. So it seems highly unlikely that Bashir would casually mention to Alt-O'Brien that the station doesn't orbit Bajor in our reality. Such an admission would surely raise the question "Why?"—forcing Bashir to lie, since he wouldn't want to say that it's out in space because it sits near the wormhole. In other words, Alt-O'Brien *should* think that the station in our reality orbits Bajor. This is a problem. Even if he could get his vessel close enough to the alternate reality's Terok Nor to transport, when he beamed into our reality expecting to find a station in orbit around Bajor, he would materialize in open space!

• After arriving in the alternate universe, Sisko easily disarms Alt-O'Brien. There were plenty of opportunities to do this before transporting to the alternate universe, and one might wonder why Sisko didn't do this sooner. Of course, if he had, it would have been a short show!

• During this episode there's a woman in the alternate universe who looks just like our Jadzia Dax. Granted she doesn't act like our Dax, but Sisko does address her as "Dax," and everyone seems to think that *is* her name. One question: Is the lovely, little Trill Symbiosis Commission in business in this alternate reality? Or did Alt-Jazdia kill someone to get the Dax symbiont? Is that why she's here with the Terran rebels? Is she hiding from the law?

• After capturing Sisko, Alt-Kira has him taken to her quarters. She then leaves to consider what she will do with him. The next time we see Sisko, Garak has brought Jennifer to visit with him. Sisko asked to see her, and *somebody* decided it would be okay. Who in the "worlds" decided that *this* was a good idea?! Sisko is the *leader* of the Terran rebellion. Jennifer is working on a new type of sensor that will reveal the presence of the rebel hiding places in the Badlands. This is the key to *annihilating* the rebellion. What possible good could come from allowing Sisko to meet with her? Answer: none!

• At the end of the episode Sisko walks in to find Alt-Dax and Jennifer "getting along." Somehow, I *don't* think so. Jennifer developed a well-defined hatred for her husband because he was always chasing after other women. Now that she meets one of those other women she "gets along" with her?

• I realize that I may not measure up to the brave and valiant standards of Starfleet officers. But if my wife died and I traveled to an alternate universe and found her alive and rescued her...I would bring her home with me!

• I wonder how long it's going to be before Alt-Kira, the Alt-Cardassians, and the Alt-Klingons get tired of our intrusion into their reality and decide to stage a little intrusion of their own.

EQUIPMENT ODDITIES

• Just before beaming down to meet the rebels, Sisko rides on a turbolift aboard Alt-O'Brien's ship. If the lights in the background aren't decoy information, the turbolift appears to travel six or seven decks during their conversation. It sure doesn't seem like Alt-O'Brien's vessel has seven decks from the external shot we see. Three, *maybe* four, but not seven.

CONTINUITY AND PRODUCTION PROBLEMS

• Twice in this episode Alt-O'Brien and Sisko use the transporter on Sisko's ship. Both times, reflecting on the panels in the background, there is a horizontal band of light that looks funny as the transport progresses. It seems to be in front of the pair instead of behind them as they fade away.

• Didn't the people at Paramount have fun during this episode?! Lots of *strategic* camera panning and placement here! (In fact, the frequent placement of the camera to enjoy the full saunter of Alt-Kira's leather-clad posterior orig-

inally inspired me to do "The Boys in Wonderland Tote Board.") For instance, to rejoin Sisko and Alt-Dax—after the interlude where Alt-Dax made Sisko glad that he was still alive—the camera starts on our favorite Trill's shoulder. Alt-Dax then runs her hand all the way down her side, giving the camera the flimsiest excuse to do a leisurely body pan traversing the length of her body to arrive at Sisko, who just happens to be seated strategically near her feet. (And—honestly—he *does* look happy to be alive!)

• Toward the end of the episode Alt-Kira and her forces have a corridor phaser fight with Sisko and company. At one point Alt-Kira's forces pour into a hallway junction and form a wall of phasers and disrupters, with several Bajorans kneeling on the front row. Alt-Kira, Alt-Garak, and several other Security personnel line the back. After Sisko and company sneak off to the ore processing center, Garak yells, "Pursue!" Watch the male Bajoran on the front row as he stands. He hops up and then hops *twice* to his left before moving forward. (I assume he's trying to get around the camera setup, but it really looks funny!)

TRIVIA ANSWERS
1. Twenty-seven.
2. Alpha, 9-1-7-5, blue.

IMPROBABLE CAUSE

Star Date: unknown

An explosion in Garak's shop begins an ever-deepening investigation for Odo. When all the leads dry up, Odo calls in a favor from a member of the Cardassian government. The contact tells Odo that five other Cardassians lost their lives on the same day as the attempt on Garak's. Seeing the list, Garak reveals that every one was a close associate of Enabran Tain—former head of the Obsidian Order. (See "The Wire.") Fearing for Tain's life as well, Garak convinces Odo to procure a runabout so Garak can travel to one of Tain's safe houses and warn his former superior. As they approach the system, a Romulan warbird decloaks and captures them in a tractor beam.

On the warbird, Tain reveals that the Romulan Tal Shiar and the Cardassian Obsidian Order have decided to stage a preemptive strike against the Dominion. Using a fleet of ships secretly constructed in the Orias System (see *"Defiant"*), they will attack and destroy the Founders' home planet. Wanting to return to his former position at the Obsidian Order

Trivia Questions

1. The Flaxian named Retaya was a suspect in the murder of whom on Japori II?

2. Where is the runabout stored on the Romulan warbird?

after the successful completion of the mission, Tain had the Romulans kill all his old associates. Now that Garak has come, however, Tain offers Garak a place beside him. Surprisingly, Garak accepts.

GREAT LINES

"Well, the truth is usually just an excuse for a lack of imagination."—Garak to the senior staff. (Not that I agree with the sentiment, but it sums up Garak's evasiveness and deception to a tee! Nominated by Seth Farrow of Independence, Missouri.)

PLOT OVERSIGHTS

• The episode begins with Bashir and Garak enjoying lunch together. During their discussion, Garak attempts to prove that humans rush through their meals by motioning to a nearby table and commenting that the Talarian is only half finished while the human's plate is empty. Garak sits opposite Bashir. The table in question is directly behind Bashir. The human at the table sits with his back to Bashir. From my perspective it doesn't look like Garak can even see the human's plate!

• The security for access to the runabouts leaves much to be desired. At first Odo believes a Flaxian is responsible for blowing up Garak's shop. When the Flaxian departs the station, Odo boards a runabout to follow. He finds Garak seated inside. Garak! The former Cardassian spy! Just sitting there?! Can anyone just wander onto these vessels anytime they choose?

• Odo seems to be broadening out the targets of his snide humor. Usually it's just reserved for Quark. But in this episode our favorite Changeling comments that one would think the Tal Shiar would appreciate a good tailor—given the look of their uniforms. (Not a nit, just an observation.)

CHANGED PREMISES

• While having lunch with Bashir, Garak motions toward a table behind the good doctor and identifies its occupants as a Talarian and a human. Bashir looks back and seems to agree with these labels. The Talarians first appear in "Suddenly Human." They look nothing like the occupant identified by the camera as a Talarian. That person looks more like a Dopterian (as seen in the episode "The Forsaken") or a Kobheerian (as seen in the episode "Duet"). (I realize that there may be Talarians who look like Dopterians or Kobheerians, but the creators make the rules in the *Star Trek* universe, and one of the principles they follow for good storytelling is similar makeup for all members of the same race. This allows the audience to identify a person's race from sight alone.)

• After finishing the biomolecular

scan of the blast site, O'Brien brings the results to Odo. The scan turned up traces of living tissue, and Odo deduces that the device that caused the explosion in Garak's shop used a "pheromonic sensor." O'Brien doesn't know what that is, so Odo explains it to him. In this episode O'Brien plays the "cabbagehead." He's the one chosen by the creators to play dumb so the audience can listen in on Odo's explanation. (Elias Saltz of Oxford, Ohio, first submitted the term "cabbage-ism" to the Nitpickers Guild and it has grown from there!) Interestingly enough, in "The Nagus," Odo plays the cabbagehead and O'Brien plays the authority in a very similar situation! Just after an attack on Quark, Sisko, O'Brien, and Odo stand near the blast site. O'Brien scans the area with his tricorder and pronounces it the work of a Ferengi locator bomb designed to lock onto a person's pheromones. At this Odo comments, "You mean they're attracted to body odor," apparently unaware that such a device exists.

EQUIPMENT ODDITIES

• This may not be the first time it's happened, but it's the first time I noticed. Someone changed the headrests on the pilot chairs of the runabout when we weren't looking. (I guess O'Brien took my comments to heart! Wink, wink. See "The Maquis, Part I.")

TRIVIA ANSWERS
1. Dakora Assan.
2. Launching Bay 3.

THE DIE IS CAST

Star Date: unknown

As the fleet of Romulan and Cardassian warships heads toward the Founders' home planet, Enabran Tain asks Garak to interrogate Odo for any additional information he might have on the Changelings. Torturing Odo with a device that prevents shape shifting, Garak learns only that our favorite Changeling still wants to be with his people even after all the atrocities they have committed.

Meanwhile, the fleet arrives at their destination and waltzes right into a trap. One hundred fifty Jem'Haddar ships pour out of the nearby nebula and start blasting away. Garak hurries to Odo's quarters. He knocks out the guard, opens the door, and tells Odo it's time for them to leave in the runabout. Tain's Romulan associate, Colonel Lovok, then appears and gives Odo a data pad to access the runabout's launching bay. He is actually a Changeling. The operation was Tain's idea initially, but the Founders encouraged it every step of the way to deal a fatal blow to the Tal Shiar and the Obsidian Order.

After departing in the runabout, Odo

Trivia Questions

1. What starship is searching for Odo's runabout in the Algira Sector?

2. Quark wants to turn Garak's burned-out shop into what?

and Garak come under attack by the rampaging Jem'Haddar. Thankfully, the *Defiant* quickly appears to rescue the pair and return them safely to the station. Against orders, Sisko brought the ship in the Gamma Quadrant to find his missing Security chief.

RUMINATIONS

This episode contains some beautiful visual and special effects. Under Garak's torture Odo becomes flaky and ghoulish-looking. Except this time—as opposed to the melting scenes in "The Forsaken" and "The Alternate"—Odo's outfit changes as well! When Garak finally turns off his machine so Odo can return to his liquid state, not only does the humanoid shape pour into the bowl but the flakes on the carpet actually rush over and jump in, too. (Very nicely done!) And the battle sequence between the Jem'Haddar and the Romulan/Cardassian fleet is gorgeous! (Must be lots of money in those seconds.) Finally, it's always great to see those phasers fire on the Defiant. *I like that weapon o' mass destruction!*

PLOT OVERSIGHTS

• Shortly after the armada heads for

the Founders' home planet, Admiral Toddman calls DS9 to advise Sisko and company of their responsibilities during the crisis. He says he wants the *Defiant* to guard Bajor. (I would agree wholeheartedly with this idea. In fact, we'll learn in a few moments that Starfleet is sending a fleet of nine ships to DS9. All I can say is: *It's about time!*) Toddman then goes on to say that the Romulan/Cardassian armada has a good chance for success. He specifically notes that the armada has modified their cloaks so the Founders cannot detect their approach! I must have really misunderstood the first few minutes of this episode because I could have sworn that DS9 detected their approach. Didn't they? Didn't Dax track the approach of this wave of tachyon particles? Didn't this wave alert the station that something was coming?

• The term "officer" seems to be very generously applied in this episode. Admiral Toddman tells Sisko, "I'm sorry about your officer." Moments later, Sisko says he's not going to abandon one of his officers. Strangely enough, both men are talking about...Odo! I don't believe Odo ever went to Starfleet Academy, and I've never seen any dialogue to indicate that Odo is actually part of the Bajoran militia. As I understand it, Odo was drafted by Dukat to solve a murder (see "Necessary Evil") on Terok Nor. Then Dukat kept him on as Security chief. (For what reason I'm not sure, because he didn't solve the murder!) Then Sisko kept him on when Starfleet took command of the station. When has this guy ever had any military training? Or doesn't that matter anymore? If you're

part of the senior staff, do you automatically get the term "officer" applied to you? (I realize you can use the term "officer" to refer to a policeman—which, of course, is Odo's occupation. But in the context of this dialogue—between Starfleet officers—the term "officer" takes on a different connotation, especially when spoken by Admiral Toddman.)

• Sisko tells his senior staff that if they go on a mission to rescue Odo—and they are fortunate enough to return—they probably will all face a general court-martial. And why not? They are leaving Bajor undefended in the middle of an aggression against the Dominion. There are no doubt *billions* of lives at stake. Of course, Sisko goes anyway, and Toddman conveniently decides not to press charges. (Granted, the *Defiant* couldn't do much if a fleet of Jem'Haddar ships attacked Bajor anyway, but that's not really the point.)

• And speaking of Sisko running off to the Gamma Quadrant with his senior staff, we are once again forced to ask: *Who's running the station?!*

• On the way to the Founders' home planet, Lovok explains that there are no Jem'Haddar bases anywhere near their destination. The *first* time I saw this episode I thought, "It's a trap. Nobody is that stupid. *Nobody* would leave his or her home planet *undefended*." Yet the Tal Shiar and the Obsidian Order seem to think this is perfectly reasonable. (On the other hand, I have always been less than impressed with the defenses for Earth. Maybe the Tal Shiar and the Obsidian Order have grown soft while fighting the Federation.)

• Garak's torture of Odo raises a few questions. After the Romulans set up the little quantum stasis gizmo, Garak acts as if Odo no longer poses a threat because the Changeling can no longer change. Yet at the end of the episode Odo open-palms Garak—knocking him unconscious and leaving a nasty bruise—all without shape shifting. Wouldn't you say that even as a humanoid, Odo poses a considerable threat? Also, one wonders why Odo didn't just walk over to the silly little machine and knock it over. (Would it violate some sort of Cardassian torture code that Odo has sworn to uphold?)

• The graphics of the Jem'Haddar attacking the Romulan/Cardassian fleet are truly gorgeous. But why aren't the Romulans and Cardassians firing back? They're just sitting there getting pummeled. They might have a better chance if they'd launch a few photon torpedoes and fire a few phasers!

• I referenced this episode in my discussion about the Changelings' ability to perfectly imitate a humanoid face at the end of "The Search, Part I" and the beginning of "The Search, Part II." Just an additional note: Obviously the Changeling who plays Lovok in this episode has no problem creating a humanoid face. Granted, he's a more skilled Changeling than Odo, but Odo *has* been practicing. Shouldn't we start to see some improvement in Odo's humanoid features? Or has he gotten used to the way he looks by now?

• Providing for Odo and Garak's escape, Lovok says that no Changeling has ever harmed another. Yet, as Odo and Garak leave the battle scene, the Jem'Haddar attack their runabout. As I see it, there are two possibilities here. Either that little statement "No Changeling has ever harmed another" applies only to *personal* injury and the Changelings have no problem with the Jem'Haddar killing Odo, or the Jem'Haddar are like sharks. Once you get them in a feeding frenzy, you can't stop them. (Even with these explanations it still seems odd to me that the Changeling would provide for Odo's exit from the warbird and not ensure safe passage through the war zone. What was Lovok going to tell the others if the runabout had been destroyed? "Well, it wasn't my fault. I got him off the ship. How was I supposed to know that he couldn't fly to safety through a pitched battle between 150 frenzied Jem'Haddar attack craft and a fleet of Alpha Quadrant warships?")

• It's *very* considerate of the Jem'Haddar not to attack the *Defiant* while her shields are down and she's transporting Odo and Garak to safety. I wonder if Sisko sent them a thank-you card.

EQUIPMENT ODDITIES

• At the beginning of the episode, the Romulan/Cardassian armada makes a close pass-by of the station on the way into the wormhole. Just before entering, the ships decloak and then recloak on the Gamma Quadrant. Several nitpickers found this odd. Why not just enter the Gamma Quadrant invisible? (I'm guessing that there's some reason you can't fly a cloaked ship through the wormhole. Maybe if the wormhole can't see you, it won't open?)

• As Garak and Tain reminisce, Lovok enters the room to say that the armada has recloaked in the Gamma Quadrant and is traveling at warp 6 toward the Founders' home planet. When Garak finds this a bit slow, Lovok explains that they cannot travel any faster without the warp drive being detected even with the cloak. Yet at the very beginning of the episode, Dax picked up the approach of the armada well before they decloaked. Granted, she wasn't reading their warp signature, but there was so much stuff flashing across her screen that Sisko called O'Brien to the bridge to get his opinion. (Of course, they couldn't figure out what it was before the armada decloaked, but I doubt the Founders would have that problem!)

• While speaking with Admiral Toddman, Lieutenant Commander Eddington says that the message they received from Odo stated the runabout had been caught in a tractor beam. Presumably this refers to the scene in the previous episode ("Improbable Cause") when the Romulan warbird decloaked and grabbed the runabout in its clutches. In that scene Odo tells Garak to take the helm because he's going to try to send out a distress signal. Garak hops in the chair and soon reports that they can't break away. At this Odo says that the Romulans are jamming their transmissions. Garak asks if the message got through. Odo says he doesn't know. When I watched "Improbable Cause" I was certain it hadn't. The Romulans have done this type of abduction before. In "The Mind's Eye" they grab La Forge's shuttlecraft and *nobody* knows about it until La Forge comes very close to killing a Klingon com-

mander of a colony. Yet apparently—in this episode—the message does get through! (Pretty sloppy of the Tal Shiar, if you ask me.)

• Shortly after arriving at the Gamma Quadrant, Sisko cloaks the *Defiant* and sets course for the Founders' home world at warp 8. Remember our discussion above about the Romulans going only warp 6 so the Jem'Haddar couldn't detect the warp drive through the cloak? (And remember, that was with a specially modified cloak.) The *Defiant* has a Romulan cloak, right? Doesn't it seem likely that if the Romulan warbirds are detectable when going faster than warp 6, the *Defiant* will be detectable when going faster than warp 6? Does it seem like a good idea to go warp 8?

• Romulan computer analysis leaves much to be desired. On the way to the Founders' home planet, Lovok explains that the armada should be able to destroy the planet's crust in one hour according to computer analysis. When the armada actually arrives, the first volley—lasting only a few seconds—destroys *30 percent* of the planet's crust. (I would project total destruction of the planet's crust in substantially less than an hour!)

• After the armada completes its first volley, a female Romulan reports that she is still reading life signs on the surface of the Founders' home planet. Garak somehow concludes that the Founders must be using an automated transponder to send this signal. Does that mean there's a transponder on the surface of a planet that just got pulverized by enough force to destroy 30 percent of the crust but it's still working?! Wow! These Founders know how to build hardy machines!

CONTINUITY AND PRODUCTION PROBLEMS

• It's a minor error—and it happens all the time in scenes that use liquids—but it's worth noting. As the opening credits roll, Garak enjoys a glass of some kind of drink with Tain. They reminisce and discuss Garak's return. At one point Garak asks Tain if he remembers a Gul named Dukat. At this point Garak's glass is approximately half empty. Tain does remember Dukat and wonders if Garak would like to have him eliminated.

Garak says that the thought had crossed his mind. Now Garak's glass has gained a noticeable amount of liquid!

• Admiral Toddman bears a striking resemblance to the commander in chief at the beginning of *Star Trek VI: The Undiscovered Country*.

• At the end of the episode—as Odo and Garak flee the battle scene in a runabout—the stars don't move in the runabout window, even when Odo executes a hard turn to port!

TRIVIA ANSWERS

1. The *Portland*.
2. An Argilian massage facility.

272

★ EXPLORERS

Star Date: unknown

fter attending the reopening of a library on Bajor, Sisko returns with plans for an ancient Bajoran spaceship that utilizes solar sails. Some scholars believe that these ships took ancient Bajorans to other planets in the Bajoran System and possibly as far as Cardassia. Aside from the pure joy of the challenge, Sisko decides to build the ship to see if he can transverse the Denorias Belt, the only real navigational hazard between Bajor and Cardassia. If so, it would be possible to make the rest of the trip. Jake even agrees to go along on the adventure. Sisko soon discovers why. The Pennington School in New Zealand on Earth has granted the young man a writing fellowship. After discussing it with Sisko, however, Jake decides to wait a year before leaving. He wants to gain more experience to enhance his writing, and he wouldn't mind seeing his father involved in a steady relationship before he leaves.

The trip proves astonishing. After some mechanical difficulties the craft unexpectedly jumps to warp—pushed there by tachyon eddies. It flashes past the Denorias belt and on to Car-

dassian space. Once it drops to sublight speed, three Cardassian warships approach, and Gul Dukat greets them with congratulations.

RUMINATIONS

In my review of the previous episode ("The Die Is Cast") I noted that the stars in the window of Odo's runabout don't move even though he executes a hard turn to port. In this episode the creators show their skill at doing it right. Just after the drunken serenade between Bashir and O'Brien, the episode returns to Sisko and Jake struggling to continue their voyage. Sisko says "Coming about," and the vessel leans to the right as he makes an adjustment. Notice the stars in the window ahead of Sisko's position. They move just as they should if the ship is really tipping! (I know, the stars wouldn't really be moving. The ship would be moving and the stars would only appear to drift because they would remain stationary. Gotta watch you nitpickers, you write letters!) Here's the problem. The easiest way to do this shot would be to tip the camera. Simple and straightforward, right? No muss, no fuss. The only problem is that the

Trivia Questions

1. What is Bashir's prescription for Leeta's cough?

2. Bashir attended a party at Bruce Lucier's home with whom?

stars would tip, too! To make the stars look right, you have to tip the stars in the opposite direction when you tip the camera. Or...you could build hydraulics into the set to actually tip the vessel. Since I don't deal in reality, I don't really care how the creators did it. (There are plenty of fan books out there that deal in this type of information.) All I know is it looks great!

A milestone to note: I believe that this is the first time in any incarnation of Star Trek that the word "bathroom" appears in a script. (I didn't say it was a great milestone.)

Oh, and one last thing: This episode opens with a Dabo girl named Leeta bidding for Bashir's attentions. Dressed in a skin-tight body suit that's peeled back at the top to show her generous cleavage, she first introduces herself to the good doctor and then makes a pitiful attempt to produce a sickly cough. Bashir immediately turns on the charm and orders a drink to begin her "treatment." I'm confused. It's obvious that the poor girl is freezing in that outfit. Why order a drink? Get her a warm, high-neck, long-sleeve sweater. That would cure Leeta's "chest cold" almost instantly! (Snicker, snicker.)

PLOT OVERSIGHTS

• Sisko must be having a slow month. He builds an entire space ship with primitive tools in fewer than three weeks! The episode begins with an announcement that the USS Lexington will be docking at the station in three weeks, and Sisko leaves in his solar sailer before it arrives. He must have spent all day, every day on it.

(It's a spaceship, for crying out loud!) Hmmm. I wonder what else he might have to do. Well...there're day-to-day operations on the station. There's preparing for a Dominion attack. There's getting Bajor ready to enter the Federation. Did he have too much vacation time accrued and needed to "use it or lose it"?

• Then again, maybe DS9 isn't as busy as it used to be. Earlier this season, during "Defiant," the station sounded positively packed to the gills with cargo. But in this episode Sisko has the crew clean out a cargo bay so he can play.

• One wonders how the Bajorans managed to get these little solar sailing ships into orbit eight hundred years ago. Did they launch them with rockets, or did they have some sort of orbiting platform?

• Oddly enough, O'Brien the "model ship builder as a child," O'Brien the "fixer of stations," O'Brien the chief of Operations on DS9 and—evidently—the chief engineer of the Defiant can't figure out why Sisko wants to build this ship in the first place. O'Brien suggests that Sisko simply use a computer model to prove it's spaceworthy. Well, if that's the way he feels, why doesn't he just move back to Earth with Keiko, make a computer model of DS9 and spend his days pretending to fix the station?

• At one point Sisko tells Jake to listen. Jake says he doesn't hear anything. "Exactly," Sisko replies, "not even the hum of an engine." No, but the sound effects guys felt the need to put in that low, droning noise in the background!

• Jake says that Pennington found out about him because he showed one of his stories to Keiko, and Keiko showed it to a friend who knew someone at the school. This must have been *before* Keiko took off for Bajor.

• Mitzi Adams assures me that tachyons could not accelerate mass from sublight to superlight speeds.

• Gul Dukat's congratulations at the end of the episode seem a bit out of character for the Cardassians. In essence he says, "Great! You made it! Now we look like idiots!" (Must be because of the new peace treaty with Bajor and the recent pummeling by the Dominion.) And personally? I felt the plasmaworks were a bit much on the end, but hey, I guess those Cardies really know how to throw a party.

CHANGED PREMISES

• Before Sisko departs in his little craft, Gul Dukat calls to warn the commander about the dangers of the trip. Specifically he says that it's a long way to the Denorios Belt. He must have forgotten that O'Brien moved the station to the mouth of the wormhole in "Emissary." That episode establishes that the wormhole is *in* the Denorios Belt. Strangely enough, *everyone* in this episode seems to think it's a long way to the Denorios Belt! (There is only one explanation that I can imagine. "Emissary" establishes that the wormhole is in the "Denorios Belt," while this episode says it's a long way from the station to the "Denorios Belt." See the difference? So...it's possible that this isn't a nit. It's possible that the creators are just playing with our minds!)

EQUIPMENT ODDITIES

• Just before telling his father that he'd like to go along with him on the solar sailing adventure, Jake receives a message from the Pennington School. He tells the computer to display it on the screen. Apparently the message is text only because Jake bends over and reads it. Text only? In this futuristic setting that uses audiovideo communications almost exclusively? (Of course, this is very convenient because it means that we don't learn immediately that Jake has been accepted to Pennington!)

• I love the little self-leveling navigation device that Sisko installs on his solar sailor when Jake comes to sign on for the mission. It appears to have a weight on the bottom and it's configured to swing freely in all directions. Evidently it was designed to stay upright and give the vessel's occupants some idea of the pitch and yaw of the craft. But, but, but this is a spaceship, and originally it didn't have any artificial gravity, right? So what good does this thing do? Without gravity it would be wandering aimlessly around on its axes. "Ah!" you might say, "maybe the ancient Bajorans didn't use that device. Maybe Sisko installed it because he's added the artificial gravity net." Well, if that's true, there's no reason for the thing to swing freely because it's *always* going to be pulled down to the floor because that's where the gravity net is installed. (In fact, you can see this happen in the scene I described above under "Ruminations." It's a bit difficult because Jake is in the way at first, but if you watch the device as the ship tips to the right you'll see that it always stays parallel with the floor—which would indicate that the creators tipped the camera, not the set. Wink, wink.)

• I find it interesting that Sisko was going to take this trip alone, but the ship seems to require two people to deploy the sails properly.

• Just before Sisko jettisons the sprit, he and Jake take some pressure off the sails by cranking the cranks. It appears that Jake forgets to *unlock* the crank before turning it. No wonder he's struggling!

• Many nitpickers had real problems when this dinky little craft jumped to warp. First, the craft has no structural integrity field, and it's made—at least in part—from wood. Can you say, "crinkle, splinter, crunch"? Second, no mention is made of an inertia damping field. This wonderful little device *somehow* overrides the normal effect of inertia on Starfleet crew members when a starship rapidly accelerates to warp. Without it—the *Technical Manual* descriptively advises—the crew on board a starship would turn into "chunk salsa." Sisko's little craft seems to be missing an IDF. Can you say, "splat, smear, dip"?

• But—just for the sake of argument—let's say that this little craft *did* manage to get to Cardassia. How was it supposed to land on the planet? Drop like a rock until it made a large crater on the surface? (In fact, Gul Dukat at the end of the episode mentions the discovery of a crash site. No doubt these crash sites were the original instigators of the deep primal fear and hatred that the Cardassians hold for the Bajorans. Look at it from the Cardies' point of view. It's eight hundred years ago. You're having a lovely dinner with the family eating raw taspar eggs. Suddenly you hear howling from the sky. A blazing eruption fills the night. Your neighbors' huts are blown to oblivion, and you're picking body parts out of your garden for weeks! In the resulting months you sift through the wreckage and keep finding the same symbol: an oval with a smaller circle at the bottom. You have no way of knowing whence the destroyer came...but you remember that symbol. That symbol. The oval with a smaller circle at the bottom. You *remember*.)

CONTINUITY AND PRODUCTION PROBLEMS

• Once Avery Brooks grows his own goatee in later episodes, the one he sports in this episode looks obviously fake.

TRIVIA ANSWERS

1. Fanalian tonic, very hot.
2. Erib, an Andorian.

FAMILY BUSINESS

Star Date: unknown

A liquidator named Brunt from the Ferengi Commerce Authority (FCA) arrives at Quark's to serve a writ of accountability. After the appropriate payment, Brunt discloses that Quark's mother, Ishka, has been caught acquiring profit. According to Ferengi law, Quark must force a confession from her and return the latinum. If he doesn't, the FCA will sell her as an indentured servant and make Quark repay the profit. Traveling to the Ferengi home world with Rom, Quark finds Ishka as stubborn as ever—fully committed to proving that females are just as capable in business as males. Now, she's even taken to wearing clothes. (Gasp!)

Moreover, as Quark begins his own investigation, he discovers that Ishka has earned much more profit than the measly three bars of latinum that the FCA claims. She's made enough that if she doesn't sign the confession, Quark will be ruined. After a bitter fight, Quark storms off to the FCA to tell them the extent of Ishka's activities. Then Rom intervenes, claiming Ishka has promised Quark half the profits. She hasn't. Rom just wants to get the two talking again. In the end, Ishka signs the confession and repays all the profit—all the profit that Quark and the FCA could *find,* that is.

Trivia Questions

1. Who was Ishka's father?

2. What is the name of Captain Yates's brother's baseball team?

RUMINATIONS

This episode contains a lovely bit of continuity. At one point, Sisko meets a freighter captain named Kasidy Yates. She has a brother who lives on the colony on Cestus III. Cestus III was the site of the Gorn retaliation in "Arena." Evidently the Federation and the Gorn worked out their differences!

One other bit of note: The music during the preview for this episode sounds very reminiscent of the music from *Psycho. A little joke from the creators!*

PLOT OVERSIGHTS

• First, Quark decides to go back to the Ferengi home world. Then Rom decides to go back to the Ferengi home world. I wonder: Who's taking care of Nog? Or is he just going to fend for himself? (At least he can get in some good study time while the bar is closed. You might recall that he's preparing for the Starfleet Academy entrance exams.)

CHANGED PREMISES

• It's interesting that Quark is so appalled at a Ferengi female acquiring profit in this episode since he protected Pel—a Ferengi female posing as a male—at the end of "Rules of Acquisition" and he even gave her a stake of ten bars of gold-pressed latinum. (Of course, Ishka *is* his mother, and that may have a lot to do with it!)

EQUIPMENT ODDITIES

• Here's a new one for you: Sisko gets to name his runabouts! Near the beginning of the episode Kira tells him the new runabout is available for inspection, and he tells her he wants to name it the *Rubicon*. This is the first time this has ever happened. Since the runabouts belong to Starfleet, Starfleet Command usually reserves this privilege for themselves.

• With the closing of the bar, O'Brien and Bashir find themselves cut off from their dartboard. In one scene O'Brien attempts to pick the lock on the main door of Quark's. Watch the "glass" panel behind O'Brien on the close-ups. As his left elbow hits it, you can clearly see that it's made from some type of flimsy plastic!

• And speaking of picking the lock on Quark's, is the bar surrounded by some type of security field? Are all the transporters broken on the station? Is there some reason Chief of Operations and Resident Transporter Guru Miles Edward O'Brien doesn't simply *beam* himself inside?

• This episode clinched the fact that O'Brien has solved the antigrav problem on the station. In "Melora" Bashir said that standard antigrav units wouldn't work on DS9, and that's why he had to replicate an old-style wheelchair. In this episode Captain Yates tells one of her men to fetch an antigrav sled.

• Ferengi doors appear to have the same intelligence as the doors of all the other races seen on *Star Trek*. At the end of the episode Brunt leaves Ishka's home. The doors open and the doors close. Then Quark leaves. The doors open. Rom hangs around for a few moments. The doors stay open. Rom finally leaves. The doors stay open. Rom stops in the outer courtyard. The doors stay open. Rom walks off. The doors *still* stay open—apparently because Ishka is wistfully staring out the opening and they know it would be rude to close!

TRIVIA ANSWERS

1. Adred.
2. Pike City Pioneers.

SHAKAAR

Star Date: unknown

When Kalem Apren—first minister of the provisional government on Bajor—dies, Kai Winn is appointed interim first minister until new elections can be held in a month. Almost immediately Winn decides to move several soil reclamators from Dahkur Province to Rakantha Province—formerly a rich farming area. Like much of Bajor, the Cardassians poisoned its soil as a parting gift. Winn wants to use the reclamators to restore Rakantha so it can quickly produce several valuable export crops, thereby attracting interstellar commerce. Unfortunately, the reclamators were promised to the farmers in Dahkur Province for a year, and they are unwilling to give them up. To make matters worse, Winn has dealt heavy-handedly with them—ordering the reclamators' return instead of asking.

Since a Bajoran named Shakaar leads the farmers, Winn turns to Kira for help. She fought in Shakaar's resistance cell during the occupation. Kira manages to set up a meeting between Winn and Shakaar, but then Winn sends in the militia instead. For

weeks Bajor totters on the brink of civil war until the military refuses to back Winn any longer over such a trivial matter. Instead the military backs Shakaar in the election for the new first minister. Not wanting her dictatorial blunders to be made public, Kai Winn fades into the background.

Trivia Questions

1. Where do Shakaar and the others make their stand?

2. Lenaris Holem served in what resistance cell?

RUMINATIONS

The subplot of this episode concerns O'Brien playing darts "in the zone." He's got a winning streak going that seems unstoppable. In fact, when Quark offers odds of ten to one on the next challenger—sight unseen—O'Brien suggests he increase them to fifteen to one. Then in the fateful game, Quark brings O'Brien a mug of synthale. Reaching back, O'Brien pops his shoulder out of place and must forfeit the match. The first time I saw this episode I really thought O'Brien and Bashir were playing a joke on Quark for taking bets on the dart game. But the episode ended without this revelation, so I guess I was mistaken.

PLOT OVERSIGHTS

• The first time we see Kira, she is

in her quarters before an open fire, praying for Bareil. At the end of the episode Kira blows out the flame, signifying the end of her mourning for her former love. These two moments raise a few questions. An open flame seems a rather luxurious commodity on a space station. It consumes oxygen. It is very dangerous, given that the station is a closed system. (On the surface of a planet you can exit a burning house!) Did this flame really burn for weeks unattended? Are the fire suppression systems so stable that DS9 regulations allow this? Then again, perhaps it's a concession to the expression of certain aspects of the Bajoran religion—in this case praying for the dead.

• In my review of "The Collaborator," I stated my reasons for finding the Bajoran religious practices a bit odd. This "praying for the dead" constitutes another strange practice. Praying for the dead does exist in many religions on Earth, but I believe it's usually motivated by a desire to see the deceased's position in the afterlife improved. I can't recall ever hearing of an Earth religion that proposes intercession for those members who achieve the highest state postulated by the system. Kai Winn herself states that Bareil is "walking with the Prophets." Sounds like Bareil has graduated to the big time! Look at it this way: Just what do you request for the dead guy who has everything? Let's say that Kira prays, "Prophets, strengthen Bareil today in everything he sets his hand to do. Give him wisdom." Since Bareil is walking with the Prophets, doesn't he already have

wisdom? Doesn't he already have strength? Or does the Bajoran religion have some sort of graduated system in its corollary to heaven?

• After hearing Kira offer to set up a meeting with Shakaar, Kai Winn dismisses Kira and asks that she convey best regards to "Commander Sisko." Normally Winn is careful to call him "Emissary."

• So...did Kira request a leave of absence from Sisko? Or did she just disappear for two weeks from the station while she acted in rebellion against the duly appointed government of Bajor? The last time she did this (see "Progress"), Sisko came within inches of booting her off the station.

EQUIPMENT ODDITIES

• Is it really that hard for the Bajorans to build a few more of these soil reclamators? And what about the Federation? In this episode we learn that Federation doctors came to fit the victims of the Cardassian occupation with prosthetics. If the Federation is willing to provide artificial limbs, why not soil reclamators? (Or is the problem really just Kai Winn and her need to be obeyed?)

• It's amazing that the Bajoran militia chased Shakaar and his people through the hills for two weeks, seemingly unable to capture them—especially when you consider that Kira is *wearing her communicator!* Doesn't that device pinpoint her location, or has Kira turned it off?

• It's also amazing that the Bajoran militia seem bereft of any air support for this search. Shakaar and his people are climbing over mountains that have little or no vegetation. One would think that a craft similar to a helicopter could make short work of this. Of course, that raises another question: Why couldn't the Cardassians find this resistance group during the occupation? (Supposedly Shakaar and company are doing the same thing that they did with the Cardies.)

CONTINUITY AND PRODUCTION PROBLEMS

• The closed captioning has Kira saying "Shakaar" just after he surprises her by grabbing her shoulder and twisting her about.

• So, um...his Shakaar guy, does he remind anyone else of a certain anaphasic energy being who was enjoying the carnal delights of Dr. Beverly Crusher in "Sub Rosa" *(TNG)*?

• During a meal between Kira and her former resistance fighter friends, a woman named Lupaza asks who wants a piece of tuwaly pie. In the closed captioning a man named Furel responds, "If you haven't put too much rejka in it."

• At one point the Bajoran militia close in on Shakaar and his people. Kira sets up a false sensor echo to throw them off the trail. One of the men in the militia scans the area and then says, "New reading: 700 meters. That way." The closed captioning has "700 yards."

TRIVIA ANSWERS

1. Tanis Canyon.
2. Ornathia.

★ FACETS

Star Date: unknown

Dax undergoes zhian'tara, a unique Trill rite in which a Guardian (see "Equilibrium") uses his telepathic abilities to transfer the memories of each of Dax's previous hosts, one at a time, into Jadzia's closest friends. This allows Jadzia to interact with them one on one. All goes well until Joran (again see "Equilibrium") tells Jadzia that she is nothing more than a pretty little girl who clearly doesn't measure up to the greatness of her previous hosts.

The words strike home. Jadzia has always wondered why Curzon didn't object when she reapplied to the initiate program after washing out. Curzon in Odo's body confirms her worst fear. Curzon claims he didn't object simply because he felt sorry for her. He also makes the surprise announcement that he and Odo both like what they have together and he's not returning to Dax. Under Sisko's urgings, Jadzia confronts Curzon, forcing him to face his selfish motives and reveal the real reason he didn't object to Jadzia's readmission. Only then does Curzon admit that he drove her

hard so no one would know he was in love with her. When Jadzia washed out, he felt guilty for what he had done and was greatly relieved when she reapplied. His deceit admitted, Curzon returns to Dax.

RUMINATIONS

*T*here are several things worth noting in this episode. It opens with Nog running a runabout simulation on the holosuite. He's trying to qualify for a Starfleet Academy preparatory program. Jake comes in and starts beating on the windshield of the runabout. Nog tells the computer to end the simulation and promptly plops to the floor on his backside. This is precisely what I've always felt should happen if a person ended a holosuite (or holodeck) program while sitting down. (See page 226 of The Nitpicker's Guide for Next Generation Trekkers, Volume II!)

Many nitpickers have probably wondered at how quickly Leeta becomes a close friend to Dax—thereby warranting her inclusion in this ceremony. This bothered me at first as well. Then I ran the timeline. We first meet Leeta at the beginning of "Explorers." (You

Trivia Questions

1. What did Bashir have for breakfast?

2. Who was Lela's supervisor as an initiate?

remember—the Dabo girl with the "chest cold" and in desperate need of a sweater.) "Explorers" takes at least three weeks. Then comes "Family Business." It appears to take at least a week. Then comes "Shakaar." It takes at least another two weeks and keeps Kira off the station almost the entire time. That means Dax has about six weeks to get to know Leeta. And—if they really hit it off—they could grow this close that fast. (Of course, that doesn't explain why we never see Leeta again until "Bar Association"! I guess Dax just wanted her for her body.)

Also, the creators used this episode to revisit a problem in a previous NextGen script. In "The Royale," Picard ponders Pierre de Fermat's Last Theorem, and the good captain mentions that it has remained unsolved for eight hundred years. This is no longer true. It is my understanding that Andrew J. Wiles presented a proof for Fermat's Last Theorem in June 1993. Although the original proof contained some problems, they were subsequently corrected with assistance from Richard Taylor, and the current Wiles-Taylor proof has been declared valid. This, of course, makes Picard's statement wrong! So, in this episode, the creators have Jadzia say that she's still working on Tobin's proof for Fermat's Last Theorem. To make Tobin feel more comfortable she tells him that it's the most original proof she's seen since Wiles's more than three hundred years ago.

As usual, the creators did a wonderful job on the visual effect showing Curzon-Odo change into something more appropriate during his visit to Quark's. I wasn't sure if this last one was a production problem or an effort by the creators to spice up the scene a bit. At the end of the program, Rom presents Nog in his fake Starfleet Academy uniform. Rom runs into the bar and yells, "He's coming!" before running out to get his son. The scene cuts to a reaction shot from the crowd, and in the background you can see Leeta fluffing her cleavage! (There are three possible explanations for this: Leeta might feel that the Ferengi beside her is getting too generous of a view. Or Chase Masterson—the actress who plays Leeta—didn't realize the camera was rolling and she was prepping for the next shot. Or Dabo girl outfits need frequent readjustment to keep Quark's an "R"-rated establishment.)

GREAT MOMENTS

I love it when Rom gives Quark a good shellacking for rigging the holosuite so that Nog would fail his spatial orientation test.

PLOT OVERSIGHTS

• I wonder why Verad didn't get to participate in the zhian'taraz. True, he stole Dax and almost cost Jadzia her life. It's also true that he had the symbiont for a short time only, but he *was* a host, was he not? (See "Invasive Procedures.")

• As mentioned in the review for "Q-Less," Dax engages in behavior during this episode that I find somewhat shocking. According to "Ménage à Troi" (TNG), Ferengi males consider their ears one of their most erogenous zones. That episode also reveals that stroking a Ferengi's cartilage—giving oo-mox—amounts to sexual foreplay.

Yet when Quark won't agree to be a part of the zhian'tara, Dax—in what seems like a radical character departure—grabs Quark's ears and pleasure-numbs him into submission. Now, I realize that Quark is a Ferengi and we're just supposed to think that anybody can do anything to him because he's a Ferengi and he probably deserves it. But it still boggles my mind that a sophisticated, intelligent woman like Dax would stoop to this depth just to get a favor. I have to wonder why Bashir doesn't suddenly jump up and say, "Wait a minute: I've decided I'm not going through with this zhian'tara thing either, unless, of course, you'd like to come over here and *convince* me!"

• Does Joran seem a bit more *wacko* since the last time we saw him? At the end of "Equilibrium" he came up to Jadzia and placed his head on her chest. In this episode he tries to strangle her!

CHANGED PREMISES

• The entire last half of this episode has Jadzia obsessing over the reason that Curzon washed her out of the Trill initiate program. She says she never knew why he did it. Then Curzon-Odo says he just felt sorry for her and he's troubled that she didn't have his respect. Then we hear the big revelation that Curzon loved Jadzia. I must have missed something along the way. Curzon is one of Dax's former hosts, is he not? Isn't Jadzia supposed to have the memories of Curzon available to her? In "Dax" we see that Jadzia remembers Curzon's love affair with General Tandro's wife. Also, during the same episode, Selin Peers testifies that a host would retain the details and feelings of the previous hosts' lives. Six episodes from now—in "Rejoined"—we'll see that Jadzia has a great emotional attachment to a woman who carries Kahn, a symbiont who once lived inside a woman married to Torias. So why doesn't Jadzia know how Curzon felt about her? (Answer: There wouldn't be a second half to the episode if she did!)

• Transferring former host Lela from Dax to Kira, the Guardian goes through a long incantation that ends with, *"Jadzia zhian'tara vok tu Dax zhian'tani res zhian'par Lela gaur'koj."* (The capitalization probably isn't correct because closed captioning doesn't *have* capitalization normally, but hey.) However, during the transfer of Curzon from Dax to Odo, the Guardian says, *"Jadzia zhian'tara vok tu Dax zhian'tani res zhian'par Odo gaur'koj."* (See the difference, huh, huh? Do ya? Do ya?) In the first instance, the Guardian names the host that will be transferred. In the second, the Guardian names the receptacle it will be transferred into. One would think that the two incantations would be the same—naming Curzon, not Odo, in the second one. Do these incantations do anything? Or are they just to set the mood? Or was it necessary to change the second incarnation because Odo is a shape shifter?

• I wonder who got to keep the gold that Curzon won while playing Tongo. He was in Odo's body, but it really belongs to Dax.

TRIVIA ANSWERS
1. Two Delvin fluff pastries.
2. Jobel.

THE ADVERSARY

Star Dates: 48959.1—48962.5

At a reception to honor newly promoted Captain Sisko, Ambassador Krajensky approaches and tells him of a coup on the Tzenkethi home world. Krajensky wants the *Defiant* to make a tour of the Federation colonies near Tzenkethi space in case anyone in the new government has aggressive tendencies. En route, O'Brien discovers that every major system on the ship has been invaded by alien control mechanisms protected by force fields. Since one of the devices is in the warp plasma conduit, Dax scans the crew for tetryon particles, finding them on Krajensky. Immediately the ambassador morphs into a gelatinous state and escapes through an air duct. He is a Changeling, come to start a war between the Federation and the Tzenkethi by using the *Defiant* to attack a Tzenkethi colony.

As O'Brien works in Main Engineering, Sisko and the others sweep the entire ship with phasers. And just to be safe, Sisko engages the autodestruct. In Engineering, two Odos appear—one real, the other an imitation. They watch O'Brien disable the force

Trivia Questions

1. What champagne does Quark serve at Sisko's reception?

2. What plans does Sisko have for Yates when she returns?

fields around the alien devices, setting the stage to regain control of the ship. At this, the Changeling attacks. Odo counterattacks—wrestling the Changeling into the warp core and exposing the being to a lethal dose of radiation. Dying, the Changeling tells Odo, "You're too late. We're everywhere." Unfortunately, there's no way to stop the autodestruct, and the series ends in a massive matter/antimatter *explosion*! (No, no, no. Of course not! O'Brien saves the day.)

GREAT MOMENTS

The death of the Changeling is a gorgeous visual effect. Very nicely done!

PLOT OVERSIGHTS

• The episode begins with Ambassador Krajensky delivering mission orders to Sisko. Pardon my suspicious nature, but did it occur to *anyone* on the senior staff to double-check this stuff with Starfleet Command? Evidently not, because later Sisko, Kira, Bashir, Eddington, and Odo discuss that they can't be sure there was a coup. And at the end of the episode we found out there wasn't! In "Improbable Cause" and "The Die Is

Cast" we saw a Changeling infiltrate the Tal Shiar and spur on a fool's mission to wipe out the Founders. Odo supposedly filed a full report with Sisko and company. Did nobody make the connection?

• Again we must ask: Does the senior staff *do* anything on the space station? Here they go again—tramping off on a two-day mission just because Starfleet supposedly wants to show the flag. And even if we agree that Starfleet underlings can handle the senior staff's responsibilities while they are gone, why do Kira and Odo come along? This is a purely *Starfleet* mission. Kira's *job* is to be the Bajoran liaison officer to DS9! Did she take a leave of absence to do this? And what about Odo? He's the station's chief of Security! He doesn't belong on this mission. (Yes, Kira and Odo went along during "The Search, Part I," but Kira mentioned the importance to Bajor of establishing a peaceful relationship with the Dominion. Yes, Kira and Odo were on board during "Past Tense, Part I" and "Past Tense, Part II," but Sisko said they were all called to Earth for a conference. Yes, Kira was on board during "Destiny," but that was a joint Bajoran/Cardassian/Federation project to set up the communications relay on the Gamma side of the wormhole. Yes, Kira was on board during "The Die Is Cast," but that was an unauthorized mission to rescue Odo. None of these missions was purely Starfleet. However, the mission in "Meridian" was, and guess what? Neither Kira nor Odo came along. That made sense! The *Defiant* is a *Starfleet* vessel.)

• Again, we must ask: Does it really make sense to leave Bajor defenseless when the hostile intentions of the Dominion are known? Doesn't Starfleet have any other ships it could send on this mission? (I realize Starfleet didn't really send the *Defiant* on this mission, but Sisko seems very comfortable with these orders, even though they will render Bajor vulnerable to attack.)

• O'Brien has to be the most overworked engineering specialist in Starfleet. Not only is he in charge of keeping an entire station running, but now he apparently has to keep the *Defiant* in tip-top condition all by himself! We get to see Main Engineering on the *Defiant* for the first time in this episode, and *nobody* is there but O'Brien. (You may recall that Main Engineering on the *Enterprise* was almost always filled with people.)

• Twice in this episode O'Brien hears the Changeling banging around while he works. Both times he calls out, but no one answers. Wouldn't want to ask the computer to scan for life signs, would we?

• The second time O'Brien hears someone banging around, he's working in a Jefferies tube. Getting no answer from his call, he crawls to a nearby junction and is startled to find Bashir in front of him. Bashir says he was connecting his new diagnostic console into the medical bay's power grid and leaves. Is there really no procedure to follow for something like this? No requisition? No work order? No notifications? (One gets the impression that this ship is just a toy for the people on the senior staff to play with.)

• When there's a problem in the communications system, O'Brien tells Dax that he could use some help, and the two leave the bridge. While no one would fault O'Brien for wanting to spend time in a Jefferies tube with Dax, the request does seem out of character for our beloved chief of Operations. Remember "The Die Is Cast"? In that episode the *Defiant* sits in the Gamma Quadrant, vulnerable to Jem'Haddar attack with a sabotaged cloak that O'Brien says will take ten hours to fix. Sisko gives him two, and the chief storms off the bridge to get busy. Three hours later, O'Brien returns to the bridge after restoring the cloaking device. The entire time he worked alone! The only time I can remember him working with someone else on board the *Defiant* was during "Destiny," and that was with a Cardassian engineer. (Of course, this "need" for Dax's help becomes important later, as we shall see.)

• Confining nonessential personnel to their quarters, Odo ushers two men and a woman into one of the *Defiant*'s living spaces before a force field engages and the door closes. If these quarters are like the other ones we've seen on the *Defiant,* that makes three people in a room with two bunks. Right.

• To make it difficult for O'Brien to regain control of the ship, the Changeling bludgeons Dax. Kira comments on this clever tactic because without Dax, O'Brien's job will be much harder. Thankfully, the Changeling seems to be less clever than everyone thinks. If he's so set on stopping O'Brien, why doesn't he just *stop*

O'Brien?! Why quit with Dax? (Because if the Changeling did what he is capable of doing, there wouldn't be a show. Everyone would be dead. And the Federation would be at war with the Tzenkethi!)

• Once Sisko hears of the attack on Dax, he tell Kira that he will order the ship's destruction before allowing it to start a war. Now, there's an interesting tactic! Sisko knows he's dealing with an entity that can be anywhere or anything, and our good captain tells everyone on the bridge his plans.

• Sisko needs to do a little work on his reflexes. In a Jefferies tube junction the Changeling attacks Sisko's buddy before shoving Sisko against the wall and darting down a tube. Sisko sits there for a second. Then he gets up and checks the downed officer. Then he alerts everyone to the Changeling's presence. Then he finally gets around to firing down the tube and going after the threat to the ship. Wouldn't it have been better to fire down the tube immediately? Maybe he could have winged the Changeling and slowed it down a bit. (Then again, maybe it's not his fault. See the next nit.)

• Sisko decides they need to search the ship in teams to find the Changelings. For a moment, let's grant that this is a reasonable plan. (It does seem a bit futile, given the abilities of the Changeling. But hey, the creators have to fill the hour somehow.) Sisko puts everyone into two-person teams. He does a more than adequate job explaining that this will ensure that the Changeling cannot assume the identity of either of the people in the team.

So what happens next? Kira allows herself to get separated from her partner. Likewise Odo and Eddington allow themselves to be separated. Is the Changeling saturating the ship with some type of ambient stupefication field during this episode?

• Did the blood sample scene remind anyone else of John Carpenter's *The Thing*?

• At one point Sisko and the others believe Eddington is the Changeling. They lead him to a holding room and are about to shove him inside when suddenly the door across the hall flies open. The real Bashir stands there looking at the Changeling who has been posing as Bashir. Everyone gawks at each other for a time until the Changeling decides to leave and Sisko fires a "missed it by that much" shot from his phaser rifle. Next time you watch this episode start shouting, "Shoot him! *Shoot* HIM!" as soon as the real Changeling appears and see how many times you can repeat it before anyone takes action.

• As stated above, Kira really has no place on this mission, yet this episode also reveals that she's first officer! (Look at it this way: Quark has military training, too, but nobody would consider making him an officer on the *Defiant*.) Okay, maybe she knows how to operate the controls, but does she really know everything about Starfleet tactical maneuvers and their corresponding names? ("Okay, okay! So I don't know what it's called! Just turn the ship to port and start going down!")

• Big time jump in this episode. On the bridge, Sisko gives the final order

to self-destruct in ten minutes. The computer starts the countdown at nine minutes, fifty-five seconds. Kira sits down at the helm. We see a reaction shot from Eddington. Sisko calls O'Brien and asks for good news. O'Brien says he might be about to shut down all the force fields. The computer says *seven* minutes to self-destruct! Whoa! Wait a minute. What happened to the other two and a half minutes?

• After his release, the real Bashir shows up on the bridge to give Sisko an update on Dax. Apparently he has no escort. Has Sisko given up on the buddy system?

• As Spock does at the end of "Whom Gods Destroy" when he must choose between duplicate Kirks, O'Brien faces a conundrum at the end of this episode. He must choose between the real and the fake Odo. Next time you watch this episode start shouting, "Shoot them both! Use your stun setting and *shoot them both!*"

• At the very end of the episode, Odo claims that just before the Changeling died he said, "You're too late. We're everywhere." I'm no expert lip-reader, but it looks like he says only, "We're everywhere."

CHANGED PREMISES

• Supposedly "No Changeling has ever harmed another." We've heard that phrase over and over from Changelings in episodes such as "The Search, Part II" and "Heart of Stone." But in this episode a Changeling looks like he's ready to allow Odo to die because the Changeling won't return control of the ship. Only with some semantic tomfoolery could you make the case that this doesn't constitute a Changeling harming Odo. And, what about that "ramming my fist into your chest" thing that the Changeling does to Odo at the end of the episode? Wouldn't that be considered "harming" Odo? Have the Changelings decided that Odo isn't one of them anymore? (Certainly Odo's status in Changeling society will be at an all-time low when word of the Changeling's death reaches the Founders!)

EQUIPMENT ODDITIES

• Just a minor item: When Dax scans the senior staff for tetryon particles, she closes and reopens the tricorder between each scan. Why? Isn't there a reset button for the sensors? (She's probably just nervous.)

• The *Defiant* must be a highly automated ship. After the discovery of the Changeling, Sisko orders Odo and Eddington to confine all nonessential personnel to their quarters. Yet earlier we learn that there are only forty-seven people on board! With only forty-seven people to begin with, how many are really "non-essential" for running this starship? (I know for sure

that O'Brien could use some help in Engineering!)

• As the teams depart to search the ship, everyone picks up a phaser rifle from the table behind the captain's chair on the bridge. Oddly enough, after everyone leaves, there's a phaser rifle left—apparently unattended! Is that one for the Changeling to use?

• Attempting to break out of his confinement, the real Bashir somehow shorts out the door to his holding area, and the door opens. He then leans into the opening, and the force field shimmers. Then he *continues* to lean on the force field, and it quits shimmering. First, force fields usually sting. Second, they usually keep shimmering as long as something is in contact with them. (See Joran's possession of Sisko in "Facets" for an example.)

• Does anyone else find it odd that the Changeling took over every system on the ship but *forgot* to disable the self-destruct?

TRIVIA ANSWERS

1. Château Cleon, 2303.
2. He is going to take her to the holosuite for the seventh game of the '64 World Series.

SISKO'S TOP TEN REASONS FOR SHAVING HIS HEAD

Between the third and fourth seasons of *Star Trek: Deep Space Nine* the creators decided that Sisko needed a new look. It came as quite a surprise and inspired this sidebar. I apologize in advance for this. It was one of those things I just had to do.

10. The station was experiencing a severe infestation of Cardassian vole lice.

9. Hoping the Jem'Haddar will mistake him for a Changeling.

8. Went to a Bolian barber who took too much off the top and had to even it up.

7. Wanted to make Worf feel welcome.

6. Mistook Captain Yates's Nair (hair remover) for shampoo after she spent the night.

5. Wondered if the reflection might brighten up his office.

4. Thought Odo needed an easier humanoid head to imitate.

3. Quark finally convinced him he could turn a tidy profit selling locks of the emissary's hair to Bajoran religious adherents.

2. Television signals carrying reruns of *Spenser for Hire* finally reached the station and Sisko couldn't help but notice the resemblance.

And Sisko's number one reason for shaving his head:

1. Figured that other bald actor's *Star Trek* series was a hit. Couldn't hurt.

FOURTH

SEASON

THE WAY OF THE WARRIOR

After chasing Odo for almost three and one-half hours in a simulated station attack by a Changeling, Sisko retires to his quarters to prepare for a dinner date with Captain Kasidy Yates. Unfortunately, shortly after Yates arrives, Dax summons Sisko to Ops. The new Klingon flagship *Negh'Var* has just arrived. Its commander, General Martok, has requested shore leave privileges for his troops. Sisko graciously offers them, only to watch at least twenty more Klingon ships decloak around the station. When questioned about the presence of the large Klingon fleet, Martok claims that Gowron has sent them to help defend the sector from an attack by the Dominion.

To find out the Klingons' true purpose, Sisko contacts Starfleet and recruits Lieutenant Commander Worf (from *NextGen*) for a special assignment. Worf soon arrives from the Klingon monastery on Boreth, where he had taken an extended leave. He has decided to resign from Starfleet but will perform his duty until then. Through an old family friend, Worf

Trivia Questions

1. What is the name of the masseur who gives Dax a rubdown?

2. What cruiser does Dukat use to evacuate the Detepa Council?

learns that the Klingons are preparing to attack Cardassia. With the fall of the Obsidian Order (see "Improbable Cause" and "The Die Is Cast"), the civilian government recently wrested power from Central Command. Gowron believes that the Dominion has engineered the takeover. He intends to conquer Cardassia, thereby eliminating the Dominion foothold in the Alpha Quadrant.

Sisko tries to dissuade Martok from attacking, but when the general returns to his ship, he gives the order to begin. Through Garak, Sisko warns Dukat that the Klingons are coming. When it appears that Cardassia will fall, Sisko takes the *Defiant* through the battle zone to rescue the leaders of the Cardassian civilian government—the Detepa Council—and escort them with Dukat to the station. Just to be sure, Sisko has Bashir perform blood tests on everyone. The doctor finds no Changelings among them.

Gowron angrily returns to DS9 to capture the Detepa Council. (He had earlier arrived at the station just before the battle with an invitation for Worf to join them. When Worf refused, Gowron proclaimed him persona non

293

grata in the Klingon Empire.) After a fierce battle between the newly upgraded station and a fleet of Klingon vessels, Sisko and Worf persuade Gowron to call off the offensive.

With gratitude, the Detepa Council returns to Cardassia Prime. Worf decides against resignation, taking a position as the Strategic Operations officer on DS9. And the Klingons? They begin fortifying the Cardassian outposts they captured during the offensive. Apparently Gowron intends to make the Klingon Empire's presence felt in the sector for some time to come.

RUMINATIONS

The visual effects crew certainly worked overtime on this episode! It is loaded with fabulous ship-to-ship and ship-to-station battle scenes.

Also, as I mentioned in my review of "Emissary," there's nice closure in this episode. Near the end Sisko tells Gowron that the station has five thousand photon torpedoes armed and ready. The sensors on Gowron's ship confirm this, but General Martok blusters that it's a trick—an illusion created by thoron fields and duranium shadows. We find out in just a few moments that Sisko is correct when he replies, "It's no illusion." In "Emissary," however, it was just an illusion, so it's very nice to see that DS9 finally has the weaponry it needed and deserved as the guardian of the wormhole.

Finally in this episode, we learn that Odo now can manufacture a glass and simulated liquid to give the appearance of sharing a drink with another person. Odo even demonstrates, and he can

refill his glass at will. I couldn't help but think that this effectively kills all continuity errors when it comes to cups with liquid and our favorite constable. Score one for the creators. (Wink, wink.) Oh, one other thing: If Odo can make a glass with liquid in it, can the plate of food be far behind? (Granted, he would have to ensure that he was always touching the plate, but he could accomplish that by running a thin portion of himself down his chair leg, across the floor, up the table leg, onto the table-top and across to the plate.)

GREAT LINES

"Nice hat."—Worf to Kira after being introduced to DS9's first officer and noting that she wears a medieval costume. (This, of course, is a cute moment because Kira has momentarily forgotten about her attire, and Worf's comment brings it shockingly back to her remembrance. Nominated by Austen O'Kurley of Bruderheim, Alberta.)

PLOT OVERSIGHTS

• The episode opens with Sisko and Kira marching down a hall in search of Odo. They pause at a door, go through a dramatic countdown, dive inside, and sweep the room with phaser fire. Then they enter the next room. Odo slides out of a chair, knocks them off balance, and flees the room as a bird, heading for the promenade. First, why do Sisko and Kira sweep only the rooms with phaser fire? Why not the corridor as well? Couldn't Odo duck around a corner and flatten into the wall (as he did in "The Siege")? And why do they bother to do the countdown thing before bursting into the room? Why not just burst in and shoot? (Are they determined to give Odo enough time to get comfortable?) Also, Sisko and Kira seem to have plenty of time to bring their weapons into position and fire as Odo slides off the chair, but they just stand there and watch him until he knocks them off balance. A similar set of problems occurs when the action moves to the promenade and Bashir's team takes over the search. They run through the promenade waiting to get into position—waiting for Bashir's signal to fire. Why? Shouldn't they sweep everything as they go?

• Unfortunately, there is a larger issue here. Frankly—without the benefit of some type of sensors and computerized tracking—I can't see any way that Sisko and company would have a chance of finding a Changeling who really wanted to hide out on the station. Even in the open stretches, the Changeling could morph into something that's much faster than a humanoid. In addition, the station contains too many places that restrict humanoid movement—the conduits, for example. These same places pose no problem for a Changeling (as we saw in "The Adversary"). Remember, any time the Changeling disappears from view, you have no way to figure out what the Changeling has become. In short, you would have to start at one end of the station and send teams down *every* corridor and *every* conduit *simultaneously*—all the while sweeping *every* room they encountered along the way.

• After the simulated Changeling attack, Sisko says that *if* the Dominion tries to infiltrate the station he wants to be ready for them. Sisko is being overly optimistic. The Dominion has *already* infiltrated the station. Look at the evidence. A Changeling demonstrated profound knowledge of the station inhabitants and station life in "Heart of Stone," and in "The Adversary" a Changeling knew that O'Brien forgot to bring a fork to eat his lamb stew the last time he went kayaking with Odo. (On this last item, I realize that one of the Odos said that anyone would have gotten that information, but my question is: "How?" Is the senior staff on the station so famous that reporters for *Deep Space Whispers*—the top-selling tabloid newspaper on Bajor—comb the station constantly?)

• I'm more than willing to be corrected, but I don't recall Bajor ever signing a peace treaty with the Klingons. Yet in this episode a Klingon tells Odo that as long as he wears a Bajoran uniform, they are allies. I understand that the Federation and the Klingon Empire are allies (at least they used to be), but Bajor isn't part of the Federation, is it?

• Sisko and company face a conundrum after discovering the true purpose of the Klingon armada. The Federation Council decides to do nothing. Yet Sisko feels compelled to warn the Cardassians. But if he warns the Cardassians, it would constitute a betrayal of an ally—the Klingon Empire. Believing that he and his staff are smarter than the Federation Council—though the council members undoubtedly have hordes of advisers and most likely have access to additional information—Sisko comes up with a way to warn the Cardassians through unofficial channels. He invites Garak to the wardroom to measure him for a new suit. The staff then discusses the fact that more than one hundred Klingon ships will reach Cardassian space in one hour. Garak leaves and immediately calls Dukat. Dukat asks Garak why the Klingon would invade Cardassia. Garak responds that—according to his sources—the Klingons believe that the Founders have taken over the Cardassian Empire. Garak must have other sources beyond Sisko and crew because they never mentioned the motivation for the Klingons' attack. (In other words, how did Garak know this piece of information?)

• When making arrangements to rendezvous with Dukat and the Detepa Council, Sisko says he doubts the Klingons will fire on a Federation ship. Hold it! Let's back up a little bit to see if this statement makes any sense. Earlier in the episode, Captain Yates departs the station in her ship, the *Xhosa*. A Klingon vessel captures the *Xhosa* with a tractor beam. Sisko comes rushing to the rescue and threatens to fire on the Klingon vessel. Kaybok—the commander of the Klingon vessel—backs down and releases the *Xhosa*. A short time later, General Martok shows up in Sisko's office with Kaybok's knife. Dax explains that Martok killed Kaybok for not obeying orders—for *not firing* on a Federation ship! One would think that this tidbit of information was passed through the troops. Now, what do you think are the chances that the

Klingons won't fire on the *Defiant*?

• I wonder why Dax suddenly got a promotion to lieutenant commander.

• This episode illuminates an important difference between Picard and Sisko. Sisko decides to rescue the Detepa Council. He knows he'll be flying through a war zone. The *Defiant* gets all the way to the rendezvous site and then discovers three Klingon vessels attacking the Cardassian ship that carries Dukat and the council. This *was* a foreseeable eventuality, was it not? Yet Sisko pauses to consider what he will do next. Picard would have already anticipated this option and decided what his response would be. (Yes, there were times when Picard took his time making a decision in private. But when he stepped onto the bridge he was always on-line and ready to go.)

• During the battle that commences between the *Defiant* and the Klingon ships, Dax authorizes phaser fire while Sisko is on the bridge. Is this really her job? Sisko didn't tell her to take over.

• There's a male bonding scene of sorts during the great battle at the end of the episode when Bashir saves Odo from a Klingon attacker. One question, though: The Klingon is attacking Odo with a bat'leth, right? Would a bat'leth really hurt Odo? (Answer: No. He's a Changeling. A thief threw a mace through Odo's face in "Emissary" and the young Jem'Haddar jumped completely through him in "The Abandoned.")

• Doesn't it seem like there are very few Klingon warriors actually boarding DS9, given the presence of "dozens" of warships? And why aren't they concentrating on taking over Ops with a Mongolian horde technique? (I know they beamed twenty or so people up there, but it just seems to me that, strategically, that's where you would want to concentrate your efforts. It would make more sense to keep pumping people in there until you overwhelmed Sisko and company.)

• At the end of the episode O'Brien makes a big deal out of Worf wearing a red uniform. Didn't Worf wear red during the first season of *NextGen*?

• So Worf is "Strategic Operations" officer, eh? Makes one wonder how the Bajoran sector survived an entire three seasons of *Star Trek: Deep Space Nine* without someone occupying this very important—and previously unheard-of—position! (Does this sound like a "make-work" posting to anyone else?)

• And speaking of O'Brien, he can be a real bootlicker at times. Not only does he compliment Worf on how he looks in red, he also tells Worf that the Klingon couldn't have a better teacher to learn command. He's referring to Sisko. That's funny—I seem to recall him telling Picard in "The Wounded" that he counted himself lucky to have served with the "two finest captains in Starfleet" (meaning Benjamin Maxwell and Jean-Luc Picard).

CHANGED PREMISES

• Just after the opening credits we see Bashir and O'Brien enjoying some down time in Quark's. O'Brien places a small round object on the back of his hand and pops it into his mouth. Bashir is suitably impressed and attempts to duplicate the feat. At one point during the scene, Bashir asks Quark for some yamok sauce to go with their "sand peas." Presumably this is what the two gentlemen are popping into their mouths. Interestingly enough, they are not "instantly reaching" for their drinks each time they eat one. Pel introduces Quark to Gramilian sand peas in "Rules of Acquisition" as a way to boost drink sales. Supposedly the peas inhibit the production of saliva. The episode demonstrates that every time you eat a sand pea, you instantly reach for your drink. (Yes, it is possible that O'Brien is playing with another type of sand pea, but that seems like a stretch to find an explanation.)

• At the beginning of his meeting with Sisko and Kira, General Martok cuts his hand and asks them to do the same. The drops of blood on the table remain blood, thereby proving everyone is who they claim to be and not Changelings in disguise. (You may recall that "The Adversary" established that if any part of a Changeling separates from the whole, that part reverts to its gelatinous state.) I think this episode once and for all establishes that the creators of the television episodes have no intention of following the Klingon blood color established by *Star Trek VI: The Undiscovered Country*. (See "The House of Quark" for more information.) General Martok's blood is red.

• Shortly after boarding the *Defiant,* Worf says he's never before been on a Federation starship that had a cloaking device. He's says it's "a little strange." Worf must have forgotten that the *Enterprise* had a cloaking device for a short time during the episode "The *Pegasus*."

• This episode presents yet another type of kanar. You may recall that the Cardassian drink kanar makes its first appearance in "The Wounded" *(TNG)*. In that episode it's clear. Next, we see Garak drinking kanar in "The Wire." In that episode it's light bluish. Next we see Quark bring a bottle of kanar to the quarters of the Cardassian scientist in "Destiny." In that episode kanar appears to be a dark liquid. Finally, in this episode, Garak walks into Quark's and orders a bottle of kanar. It comes in the same bottle as the dark liquid but now is pinkish.

EQUIPMENT ODDITIES

• Evidently Klingon cloaks are better than Romulan cloaks. In this episode an armada of more than twenty Klingon vessels approaches the station, and no one is the wiser until they decloak. In "The Die Is Cast" an armada of twenty Romulan and Cardassian vessels approached the station, and Dax registered a tachyon surge *before* they decloaked. (Speaking of cloaked ships, several nitpickers had the same wonderment: Can cloaked Klingon vessels detect other cloaked Klingon ships? If not, how do they fly in close formation—as seen in this episode—without running into each other?)

• One hour after departing DS9, Captain Yates issues a distress call. Sisko and company hop in the *Defiant* and charge to the rescue. Dax locates Yates's ship—the *Xhosa*—using the forward scanners. Kira chimes in that she's picking up another ship. It has a tractor beam on the *Xhosa*. Sisko orders the image onscreen and Kira reacts with surprise when she sees that the other ship is a Klingon Bird-of-Prey. Why didn't the sensors tell her that the other ship was a Bird-of-Prey? Other episodes—"The Maquis, Part I," for instance—have shown that runabout sensors can identify vessel type and affiliation well outside visual range. Are the *Defiant*'s sensors inferior to a runabout's sensors?

• When it becomes evident that the Klingons will soon attack the station, Quark closes up shop and turns to stand guard in front of his locked doorway. Odo wanders by and asks how Quark intends to defend himself. Our favorite Ferengi barkeep proudly opens a box he carries, only to find that Rom has taken his disrupter pistol to use for parts. Just how much do these disrupter pistols weigh? Why didn't Quark notice the box was empty the minute he picked it up?

• For some reason the Universal Translator doesn't seem to be working during this episode. At one point Gowron tells Sisko "It is a good day to die" in Klingon, and Worf has to translate. (Maybe Gowron had pressed the button labeled "Push Here to Demonstrate the Linguistic Ineptitude of Opponent.")

• Well, it's nice to see that the more things change, the more they stay the same. It's true. The station now has integrated phaser banks on every level. It's true. The station now has five thousand photon torpedoes. All I can say is, they need them all because the targeting systems can't hit the broad side of the barn! Much of the exterior footage shows slow-moving Klingon vessels, and photon torpedoes screaming off into empty space. For every six or seven torpedoes, one finally hits something! (Of course, if you've got five thousand of them and the Klingons have only several dozen ships...)

• Then again, maybe these photon torpedoes are some kind of super-duper photon torpedoes. They appear to have a lousy guidance system, but they really pack a punch. Every time *one* of them hits a Bird-of-Prey, the ship *blows up*!

CONTINUITY AND PRODUCTION PROBLEMS

• During a Dax-sponsored holosuite trip to the Hoobisian Baths on Trill, Kira tells her host that she doesn't need a massage because the masseur is a puppet made of holographic light and replicated matter. Her arms are pulled away from her body. The shot changes, and suddenly her arms are tight against her sides, with her hands in her lap.

• Boy, Alexander sure has changed, hasn't he? While unpacking, Worf pulls out a picture of himself and his son, and Alexander doesn't look anything like he used to!

• Not really a nit, just an observation: Worf's martial arts suit is black in this episode. During *NextGen* it was white. (Or some other light tint. I don't do colors that well.)

• Can't say for sure on this next one, but it sure looks like it. Pay special attention to Worf's new stubby weapon as he practices with Dax's Klingon exercise program on the holosuite. After Dax walks in and tells Worf that he shouldn't drop his left arm, does it look like Worf's weapon is bent upward?

• Just after Sisko gives the order to attack the Klingon vessels that are pummeling the ship that carries the Detepa Council, the closed captioning has someone saying, "Aye, Captain."

• After Garak orders kanar, Quark pours him a glass of root beer. Garak finds the drink revolting. No wonder. Look at the glass: The stuff is completely flat! It doesn't even form a head when Quark pours it out of the jug. (The sound effects guys did try to help this problem by dubbing in a fizzing sound, but as soon as you get a clear view of the glass, it's pretty obvious that the stuff ain't got no zip.) Apparently Quark keeps his stock of root beer in an open pitcher! No wonder it doesn't taste any good. It doesn't have any bubbles to tickle the nose!

• At the very end of the big hand-to-hand fight in Ops, Dax sweeps a Klingon off his feet with a bat'leth before turning to ferociously survey the room. The camera angle changes to Sisko and then pans over to Dax. Now she's empty-handed. There is time for her to throw the bat'leth to the ground, but there is no clattering sound to indicate that's what she did. (Granted, it's not really a nit. It just looks funny.)

TRIVIA ANSWERS
1. Malko.
2. The *Prakesh*.

Star Date: unknown

As the episode begins, Jake Sisko—as an old man—answers the door in his Louisiana home. He finds a young lady named Melanie who has come to ask him why he stopped writing. Normally, Jake would send her away unanswered. But today he can tell the story.

Jake says that when he was eighteen, he accompanied his father onto the *Defiant* to watch the wormhole undergo an inversion. Unexpectedly, the event caused an overload in the warp core. As Jake watched, an energy discharge snaked out and pulled his father into subspace. Unfortunately, the crew had no way to retrieve their captain despite his sporadic reappearances in normal space. After one such appearance, Jake dedicated his life to finding a way to rescue his father—sacrificing his writing for its pursuit.

Jake tells Melanie he's finally found the answer. The accident created a subspace link between himself and his father. This link is causing Benjamin Sisko's sporadic reappearances. The next one will be today. Jake has

taken poison to end his life, to break the link and send his father back to the moment of the accident. After Melanie leaves, Benjamin Sisko does appear. Though he's horrified at what Jake has done, the plan does work and allows Sisko to avoid being pulled into subspace in the first place.

RUMINATIONS

A two-hundred-twenty-word plot synopsis doesn't do this episode justice. This is a wonderful episode, filled with courage and sacrifice. It has become one of my favorites of all the incarnations of Star Trek. *Everyone involved turns in a beautiful performance. I especially like the interplay between the elder Jake and Melanie and the way the background music plays off their interactions. Well done!*

PLOT OVERSIGHTS

• Gotta hand it to those Federation scientists. They discover a wormhole just over three years back and already they know that it undergoes an inversion *every* fifty years!

• A short time after the accident, Sisko appears momentarily in Jake's

---

Trivia Questions

1. What does Quark ask Nog to bring up from the stockroom?

2. What literary award does Jake win for his *Collected Stories*?

bedroom. The next time, he materializes in a hallway. This time he sticks around long enough for Jake to take him to the infirmary. When asked what he remembers last, Sisko relates the accident. So...why didn't he say anything about appearing in Jake's bedroom? (He did seem to recognize Jake and his surroundings.)

• In relating his story to Melanie, the elder Jake says that after his father's death, the Bajorans took it as a sign that the Federation could not protect them, so they signed a mutual defense pact with the Cardassians. This made the Klingons mad. Jake then says that the Federation eventually turned control of DS9 over to the Klingons. I would imagine that this action made the Bajorans mad! After all, the Cardassians built the station, and it currently belongs to Bajor. All this and the Federation turns control over to the *Klingons*? (Unless, of course, the Klingons had already conquered the Bajorans and the Cardassians, although Jake never mentions this.)

• Not a nit, just a wonderment. As a person who loves to write—as a person who would love to get some of my own fiction published someday—I found this episode very encouraging. Evidently—even with the advent of ubiquitous computer systems small enough to carry around like paperback novels—there will still be *real* books printed. In this episode we see that Jake has two real books to his name. Yes, it's more efficient simply to download the contents of a book into a padd (and during "Profit and Loss" we see that O'Brien has given *I, the Jury* by Mickey Spillane to Odo

in just such a format). Yes, it allows for a much cheaper dissemination of writing endeavors because electricity and RAM are less expensive than printing. But there's just something satisfying about holding a real book and leafing through the pages, isn't there?

• The accident occurs when Jake is eighteen. The wormhole experiences an inversion every fifty years. Keep those two pieces of information handy while we add a few more. The elder Jake tells Melanie that he went back to school at age thirty-seven. This was sometime after his father appeared in his home in Louisiana. Next we see Nog helping the elder Jake to return to the wormhole in the *Defiant*. The wormhole is about to undergo an inversion, and the elder Jake hopes to rescue Sisko. The rescue attempt fails, but the elder Jake is sucked into subspace for a time and can converse with his father. Sisko asks how long it's been since the last time. Elder Jake says fourteen years. That would make elder Jake no more than fifty-one years old, since we know he went back to school at thirty-seven after the last visit. Here's the problem: Remember the two pieces of information above. The wormhole cycles every fifty years, and Jake was eighteen during the previous cycle. That means Jake should be sixty-eight, not fifty-one. (It is possible that there was a visit from Sisko between the first home visit in Louisiana and the visit on the *Defiant*. But if there was, why didn't Sisko know that his son had stopped writing and taken up the study of subspace mechanics?)

• The elder Jake says that if he dies while he and Sisko are together, Sisko will return to the moment of the accident. Actually, I think he meant to say that Sisko would return to the moment just *before* the accident. If you returned to the moment of the accident there wouldn't be time to prevent it and you would just start the whole cycle all over again!

EQUIPMENT ODDITIES

• Are the sensors better on the *Defiant* than on the station? Is that why the crew putter out to the wormhole as it undergoes inversion? The station sits right beside the wormhole. Was that not close enough?

• I've just about decided to start a list called "The Most Useless Inventions of the Twenty-fourth Century." Among the most prominent would be the warp-core ejection system! Seems like every time it's needed, it's off-line, it's stuck, it's jammed, it's not working, it's in a bad mood, they can't find the code, blah, blah-blah, blah-blah, blah, blah! (One would think that Starfleet officers would get tired of this. I think they should change the design. They *should* attach the warp core with some of those big bolts that were used on the original *Enterprise* and hang one of those huge monkey wrenches on the wall. It would be much more efficient than the automated system, and it would finally solve the Great Monkey Wrench Mystery from *Classic Trek*.)

CONTINUITY AND PRODUCTION PROBLEMS

• This isn't really a nit, just an observation. One of Sisko's appearances occurs while Jake is married to a Bajoran female named Korena. After meeting her father-in-law, she rushes to the bookcase and brings back two of Jake's published works. Taking them, Sisko holds *Anslem* in his left hand and Jake's *Collected Stories* in his right hand. The scene cuts to a reaction shot of Korena and then back to Sisko and Jake. Now the books are reversed—*Collected Stories* in the left, *Anslem* in the right. (It's not a nit because there is time for Sisko to switch them. After all, who knows? Maybe he took up book-juggling to pass the time in subspace.)

• As you are no doubt aware, the future uniforms and combadges used in this episode originally appeared in the episode "All Good Things" *(TNG)*.

• The elder Jake finishes another collection of stories before Sisko appears for the last time. In fact, Jake gives his handwritten copy to Melanie. He must write really small, because the stack of papers looks like it's less than one-half inch thick! (The manuscript for this book was a stack of paper more than two inches high.)

TRIVIA ANSWERS

1. Five kegs of Takarian mead.
2. The Betar Prize.

HIPPOCRATIC OATH

Star Date: 49066.5

Responding to an anomalous reading in the Gamma Quadrant, Bashir and O'Brien drop into orbit around a planet, only to have their runabout knocked from the sky by a plasma field. On the surface, Jem'Haddar soldiers quickly capture the pair. Learning that Bashir is a doctor, their leader, Goran'Agar, spares their lives. Then he takes Bashir to a makeshift laboratory and explains.

All Jem'Haddar are addicted to "Ketracel-White." Without it, they die. The Vorta—of the Dominion—control the White, so they control the Jem'Haddar. Yet three years ago Goran'Agar crash-landed on this planet. He lived for thirty-five days without White and is no longer addicted. He brought his Jem'Haddar squad here to break their addiction as well, but it hasn't worked. Now Goran'Agar wants Bashir to accomplish this feat instead. Over O'Brien's objections, Bashir agrees to try. The doctor believes that Goran'Agar is developing a moral structure just as other Jem'Haddar might if he can free them. Eventually O'Brien escapes and destroys Bashir's equipment to force

the doctor to come with him. Goran'Agar returns and realizes there will be no cure when the supply of White runs out. He escorts the pair back to their runabout before turning to seek out his own men. He will give them a chance to die quickly in battle.

PLOT OVERSIGHTS

• Again, we have Starfleet officers tooling around in the Gamma Quadrant, doing surveys just for the fun of it. If you recall, during the episode "The Jem'Haddar," Third Talak'Talan told the crew of DS9 that the Dominion would be offended if anyone came through the wormhole. So I guess Bashir and O'Brien aren't worried about offending the Dominion. Now, I know the creators try to cover this problem by having Bashir mumble that the nearest Dominion outpost is six weeks away. But this justification raises some questions. When and how did Starfleet map Dominion territory? And even if they bought a map from somewhere, the Jem'Haddar told the crew of DS9 to *stay out of the Gamma Quadrant*! If Bashir and O'Brien run into a Jem'Haddar patrol, are they going to whip out their *Rand

Trivia Questions

1. What is the name of the individual involved with the Markalian smuggling operation?

2. Kira believes that Quark has more in common with what animal than Starfleet?

303

McNally Atlas (Galactic Edition SD49001, Gamma Quadrant, Volume II) and say, "No, no, no. We're not in your territory. See, see. It says so right here."? (Wanna guess what the Jem'Haddar response would be to such a tactic? BLAM, BLAM, BLAM!)

• Happily, we finally get a job description for Worf in this episode. Sisko says that his primary duty is to "coordinate all Starfleet activity in this sector." Sisko tells Worf this as part of the subplot for this episode. He's trying to get Worf to leave Odo alone. For some reason Worf decides to be a busybody in this episode and do Odo's job as well. (No doubt because Worf really doesn't *have* a job! He just has this fancy-schmancy title.) In this episode Odo is running an undercover operation to break a Markalian smuggling ring. A criminal named Regana Tosh has come to the station to sell Quark an illegally acquired Tallonian crystal. Odo has arranged for Quark to purchase the crystal so he can sneak on board Tosh's ship disguised as a bag of latinum. Odo then plans for Tosh to transport him to the ringleaders of the smuggling operation, whereupon Odo will morph back to his humanoid self and bring them to justice. Of course, Worf doesn't know about Odo's investigation, and Odo doesn't see fit to tell Worf. Consequently Worf tries to arrest both Quark and Tosh during the sale of the crystal. Disgusted, Odo changes from the bag to his humanoid self. He says that he should arrest Worf for interfering with an investigation. He grouses that he'll have to settle for the middleman. He hauls Tosh off to jail. Worf ends

up looking like an idiot, and Sisko comforts him by saying that it will take some time for the Klingon to fit in.

But wait: Let's look at this situation from a different angle. What is Odo's title? Chief of Security for Deep Space 9, right? What is he supposed to do? Police the station and arrest anyone exhibiting criminal activity. Wouldn't his jurisdiction be limited to the station? Or has Bajor extended his area of influence to include the entire sector? Why is he *personally* running an investigation to break a smuggling ring, anyway? Seems to me that his only concern should be when individuals come to the station to sell their illegal goods. In other words, he *should* settle for arresting Tosh, because that's the only thing that happened within his jurisdiction! (Think of it this way: Do local sheriffs hop on planes bound for Colombia to crack drug smuggling rings?) On the other hand, the coordination of Starfleet resources to break the smuggling ring might very well fall under *Worf's* authority. He's supposed to "coordinate all Starfleet activity in this sector." Just what does that mean? Would it not include Starfleet's legal enforcement aspects as well? So *maybe* we should really be asking why Odo is rooting around in Worf's domain to begin with and not the other way around. *Maybe* Sisko should be telling Odo to stick to the business of keeping the station safe and free of criminal activity and leave the smuggling-ring-busting to the people whose authority extends beyond the pylons of DS9!

• I'm confused. When we first see the Jem'Haddar in "The Jem'Haddar," they zip to a standstill and become visible.

Then, in "The Abandoned," a young Jem'Haddar shows up in Sisko's office the same way—invisible at first, then slowing down and becoming visible. Okay, I thought, they must move so fast that they become invisible. It has to be an innate ability, because the young Jem'Haddar didn't have any Jem'Haddar equipment. Well...at the end of this episode Goran'Agar *trudges* away from Bashir and O'Brien and fades from view. Okay, I thought, the Jem'Haddar must have some sort of innate ability to camouflage themselves. But if that's true, why are they visible when they are hunting O'Brien near the end of the episode?

• At the end of this episode O'Brien tells Bashir that the doctor can bring him up on charges for disobeying orders. Bashir says that's not really his style. One also wonders if O'Brien could bring Bashir up on charges of aiding and abetting the enemy. I guess that whole charges thing really isn't O'Brien's style either.

CHANGED PREMISES

• Well, the creators decided to settle O'Brien's rank once and for all. They have Goran'Agar identify him as a chief petty officer. I suppose I could mention again that Riker calls him "Lieutenant" in "Where Silence Has Lease" *(TNG)*, but honestly, what would be the point?

• Someone renamed those big hydraulic platforms on the habitat ring— the ones used by the runabouts. "Emissary" establishes that they are called "pads" and are identified using letters (e.g., "Pad C"). Throughout the first three seasons, these platforms are variously called "pads" or "landing pads" or "runabout pads." (See "Battlelines," "The Maquis, Part I," and "In the Hands of the Prophets" for an example of each, respectively.) In all but one case they are identified with the letters "A" through "C." (In "Q-Less" there is mention of a "Landing Pad 5." It's possible that this is not a hydraulic platform since it looks like there are only *four* platforms!) At the very end of this episode, however, one of the platforms is identified as "Docking Platform 2."

CONTINUITY AND PRODUCTION PROBLEMS

• Bashir picks the oddest time in this episode to turn his back on a ruthless Jem'Haddar soldier. During the first conversation with Goran'Agar, Bashir talks of the drug the Jem'Haddar need. Then he learns that Goran'Agar and the others are trying to escape from the Dominion. Goran'Agar asks if Bashir disapproves. Bashir says that he's just surprised. At this Goran'Agar walks up to Bashir while expressing his disgust that Bashir should be surprised that a Jem'Haddar soldier would want more than the life of a slave. As Goran'Agar approaches, we see that Bashir has spun 180 degrees, turning his back on the conversation!

TRIVIA ANSWERS
1. Regana Tosh.
2. A Rakonian swamp rat.

INDISCRETION

Star Date: unknown

Scrap metal merchant Razka Karn contacts Kira concerning a metal fragment he has purchased from a Ferengi trader. He claims it came from the *Ravinok,* a Cardassian transport that disappeared six years ago while en route to a labor camp with thirty-two Bajorans. For some time Kira has searched for the *Ravinok.* Her resistance recruiter, Lorit Akrem, was on board. Before Kira leaves DS9, however, Sisko informs her that the new leader of the Cardassian civil government has asked to send a representative along for the search. It turns out to be Gul Dukat.

Soon the pair trace the *Ravinok* to a planet in the Dozaria System. There they find the Breen—a race whose home world is a frozen wasteland—using the survivors of the transport's crash to mine dilithium from caves beneath the hot, arid surface. Along the way, Kira also discovers that two civilians were on board the *Ravinok*—a Bajoran woman who died in the crash named Tora Naprem, and her thirteen-year-old daughter, Tora Ziyal. Naprem was Dukat's mistress during the occupation, and Ziyal his

daughter. Dukat has come to close the book on his disgrace. He plans to kill Ziyal if she still lives. Kira convinces Dukat otherwise. Grateful, Dukat returns to Cardassia, taking Ziyal with him.

Trivia Questions

1. What ship brings Dukat to DS9?

2. Who awards the job on Bajor to Captain Kasidy Yates?

GREAT LINES

"Could you muster up a bit more enthusiasm?"—A disgruntled Kasidy Yates to Sisko after she decides to take a job on Bajor. She had just told Sisko that she intends to move onto the station, and all he could say was "It's a big step." (Through this whole exchange I kept thinking, "You are *dead,* buddy. Dead, dead, dead, dead. As soon as you said that 'It's a big step' thing, you bought the farm. Might as well call the mortician and get it over with!")

PLOT OVERSIGHTS

• Well, it's nice to see that Sisko found something for Worf to do. In this episode, Worf tells Kira that she has an incoming message, and later he advises Sisko that a Cardassian transport has arrived. It's nice to see that even though Worf's on the command track now and wears a red uniform, he's not above working as a recep-

306

tionist when needed. (Sorry, that was catty. I apologize. It does make one wonder, though: Just how many rating notches did this episode improve because Worf had these two bit parts?)

• As usual in *Star Trek,* I am always amazed when ships land far, far away from their destinations—forcing their occupants to slog it out through inhospitable terrain. (And in case you're thinking that Kira didn't know where the *Ravinok* crashed and therefore *couldn't* park any closer, see below under "Equipment Oddities.")

CHANGED PREMISES

• Does phaser fire damage look the same as disrupter fire damage? After finding the *Ravinok,* Kira proclaims that the side of the ship shows phaser hits. Yet "Hero Worship" establishes that the Breen—later seen as the captors of the *Ravinok*'s occupants—use disrupters. (Pick, pick, pick, pick, pick.)

EQUIPMENT ODDITIES

• Kira evidently isn't as worried as Sisko about Dukat stealing Federation technology. In "The Maquis, Part I," when Dukat came along for a runabout ride, Sisko shut off all his control panels. In this episode Kira leaves them illuminated.

• Finding the crash site accompanied by only twelve graves, Kira and Dukat begin a search for the forty other occupants of the vessel. Dukat suggests scanning from orbit, but because of the ionic interference Kira decides a foot search would be better. Why not a low-altitude visual sweep in the runabout? Surely this would be faster than trudging through the sand. (The same would apply for finding the crash site, would it not?)

• To facilitate the foot search Kira tunes her tricorder to pick up tritonium isotopes. She says Bajoran resistance fighters carried subdermal implants. When captured, they could activate these implants and leave a trail for potential rescuers to follow. Dukat seems completely unaware of this tactic. You might remember that Dukat was in charge of the Cardassian occupation of Bajor. Are we to believe that not one captured resistance fighter ever broke under torture and told his captors of these subdermal implants? Are we to believe that they somehow remained hidden from all the testing and scanning that the Cardassians perform on their prisoners?

• Deciding to stop for the night, Kira tells Dukat that she can't see two meters in front of her. This bit of dialogue finally gave Paul M. Steele of Fort Belvoir, Virginia, a chance to ask a question he's pondered about *Star Trek* for some time: namely, Why doesn't Starfleet have night vision technology? (Paul tells me that even today we have lightweight night vision goggles that allow soldiers to walk and even fly helicopters at night under totally overcast skies with no moonlight! By the way, Paul should know: He works at the U.S. Army Night Vision Laboratory. I *love* this Guild!)

• Evidently, military supplies aren't going to change much in the next three hundred years. Jim Ferris of Holly, Michigan, recognized the field rations in this episode as standard military MREs ("Meals Ready to Eat"). The bedrolls are standard issue as well.

CONTINUITY AND PRODUCTION PROBLEMS

• As soon as I heard Razka Karn's voice I started mumbling, "Who is that guy? Who *is* that guy?!" Then it hit me. He sounds just like Sirna Kolrami from "Peak Performance" *(TNG)*. Those random genetic combinations continue to amaze. (Roy Brocksmith really does have a great voice, doesn't he?)

• The markings on Dukat's uniform in this episode are the same as those previously seem only on Cardassians of the rank "legate." (See "The Maquis, Part II," "Second Skin," and "Life Support.") Did Dukat get a promotion? Or is "legate" an honorific of office rather than a rank? (An abbreviation of "delegate," perhaps?)

• As Kira and Dukat meet with Karn in the Badlands, there are two different shots showing a normal starfield out the window of the runabout. Since the Badlands are rife with plasma storms, the windows should show the same type of background as we see in the exterior establishing shot of the two ships. Watch for the window after Karn says that Dukat's new attitude "almost" makes him forget the occupation and just after Kira decides to go to the Dozaria System.

• The elusive Breen—mentioned in "Hero Worship" *(TNG)*, "The Loss" *(TNG)*, and *Star Trek Generations*—finally make an appearance, and in a fate stranger than Hollywood, we see that they come from…*Star Wars*! Princess Leia stole one of their helmets to use as a disguise when she infiltrated Jabba the Hutt's castle in *Return of the Jedi*. (Actually, the helmets that the Breen wear in this episode are a bit different, but they are similar enough that several nitpickers wrote to mention it.)

• After reacting badly to Yates moving onto the station, Sisko goes to apologize in a cargo bay. As he begins, Yates hands him a small plastic barrel. He launches into his song and dance. The cameras cut to a close-up, and the handle on the barrel suddenly pops up. Moments later it pops back down—all without any perceptible help!

• It looks like Kira finally got some major heels to match her rank. Watch as she and Dax walk down the upper level of the promenade at the end of this episode. They stand shoulder to shoulder! Now, friends, I've seen both Terry Farrell and Nana Visitor at conventions, and I can assure you that they are nowhere near the same height. Farrell is an amazon! (She's six feet tall.) And—apart from the Ferengi—Kira is the shortest person in the cast. You can't see the back of the ladies' feet in the promenade scene, but I'd be willing to bet that Farrell has *no* heel on her shoes and Visitor has five or six inches' worth! (In person, these two look more like Mutt and Jeff—with all due respect to a pair of fine actresses.)

TRIVIA ANSWERS
1. The *Rabol*.
2. Minister Azin

REJOINED

Star Date: 49195.5

A team of Trill scientists arrive on the station to conduct studies on the creation of an artificial wormhole—led by Dr. Lenara Kahn, formerly Nilani Kahn, wife of Torias Dax. When a shuttle accident killed Torias, the Dax symbiont was placed in Joran for a short time (see "Equilibrium") before the Symbiosis Commission moved it to Curzon. After a full life, Curzon died, and the Dax symbiont joined with Jadzia. As a widow, Nilani retained the Kahn symbiont until her death, when it joined with Lenara. Almost immediately both women find they are having difficulty separating their lives from the memories of Torias and Nilani. Recognizing this type of "reassociation" as a normal problem, Trill society long ago developed a taboo against continuing a love relationship begun by another host. Violating the taboo carries a strict punishment: The perpetrator is exiled from the Trill home world, denying the symbiont any further opportunity to join with another host.

Though the wormhole tests enjoy some degree of success, an accident almost costs Kahn her life—convincing Dax that she doesn't want to lose Kahn again. Kahn feels the same way, though she cannot endure the punishment her reassociation with Dax would bring. With regret, she accompanies the other scientists back to the Trill home world.

PLOT OVERSIGHTS

• So...aside from the fact that it's a plot contrivance to get Kahn and Dax together, is there some reason that the Trill science team needs to do these experiments at DS9?

• After learning of Kahn's imminent arrival and hearing Sisko's suggestion that she take a leave of absence, Dax jokingly asks if she's that dispensable. Sisko replies with a smile that they'll never notice she's gone. Why should they? The senior staff doesn't *do anything* on this station. That much is perfectly clear. Anytime they feel like it, they hop into the *Defiant* and tool off for the regions beyond. (I'm just joking!)

• Well, it's nice to see that Worf has managed to find something else to do with his time. In the previous episode he worked as the Ops receptionist. In this episode he escorts people to their

Trivia Questions

1. What three Bajoran foods does Dax identify at the reception?

2. Who broke his leg during this episode?

309

quarters and captains the *Defiant* for a research mission. I guess the sector must be pretty quiet and there really isn't any need for him to do any active strategic coordination in his capacity as the Strategic Operations officer!

• In discussing "reassociation" with Kira, Bashir says it's not really a rule. It's more of a taboo. I'm having a bit of difficulty in finding any more than a euphemistic difference between these two words when applied to this context. This "taboo" carries a death sentence that is implemented by Trill society as a whole. The persons committing this "taboo" are exiled from the Trill home world. To be effective, this exile would have to be backed by the legal enforcement structure within the Trill government. Does this not sound like a rule—nay, even a *law*?

• So let's talk about why reassociation is supposedly taboo. Bashir tells Kira that the whole point of joining is for the symbiont to accumulate experiences over many lifetimes. He also says that to move on from host to host the symbiont has to learn to let go of the past. This "letting go" includes parents, siblings, spouses, and children. First, the Dax symbiont has never had a problem letting go of the past. I cite as an example "Invasive Procedures." Verad comes to the station and steals Dax. Verad Dax's response? *Token* remorse. Evidently the Dax symbiont didn't care that the theft was illegal and would result in Jadzia's death. As long as it still had access to opposable thumbs, it was happy! Second, if the symbiont is supposed to let go of the past, wouldn't this also include close friends? Close

friends such as Sisko? And what about a godson? Shouldn't Dax's little adventure during "Blood Oath" be considered a reassociation?

• At the reception in honor of the Trill scientists, Sisko states that they will attempt to create the first artificial wormhole. He seems to have forgotten that the wormhole right next door—the one that takes them to the Gamma Quadrant—is *artificial*.

• After discovering that some data were lost during the download of the Trill routines to the main computer on the *Defiant*, Trill scientist Dr. Hanor Pren leaves the bridge to fetch some diagnostic routines. This action leaves Dax and Kahn on the bridge alone. If Trill reassociation is so taboo, wouldn't it make sense to provide these two with a constant chaperon?

• While Dax and Kahn enjoy dinner together in Quark's, Pren notices that they hold hands. Later, on the *Defiant,* Pren tries to discuss the matter with Kahn's brother, Dr. Bejal Otner. Pren notes that Dax and Kahn are very friendly and tells Otner that they had dinner alone. Otner reacts instantly, asking Pren what he's trying to say. Pren retorts that he shouldn't have to say anything. At this Otner responds, "Then don't!" One gets the impression that Otner doesn't want to talk about what Pren did or did not see. Obviously Otner cooled down later and got all the details from Pren because the next day he confronts Kahn over the fact that Pren saw them holding hands. (He couldn't have known Pren saw them holding hands unless he went back and talked with Pren about it.)

• Rushing to rescue Kahn, Dax arrives at Main Engineering with a damage control team. (It consists of two people carrying little fire extinguishers. No doubt they are hoping for a *small* fire.) Dax tells the pair to stand back as she opens the door. The guy on the team nods and stays right where he is!

• To save Kahn from the ruptured plasma conduits in Main Engineering, Dax reconfigures a force field so she can use it to walk over the damaged conduits and drag Kahn into an access hatch. She tells Eddington to give her ten seconds after the force field engages and then vent the atmosphere in the room to put out the plasma fire. Of course, the trip across the force field actually takes thirty seconds.

CHANGED PREMISES

• Deciding to stay at her post even though Kahn is coming to the station, Dax says that she has never let her past lives interfere with her job and she's not going to start now. Don't you just love people who make grand pronouncements about their work record when the truth isn't nearly as spotless as they proclaim? If Dax has *never* let her past lives interfere with her job, what was that deal with running off with the Klingons intending to murder the Albino in cold blood? (See "Blood Oath.") If I recall, Sisko did not want her to go, but she went anyway. Seems to me that this would constitute letting a past life interfere with your job! Of course, Sisko conveniently forgets this incident as well and acts like Dax is absolutely correct in her protestations.

• And while we're on the topic of this

"rejoining" thing, what about Odan in "The Host" *(TNG)*? He's having a relationship with Crusher. The host dies. Crusher implants the symbiont in Riker. Riker takes up the relationship with Crusher. Riker almost dies. Crusher puts the symbiont in another Trill host. *That* Trill host tries to get something going with Beverly. See a pattern here? Sounds like rejoining to me, and Odan doesn't seem to have any qualms about it!

• In "The Search, Part I" we meet Lieutenant Commander Michael Eddington of Starfleet Security. As late as "The Adversary," Eddington reaffirms his role as a Security officer. Suddenly, in this episode, Eddington substitutes for O'Brien in Main Engineering on the *Defiant*. Did he decide to switch careers from Security to Engineering? (And why isn't O'Brien along on this mission, by the way? Was it important enough for Worf to command but not important enough for O'Brien to engineer?)

EQUIPMENT ODDITIES

• After downloading the routines and data to the main computer on the *Defiant,* the Trill science team discover that some of it has been lost. This is appalling! What good is a data transfer if stuff is going to be lost? What happened to verification protocols and check sums in the twenty-fourth century? When I was a programmer, there were times when I had to send the latest version of software over phone lines to a parent company in Minneapolis. Either it went through or it didn't (and sometimes it took more than thirty minutes to send), but if it went through, it didn't have lost data. The software was simply too huge to put up with that type of foolishness.

• After getting some more odd readings from the Trill download, Dax tells Kahn not to panic. It could just be transtater failure, she says. It happens all the time, she says. *All the time?* The ship is docked at the station, free of any stress, and portions of its system are *failing*? This does not inspire confidence! (By the way, concerning these "transtaters," any chance that these are the same circuits referred to in the *Classic Trek* episode "A Piece of the Action"? The ones that Kirk claims are the key components of virtually all twenty-third-century Starfleet equipment?)

CONTINUITY AND PRODUCTION PROBLEMS

• The Trill ship that docks at DS9 during this episode looks stunningly similar to the Wadi ship that docks during "Move Along Home." That's very interesting—given that the Wadi are from the *Gamma* Quadrant.

• I knew it! I knew it! I *knew* it! I knew Kira was wearing tall heels during the last episode! In this episode—as she and Bashir walk out of Quark's just after the opening credits—you can see them clearly.

• Just before the first attempt to open a wormhole, Dax goes over to Kahn's station. Both women face the displays on the wall. The scene cuts to the other two Trill scientists as they worry over the goings on between the pair. In the background you can see that Dax has instantly rotated 180 degrees to face the center of the bridge.

TRIVIA ANSWERS

1. Hasperat, Moba fruit, and Veklava.
2. Ensign Tyler

Star Date: unknown

After a long-promised shuttle arrives from his cousin Gaila, Quark decides to transport Nog to Earth so the young male can enter Starfleet Academy. All is not as it seems, however. Rom soon discovers Quark is smuggling kemacite—an unstable, contraband substance. Rom also discovers that cousin Gaila rigged the shuttle to lock itself into warp. When it threatens to fly itself apart, Rom ignites the kemacite in the hold. The resulting inversion wave not only knocks the craft out of warp but also throws the shuttle back to the year A.D. 1947, where it crashlands near Roswell, New Mexico.

The three Ferengi awake at a U.S. military base. Once Rom fixes an initial glitch in their Universal Translators, Quark seizes the profit potential. He proposes to sell twenty-fourth-century technology to twentieth-century Earth. He intends to take over the planet and then supply the Ferengi home world with warp technology centuries ahead of its time. Unfortunately, the U.S. military personnel see only the danger of invasion and begin torturing

Trivia Questions

1. According to Rom's guidebook, when was Gabriel Bell born?

2. What is the first letter on the eye chart in the room where Quark, Rom, and Nog are detained?

Quark for information. Thankfully, a kindly professor and his fiancée nurse intervene. They help the three Ferengi and stowaway Odo return to Quark's shuttle, where Rom uses the power of an atomic bomb test to fly everyone back to the twenty-fourth century.

RUMINATIONS

Originally, The Nitpicker's Guide for Next Generation Trekkers, Volume II, *contained a discussion concerning Earth's role in the founding of the Federation. (It was cut for space.) Many nitpickers had taken me to task for my comments in* The Nitpicker's Guide for Next Generation Trekkers *over my lack of knowledge that Earth was a founding member of the Federation. The discussion deleted from the NextGen II Guide noted that in 178 episodes of* Star Trek: The Next Generation *you cannot find one piece of dialogue that states this fact clearly. I am happy to report that the creators answered this oversight in this episode, sort of. On the way to Earth, Nog wonders that humans could go from nothing to leaders of a vast interstellar Federation in just five thousand years.*

(Okay, so it would have been more satisfying if the creators had said "founders" of a vast interstellar federation instead of just "leaders," but at least we're getting closer!)

PLOT OVERSIGHTS

• From the sounds of it at the beginning of this episode, Nog has made it into Starfleet Academy. That's pretty astonishing, given the trouble Wesley Crusher had in "Coming of Age" when he competed against four other topflight candidates for one entry slot and *lost*! (I suspect quotas at work here.)

• I am ever amazed at the good fortune of the navigators in *Star Trek*. To quote Douglas Adams, "Space is big, really big!" I understand that Rom had the shuttle pointed at Earth's star system when he ignited the kemacite. But did he really have it pointed directly at the *planet* Earth?! What if he couldn't get them out of warp? Would *Quark's Treasure* just plow into the planet? One would think a more sensible plan would be to set the trajectory of the shuttle so it wouldn't smash into something if the inversion wave didn't work. At least then you might have a second chance. On the other hand, if Rom simply pointed the shuttle in the general direction, how in the world did he hit that little BB called Earth in the sea of space?

• My appreciation for Nog's study skills went up several notches during this episode. Before he leaves for Earth, Bashir and O'Brien give him a going-away present—a guidebook to Earth. Supposedly it contains all the information he would ever want to know on geography, customs, histo-

ry, etc. During the shuttle trip we do see Nog studying the book. He mentions that humans only recently acquired currency (within the past five thousand years). He finds Sisko's picture—taken during the Bell Riots in A.D. 2024 (See "Past Tense, Part II.") Obviously Nog has decided to overview the entire panorama of human history. Here's what's amazing: A bit later, Nog correctly identifies the time frame for the uniforms he sees on the soldiers and even knows that aboveground nuclear testing was carried on during the midpart of the twentieth century! Were these two items part of the historical overview, or did Nog study the *entire* history of Earth? Or did he just *happen* to decide to study in depth the goings-on in the midtwentieth century?

• I think we can safely say that Starfleet uses some type of language we'll call Federation Standard. I know it looks like English and it sounds like English (unless you're in France or Germany or Spain or Japan...). However, I believe this episode provides plentiful circumstantial evidence that it's *not* English. Try this on for size: Rom has a guidebook that provides a complete history of the Earth. This guidebook is in Quark's shuttle. The shuttle is in the hands of the U.S. military. The U.S. military has searched the shuttle. Now, what would you do if you were a military guy—fearing a potential invasion by aliens—and you came across something that said "EARTH" on the front? Wouldn't you start dinking around with it? Knowing Starfleet, the user interface would be supersmooth and easy. And think of the information the guidebook would provide! Strangely enough, no one ever mentions the guidebook to the general in charge of the operation. The reason? The front of the guidebook is really written in Federation Standard and reads, "S^DK&JU8H." (I suspect that the reason it looks like it says "EARTH" when you see the guidebook on television is due to some spatial metaphasic translation discriminator coded into the vertical blanking of the video signal.)

• At one point the kindly professor and his fiancée nurse leave the room where Quark, Rom, and Nog are held. A dog remains behind. The dog subsequently morphs into Odo. First, why would the kindly professor and his fiancée nurse leave the dog behind? It looks like a military police dog. Shouldn't someone be keeping track of a guard dog? This isn't home sweet home—this is a military installation! Second, Odo morphs from a dog to a humanoid right in front of a one-way mirror, yet no one seems to notice. Has the military really suspended all surveillance of these aliens? Did the general decide that just because they speak English, they don't need to be watched?

• And speaking of Odo, does it really fall within his jurisdiction to catch Quark smuggling kemacite into the Orion System? Shouldn't he be back on DS9 minding the store? A subspace call to the authorities on Earth would take care of the smuggling problem. (As I asked in my review of "Hippocratic Oath," do local sheriffs go to Colombia to crack drug smuggling rings?)

• At one point Quark speaks of sell-ing his shuttle to the Ferengi home world so they will have warp drive centuries before the humans, Klingons, or even Vulcans. In other words, Vulcan didn't have warp drive prior to 1947? Hmmm. According to *The Star Trek Encyclopedia,* the Romulans left Vulcan "over a thousand years ago." Now, even if those words refer to the time frame of the 24th century, that still means the Romulans left Vulcan sometime in the 14th century—about six hundred years before A.D. 1947! If Vulcan didn't have warp drive yet, it was a *very long* trip! (It would take at least four and one-half years for humans to get to their closest neighboring star system without warp drive!)

• After visiting the Ferengi trio, Odo says he will have their ship ready to go in six hours. I'm telling ya, those engineering correspondence courses can do wonders.

• Of course, one might muse that if this plan for selling the Ferengi home world warp technology is so great, why hasn't someone in the Ferengi Alliance whipped around the sun as Kirk and crew did in *Star Trek IV: The Voyage Home*? Don't the Ferengi know about this method of time travel?

• When the president orders the general in charge of the operation to get more information from Quark and company, Captain Wainwright takes them to a room for questioning. Eventually Nog comes up with a plan to help himself, his father, and his uncle escape. He tells Wainwright that a fleet of three hundred Marauder-class attack cruisers orbits the planet and soon will drop their cloaks. Then this fleet will begin transporting Klingon

shock troops to the surface. Wainwright seems convinced that this is
the truth and allows Nog to indicate on
a large wall map where the first assault
will take place. Nog then elbows Wainwright in the stomach and attempts
to take his gun, but a guard intervenes.
That's when the kindly professor and
his nurse fiancée come to the rescue.
Interestingly enough, at the end of the
episode, Wainwright seems to forget
Nog's fabrication about the invasion
fleet. He stands beside the general
as *Quark's Treasure* takes off for parts
unknown and says nary a word. (One
would think such information would
be vital to national security.)

• Quark finally goes to jail on charges
of kemacite smuggling. Of course,
he's out of jail in the very next episode.
(And in case you're thinking, "But
Quark said all the kemacite was destroyed, so there's no evidence," I remind you that Odo was there *every*
time the kemacite was discussed in
the shuttle. At the very least, his testimony on the use of the kemacite remains to return to the twenty-fourth
century should be enough to get a
conviction.)

CHANGED PREMISES

• Rom's amazing transformation into a technological whiz kid reaches
completion in this episode. All of a
sudden he can spout technobabble
with the best of them. Not only that, he
also figures out how to leap four hundred years into the future using a damaged shuttle, a primitive atomic bomb,
the last dredges of kemacite, some
twine, a bit of baling wire, and a wad
of bubble gum! All this from a guy Odo

describes in "Babel" as an idiot who
couldn't fix a straw that was bent.
(Okay, okay. I was exaggerating about
the twine, baling wire, and gum.)

EQUIPMENT ODDITIES

• I spent quite a bit of space on the
topic of the Universal Translator in my
review of "Sanctuary." As I said in
those paragraphs, I believe the UT is
something best left unexplained. Unfortunately, the creators seem determined to enlighten us. Much of what
I said during my review of "Sanctuary" also applies here, so I'll spare
you the repeat, though I did have one
further comment. Let's see...UTs in
the ear. Can you say, "Babel fish"?
(from Douglas Adams's *Hitchiker's
Guide to the Galaxy*).

• If replicators can make complex
foods, why can't they replicate gold?
And if they can replicate gold, why is
Quark interested in selling Earth technology *for* gold? Why not just replicate all you want?

CONTINUITY AND
PRODUCTION PROBLEMS

• At the beginning of the episode,
Nog sells his childhood possessions
to raise capital as per Ferengi traditions. Dax buys Nog's favorite holosuite program (a visit with the pleasure
goddess of Rixx) for ten strips of latinum as a gift for Bashir. As she places
the latinum in Nog's hand you can see
that there are only three or four strips,
yet Nog seems content with the exchange. Do the Ferengi have latinum
pieces that are worth two or three
strips apiece? (Sort of like different
denominations of coins?)

• When Rom discovers that he can't take the shuttle out of warp, start watching Quark's right ear. It looks like the makeup artists forgot to cover the innermost part of the latex prosthesis. Moments later, the problem is corrected.

• When Odo surprises Quark by morphing from a dog to a humanoid, the Changeling's left hand rest on Quark's shoulder. Then the shot changes and suddenly Odo's hand disappears.

• Trying to extract information from Quark, mean old Captain Wainwright has the kindly professor's nurse fiancée administer sodium pentothal to Quark. Coming back from a commercial, we see her stick the needle in Quark's arm. Note that the syringe has markings, on the side that faces the back of her hand, to show the amount of dosage. The camera pans up to show Quark screaming and then pulls back as the kindly professor's nurse fiancée raises the empty syringe. Note that the markings to show the dosage amount have *disappeared*! There're two possible explanations for this: The syringe she stuck in Quark's arm isn't the same one she pretends to pull out; or, while the syringe was in Quark's arm, she twisted it around so the marking faced the other way! (No wonder Quark is screaming!)

• Since I am no expert in military costuming, I defer to Dr. Gordon J. Malkowski of San Antonio, Texas, who wrote, "The general is wearing the Air Corps branch insignia on the lower lapels of his coat, which is possible but unlikely. However, his aviator's wings should be command pilot wings, unless he just learned how to fly. The captain is wearing an enlisted rather than an officer's garrison cap. In any event, his rank is missing from his cap. In all but two scenes, his collar rank insignia is turned sideways. Nurse Garland should be a commissioned officer rather than a private. If she was an enlisted medical corpsman, she should have been much higher in rank. For that matter, they were dealing with extraterrestrials. Why was there not a medical doctor present?"

TRIVIA ANSWERS
1. April 24, 1987.
2. "M."

STARSHIP DOWN

Star Date: 49263.5

Responding to a request from the Karemma Commerce Ministry, Sisko takes Quark and the *Defiant* to a remote system in the Gamma Quadrant for a secret meeting. The Federation has recently concluded a trade agreement with the Karemma, using the Ferengi as intermediaries. In the mess hall, Sisko and Quark meet with Hanok, who claims there is no profit in trading with the Federation. He begins quoting surcharges and tariffs added to the last shipment of Karemman fleece. All come as a surprise to Sisko. In fact, Quark has been cheating both sides to line his pockets.

Meanwhile, two Jem'Haddar ships show up to punish the Karemma for doing business with the Federation. Sisko tries to protect the Karemma ship, but its crew drive the vessel into the atmosphere of a nearby gas giant instead. When the Jem'Haddar follow, Sisko decides to take the *Defiant* in as well. Crippling attacks by the Jem'Haddar leave Bashir and Dax in a turbolift, Sisko with a concussion, Kira on the bridge tending his wounds, and Worf in command in the engine room—though one of the

Jem'Haddar ships is destroyed during the assaults. Eventually Worf dispatches the other.

At the same time—back in the mess hall—Quark and Hanok defuse an unexploded Jem'Haddar photon torpedo and become friends.

RUMINATIONS

I found the story Kira tells Sisko about the three brothers who go to Jo'Kala interesting. Very interesting. They find a kava root in the field and take it to market to sell. For several years my parents served as missionaries in Fiji, where kava is the national drink. In fact, it does grow as a root and is mashed into kava powder to prepare the drink—one that can make humans quite *mellow, by the way!*

PLOT OVERSIGHTS
• The episode opens with the *Defiant* in the Gamma Quadrant, again with only a hairbreadth of an excuse. Supposedly the Karemma have asked for a meeting. It appears that less than a minute after the meeting begins, Hanok and Sisko have already decided the problem is Quark and are well on the way to a solution! Seems

Trivia Questions

1. On a shipment of Karemman fleece, Quark added a 6 percent tariff to offset the income loss of what group?

2. Who assists Dax in Jefferies Tube 4?

318

to me that the same thing could have been accomplished with a subspace memo. Or—if the memo doesn't strike your fancy—how about this? Hanok says that the Karemma uses the Ferengi as intermediaries because they know the Dominion would never allow the Karemma to trade directly with the Federation. At this Quark pipes up and says he's happy to report that not one Ferengi ship has ever been stopped. So, why doesn't Sisko get Quark to arrange for a *Ferengi* vessel to ferry him to the meeting? If he's dead set on going into the Gamma Quadrant—despite the strict and unequivocal pronouncements by the Dominion that he and his company should stay out—why not travel there with a bit of stealth? Why would you want to haul the warship *Defiant* in there? (This is like beating a wasp nest with a stick just to see how loud a buzz you can get from the hive!)

• Hanok begins the meeting by noting that certain surcharges and tariffs make it unprofitable to do business with the Federation. The first one he cites is a 4 percent surcharge that Quark has added to inspect the cargo for Changeling infiltrators. Sisko reacts with "*What!*"? He acts as if this is a bad thing. Inspecting cargo for Changeling infiltrators is not a bad thing. Inspecting cargo for Changeling infiltrators is a *good* thing. If there had been better and more frequent inspections, perhaps Changelings wouldn't have made it all the way to Earth! (See "Homefront.")

• Several nitpickers noted that this episode feels like a cross between "Balance of Power" *(TOS)*, the end of

Star Trek II: The Wrath of Khan, and "Disaster" *(TNG).*

• To cut through the sensor interference generated by the atmosphere of the planet, Kira and Dax devise an echo-location system using tetrion particles. (Read that: active sonar). Kira states that every time the ship sends out a pulse they will have to change their speed and alter their course to avoid detection. So what happens a few moments later? A display shows them creeping along in a straight line, sending out pulses. And a few moments after this, the ship actually comes within 10 kilometers of an unidentified ship *and holds position* as it continues to send out the pulses! Did they think Kira was just joking? Did they forget what she said? In any case—after executing this less-than-intelligent maneuver of holding position and broadcasting their location—the Jem'Haddar ride up on the *Defiant*'s tail and blast the stuffing out of the ship!

• After getting pummeled by the Jem'Haddar, the *Defiant* begins to lose altitude. The helmsman first reports a hull pressure of 2 million GSC. Then she reports a hull pressure of 9 million GSC. I assume GSC stands for "grams per square centimeter." Just how much pressure is this? Well, David Brown—one of Mitzi Adams's coworkers—tells me that 1 "atmosphere" on Earth equals 1,000 GSC. The pressure on the hull is *9 million* GSC—approximately 9,000 times what we experience on Earth. Remember that figure ('cause there's going to be a test). After enduring this enormous pressure for a short while, a bulkhead on deck 2 finally gives way, and the atmosphere of the star roars in. An emergency force field pops up, but it can hold for only a short time. In peril are six persons in sick bay, Dax, and a crew member who assists her in Jefferies Tube 4. Bashir gets everyone to the next sealable bulkhead when Dax and the crew member crawl out of the Jefferies Tube. Then the force field blows. Both Dax and the crew member are knocked to the ground as Bashir watches from the open doorway. He pulls the crew member through the doorway. He hears Jadzia yell for his help. He hits the button to seal the area, steps inside as the atmosphere of the planet floods the area, drags Dax into an open turbolift, and closes the door. Now...dear friends, let's think about this.

When the force field goes down there is a direct vent from the atmosphere of the planet to the interior of the ship. What was that exterior pressure on the hull? That's right! *Nine million* GSC! And what do you think the interior pressure of the hallway was before the bulkhead blew? Probably about 1,000 GSC. What do you think will happen now that there is an open vent between the exterior and the interior of the ship? That's right! The pressures between the two areas will equalize—*rapidly*. Since there's a whole lot more atmosphere at *9 million* GSC outside the ship than there is at 1,000 GSC inside the ship, the pressure in the hallway will rise to *9 million* GSC *almost instantly*. Dax and the crew member would not be thrown to the floor, they would be *steamrollered* to the floor and squished into a big, dark stain on the carpet.

Bashir could not stand in the open doorway and watch—aghast—because the pressure wave would hurl him against the opposite wall and crush him into a work of modern art. And even if Bashir could manage to survive long enough to drag Dax into an open turbolift and shut the door, what good would that do? The pressure inside the turbolift would be—what was that figure again?—*9 MILLION GSC*!

• And—if all of the above wasn't bad enough—the creators actually expect us to believe that all the poisonous fluorine gas in the hallway somehow *forgot* to wander through the *open door* of the turbolift (even though the breathable atmosphere was only at 1,000 GSC and the fluorine was at...never mind, you get the idea). This considerate behavior by the fluorine is really very fortunate, because otherwise Dax and Bashir would have quickly succumbed to fluorine poisoning.

• And speaking of the fluorine gas, just where did it come from? Daniel B. Case of Clarence, New York, assures me that fluorine is highly reactive. There is practically no chance of it existing in any measurable quantities in the atmosphere of a gas giant.

• I love Worf's evasive maneuvers after he takes over the ship in the engine room. Two Jem'Haddar torpedoes approach. To avoid the first, he orders a hard-a-port. To avoid the second, he stands there and waits for it to hit the ship!

• Speaking of this second torpedo that Worf lets hit the ship, isn't it just really, really *convenient* that it forgets to explode?

• And what is the deal with these little guys under O'Brien's command in the engine room? Worf comes down and takes command. They're in the middle of a crisis. They are very close to losing the ship, and O'Brien has to tell Worf to go nicey-nice on these guys or they will get their feelings hurt? Also, everyone in the engine room looks like a noncom. Main Engineering on the *Enterprise* was *crawling* with ensigns and lieutenants. What's going on here? And another thing about O'Brien's pep talk to Worf. Are we to believe that the entire time Worf was the chief of Security on the *Enterprise* he never learned how to deal with noncoms?

CHANGED PREMISES

• During "The Adversary" we learned that Kira was the first officer of the *Defiant*. (I found this hard to believe, but the episode does make this claim.) Yet in this episode, when Sisko goes down, Worf takes command of the ship. This actually makes *a lot* more sense, because Worf is a Starfleet officer. (It *is* a change, however, and it is therefore my duty to note it.)

EQUIPMENT ODDITIES

• For some reason—when shutting off all nonessential systems to "run silent, run deep," Kira and Worf have to walk around to several different stations and manually shut them off. Are the automated shutdowns not working?

• The torpedo dud mentioned above just happens to pierce the bulkhead of the *Defiant* in the area of the mess hall. Quark and Hanok take it upon themselves to defuse the torpedo before it decides to start working. After Hanok opens the access panel (which just happens to be on the upper side of the torpedo, wink, wink), Quark pulls out a tricorder to take a reading. Interestingly enough, he's not taking a reading of the torpedo. He's taking a reading of himself, because he's holding the tricorder backward!

CONTINUITY AND PRODUCTION PROBLEMS

• To defuse the dud torpedo, Quark pulls out the firing diode. The torpedo goes dark. When the damage control teams arrive, however, the torpedo has illuminated again. (Somebody better check that thing!)

TRIVIA ANSWERS
1. Tarkalian sheepherders.
2. Muñiz.

THE SWORD OF KAHLESS

Star Date: unknown

Kor (see "Blood Oath") comes to the station to enlist Dax's help. While serving on Vulcan as the Klingon ambassador he came across a piece of cloth that he believes once held the fabled sword of Kahless. Following its discovery during a mining operation on an uncharted planet, the Vulcans brought the cloth back from the Gamma Quadrant. During analysis, Dax finds both Klingon and Hur'Q DNA along with metallic traces of a fourteen-hundred-year-old bat'leth. Since the Hur'Q stole the sword from Kronos a thousand years ago, Kor is certain that he knows its location and wants Dax to assist him in his quest. He invites Worf to come along as well.

Arriving at the planet, the trio quickly recover the sword of Kahless. Unfortunately, Kor's drunken revelry at taverns across the quadrant brings unwanted guests to the celebration. Toral, the illegitimate son of Duras (see "Redemption," *TNG*), appears with a band of Klingons to steal the sword for himself. Eventually Kor, Worf, and Dax escape, but not before the trio realizes the effect that the an-

Trivia Questions

1. What were the Vulcans mining when they discovered the ancient Hur'Q ruins?

2. Where did Toral learn of Kor's quest to find the sword?

cient bat'leth has on Klingons. Everyone who sees it becomes enthralled with visions of grandeur. Knowing its return would plunge the Klingon Empire into bloody civil war, Worf and Kor beam the sword into space, leaving it to be rediscovered when destiny appoints.

PLOT OVERSIGHTS

• After his introduction to Kor by Dax, Worf mentions a list of the great warrior's accomplishments. The first of them, "your confrontation with Kirk on Organia," seems a bit overplayed for the events seen in "Errand of Mercy" (*TOS*). In that episode Kirk and Spock were caught on the surface of Organia just as Kor arrived with troops to subdue the planet. Kirk and Spock went underground, dressing like Organians. But even after Kirk and Spock blew up a munitions dump, Kor couldn't locate the culprits. He only arrested them after the Organians ratted on our heroes. Then Kirk and Spock attacked Kor's headquarters and actually managed to make it all the way to Kor's office. Of course, the Organians—who were really powerful beings who simply had taken on corporeal form—got fed up with the shenanigans on both sides and stepped in. They forced a truce not only between Kirk and Kor but also between the Federation and the Klingon Empire. So why do the Klingons consider Kor's performance on this planet worthy of veneration? What did Kor do that was so spectacular? (Maybe they've only heard Kor's version on Kronos. "There we were, face to face, circling each other, blood lust in our veins despite the interference of the "smiles and smiles" lily-livered Organians. Without warning, Kirk *lunged* at me like a Marclosian wind devil! I grabbed him, hurling him against the wall—searing heat racing along my arms at even this momentary contact. Teeth bared, eyes flashing with the fear of an outmatched opponent, he came at me again. We fell to the floor—the very flesh on our hands boiling, our breath blistering each other's face with...")

• I hate to bring this up, but Worf apparently isn't too busy with his new assignment as "Strategic Operations" officer. At a moment's notice, he takes off on an adventure with Dax and Kor.

• Supposedly, a Vulcan geological survey team brought back the piece of cloth from the Gamma Quadrant. Dax says the cloth was discovered while the team was mining bakrinium on an uncharted planet. This forces us to ask the question again: What about Third Talak'Talan's statements in "The Jem'Haddar"? Why are the Vulcans going out of their way to "offend" the Dominion? Does this seem logical?

• My appreciation for Vulcans dropped yet another notch as this episode proceeded. On the planet, a force field protects the chamber that houses the remnants of the central museum. Kor says the Vulcans couldn't penetrate it. Dax and Worf accomplish this feat in all of about thirty seconds! (Remember that Dax didn't know she would be dealing with a force field before she got there, so she didn't bring along any special equipment.) That's funny. I thought the Vulcans were the whiz-bang, technoheaded, science-groking titans of the Federation. And they couldn't get through a puny force field?!

• Well, if Worf wasn't in deep, deep doo-doo with the Klingon High Command before this episode, he certainly is now. How could he ever explain to Gowron that he helped recover the fabled sword of Kahless and then set it adrift in space? (Somehow, I don't think "It made us act bad and we felt bad" is going to cut it!)

• And speaking of setting the sword adrift in the Gamma Quadrant, I wonder what would happen if the Changelings happened to find it and sent one of their own to Kronos to pose as Kahless? (When Johnson Lai of Ajax, Ontario, proposed this scenario to me, I thought, "Oops!")

CHANGED PREMISES

• When our heroes first find the legendary sword of Kahless, Kor holds it for a moment before giving it to Worf. Clutching the sword, Worf recites its legacy. With this sword, he claims that Kahless killed Molor, conquered the Fek'Ihri, and forged the first empire. Remember that "killed Molor" thing as we go back to the *NextGen* episode "Rightful Heir." In that episode Kahless supposedly comes back from the dead at the monastery on Boreth. He marches into a room that contains a thronelike chair and grabs a bat'leth that rests on the seat. One of the clerics reacts with indignation at the sight, at which point Kahless asks, "Who here knows the story of how *this* sword was forged?" (Emphasis mine.) Kahless tells the story. Then he refers to the blade that he holds as the bat'leth that killed Molor! So...it appears that there are *two* swords of Kahless.

EQUIPMENT ODDITIES

• This episode contains two BILCs. (Walbert Ng of Elmhurst, New York, originally submitted the term "BILC." It's an anagram for "Because It Looks Cool.") After deciding to abandon the sword to the galaxy, the hearty trio affixes the sword to a cylindrical tower on the transporter platform. This is very convenient for the director because it just happens to put the bat'leth into perfect position to film a dramatic beam-out, with Worf and Kor in the background. However, it does beg the question: Was this just done for ceremony? Why not just lean the sword against the interior of the transporter chamber? (For the other BILC, see below.)

CONTINUITY AND PRODUCTION PROBLEMS

• When discussing which runabout they might take to the Gamma Quadrant, Worf tells Sisko that the *Rio Grande* is available. The closed captioning says, "*Mekong.*"

• After Kor goes off to find another rat on which our heroes can feast, Dax changes Worf's bandage. She inserts a piece of cloth into the tear on his uniform. As she withdraws her right hand and places it on Worf's shoulder, you can see blood on the middle joints of her fingers. Then the shot changes, and Dax moves this same hand around to Worf's back. Now the blood has disappeared. (I know. Pick, pick, pick, pick, pick.)

• At the very end of the episode we see the runabout departing and the sword of Kahless rotating away from the camera. Amazingly enough, it rotates in a perfect circle, *on edge*! If we assume that the bat'leth materialized in the same position in which it left the ship, the sword of Kahless would have hung in space with its prongs facing up. Somehow, from this position, it began moving and rotating. Did Dax nudge it with the tractor beam before pulling away? Are we supposed to believe that a piece of cosmic dust hit it *exactly* on edge and started it turning? What are the chances of *that* happening? Or did Worf program the transporter to materialize the bat'leth rotating, in flight? (Of course, the real explanation for why the sword began rotating is...*BILC*!)

TRIVIA ANSWERS

1. Bakrinium.
2. In a tavern on Tora IV.

TREK SILLINESS

THE TOP TEN ODDITIES OF THE FIRST
FOUR SEASONS OF STAR TREK: DEEP SPACE NINE

1. *Cosmology 101.* At times, reality holds little visual appeal. Take comets, for example. As they approach a star, they develop a beautiful tail because the star affects the exterior surface of the comet, forming a stream of gases and particles. (Note that this stream *always* points away from the star.) In deep space, however, the comet is nothing more than a chunk of ice and rock. Not exactly thrilling, but that's reality for you. Apparently this wasn't good enough for the creators, so they made up their own version of comets! The *DS9* comets not only have tails all the time, the tails always point in the direction of the creators' choosing. (Imagine…wink, wink.) Take the title sequence, for instance. We see a comet approach. It passes. The camera turns, and we are looking directly at the backside of the comet from inside the tail. A very nice visual effect. There's only one problem: There should be a star directly in front of the comet, and there isn't! Even more interesting, when the station appears, we see that the major light source comes from the left. Okay, so the star is off to the left. But that means this comet somehow formed a tail that pointed perpendicular to the light coming from the nearest star!

2. *Space station design.* Several episodes lend the impression that the Cardassians are quite a meticulous race—planners, filers, detailists. Why, then, would they build a space station with an inherent limitation on the size of ships that can dock? Consider the pylons—those arcing fangs that grow from the docking ring. Apparently these pylons are used by the larger ships that need to dock. Why, then, do these pylons curve inward? Doesn't that inherently limit the amount of usable space? Wouldn't it be better if the pylons curved *outward*? Doing that would dramatically increase the area surrounding the tip of each pylon. And—lest you think the extra space would never be needed— I remind you that a Romulan warbird is *four times* the size of the *Enterprise*. When we saw the *Enterprise* docked at an upper pylon at the beginning of "Emissary," it appeared to take up a full third of the available space. In other words, *if* a warbird could dock at one of the pylons, the other two would be unusable. (And if you're wondering about the complications outward-arcing pylons would cause on the defensive shield bubble, the pylons could begin at the central core and slope out. This would also have the benefit of delivering travelers to the promenade more quickly!)

3. *Now they move, now they don't.* The personnel on the station can't seem to make up their minds over whether they want the station to rotate. Almost every time we look out the window in Sisko's office, the stars gently drift from right to left. Almost every time we look out every other window, they don't!

4. *Senior staff job descriptions.* Does the senior staff really *do* anything on this station? (Apart from O'Brien, of course, who is positively worked to death.) It seems like any time they feel like it the senior staff all hop on a runabout or the *Defiant* and set off on some adventure. Bored with station life, are we?

5. *Whacking the Dominion hive.* After two seasons of happily tromping back and forth between the Alpha and the Gamma quadrants, our heroes faced a difficult challenge. At the end of the second season—during "The Jem'Haddar"—Third Talak'Talan informs the crew that the Jem'Haddar has captured Sisko and wiped out the Bajoran colony in the Gamma Quadrant. He goes on to say that the Dominion will no longer tolerate interference. Third Talak'Talan then defines "interference" as traveling through the wormhole. He says that this would offend the Dominion. Amazingly enough, we watch for the next two seasons as Starfleet personnel invade the Gamma Quadrant any time they jolly well please!

6. *The violations of Sisko.* It amazes me how many times Sisko can disobey orders and still retain his commission. (Even stranger, he not only retains his commission, he also gets promoted!) In "The Circle" Sisko is ordered to withdraw from the station. Instead, during "The Siege," he comes up with a flimsy excuse and engages in a battle with Bajorans over control of a station that the Bajorans own! In "The Die Is Cast" Admiral Rollman orders Sisko to stay put and defend Bajor, but he decides to take off for the Gamma Quadrant to find Odo. In "The Way of the Warrior" the Federation Council decides not to intervene. They decide not to warn Cardassia that the Klingons are coming. Sisko's response? He purposefully leaks word of the invasion fleet to Garak, knowing that Garak will warn Cardassia. Not only that, he also take the *Defiant* into Cardassian territory to rescue the Cardassian leaders! Yes, we've seen captains pull these stunts before, but the consequences of Sisko's actions involve more than just his small sphere of influence. In "The Siege," if the Circle had taken control of Bajor, Sisko's actions would have permanently soured the potential for any future relationship between Bajor and the Federation. In "The Die Is Cast," if the Jem'Haddar had attacked Bajor during that critically vulnerable time between Sisko's departure and the arrival of the nine Starfleet ships, *millions*—most likely *billions*—of Bajorans would have died. In "The Way of the Warrior," Sisko came this close to starting a war between the Federation and the Klingon Empire! These are not minor consequences. Sooner or lat-

er, a person who disobeys orders consistently will make a fatal mistake. There's no guarantee that everything will work out for the best the next time Sisko decides to violate an order. Starfleet should know that. (Granted, it might be next to impossible to remove him from command of the station, given the Bajoran belief that he's the "emissary." But you don't let the guy keep his warship and you don't let him remain a captain if you were silly enough to promote him in the first place!) One final rant before I get off this soapbox. I wonder why Starfleet didn't promote Captain Maxwell of the *Phoenix* to admiral. (See "The Wounded.") After all, Maxwell probably was right. The Cardassians were massing for war. And Maxwell did alert the Federation in time through his actions. By the standards applied to Sisko, Maxwell is a hero! (Please don't misunderstand. I like Sisko. I just think it's a bit unbelievable that Starfleet hasn't busted him down to ensign!)

7. *There's the Trill and then there's the Trill.* I spent a lot of space in the *NextGen II Guide* talking about the changes between the Trill of *NextGen* and the Trill of *DS9*. (For a quick revisit, see "Dax.") I wonder: Would it really have been that hard to come up with another name for Dax's race?

8. *The ever-changing mass of our favorite shape shifter.* It does! Sometimes Odo is described as heavier than he looks. At other times characters carry him with one hand. (For more information see "Emissary," "Past Prolouge," "Vortex," "The Circle," and "Second Skin.")

9. *Quark's pardons.* I am also amazed that Quark still walks the halls of the promenade. In "Babel" Quark breaks into crew quarters to illegally use a replicator. This spreads the aphasia virus throughout the entire station. His punishment? Nothing! In "The Siege" he sells nonexistent tickets to individuals attempting to flee the station. This is called fraud. His punishment? Nothing! In "Invasive Procedures" he arranges for mercenaries to gain access to the station. This almost results in the death of Dax, and Kira tells him in no uncertain terms that he is through on the station. What happens to Quark after the episode? Nothing! In "Meridian" Quark breaks into the station files and extracts Kira's personnel records. His *legal* punishment? Nothing! In "Little Green Men" Odo witnesses the fact that Quark attempts to smuggle kemacite to the Orion System. At the end of the episode, Odo does haul Quark off to jail, but guess what comes of it? Nothing!

10. *The heels of Kira.* For some reason, just after the start of the fourth season, the creators decided that Kira wasn't tall enough! So they gave her these huge heels. It seems very odd to suddenly see her walking head to head with Dax.

OUR MAN BASHIR

Star Date: unknown

As the episode begins, Bashir enjoys a holosuite adventure that casts him in the role of a flamboyant spy during the Cold War on Earth ("licensed to kill," if you get my drift). Ever since the new program arrived, Bashir has spent all his free time acting out its story line. (No doubt his valet, Miss Mona "Wonder Bra" Luvsitt, has a tad to do with his preoccupation.)

Meanwhile, Sisko, Kira, Dax, Worf, and O'Brien return from a conference. Nearing DS9, they discover that someone has sabotaged the runabout. (It turns out to be a Cardassian group called "the True Way," but they're just a plot device to get the fun started.) Eddington, in Ops, attempts to beam the officers off the runabout. Unfortunately, the runabout explodes, leaving them stranded in the pattern buffer. With no other option, Eddington tells the computer to store the patterns in all available memory. The computer stores the officers' physical patterns in Bashir's program while saving their neural energy everywhere else. Thus begins a delightful James Bondian

romp in which Bashir must keep anyone from dying lest their patterns be lost. Eventually Rom manages to hotwire the *Defiant's* transporters to the holosuite memory core, restoring everyone to their normal selves.

Trivia Questions

1. In what Earth year does this holosuite adventure occur?

2. From where do the rubies in Dr. Noah's latest acquisition come?

RUMINATIONS

This was a very cute episode—a refreshing change of pace (though the "holodeck/holosuite gone awry" aspect of it was a bit stale).

And in the category of "did you notice?" Toward the end of the episode, the evil Dr. Noah (Sisko) handcuffs Bashir and Garak to a laser that will soon fire, penetrating the Earth's crust and filling the chamber with lava. The timer starts at "0:04:59" and counts down. Just before our heroes escape from the chamber, the timer reads "0:00:08," "0:00:07," and "0:00:06." Would that middle number be just a coincidence? (Jonathan Strawn of Albuquerque, New Mexico, tells me that this bit comes straight out of the Bond movie *Goldfinger*. A homage, if you will!)

PLOT OVERSIGHTS

• Again, almost the entire senior staff

strolls off to some conference, leaving DS9 without the knowledge and experience of its most seasoned officers. At least they left the *Defiant* behind this time! (More on that below.)

• Someone needs to have a chat with Lieutenant Commander Michael Eddington concerning his hands and the female anatomy. When the primary energizing coils on the transporter in Ops surged, both Eddington and the young lady who is seated next to him duck behind a console. The next time we see him he's getting up with his left hand on her chair, fingertips pressing into her posterior! (I'm sure it was an accident. Uh-huh, uh-huh.)

• Just after the computer transfers the physical patterns of Sisko and crew to the holosuite computer, Bashir hears a thump from behind a false wall in his apartment. The entire wall rotates, to reveal a circular bed on which a scantily clad Colonel Anastasia Komananov (read that: Kira) has draped herself. (Yessirree bob, the boys did have fun on this episode.) Komananov rouses and says she must have fallen asleep. Who's she trying to kid? It's obvious she got tired of waiting for Bashir to find her, so she kicked the wall and then faked her repose.

• Where are all those little Engineering guys we saw in "Starship Down"? Why aren't they helping Rom with this problem?

• Noah handcuffing Bashir and Garak to a laser drill in caves underneath his hideout raises an interesting question: Just how long is that elevator shaft? Noah's hideout is approximately five *miles* above sea level. Yet once the laser in the cave starts drilling it supposedly hits magma almost instantly. That means Noah and associates had escorted the captive Bashir and Garak at least five miles to the place of their incarceration and predicted demise! Hmmm.

• I suppose I could make some completely uncalled-for comments about the fact that Professor Honey Bare (Dax) carries a handcuff key around in the pocket of her lab coat, but I believe I shall postpone.

• Speaking of which..."Professor Honey Bare?" *"Honey...Bare?!"* (Snicker, snicker.)

• There's a dramatic moment at the end of the episode when Garak decides to call it quits and leave the holosuite. Bashir doesn't know if this will endanger the physical patterns of his friends and threatens to shoot the Cardassian tailor if he tries. At this, Garak turns and manages to say, "Computer, show me the mech—" before Bashir shoots him! Good thing Garak didn't just say, "Computer, exit!" (Is it possible that Garak *purposely* used the longer form of the request to give Bashir time to react?)

CHANGED PREMISES

• Well, well, well, well, well. Here's a hot news flash for you. Breaking into a holosuite during someone's program is not only rude, it's also illegal, according to our dear Julian Bashir in this episode. This makes perfect sense! These holosuites *are* used by individuals to act out their fantasies, right? Would you want someone strolling into your bedroom? The only problem here is that personnel on the *Enterprise*-D used to break into other people's holodeck experiences somewhat frequently. Is it illegal to violate someone's privacy in one of Quark's holosuites but *legal* to do so on a starship's holodeck? (For instance, in "Hollow Pursuits," La Forge just strolls in on Barclay's fantasy—an action that I found very odd in *The Nitpicker's Guide for Next Generation Trekkers*.)

EQUIPMENT ODDITIES

• Does anyone else find it amazing that a powerless shuttle glides to a stop while still in space without any visible firing of thrusters to reverse the forward momentum?

• O'Brien and his teams must have slacked off their routine maintenance programs. In this episode Eddington tries to beam Sisko and company from an exploding runabout. Some of the energy travels back along the transporter beam and blows up the primary energizing coils. Something is very, very wrong here. The crew of the *Enterprise*-D did this *all the time*. (See the *NextGen* episode "A Matter of Perspective" for an example.) In addition, the crew of DS9 have done it several times without adverse effect. (See "Past Prologue" for an example.) The transporter in Ops has even managed to successfully receive a transport from another transporter even though that transporter was based on a ship and the ship had exploded into teeny-tiny bits! (See "Dramatis Personae.")

• I'm sure there is some complicated technobabble reason but why didn't Eddington just transfer the pattern buffer to the *Defiant* right after the coils burned out.

• Cardassian pattern buffers seem to lose their cohesion very quickly. The *Tech Manual* says the pattern buffers on the *Enterprise* can cycle their contents for almost seven minutes without degradation. (Where is Scotty when you need him? See the *NextGen* episode "Relics.")

• At one point Quark makes the connection that the computer used all available energy to store the neural patterns of Sisko and company. So why did the *lights* go out? Do you really *need* a computer on board this station to run the lights? (Or does the computer just automatically turn off the lights whenever there's trouble so everyone understands how bad things really are?)

• Attempting to find a way to reintegrate Sisko and company's neural and physical patterns, Rom comments that his equipment isn't designed to interface with Starfleet equipment. Oddly enough, his holosuite computer contains a Starfleet module! (Watch for it when Eddington finds the physical patterns.)

• After starting the five-minute timer on the laser, Dr. Noah exits with Falcon (O'Brien). Just before they go, a close-up shows the timer ticking off the seconds between "0:04:59" and "0:04:57." Then the shot changes and you can see the timer in the corner. For some reason, it's running at twice the normal speed!

• So, um...Bashir shoots Garak with a holosuite-created gun, right? A gun that shoots bullets and is normally lethal, but the holosuite somehow overrides this lethal component with its mortality fail-safes. Wouldn't it be simpler to make the gun nonlethal in the first place and just simulate the firing of the weapon? (The *NextGen* episode "The Big Good-bye" contains another example of this. On the other hand, I suppose we could say that Bashir made the weapon and bullets with a replicator and brought them inside, but this seems needlessly dangerous.)

• After Eddington and crew transfer the neural and physical patterns of Sisko and company to the *Defiant,* the ship's transporter puts the senior officers back together. Interestingly enough, on the holodeck we see the characters *transporting* out instead of just fading from view. Are the creators trying to tell us that Rom somehow figured out a way to beam physical patterns off a hologrid? Somebody should tell Moriarty about this! (In the *NextGen* episode "Ship in a Bottle" the fearless, "best o'their fields" crew of the *Enterprise* attempted this and failed.)

• Several nitpickers wondered why Sisko and company didn't materialize on the transporter pads wearing the clothes they wore on the holodeck. Or, if their stored physical pattern included their uniforms, why they didn't look like they had holodeck clothes on *over* their Starfleet uniforms!

• Of course, if you can actually *do* this—if you can actually store some-

one in memory and reanimate that person later—the crew of DS9 have discovered eternal life! (Just keep several copies of yourself around in case you ever get killed.)

CONTINUITY AND PRODUCTION PROBLEMS

• Two points of interest about the preview for this episode. The explosion of the runabout actually comes from "Armageddon Game." Also, one of the clips shows Bashir shoving a clip into a pistol. In the actual episode, he is *removing* the clip from the pistol!

• When the creators offer us the close-up of the tassel-covered, bikini-clad go-go dancer in Club Ingenue, the music in the background actually has words. The closed caption reads, "Girl, you really got me now. You got me so I can't sleep at night. Girl, you really got me now. You got me so I can't sleep at night." (There was no question in my mind that your life would be substantially richer for having learned this.)

TRIVIA ANSWERS
1. In A.D. 1964
2. The hydrothermal deposits on the Tibetan Plateau.

HOMEFRONT

Star Date: 49170.65 plus two days (see below)

With the wormhole exhibiting strange activity—opening and closing for no apparent reason—a priority 1 message arrives from Starfleet Security on Earth. It contains a two-day-old Security log of a meeting between the Federation and the Romulans. Someone planted a bomb that went off during the conference, killing twenty-seven people. Further analysis of the tape shows a vase beginning to shape-shift just before the explosion. The evidence is clear: The Changelings have infiltrated Earth. As per Starfleet Security's instructions, Sisko and Odo board the *Lakota* for passage to Earth. Once there, Admiral Leyton puts Sisko in charge of Earth's security.

Sisko soon convinces Federation president Jaresh-Inyo to increase security at Federation and Starfleet offices. As a result, Starfleet institutes a series of blood screenings, and all Federation and Starfleet facilities are fitted with wide-beam phaser pods that can sweep an entire room. Even so, a Changeling somehow manages to temporarily assume Leyton's identity and clear all the checkpoints.

Only Odo's sense of the Changeling's animosity uncovers the ruse. Then, without warning, every power relay on Earth stops working, leaving Earth defenseless. Expecting a Jem'Haddar attack, Leyton, Sisko, and Odo convince Jaresh-Inyo to declare a state of emergency. As the episode ends, the transporters on the *Lakota* begin filling the streets of every city on Earth with phaser-equipped Starfleet officers.

PLOT OVERSIGHTS

• In the first part of the episode, we learn that Dax periodically moves the furnishings in Odo's apartment a few centimeters just to bug him. Near the beginning of the episode, Odo storms into Quark's looking for her. I guess he forgot he could ask the computer to give him Dax's location.

• I could comment again about the conservation of matter and the fact that Sisko carries Odo with one hand in this episode, but I'll simply point you to my discussions in other episodes. (See "Emissary" and "Vortex.")

• Every time Nog is around Sisko in this episode, our good captain seems much too uncomfortable. It's like he

Trivia Questions

1. Sisko served as Leyton's executive officer aboard what ship?

2. Where do Sisko and his father, Grandpa Joe, go for a walk?

actually fears a confrontation with Nog when the half-pint Ferengi asks Sisko for a recommendation to the Starfleet Academy's "Red Squad"—an elite group of cadets that receive special training and missions.

• Despite all the security precautions, a Changeling still manages to temporarily assume Admiral Leyton's identity. How? Shouldn't every person be blood-tested again once they leave the company of their fellow Starfleet officers and then return? They really aren't doing something silly, like just testing everyone once a week, are they? (Or is Grandpa Joe Sisko right?! You may recall that when Sisko was trying to make him take a blood test, he suggested a Changeling could steal a human's blood and then produce it at will anytime someone came along with a hypo. Of course, if that's what happened, *if* the Changeling who posed as Leyton actually *passed* a blood test, why is Sisko so insistent that his father take one?)

• After being exposed by Odo, the Changeling who poses as Leyton shoves Odo to the ground and runs away—turning into a bird in midflight. I doubt I am alone in wondering why Odo didn't leap to his feet and chase after him.

• Near the end of this episode, Sisko and Odo offer that the Dominion may have cloaking technology. They recount the events in "The Die Is Cast" and speculate that the Dominion may have salvaged it from the destroyed Romulan and Cardassian fleet. In my humble opinion, the Dominion doesn't need Romulan cloaking technology because they had cloaking technolo-gy long before the Tal Shiar and the Obsidian Order decided to attempt to obliterate the Founders. Remember the end of "The Jem'Haddar"? Sisko deduces that Eris is a member of the Dominion and tries to take her captive in Ops. Eris simply taps her forearm and transports away. O'Brien can neither trace the transporter signal nor find any nearby ships. So where did she go? Possibly she had a personal transporter and beamed herself someplace else on the station to await extraction. Possibly she had a personal transporter that transported her all the way back to the Gamma Quadrant. More likely, though, she was beamed off the station by a ship that belonged to the Dominion. And since O'Brien couldn't find the ship, it seems reasonable to conclude that the Dominion has cloaking technology.

• Attempting to convince Federation president Jaresh-Inyo to declare a state of emergency, Odo contends that destructive fear will grow in the "...people all over this planet, huddled in the dark..." if the president doesn't give them a sign of hope. Excuse me. I have no desire to defuse such an emotional moment, but ...I believe that only *half* the people on the planet are huddled in the dark. The others have daylight!

• Despite Odo's exaggerated claims concerning the dark, huddled masses of Earth, Jaresh-Inyo declares a state of emergency on Earth. From a jurisdictional viewpoint, does this seem right? Doesn't Earth have a government of its own? Is it completely ruled by the governing body of the Federation? (Look at it this way: Suppose the United Nations was really in charge of Earth: Would it be right for them to place New York State under martial law? Wouldn't that be the jurisdiction of the governor?)

CHANGED PREMISES

• In this episode Bashir and O'Brien, dressed as Spitfire pilots, approach the bar in Quark's. They've just come from a holosuite simulation of the Battle of Britain. O'Brien yells for Quark as they draw near, using the term of affection "barkeep." Evidently this doesn't bother Quark any longer. In "Captive Pursuit" O'Brien calls Quark "barkeep" and Quark reacts quite vehemently to the term.

• Shortly after greeting Sisko's arrival on Earth, Leyton says that Earth is in danger—maybe the greatest danger since the last world war. Obviously Leyton isn't too well versed in recent history. V'ger almost wiped out all life on Earth in *Star Trek: The Motion Picture*. The whaleship almost did it again in *Star Trek IV: The Voyage Home*. Alien parasites almost took over Starfleet in "Contagion" *(TNG)*. And the Borg almost assimilated humanity in "The Best of Both Worlds, Part 2" *(TNG)*. (Of course, the same type of objection could be raised to Jaresh-Inyo's statements at the end of the episode when he says that—with the exception of the Borg incidence—there hasn't been a state of emergency declared on Earth in a century.)

• The Federation must be downsizing. In this episode the president's office is much smaller than the one shown in *Star Trek VI: The Undis-*

covered Country. In that episode the president's office was as big as Ten-Forward on the *Enterprise*-D! (And looked just like it! Wink, wink.)

EQUIPMENT ODDITIES

• Attempting to protect Starfleet headquarters from Changeling infiltration, Sisko oversees the installation of phaser pods in all the offices. We join the action as Sisko and Commander Benteen finalize the firing setting for the phaser. This raises some questions: Hasn't Sisko and his crew already done this work on DS9? Don't they already know that the phasers should be set to level 3.5? During this episode Sisko states that phaser sweeps have been effective on the station. If Sisko doesn't know the right setting to use on the phasers, how does he know that the sweeps were effective? After all, if you don't have the phaser set high enough, the Changeling can simply remain whatever it has changed into.

• At the end of this episode Leyton and Sisko speak of using the communication and transporter systems of the *Lakota* exclusively to implement their plan to protect Earth. I hate to ask this, but is this the *only* ship that's currently in orbit? (It's the *Star Trek* movies all over again! In several of these, the *Enterprise* was always the only ship in range to help with a problem.)

CONTINUITY AND PRODUCTION PROBLEMS

• The star date on the security log is 49170.65. Worf says the conference occurred two days ago, so that would put this episode's star date just a bit after 49170.65. Either this date is wrong, or this episode is out of sequence. "Rejoined" carries a star date of 49195.5.

• Speaking of the Security log, if you do a frame-by-frame advance as Worf replays the close-up of the pottery, you will notice that the clock jumps from time index 5917.99 to 5918.12. (The counter skips in other spots as well, but only one or two digits at a time. This would be expected when you are measuring one one-hundredth of a second on a readout but only recording the image at twenty-four or thirty frames a second.)

• Is it just me, or does Grandpa Joe look an awful lot like Admiral Cartwright from *Star Trek VI: The Undiscovered Country*?

• For some reason, the creators have Sisko wear a *NextGen*-style uniform as soon as he arrives on Earth.

• Is it just me, or does Admiral Leyton's executive officer, Commander Benteen, look an awful lot like Dr. Leah Brahms? (See the *NextGen* episodes "Booby Trap" and "Galaxy's Child.")

• At one point Nog visits Sisko in his office. (If security is supposed to be so tight, one could ask how a *cadet* manages make it all the way to the office of the head of Starfleet Security on Earth without being announced or escorted, but that's another issue.) Sisko and Nog speak for a moment near the doorway of Sisko's office. The doors are open. Sisko walks back to his desk and sits. Nog follows. Subsequent shots show that the doors

have closed. However, if the doors made any sound at all when they closed, it was very-berry soft.

• When Grandpa Joe refuses to take a blood test, Sisko tries to convince him otherwise. The discussion soon becomes heated, and Grandpa Joe accidently cuts himself while preparing food for his restaurant. He walks over to a sink to wash his finger and then asks Jake to bring the dermal regenerator. However, when he sees Sisko inspecting the knife to see if his blood is real, Grandpa Joe becomes irate. He accuses Sisko of seeing shape shifters everywhere and suggests that a clever shape shifter might just steal a human's blood and keep it on hand to release in case someone ordered a blood test. The scene stays tight on Grandpa Joe's face during this speech, and either Grandpa Joe's got an eye twitch or he's reading from a set of cue cards.

• And speaking of this scene, Grandpa Joe starts out with a cloth napkin wrapped around his injured finger. He appears to drop the napkin when he grows angry. All through the speech, his left hand—clearly empty—grasps an upright bar. Then Grandpa Joe has a mild stroke. As he heads for the floor, the shot changes, and suddenly the napkin has again wrapped itself around his finger.

TRIVIA ANSWERS
1. The *Okinawa*.
2. Audubon Park.

PARADISE LOST

Star Date: unknown

As the days pass, Sisko becomes more and more puzzled by the events that led to martial law on Earth. He wonders how Changelings could have accomplished the power outage in the first place. And his suspicions heighten when Odo uncovers a transporter log showing the elite Red Squad returning to Starfleet Academy only twenty-six minutes after the state of emergency was declared. Under the ploy of dissatisfaction with Red Squad's performance, Sisko manages to trick one of its members, Cadet Riley Shepard, into disclosing the truth. In fact, Red Squad caused the outage—acting on orders from Starfleet Command. All indications point to Admiral Leyton. Evidently Leyton and others staged the incident to convince Federation president Jaresh-Inyo to declare the state of emergency.

Unfortunately, Shepard and the rest of Red Squad disappear before Sisko can force them to appear before Jaresh-Inyo. Sisko then calls Kira to say he suspects someone faked the wormhole openings to raise suspicions about a cloaked fleet of Jem'Haddar warships. Quickly locating the conspirator, the senior staff board the *Defiant* to bring him to Earth. At this Leyton sends the *Lakota* to blockade the *Defiant*. But when he subsequently orders Commander Benteen to destroy and not just disable the vessel, Benteen balks—allowing the *Defiant* to reach Earth with the evidence needed to expose the conspiracy.

Trivia Questions

1. Besides Sisko, who are five other officers who served under Leyton on the *Okinawa*?

2. What drink does Leyton offer Sisko to calm his nerves?

PLOT OVERSIGHTS

• I'm thinking about applying to Starfleet Academy. I think I can pass the intelligence requirements. Sisko debriefs Red Squad member Cadet Riley Shepard concerning the power outages. The young man rehearses the operation in detail. Then Sisko goes to Jaresh-Inyo with his suspicions that Starfleet sabotaged the power grid. Jaresh-Inyo can't believe it and asks for proof. Sisko says he will get some. In other words, Sisko didn't record the conversation he had with Shepard?! (Okay, okay. It may not have been admissible in court, but it would have been enough for Jaresh-Inyo to test the waters by asking Leyton to withdraw the troops.)

• Trying to stop Sisko from thwarting his plans, Leyton frames our good captain as a Changeling and throws him in a holding cell. Odo soon comes to break Sisko out and in the process demonstrates that he knows the Vulcan neck pinch. (Must have ordered the correspondence course from Spock.)

• Gotta hand it to Sisko on this one. He can be a "sneaky" guy when he wants to. After Odo busts him out of the joint, Sisko grabs a phaser and manages to make it all the way to Admiral Leyton's office without being stopped!

• Okay, so let's talk about the battle between the *Defiant* and the *Lakota*. First and foremost, *it was gorgeous!* Beautiful graphics. Kudos to the creators. Unfortunately, I do have a few nits to report. (I'm sure you guessed there would be.) First, the battle never had to happen! Worf commands the ship. He has a mission. His mission is to make it to Earth with and deliver the conspirator, Lieutenant Arriaga. As the *Defiant* tools along, Dax reports that the *Lakota* has hailed them, ordering them to drop out of warp and prepare to be boarded. Kira then chimes in that the *Lakota* has raised its shields and powered up its phasers. In other words, it means business. What is Worf's response? He keeps flying straight into the *Lakota*'s weapons range. Why not just flip on the cloak, execute a few turns, and ditch the *Lakota*? (I know it's illegal, but that's never stopped this crew before.) Of course, once the *Defiant* wanders into the *Lakota*'s weapons range and takes a few hits, Kira finally suggests the cloak. To this, Worf responds that

they would have to drop their shields. So why not jump to warp, get out of weapons range momentarily, drop your shields, cloak, do a few fancy turns, and...*ditch the* Lakota?! (I think Worf just really wants to fight.)

• And while we're on the subject of the fight, the *Defiant* executes a beautiful barrel roll over the top of the *Lakota* with guns blazing. It is a lovely sight to behold. It is also a very poor tactic strategically. The roll places the *Defiant* upside down, parallel to the flight plane of the *Lakota* directly above the *Lakota*'s phasers, as the *Defiant* displays the largest possible target profile! Guess what happens next? The *Lakota* opens fire. (I am told that in three-dimensional warfare the smartest tactic is keep your ship profile to a minimum, making yourself a more difficult target to hit. In the case of the *Defiant* you would always want one on the ship's *edges* to face the opponent. In fact, one could speculate that this is *precisely* why the ship is so flat in the first place! You could still do all the fancy flying. You would just be slipping and slicing as opposed to barrel-rolling over the top of your enemy's vessel.)

CHANGED PREMISES

• In "The First Duty" *(TNG)*, as Wesley Crusher testifies about the activities of Nova Squadron, the wall display behind him shows the Starfleet Academy logo at one point. On it we see the motto *Ex astra, scientia.* Presumably the creators intended this to mean "From the stars, knowledge." However, in this episode—as Sisko discusses Red Squad with the admiral in charge of the academy—the same logo now reads *Ex astris, scientia*. Why the change? Well, I'm no Latin scholar, but those who are tell me that the second version is correct! (One wonders how many decades Starfleet Academy was in business before the Latin professors noticed the mistake. By the way, after Alexander Foertch of Nuremberg, Germany, wrote me concerning the mistake in "The First Duty," I decided the Nitpicker's Guild needed a Latin slogan as well. I settled on *Ex Astro Trekkio, nitpickius*.)

• As Sisko initially searches for the name of a person in Red Squad, Nog tells the captain that the names of Red Squad members are secret. That's when I frowned. Last episode, Nog said that Red Squad was a way of rewarding excellence. But not only did he need good grades, he also had to be recommended by a high-ranking officer. He claimed the cadets in Red Squad got special classes, simulated missions, off-campus training sessions, "all kind of things." Wait a minute: Red Squad gets "all kinds of things" and their membership is secret? Red Squad's membership is secret but you need a recommendation from an officer who isn't in Red Squad to get in? And besides, what's the point of "rewarding excellence" if nobody knows who's being rewarded? And another thing: How do you keep a group's membership secret if they keep disappearing at the same time? ("Hey, where's Bob, Nick, and Smulrk?" "I don't know. They didn't come to class today. I heard Red Squad is doing a special training session in Tibet, but that can't be it.")

EQUIPMENT ODDITIES

• At the beginning of the Changeling chat above, Sisko doesn't believe that O'Brien could be on Earth. Sisko says there's no way the *Defiant* could get from the station to Earth that fast. Later we see Sisko talking with Kira on DS9. The conversation seems instantaneous in its interaction. In addition, it's pretty obvious that Sisko hasn't asked his senior staff to join him on Earth yet. (If he had, they wouldn't be on the station, they would be in transit.) Most likely, then, when telling the Changeling that the *Defiant* couldn't get to Earth *that* fast, Sisko is imagining the senior staff disembarking on their own for Earth because of some emergency. It makes sense that if the senior staff heard that Earth was defenseless, they would hop in the *Defiant* and come to protect it. (After all—as we have seen over and over—they really don't have *jobs* on the station, and they can leave whenever they feel like it!) The power outage occurred at least four days prior to the Changeling chat, according to dialogue. Sisko then would be incredulous that the *Defiant* could make it to Earth in only four days. This actually jibes with dialogue in other episodes. "The Search, Part I" seems to indicate that the trip from Earth to the station takes about a week. (Yes, the dialogue in "The Search, Part I" could mean that the trip takes less than four days but then Deep Space 9 wouldn't be very deep in space, now, would it?)

So...just for the sake of argument, let's say it takes only four days to fly from DS9 to Earth. I realize you've probably been wondering if there's a point to this discussion. There is. Remember the instantaneous conversation with Kira? If the *Defiant* takes four days to make the trip from Earth to the station and subspace communications make the trip with a one-second or less delay, just how fast do subspace communications travel? Answer: Subspace communications must be 345,600 times faster than the *Defiant*! (That's 4 multiplied by 24 multiplied by 60 multiplied by 60.) *And,* if the trip to Earth takes longer than four days, the problem just gets worse. Now, the *Tech Manual* says that subspace communications travel approximately *sixty* times faster than the fastest Starfleet starship either existing or predicted. Either the *Defiant* is a lot slower than the fastest starship predicted, or subspace communications have received an amazing performance upgrade.

• The *Lakota* appears to be an Excelsior-class vessel, just like the *Enterprise*-B in *Star Trek Generations*. But the *Lakota* differs from the normal Excelsior-class vessel in that it features a ridge around the belly of the star-drive section. In my review of *Star Trek Generations* for the *NextGen II Guide,* I found it odd that we never saw this particular Excelsior-class configuration in the entire run of the *NextGen* television series. Since the *Enterprise*-B supposedly existed more than seventy years prior to *NextGen,* I couldn't figure out why we hadn't seen the design before. I even spec-

ulated that Starfleet had abandoned it for some reason. I guess they hadn't. It just *happened* that we never saw it. (Wink, wink.)

• You may have noticed that I rarely talk about the user interfaces of Starfleet combadges any longer. I hit the topic pretty hard in the *NextGen Guide,* and even I have a limit on how long I'll flail a dead horse. The end of this episode *did* catch my eye, however. In the very last scene, Sisko, Odo, Jake, and Grandpa Joe chat in Grandpa Joe's restaurant. Then everyone gets into transport position and Sisko says, "Three to beam up." He doesn't page the ship. He doesn't tap his combadge. He just says, "Three to beam up." (I guess Kira was eavesdropping on the entire conversation.)

CONTINUITY AND PRODUCTION PROBLEMS

• For some reason, neither Nog nor Shepard has those bars on the collar that we saw on the cadet uniforms in "The First Duty" *(TNG)*.

• The first two times the creators use the establishing shot of Starfleet Headquarters, the same two pairs of individuals walk toward each other. Quite a coincidence, eh?

TRIVIA ANSWERS

1. Daneeka, McWatt, Swonden, Orr, and Moodus. (Arija Weddle tells me that at least some of these names come from Joseph Heller's *Catch-22*.)
2. Bolian tonic water.

CROSSFIRE

Star Date: unknown

Shakaar's arrival on the station complicates matters for Odo—in more ways than one. Once the leader of Kira's resistance cell, now the first minister of Bajor (see "Shakaar"), he has come to DS9 to negotiate with the Federation, hoping to accelerate the process of his planet's admission. Unfortunately, Odo has received word from his contacts inside the civilian government on Cardassia that a terrorist group called "The True Way" has placed an operative on the station to kill Shakaar. In addition, Shakaar and Kira suddenly find that they are falling in love.

Distracted by his own unrequited feelings for Kira, Odo makes a simple mistake that allows the assassin to make an attempt on Shakaar's life. When Odo goes to discuss the matter with Kira he finds that she has spent the night with Shakaar. Worse yet, upon returning to his office, he learns that Worf has apprehended the operative and obtained a confession. Incensed by his own foolishness, Odo rampages through his quarters before collapsing to sulk. Quark soon arrives,

Trivia Questions

1. Who was caught scrawling graffiti on a wall in Section 4?

2. Who does Odo relieve outside of Kira's quarters?

summoned from his quarters below by the noise. With a bit of carefully worded help from Quark, Odo realizes he must either tell Kira how he feels or walk away. He opts for the latter, ordering soundproofing for his floor as his way of thanking Quark.

PLOT OVERSIGHTS

• This problem shows up in other episodes, but I'll mention it here. Shakaar's ship docks at the outer ring in the middle of one of the pylon supports. Shakaar disembarks through an airlock. Then Sisko escorts him down a short hall, and the entire entourage turns to the left. Moments later we see everyone walking onto the promenade through one of its large airlock doors. Did Sisko, Shakaar, and the others *walk* all the way from the docking ring to the promenade? Just how far is this, you ask? Well, in "Emissary" we saw that the saucer section of the *Enterprise* was approximately the same size as the habitat ring on the station. The habitat ring is the inner ring. From the *Tech Manual* we know that the *Enterprise*'s saucer section is about 560 meters in diameter. That means it's probably more than 800 meters from the docking ring to the promenade. (That's about half a mile!) Maybe they needed the exercise. Or maybe the crossover bridges have those people mover things like we have in our airports. Or maybe Sisko and the others suffered another techno-amnesia attack and forgot they have turbolifts.

• With Lieutenant Commander Eddington away from the station, Sisko asks Worf to assist Odo in protecting Shakaar. I guess performing the duties of the "Strategic Operations officer" doesn't really take that much time!

• During a discussion with Worf, Odo states that he has a daily routine he follows unwaveringly. He says the shopkeepers on the promenade joke that they can set their clocks by him. Um...is this supposed to be a good thing? Do you really want a Security officer who is predictable? Also, during "Fascination," Odo told the officer who would fill in for him during the Bajoran Gratitude Festival that he made it a policy to drop by Quark's three or four times a day at *random* intervals. How do you set your clocks by someone who strolls by at random intervals?

EQUIPMENT ODDITIES

• The assassination attempt on Shakaar deserves some scrutiny. To review, Shakaar and Kira watch the wormhole open at the tip of one of the upper pylons. Odo accompanies them. Afterward, the trio board a turbolift. Odo communicates to Worf that they are heading to the docking ring. He tells the turbolift to take them to Level 2-D. It begins moving. Using Worf's voice, the assassin then calls

Odo and says that there is another turbolift stuck on Level 41. Supposedly the turbolift carrying Shakaar must be rerouted. Distracted by the burgeoning relationship between Kira and Shakaar, Odo releases the controls without waiting for Worf to verify his Security code. The assassin immediately sends the turbolift plummeting down the tube. Thankfully, Odo morphs into a type of jack that spreads on the sides of the turbolift, binding it in its shaft.

First, Odo identifies their destination as both the docking ring and Level 2-D. Yet in "Playing God," an area near the center of the docking ring was identified as Level 22, Section 14. If the docking ring really has a Level 2, and if Level 22 is near the center of the ring, then the docking ring is probably more than forty levels tall! As tall as the *Enterprise!* This does not seem right!

Second, I praised the creators in "The Forsaken" for showing that there is only one set of doors on the turbolifts. In that episode Odo and Lwaxana ride on a turbolift, and you can see the decks flying by. Unfortunately, the creators do not show the same thing in this episode. Suddenly the turbolift featured here has an interior set of doors. Of course, these doors are not visible when the exterior doors shut moments earlier in the scene.

Third, I am very surprised that Cardassian turbolifts don't have an emergency stop mechanism like the plain old unsophisticated elevators we use today.

Fourth, Sisko explicitly refers to this incident as a "free fall." This raises a question. Why is there artificial gravity in the turbolift shafts? If Cardassian technology is anything like Federation technology, artificial gravity nets would be installed in the flooring on each level. For a turbolift to "fall" down a shaft, a heavy-duty artificial-gravity generator would have to be placed at the bottom of the turbolift shaft. This seems counterproductive, since every time the turbolift goes up, the machinery would have to expend energy to fight *against* the gravity. Why not just let it float free? (Because then we could not have these tense "elevator plummeting like a rock" scenes!)

CONTINUITY AND PRODUCTION PROBLEMS

• Does Shakaar's ship look strangely familiar? Sort of like the Wadi ship from "Move Along Home"?

• At one point Kira takes Shakaar on a tour of the station. Eventually they arrive at an upper pylon, where they gaze out the airlock and watch the wormhole open. The opening of the wormhole points up and to the left. Yet, in the opening sequence, the wormhole opens pointing up and to the *right* from the perspective of the

station. Seems to me that if the wormhole and the station stay somewhat stationary in their respective positions, *every* viewing cubby on DS9 should show the wormhole opening up and to the right. The only possibility would be if the station orbited the wormhole. Somehow I don't think it does that. (And, if you think about it, it doesn't even matter if the station is rotating. Think of it this way. Turning from side to side at night won't make the craters on the moon reorient themselves.)

• Shakaar seems to be missing his earring at the very end of the episode.

• And speaking of Shakaar and Kira having a conversation in Quark's at the end of the episode, where are all the Bajorans? Throughout this episode we saw Bajorans swarming Shakaar wherever he appeared. At the end of the episode, however, he sits with Kira in a crowded bar and no one approaches.

TRIVIA ANSWERS

1. Oguy Jel. (This is item seven on Odo's criminal activity reports, by the way. Hmmm. See the sidebar "47.")
2. Ensign Jimenez.

Star Date: unknown

As a favor to Shakaar, Kira agrees to go to a conference on the remote Cardassian outpost of Korma. Surprisingly enough, Dukat arrives in a freighter to ferry her there, having recently been demoted for bringing his half-Bajoran daughter, Tora Ziyal, back to Cardassia. (See "Indiscretion.") At Korma, Dukat and crew find the outpost destroyed, the work of a Klingon Bird-of-Prey that warps off to its next target. Seeking justice for the fifteen Bajoran diplomats who died in the attack, Kira helps Dukat install one of the outpost's System 5 disrupters in a cargo bay. Then they head for Loval, suspected as the locale for the next attack.

Soon the Klingons do appear. Kira scores a direct hit, but the Bird-of-Prey quickly swings around to make the kill. Desperate, Kira uses the transporters to swap the crews of the two ships. To her surprise, Dukat immediately destroys the freighter, killing all the Klingons on board. He then contacts the Detapa Council, expecting congratulations and a promotion. The council does offer Dukat his old job but forbids him from launching any

further attacks. They seek a diplomatic solution instead. Incensed, Dukat decides to fight the Klingons himself and asks Kira to join him. She refuses but offers to care for Ziyal on DS9 as he wages his campaign.

PLOT OVERSIGHTS

• The Federation seems a bit naive about what the Cardassians do and do not know of both Federation and Klingon technology. As the episode begins, Worf comes to the infirmary with a list of technological advancements that the Federation has shared with both the Klingons and the Bajorans. He gives them to Kira, stating that the Federation does not want the Cardassians to learn of them. Yet, in "The Maquis, Part I," we saw that Gul Dukat already knew how to operate a runabout—from all appearances, a relatively new class of vessel. And in this episode Cardassians seize a Klingon Bird-of-Prey (with Kira's help, no less) and quickly repair it to full operating status. Doesn't this give the impression that the Cardassians are already very familiar with Klingon and Federation technology? (Also—at the time of this writing—the *Voyager* episode "Dread-

Trivia Questions

1. What is the name of Dukat's freighter?

2. What is the power capacity of a standard-issue Cardassian phase disrupter rifle?

nought" has just aired, and in it we see very sophisticated Cardassian technology supposedly developed several years ago.)

• One wonders why Kira didn't just borrow a runabout to go to the conference. Isn't that standard operating procedure for the senior staff of DS9? (Yes, but then Kira wouldn't go to the conference with Dukat!)

• The Klingons in this episode seem downright Starfleet in some of their actions. When Dukat's freighter arrives at Korma, a Bird-of-Prey looks them over and then wanders off. Dukat *fires* on them with the freighter's wimpy phasers; the Bird-of-Prey turns, flies over them, and goes to warp without firing a single shot! This is *amazing* restraint for the Klingons! (I realize the creators try to cover this by having Dukat mumble that destroying a helpless freighter wouldn't be very honorable, but I'm not buying it. Usually Klingons don't hesitate to attack.)

• Kira's actions in this episode seem suspect. She tells Dukat that she's assisting him only because the Klingons killed fifteen Bajorans on Korma. At the same time, she seems very aware that the success of the mission will restore Dukat's prestige. Later she admits to Ziyal that she can only see a murderer when she looks at Dukat. So...is Kira really so single-focused that she must have vengeance for the lives of the Bajorans at *any* cost? Even the *exaltation* of Dukat? This is the Cardassian who headed the occupation on Bajor and directly contributed to the deaths of *millions* of Bajorans—Hitler, if you will. Even odder, at the end of the episode, Kira seems to be on Dukat's side—encouraging him to fight the Klingons and, by default, encouraging him to reinvigorate the Cardassian Empire. If Kira lived on "hate and adrenaline" all those years as a resistance fighter, if she spent decades despising the Cardassians, wouldn't she be a bit more smug about this? (More like: "Serves you right, Dukat. How does it feel to be on the other side of the oppression?")

CHANGED PREMISES

• At some point in the past seventy years the crew complement on a Klingon Bird-of-Prey tripled! In *Star Trek III: The Search for Spock* we learn that the crew complement of a Bird-of-Prey is about a dozen Klingons. In this episode Kira says that all thirty-six of the Klingons were transported over to the freighter. (A bigger version of a Bird-of-Prey, maybe?)

EQUIPMENT ODDITIES

• Dukat first attempts to engage the Klingons with the phasers he carries on his freighter. On the viewscreen we see the phasers firing, after which the Bird-of-Prey turns slowly, makes a pass directly over the freighter, and warps away. A few items about this scene: First, the phasers hit the Bird-of-Prey at a very odd angle. It looks like the beam comes from almost directly underneath the Klingon ship! Yet, from the perspective of Dukat's viewscreen, it looks like the Bird-of-Prey sits quite a distance from the freighter. For the picture on the viewscreen to be correct the freighter would have to be directly under the Bird-of-Prey. (Perhaps the viewscreen has Cardassian script that reads, "Objects in viewscreen are closer than they appear"?) Second, when the Bird-of-Prey makes its overpass there's not even a scorch mark where the phasers hit, and from the dialogue we know that the Bird-of-Prey had dropped its shields! That freighter must have really, *really* pitiful phasers.

• At one point Kira gives Ziyal a comparison between a Cardassian and a Federation phaser rifle. Where did Kira get a Federation-issue Type III phaser rifle? Did Dukat just happen to have one on board? It seems unlikely Sisko would give one to Kira. She's not Starfleet! And besides, she was supposed to be going to a conference, not into battle. (At the very most I would have expected her to be

carrying a Bajoran phaser rifle. After all, she carries a Bajoran phaser.)

• The sensors on the Bird-of-Prey that Dukat and Kira meet at Loval must not be working. The Bird-of-Prey locks a tractor beam on the freighter, and as it approaches, Dukat tells Kira to open the cargo bay doors. Shouldn't the sensors on the Bird-of-Prey pick this up? And what about the disrupter in the cargo bay? With the bay doors open, wouldn't the Bird-of-Prey see the weapon and register its power buildup? Evidently not, because the Klingon vessel just keeps coming!

TRIVIA ANSWERS
1. The *Groumall*.
2. 4.7 megajoules. (See the sidebar "47.")

THE SONS OF MOGH

Star Date: 49556.2

Excommunicated from the Klingon Empire by Worf's actions in "The Way of the Warrior," Kurn comes to the station to ask his brother Worf for *Mauk-To'Vor*. According to Klingon beliefs, Worf must ceremonially slay his brother so that Kurn can regain his honor and enter *Sto'Vo'Kor*. Worf agrees, but just after he delivers the death blow, Dax and Odo barge into his quarters. An emergency transport saves Kurn's life.

Meanwhile, Kira and O'Brien witness an unexplained explosion while coming home from an inspection tour of the Bajoran colonies closest to the Cardassian border. When they return to investigate further in the *Defiant,* another explosion nearly destroys a cloaked *Vor'Cha*-class cruiser. After Kira tows it back to DS9 so Bashir can tend to the wounded, Worf and Kurn sneak on board the cruiser and learn that the Klingons have mined the area just outside Bajoran space. Though Kurn now considers his dishonor complete, Kira uses the information to detonate the cloaked mines and avert the threat of Klingon-enforced isolation. Worf

then acts on Dax's suggestion to end Kurn's life without killing him—allowing Bashir to erase Kurn's memory, reconfigure his DNA, and surgically alter his appearance. In short order, an old family friend named Noggra arrives on the station to provide a new identity for Kurn as his son Rodek.

Trivia Questions

1. What is the name of the *Vor'Cha*-class cruiser?

2. Whom does Worf claim to be while on the cruiser?

RUMINATIONS

My, oh, my, oh, my, oh, my! Dax certainly is purring over Worf at the beginning of this episode! (Again . . . must be the new and improved Dax.) In nitpicking lingo, this is called a KMYF moment. (KMYF is an acronym for "Kiss Me, You Fool," a term first identified by Darrin Hull of Willard, Missouri, in response to the mannerism of Captain Kathryn Janeway of Star Trek: Voyager. There is an ongoing effort within the Nitpicker's Guild to identify a KMYF moment for Janeway in every episode of that series. However, none of the KMYF moments is as blatant as the one here!)

By the way, the replacement for the Orinoco—lost at the beginning of "Our Man Bashir"—makes its first appearance in this episode. Kira and O'Brien return to DS9 in the Yukon.

346

Two other items before the nitpick-ing begins: It was good to hear Sisko yell again. For the past several episodes, whenever Sisko got mad he would go into this impassioned speech mode with a quivering voice. In this episode he just yells! Also, it was good to finally see a bunch of ships around the station during the external shots littered throughout the episode! (See Continuity and Pro-duction Problems for "Fascinations.")

PLOT OVERSIGHTS

• Directly after Worf stabs Kurn, Dax and Odo rush into Worf's quarters. Af-ter Dax and Kurn beam to the infirmary, Odo tells Worf that he'd better hope Kurn doesn't die or the Klingon will be charged with murder. Odo then stalks out. So...in the twenty-fourth century there's no charge for *attempted* mur-der?! Worf did stab his brother with a knife, after all—in the *heart*!

• After returning to DS9, Kira and O'Brien give Sisko a report on the unidentified explosion they encoun-tered. Oddly enough, they give him the report in the replimat. It's a nice change of pace for the episode, but is this really the best place to be talking about this type of information?

• At the end of the aforementioned meeting in the replimat, Sisko tells Ki-ra to take the *Defiant* and check it out. I wonder how Starfleet feels about Sisko turning over its most heavily armed starship to a member of the Bajoran militia. (I realize that Sisko doesn't want Worf to go along, but shouldn't Dax command the ship, with Kira along as an adviser? See "Star-ship Down.")

• At one point Kurn complains to Worf that the Bajoran Security officer uniform he wears is "uncomfortable." I'm not quite sure what he means. You might recall that earlier in the episode Kurn berated Worf for living in soft ac-commodations—soft bed, soft blan-ket, soft couch. So, if Kurn is uncomfortable with the Bajoran uni-form, perhaps it's really too *soft* for him? (One wonders if Klingon uni-forms are lined with tacks on the in-side just to test the "warriorness" of the wearer!)

• Klingons are obviously "challenged" when it comes to thinking three-di-mensionally. When I first heard Sisko say that the cloaked Klingon mines could be used to cut off the entire Ba-joran System, including DS9, I thought, "Wow! That's a lot of mines!" To cut off the entire Bajoran System, I knew the Klingons would first have to map a sphere that enclosed the entire Bajo-ran System—including DS9. Then the Klingons would have to populate the surface of that sphere so that no point on the sphere was more than 5,000 kilometers from a mine. (Actually, every point on the sphere would have to be fewer than 5,000 kilometers from a mine, since one of the mines detonat-ed 5,000 kilometers from the *Yukon,* and it sustained no damage. But "no point farther than 5,000 kilometers" will do for our purposes.)

In addition, "Emissary" establishes that DS9 is 160 million kilometers from Bajor. (Unfortunately, we are not told where Bajor is in its orbit at the time this statistic is given. In other words, we don't know if this is Bajor's farthest or nearest or average distance to the station. However, "Past Prologue" mentions a Bajor VIII, so no matter where Bajor was in its orbit during "Emissary," 160 million kilometers probably is already much too small for the diameter of a sphere that will enclose the Bajoran System and DS9...but it will do for our purposes!)

Okay, so we have a sphere 160 million kilometers in diameter and we have to cover its surface so no point on the sphere is more than 5,000 kilometers from a mine. Wanna guess how many mines you would need?

I was a bit rusty with my high school math, so I posed this question to Dr. David Brown. He told me that the formula for the surface area of a sphere is $4\pi r^2$ (where r is the radius of the sphere). That means the surface area of this sphere would be roughly 80 quadrillion square kilometers! For our purposes here, we will consider this surface area flat, not curved. (Considering the area flat instead of curved does introduce a small margin of error, but as we will see, it won't make any difference!) So, if you've got an area of eighty *quadrillion* square kilometers and you want to cover it so no point on the surface is more than 5,000 kilometers from a mine, how many mines would you have to have?

David came up with a very simple way to get a rough estimate. Imagine a square 10,000 kilometers on a side. If we place one mine in the center of each square, then every point within the square will be approximately 5,000 kilometers from the mine! (Yes, the corners will be farther than 5,000 kilometers, and it would be better to use something like a hexagon, but let's keep this simple, okay?) Since the area of each of these squares is 100 million square kilometers, we can quickly determine the approximate number of mines needed. All we have to do is figure out how many squares will fit in the allotted area. (Drumroll, math maestro!) The number of mines needed would be eighty *quadrillion* divided by 100 million. Answer: about 800 *million* mines!

Now, let's say that Gowron has 100 ships deploying these mines. If they can drop a mine every 5 minutes (Earth standard), how long will it take to populate the entire sphere? Answer: 76 *years* (Earth standard)! (That's 800 million divided by 100 to split it up among the ships; divided by 12 to get the number of hours; divided by 24 to get the number of days; divided by 365 to get the number of years.) Somehow I don't think this plan is feasible.

As it turns out, the Klingons didn't have to work that hard because they didn't populate a sphere that enclosed the Bajoran System and DS9. In the ward room, when Worf displays a map of the location of the mines, we see that all the mines are laid out in the same plane as the planetary system! And when Kira detonates the mines we see the same thing. They are all laid out in a nice, flat plane. In other words, the Klingons *forgot* that space has three dimensions! They just circled around Bajor and DS9—never expecting anyone to fly over the top of their minefield. (Ding, ding, guys! Not gonna win any wars *that* way.)

• Once again O'Brien gives a heading that is technically correct but needlessly confusing. When the detonating mines flush out several cloaked Birds-of-Prey, O'Brien gives their heading as "327 mark 215." It would be a whole lot simpler and clearer to say, "147 mark 305." (See "Melora" for more information.)

• Finally, at the end of this program, Worf makes a unilateral decision to have Bashir erase Kurn's memory and give him a new identity. I realize that Kurn has bowed to Worf as the older brother and said that he will do whatever Worf commands. But does Federation law really allow a family member to make this kind of medical decision without verbal or written consent from the patient?

CHANGED PREMISES

• I could say something about the fact that Kurn's blood is red when Worf stabs him, but I decided not to talk about that issue any longer. (See Changed Premises for "The Way of the Warrior.")

• I'm a bit confused over the Odo/Worf relationship. They start out rocky in "The Way of the Warrior." Then Worf plays the intrusive busybody in "Hippocratic Oath," attempting to tell Odo how to do his job. The end of that episode has Odo vindicated and Worf apologizing. Then comes "Crossfire." At the beginning of that episode Odo and Worf appear friendly toward each other. In fact, when Odo falters on the job, Worf steps in and catches a criminal intent on assassinating Shakaar. In spite of Odo's sloppiness, Worf congratulates Odo for the training he has given the Bajoran Security officers. Now we come to this episode. Needing something for Kurn to do, Worf goes to Odo

and asks him to bring him on as part of the Bajoran Security team on the station. Odo eventually does, but in the process makes some odd statements. First he tells Worf that he knows how hard it was for Worf to come to him for a favor. That's odd because in "Crossfire" they seemed to be well on their way to understanding each other. Did something happen between then and now to sour their relationship again? Second, after Odo agrees to give Kurn a chance, Worf says he is indebted to the Changeling. "Yes, you are," Odo replies. "And Mr. Worf, you'll find I am a man who collects on his debts." Excuse me? Isn't this the same Klingon who pulled Odo's shape-shifting posterior out of the fire only two episodes ago? I'd say that Odo giving Kurn a job just evens the score!

• The male Boslic captain seen in this episode bears little resemblance to the female Boslic freighter captain seen in "The Homecoming" and "The Abandoned," but maybe this is a case where individuals of the same race actually have different facial features! (Or maybe the female Boslic freighter captain wasn't really Boslic. Sort of like the old problem in describing a "large animal hospital." Is it a hospital for large animals, or a large hospital for animals of all sizes?)

• As stated in the summary above, when Kira and O'Brien take the Defiant to investigate the strange explosions, they encounter a badly damaged Klingon Vor'Cha-class cruiser. At first the spokesperson for the cruiser orders them away. Then the spokesperson asks for access for the

Defiant's medical facilities. Kira replies that their facilities are limited but offers to tow them back to DS9. After a moment's hesitation the spokesperson accepts her offer. This is very, very strange behavior for Klingons. In "Ethics" *(TNG)*, we learn that there are significant gaps in Klingon medical science. As the reason, the episode states that Klingons believe injured warriors should be left to die. "Ethics" *(TNG)* also describes a Klingon ritual called the *Hegh'bat*. An injured Worf tells Riker that it is invoked when a Klingon can no longer stand and face his enemy. A family member or close friend gives the warrior a ritual knife. The warrior plunges it into his chest. The family member or close friend pulls out the knife and wipes the blade clean on his sleeve. Given the information in "Ethics" *(TNG)*, does it seem right that a damaged Klingon vessel would ask a Starfleet warship for access to medical facilities or allow itself to be towed back to DS9 so Bashir could attend to its wounded? (Of course, if the cruiser hadn't done this, then Worf and Kurn couldn't have found the location of the mines...yada, yada, yada.)

EQUIPMENT ODDITIES

• What happened to those big toad-sticker knives the Klingons used to carry? Twice in this episode—when Kurn initially boards the station and when a warrior on the *Vor'Cha*-class cruiser attempts to stab Worf—Klingons carry these dinky little knives. (I liked the other style better. It looked like a knife that could get some real work done!)

• Not a nit, just an observation. It's good to see that O'Brien knows how to take a hint. In "Tribunal," near the end of the second season, O'Brien and Keiko go on vacation. A short while after the trip begins, O'Brien starts kissing Keiko, who is seated in a pilot's chair. Unable to find a suitable posture to receive this amorous advance, Keiko eventually bursts into laughter, asking if the chairs recline. Smiling, O'Brien says no. Evidently O'Brien thought it was a good enough idea that he passed on a recommendation to Starfleet concerning this matter, because when we first see the interior of the *Yukon*—the newest runabout addition to DS9—Kira is sleeping on a *fully reclined* chair in the pilot area.

• I'm an not impressed with these cloaked Klingon mines. They seem to have a high failure rate! Remember that space is big. Kira and O'Brien mosey back to Bajoran space, and a mine detonates only 5,000 kilometers from their position. That's spitting distance in cosmic terms. They fly the *Defiant* to that location, and another mine goes off directly in front of them. Later we learn that the Klingons have placed mines all around Bajoran space. Now, what are the chances that Kira and O'Brien just *happened* to come upon the only two mines that fail, and the only two mines that fail just *happened* to be in the same very small area of space? I would say, "Slim to none." That means that these mines must be failing *all over* the area just outside Bajoran space! (As I said, pretty high failure rate.)

CONTINUITY AND PRODUCTION PROBLEMS

• Just before Worf snaps Dax's *bat'leth,* the position of his *mek'leth* changes with the camera angle. In one shot, no portion of the *mek'leth* protrudes into the *bat'leth.* Then the shot changes and suddenly the *mek'leth* is set to snap the *bat'leth* in two.

• After Bashir saves Kurn's life, Worf visits his brother in the infirmary. Kurn slowly revives and is instantly disappointed that he has not gone to *Sto'Vo'Kor.* Worf attempts to explain what happened, but Kurn upbraids Worf, wondering why Worf isn't standing over him with a *mevak* dagger, ready to slit his throat and bring him the death he deserves. During this exchange, the camera shows us a close-up of Kurn, and it appears that his nosepiece has come loose from his forehead prosthetic. Every time Kurn crinkles his nose, the very top of his nose moves freely, as if it's disconnected.

• As Worf tries to convince Kurn to help him sneak onto the Klingon cruiser, the camera gives us close-ups of their teeth. For some reason, both have grungy-looking top rows and straight, shiny bottom rows. (Just like D'Ghor from "House of Quark"! Maybe it's Klingon genetics?)

TRIVIA ANSWERS

1. The IKS *Drovana.*
2. Commander Sorval, son of M'Tokra.

Star Date: unknown

When Quark announces that he's cutting his employees' salaries by a third, Rom balks. It *is* true that a month-long Bajoran ritual of cleansing has drastically reduced the bar's business, but Rom knows—in reality—that Quark has implemented the pay reductions to boost his profits. Acting on a suggestion from Bashir, Rom does the unthinkable as a Ferengi: He starts a union. At first Quark reacts with disbelief and mockery but soon sobers when all the bar's employees go on strike. Soon Liquidator Brunt of the Ferengi Commerce Authority (see "Family Business") shows up with two Nausicaan thugs, determined to end it.

Brunt begins by trying to scare the strikers into returning to their jobs. When that fails, he decides to make an example of someone. He chooses Quark. The Nausicaans maul Quark, landing him in the infirmary with a crushed eye socket, two broken ribs, and a punctured lung. Even this tactic doesn't intimidate Rom, but Quark quickly cuts a deal: He will agree to all the workers' demands if they will make a show of dissolving the union so Brunt will leave. As the episode concludes, the bar reopens for business—minus one employee. After the strike, Rom decides to take a job as a diagnostic and repair technician for the station.

Trivia Questions

1. Supposedly O'Brien is a direct descendant of what king?

2. What in full is Kira's dialogue for this episode?

PLOT OVERSIGHTS

• The episode begins with the *Defiant* returning from a five-day mission in the Gamma Quadrant. Sure...*why not*? Why not go tooling around in the Gamma Quadrant anytime they feel like it? After all, Third Talak'Talan was probably just joking when he told the senior staff of DS9 the Dominion would be offended if anyone came through the wormhole. And those Dominion guys can't be as bad as everyone says. I'm sure by now—if they *really* meant what they said—they would have sent off a vitriolic subspace memo with all the comings and goings through the wormhole in recent months. I mean, it just wouldn't be *polite* for the Dominion to sit there and fume until they finally got mad enough to roar through the wormhole and blast the station into oblivion. *I'm sure* before they did that they would have Third Talak'Talan come back and say, "Okay, now look. We really meant what we said. Okay? So you guys better not keep coming through the passage or...or...well, *you* know!"

• Reporting on the success of the aforementioned excursion, Dax says that they spent five days in the Gamma Quadrant and there was no sign of the Jem'Haddar. This does not seem like cause for celebration. The Jem'Haddar might have been there even though there wasn't any sign of them! You may recall that Eris disappeared from the station at the end of "The Jem'Haddar." She transported into space! Since it seems unlikely that she transported all the way back to the Gamma Quadrant, there's a good possibility that the Jem'Haddar have *cloaking technology*.

• The whole episode revolves around the fact that Quark is implementing Ferengi labor practices in his bar. Does this seem right? The first season of *DS9* is very clear about the fact that Odo is unhappy that he has to abide by new Federation regulations on the station. Wouldn't the Federation rule book extend not only to security but to labor practices as well?

• This Sisko guy, he's tough. When Worf and O'Brien get into a scuffle over the strike, Bashir is injured and Odo throws them all in the same cell. Sisko decides to let them stay there all night. Three guys. One cell. One bed and apparently no bathroom. All night.

• Attempting to force Quark to settle the strike, Sisko tells the Ferengi barkeep that the Federation will no longer be generous landlords. No longer will they lease him the space on the promenade free, no longer will they provide him with free repairs or free energy. In fact, Sisko calculates the back rent, repair costs and energy use for the past five years and threatens to demand payment from Quark if the strike isn't settled soon! First, doesn't Bajor own this station? Wouldn't that make the Bajorans the landlords? Second, if the Bajorans really *are* the landlords and the Federation is simply managing the property for them, why hasn't the Bajoran civilian government demanded at least *some* compensation from Quark? Who pays the salaries of the Bajorans who work with O'Brien on Quark's equipment? Third, Quark says that the Federation holds his lease. Well, if there's a lease, there's an agreed-upon payment for the space. Quark would be a fool if he didn't hold back that amount every month, even if Sisko told him to ignore the lease agreement. The only way a good businessman would release those funds back into circulation would be if Sisko modified the lease agreement to show that the space was free. But if the lease agreement stipulates that the space is free, how can Sisko demand back rent? And finally, Sisko is a bit generous in his demands for *five years* of back rent, or the creators have broken their tradition of one season equaling one year. This episode occurs halfway through the fourth season. Traditionally that would mean that the Federation has had a presence on the station for only *three and one-half years*!

CHANGED PREMISES

• O'Brien certainly has come a long way in his attitudes toward station hardware. In the first season he was always fussing and fuming about the equipment. For instance, in "The Forsaken," he says that working with the *Enterprise* computer was like dancing a waltz, whereas working with the DS9 computer is like a wrestling match. But in this episode, O'Brien tells Worf that working on the station is "a lot easier" than working on the *Enterprise*. He complains that on the *Enterprise* he just sat around bored, waiting for something to break down. (I guess he was the future equivalent of the Maytag repairman.)

EQUIPMENT ODDITIES

• When did Quark install holographic generators inside the bar? Shortly after the strike begins, Odo comes to the bar and finds it staffed with multiple versions of Quark. The real Quark says that he purchased a holographic waiter program from a Lissepian. Buying a program is all fine and good, but you've got to have some hardware to run it. Specifically, you have to have a holographic generator like the ones in the holosuites. Until now we've never had any indication that holographic generators could project out of their respective holosuites or holodecks. Likewise, we've never seen that these holographic generators are portable.

(For instance, allowing the holographic doctor to move around the ship in *Voyager* required the installation of projectors in all rooms he would inhabit.) Since Rom is on strike and Quark has never shown any proclivity for technical things, one wonders how this upgrade occurred (especially with O'Brien's support of the strike). And—make no mistake—it *is* an upgrade. In the first place, Quark would never pay for a holographic generator in the bar area and then not use it. In this episode we learn that Quark doesn't have to reimburse the station for the energy the bar consumes. If Quark had a holographic generator in the bar capable of creating holographic waiters and he doesn't have to pay for the energy it uses, why hasn't he fired his staff long ago? (I realize that the particular program he purchased has some problems, but the idea of holographic waiters seems very sound financially, and the prospect of doing away with a dozen or so employees would be a great incentive.)

TRIVIA ANSWERS

1. Brian Boru.
2. "Just get two mugs of synthale, a double order of hasperat, and, uh...hold the conversation."

ACCESSION

Star Date: unknown

After a two-hundred-year-old Bajoran lightship (see "Explorers") comes through the wormhole, its pilot—Akorem Laan—announces that he is the emissary. Akorem recounts how his damaged vessel drifted into the wormhole, where the "Prophets" met with him and healed his injuries before they returned him to Bajoran space. Believing he was the first to meet with the Prophets, Akorem lays claim to the title previously bestowed on Sisko by Kai Opaka. (See "Emissary.") Sisko is happy to withdraw.

Akorem's first pronouncements as the emissary quickly cause Sisko to reconsider, however. Seeking a reason for the time frame that the Prophets chose for his return, Akorem finds that Bajorans no longer follow their "D'jarras"—a rigid caste system abandoned during the Cardassian occupation. The D'jarras dictated an individual's place in Bajoran society based on bloodline. Akorem calls for a return to the D'jarras—an action Sisko knows would irreparably damage Bajor's petition to join the Federation. (The Federation Charter opposed caste-based

discrimination.) Desperate to find a solution, Sisko suggests that he and Akorem return to the wormhole to ask the Prophets who is the true emissary. The aliens who live inside affirm "the Sisko" and seem to indicate that they sent Akorem to convince Sisko of his true place in Bajoran society. They then return Akorem to his own time.

GREAT LINES

"See Brak acquire. Acquire, Brak, acquire."— Quark, recounting a book he used to read to Nog as a child.

GREAT MOMENTS

There're a wonderful few moments when Worf finds out that Keiko is pregnant. Recalling his experience helping Keiko deliver Molly in the NextGen episode "Disaster," Worf quickly announces that he will be away from the station—visiting his parents—when her due date arrives!

PLOT OVERSIGHTS

• After Vedek Porta kills a member of his order for refusing to honor the D'jarras, Sisko inserts himself into the fray by challenging Akorem's claim as the emissary. Excuse me, but I be-

Trivia Questions

1. What is the name of Kira's D'jarra?

2. Whom did O'Brien insult in "his own keep"?

355

lieve this would be a direct violation of the Prime Directive, would it not? The role of the emissary and his call for a return to the D'jarras are entirely internal matters to Bajor. The Federation has no right to intervene. (Of course, that's never stopped Sisko before!)

• Okay, so Sisko decides he's going to challenge Akorem's claim to be the emissary. Sisko takes Akorem into the wormhole. The aliens choose Sisko. Sisko suggests that the aliens send Akorem back to his own time frame. They do so. Sisko goes back to the station and makes a speech explaining everything. Now, think about this whole sequence from Kai Winn's perspective. A new emissary appears. Sisko resigns the office. The new emissary calls for a return to traditional values—first and foremost among them, a return to the D'jarras. Winn is hip to this because she has always been a traditionalist. All of a sudden, the *Starfleet* officer in charge of DS9 is unhappy. He says that returning to traditional values will disallow Bajor's entrance into the Federation—the same Federation that probably has some interest in maintaining its access *to the wormhole*. Next, this *Starfleet* officer says that *he* might really be the emissary after all, so he takes Akorem into the wormhole. What happens after that? The *Starfleet* officer—the *Federation's* top official in the sector—comes back out of the wormhole *alone* and says that the aliens really want *him* to be the emissary, and they sent Akorem back to his own time. I don't know about you, but if *I* were Winn, I'd be just a tad

suspicious about this whole deal! (The sad part is that Sisko could have easily prevented any suspicions. All he had to do was return Akorem to the station for a farewell speech and *then* let the aliens send him home.)

CHANGED PREMISES

• At some point all the Bajorans on the station decided to change the way they clap! In this episode, as Akorem walks up to the podium on the promenade, all the Bajorans in the audience clap by slapping the back of one hand against the palm of the other. However, during "In the Hands of the Prophets," most of the Bajorans on the promenade—including Vedek Winn—clap by slapping the back of their wrists.

• The aliens who live in nonlinear time inside the wormhole seem to change their purpose in this episode. Originally, "Emissary" painted these aliens as unconcerned with corporeal life forms. The orbs they sent out—the same orbs that eventually found their way into Bajoran veneration as religious artifacts—were simply meant to seek out other noncorporeal life. According to "Emissary," the Bajorans encountered these probes and built an entire theology around them, calling their makers the "Prophets" and worshiping them as gods. As I noted in my discussion of "Emissary," this idea resonates with a classic science-fiction concept: Advanced races will appear as gods to less advanced races whether they intend to do so or not. All this time, I thought the aliens who lived in the wormhole were just that: *Aliens who lived in the worm-*

hole. I thought they existed in their nonlinear time and couldn't give a rip about corporeal beings. And certainly they didn't pay much attention to all these "prophecies" written by Bajorans who had spent too much time snorting the celestial orbs. Yet, in this episode, the aliens suddenly seem to confirm that Sisko is the emissary! I realize that they don't come out and say it. But they do say that they sent Akorem to DS9 "for the Sisko." Now, what could that enigmatic phrase mean? If it means that the aliens sent Akorem to the station to challenge Sisko's claim as emissary so that Sisko would really want the position, then the aliens must know about the Bajoran prophecies and have a *real interest* in seeing them fulfilled in the appropriate manner! (And what was that "We are of Bajor" bit? The aliens said it twice to Sisko—even going so far as to say to him, *"You* are of Bajor." Are the creators trying to say that the nonlinear time aliens are really distant-future descendants of the Bajorans?)

EQUIPMENT ODDITIES
• Disturbed by Akorem's announcement that Bajorans should return to their D'jarras, Sisko experiences a sleepless night. He decides to go for a walk on the promenade, and in short order we see him strolling past Quark's. Oddly enough, all the lights are on, even though the promenade is clearly closed for the evening.

Compare this to "Necessary Evil." Just after the title sequence in that episode, we see Odo presiding over the promenade as it literally shuts down for the night.
• At the start of "Playing God," Bashir asks the computer to locate Dax. The computer responds that Dax is on "Level 7, Section 5." Bashir quickly interprets this as Quark's bar for a young Trill initiate named Arjin. In this episode, however, O'Brien asks for Bashir's location, and the computer answers, "Dr. Bashir is in Quark's bar." Obviously someone reprogrammed the computer to give more user-friendly answers. (Must have something to do with its new voice. Anybody else notice that for the past several episodes Majel Barrett-Roddenberry has not provided the voice of the computer?)

CONTINUITY AND PRODUCTION PROBLEMS
• Near the beginning of the episode Sisko ruminates with Dax over his role as the emissary. He says it's not so bad, but it's just hard getting used to being a religious icon. Off-camera, Dax replies, *"Really...I* think I'd like it." At this point the closed captioning reads, "I'll have to take your word for it."

TRIVIA ANSWERS
1. Ih'valla.
2. King Leinster.

HODGEPODGE TOTE BOARD

1. Number of episodes in which Sisko plays with his baseball: thirteen
2. Number of times we see Odo shape-shift: thirty-six
3. Number of times Quark reacts with a drink in his mouth: four
4. Number of characters who made their first appearance in *NextGen:* ten
5. Number of times an individual fires upward on the station and no chickens fall: two
6. Number of episodes in which someone yells, "Dabo!": fifteen
7. Number of times we see characters holding jumja sticks: seven
8. Number of times the creators use Quark to take a dig at current-day businesses: four

REFERENCES

Note: This tote board is current only through the first eighty-four episodes, ending with "Paradise Lost."

1. "Emissary," "The Nagus," "The Homecoming," "Rules of Acquisition," "Second Sight," "Whispers," "Profit and Loss," "The Jem'Haddar," "The Abandoned," *"Defiant,"* "Improbable Cause," "Hippocratic Oath," and "Starship Down"

2. "Emissary": Odo shape-shifts to allow a mace to pass through his face and transforms from a bag to a humanoid. "Past Prologue": mouse to humanoid. "A Man Alone": chair to humanoid. "Babel": cart and gizmo to humanoid. "Captive Pursuit": painting to humanoid. "The Nagus": Odo shape-shifts under an airlock door. "Vortex": broken piece of glass to humanoid. "The Forsaken": humanoid to goop. "Dramatis Personae": Odo's face butterflies. "The Circle": slab to mouse. "The Siege": wall to partial humanoid, humanoid to trip wire. "Invasive Procedures": humanoid to goop, table to humanoid. "The Alternate": humanoid to angry blobby humanoid, the Big Blob to humanoid. "Shadowplay": humanoid to top. "The Search, Part I": humanoid to goop. "The Search, Part II": bird to humanoid, hand to lock opener. "Second Skin": bag to humanoid. "The Abandoned": Odo shape-shifts to become permeable so the young Jem'Haddar can jump through him. "Heart of Stone": shield to humanoid. "The Die Is Cast": humanoid to goop. "The Adversary": humanoid to conduit-running goop, goop to humanoid. "The Way of the Warrior": chair to bird, Rosetta stone to humanoid. "Hippocratic Oath": bag of latinum to humanoid. "Little

Green Men": dog to humanoid, humanoid to dog, tire to humanoid. "Home-front": briefcase to humanoid, seagull to humanoid, plant to humanoid.

3. When he samples the Wadi's alpha-currant nectar in "Move Along Home." When Rom suggests that he could take over the bar in "The Nagus." When Sarkonna says she would like to purchase weapons in "The Maquis, Part I." When Boheeka discovers that the requisition code he received from Quark is for a classified piece of Obsidian Order biotechnology in "The Wire."

4. Picard in "Emissary." O'Brien in "Emissary" and beyond. Lursa and B'Etor of the House of Duras in "Past Prologue." Keiko in "A Man Alone" and beyond. Vash and Q in "Q-Less." Lwaxana in "The Forsaken" and "Fascinations." Admiral Nechayev in "The Search, Part II." Worf in "The Way of the Warrior" and beyond.

5. Sisko fires upward to stop the mob heading for Odo in "A Man Alone." T'Kar fires upward in Ops in "Invasive Procedures."

6. "Emissary," "A Man Alone," "Babel," "Captive Pursuit," "Move Along Home," "Progress," "If Wishes Were Horses," "The Homecoming," "Cardassians," "Sanctuary," "The Abandoned," "Visionary," "Distant Voices," "The Way of the Warrior," and "Starship Down."

7. Nog has one in both " A Man Alone" and "The Nagus." O'Brien "enjoys" one during "In the Hands of the Prophets." Morn walks by with one during "In the Hands of the Prophets." Bashir gives one to Kira in *"Defiant."* Jake gives Kira a jumja stick and carries one of his own during "Fascination."

8. During "If Wishes Were Horses," Quark smells the scent of opportunity. He says "Family entertainment. That's the future, Odo. There's a fortune to be made. Little holocreatures running around. Rides and games for the kiddies. Ferengi standing in every doorway selling useless souvenirs." (Kinda sounds like Disney World, doesn't it?) In "The Siege," Quark overbooks the seats on the runabouts and claims it's an accepted Ferengi trade practice. In "The Jem'Haddar," Quark wants to sell merchandise (collectibles!) over the station monitors. Listen to his description: "Andorian jewelry. Vulcan IDIC pins, Bolian crystal-steel. With my low overhead, I could offer these items at a significant discount." (Sound like QVC?) And finally, during "The House of Quark," Quark says he should have gone into insurance— "Better hours. More money. Less scruples."

RULES OF ENGAGEMENT

Star Dates: 49648.0–9665.3

As the episode begins, Worf faces an extradition hearing. The Klingon Empire has charged him with murder and wants the Federation to relinquish him to its custody so he can stand trial under Klingon law. The incident in question occurred while Worf captained the *Defiant* as it escorted the sixth of seven Cardassian relief convoys to Pentath III, site of a plague outbreak. Because of Pentath III's proximity to the Cardassian/Klingon border, the Cardassians had requested help in protecting the shipments from Klingon raiders.

Two days into the mission, two Klingon warships attacked without provocation—decloaking, firing, cloaking; attempting to draw the *Defiant* away from the convoy. Sensing a pattern, Worf ordered the *Defiant* to come about after one of the Klingon ships cloaked. Quickly locking onto an unknown decloaking vessel, Worf then ordered a spread of quantum torpedoes. The decloaking ship turned out to be a transport vessel supposedly carrying 441 Klingon "civilians"—all of whom were killed. As the hearing nears a conclusion, Odo uncovers the truth. The list of the casualities actually came from a crash of a Klingon transport in the mountains of Galorda Prime three months prior. The transport vessel Worf destroyed was empty—a ruse to embarrass the Federation and force it to withdraw its assistance from the Cardassians.

Trivia Questions

1. From what illness do the Cardassian colonists on Pentath III suffer?

2. With whom does Morn speak at the bar?

PLOT OVERSIGHTS

• In his opening statement, Klingon advocate Ch'Pok says that the Klingon Empire makes—among others—the allegation that Worf knowingly fired upon and destroyed a Klingon civilian transport ship. Surprisingly enough, Ch'Pok begins his presentation of evidence by saying that he will accept all the logs recorded by the *Defiant* officers, thereby agreeing to the Federation's recital of the facts. But the Federation's recital of the facts says that Worf fired on the transport ship as it was decloaking. *Everyone* on board the *Defiant* agrees that the crew did not know it was a civilian transport ship until the ship exploded. You can't "knowingly" fire on a civilian ship if it hasn't been identified yet! (Actually, the whole legal basis of this episode is tricky. Both Reid

E. Joiner of Arkadelphia, Arkansas, and Mark Luta of Eugene, Oregon, sent me excellent discussions on murder and extradition, but space does not allow their inclusion.)

• Responding to the charge that Worf knowingly destroyed a Klingon civilian transport ship, Sisko says in his opening statement that Worf believed it was a warship; that the destruction of the civilian transport ship was an *unavoidable* accident. Yet at the end of the episode, Sisko chews on Worf because he didn't identify his target before firing. In other words, it was avoidable. Worf was negligent.

• Ch'Pok's reasoning to have Worf prosecuted under Klingon law seems to be internally inconsistent—a characteristic that Admiral T'Lara, a *Vulcan,* should notice but fails to for some reason. (Hmmm.) Ch'Pok continually harps on the fact that Worf's actions resulted in the deaths of civilians. He appears to be labeling this "a bad thing." Yet, in the course of the presentation of the evidence, Ch'Pok draws out the fact that Emperor Sompek ("...one of our greatest heroes") ordered his men to burn the city of Tong Vey to the ground and kill its men, women, *and* children. Also, toward the end of the episode, Ch'Pok states that a true Klingon rejoices in the death of all his enemies whether they be young or old, armed or weaponless. So, on one hand, Ch'Pok exalts the fact that Klingons kill civilians if they are the "enemy" while on the other suggesting that Worf should be returned to the Empire to stand trial for killing Klingon civilians in a battle where the Klingons attacked him

without provocation! (My point is that even if Worf was shown to be negligent in firing on the ship without identifying it, Admiral T'Lara should never have considered extradition since, according to Klingon tradition, firing on civilians is perfectly acceptable.)

• Can someone tell me why O'Brien is at the helm during the mission to escort the Cardassian convoy? Isn't he the chief of Engineering for the *Defiant*?

• Throughout this episode Sisko suspects that the Klingons are really interested in embarrassing the Federation so that Starfleet will cease its escorts of the Cardassian convoys to the Pentath system. In the first place, the Klingons seem a bit slow on the uptake if this is what they are really attempting to accomplish. The *Defiant* was escorting the *sixth* convoy—the *sixth* of seven! Besides, I fail to understand how this embarrassment over Worf would cause the Federation to halt a humanitarian effort. Let's say that Worf really was negligent. Let's even say that he intentionally fired on a civilian ship, killing 441 Klingons. Would this really paralyze Starfleet and turn them into a bunch of hand-wringers? Was Starfleet paralyzed when Captain Maxwell mounted his own campaign against the Cardassians, destroying an outpost and two ships? Of course not! Starfleet sent Picard to get him and bring him back for trial. And that was that! (See the *NextGen* episode "The Wounded.")

• At one point Ch'Pok gets way out of line in his questioning of Worf. Sisko objects. Admiral T'Lara calls Ch'Pok's name as a rebuff. Ch'Pok continues.

Admiral T'Lara warns Ch'Pok that he is stepping well beyond the bounds of protocol. Ch'Pok continues. Admiral T'Lara says that the bickering will stop or she will hold both him and Worf in contempt. Ch'Pok continues. Finally Worf gets upset and hits Ch'Pok. I suspect that T'Lara learned her extradition hearing demeanor from the "Judge Ito Correspondence School of Judicial Courtroom Conflict Resolution."

CHANGED PREMISES

• I must admit that this entire idea of Klingon "civilians" came as something of a surprise to me. *The Star Trek Encyclopedia* identifies Klingons as a "humanoid warrior race." In "Ethics" *(TNG)* we learn that Klingon tradition stipulates that the son of a Klingon is a man the day he can hold a blade— a battle implement, mind you. Speaking of his own race during this episode, Ch'Pok generalizes them as "a violent, warrior race." A people with a predatory instinct, a blood lust. He also identifies Worf as a Klingon warrior, "one of us…a killer." He later says, "A true Klingon rejoices in the death of his enemies—old, young, armed, unarmed. All that matters is the victory." During the hearing Worf says, "I am a Klingon. We live for battle." From all appearances, "warrior" is a term that applies to every full-blooded member of the race. Yet this episode features a transport ship full of "civilians." (You might also recall that during the *NextGen* episode "Sins of the Father," Worf's former nanny Kahlest killed a Klingon warrior who was attacking Picard. This…from the *nanny*!)

CONTINUITY AND PRODUCTION PROBLEMS

• Most of the footage of Worf and Dax fighting on the holosuite comes from "The Sons of Mogh."

• I was worried there for a while. I thought the creators might make it through the first four seasons of *Star Trek: Deep Space Nine* without a blatant problem concerning the rank pips. (That's just no fun at all for us nitpickers!) I am happy to report that Sisko receives a sudden demotion in this episode to commander, only to receive a sudden promotion back to captain only minutes later. While questioning Dax, Ch'Pok brings up Worf's habit of fighting the Battle of Tong Vey in one of Quark's holosuites. He tries to get Dax to admit that Worf gives the order at the end of the simulation to slaughter everyone in the city. Dax protests, and Ch'Pok asks Admiral T'Lara to instruct Dax to answer the question. At this point there is a reaction shot of Sisko, and he has only three pips on his dress uniform. The three remain until the commercial break, after which they return to their normal four.

TRIVIA ANSWERS
1. Rudellian plague.
2. Ralidia.

HARD TIME

While visiting Argratha, O'Brien becomes intrigued with Argrathi technology. The suspicious Argrathi quickly convict him of espionage, punishing him with a virtual imprisonment of twenty years. Though O'Brien spends only a few hours on the correctional table, the Argrathi fill his head with memories of two decades of harsh detention.

Back on the station, O'Brien's "old" prisoner habits surface. He hoards food and sleeps on the floor. Worse, he refuses counseling, becoming belligerent when confronted by Bashir. As a result, Sisko puts O'Brien on medical leave. A frustrated O'Brien returns to his quarters, only to come very close to striking Molly when she demands too much attention. Aghast, O'Brien heads for a cargo bay, taking out his rage on a stack of containers. Then the rage turns inward and he grabs a phaser to commit suicide. When Bashir finds him, O'Brien—holding the phaser to his throat—explains that the Argrathi also provided him a virtual cellmate named Ee'Char. Over the "years," he and Ee'Char became best friends until one night when O'Brien mistakenly thought Ee'Char was selfishly hoarding food. In the fight that followed, O'Brien accidently killed Ee'Char. O'Brien has been struggling to forgive himself for the brutal act. With Bashir's help, he begins to find healing.

Trivia Questions

1. Where does O'Brien believe that he was held on Argratha?

2. What is the number on the weapons locker from which O'Brien gets a phaser?

RUMINATIONS

There are some items that only a nitpicker would notice and for which the creators deserve credit. Twice in the episode the public address system in O'Brien's "prison" announces, "Illumination will be suspended in twenty seconds." Guess what? Both times, twenty seconds later, the lights go out. Kudos!

PLOT OVERSIGHTS

• Did this episode remind anyone else of a cross among "The Inner Light" *(TNG)*, "Frame of Mind" *(TNG)*, and "Ex Post Facto" *(VOY)*?

• Okay, so O'Brien comes back to the station, and part of the agreement for him to go back to work is that he will visit with Counselor Telnorri three times a week. A bit later we learn that

O'Brien hasn't seen Telnorri in *ten* days, and Bashir has finally gotten around to confronting the chief on the issue. Does this seem right? Maybe you let the guy miss one session, but…three, possibly four before you do something about it?

• I'm always intrigued by the way colloquialisms remain in language. At the end of this episode Bashir tells O'Brien that if he "pulls the trigger" on his phaser and commits suicide the Argrathi will have destroyed a good man. One question: How do you pull a button? (In case you don't know, the trigger on the phaser is a small, rectangular button.)

• Someone needs to teach Bashir a few principles of safe weapons handling. After taking the phaser away from O'Brien, Bashir points it right at him while resetting it! (Of course, O'Brien isn't much better when—moments later—he holds a loaded hypospray while hugging his daughter and he keeps the business end toward her back.)

CHANGED PREMISES

• I realize that O'Brien wakes up somewhat addled by his mental imprisonment, but he seems stunned at first by the notion that it would be possible to create years of false memories within the humanoid brain. Obviously he forgot Picard's experience during "The Inner Light" (an experience that occurred while O'Brien served aboard the *Enterprise*).

• It's very fortuitous that no one remembered Vulcans can erase memory (as Spock did for Kirk in the *Classic Trek* episode "Requiem for Methuselah") or that Bashir has never heard of the Pulaski Memory Excision technique (employed in the *NextGen* episode "Pen Pals"). Otherwise it would have been a short show. (Actually, I think it *was* a short show. At the end, the creators included a one-minute May sweeps promo for the "month of blockbuster adventure" that lay ahead. Normally the previews for the next episode run only thirty seconds.)

• Of course, one could wonder what O'Brien was doing in the Gamma Quadrant in the first place (the runabout that brought him home came out of the wormhole), given Third Talak'Talan's statements in "The Jem'Haddar." But one has probably beaten that dead horse long enough.

EQUIPMENT ODDITIES

• In the cargo bay, O'Brien extracts a phaser from a weapons locker that hangs on the wall. It is a small affair, made from some type of plastic, with a latch at the top. When undone, the entire front of the locker folds down. Along the bottom edge of the front, the locker has an official-looking metal plate that runs the entire length. Oddly enough, if you look closely when O'Brien opens the locker, you will see that the plate covers words that were formed into the front piece when it was manufactured. The words appear to be "Action Pack." I needn't tell you that this raises many, many questions about the financial stability of the Federation. (For instance: With replicator technology, why wouldn't the Federation manufacture an entirely new case instead of cobbling up a metal strip to cover the words from an obviously recycled case? Is the Federation really in such dire straits when it comes to container technology?) Instead of spoiling your fun, however, gentle readers, I leave it to you to come up with additional questions and the possible ramifications of their answers.

• Ya gotta say one thing for this O'Brien guy: When he means to commit suicide, he *means* to commit suicide. After retrieving the phaser, he sets it to the maximum: level 16 (if the *Tech Manual* is to be believed). At that level, the phaser would not only kill O'Brien, it also would probably take out the bulkhead of the cargo bay!

CONTINUITY AND PRODUCTION PROBLEMS

• It's nice to see that the Bolian woman's "bar probation" is finally over. In "Captive Pursuit" Quark tosses a Bolian woman from the bar after she illegally moves a wager during play. He tells her that she is not welcome in his establishment. In this episode she's back, sitting at the bar when O'Brien comes in for his synthale. At least it looks like her.

TRIVIA ANSWERS

1. Detention Area 4.
2. 47. (See "47." By the way, a weapons locker that looks identical to this one with a "47" on it as well shows up in the next episode, "Shattered Mirror.")

SHATTERED MIRROR

Star Date: unknown

Coming from the parallel universe featured in "Crossover" and "Through the Looking Glass," Jennifer Sisko brings news that the human rebels have taken control of Terok Nor. Happy for the good news, Sisko does not realize the real reason for Jennifer's visit. She has come to lure Jake back to the parallel universe, knowing that Sisko will follow.

When Sisko arrives on Terok Nor, "Smiley" O'Brien explains that they needed his help and knew he wouldn't come on his own. The rebels *have* indeed taken the station, but an Alliance fleet—led by Regent Worf—is on the way to reclaim it. Their only hope is the *Defiant*. Alt-O'Brien then reveals that the last time he came to the station to get Sisko (see "Through the Looking Glass"), he downloaded the schematics for the powerful warship. The rebels have constructed their own version, but it faces the same structure problems as the original—it is overpowered, capable of shaking itself to pieces. Sisko agrees to help stabilize the craft and—with the rebels' assistance—succeeds

just as the Alliance fleet attacks. Sisko takes command of the rebels' *Defiant* and defeats the fleet. Meanwhile, Intendant Kira escapes and—while fleeing the station—fatally wounds Jennifer. Grieving his wife's death a second time, Sisko and Jake return to our universe.

GREAT LINES

Isn't that a coincidence! I was hoping you weren't married."—Intendant Kira to her guard after she tries to seduce him and he replies that she sentenced his wife to death. This is another one of those great turn-arounds where the character should be humbled by the comments of another but instead makes a tart reply.

GREAT MOMENTS

The battle scenes in this episode are absolutely fabulous—the most intricate so far in any television incarnation of Star Trek.

PLOT OVERSIGHTS

• The entire premise of this episode demands some scrutiny. First, Alt-O'Brien—evidently when he visited DS9 during "Through the Looking Glass"—somehow managed to down-

Trivia Questions

1. What is the name of the Bajoran minister who comes to speak with the emissary?

2. Who gives Kira the most exquisite massages?

load the complete schematics for the *Defiant*! This does not seem like information that should be readily available. But perhaps he was able to use his intuitive knowledge of *our* O'Brien to accomplish this incredible feat. Second, having absconded with the aforementioned plans, these rebels; these guys who have spent their lives working in ore processing or serving Alt-Sisko as little better than pirates; these shorthanded, resource-challenged humans *somehow* manage to build an exact duplicate of the *Defiant*! Where did they get the materials? And how did they slap this warship together so quickly? And even if they could duplicate the ship down to the last optical transtator cluster of FTL nanoprocessor units in the *Defiant*'s computer core, *who programmed the thing*? Every display is obviously a Federation-style display (even the ones in the rebel raider, but that's another topic). Displays require user interfaces. User interfaces require software engineers—in the case of the Federation, *teams* of engineers. Are we to believe that Alt-O'Brien was actually able to cart back the entire core-memory programming for a Federation starship when he kidnapped Sisko? (Or do the creators expect us to believe that Jennifer Sisko could duplicate all the programming written by the staff at Utopia Planitia?)

• Every time we see Intendant Kira in this episode she wears her headband and her Bajoran earring. Given that she is a prisoner for most of the episode, I find this interesting, since the headband could probably serve as a garotte, and Intendant Kira no doubt knows 8,153 ways to kill or seriously debilitate another humanoid with that earring!

CHANGED PREMISES

• In talking with Sisko about Jennifer, Jake mentions that he's been telling her everything that has happened to him in the past nine years. At first this seems to be a reference to the time that has passed since his mother's death. But our Jennifer Sisko supposedly died three years before Jake and Sisko came to DS9. Since this is the fourth season, they have been at DS9 for four years. Three plus four make seven...not nine. (Unless, of course, Jake means Bajoran years.)

EQUIPMENT ODDITIES

• The "rebel raider" in this episode is the same model of ship that was used by the Maquis in "The Maquis, Part II." Oddly enough, the cockpits are different.

• Preparing the *Defiant* to face the Alliance fleet, Sisko commands, "Aft thrusters at one-quarter impulse." Those are some high-powered thrusters if they can actually propel the *Defiant* at 18,750 kilometers per *second*! (Full impulse, according to the *NextGen Tech Manual*, is one-quarter the speed of light.) Normally only the impulse and warp engines can drive a starship this fast.

• What happened to the shield bubbles? During the gorgeous battle scenes in this episode, the characters speak of the shields, yet not one shot of a weapon hitting a ship includes the shield bubble effect we've all grown to love over the past nine years of *Star Trek*. I suppose we could say that the Alliance doesn't use shield bubbles, but shouldn't the *Defiant*, since it's supposedly an exact copy of our *Defiant*? (Of course, if the shield bubbles existed, then we couldn't have those wonderful shots of the ships flying in and around the station, because the ships would bounce off the station's shields. The same holds true for Sisko's close-quarter flying of the *Defiant* next to the Klingon battle cruiser!)

CONTINUITY AND PRODUCTION PROBLEMS

• When we first see Jake in the parallel universe, he talks with Alt-Nog. Given that Nog has his arms around two scantily clad bar babes, the boys at Paramount strategically framed the close-ups of Nog so that the chest of the woman on Nog's left occupies the entire right third of the screen! Crisscrossing this woman's chest is a ragged plastic/leather strap that winds around her neck before proceeding out to her sides and around to her back. In the close-ups the right side of this strap angles out almost identically to the left. However, in the medium shot, when Nog tosses her to Jake, the strap suddenly hangs in front of her cleavage.

• For the entire episode, Worf has Garak at his side, with the Cardassian attired in a rigid metal collar and attached chain. At one point Garak makes the mistake of suggesting that the Alliance fleet increase their speed to warp 9. Worf whips the chain, attempting to make it look like he has

pulled it taut and has caused Garak great discomfort. There's only one problem: The chain still hangs, arcing down. Taut chains do not arc down like that over such a short distance. It looks like Worf and Garak are just putting on a show, but why would they do this? (Maybe they've decided to audition for "The Gong and Dagger Show"?) And speaking of putting on a show, Garak acts like he's choking several times when Worf pulls the collar forward by yanking on the chain. Shouldn't this *relieve* the pressure on Garak's windpipe? Or is Cardassian physiology different?

• After Worf gives the order to increase speed to warp 9, a Klingon subordinate steps away from the forward viewscreen on the bridge of the battle cruiser. In the background, we see a static star field when the ship supposedly is already traveling at warp.

• It's always fun to watch a guest actor or actress attempt to duplicate the "everybody lurch to the right so we can make the viewer think an explosion just rocked the station" motion normally executed with such practiced ease by the stars of the series. Toward the end of this episode, Intendant Kira marches Jennifer and Jake down a hall when the attacking Alliance fleet hits the station with their phasers. Intendant Kira takes one stumble, as does Jake. Jennifer bobs back and forth like she's auditioning to be a flygirl.

TRIVIA ANSWERS
1. Gettor.
2. Marani.

THE MUSE

Star Date: unknown

A mysterious woman approaches Jake in the replimat, and—seeing his padd—notes that he is a writer. The woman introduces herself as Onaya, claiming that she can help him draw his talents to the surface. When Sisko leaves for a three-day vacation with Kasidy Yates, Jake visits Onaya in her quarters. She encourages him to begin work on the most ambitious novel he can imagine. As Jake writes, Onaya rubs his head, increasing his neural activity, and feeding on his creative energy. By the time Sisko returns, Jake is in the infirmary on the verge of synaptic collapse. Unfortunately, Onaya isn't through with him and soon lures him back. Just in time, Sisko locates the pair and saves his son's life while Onaya—transmutating into energy—slips away to find her next creative endeavor.

At the same time, a pregnant Lwaxana Troi visit the station. She has married a Tavnian named Jeyal. Once Jeyal determined the child was a male, he invoked Tavnian tradition to take the son and raise him apart from Lwaxana. Odo comes to Lwaxana's rescue, marrying her in a legal Tavnian wedding to nullify Lwaxana's marriage to Jeyal so that she may raise the child on her own. As the episode ends, Lwaxana books passage to Betazed.

Trivia Questions

1. What does Jake order from the replicator in the replimat?

2. Whom does Onaya backhand in the infirmary?

RUMINATIONS

At the end of this episode there is a very nice tie-in to a prior episode this season. In one of the final shots of this episode we learn that the novel Jake began is called Anslem. You may recall that this is the name of the novel that Jake publishes during the events of "The Visitor."

PLOT OVERSIGHTS

• Concerning Lwaxana's pregnancy via the Tavnian male, there is a nit that many Guild members have submitted in various forms. This seems as good a place as any to discuss it. On Earth—if I have my biology correct—we say that two entities are members of the same species if they can mate and produce fertile offspring. Interestingly enough, in *Star Trek* we see many mixed-race individuals—all apparently healthy—and not once have we heard that any of these offspring are infertile. In fact, Deanna

369

Troi—half human, half Betazoid—conceives in "The Child" *(TNG)*, and no one finds this unusual (apart from the rapid growth of the child, of course). Evidently the creators of *Star Trek* believe that most of the humanoid races scattered across the far reaches of the Alpha and Beta quadrants are all part of the same species. (I have not forgotten the events in the *NextGen* episode "The Chase" that suggest that humans, Cardassians, Klingons, and Romulans have a common ancestor. However, if a common ancestor is sufficient to make humans and Klingons part of the same species, then why is Troi surprised to learn that K'Ehleyr is half human and half Klingon, commenting in the *NextGen* episode "The Emissary" that she didn't think that was possible?)

• We should probably add Tavnians to the list of races that Betazoids cannot read telepathically. One would think that if Lwaxana could sense that Jeyal intended for them to live according to Tavnian traditions after they married, she wouldn't have gone through with the wedding!

EQUIPMENT ODDITIES

• As part of the Tavnian wedding ceremony, Lwaxana holds a sphere. The upper half of it glows. Evidently she didn't use Energizer batteries in it, because halfway through—as Odo speaks of how Lwaxana didn't recoil from him and wanted to see more—the light becomes noticeably dim. Thankfully, someone in attendance just happens to have the right-size batteries in his or her pocket, and they manage to slip them covertly to Lwaxana because—by the time Odo speaks of the day he stopped being alone—the sphere has returned to its former glory!

CONTINUITY AND PRODUCTION PROBLEMS

• The opening exterior shot of this episode—featuring a Bajoran transport flying between the habitat and docking rings with two other Bajoran transporters already docked—comes from "The Siege."

• Not really a nit, just an amazement. In "The Visitor," see Jake working on a padd, with "4747" in the corner, writing a short story. Interestingly enough, in this episode Jake works on a story as well, on a padd, with "4747" in the corner *and the padd is displaying the same text!* (No, it's not impossible; some writers do rewrite their stuff over and over. Just thought I'd note it.)

• The actor who plays Jeyal in this episode also played the part of Kang in "Day of the Dove" *(TOS)* and "Blood Oath." (There's no mistaking that voice!)

TRIVIA ANSWERS
1. Orange juice.
2. Nurse Tagara.

FOR THE CAUSE

Star Date: supplemental

D uring a Security briefing, Lieutenant Commander Eddington informs the senior staff that—in response to an urgent request from the Cardassians—the Federation will soon deliver twelve industrial replicators to the beleaguered empire. The shipment will pass through DS9 in three days, and Starfleet Intelligence believes that the Maquis will try to stop it.

After the briefing, Eddington and Odo approach Sisko with another matter. They suspect that Kasidy Yates—Sisko's "significant other"—is a Maquis smuggler. Odo points to the amount of time it has taken her to make certain deliveries. Eddington says that a recently acquired, partial list of Maquis contacts in the Bajoran Sector hints at her as well. Sisko sends Worf in the *Defiant* to confirm the suspicions and, a short time later, Yates's ship, the *Xhosa*, does transfer cargo to a Maquis raider in the Cardassian Badlands. On Yates's next run, Sisko takes command of the *Defiant*, intending to capture both the *Xhosa* and the Maquis raider. When the rendezvous doesn't occur, Odo becomes suspicious, speculating that the real reason for this particular run was to draw Sisko from the station. By the time the *Defiant* returns to DS9, Eddington has absconded with the replicators. He later contacts the station to proclaim his allegiance to the Maquis. As the episode concludes, Yates is arrested for smuggling.

Trivia Questions

1. What experiment in cooking does Sisko attempt in this episode?

2. Where are the C.F.I. replicators stored on the station?

RUMINATIONS

I must admit that after "Way of the Warrior," I became convinced that Kasidy Yates was a Changeling. I thought the creators were setting us up for a "wrench Sisko's heart out through his throat" episode. While she didn't turn out to be a Changeling, the creators eventually did give us the episode. (Wouldn't want to have the lead character in a Star Trek series in a loving, caring, gentle, understanding, long-term relationship, now, would we? I suppose it was daring enough to have a lead character who was actually married—at one time— with a son born in wedlock.)

PLOT OVERSIGHTS

• This episode also contains a subplot concerning Garak the tailor, DS9's only Cardassian merchant. You might recall that Kira offered to let Dukat's daughter, Ziyal, stay on the station when Dukat flew off to be a terrorist at the end of "Return to Glory." In this episode, Garak and Ziyal get to know each other—being the only Cardassians on the station. In time, Ziyal invites Garak to enjoy a Cardassian sauna with her in one of Quark's holosuites. Garak accepts the invitation but determines not to go. He suspects that Ziyal is planning to kill him and present his head to Dukat for a birthday present. Then Kira comes into the tailor shop and threatens Garak if he does anything to hurt Ziyal. From this, Garak decides that it is safe to get acquainted after all, since Kira wouldn't say anything if Ziyal had ill in mind for Garak. Quark happens to be a customer in Garak's shop at the time and counters that Kira's threats might be designed to put him at ease so that Ziyal *can* kill him. Garak—the master spy, the weaver of intricate lies, the overlord of intrigue—acts like this thought *never* occurred to him. Does this seem right? (Just love-numbed, I guess.)

• Is Dax on some really important mission during this episode? She shows up in the briefings but is conspicuously absent the rest of the time. O'Brien pilots the *Defiant*. While seizing the station, Eddington apparently doesn't have to contend with her. When Eddington sends Lieutenant Reese to take over Ops, she apparently isn't there because no one finds this odd enough to investigate. And, even at the end, when everyone is scrambling to locate Eddington and the replicators, she's not in Ops!

CHANGED PREMISES

• Does anyone else find it odd that Kasidy Yates will probably go to prison for delivering *medical* supplies to the Maquis—something Starfleet has always seemed content to give to every Tosk, Dick, and Harry who comes along—but Quark spends only a short time in one of Odo's cells for brokering a *weapons* deal with the same organization in "The Maquis, Part II"?

EQUIPMENT ODDITIES

• Early on, we enjoy some type of spectator sport match between Kira and an unidentified opponent. It looks like a combination of handball and racquetball, with the back wall removed in favor of a force field. At various times in the series, Bajoran characters *have* referred to a game called "springball." (I believe the first mention comes between Kira and Vedek Bareil in "Shadowplay.") While no dialogue indicates that the game in this episode is, in fact, springball, for my purposes here I will refer to it as such (to keep from simply calling it "the game").

On to the nit. The court used in the springball match has scoring indicators on the front wall: Kira's on the left, the other guy's on the right. The first time we see a full shot of the court, the indicators show Kira with two points and the guy with one. There are apparently five points in a match. Kira scores a point, and a close-up shows her indicator going from three to four. (Don't ask me when she scored the third point!) Next we see Kira take off her helmet to wipe the sweat from her brow. If you will watch carefully in the upper left-hand portion of the screen, you will see that, for some reason, her indicator has reverted to three points. Play continues and the guy trips Kira. Now the indicators show that Kira has three and the guy has two! (Don't ask me when he scored his second point.) Play continues, the guy scores a point while we are watching. His indicator goes from one to two! So not only did he make the second point when we weren't looking, he also lost it and had to make it again. Kira then wins the match with a final point even though the last time we saw her indicator it showed only three points and the game looks like it goes to five points. (Then again, no one ever said Bajorans were good at math!)

• Ya gotta hand it to Sisko. He knows how to make a *dramatic* arrest. At the end of the episode, Sisko talks with Yates in a cargo bay. When they conclude, Sisko steps back, taps his communicator, and says, "Lieutenant Reese." The hallway doors pop open. Reese and two other Starfleet Security officers march in and take Yates away. Note that the guards were standing right in front of the door. Note that not one of them had an arm extended as if he had pressed a button to enter. Note that Sisko didn't call Ops, he called Reese, who was standing

outside. Obviously Sisko programmed the doors to pop open as soon as he paged Reese. Either that or he had Odo monitoring the conversation so the Changeling could open the doors from the Security office.

CONTINUITY AND PRODUCTION PROBLEMS

• Ziyal sure has changed since the last time we saw her! (She's played by a different actress.)

• At one point Sisko cooks a meal for Jake and Yates. Since the combination has never been tried before, both Jake and Yates are hesitant to sample the cuisine. Jake tells Yates to go first. She indicates with a disapproving grunt that he should go ahead. The shot then cuts to Sisko, and the closed captioning adds Jake saying, "Hey, I'm being polite—you're the guest." To which Yates replies, "'Guest, not guinea pig, Jake."

• To seize control of the station, Eddington stuns Kira. She appears to be standing straight when the phaser beam hits her chest. However, when the camera angle reverses, her legs are suddenly bent and she falls backward.

TRIVIA ANSWERS

1. Bajoran ratamba stew over spinach linguine.
2. Cargo Bay 17.

TO THE DEATH

Star Date: 49904.2

Returning from a mission with the *Defiant*, Sisko and crew find the station recovering from an assault by the Jem'Haddar. Without warning, a raiding party beamed onto the station from a commercial transport, stole several pieces of equipment, and escaped into the wormhole. Following the transport's ion trail, Sisko gives chase in the *Defiant*.

Soon the *Defiant* locates a damaged Jem'Haddar warship. With a Security detail nearby, Sisko beams on board seven survivors: six Jem'Haddar soldiers and their Vorta field supervisor, Weyoun. Weyoun explains that the Dominion has located an Iconian "gateway" on a distant world—a device that allows travel to other planets without the use of starships. (See the *NextGen* episode "Contagion.") However, the Jem'Haddar who escorted the Dominion scientists sent to investigate the gateway have rebelled and now are attempting to activate it on their own. Weyoun wants Sisko's help to destroy the gateway—though it is guarded by 150 Jem'Haddar renegades. Sisko agrees, realizing the threat to the Federation.

Trivia Questions

1. What was the name of Lela Dax's son?

2. What is the location of the Iconian gateway?

With a functioning gateway, the renegade Jem'Haddar might convince other Jem'Haddar to join them. Then no place in the galaxy would be safe from their incursions. The mission requires a fierce battle, but Sisko and company are victorious.

As the *Defiant* returns to the Alpha Quadrant, the Jem'Haddar whom Sisko rescued stay behind to finish off the renegades.

PLOT OVERSIGHTS

• Once the *Defiant* cloaks in the Gamma Quadrant and begins looking for the Jem'Haddar who attacked the station, Odo comments that he's surprised something like this hasn't happened sooner. (Hear, hear. Me too!) He says that being at the edge of the wormhole makes DS9 a tempting target. Sisko responds that he wishes the *Defiant* could guard the station twenty-six hours a day. Worf disagrees, mumbling that it would be a mistake to put the *Defiant* on guard duty. O'Brien comments that Worf might feel different if he had family living on the station. Worf then retorts that adopting a "siege mentality" is ultimately self-defeating. A siege men-

374

tality?! Didn't Odo just remind everyone that the station sits at the edge of the wormhole? A wormhole, I might add, that represents the *only* avenue whereby the Jem'Haddar can attack the Alpha Quadrant. In other words, DS9 is the extreme forward position—the front line of defense—hard against an aggressive foe who has pledged to destroy the Federation; a foe who has already demonstrated its propensity to viciously attack without warning. How is this a "siege mentality"? The station isn't all there is of the Federation. We've seen other Federation starships exploring the galaxy—sometimes even in the Gamma Quadrant. DS9 just happens to be a crucial piece of real estate. It makes *perfect* sense for it to have constant protection. (Personally, I think Worf is just barking about "siege mentality" because he's worried that Sisko will restrict him to flying the *Defiant* in circles around the station, and that just doesn't seem very "warrior-like" to our favorite Klingon! Of course, if I wasn't a nitpicker and I actually dealt in reality, I might suggest that this dialogue is an attempt by the creators to justify the fact that Starfleet constantly—and unnecessarily—leaves the station exposed to attack. I might also suggest that this little exchange could indicate an underlying structural problem with the show. But since I don't deal in reality…)

• This episode reminds us several times that the Jem'Haddar are addicted to a substance known as Ketracel-White. Without it, they go into withdrawal and die. Watching the show, I kept wondering, "How are the renegades supplying themselves with this drug?" The end of the episode might provide a clue. The leader of the Jem'Haddar whom Sisko rescued is named Omet'iklan. After destroying the gateway, Omet'iklan kills Weyoun, and a Jem'Haddar soldier takes the Ketracel-White generator used by Weyoun to supply the Jem'Haddar with the drug earlier in the episode. This would seem to indicate that the remaining Jem'Haddar will use the Ketracel-White generator to keep themselves supplied. Let's back up a minute, though. The whole point of addicting the Jem'Haddar to the Ketracel-White is to control them and ensure their loyalty. The *only* way to do that would be to tightly regulate the supply of Ketracel-White. In fact, we do see in this episode that Weyoun orders the manufacture of the Ketracel-White from the generator and then must provide a handprint to access it. This seems reasonable. As intelligent as the Founders and the Vorta appear to be, one would think that they would rig these Ketracel-White generators with some very, very sophisticated theft-deterrent systems. Otherwise you could very easily end up with squadrons of Jem'Haddar with their own generators, and you would lose control. So I ask again: How are the renegades supplying themselves with Ketracel-White?

• Supposedly the *Defiant* can't attack the gateway from orbit because it's made of solid neutronium. I'm told by several nitpickers that even a teaspoonful of neutronium weighs *a lot* (like…as much as the Earth)! It boggles the mind to think that an entire building could be made of the stuff and those standing around the building wouldn't be crushed by the gravitational effects.

• Also, isn't it just supremely considerate of the renegade Jem'Haddar to wear black vests so that Starfleet personnel can tell the good guys from the bad guys?

CHANGED PREMISES

• In this episode we learn that the Jem'Haddar do not sleep, do not eat, never relax, and have no women. (Bummer, dude.) Why then does the young Jem'Haddar child in "The Abandoned" say, "I need food"? Do the Jem'Haddar stop eating once they are fully grown?

EQUIPMENT ODDITIES

• Just before the ground assault begins, O'Brien hands out weapons to everyone on the teams. At one point, Omet'iklan appears with his men. O'Brien hesitates, but Sisko nods his approval and O'Brien starts handing them fully charged Type III phaser rifles as well. Two items here. When O'Brien hands the first phaser rifle to a Jem'Haddar soldier, you can see that there is another phaser rifle resting directly above it on the wall. However, when the shot returns to O'Brien, this second phaser rifle has disappeared! (I bet the inventory auditors love it when that happens.) Also, Omet'iklan comes to the weapons giveaway with four other Jem'Haddar. That makes five if I've done my math correctly (Omet'iklan killed the sixth earlier in the episode.) The odd thing is this. O'Brien gives the Jem'Haddar only three rifles, yet later we see that *all* of the Jem'Haddar have them—as does everyone else on the

assault teams. Where did the other two rifles come from? Was someone else handing out rifles as well?

• I supposed I could point out that the Iconian gateway in "Contagion" *(TNG)* didn't put out a dampening field because Picard fired his phaser. But maybe the one in this episode is an older version with thinner shielding or something. (Shortly after arriving on the planet's surface, Sisko and company discover that their rifles don't work. The episode seems to suggest that it's because of the gateway.)

CONTINUITY AND PRODUCTION PROBLEMS

• A Jem'Haddar soldier named Toman'torax—once on board the *Defiant*—takes great delight in taunting Worf. Our favorite Klingon finally has enough and backhands Toman'torax. (This nit may be a bit difficult to follow, so pay attention out there!) Toman'torax swings his left fist at Worf. Worf ducks and plows into Toman'torax (let's call him "Tom" for short). At this point, Worf has his left shoulder in Tom's left armpit, and Worf's head is against Tom's back because Tom is turned sideways. The shot changes and suddenly Worf has his *right* shoulder in Tom's stomach and Worf's head is in under Tom's *right* arm because Tom is now facing Worf. Somehow, in the flicker of an eye, Worf manages to leap to the other side of his opponent's body. Gotta admire those Klingon reflexes.

TRIVIA ANSWERS
1. Ahjess.
2. Vandros IV.

THE QUICKENING

Star Date: unknown

En route to a biosurvey in the Gamma Quadrant, Kira, Dax, and Bashir intercept a distress call from the Teplan System just outside Dominion territory. They find a planet ravaged two centuries ago by the Jem'Haddar. But not only did the Dominion send the Jem'Haddar to destroy the inhabitants' infrastructure, they also infected the survivors with a virus to make them an example to others. The disease causes lesions that turn red when a person "quickens." A short time later, the person dies in agony. Everyone on the planet is born with the lesions, and no one can tell when the quickening will come for them.

Bashir goes to work, attempting to find a cure for the disease. Within a week he develops an antigen. Unfortunately, the Dominion designed the virus to mutate in the presence of electromagnetic fields. Bashir's own diagnostic instruments kill everyone he attempts to treat. After this, the inhabitants reject Bashir's help—all except a pregnant woman named Ekoria, who hopes to live to see the birth of her baby. With Bashir's help,

Trivia Questions

1. What is the name of the woman Bashir and Dax bring to Trevean's hospital?

2. For where do the Jem'Haddar set course after leaving the Kendi System?

she does. And though Ekoria dies shortly after birth, her son is born without lesions due to the antigen injections. While it is not a cure, it does give the inhabitants hope that the next generation will live free of the virus.

RUMINATIONS

This episode features some beautiful new matte paintings for the surface of the planet in the Teplan System. Also, I know this next comment is very tacky and uncalled for and insensitive and qualifies for just about every other derogatory label I can imagine. But the first time I watched this episode and saw the guy pushing the cart with a recently deceased body in it, all I could think of was, "Bring out your dead. Bring out your dead." (From Monty Python's The Search for the Holy Grail.)

PLOT OVERSIGHTS

• Sometimes Starfleet medical practices mystify me. Bashir and Dax beam down to the planet. A woman who has quickened approaches in great pain, asking to be taken to Trevean's "hospital" (in reality, an assisted-suicide center). Dax runs off to find help. Bashir whips out a hypo and injects the woman with a painkiller. Dax returns with transportation. Bashir says the woman isn't responding well to the medication because her physiology is so different. Note that Bashir makes the determination that the woman's physiology is different *after* he injects her. He doesn't even do a tricorder scan before he hypos her! He just waltzes up to an alien humanoid on a previously unencountered world and starts shooting her full of drugs! Does this seem right?

• One of the men who die because of exposure to the EM fields of Bashir's instruments is named Epran. When his heart stops, Bashir rushes over and begins giving him heart massage by pressing Epran's chest. Struggling to save Epran's life, Bashir shouts, "Breathe! Breathe!" Now, I'm no doctor, but I don't think pounding on someone's chest is sufficient to get him or her to breathe. I believe you have to do mouth-to-mouth resuscitation as well. (Granted, I can understand Bashir's hesitancy to engage in this, given the lesions all over the guy's face, but still...)

CHANGED PREMISES

• Never one to let a dead horse decay without giving it one last *kick,* I suppose I should—once again—mention that Third Talak'Talan in "The Jem'Haddar" wasn't real keen on the idea of the Federation coming through the wormhole into the Gamma Quadrant, but apparently the senior staff on DS9 isn't bothered by offending the Dominion (as evidenced by this episode).

• And speaking of whacking the Dominion hive (see "Trek Silliness"), at one point Kira prepares to leave orbit when Bashir says he wants to try to find a cure for the disease. Kira suggests that they return to DS9 and advise Starfleet. She asserts that Starfleet will organize a relief mission to the planet. Earlier in the episode we learned that the planet resides in a system just outside Dominion space. Would Starfleet really send a starship to assist these people after the Dominion singled them out for punishment?

EQUIPMENT ODDITIES

• With just a bit of modification, the center portion of the quantum stasis field generator used by Garak in "The Die Is Cast" reappears in this episode as a protein sequencer.

• Bashir must be taking magic lessons from Dax (first seen performing magic at the beginning of "Rejoined"). Needing tissue samples from individuals who have already quickened, Bashir tries to win the inhabitants' trust by healing a young boy's broken arm. At the beginning of the sequence, Bashir has his medical kit slung over his shoulder. You can clearly see the end of his medical tricorder resting in a slot at the very top of the kit, with the opening for the slot built into the left side. The camera angle changes. Bashir walks over and sets down the kit on a concrete abutment. His hands are empty. Now the slot is empty as well. Bashir opens the lower half of the kit, reaches behind himself, reaches forward, and suddenly has a tricorder in his hand. It's as if the tricorder wasn't in the kit to begin with but was waiting for him, and was hidden somewhere on the abutment. Yet, a moment earlier, the tricorder was in his kit as Bashir stood *several feet* away from the abutment. How did he do this? (I'm usually pretty good at figuring out magic tricks, but I've watched the tape several times and I'm not too proud to say that Bashir has me stumped!)

• Near the end of the episode, Kira and Dax return to DS9. Bashir stays behind to do what he can to help Ekoria stay alive until she delivers her baby. Leaving the runabout, Bashir steps onto the transporter pad with six containers next to him. Apparently the transporter didn't think he needed all that junk because he materializes on the planet with only four!

CONTINUITY AND PRODUCTION PROBLEMS

• Comparatively speaking, this episode is loaded with closed-captioned dialogue that's either changed or deleted altogether from the audio track. After trading her hair clip for transportation to Trevean's hospital, Dax tells Bashir, "I gave her my clip," but the closed captioning reads, "You'd be amazed what they'll do for a latinum hair clip."

• Then, a bit later, as Bashir and Dax silently work on isolating the virus, the closed captioning reads: "If I adjust the polarization filter, I might be able to increase the contrast in this tissue sample." (Presumably this was Bashir speaking, followed by Dax's reply.) "Maybe I could devise some kind of photoactive marker." (Personally, I found this to be a very satisfying cut. I've never been a big fan of "tech-nobabble as dialogue"—also known as TAD in nitpicker jargon.)

• *Then*, after Bashir heals the boy's broken arm, Trevean retorts that fixing a broken arm and curing the blight are two different things, but the close captioning prefixes his comments with "Don't be deceived."

• *And then*, after Ekoria makes a snide comment about not wanting to drink a pungent concoction that Bashir prepares, the closed captioning has the good doctor saying, "Ha-ha-ha."

• *And finally,* at the end of the program, as Trevean holds up the healthy newborn for all to see, the closed captioning reads, "Come, come. Take a look for yourself. It's a miracle. See what the doctor has done for the baby—for all of us. Take a close look. There's not a mark on this child. Come—take a look at our future."

TRIVIA ANSWERS
1. Norva.
2. The Obatta Cluster.

BODY PARTS

Star Date: unknown

When Quark returns to Ferenginar, an annual insurance physical reports that he has Dorek syndrome—a rare Ferengi disease with no cure—and only six or seven days to live. Since Quark owes a considerable amount of debt, Rom suggests that he sell the vacuum-desiccated remains of his body on the Ferengi futures exchange. Amazingly enough, an anonymous buyer bids 500 bars of latinum. Quark jumps at the offer and only afterward learns from Bashir that the doctor on Ferenginar made a mistake. Quark doesn't have Dorek syndrome. The problem is Brunt. (See "Family Business" and "Bar Association.") He's the one who purchased Quark's remains, and he intends to see that Quark honors the contract. Otherwise Brunt will seize all of Quark's assets, kick his mother out onto the street on Ferenginar, and ensure that Quark is banned from all contact with other Ferengi. Eventually Quark does break the contract and Brunt does seize all his assets. However, Sisko and company come to Quark's rescue—restocking

the bar with station furniture, a case of Alvanian brandy, and a set of ugly glasses.

Meanwhile, Keiko is injured while on a trip to the Gamma Quadrant, and Bashir must transplant the O'Briens' baby into Kira, who will carry it to term.

Trivia Questions

1. Where did Keiko want to go on Bajor to get a fungus sample?

2. Name three Ferengi relatives to whom Quark owes money.

RUMINATIONS

At one point Quark dreams that he goes to the Divine Treasury (Ferengi Heaven) and meets with Gint—the first grand nagus. The two get into a discussion about the Rules of Acquisition. I think somebody was having a little fun when they wrote this discussion. Quark claims that Gint of all people can't expect Quark to break the rules. Gint wonders why not. After all, they're just written in a book. "A bunch of us just made them up," Gint says. (Would this be a reference to the creators?) Quark wonders if Gint is saying that the rules don't matter. Gint replies that they do matter, that's why they're a best-seller. (Coincidentally, there is a book available from Pocket Books called The Ferengi Rules of Acquisition, and I would imagine it's a best-seller!) Gint goes on to explain that the rules are just guide posts. Quark wonders why they were called rules. Gint responds by asking who would buy a book called *Suggestions for Acquisition*. Quark realizes that calling them "rules" was a marketing ploy. (No doubt!) Gint agrees, quoting Rule of Acquisition 239: Never be afraid to mislabel a product. (I find this last comment a scream, given that—the last I heard—the copy of The Ferengi Rules of Acquisition *that I purchased for $6.00 only had 70 out of 285 rules, generously spaced over 84 pages!*)

PLOT OVERSIGHTS

• What is it about this station? You've got Nog, who's an outcast from Ferengi society. You've got Garak, who's an outcast from Cardassian society. You've got Rom, who's an outcast from Ferengi society. You've got Odo, who's an outcast from Changeling society. You've got Worf, who's an outcast from Klingon society. You've got Dax, who was a hairs breadth away from being an outcast from Trill society. And now *Quark* is an outcast from Ferengi society. (It's almost as if the creators believe that everyone should become like us.)

CHANGED PREMISES

• I don't suppose I really *need* to bring this up again, but the level of arrogance of the senior staff on the station has surprised me yet again. Not only are they not concerned about offending the Dominion (see "The Jem'Haddar."), they also take a *pregnant* woman along with them into the Gamma Quadrant.

• Several times the episode men-

tions that Quark is offering a complete set of 52 discs of his remains. Either Quark plans to have significantly bigger portions in the discs that he is selling of himself, or Plegg was one *big* Ferengi. You may recall that Odo stopped Quark from selling discs of Plegg at the beginning of "The Alternate" because Odo had discovered that Plegg was still alive. Astonished, Quark protests, claiming that he was a victim of fraud, that he had *five thousand* pieces of Plegg in his storeroom. (In case you are wondering, "pieces" and "discs" are used interchangeably.)

EQUIPMENT ODDITIES

• I wonder what happened to the communications relay that the joint Cardassian/Bajoran/Starfleet team placed at the mouth of the wormhole in the Gamma Quadrant during "Destiny"? Supposedly that relay would allow ships in the Gamma Quadrant to communicate with DS9. Yet, in this episode, Dax reports that "something" is coming through the wormhole as the runabout that carries Kira, Bashir, and Keiko appears. Doesn't the relay have sensors to detect the approach of a ship? Couldn't it "relay" a message from the runabout so that the DS9 infirmary would be ready to receive Kira and Keiko *before* the runabout enters the Alpha Quadrant? (I would remind you that Bashir contacts the station shortly after the runabout comes out of the wormhole, so at least the short-range transmitters are working.)

• And speaking of the runabout, Worf identifies it as the *Volga*. Ever since the beginning of the series, the station has had three runabouts. As of "The

Sons of Mogh," those three runabouts were: the *Rio Grande,* the *Rubicon,* and the *Yukon*. Did DS9 inherit another runabout? Or did one of the other runabouts get destroyed and the *Volga* is the replacement? (If another runabout was destroyed, you can bet that it wasn't the *Rio Grande*; that runabout seems to enjoy a charmed existence. It was one of the original three! If you are interested in reading more about the runabouts of the station, see "The Damage Tote Board.")

• I suppose it would be useless to mention that if the runabout had harness restraints, Keiko might still be carrying her baby (since Bashir reports that an explosion slammed her into a bulkhead).

• To discuss the methods that Garak might use to kill him, Quark meets with the Cardassian tailor. After Garak snaps the neck of a Quark hologram and leaves it face down in a plate of food, the real Quark asks Garak to get rid of the body because it's bothering him. Garak obliges, instructing the computer to remove the corpse. Surprisingly enough, the plate of food disappears as well. (It must realize that Quark is offended by half-eaten meals.)

CONTINUITY AND PRODUCTION PROBLEMS

• In the first shot of the bar, Quark descends a staircase. Two Starfleet officers sit in the foreground of the shot. The closed captioning appears to have a comment by one of these individuals. It reads, "Hey, how are you? Thanks for ordering me a drink."

• Just before the bid for five hundred bars of latinum arrives at the station, Quark walks by a bookcase in his quarters. The top shelf on the right side contains a round cylinder. Keep your eyes on it. After the bid comes in, Quark walks over to his desk, and the cylinder has moved noticeably to the left! (This *apparently* without anyone touching it. I suspect a Changeling.)

• During the final scene in the bar, the camera begins a wide-angle sweep of the room, eventually resting on Quark as Rom descends a staircase. The camera starts this sweep on the wall at the end of the bar nearest the main entrance and dips down to pan over the room. As it dips down, you can see the moving shadow of what appears to be a reflective panel attached to the camera.

• And speaking of this camera pan, it ends with Quark sitting on the step that leads to the raised area that used to contain the Dabo table. Then the scene cuts to a closeup of Quark, pans down, and Quark sits on the actual raised area.

• And while we're on the subject of the camera pan, it clearly shows a chair directly behind Quark as he dejectedly sits on the step. Rom comes in and comments that "they" took everything. Quark agrees, saying that Brunt even wants him to send the shirt he wears in the morning. Well…"they" didn't take *everything*. They left the chair! (A chair that seems to disappear in subsequent closeups. Hmmm.)

TRIVIA ANSWERS
1. The cliffs of Undalar.
2. Moogie, Uncle Gorad, and Cousin Gaila.

BROKEN LINK

Star Date: 49962.4

When Odo collapses in Garak's shop, Bashir finds that the station's resident Changeling is losing his ability to retain a solid shape. Bashir has so little knowledge of Changeling physiology that Odo admits the obvious: He must return to his people, the Founders of the Dominion, to seek their help. Since the location of the Founders' new home world is unknown (see "The Die Is Cast"), Sisko flies into Dominion space—without the *Defiant*'s cloak engaged —all the while transmitting a plea for help. The Jem'Haddar soon arrive with a Changeling who tells Odo that he must return to the Great Link (see "The Search, Part II") or he will die. The Changeling also advises Odo that when he merges with the Great Link, the rest of the Changelings will judge him for killing another Changeling during the events of "The Adversary" and they will punish him as they see fit.

Even so, Odo joins with the Great Link, submitting to his people's punishment. They find him guilty of harming another Changeling and turn him into a "solid," a human. Back on the station, a distraught Odo recalls that during his time in the link, he sensed some of the Founders' plans for conquering the Alpha Quadrant. Specifically, he remembers that Gowron—the head of the Klingon Empire—is a Changeling.

RUMINATIONS

There's a wonderful little homage near the end of this episode that I noticed but almost didn't include in this review. Then Vicki Strzembosz of Oak Lawn, IL, mentioned it in her comments and I thought if two nitpickers noticed, no doubt, others would as well! It occurs as the Defiant transports Sisko, Bashir, and now-human Odo back to the ship. Odo lies on his back in the foreground. Bashir kneels beside him. Sisko stands near the center of the screen with the female Changeling to his left. She looks at Odo. Just before dematerializing, Odo raises his left hand—index finger extended—toward the female Changeling while she stares without any response. Does Odo's pose remind anyone else of the section of the Sistine Chapel that depicts God stretching out to animate man? Some very nice parallels here.

Trivia Questions

1. When does Odo walk by Chalan Aroya's Celestial Café each morning?

2. Whom does Odo suspect that Garak killed by staging a transporter "accident"?

383

(Except, of course, in this instance, "god" couldn't give a rip about the new creation!)

PLOT OVERSIGHTS

• How the mighty have fallen! This episode begins with Garak—former operative for the Obsidian Order; at one time closer than anyone else to the head of that same order, Enabran Tain; spy par excellence; assassin extraordinaire—playing matchmaker, trying to fix up Odo with a Bajoran woman who's just moved to the station. And if that weren't bad enough, Garak actually tries to report a "crime" to Odo: the fact that Odo didn't ask the woman out on a date. (Ick, pthooey, ick.)

• After his attack in Garak's shop, Odo collapses to the floor, apparently unconscious yet still in his humanoid form. Doesn't it seem reasonable that Odo should revert to his natural liquid state under these conditions? (Of course, the same comment could be made for the episode "Vortex" after Odo is knocked unconscious by a rock.)

• The creators finally come out and say it in this episode. They finally have Bashir comment that when Odo shape-shifts, he changes not only his density but also his mass. (You may recall that this fact has puzzled me more than once in this *Guide*.) Now, density I can understand. (As I said in "Past Prologue," it is possible for Odo to become a rat; he would just be one hot and heavy rat.) But I'm still trying to figure out how Odo would change his *mass*. The molecules have to go somewhere. The creators have never given us any indication that Odo's

basic matter is any different from ours. (Bashir calls Odo's makeup "Changeling protoplasm," not "protomatter," or even something like "transmutational mogrificating bifibrilactile molecular mush.") So does he supposedly phase a portion of his body into subspace when he shapeshifts? (Not that we have to worry about this anymore, given the events in this episode!)

• In discussing the trip to the Dominion, Bashir comments that the *Defiant* will attract attention as soon as it flies into the "Dominion's *air*space." Interesting choice of words, given that there is no air in space!

CHANGED PREMISES

• Just before the *Defiant* leaves for the Gamma Quadrant, Garak shows up at the docking port, asking to come along. Worf—on the bridge—grouses that he doesn't want any Cardassian spies on board. Sisko agrees to talk with Garak but has him delivered to the mess hall instead of brought to the bridge. If I didn't know better, I would think that Sisko was trying to keep Garak off the bridge so he wouldn't be exposed to sensitive technology. Of course, that doesn't explain why Sisko had Garak on the bridge of the *Defiant* during "Second Skin"! (I'm thinking that Sisko is just posturing for Worf's benefit.)

• Wow, those Changelings evidently have been doing that wild-and-crazy-linkin' thing and making lots o' little Changelings. The last time we saw the Great Link (in "The Search, Part II"), it looked like a small lake. In this episode the Great Link stretches to the horizon in at least two directions, like a massive ocean!

EQUIPMENT ODDITIES

• In the early part of this episode, Sisko replays a message the Federation has received from Gowron. It features a running clock in the corner of the screen. Running clocks are always fun for nitpickers, and this clock doesn't disappoint. Just before the first cutaway for reaction shots, the clock reads "1:40:29" and some hundredths of a second in change. After thirteen seconds we return to the recording and the clock reads "1:40:30," as if virtually no time has elapsed. By the next cutaway the clock reads "1:40:38." Yet when we return to it the clock has somehow gone backward in time to read "1:40:36."

• I'm always amazed that the transporter and/or transporter chief know exactly whom to beam. After Odo is turned into a solid, a Changeling approaches from the Great Link. She tells Sisko to take Odo and go. Sisko slaps his communicator, contacts Dax, and then says, "Three to beam up." Somehow, whoever is running the transporter knows to pick Sisko, Bashir,

and Odo, even though Sisko has not told the *Defiant* that Odo is now a human and not a Changeling. In other words, the transporter operator looks at the console and sees two Starfleet combadge signals, a naked guy, and a Changeling. Now, I suppose the transporter chief could just guess and beam up the three humans, but wouldn't he or she be expecting a Changeling to return? Or was Dax eavesdropping on the conversation?

• One wonders if any of the Starfleet officers had the presence of mind to sneak a tricorder scan out of a few of the *Defiant*'s windows so that Starfleet could later identify the location of the Changelings' new home world. (When Kevin Loughlin of Kitchener, Ontario, suggested this, I thought, "Now, there's a thought!")

CONTINUITY AND PRODUCTION PROBLEMS

• I believe the external graphic showing the *Defiant* heading for the wormhole comes from the title sequence.

TRIVIA ANSWERS
1. 0937.
2. Romulan subcommander Ustard.

TRIATHLON TRIVIA ON PEOPLE GROUPS

MATCH THE GROUP TO THE DESCRIPTION TO THE EPISODE

GROUP	DESCRIPTION	EPISODE
1. Andorians	A. An officer threw a drink in Sisko's face	a. "A Man Alone"
2. Arbazan	B. Can't see red or orange	b. "The Adversary"
3. Argilians	C. Their ship captain traded for yamok sauce	c. "Armageddon Game"
4. Argosians	D. Stole the sword of Kahless	d. "Battlelines"
5. Betazoids	E. They supply weapons to the Circle	e. "The Circle"
6. Bolians	F. Dax makes Sisko look like one	f. "Dax"
7. Breen	G. Enslaved survivors of the Ravinok	g. "The Die Is Cast"
8. Delavians	H. It's illegal to have their crystals	h. "Distant Voices"
9. Dopterians	I. Kira's eyes shine like their fire diamonds	i. "Dramatis Personae"
10. El Aurians	J. Makers of great chocolates	j. "Emissary"
11. Elaysians	K. Their bolites turn people different colors	k. "Explorers"
12. Fanalians	L. Known for their massage facilities	l. "Fascination"
13. Flaxians	M. They can suffer from Zanthi fever	m. "The Forsaken"
14. Granarians	N. One comes to murder Garak	n. "Hippocratic Oath"
15. Haligians	O. Lense mistook Bashir for one	o. "The Homecoming"
16. Hur'Q	P. Their tonic can cure a "chest cold"	p. "Improbable Cause"
17. Jem'Haddar	Q. Li tried to stow away with them	q. "Indiscretion"
18. Karemma	R. Love to play games	r. "Invasive Procedures"
19. Kellerun	S. They breathe hydrogen	s. "The Jem'Haddar"
20. Kibberians	T. Makers of beautiful silk	t. "Life Support"
21. Kobheerians	U. Their horn flies swarm	u. "The Maquis, Part II"
22. Kressari	V. Martus's race	v. "Melora"
23. Letheans	W. Odo learned their neck pinch	w. "Move Along Home"
24. Lissepians	X. Their transport carried dolamide	x. "Paradise Lost"
25. Lothars	Y. One tried to steal Lwaxana's brooch	y. "Progress"
26. Riseans	Z. Dax is one	z. "Rejoined"
27. Senarians	AA. Oppressed the Skrreeans	aa. "Rivals"
28. T'Rogorans	BB. Paid Quark a surcharge for cargo inspection	bb. "Rules of Acquisition"
29. Tallonians	CC. Ruled by an autarch	cc. "Sanctuary"
30. Tholians	DD. Sexually repressed according to Bolians	dd. "The Search, Part I"
31. Trill	EE. Their tonic water calms the nerves	ee. "Second Skin"

32. Tygarians	FF. Soldiers for the Dominion	ff. "Starship Down"
33. Tzenkethi	GG. Inhabitants of a low-gravity world	gg. "The Sword of Kahless"
34. Valerians	HH. Known for their tongue sauce	hh. "The Way of the Warrior
35. Vayans	II. Dax gave their perfume to Kahn	
36. Vorta	JJ. Telepathic assassins	
37. Vulcans	KK. The Karemmas' Dominion contact	
38. Wadi	LL. Known for their good egg broth	
39. Xepolite	MM. Used harvesters as weapons	
40. Yalosians	NN. Demilitarized zone weapons smugglers	

SCORING

(BASED ON NUMBER OF CORRECT ANSWERS)

0-10	Normal
11-19	Good
20-29	You certainly know your groups
30-40	Master Groupie

GROUPS ANSWER KEY: **1.** O k **2.** DD m **3.** L g **4.** A f **5.** M l **6.** EE x **7.** G q **8.** J p **9.** Y m **10.** V aa **11.** GG v **12.** P k **13.** N p **14.** K a **15.** HH t **16.** D gg **17.** FF s **18.** BB ff **19.** MM c **20.** I bb **21.** F ee **22.** E e **23.** JJ h **24.** C y **25.** S v **26.** II z **27.** LL r **28.** AA cc **29.** H n **30.** T hh **31.** Z j **32.** Q o **33.** CC b **34.** X i **35.** U d **36.** KK dd **37.** W x **38.** R w **39.** NN u **40.** B p

INDEX

A

"Abandoned, The," 63, 125, 214-216, 296, 305, 349, 358, 359, 376
"Accession," 355-357
Adams, Douglas, 128, 132, 316
Adred, 278
"Adversary, The," 63, 95, 104, 192, 200, 228, 247, 285-289, 295, 297, 311, 321, 358, 383, 386
Ahjess, 376
Ah-Kel, 52-55
Akorem Laan, 355-357
Akrem, Lorit, 125, 306
Albeni meditation crystal, 32
Albino, 162-164, 166, 188, 223, 311
Aldara, 16
Alexander, 299
Alixus, 144-147, 188
"All Good Things," 162, 185, 302
Alpha Quadrant, 45, 48, 177, 199, 200, 201, 381
Alsia, 133
"Alternate, The," 37, 80, 134-136, 142, 160, 268, 358, 381
Altovar, 258, 259
Altrina, 125
Anara, 74
Andevian II, 74, 228
Andorians, 386
Anetra, 148
"Angel One," 32, 38
Apren, Kalem, 279
Aquino, Ensign, 84
Arawath colony, 173

Arbazans, 72, 386
"Arena," 277
Argilians, 386
Argosians, 386
Argrathi, 363, 364
Arjin, 151-155, 191, 357
Arlin, Lysia, 125, 150
"Armageddon Game," 37, 137-139, 160, 161, 164, 188, 228, 331, 386
Arriaga, Lieutenant, 337
Ashrock, 125
Assan, Dakora, 267
Audubon Park, 335
Awa, Drofo, 171
Azetbur, 244
Azin, Minister, 308

B

"Babel," 21-24, 101, 228, 246, 316, 327, 358, 359
Bajor, 3, 5, 10, 13, 19, 21, 35, 36, 49, 50, 64-66, 86, 91, 94, 98-99, 127, 179-181, 195-197, 205, 228, 243, 244, 246, 248, 269, 279-281, 286, 347-348
Bajor: Terok Nor episodes, 88
Bajoran System, 346-348, 350
Bajor VIII, 348
Bakrinium, 324
"Balance of Power," 319
Balosnee VI, 228
Baltrim, 66, 108-109
"Bar Association," 283, 352-354, 380
Bareil, Vedek, 62, 82-85,

94, 96-98, 100, 159, 179-181, 230-232, 243, 244, 280, 372
Barrett-Roddenberry, Majel, 357
"Battle, The," 116
"Battlelines," 56-58, 125, 159-161, 305, 386
Bek, Prylar, 179
Belar, Joran, 207-210, 282, 284, 289, 309
Belar, Yolad, 208, 210
Bell, Gabriel, 234, 236, 240, 242
Bell Riots, 234, 237, 240, 314
Benial, Gul, 213
Benteen, Commander, 335
"Best of Both Worlds, The, Part 2," 3, 6, 8, 9, 42, 92, 113, 146, 334
Betar Prize, 302
Betazoids, 370, 386
B'Etor, 13-16, 359
"Big Good-bye, The," 69, 331
Bilecki, Lieutenant, 101, 125
Bilitirum, 13, 14, 16
"Blood Oath," 159, 162-164, 166, 223, 228, 310, 311, 370
Blue Horizon, 228
Boday, 62, 125
"Body Parts," 380-382
Boheeka, 172-174, 359
Bokai, Buck, 67-69
Bok'Nor, 165, 167
Bolians, 365, 386
"Booby Trap," 335
Boone, 182, 183
Borath, 125, 201
Boreth, 324
Borg, 3-5, 9, 42, 123, 153, 215, 256, 334

Boru, Brian, 354
Boslic, 349
Brahms, Dr. Leah, 335
Brax, 228
Breen, 306-308, 386
Brentalia, 49
Broik, 125
"Broken Link," 383-385
"Brothers," 39
Brunt, 277, 278, 352, 380
Bryma colony, 171
Brynner, Chris, 234, 235, 239, 242

C

Callinon System, 198
Calondia IV, 228
Calondon, 97
Campor III, 228
"Captain's Holiday," 29
"Captive Pursuit," 25-28, 33, 53, 61, 63, 80, 119, 125, 160, 188, 334, 358, 359, 365
Cardassia III, 228
Cardassia IV, 91, 92, 228
Cardassian Outpost 47, 191
Cardassians, 3, 7-11, 13, 19, 21, 30, 31, 54, 65, 73, 74, 78, 79, 93, 94, 98, 106-109, 117, 137, 151, 155, 156, 165-173, 175, 182-184, 201, 219, 225-227, 243, 244, 246, 248, 250, 268-270, 275, 276, 281, 293-296, 301, 306, 307, 326, 341-345, 360, 361, 370
"Cardassians," 106-109, 113, 125, 136, 139, 164, 183, 359
Cardassia Prime, 228
Carrington Award, 252
Cartwright, Admiral, 335
"Catspaw," 46
Celestial Temple, 3, 9, 10, 59, 82, 83, 248
Cestus III, 228, 277

"Chain of Command, Part 1," 54
"Chain of Command, Part 2," 184, 226
Changelings, 52, 53, 63, 195, 197, 199-201, 214, 245-247, 268, 285-289, 295, 297, 332-334, 336-338, 383-385
"Chase, The," 9, 113-114, 370
Chekote, Admiral, 96
Ches'sarro, 119
"Child, The," 370
Children of Tarma, 37
Ch'Pok, 360-362
"Circle, The," 62, 94-97, 107, 125, 149, 167, 180, 252, 326, 327, 358, 386
Circle separatist group, 91-92, 94, 95, 98, 106, 107, 167
"City on the Edge of Forever, The," 236, 237, 241
"Civil Defense," 62, 125, 160, 217-220, 243
Classic Star Trek, 110, 236, 241, 261, 263, 312, 364
"Code of Honor," 202
"Collaborator, The," 63, 179-181, 222, 280
Colyus, 148-150
"Coming of Age," 314
"Contagion," 334, 374, 376
Corvan gilvos, 49
Croden, 7, 52-55
"Crossfire," 243, 340-342, 349
"Crossover," 175-178, 205, 261-262, 263, 264, 366
Crusher, Dr. Beverly, 36, 104, 259, 281, 311
Crusher, Wesley, 314, 337

D

Dahkur province, 279
Dakeen Monastery, 181
Dal'Rok, 59-61, 67
Danar, Gul, 14, 15

Daneeka, 336
Darhe'el, Gul, 78-81
"Darmok," 37, 139
Data, 6, 9, 92, 168, 188, 244
"Datalore," 112
Davlos III, 228, 257
"Dax," 7, 15, 35-38, 50, 68, 69, 96, 123, 125, 154, 159, 228, 284, 327, 386
Dax, Curzon, 35-37, 68, 102, 123, 151, 152, 154, 162, 163, 166, 208, 282-284, 309
Dax, Torias, 284, 309
Day, Colonel, 98, 100
"Day of the Dove," 164, 370
Dayos IV, 228
Defiant, 62, 112, 125, 160, 188, 191, 195-198, 200-202, 207, 208, 213, 223, 224, 225, 227, 230, 233, 235, 240, 249, 250, 268-271, 285-287, 289, 296, 297, 309, 310, 318-321, 326, 336-339, 347, 352, 360, 361, 366-368, 371, 374, 384, 385
"*Defiant*," 19, 160, 191, 224-227, 228, 249, 266, 274, 358, 359
Dejar, 249
Delavians, 386
Della Santina, Robert, 17, 125
Delvok, 114
Demilitarized zone (DMZ), 165-171, 226
Denorias Belt, 3, 273, 275
"Descent, Part II," 215
"Destiny," 63, 142, 160, 173, 174, 248-250, 258, 287, 298, 381
Deuridium, 39, 40
D'Ghor, 160, 203-206, 351
"Die is Cast, The," 160, 161, 200, 268-273, 285-287, 293, 298, 326, 332, 358, 378, 383, 386
"Disaster," 19, 32, 49, 183, 319, 355
"Distant Voices," 160, 258-260, 359, 386

D'jarras, 355-357
Doek, Romah, 93
Dominion, 185-188, 195-
197, 199, 200, 207-208,
221, 248, 254, 257, 266,
268, 269, 293, 295, 303,
319, 326, 333, 352, 378
Dopterians, 72, 267, 386
Doral, 19, 62, 221-223
Dorek syndrome, 380
Dorvan V, 166, 167
Dosi, 115, 116
Dozaria System, 306, 308
"Dramatis Personae," 75-
77, 86, 160, 228, 330,
358, 386
Draxman, Admiral, 125
Draylon II, 127, 228
"Drumhead, The," 9
"Duet," 78-82, 159, 213, 228
Dukat, Gul, 9, 62, 79, 80,
96, 106-109, 117, 118,
157, 165-166, 168-171,
174, 183, 217, 219, 220,
224-227, 269, 272, 273,
275, 276, 293, 296, 306-
308, 343-345, 372
Duonetic field, 144-145, 147
Duras, 322
Duras sisters, 13, 80
Durg, 43

E

Earth, 228, 313, 332-334,
336, 338314
Eddington, Lieutenant Com-
mander Michael, 195,
271, 288, 289, 311, 328-
331, 341, 371-373
Ee'Char, 363
Ekoria, 377, 379
Elaan, 110
"Elaan of Troyius," 110
Elasians, 110
El Aurians, 131, 386
Elaysians, 110, 386
"Elementary, My Dear
Data," 8

Elemspur Detention Center,
211, 212
Elig, Dekon, 21, 23
Emi, 63, 253
"Emissary," 3-12, 26, 31, 32,
35, 37, 54, 59, 61-63, 69,
73, 80, 84, 92, 96, 108,
117, 123, 125, 128, 153,
160, 205, 228, 232, 248,
251-252, 258, 275, 294,
296, 305, 325, 327, 332,
340, 347, 348, 355, 356,
358, 359, 386
"Emissary, The" (*Next/Gen*),
370
"Encounter at Farpoint," 145
"Enemy, The," 181
Ennis, 56, 57
"Ensign Ro," 9, 205
"Ensigns of Command," 34,
168
Entek, 211-213
Enterprise, 4, 6, 9, 74, 87,
145-147, 150, 153, 189,
195, 198, 225, 247, 286,
297, 325, 330, 334, 340,
354
Epran, 378
Epsilon 119, 121, 122
"Equilibrium," 62, 125, 152,
159, 207-210, 209-210,
282, 284, 309
Erib, 276
Eris, 185, 186, 188, 189,
197, 333, 353
"Errand of Mercy," 164, 322
"Ethics," 350, 362
Evek, Gul, 165, 182, 184
"Evolution," 259
"Explorers," 7, 65, 111, 122,
273-276, 282-283, 355,
386
"Ex Post Facto," 38, 363

F

"Facets," 11, 31, 34, 63, 68,
159, 209, 282-284, 289
Falow, 44, 45, 47

"Family," 4
"Family Business," 116,
160, 161, 191, 228, 277-
278, 283, 352, 380
Fanalians, 386
"Fascination," 63, 125, 159,
160, 228, 230-233, 341,
347, 359, 386
Fek'Ihri, 323
Fenna, 62, 121-123
Ferengi, 48-51, 72, 99, 115,
139, 197-198, 318-319
*Ferengi Rules of Acquisi-
tion, The,* 380, 381
Fermat's Last Theorem,
283
Ferris VI, 228
"Firstborn," 13
"First Contact," 38
"First Duty," 337-339
Flaxians, 386
"Force of Nature," 124, 197,
198, 227
"Forsaken, The," 60, 71-74,
77, 84, 100, 136, 159,
160, 219, 228, 267, 268,
341, 354, 358, 359, 386
"For the Cause," 371-373
Founders of the Dominion,
195, 196, 199, 201-202,
214, 215, 268, 269, 271-
272, 333, 375, 383
"Frame of Mind," 363
Frenchotte, 155
Frin, 125, 220
Frunalians, 10
Furel, 281

G

Gaila, 313
"Galaxy's Child," 335
Gallitepp, 78, 79
Galorda Prime, 360
Galorndon Core, 181
"Gambit, Part I," 42
Gamma Quadrant, 25-27,
29, 30, 45, 48, 52, 53, 56,
112, 115, 128, 142, 177,

187, 195, 196, 198, 221, 222, 227, 248, 270, 271, 287, 318, 323, 326, 352, 353
Ganges, 146, 160, 161
Garland, Nurse, 125
Gasko, 145, 146
Gemulon V, 147, 228
Gettor, 368
Ghemor, Iliana, 211, 213
Ghemor, Legate Tekeny, 211, 213
Gilora, 63, 160, 249, 250
Gint, 380-381
Gocke, Bill, 17
Goran'Agar, 303, 305
Gorn, 277
Gosheven, 168
Gowron, 11, 96, 203, 206, 293, 294, 298, 323, 348, 383, 384
Granarians, 386
Great Link, 383-385
Grem, Alenis, 125, 211
Grilka, 63, 203, 204, 206
Groumall, 345
G'Trok, 122, 125
Guinan, 131, 259
Gupta, Admiral, 143

H

Halanans, 121
Haligians, 386
Haneek, 127-130
Hanok, 318-319, 321
"Hard Time," 363-365
Harvesters, 137-139
"Heart of Glory," 163, 189
"Heart of Stone," 22, 62, 72, 125, 200, 245-247, 252, 288, 295, 358
Hedrikspool, 150
Helewa, Isam, 178
"Hero Worship," 307, 308
"Hide and Q," 135
"Hippocratic Oath," 192, 228, 303-305, 315, 349, 358, 386

Hitchiker's Guide to the Galaxy, The (Adams), 128, 132, 316
Hogue, 125, 156
Holem, Lenaris, 279
"Hollow Pursuits," 330
"Homecoming, The," 41, 91-93, 107, 123, 125, 136, 157, 159, 167, 173, 228, 349, 358, 359
"Homefront," 63, 99, 192, 319, 332-335, 359
"Home Soil," 123, 128
Hon'Tihl, 77
Hortak, 216
"Host, The," 7, 36, 37, 104, 136, 149, 223, 311
"House of Quark, The," 49, 63, 125, 160, 203-206, 208, 231, 297, 351, 359
Hovath, 59-61
Hudson, Commander Calvin, 165-171
Hur'Q, 322, 386
Hutet labor camp, 92

I

Ibudan, 17-20
"If Wishes Were Horses," 63, 67-70, 73, 100, 359
Ih'valla, 357
IKS *Drovana*, 351
Iloja of Prim, 250
Ilvian Proclamation, 181
"Improbable Cause," 159, 228, 266-267, 271, 285, 293, 358, 386
"Indiscretion," 63, 125, 306-308, 343, 386
Inglatu, 125
"Inheritance," 38
"Inner Light, The," 120, 363, 364
"In the Hands of the Prophets," 19, 63, 82-85, 96, 159, 305, 356, 359
"Invasive Procedures," 63, 102-105, 125, 154, 159,

208, 209, 219, 228, 232, 283, 310, 327, 358, 359, 386
Ishka, 277-278
Itamish III, 189

J

Jaheel, Captain, 21, 22
Janeway, Captain Kathryn, 255-256, 346
Japori II, 228
Jaresh-Inyo, 332-334, 336
Jaro Essa, Minister, 91, 93-95, 97, 180
Jasad, Gul, 11, 125
Jel, Oguy, 342
Jem'Haddar, 128, 132, 185-189, 195-197, 201, 225, 227, 268, 270, 271, 303-305, 318, 319, 326, 353, 374-377, 383, 386
"Jem'haddar, The," 118, 146, 185-189, 195, 221, 248, 298, 303, 304, 323, 326, 333, 353, 358, 359, 364, 378, 386
Jeraddo, 50, 66
Jeyal, 369, 370
Jimenez, Ensihn, 342
Jobel, 284
Joseph, 145
"Journey's End," 165, 166

K

Kag, Faren, 61
Kahless, 322-324
Kahlest, 362
Kahn, Lenara, 63, 284, 309-312
Kahn, Nilani, 125, 309
Kajada, Ty, 39, 40, 42
Kalla Nohra, 78, 79
Kang, 162, 164, 370
Karemma, 197-198, 318-319, 386

Karina, 257
Karn, Razka, 306, 308
Kaval, 81
Kaybok, 296
Keena, 66, 108
K'Ehleyr, 370
Kellerun, 137-139, 386
Kelly, Ensign, 100
Kendra Massacre, 179, 181
Kentanna, 127
Keogh, Captain, 187, 189, 198
Khefka IV, 102, 103, 228
Kibberians, 386
Kirk, Captain James, 146, 175, 236, 241, 261, 312, 322-323
Klaestron IV, 35-38, 228
Klingons, 11, 48, 53, 75, 76, 96, 102, 108, 113, 155, 162-164, 175, 203-206, 223, 293-299, 301, 311, 315, 322-324, 326, 343-350, 360-362, 370
Kobheerians, 267, 386
Kobliad, 39, 40
Kohn-Ma, 13, 15
Kolos, 125
Koloth, 162-164
Kolrami, Sirna, 308
Kor, 162-164, 322-324
Kora II, 228
Korena, 302
Korinas, 225, 226
Korma, 343, 344
Korvat colony, 164, 228
Kot, Fallit, 110-113
Kovat, Conservator, 182
Kozak, 160, 203-206
Krajensky, Ambassador, 285
Krax, 48-50, 160
Kressari, 94, 95, 167, 386
Krim, General, 98
Kronos, 322, 323
Kurill Prime, 189
Kurn, 346-347, 349-351

L

Laira, 93
Lakota, 332, 334, 336, 337, 339
Lang, Professor Natima, 156-158
Lapolis System, 12
Largo V, 228
Leanne, 63, 125
Leeta, 34, 274, 282-283
Leinster, King, 357
Lela, 284
Lense, Elizabeth, 7
Letheans, 160, 258-260, 386
Leyton, Admiral, 332-337
"Liaisons," 244
"Life Support," 63, 125, 159, 228, 243-244, 248, 255, 308, 386
Ligobis X, 124, 228
Ligon II, 201
Lissepians, 386
"Little Green Men," 125, 192, 228, 313-317, 327, 358-359
Locutus, 8, 9
"Loss, The," 308
Lothars, 386
Loval, 343, 345
Lovok, Colonel, 268-271
"Lower Decks," 54
Lunar V base, 98-99
Lupaza, 281
Lursa, 13-15, 359

M

Madred, Gul, 226
Magratheans, 130
Maihar'Du, 116, 251, 252
Makbar, Chief Archon, 183, 184
Malko, 125, 299
"Man Alone, A," 17-20, 28, 42, 49, 50, 63, 72, 83, 125, 152, 209, 222, 358, 359, 386
Maquis, 19, 165-167, 169-171, 182, 224, 226, 245, 246, 371, 372
"Maquis, The, Part I," 34, 62, 63, 79, 125, 165-168, 181, 267, 298, 305, 307, 359
"Maquis, The, Part II," 169-171, 174, 226, 246, 308, 367, 372, 386
Marani, 368
Marayn, Gul, 125
Marcus, Dr. David, 123
Mardah, 216
Mareel, 101-104
Marritza, Aamin, 78-81
Marta, 215, 216, 231
Martok, General, 11, 293, 294, 296, 297
Martus, 131-133
"Matter of Honor, A," 114
"Matter of Perspective, A," 330
Mauk-To'Vor, 346
Maxwell, Captain Benjamin, 297, 327, 361
McCoullough, Captain, 47
McCoy, Dr., 53, 69, 236, 261
McWatt, 339
Mekong, 147, 160, 161, 247, 324
Melanie, 300-302
"Melora," 42, 110-114, 117, 125, 155, 160, 166, 278, 386
"Ménage à Troi," 31, 283
Meridian, 221-223, 228
"Meridian," 19, 62, 125, 191, 221-223, 228, 262, 286, 327
Merik III, 228
Migdal, Proka, 109
Mikor, 227
"Mind's Eye, The," 38, 271
Minezaki, 184
Miradorn raiders, 52, 55
"Mirror, Mirror," 175, 177, 261, 263

Mollibok, 60, 64-66, 108
Molor, 323, 324
Moodus, 339
Mora, Dr., 80, 134-136, 160
Moreau, Marlena, 177
Morn, 61, 62, 359, 360
Moudakis, 20
"Move Along Home," 41,
  44-47, 63, 85, 125, 312,
  342, 359, 386
M'Tokra, 351
Muniz, 125, 321
"Muse, The," 369-370

N

"Nagus, The," 26, 48-51, 63,
  66, 100, 118, 135, 159,
  160, 165, 228, 267, 358,
  359
Nalas, Li, 91-93, 95, 97-100
Nanut, 91
Naprem, Tora, 306
Natima, 63
Nausicaans, 352
"Necessary Evil," 63, 113,
  117-120, 159, 160, 269,
  357
Nechayev, Admiral, 171,
  216, 359
Neela, 63, 82-85
Negh'Var, 293
Nehelik Province, 55
"New Ground," 49, 141
New Halana, 228
New Mecca, 228
"Night Terrors," 142, 188
Nimoy, Leonard, 163
Nitpicker's Guide for Next
  Generation Trekkers, The,
  Volume I, 8, 36, 244, 330
Nitpicker's Guide for Next
  Generation Trekkers, The,
  Volume II, 7, 8, 37, 167,
  244, 282, 313, 327
Noggra, 346
Nol-Ennis, 56, 57
Nonlinear time, 4, 6, 252
"Non Sequitur," 235

Norva, 379
Novat clan, 59-60

O

Oak, Kubus, 179, 181
Obatta Cluster, 379
Obsidian Order, 157, 172,
  173, 211-213, 224-227,
  266, 268, 269, 293, 333
Odan, 36, 37, 104, 223, 311
Odyssey, 185-187, 189,
  198
Okalar, 125
Omarion Nebula, 195
Omet'iklan, 375, 376
Onaya, 369
"11001001," 11
Oo-mox, 30-31, 158, 283
Opaka, Kai, 3, 10, 56-58,
  82, 179, 181, 355
Organians, 322-323
Orias III, 229
Orias System, 224-226, 266
Orinoco, 160, 161, 346
Ornathia, 281
Orr, 339
Otner, Dr. Bejal, 310
"Our Man Bashir," 160, 161,
  328-331
"Outcast, The," 58

P

Pa'Dar, Kotan, 106-108,
  125
Paqu clan, 59-60
Parada IV, 191, 229
Paradans, 140-143, 250
"Paradise," 46, 62, 144-147,
  184, 188
"Paradise Lost," 192, 200,
  336-339, 386
"Parallax," 255-256
"Parallels," 58
Paris, 255-256
Parn, Legate, 169, 171

"Passenger, The," 39-43,
  54, 57, 76, 160, 164, 190
"Past Prologue," 13-16, 25,
  33, 36, 54, 72, 76, 80,
  104, 125, 135, 139, 149,
  159, 161, 205, 327, 330,
  348, 358, 359, 384
"Past Tense, Part I," 118,
  125, 159, 234-238, 255,
  286, 314
"Past Tense, Part II," 239-
  242, 286
Pazlar, Melora, 110-114,
  119
"Peak Performance," 308
Peers, Selin, 125, 284
"Pegasus, The," 297
Pel, 63, 115-116, 160, 278,
  297
Pelios Station, 105
Pennington School, 273,
  275
"Pen Pals," 364
Pentath III, 360, 361
Perikian peninsula, 95
Picard, Captain Jean-Luc,
  3-5, 9-11, 54, 69, 73, 92,
  96, 101, 119, 146, 163,
  166-167, 184, 205, 226-
  227, 283, 296, 297, 359,
  362, 376
"Piece of the Action, A," 312
Piersall, Lieutenant J.G.,
  122
"Playing God," 63, 98, 151-
  155, 159, 160, 163, 191,
  209, 210, 216, 228, 230,
  232, 341, 357
Plegg, 381
Porta, Vedek, 355
Portland, 272
"Power Play," 225, 247
Prakesh, 299
"Preemptive Strike," 165,
  167
Preloc, 174
Pren, Dr. Hanor, 310
Prime Directive, 25, 356
Primmin, George, 39, 40, 45
"Profit and Loss," 63, 125,
  156-158, 228, 301, 358

"Progress," 50, 62, 64-66, 99, 108, 125, 159, 191, 251, 280, 386
"Prophet Motive," 63, 160, 228, 251-253
Prophets, the, 3, 4, 83, 84, 135, 248, 250, 280, 355, 356
Protouniverse, 151-155
P'Trell, Chirugeon Ghee, 253

Q

Q, 135, 159, 359
"Q-Less," 29-33, 63, 72, 125, 159, 228, 232, 283, 359
"Qpid," 29, 30
"Quickening, The," 377-379
Quintana, Ensign, 223

R

Rabol, 308
Rahkar, 52-55, 229
Rakantha Province, 279
Rak-Miunis, 213
Ralidia, 362
Ranor, Gul, 227
"Rascals," 58, 101, 225
Ravinok, 306, 307
Redab, Vedek, 125
"Redemption," 13, 322
"Redemption II," 13, 96
Red Squad, 333, 336, 337-338
Reese, Lieutenant, 372, 373
Regulas III, 229, 231
"Rejoined," 63, 125, 284, 309-312, 378, 386
Rekelen, 156
"Relics," 330
Ren, Surmak, 21, 22, 24
Renhol, Dr., 207
"Requiem for Methuselah," 364
"Return to Glory," 372

"Return to Grace," 343-345
"Reunion," 163
Reyab, 43
Rhit, Prylar, 180
Rhymus Major, 229
Rigel VII, 40
"Rightful Heir," 323-324
Riker, 160, 311
Riker, Thomas, 19, 224-225, 227
Riker, Will, 6, 104, 224, 237
Rio Grande, 101, 145-147, 153, 160, 161, 324, 382
Riseans, 386
"Rivals," 16, 46, 63, 131-133, 160, 191, 386
River Glyrhond, 61
Rochani III, 229
Rodek, 346
Rollman, Admiral, 16, 326
Romulans, 96, 145, 191, 195, 199, 200, 227, 237, 254, 256-257, 266, 268-271, 298, 315, 332, 333, 370
"Royale, The," 283
Rubicon, 161, 278, 382
Rudellian plague, 362
Rugal, 106-109
"Rules of Acquisition," 62, 63, 115-116, 125, 160, 278, 297, 358, 386
"Rules of Engagement," 360-362
Rurigan, 148, 149
Rutledge, 145, 146

S

Sakonna, 165, 166, 170, 359
"Samaritan Snare," 38, 145, 147
Samuels, William, 165, 168
"Sanctuary," 27, 33-34, 65, 127-130, 159, 216, 228, 316, 359, 386
Sanctuary districts, 234-237, 239, 242

Sarda, Miss, 28, 63, 125
Scott, 261, 330
"Search, The, Part I," 35, 160, 195-198, 204, 220, 225, 227, 231-232, 270, 286, 311, 338, 358, 386
"Search, The, Part II," 63, 125, 191, 197, 199-202, 207, 227, 270, 288, 358, 359, 383, 384
Sebarr, 233
"Second Chances," 224
"Second Sight," 37, 62, 121-124, 126, 159, 228, 308, 358, 386
"Second Skin," 126, 211-213, 219, 228, 327, 358, 384
Sefalla Prime, 229
Senarians, 386
Setlik III, 92, 145
Seyetik, Gideon, 121-123, 128
Seyetik, Nidell, 121-124
"Shadowplay," 50, 126, 148-150, 180, 188, 228, 358, 372
Shakaar, 279-281, 340-343, 349
"Shakaar," 65, 191, 212, 279-281, 283, 340
Shakaar resistance, 78, 79
"Shattered Mirror," 365, 366-368
Sheliak, 34, 168
Shel-La, Golin, 56, 57
Shepard, Cadet Ripley, 336, 339
"Ship in a Bottle," 8, 331
"Siege, The," 98-101, 104, 107, 126, 135, 159-161, 167, 294, 326, 327, 358, 359, 370
"Sins of the Father," 362
Sirco Ch'Ano, 125
Sisko, Jennifer, 5, 10, 62, 121, 263, 264, 366-368
Skrreeans, 33-34, 127-130
Solais V, 229
Solar sails, 273-276
Sompek, Emperor, 361

"Sons of Mogh, The," 161, 346-351, 362
Soren, 131
Sorval, Commander, 351
Spock, 69, 175, 177, 241, 288, 322, 337
Stakoron II, 51, 229
Starbase 74, 11
Starfleet Academy, 122, 145, 313, 314, 333, 336-338
"Starship Down," 62, 126, 318-321, 329, 347, 358, 359, 387
"Starship Mine," 105
Star Trek: The Motion Picture, 334
Star Trek: The Next Generation, 3-5, 9, 29, 32, 47, 101, 111, 112, 165, 185-186, 190, 197, 201, 215, 224, 233, 237, 243-244, 313, 323-324, 330, 331, 335, 339, 355, 361, 364, 370, 374
Star Trek: The Next Generation Technical Manual, 7, 140, 247, 276, 330, 339, 340, 365, 367
Star Trek: Voyager, 38, 87, 96, 235, 255-256, 346, 354
Star Trek Encyclopedia, The, 8, 14, 36, 40, 69, 196, 232, 247, 315, 362
Star Trek Generations, 13, 131, 186, 250, 308, 339
Star Trek II: The Wrath of Khan, 31, 146, 319
Star Trek III: The Search for Spock, 123, 344
Star Trek IV: The Voyage Home, 7, 171, 235, 315, 334
Star Trek VI: The Undiscovered Country, 69, 164, 205, 244, 272, 297, 334, 335
Star Wars, 308
Stoll, 32
"Storyteller, The," 19, 49,

59-61, 63, 67, 69, 95, 99, 126
Sto'Vo'Kor, 346, 351
"Sub Rosa," 281
"Suddenly Human," 10, 267
"Survivors, The," 73
"Suspicions," 259
Sutter, Clara, 150
Swonden, 339
"Sword of Kahless, The," 161, 322-324, 387
Symbiosis Commission, 207-209

T

Tagara, Nurse, 370
Tahna Los, 13-16, 25, 33, 54, 125
Tain, Enabran, 172, 173, 266, 268, 270, 272, 384
Talarians, 10, 266, 267
Tallonians, 386
Tal Shiar, 266-269, 271, 286, 333
Taluno, 11
Tamal, 125
Tandro, Enina, 35-38, 123, 284
Tandro, General Ardelon, 35, 123, 284
Tandro, Ilon, 35, 37
Tanis Canyon, 281
"Tapestry," 119
Tarellians, 243-244
Tasha Yar syndrome, 75
Tau Cynga V, 168
Tavnians, 369, 370
Taya, 148-150
Telepathic energy, 75-77
Telnorri, Counselor, 363-364
Teplan System, 377
Terok Nor, 106, 175-177, 263, 264, 269
Teros, Nathaniel, 114
Terosa Prime, 229
Terrellians, 244, 255
Thed, Villus, 124

Third Talak'Talan, 186-187, 221, 248, 303, 323, 326, 352, 364, 378
Tholians, 386
"Tholian Web, The," 196
Thoron field, 11
"Through the Looking Glass," 62, 261-265, 366
Tibetan Plateau, 331
"Time and Again," 256
"Time's Arrow, Part II," 235
Timor, 126
Tiron, 62, 126, 222
Tixaplik, Plix, 130
T'Kar, 103, 105, 359
T'Lani, 37, 137-139, 160, 161
T'Lani III, 137, 138, 164, 229
T'Lara, Admiral, 361, 362
Tobias, 68
Tobin, 68, 283
Toddman, Admiral, 269, 271, 272
Toh'Kaht, 75
Toman'torax, 376
Tong Vey, 361, 362
Toran, Gul, 156, 157
Toran, Minister, 65
Torias, 284, 309
Torvin, Dr., 210
Tosh, Regana, 304, 305
Tosk, 25-28, 33, 160
"To the Death," 374-376
Tozhat resettlement center, 106, 108
Trakor, 248-250
"Transfigurations," 28
Trevean, 377, 379
"Tribunal," 19, 34, 182-184, 219, 229, 350
Trill, 36-37, 102-104, 151, 152, 207, 208, 222, 309-312, 327, 386
T'Rogorans, 34, 127, 128, 386
Troi, Deanna, 32, 142, 369-370
Troi, Lwaxana, 71-74, 100, 160, 230-232, 341, 359, 369-370

"Trouble with Tribbles, The,"
164
True Way, 328, 340
T'Rul, 195
Tumak, 127
Tumek, 126, 204, 206
Turrel, Legate, 243, 244
Tygarians, 387
Tyler, Ensign, 312
Tzenkethi, 285, 287, 387

U

Uhura, 261
Ulani, 250
Undalar cliffs, 382
"Unification II," 10, 109
Universal Translator, 27-28,
79, 118, 127-129, 164,
298, 316
"Unnatural Selection," 146
"Up the Long Ladder," 19
Urudium, 218
USS *Constellation*, 216
USS *Crockett*, 147
USS *Lantree*, 146
USS *Lexington*, 7, 122, 202,
274
USS *Melbourne*, 8, 9
USS *Okinawa*, 335, 336
USS *Phoenix*, 327
USS *Prometheus*, 121, 122,
124
USS *Reliant*, 146
USS *Saratoga*, 3, 7-9
Ustard, 385
Uxbridge, Kevin, 73

V

Vaatrik, 117-120
Vaatrik, Mrs., 63, 117-120,
160
Valerians, 387
Vantika, 39-42
Varani, 129
Varis Sul, 60, 63, 126

Vash, 29-32, 63, 359
Vayans, 387
Vekor, 42
Verad, 102-105, 283, 310
Vertiron nodes, 154, 191
V'ger, 334
Vilix'Pran, Ensign, 126, 247
"Visionary," 34, 159, 191,
229, 236, 254-257, 369,
370
"Visitor, The," 192, 300-302,
369
Volan III, 171
Vole infestation, 151, 155
Volga, 381, 382
Vorta, 198, 303, 375, 387
"Vortex," 7, 52-55, 95, 160,
213, 229, 247, 327, 332,
358, 384
Vulcans, 44-45, 54, 108,
112, 165, 315, 322-323,
364, 387

W

Wadi, 44-46, 85, 312, 342,
359, 387
Wainwright, Captain, 315-
317
"Way of the Warrior, The,"
11, 62, 126, 232, 293-299,
326, 346, 349, 358, 359,
387
Webb, Jeannie, 242
Weld, Dr., 134, 136
Weyoun, 374, 375
"When the Bough Breaks,"
92, 123
"Where Silence Has Lease,"
237, 305
"Whispers," 140-143, 144,
161, 191, 229, 250, 358
"Whom Gods Destroy," 288
Winn, Kai, 82-85, 94, 179-
181, 243, 244, 279, 280,
356
"Wire, The," 65, 149, 172-
174, 266, 359
Woban, 60, 126

Wolf 359, 3-7, 9, 123, 153
Wormhole, 4, 6, 31, 54, 82,
83, 94, 153-154, 187, 195,
198-200, 202, 208, 248-
250, 270, 275, 300-302,
310, 326, 332, 342, 374-
375, 378, 381
"Wounded, The," 174, 297,
298, 327, 361

X

Xepolite, 387
Xhosa, 296, 298, 371

Y

Yadera Prime, 229
Yalosians, 387
Yangtzee Kiang, 56, 160,
161
Yarka, Vedek, 248, 250
Yates, Kasidy, 62, 63, 277,
278, 293, 296, 298, 306,
308, 369, 371-373
Yeto, 63, 126
Yiri, General, 157
Yridians, 167
Yukon, 161, 346, 347, 350,
382

Z

Zalkonians, 28
Zanthi fever, 230
Zarale, Gul, 91
Zef'No, 126
Zek, Grand Nagus, 48-49,
62, 63, 115-116, 251-252
Zhian'tara, 282-284
Zimm, Ermat, 230
Ziyal, Tora, 306, 343-345,
372, 373
Zlangco, 126
Zyree, 116

ATTENTION
ALL NITPICKING TREKKERS!

JOIN THE NITPICKER'S GUILD TODAY!

J ust send in a mistake that you've found in an incarnation of Star Trek—the original series, the movies, *Next Generation, Deep Space Nine* or *Voyager*—or even a mistake that you've found in any of the *Nitpicker's Guides*. Simply mailing that entry will make you an official member of the Nitpicker's Guild! (Please understand. I get *a lot* of mail and I try to read every letter, but it is very difficult to send out personal responses.)

Send your mistake to:
Phil Farrand, Chief Nitpicker
The Nitpicker's Guild
P.O. Box 6248
Springfield, MO 65801-6248

Note: All submissions become the property of Phil Farrand and will not be returned. Submissions may or may not be acknowledged. By submitting material, you grant permission for use of your submission and name in any future publication by the author. Should a given mistake be published in one of the mediums of the Nitpicker's Guild, an effort will be made to credit the first person sending in that mistake. However, Phil Farrand makes no guarantee that such credit will be given.